The Editor

MICHAEL GORRA is the Mary Augusta Jordan Professor of English at Smith College. He is the recipient of fellowships from the National Endowment for the Humanities and the Guggenheim Foundation and, for his work as a reviewer, of the Balakian Award from the National Book Critics Circle. His books include *Portrait of a Novel: Henry James and the Making of an American Masterpiece*, *The Bells in Their Silence: Travels through Germany*, *After Empire: Scott, Naipaul, Rushdie*, *The English Novel at Mid-Century*, and, as editor, *The Portable Conrad* and the Norton Critical Edition of William Faulkner's *As I Lay Dying*.

A NORTON CRITICAL EDITION

William Faulkner

THE SOUND AND THE FURY

AN AUTHORITATIVE TEXT

BACKGROUNDS AND CONTEXTS

CRITICISM

THIRD EDITION

Edited by

MICHAEL GORRA
SMITH COLLEGE

W · W · NORTON & COMPANY · *New York* · *London*

W. W. Norton & Company has been independent since its founding in 1923, when William Warder Norton and Mary D. Herter Norton first published lectures delivered at the People's Institute, the adult education division of New York City's Cooper Union. The firm soon expanded its program beyond the Institute, publishing books by celebrated academics from America and abroad. By midcentury, the two major pillars of Norton's publishing program—trade books and college texts—were firmly established. In the 1950s, the Norton family transferred control of the company to its employees, and today—with a staff of four hundred and a comparable number of trade, college, and professional titles published each year—W. W. Norton & Company stands as the largest and oldest publishing house owned wholly by its employees.

The text of this book is composed in Fairfield Medium
with the display set in Bernhard Modern.
Production manager: Sean Mintus

Library of Congress Cataloging-in-Publication Data

Faulkner, William, 1897–1962.
    The Sound and the Fury : an authoritative text, backgrounds and contexts, criticism / William Faulkner ; edited by Michael Gorra, Smith College. — Third edition.
        pages cm. — (A Norton Critical Edition)
    Includes bibliographical references.
    ISBN 978-0-393-91269-2 (pbk.)
    1. Faulkner, William, 1897–1962. Sound and the fury.   2. People with mental disabilities—Fiction.   3. African American women cooks—Fiction.
4. Aristocracy (Social class)—Fiction.   5. Illegitimate children—Fiction.
6. Brothers and sisters—Fiction.   7. Mississippi—Fiction.   8. Psychological fiction.   9. Domestic fiction.   I. Gorra, Michael Edward.   II. Title.
    PS3511.A86S7 2013
    813'.52—dc23
                                                                                    2013039746

W. W. Norton & Company, Inc., 500 Fifth Avenue, New York, NY 10110-0017
wwnorton.com

W. W. Norton & Company Ltd., 15 Carlisle Street, London W1D 3BS

    3 4 5 6 7 8 9 0

Contents

Preface to the Third Edition

"Ever tried. Ever failed," writes Samuel Beckett in his 1983 *Worstward Ho*. "No matter. Try again. Fail again. Fail better."[1] Those words might have been conceived with one of his fellow Nobel laureates in mind, for they echo the anecdote that William Faulkner liked to tell about the writing of *The Sound and the Fury*. The novel began as a short story called "Twilight," and although Faulkner didn't record the date on which he started to work, it was probably close to the one he scrawled at the top of his opening page: April 7, 1928, a Saturday, and the day on which the first of the book's four sections is set. The story told of a Mississippi family called Compson, whose four children have been told to go out and play, sent away from the house to keep them from knowing what's going on inside, where their paternal grandmother has just died. Faulkner was working as well on other pieces about those children, and would go on with them after "Twilight" had swelled out to novel-length and been published; one of them, "That Evening Sun," stands among the greatest of all American short stories. But even in its opening pages the surviving manuscript shows that Faulkner had already moved beyond or away from that kernel of narrative. For one thing, "Damuddy's" death takes place about thirty years before the date on that first page. And for another, the first-person narration of that section seems an embodiment of the words from *Macbeth* that Faulkner would soon draw upon for his title.

Before going on I had better get the Shakespeare out before us. The lines come in the fifth act, when the usurper receives the news that his wife has killed herself:

> She should have died hereafter;
> There would have been a time for such a word.
> Tomorrow, and tomorrow, and tomorrow,
> Creeps in this petty pace from day to day
> To the last syllable of recorded time,
> And all our yesterdays have lighted fools
> The way to dusty death. Out, out, brief candle!

---

1. Samuel Beckett, *Worstward Ho* (New York: Grove Press, 1983), 7.

Life's but a walking shadow, a poor player
That struts and frets his hour upon the stage
And then is heard no more. It is a tale
Told by an idiot, full of sound and fury,
Signifying nothing.[2]

That soliloquy echoes in half a dozen ways throughout the novel.
Quentin Compson, the narrator of the novel's second part, sees himself as a shadow caught by the petty creep of time; his brother Jason,
in the novel's third section, stands as the loud voice of anger itself.
Still, the speech finds its immediate burden in the novel's opening
pages. The youngest of the three Compson brothers, Benjy, is a man
who cannot speak and whose mind cannot distinguish between past
and present. He is the "idiot" of Shakespeare's lines, and for the
novel's first readers the way in which his thoughts slip from one
moment to another proved so hard to follow that some of them took
the bait that Faulkner's title offered—"Signifying nothing," as the
Providence Sunday Journal had it.[3]

    The novelist later wrote, however, that he had in fact begun not
with Benjy but instead with the image of a girl in a pear tree: the
Compson sister, Caddy. The children have been splashing around
in a creek, and Caddy has climbed up to look in the window of her
dead grandmother's room, while her more timid siblings stand below,
peering up at her muddy drawers. It was, Faulkner said, "the only
thing in literature which would ever move me very much," and
having created that image he felt impelled to explore its every implication. He tried to "tell it with one brother,"[4] with Benjy, but that
didn't work and so he went on to fail with it once more, this time with
a section written in Quentin's voice and set on a June day in 1910 in
Cambridge, Massachusetts. Try again, fail again, and now he moved
the narration back to 1928 and turned the book over to the third
brother, Jason. But it "still wasn't enough," and so he let "Faulkner try
it" with a concluding section written in an omniscient third-person,
and then threw up his hands.[5] The struggle wasn't yet over, and
fifteen years later Faulkner took the chance to fail one last time,
finally writing the family history he called "Compson: 1699–1945."

    Faulkner believed in failure—or at least he believed in risking
it. Perhaps that belief grew from his identification with his region's
history. Perhaps it came from his own family; his father had among
other things kept a livery stable and was so clearly not the success that his own banker father had been. Yet whatever the cause,

2. V.5, ll. 17–28.
3. The review was by Winfield Townley Scott, and appeared on October 20, 1929.
4. From his Class Conferences at the University of Virginia. See p. 275 of this Norton
   Critical Edition.
5. Ibid., p. 277.

Faulkner believed not only in failure's probability but also in the need to face it. He put Thomas Wolfe first whenever he was asked which of his contemporaries he admired, for he thought that the author of *Look Homeward, Angel* (1929) had dared the most, had taken the biggest chances. He had failed—but the attempt had been too big to succeed. He felt the same way about *Moby-Dick*, while marking Hemingway down a bit in contrast. The latter took few risks, his work was too controlled, and he no longer had the necessary artistic courage, the courage to risk a flop by writing the kind of book he didn't already know how to write. Faulkner himself was a gambler, and *The Sound and the Fury* now seems the novelistic equivalent of drawing to an inside straight—foolish to try, yet glorious in its achievement. He took the chance because he believed he had nothing left to lose, for by the time he wrote "Twilight," William Faulkner had become all too familiar with failure.

A high-school dropout in the university town of Oxford, Mississippi, the young Faulkner was sometimes called "Count No 'Count" because of his mannerisms and the undeserved airs he gave himself. He had joined the Royal Air Force in Toronto in the hopes of becoming a fighter pilot, but World War I ended before he finished his training and for years he claimed more military experience than he actually had. He drifted and wandered—France, New York, New Orleans—and wrote some bad poetry before publishing *Soldiers' Pay* (1926), a good first novel about a wounded veteran. But his next one, *Mosquitoes* (1927), wasn't nearly as successful, and with his third he met failure. In New Orleans, Faulkner had gotten to know Sherwood Anderson, then at the height of his fame from *Winesburg, Ohio* (1919), and the older writer had offered him a bit of advice: go back to Mississippi, and cultivate the material in his own postage-stamp of native soil. Faulkner took that advice, and even before *Mosquitoes* was published had begun two separate pieces about what he eventually called Yoknapatawpha County. One was the unfinished *Father Abraham*, which contained the germ of his later books about the Snopes family, such as *The Hamlet* (1940). The other was a sprawling multi-plotted novel called *Flags in the Dust* that stands as both a Lost Cause and a Lost Generation novel at once. Faulkner thought it was "THE book, of which those other things were but foals." His publisher didn't agree. Horace Liveright had taken Faulkner's first novels, but he sent this one back as a botch, writing in November 1927 that he was "frankly very much disappointed by it." The book had a "thousand loose ends," and he suggested that the writer would only hurt his reputation if he tried to place it elsewhere.[6]

6. Quoted in Joseph Leo Blotner, *Faulkner: A Biography*, vol. 1 (New York: Random House, 1974), 560.

It took Faulkner the better part of a year to find another house, and Harcourt, Brace accepted the novel only on the condition that it be cut. The novelist couldn't face the job of trimming it down himself, however, and turned it over to his agent Ben Wasson, who finished it in just a few weeks; now called *Sartoris*, after the family name of its main characters, the book was released early in 1929. Yet Faulkner had already outgrown it—had, in fact, gone beyond it even before Wasson set to work. Liveright's rejection must have cost him something, but it also freed him, and a few years later he would remember that in a time when hope itself appeared to have died he had begun to tell a story about a little girl and her brothers. "One day," he said, "it suddenly seemed as if a door had clapped silently and forever to between me and all publishers' addresses and book-lists and I said to myself, 'Now I can write. Now I can just write.'"[7] He worked without allowing himself to form a plan or to think about where he was going; worked without any sense of strain or trouble. He wrote *The Sound and the Fury*, and when he was done he described as "the damnedest book I ever read. I dont believe anybody will publish it for ten years."[8]

One other failure may have shaped the novel, and in particular Faulkner's conception of Caddy, the character he called his "heart's darling,"[9] and with whom each of her three brothers are differently though equally obsessed. Faulkner had no sisters—he was one of four boys—but as a child he was especially close to two girls. One was a first cousin called Sallie Murry Wilkins, the daughter of his father's sister. The other was a neighbor child and grade-school class-mate named Estelle Oldham, from whom he was inseparable until she was sent away to a Virginia boarding school in her teens. When she returned, however, Estelle quickly moved into the vivid social world of undergraduate life at Ole Miss, a world of parties and dates and dances into which the young Faulkner felt he could not follow, even as he fell ever more desperately in love. Soon she was engaged to a conspicuously eligible lawyer named Cornell Franklin. She still talked about running away with her childhood sweetheart, but Faulkner had no profession or prospects, and in 1918 she married the older man. Estelle had two children with Franklin, but the mar-riage foundered and in 1926 they separated. *The Sound and the Fury* was written after she had moved back to Oxford and yet before her divorce was final, before the terms of Faulkner's relations with

---

7. "An Introduction to *The Sound and the Fury*." See p. 229 of this Norton Critical Edition.
8. From a letter; see p. 229 of this Norton Critical Edition.
9. From his Class Conferences at the University of Virginia; see p. 276 of this Norton Critical Edition.

her were settled. But they had been married for three months by the time it was published in October 1929: a difficult marriage, troubled by both alcohol and Faulkner's periodic infidelity, yet one that endured.

Still, he never wrote definitively of the connection between Caddy and Estelle, and any biographer must be cautious. About one "original" we can, however, be more certain. One of Oxford's few surviving antebellum houses belonged to a family named Chandler, a big white place on a corner lot just a bit south of the courthouse square, and with a high iron fence around the property. It was a large household, and included a son named Edwin, a grown man who lived behind that fence, kept on the family grounds. Edwin Chandler's mental age has been variously given as between three and six, and he would like Benjy run along within the barricade, trying to follow the world outside; the neighborhood's children would often torment him on their way home from school. Faulkner himself evidently liked him, though, and after the 1934 birth of his daughter, Jill, he often took the little girl to visit.[1]

The Sound and the Fury was published by the new firm of Cape & Smith in a first printing of just 1,789 copies. It did not sell quickly. Two smaller printings followed in 1931, on the strength of the lurid *Sanctuary*, the only one of Faulkner's early masterpieces to enjoy a popular success. Sales were comparatively stronger in Britain and especially in France, but there was no further American release, and by the early 1940s the novel had fallen out of print. In 1946 the Modern Library reissued it, bound in a single volume with *As I Lay Dying*. That new edition stands with another book of that year, Malcolm Cowley's *Portable Faulkner*, at the start of the postwar boom in the novelist's reputation and audience. Fail better. The Nobel Prize followed in 1950.

This third Norton Critical Edition of *The Sound and the Fury* replaces David Minter's second edition of 1994. I have left Minter's careful annotations in place, with some minor changes, along with the note on the text and the list of variants prepared by the great textual scholar Noel Polk, but I have reorganized the second half of this volume. "Backgrounds and Contexts" includes a new section on the novel's initial reception, along with a choice of documents about Faulkner's work on and continued engagement with the book, and brief excerpts from writers ranging from C. Vann Woodward to

---

1. See Sally Wolff with Floyd C. Watkins, *Talking about William Faulkner: Interviews with Jimmy Faulkner and Others* (Baton Rouge: Louisiana State UP, 1996), 45–49.

Henri Bergson that provide a context for the novel. Some but not all of this material appeared in Minter's edition, as did a number of the articles in this book's choice of criticism. In that section I have trimmed some of the older selections and augmented others, swapped out a couple of essays for different pieces by the same hands, and brought everything up to date by including work published since the previous edition went to press.

At W. W. Norton, Carol Bemis and Rivka Genesen have been models of editorial patience and tact. At Smith, I have been helped by Jennifer Roberts in the English Department office, and by my research assistants Stephanie Friedman and Catharina Gress-Wright. My colleague Rick Millington made several invaluable suggestions about the materials to include, and I am grateful to those scholars elsewhere who have answered my questions: Minrose C. Gwin, Don Kartiganer, Jay Watson, and Terrell L. Tebbetts.

Editor's Note[†]

This new edition of *The Sound and the Fury* is based upon a comparison of Faulkner's holograph manuscript, the carbon typescript (both documents in the Faulkner Collection of the Alderman Library at the University of Virginia), and the 1929 Cape & Smith first edition. Every effort has been made to produce a text that conforms to Faulkner's "final intentions" for the novel; unfortunately, the relationships among the extant manuscript and the printed materials and the little we know about the circumstances of editing, proofreading, and publication make it impossible to reconstruct in all cases exactly what those "final intentions" were. That is, there are numerous differences between the carbon typescript and the first edition; but since neither the setting copy (the typescript actually sent to the editor and compositor) nor any set of galleys has been preserved, there is no way to determine with certainty whether any single variant is the result of Faulkner's changes on typescript or galleys, of an editor's intervention at any point in the publishing process, or of a compositor's errors in setting type. In general, this edition reproduces the text of the carbon typescript unless there was compelling reason to accept any reading from the 1929 edition. Faulkner's holograph manuscript has been consulted regularly to help solve textual problems.

There is not enough space here to provide a complete textual apparatus for this novel. The tables appended are intended merely to record, for the interested reader, a highly selective sampling of some of the more significant variations among the present text, the carbon typescript, and the first edition. Table A records differences between the present text and the 1929 first edition; Table B, differences between this text and the carbon typescript. Both tables are keyed to page and line numbers of the present text. The reading to the left of the bracket is the reading of the new edition; in Table A, the reading to the right of the bracket is that of the 1929 text; in Table B, of the carbon typescript.

---

† By Noel Polk, who prepared the current text.

TABLE A

Differences between the present text and the 1929 Cape & Smith first edition:

6.25 Are you. Are you.] Are you.	68.16 the new text; each ¶ begins flush left.]
14.24 Open] "Open	68.41 home.] home in Mississippi.
14.25 Versh.] Versh."	
14.25 Spread] "Spread	69.10 healing] heading
14.25 floor. [floor."	73.20 unitarial] Unitarian
14.26 Now] "Now	91.14– [No ¶ indentation here;
14.26 feet.] feet."	100.9 each ¶ begins flush left.]
15.26 stooped] stopped	
17.33 You] "You	93.11 to the house [The new edition restores this line to the text; omitted in the first edition.]
17.36 Quentin.] Quentin."	
17.37 Didn't] "Didn't	
17.38 on.] on."	
24.28 Didn't he didn't he] Didn't he	109.43 Harvard] Harvard like Quentin
47.1 said] said, Quentin,	109.43 ground] ground like Father
50.8 folded] wrapped	
50.31– students. They'll think	115.41 dope.] coca-cola.
32 you go to Harvard.] students.	119.32 Father's] Father's funeral
52.40 "Maybe you want a tailor's goose," the clerk said. "They] The clerk said, "These	112.47– your name. You'd be
	123.2 better off if you were down there] you
54.33– *still. My bowels moved for thee.*] *still.*	146.18 shot] coca-cola
57.17 *Jason*] *Jason a position in the bank.*	156.32 both of them] Caddy and Quentin
62.12 and Versh] Versh said	173.20 kin do dat] gwine preach today
66.6– [No ¶ indentations in	174.4 shaling] shading

TABLE B

Differences between the present text and the carbon typescript:

5.1 What] Versh, what	puffed his face. The candles went away.] He blew out the candles.
5.2 for, Versh."] for."	
6.32 Jason] Mr. Jason	
35.13– him." She set the cake	53.29 window.] window, thinking that if she had just been a boy she'd
14 on the table.] him"	
35.39 He leaned down and	

have invented windows
you could raise easily
instead of fine names
for the cars.

55.9– and through my coat
10 touched the letters I had
written.] and touched
the letters through my
coat

61.20– his black hand, in the
21 sun.] the sun, in his
dark hand.

61.30 boy."] boy. Whatever it
is, Marcus Lafayette   I
had forgotten about
that. He told me once

that his name used to
be Marcus something
else, but when they
moved away and he
went to school and
became an American,
he says, his name got
changed to Marcus
Lafayette, in honor of
France and America,
he said   Listenbee
will value it for the
giver's sake and sight
unseen, I thanks you."

62.12 and Versh] Versh

The Text of
THE SOUND
AND THE FURY

This new edition of *The Sound and the Fury* is the first corrected version of the book to appear in paperback since the book was originally published in 1929. The text is based on a comparison—under the direction of Noel Polk—of the first edition and Faulkner's original manuscript and carbon typescript.

—Publisher's Note to the 1984 Random House edition

April Seventh, 1928.

Through the fence, between the curling flower spaces, I could see them hitting. They were coming toward where the flag was and I went along the fence. Luster was hunting in the grass by the flower tree. They took the flag out, and they were hitting. Then they put the flag back and they went to the table, and he hit and the other hit. Then they went on, and I went along the fence. Luster came away from the flower tree and we went along the fence and they stopped and we stopped and I looked through the fence while Luster was hunting in the grass.

"Here, caddie." He hit. They went away across the pasture. I held to the fence and watched them going away.

"Listen at you, now." Luster said. "Aint you something, thirty three years old, going on that way. After I done went all the way to town to buy you that cake. Hush up that moaning. Aint you going to help me find that quarter so I can go to the show tonight."

They were hitting little, across the pasture. I went back along the fence to where the flag was. It flapped on the bright grass and the trees.

"Come on." Luster said. "We done looked there. They aint no more coming right now. Les go down to the branch and find that quarter before them niggers finds it."

It was red, flapping on the pasture. Then there was a bird slanting and tilting on it. Luster threw. The flag flapped on the bright grass and the trees. I held to the fence.

"Shut up that moaning." Luster said. "I cant make them come if they aint coming, can I. If you dont hush up, mammy aint going to have no birthday for you. If you dont hush, you know what I going to do. I going to eat that cake all up. Eat them candles, too. Eat all them thirty three candles. Come on, les go down to the branch. I got to find my quarter. Maybe we can find one of they balls. Here. Here they is. Way over yonder. See." He came to the fence and pointed his arm. "See them. They aint coming back here no more. Come on."

We went along the fence and came to the garden fence, where our shadows were. My shadow was higher than Luster's on the fence. We came to the broken place and went through it.

"Wait a minute." Luster said. "You snagged on that nail again. Cant you never crawl through here without snagging on that nail."

Caddy uncaught me and we crawled through. Uncle Maury said to not let anybody see us, so we better stoop over, Caddy said. Stoop over, Benjy. Like this, see. We stooped over and crossed the garden, where the flowers rasped and rattled against us. The ground was hard. We climbed the fence, where the pigs were grunting and snuffing. I expect they're sorry because one of them got killed today, Caddy said. *The ground was hard, churned and knotted.*

Keep your hands in your pockets, Caddy said. *Or they'll get froze. You dont want your hands froze on Christmas, do you.*

"It's too cold out there." Versh said. "You dont want to go out doors."

"What is it now." Mother said.

"He want to go out doors." Versh said.

"Let him go." Uncle Maury said.

"It's too cold." Mother said. "He'd better stay in. Benjamin. Stop that, now."

"It wont hurt him." Uncle Maury said.

"You, Benjamin." Mother said. "If you dont be good, you'll have to go to the kitchen."

"Mammy say keep him out the kitchen today." Versh said. "She say she got all that cooking to get done."

"Let him go, Caroline." Uncle Maury said. "You'll worry yourself sick over him."

"I know it." Mother said. "It's a judgment on me. I sometimes wonder."

"I know, I know." Uncle Maury said. "You must keep your strength up. I'll make you a toddy."

"It just upsets me that much more." Mother said. "Dont you know it does."

"You'll feel better." Uncle Maury said. "Wrap him up good, boy, and take him out for a while."

Uncle Maury went away. Versh went away.

"Please hush." Mother said. "We're trying to get you out as fast as we can. I dont want you to get sick."

Versh put my overshoes and overcoat on and we took my cap and went out. Uncle Maury was putting the bottle away in the sideboard in the diningroom.

"Keep him out about half an hour, boy." Uncle Maury said. "Keep him in the yard, now."

"Yes, sir." Versh said. "We dont never let him get off the place."

We went out doors. The sun was cold and bright.

"Where you heading for." Versh said. "You dont think you going to town, does you." We went through the rattling leaves. The gate was cold. "You better keep them hands in your pockets." Versh said. "You get them froze onto that gate, then what you do. Whyn't you wait for them in the house." He put my hands into my pockets. I could hear him rattling in the leaves. I could smell the cold. The gate was cold.

"Here some hickeynuts. Whooey. Git up that tree. Look here at this squirl, Benjy."

I couldn't feel the gate at all, but I could smell the bright cold.

"You better put them hands back in your pockets."

Caddy was walking. Then she was running, her booksatchel swinging and jouncing behind her.

"Hello, Benjy." Caddy said. She opened the gate and came in and stooped down. Caddy smelled like leaves. "Did you come to meet me." she said. "Did you come to meet Caddy. What did you let him get his hands so cold for, Versh."

"I told him to keep them in his pockets." Versh said. "Holding on to that ahun gate."

"Did you come to meet Caddy." she said, rubbing my hands. "What is it. What are you trying to tell Caddy." Caddy smelled like trees and like when she says we were asleep.

What are you moaning about, Luster said. You can watch them again when we get to the branch. Here. Here's you a jimson weed. He gave me the flower. We went through the fence, into the lot.

"What is it." Caddy said. "What are you trying to tell Caddy. Did they send him out, Versh."

"Couldn't keep him in." Versh said. "He kept on until they let him go and he come right straight down here, looking through the gate."

"What is it." Caddy said. "Did you think it would be Christmas when I came home from school. Is that what you thought. Christmas is the day after tomorrow. Santy Claus, Benjy. Santy Claus. Come on, let's run to the house and get warm." She took my hand and we ran through the bright rustling leaves. We ran up the steps and out of the bright cold, into the dark cold. Uncle Maury was putting the bottle back in the sideboard. He called Caddy. Caddy said,

"Take him in to the fire, Versh. Go with Versh." she said. "I'll come in a minute."

We went to the fire. Mother said,

"Is he cold, Versh."

"Nome." Versh said.

"Take his overcoat and overshoes off." Mother said. "How many times do I have to tell you not to bring him into the house with his overshoes on."

"Yessum." Versh said. "Hold still, now." He took my overshoes off and unbuttoned my coat. Caddy said,

"Wait, Versh. Cant he go out again, Mother. I want him to go with me."

"You'd better leave him here." Uncle Maury said. "He's been out enough today."

"I think you'd both better stay in." Mother said. "It's getting colder, Dilsey says."

"Oh, Mother." Caddy said.

"Nonsense." Uncle Maury said. "She's been in school all day. She needs the fresh air. Run along, Candace."

"Let him go, Mother." Caddy said. "Please. You know he'll cry."

"Then why did you mention it before him." Mother said. "Why did you come in here. To give him some excuse to worry me again. You've been out enough today. I think you'd better sit down here and play with him."

"Let them go, Caroline." Uncle Maury said. "A little cold wont hurt them. Remember, you've got to keep your strength up."

"I know." Mother said. "Nobody knows how I dread Christmas. Nobody knows. I am not one of those women who can stand things. I wish for Jason's and the children's sakes I was stronger."

"You must do the best you can and not let them worry you." Uncle Maury said. "Run along, you two. But dont stay out long, now. Your mother will worry."

"Yes, sir." Caddy said. "Come on, Benjy. We're going out doors again." She buttoned my coat and we went toward the door.

"Are you going to take that baby out without his overshoes." Mother said. "Do you want to make him sick, with the house full of company."

"I forgot." Caddy said. "I thought he had them on."

We went back. "You must think." Mother said.   *Hold still now* Versh said. He put my overshoes on. "Someday I'll be gone, and you'll have to think for him."   *Now stomp*   Versh said. "Come here and kiss Mother, Benjamin."

Caddy took me to Mother's chair and Mother took my face in her hands and then she held me against her.

"My poor baby." she said. She let me go. "You and Versh take good care of him, honey."

"Yessum." Caddy said. We went out. Caddy said,

"You needn't go, Versh. I'll keep him for a while."

"All right." Versh said. "I aint going out in that cold for no fun." He went on and we stopped in the hall and Caddy knelt and put her arms around me and her cold bright face against mine. She smelled like trees.

"You're not a poor baby. Are you. Are you. You've got your Caddy. Haven't you got your Caddy."

Cant you shut up that moaning and slobbering, Luster said. Aint you shamed of yourself, making all this racket. We passed the carriage house, where the carriage was. It had a new wheel.

"Git in, now, and set still until your maw come." Dilsey said. She shoved me into the carriage. T. P. held the reins. "Clare I dont see how come Jason wont get a new surrey." Dilsey said. "This thing going to fall to pieces under you all some day. Look at them wheels."

Mother came out, pulling her veil down. She had some flowers.

"Where's Roskus." she said.

"Roskus cant lift his arms, today." Dilsey said. "T. P. can drive all right."

"I'm afraid to." Mother said. "It seems to me you all could furnish me with a driver for the carriage once a week. It's little enough I ask, Lord knows."

"You know just as well as me that Roskus got the rheumatism too bad to do more than he have to, Miss Cahline." Dilsey said. "You come on and get in, now. T. P. can drive you just as good as Roskus."

"I'm afraid to." Mother said. "With the baby."

Dilsey went up the steps. "You calling that thing a baby." she said. She took Mother's arm. "A man big as T. P. Come on, now, if you going."

"I'm afraid to." Mother said. They came down the steps and Dilsey helped Mother in. "Perhaps it'll be the best thing, for all of us." Mother said.

"Aint you shamed, talking that way." Dilsey said. "Dont you know it'll take more than a eighteen year old nigger to make Queenie run away. She older than him and Benjy put together. And dont you start no projecking with Queenie, you hear me. T. P. If you dont drive to suit Miss Cahline, I going to put Roskus on you. He aint too tied up to do that."

"Yessum." T. P. said.

"I just know something will happen." Mother said. "Stop, Benjamin."

"Give him a flower to hold." Dilsey said. "That what he wanting." She reached her hand in.

"No, no." Mother said. "You'll have them all scattered."

"You hold them." Dilsey said. "I'll get him one out." She gave me a flower and her hand went away.

"Go on now, fore Quentin see you and have to go too." Dilsey said.

"Where is she." Mother said.

"She down to the house playing with Luster." Dilsey said. "Go on, T. P. Drive that surrey like Roskus told you, now."

"Yessum." T. P. said. "Hum up, Queenie."

"Quentin." Mother said. "Dont let   "

"Course I is." Dilsey said.

The carriage jolted and crunched on the drive. "I'm afraid to go and leave Quentin." Mother said. "I'd better not go. T. P." We went through the gate, where it didn't jolt anymore. T. P. hit Queenie with the whip.

"You, T. P." Mother said.

"Got to get her going." T. P. said. "Keep her wake up till we get back to the barn."

"Turn around." Mother said. "I'm afraid to go and leave Quentin."

"Cant turn here." T. P. said. Then it was broader.

"Cant you turn here." Mother said.

"All right." T. P. said. We began to turn.

"You, T. P." Mother said, clutching me.

"I got to turn around some how." T. P. said. "Whoa, Queenie." We stopped.

"You'll turn us over." Mother said.

"What you want to do, then." T. P. said.

"I'm afraid for you to try to turn around." Mother said.

"Get up, Queenie." T. P. said. We went on.

"I just know Dilsey will let something happen to Quentin while I'm gone." Mother said. "We must hurry back."

"Hum up,[1] there." T. P. said. He hit Queenie with the whip.

"You, T. P." Mother said, clutching me. I could hear Queenie's feet and the bright shapes went smooth and steady on both sides, the shadows of them flowing across Queenie's back. They went on like the bright tops of wheels. Then those on one side stopped at the tall white post where the soldier was.[2] But on the other side they went on smooth and steady, but a little slower.

"What do you want." Jason said. He had his hands in his pockets and a pencil behind his ear.

"We're going to the cemetery." Mother said.

"All right." Jason said. "I dont aim to stop you, do I. Was that all you wanted with me, just to tell me that."

"I know you wont come." Mother said. "I'd feel safer if you would."

"Safe from what." Jason said. "Father and Quentin cant hurt you."

Mother put her handkerchief under her veil. "Stop it, Mother." Jason said. "Do you want to get that damn looney to bawling in the middle of the square. Drive on, T. P."

"Hum up, Queenie." T. P. said.

"It's a judgment on me." Mother said. "But I'll be gone too, soon."

"Here." Jason said.

"Whoa." T. P. said. Jason said,

"Uncle Maury's drawing on you for fifty. What do you want to do about it."

"Why ask me." Mother said. "I dont have any say so. I try not to worry you and Dilsey. I'll be gone soon, and then you   "

---

1. Similar to the command "Get up."
2. The statue of the Confederate soldier on the town square.

"Go on, T. P." Jason said.

"Hum up, Queenie." T. P. said. The shapes flowed on. The ones on the other side began again, bright and fast and smooth, like when Caddy says we are going to sleep.

Cry baby, Luster said. Aint you shamed. We went through the barn. The stalls were all open. You aint got no spotted pony to ride now, Luster said. The floor was dry and dusty. The roof was falling. The slanting holes were full of spinning yellow. What do you want to go that way, for. You want to get your head knocked off with one of them balls.

"Keep your hands in your pockets." Caddy said. "Or they'll be froze. You dont want your hands froze on Christmas, do you."

We went around the barn. The big cow and the little one were standing in the door, and we could hear Prince and Queenie and Fancy stomping inside the barn. "If it wasn't so cold, we'd ride Fancy." Caddy said. "But it's too cold to hold on today." Then we could see the branch, where the smoke was blowing. "That's where they are killing the pig." Caddy said. "We can come back by there and see them." We went down the hill.

"You want to carry the letter." Caddy said. "You can carry it." She took the letter out of her pocket and put it in mine. "It's a Christmas present." Caddy said. "Uncle Maury is going to surprise Mrs Patterson with it. We got to give it to her without letting anybody see it. Keep your hands in your pockets good, now." We came to the branch.

"It's froze." Caddy said. "Look." She broke the top of the water and held a piece of it against my face. "Ice. That means how cold it is." She helped me across and we went up the hill. "We cant even tell Mother and Father. You know what I think it is. I think it's a surprise for Mother and Father and Mr Patterson both, because Mr Patterson sent you some candy. Do you remember when Mr Patterson sent you some candy last summer."

There was a fence. The vine was dry, and the wind rattled in it.

"Only I dont see why Uncle Maury didn't send Versh." Caddy said. "Versh wont tell." Mrs Patterson was looking out the window. "You wait here." Caddy said. "Wait right here, now. I'll be back in a minute. Give me the letter." She took the letter out of my pocket. "Keep your hands in your pockets." She climbed the fence with the letter in her hand and went through the brown, rattling flowers. Mrs Patterson came to the door and opened it and stood there.

Mr Patterson was chopping in the green flowers. He stopped chopping and looked at me. Mrs Patterson came across the garden, running. When I saw her eyes I began to cry. You idiot, Mrs Patterson said, I told him never to send you alone again. Give it to me. Quick. Mr Patterson came fast, with the hoe. Mrs Patterson leaned across the fence, reaching her hand. She was trying to climb the fence. Give it to me, she said, Give it to me. Mr Patterson climbed the fence. He took the letter. Mrs Patterson's dress was caught on the fence. I saw her eyes again and I ran down the hill.

"They aint nothing over yonder but houses." Luster said. "We going down to the branch."

They were washing down at the branch. One of them was singing. I could smell the clothes flapping, and the smoke blowing across the branch.

"You stay down here." Luster said. "You aint got no business up yonder. Them folks hit you, sho."

"What he want to do."

"He dont know what he want to do." Luster said. "He think he want to go up yonder where they knocking that ball. You sit down here and play with your jimson weed. Look at them chillen playing in the branch, if you got to look at something. How come you cant behave yourself like folks." I sat down on the bank, where they were washing, and the smoke blowing blue.

"Is you all seen anything of a quarter down here." Luster said.

"What quarter."

"The one I had here this morning." Luster said. "I lost it somewhere. It fell through this here hole in my pocket. If I dont find it I cant go to the show tonight."

"Where'd you get a quarter, boy. Find it in white folks' pocket while they aint looking."

"Got it at the getting place." Luster said. "Plenty more where that one come from. Only I got to find that one. Is you all found it yet."

"I aint studying no quarter. I got my own business to tend to."

"Come on here." Luster said. "Help me look for it."

"He wouldn't know a quarter if he was to see it, would he."

"He can help look just the same." Luster said. "You all going to the show tonight."

"Dont talk to me about no show. Time I get done over this here tub I be too tired to lift my hand to do nothing."

"I bet you be there." Luster said. "I bet you was there last night. I bet you all be right there when that tent open."

"Be enough niggers there without me. Was last night."

"Nigger's money good as white folks, I reckon."

"White folks gives nigger money because know first white man comes along with a band going to get it all back, so nigger can go to work for some more."

"Aint nobody going make you go to that show."

"Aint yet. Aint thought of it, I reckon."

"What you got against white folks."

"Aint got nothing against them. I goes my way and lets white folks go theirs. I aint studying that show."

"Got a man in it can play a tune on a saw. Play it like a banjo."

"You go last night." Luster said. "I going tonight. If I can find where I lost that quarter."

"You going take him with you, I reckon."

"Me." Luster said. "You reckon I be found anywhere with him, time he start bellering."

"What does you do when he start bellering."

"I whips him." Luster said. He sat down and rolled up his overalls. They played in the branch.

"You all found any balls yet." Luster said.

"Aint you talking biggity. I bet you better not let your grandmammy hear you talking like that."

Luster got into the branch, where they were playing. He hunted in the water, along the bank.

"I had it when we was down here this morning." Luster said.

"Where bouts you lose it."

"Right out this here hole in my pocket." Luster said. They hunted in the branch. Then they all stood up quick and stopped, then they splashed and fought in the branch. Luster got it and they squatted in the water, looking up the hill through the bushes.

"Where is they." Luster said.

"Aint in sight yet."

Luster put it in his pocket. They came down the hill.

"Did a ball come down here."

"It ought to be in the water. Didn't any of you boys see it or hear it."

"Aint heard nothing come down here." Luster said. "Heard something hit that tree up yonder. Dont know which way it went."

They looked in the branch.

"Hell. Look along the branch. It came down here. I saw it."

They looked along the branch. Then they went back up the hill.

"Have you got that ball." the boy said.

"What I want with it." Luster said. "I aint seen no ball."

The boy got in the water. He went on. He turned and looked at Luster again. He went on down the branch.

The man said "Caddie" up the hill. The boy got out of the water and went up the hill.

"Now, just listen at you." Luster said. "Hush up."

"What he moaning about now."

"Lawd knows." Luster said. "He just starts like that. He been at it all morning. Cause it his birthday, I reckon."

"How old he."

"He thirty three." Luster said. "Thirty three this morning."

"You mean, he been three years old thirty years."

"I going by what mammy say." Luster said. "I dont know. We going to have thirty three candles on a cake, anyway. Little cake. Wont hardly hold them. Hush up. Come on back here." He came and caught my arm. "You old looney." he said. "You want me to whip you."

"I bet you will."

"I is done it. Hush, now." Luster said. "Aint I told you you cant go up there. They'll knock your head clean off with one of them balls. Come on, here." He pulled me back. "Sit down." I sat down and he took off my shoes and rolled up my trousers. "Now, git in that water and play and see can you stop that slobbering and moaning."

I hushed and got in the water *and Roskus came and said to come to supper and Caddy said,*

It's not supper time yet. I'm not going.

She was wet. We were playing in the branch and Caddy squatted down and got her dress wet and Versh said,

"Your mommer going to whip you for getting your dress wet."

"She's not going to do any such thing." Caddy said.

"How do you know." Quentin said.

"That's all right how I know." Caddy said. "How do you know."

"She said she was." Quentin said. "Besides, I'm older than you."

"I'm seven years old." Caddy said. "I guess I know."

"I'm older than that." Quentin said. "I go to school. Dont I, Versh."

"I'm going to school next year." Caddy said. "When it comes. Aint I, Versh."

"You know she whip you when you get your dress wet." Versh said.

"It's not wet." Caddy said. She stood up in the water and looked at her dress. "I'll take it off." she said. "Then it'll dry."

"I bet you wont." Quentin said.

"I bet I will." Caddy said.

"I bet you better not." Quentin said.

Caddy came to Versh and me and turned her back.

"Unbutton it, Versh." she said.

"Dont you do it, Versh." Quentin said.

"Taint none of my dress." Versh said.

"You unbutton it, Versh." Caddy said. "Or I'll tell Dilsey what you did yesterday." So Versh unbuttoned it.

"You just take your dress off." Quentin said. Caddy took her dress off and threw it on the bank. Then she didn't have on anything but her bodice and drawers, and Quentin slapped her and she slipped and fell down in the water. When she got up she began to splash water on Quentin, and Quentin splashed water on Caddy. Some of it splashed on Versh and me and Versh picked me up and put me on the bank. He said he was going to tell on Caddy and Quentin, and then Quentin and Caddy began to splash water at Versh. He got behind a bush.

"I'm going to tell mammy on you all." Versh said.

Quentin climbed up the bank and tried to catch Versh, but Versh ran away and Quentin couldn't. When Quentin came back Versh stopped and hollered that he was going to tell. Caddy told him that if he wouldn't tell, they'd let him come back. So Versh said he wouldn't, and they let him.

"Now I guess you're satisfied." Quentin said. "We'll both get whipped now."

"I dont care." Caddy said. "I'll run away."

"Yes you will." Quentin said.

"I'll run away and never come back." Caddy said. I began to cry. Caddy turned around and said "Hush" So I hushed. Then they played in the branch. Jason was playing too. He was by himself further down the branch. Versh came around the bush and lifted me down into the water again. Caddy was all wet and muddy behind, and I started to cry and she came and squatted in the water.

"Hush now." she said. "I'm not going to run away." So I hushed. Caddy smelled like trees in the rain.

What is the matter with you, Luster said. Cant you get done with that moaning and play in the branch like folks.

Whyn't you take him on home. Didn't they told you not to take him off the place.

He still think they own this pasture, Luster said. Cant nobody see down here from the house, noways.

We can. And folks dont like to look at a looney. Taint no luck in it.

Roskus came and said to come to supper and Caddy said it wasn't supper time yet.

"Yes tis." Roskus said. "Dilsey say for you all to come on to the house. Bring them on, Versh." He went up the hill, where the cow was lowing.

"Maybe we'll be dry by the time we get to the house." Quentin said.

"It was all your fault." Caddy said. "I hope we do get whipped." She put her dress on and Versh buttoned it.

"They wont know you got wet." Versh said. "It dont show on you. Less me and Jason tells."

"Are you going to tell, Jason." Caddy said.

"Tell on who." Jason said.

"He wont tell." Quentin said. "Will you, Jason."

"I bet he does tell." Caddy said. "He'll tell Damuddy."

"He cant tell her." Quentin said. "She's sick. If we walk slow it'll be too dark for them to see."

"I dont care whether they see or not." Caddy said. "I'm going to tell, myself. You carry him up the hill, Versh."

"Jason wont tell." Quentin said. "You remember that bow and arrow I made you, Jason."

"It's broke now." Jason said.

"Let him tell." Caddy said. "I dont give a cuss. Carry Maury up the hill, Versh." Versh squatted and I got on his back.

See you all at the show tonight, Luster said. Come on, here. We got to find that quarter.

"If we go slow, it'll be dark when we get there." Quentin said.

"I'm not going slow." Caddy said. We went up the hill, but Quentin didn't come. He was down at the branch when we got to where we could smell the pigs. They were grunting and snuffing in the trough in the corner. Jason came behind us, with his hands in his pockets. Roskus was milking the cow in the barn door.

The cows came jumping out of the barn.

"Go on." T. P. said. "Holler again. I going to holler myself. Whooey." Quentin kicked T. P. again. He kicked T. P. into the trough where the pigs ate and T. P. lay there. "Hot dog." T. P. said. "Didn't he get me then. You see that white man kick me that time. Whooey."

I wasn't crying, but I couldn't stop. I wasn't crying, but the ground wasn't still, and then I was crying. The ground kept sloping up and the cows ran up the hill. T. P. tried to get up. He fell down again and the cows ran down the hill. Quentin held my arm and we went toward the barn. Then the barn wasn't there and we had to wait until it came back. I didn't see it come back. It came behind us and Quentin set me down in the trough where the cows ate. I held on to it. It was going away too, and I held to it. The cows ran down the hill again, across the door. I couldn't stop. Quentin and T. P. came up the hill, fighting. T. P. was falling down the hill and Quentin dragged him up the hill. Quentin hit T. P. I couldn't stop.

"Stand up." Quentin said. "You stay right here. Dont you go away until I get back."

"Me and Benjy going back to the wedding." T. P. said. "Whooey." Quentin hit T. P. again. Then he began to thump T. P. against the wall. T. P. was laughing. Every time Quentin thumped him against the wall he tried to say Whooey, but he couldn't say it for laughing. I quit crying, but I couldn't stop. T. P. fell on me and the barn door went away. It went down the hill and T. P. was fighting by himself and he fell down again. He was still laughing, and I couldn't stop, and I tried to get up and I fell down, and I couldn't stop. Versh said,

"You sho done it now. I'll declare if you aint. Shut up that yelling."

T. P. was still laughing. He flopped on the door and laughed. "Whooey." he said. "Me and Benjy going back to the wedding. Sassprilluh."[3] T. P. said.

"Hush." Versh said. "Where you get it."

"Out the cellar." T. P. said. "Whooey."

"Hush up." Versh said. "Where bouts in the cellar."

"Anywhere." T. P. said. He laughed some more. "Moren a hundred bottles lef. Moren a million. Look out, nigger, I going to holler."

Quentin said, "Lift him up."

Versh lifted me up.

"Drink this, Benjy." Quentin said. The glass was hot. "Hush, now." Quentin said. "Drink it."

"Sassprilluh." T. P. said. "Lemme drink it, Mr Quentin."

"You shut your mouth." Versh said. "Mr Quentin wear you out."

"Hold him, Versh." Quentin said.

They held me. It was hot on my chin and on my shirt. "Drink." Quentin said. They held my head. It was hot inside me, and I began again. I was crying now, and something was happening inside me and I cried more, and they held me until it stopped happening. Then I hushed. It was still going around, and then the shapes began. Open the crib, Versh. They were going slow. Spread those empty sacks on the floor. They were going faster, almost fast enough. Now. Pick up his feet. They went on, smooth and bright. I could hear T. P. laughing. I went on with them, up the bright hill.

At the top of the hill Versh put me down. "Come on here, Quentin." he called, looking back down the hill. Quentin was still standing there by the branch. He was chunking into the shadows where the branch was.

"Let the old skizzard stay there." Caddy said. She took my hand and we went on past the barn and through the gate. There was a frog on the brick walk, squatting in the middle of it. Caddy stepped over it and pulled me on.

"Come on, Maury." she said. It still squatted there until Jason poked at it with his toe.

"He'll make a wart on you." Versh said. The frog hopped away.

"Come on, Maury." Caddy said.

"They got company tonight." Versh said.

"How do you know." Caddy said.

"With all them lights on." Versh said. "Light in every window."

"I reckon we can turn all the lights on without company, if we want to." Caddy said.

---

3. A variant of sarsaparilla, a sweet soft drink similar to root beer with the predominant flavor from birch oil and sassafras. But the context suggests that they are drinking something alcoholic.

"I bet it's company." Versh said. "You all better go in the back and slip upstairs."

"I dont care." Caddy said. "I'll walk right in the parlor where they are."

"I bet your pappy whip you if you do." Versh said.

"I dont care." Caddy said. "I'll walk right in the parlor. I'll walk right in the dining room and eat supper."

"Where you sit." Versh said.

"I'd sit in Damuddy's chair." Caddy said. "She eats in bed."

"I'm hungry." Jason said. He passed us and ran on up the walk. He had his hands in his pockets and he fell down. Versh went and picked him up.

"If you keep them hands out your pockets, you could stay on your feet." Versh said. "You cant never get them out in time to catch yourself, fat as you is."

Father was standing by the kitchen steps.

"Where's Quentin." he said.

"He coming up the walk." Versh said. Quentin was coming slow. His shirt was a white blur.

"Oh." Father said. Light fell down the steps, on him.

"Caddy and Quentin threw water on each other." Jason said.

We waited.

"They did." Father said. Quentin came, and Father said, "You can eat supper in the kitchen tonight." He stooped and took me up, and the light came tumbling down the steps on me too, and I could look down at Caddy and Jason and Quentin and Versh. Father turned toward the steps. "You must be quiet, though." he said.

"Why must we be quiet, Father." Caddy said. "Have we got company."

"Yes." Father said.

"I told you they was company." Versh said.

"You did not." Caddy said. "I was the one that said there was. I said I would   "

"Hush." Father said. They hushed and Father opened the door and we crossed the back porch and went in to the kitchen. Dilsey was there, and Father put me in the chair and closed the apron down and pushed it to the table, where supper was. It was steaming up.

"You mind Dilsey, now." Father said. "Dont let them make any more noise than they can help, Dilsey."

"Yes, sir." Dilsey said. Father went away.

"Remember to mind Dilsey, now." he said behind us. I leaned my face over where the supper was. It steamed up on my face.

"Let them mind me tonight, Father." Caddy said.

"I wont." Jason said. "I'm going to mind Dilsey."

"You'll have to, if Father says so." Caddy said. "Let them mind me, Father."

"I wont." Jason said. "I wont mind you."

"Hush." Father said. "You all mind Caddy, then. When they are done, bring them up the back stairs, Dilsey."

"Yes, sir." Dilsey said.

"There." Caddy said. "Now I guess you'll mind me."

"You all hush, now." Dilsey said. "You got to be quiet tonight."

"Why do we have to be quiet tonight." Caddy whispered.

"Never you mind." Dilsey said. "You'll know in the Lawd's own time." She brought my bowl. The steam from it came and tickled my face. "Come here, Versh." Dilsey said.

"When is the Lawd's own time, Dilsey." Caddy said.

"It's Sunday." Quentin said. "Dont you know anything."

"Shhhhhh." Dilsey said. "Didn't Mr Jason say for you all to be quiet. Eat your supper, now. Here, Versh. Git his spoon." Versh's hand came with the spoon, into the bowl. The spoon came up to my mouth. The steam tickled into my mouth. Then we quit eating and we looked at each other and we were quiet, and then we heard it again and I began to cry.

"What was that." Caddy said. She put her hand on my hand.

"That was Mother." Quentin said. The spoon came up and I ate, then I cried again.

"Hush." Caddy said. But I didn't hush and she came and put her arms around me. Dilsey went and closed both the doors and then we couldn't hear it.

"Hush, now." Caddy said. I hushed and ate. Quentin wasn't eating, but Jason was.

"That was Mother." Quentin said. He got up.

"You set right down." Dilsey said. "They got company in there, and you in them muddy clothes. You set down too, Caddy, and get done eating."

"She was crying." Quentin said.

"It was somebody singing." Caddy said. "Wasn't it, Dilsey."

"You all eat your supper, now, like Mr Jason said." Dilsey said. "You'll know in the Lawd's own time." Caddy went back to her chair.

"I told you it was a party." she said.

Versh said, "He done et all that."

"Bring his bowl here." Dilsey said. The bowl went away.

"Dilsey." Caddy said. "Quentin's not eating his supper. Hasn't he got to mind me."

"Eat your supper, Quentin." Dilsey said. "You all got to get done and get out of my kitchen."

"I dont want any more supper." Quentin said.

"You've got to eat if I say you have." Caddy said. "Hasn't he, Dilsey."

The bowl steamed up to my face, and Versh's hand dipped the spoon in it and the steam tickled into my mouth.

"I dont want any more." Quentin said. "How can they have a party when Damuddy's sick."

"They'll have it down stairs." Caddy said. "She can come to the landing and see it. That's what I'm going to do when I get my nightie on."

"Mother was crying." Quentin said. "Wasn't she crying, Dilsey."

"Dont you come pestering at me, boy." Dilsey said. "I got to get supper for all them folks soon as you all get done eating."

After a while even Jason was through eating, and he began to cry.

"Now you got to tune up." Dilsey said.

"He does it every night since Damuddy was sick and he cant sleep with her." Caddy said. "Cry baby."

"I'm going to tell on you." Jason said.

He was crying. "You've already told." Caddy said. "There's not anything else you can tell, now."

"You all needs to go to bed." Dilsey said. She came and lifted me down and wiped my face and hands with a warm cloth. "Versh, can you get them up the back stairs quiet. You, Jason, shut up that crying."

"It's too early to go to bed now." Caddy said. "We dont ever have to go to bed this early."

"You is tonight." Dilsey said. "Your paw say for you to come right on up stairs when you et supper. You heard him." ·

"He said to mind me." Caddy said.

"I'm not going to mind you." Jason said.

"You have to." Caddy said. "Come on, now. You have to do like I say."

"Make them be quiet, Versh." Dilsey said. "You all going to be quiet, aint you."

"What do we have to be so quiet for, tonight." Caddy said.

"Your mommer aint feeling well." Dilsey said. "You all go on with Versh, now."

"I told you Mother was crying." Quentin said. Versh took me up and opened the door onto the back porch. We went out and Versh closed the door black. I could smell Versh and feel him. You all be quiet, now. We're not going up stairs yet. Mr Jason said for you to come right up stairs. He said to mind me. I'm not going to mind you. But he said for all of us to. Didn't he, Quentin. I could feel Versh's head. I could hear us. Didn't he, Versh. Yes, that right. Then I say for us to go out doors a while. Come on. Versh opened the door and we went out.

We went down the steps.

"I expect we'd better go down to Versh's house, so we'll be quiet." Caddy said. Versh put me down and Caddy took my hand and we went down the brick walk.

"Come on." Caddy said. "That frog's gone. He's hopped way over to the garden, by now. Maybe we'll see another one." Roskus came with the milk buckets. He went on. Quentin wasn't coming with us. He was sitting on the kitchen steps. We went down to Versh's house. I liked to smell Versh's house. *There was a fire in it and T. P. squatting in his shirt tail in front of it, chunking it into a blaze.*

Then I got up and T. P. dressed me and we went to the kitchen and ate. Dilsey was singing and I began to cry and she stopped.

"Keep him away from the house, now." Dilsey said.

"We cant go that way." T. P. said.

We played in the branch.

"We cant go around yonder." T. P. said. "Dont you know mammy say we cant."

Dilsey was singing in the kitchen and I began to cry.

"Hush." T. P. said. "Come on. Les go down to the barn."

Roskus was milking at the barn. He was milking with one hand, and groaning. Some birds sat on the barn door and watched him. One of them came down and ate with the cows. I watched Roskus milk while T. P. was feeding Queenie and Prince. The calf was in the pig pen. It nuzzled at the wire, bawling.

"T. P." Roskus said. T. P. said Sir, in the barn. Fancy held her head over the door, because T. P. hadn't fed her yet. "Git done there." Roskus said. "You got to do this milking. I cant use my right hand no more."

T. P. came and milked.

"Whyn't you get the doctor." T. P. said.

"Doctor cant do no good." Roskus said. "Not on this place."

"What wrong with this place." T. P. said.

"Taint no luck on this place." Roskus said. "Turn that calf in if you done."

Taint no luck on this place, Roskus said. The fire rose and fell behind him and Versh, sliding on his and Versh's face. Dilsey finished putting me to bed. The bed smelled like T. P. I liked it.

"What you know about it." Dilsey said. "What trance you been in."

"Dont need no trance." Roskus said. "Aint the sign of it laying right there on that bed. Aint the sign of it been here for folks to see fifteen years now."

"Spose it is." Dilsey said. "It aint hurt none of you and yourn, is it. Versh working and Frony married off your hands and T. P. getting big enough to take your place when rheumatism finish getting you."

"They been two, now." Roskus said. "Going to be one more. I seen the sign, and you is too."

"I heard a squinch owl[4] that night." T. P. said. "Dan wouldn't come and get his supper, neither. Wouldn't come no closer than the barn. Begun howling right after dark. Versh heard him."

"Going to be more than one more." Dilsey said. "Show me the man what aint going to die, bless Jesus."

"Dying aint all." Roskus said.

"I knows what you thinking." Dilsey said. "And they aint going to be no luck in saying that name, lessen you going to set up with him while he cries."

"They aint no luck on this place." Roskus said. "I seen it at first but when they changed his name I knowed it."

"Hush your mouth." Dilsey said. She pulled the covers up. It smelled like T. P. "You all shut up now, till he get to sleep."

"I seen the sign." Roskus said.

"Sign T. P. got to do all your work for you." Dilsey said. *Take him and Quentin down to the house and let them play with Luster, where Frony can watch them, T. P., and go and help your paw.*

We finished eating. T. P. took Quentin up and we went down to T. P.'s house. Luster was playing in the dirt. T. P. put Quentin down and she played in the dirt too. Luster had some spools and he and Quentin fought and Quentin had the spools. Luster cried and Frony came and gave Luster a tin can to play with, and then I had the spools and Quentin fought me and I cried.

"Hush." Frony said. "Aint you shamed of yourself. Taking a baby's play pretty." She took the spools from me and gave them back to Quentin.

"Hush, now." Frony said. "Hush, I tell you."

"Hush up." Frony said. "You needs whipping, that's what you needs." She took Luster and Quentin up. "Come on here." she said. We went to the barn. T. P. was milking the cow. Roskus was sitting on the box.

"What's the matter with him now." Roskus said.

"You have to keep him down here." Frony said. "He fighting these babies again. Taking they play things. Stay here with T. P. now, and see can you hush a while."

"Clean that udder good now." Roskus said. "You milked that young cow dry last winter. If you milk this one dry, they aint going to be no more milk."

Dilsey was singing.

4. Screech owl.

"Not around yonder." T. P. said. "Dont you know mammy say you cant go around there."

They were singing.

"Come on." T. P. said. "Les go play with Quentin and Luster. Come on."

Quentin and Luster were playing in the dirt in front of T. P.'s house. There was a fire in the house, rising and falling, with Roskus sitting black against it.

"That's three, thank the Lawd." Roskus said. "I told you two years ago. They aint no luck on this place."

"Whyn't you get out, then." Dilsey said. She was undressing me. "Your bad luck talk got them Memphis notions into Versh. That ought to satisfy you."

"If that all the bad luck Versh have." Roskus said.

Frony came in.

"You all done." Dilsey said.

"T. P. finishing up." Frony said. "Miss Cahline want you to put Quentin to bed."

"I'm coming just as fast as I can." Dilsey said. "She ought to know by this time I aint got no wings."

"That's what I tell you." Roskus said. "They aint no luck going be on no place where one of they own chillen's name aint never spoke."

"Hush." Dilsey said. "Do you want to get him started."

"Raising a child not to know its own mammy's name." Roskus said.

"Dont you bother your head about her." Dilsey said. "I raised all of them and I reckon I can raise one more. Hush, now. Let him get to sleep if he will."

"Saying a name." Frony said. "He dont know nobody's name."

"You just say it and see if he dont." Dilsey said. "You say it to him while he sleeping and I bet he hear you."

"He know lot more than folks thinks." Roskus said. "He knowed they time was coming, like that pointer done. He could tell you when hisn coming, if he could talk. Or yours. Or mine."

"You take Luster outen that bed, mammy." Frony said. "That boy conjure him."

"Hush your mouth." Dilsey said. "Aint you got no better sense than that. What you want to listen to Roskus for, anyway. Get in, Benjy."

Dilsey pushed me and I got in the bed, where Luster already was. He was asleep. Dilsey took a long piece of wood and laid it between Luster and me. "Stay on your side now." Dilsey said. "Luster little, and you dont want to hurt him."

You cant go yet, T. P. said. Wait.

We looked around the corner of the house and watched the carriages go away.

"Now." T. P. said. He took Quentin up and we ran down to the corner of the fence and watched them pass. "There he go." T. P. said. "See that one with the glass in it.[5] Look at him. He laying in there. See him."

Come on, Luster said, I going to take this here ball down home, where I wont lose it. Naw, sir, you cant have it. If them men sees you with it, they'll say you stole it. Hush up, now. You cant have it. What business you got with it. You cant play no ball.

Frony and T. P. were playing in the dirt by the door. T. P. had lightning bugs in a bottle.

"How did you all get back out." Frony said.

"We've got company." Caddy said. "Father said for us to mind me tonight. I expect you and T. P. will have to mind me too."

"I'm not going to mind you." Jason said. "Frony and T. P. dont have to either."

"They will if I say so." Caddy said. "Maybe I wont say for them to."

"T. P. dont mind nobody." Frony said. "Is they started the funeral yet."

"What's a funeral." Jason said.

"Didn't mammy tell you not to tell them." Versh said.

"Where they moans." Frony said. "They moaned two days on Sis Beulah Clay."

They moaned at Dilsey's house. Dilsey was moaning. When Dilsey moaned Luster said, Hush, and we hushed, and then I began to cry and Blue howled under the kitchen steps.[6] Then Dilsey stopped and we stopped.

"Oh." Caddy said. "That's niggers. White folks dont have funerals."

"Mammy said us not to tell them, Frony." Versh said.

"Tell them what." Caddy said.

Dilsey moaned, and when it got to the place I began to cry and Blue howled under the steps. Luster, Frony said in the window. Take them down to the barn. I cant get no cooking done with all that racket. That hound too. Get them outen here.

I aint going down there, Luster said. I might meet pappy down there. I seen him last night, waving his arms in the barn.

"I like to know why not." Frony said. "White folks dies too. Your grandmammy dead as any nigger can get, I reckon."

5. The horse-drawn hearse with glass windows.
6. According to folk beliefs, dogs often howl after a death in the family.

"Dogs are dead." Caddy said. "And when Nancy fell in the ditch and Roskus shot her and the buzzards came and undressed her."

The bones rounded out of the ditch, where the dark vines were in the black ditch, into the moonlight, like some of the shapes had stopped. Then they all stopped and it was dark, and when I stopped to start again I could hear Mother, and feet walking fast away, and I could smell it. Then the room came, but my eyes went shut. I didn't stop. I could smell it. T. P. unpinned the bed clothes.

"Hush." he said. "Shhhhhhhh."

But I could smell it. T. P. pulled me up and he put on my clothes fast.

"Hush, Benjy." he said. "We going down to our house. You want to go down to our house, where Frony is. Hush. Shhhhh."

He laced my shoes and put my cap on and we went out. There was a light in the hall. Across the hall we could hear Mother.

"Shhhhhh, Benjy." T. P. said. "We'll be out in a minute."

A door opened and I could smell it more than ever, and a head came out. It wasn't Father. Father was sick there.

"Can you take him out of the house."

"That's where we going." T. P. said. Dilsey came up the stairs.

"Hush." she said. "Hush. Take him down home, T. P. Frony fixing him a bed. You all look after him, now. Hush, Benjy. Go on with T. P."

She went where we could hear Mother.

"Better keep him there." It wasn't Father. He shut the door, but I could still smell it.

We went down stairs. The stairs went down into the dark and T. P. took my hand, and we went out the door, out of the dark. Dan was sitting in the back yard, howling.

"He smell it." T. P. said. "Is that the way you found it out."

We went down the steps, where our shadows were.

"I forgot your coat." T. P. said. "You ought to had it. But I aint going back."

Dan howled.

"Hush now." T. P. said. Our shadows moved, but Dan's shadow didn't move except to howl when he did.

"I cant take you down home, bellering like you is." T. P. said. "You was bad enough before you got that bullfrog voice. Come on."

We went along the brick walk, with our shadows. The pig pen smelled like pigs. The cow stood in the lot, chewing at us. Dan howled.

"You going to wake the whole town up." T. P. said. "Cant you hush."

We saw Fancy, eating by the branch. The moon shone on the water when we got there.

"Naw, sir." T. P. said. "This too close. We cant stop here. Come on. Now, just look at you. Got your whole leg wet. Come on, here." Dan howled.

The ditch came up out of the buzzing grass. The bones rounded out of the black vines.

"Now." T. P. said. "Beller your head off if you want to. You got the whole night and a twenty acre pasture to beller in."

T. P. lay down in the ditch and I sat down, watching the bones where the buzzards ate Nancy, flapping black and slow and heavy out of the ditch.

I had it when we was down here before, Luster said. I showed it to you. Didn't you see it. I took it out of my pocket right here and showed it to you.

"Do you think buzzards are going to undress Damuddy." Caddy said. "You're crazy."

"You're a skizzard." Jason said. He began to cry.

"You're a knobnot." Caddy said. Jason cried. His hands were in his pockets.

"Jason going to be rich man." Versh said. "He holding his money all the time."

Jason cried.

"Now you've got him started." Caddy said. "Hush up, Jason. How can buzzards get in where Damuddy is. Father wouldn't let them. Would you let a buzzard undress you. Hush up, now."

Jason hushed. "Frony said it was a funeral." he said.

"Well it's not." Caddy said. "It's a party. Frony dont know anything about it. He wants your lightning bugs, T. P. Let him hold it a while."

T. P. gave me the bottle of lightning bugs.

"I bet if we go around to the parlor window we can see something." Caddy said. "Then you'll believe me."

"I already knows." Frony said. "I dont need to see."

"You better hush your mouth, Frony." Versh said. "Mammy going whip you."

"What is it." Caddy said.

"I knows what I knows." Frony said.

"Come on." Caddy said. "Let's go around to the front."

We started to go.

"T. P. wants his lightning bugs." Frony said.

"Let him hold it a while longer, T. P." Caddy said. "We'll bring it back."

"You all never caught them." Frony said.

"If I say you and T. P. can come too, will you let him hold it." Caddy said.

"Aint nobody said me and T. P. got to mind you." Frony said.

"If I say you dont have to, will you let him hold it." Caddy said.

"All right." Frony said. "Let him hold it, T. P. We going to watch them moaning."

"They aint moaning." Caddy said. "I tell you it's a party. Are they moaning, Versh."

"We aint going to know what they doing, standing here." Versh said.

"Come on." Caddy said. "Frony and T. P. dont have to mind me. But the rest of us do. You better carry him, Versh. It's getting dark."

Versh took me up and we went on around the kitchen.

When we looked around the corner we could see the lights coming up the drive. T. P. went back to the cellar door and opened it.

You know what's down there, T. P. said. Soda water. I seen Mr Jason come up with both hands full of them. Wait here a minute.

T. P. went and looked in the kitchen door. Dilsey said, What are you peeping in here for. Where's Benjy.

He out here, T. P. said.

Go on and watch him, Dilsey said. Keep him out the house now.

Yessum, T. P. said. Is they started yet.

You go on and keep that boy out of sight, Dilsey said. I got all I can tend to.

A snake crawled out from under the house. Jason said he wasn't afraid of snakes and Caddy said he was but she wasn't and Versh said they both were and Caddy said to be quiet, like Father said.

You aint got to start bellering now, T. P. said. You want some this sassprilluh.

It tickled my nose and eyes.

If you aint going to drink it, let me get to it, T. P. said. All right, here tis. We better get another bottle while aint nobody bothering us. You be quiet, now.

We stopped under the tree by the parlor window. Versh set me down in the wet grass. It was cold. There were lights in all the windows.

"That's where Damuddy is." Caddy said. "She's sick every day now. When she gets well we're going to have a picnic."

"I knows what I knows." Frony said.

The trees were buzzing, and the grass.

"The one next to it is where we have the measles." Caddy said. "Where do you and T. P. have the measles, Frony."

"Has them just wherever we is, I reckon." Frony said.

"They haven't started yet." Caddy said.

They getting ready to start, T. P. said. You stand right here now while I get that box so we can see in the window. Here, les finish drinking this here sassprilluh. It make me feel just like a squinch owl inside.

We drank the sassprilluh and T. P. pushed the bottle through the lattice, under the house, and went away. I could hear them in the parlor and I clawed my hands against the wall. T. P. dragged the box. He fell down, and he began to laugh. He lay there, laughing into the grass. He got up and dragged the box under the window, trying not to laugh.

"I skeered I going to holler." T. P. said. "Git on the box and see is they started."

"They haven't started because the band hasn't come yet." Caddy said.

"They aint going to have no band." Frony said.

"How do you know." Caddy said.

"I knows what I knows." Frony said.

"You dont know anything." Caddy said. She went to the tree. "Push me up, Versh."

"Your paw told you to stay out that tree." Versh said.

"That was a long time ago." Caddy said. "I expect he's forgotten about it. Besides, he said to mind me tonight. Didn't he didn't he say to mind me tonight."

"I'm not going to mind you." Jason said. "Frony and T. P. are not going to either."

"Push me up, Versh." Caddy said.

"All right." Versh said. "You the one going to get whipped. I aint." He went and pushed Caddy up into the tree to the first limb. We watched the muddy bottom of her drawers. Then we couldn't see her. We could hear the tree thrashing.

"Mr Jason said if you break that tree he whip you." Versh said.

"I'm going to tell on her too." Jason said.

The tree quit thrashing. We looked up into the still branches.

"What you seeing." Frony whispered.

I saw them. Then I saw Caddy, with flowers in her hair, and a long veil like shining wind. Caddy Caddy

"Hush." T. P. said. "They going to hear you. Get down quick." He pulled me. Caddy. I clawed my hands against the wall Caddy. T. P. pulled me. "Hush." he said. "Hush. Come on here quick." He pulled me on. Caddy "Hush up, Benjy. You want them to hear you. Come on, les drink some more sassprilluh, then we can come back if you hush. We better get one more bottle or we both be hollering. We can say Dan drunk it. Mr Quentin always saying he so smart, we can say he sassprilluh dog, too."

The moonlight came down the cellar stairs. We drank some more sassprilluh.

"You know what I wish." T. P. said. "I wish a bear would walk in that cellar door. You know what I do. I walk right up to him and spit in he eye. Gimme that bottle to stop my mouth before I holler."

T. P. fell down. He began to laugh, and the cellar door and the moonlight jumped away and something hit me.

"Hush up." T. P. said, trying not to laugh. "Lawd, they'll all hear us. Get up." T. P. said. "Get up, Benjy, quick." He was thrashing about and laughing and I tried to get up. The cellar steps ran up the hill in the moonlight and T. P. fell up the hill, into the moonlight, and I ran against the fence and T. P. ran behind me saying "Hush up hush up." Then he fell into the flowers, laughing, and I ran into the box. But when I tried to climb onto it it jumped away and hit me on the back of the head and my throat made a sound. It made the sound again and I stopped trying to get up, and it made the sound again and I began to cry. But my throat kept on making the sound while T. P. was pulling me. It kept on making it and I couldn't tell if I was crying or not, and T. P. fell down on top of me, laughing, and it kept on making the sound and Quentin kicked T. P. and Caddy put her arms around me, and her shining veil, and I couldn't smell trees anymore and I began to cry.

Benjy, Caddy said, Benjy. She put her arms around me again, but I went away. "What is it, Benjy." she said. "Is it this hat." She took her hat off and came again, and I went away.

"Benjy." she said. "What is it, Benjy. What has Caddy done."

"He dont like that prissy dress." Jason said. "You think you're grown up, dont you. You think you're better than anybody else, dont you. Prissy."

"You shut your mouth." Caddy said. "You dirty little beast. Benjy."

"Just because you are fourteen, you think you're grown up, dont you." Jason said. "You think you're something. Dont you."

"Hush, Benjy." Caddy said. "You'll disturb Mother. Hush."

But I didn't hush, and when she went away I followed, and she stopped on the stairs and waited and I stopped too.

"What is it, Benjy." Caddy said. "Tell Caddy. She'll do it. Try."

"Candace." Mother said.

"Yessum." Caddy said.

"Why are you teasing him." Mother said. "Bring him here."

We went to Mother's room, where she was lying with the sickness on a cloth on her head.

"What is the matter now." Mother said. "Benjamin."

"Benjy." Caddy said. She came again, but I went away.

"You must have done something to him." Mother said. "Why wont you let him alone, so I can have some peace. Give him the box and please go on and let him alone."

Caddy got the box and set it on the floor and opened it. It was full of stars. When I was still, they were still. When I moved, they glinted and sparkled. I hushed.

Then I heard Caddy walking and I began again.

"Benjamin." Mother said. "Come here." I went to the door. "You, Benjamin." Mother said.

"What is it now." Father said. "Where are you going."

"Take him downstairs and get someone to watch him, Jason." Mother said. "You know I'm ill, yet you   "

Father shut the door behind us.

"T. P." he said.

"Sir." T. P. said downstairs.

"Benjy's coming down." Father said. "Go with T. P."

I went to the bathroom door. I could hear the water.

"Benjy." T. P. said downstairs.

I could hear the water. I listened to it.

"Benjy." T. P. said downstairs.

I listened to the water.

I couldn't hear the water, and Caddy opened the door.

"Why, Benjy." she said. She looked at me and I went and she put her arms around me. "Did you find Caddy again." she said. "Did you think Caddy had run away." Caddy smelled like trees.

We went to Caddy's room. She sat down at the mirror. She stopped her hands and looked at me.

"Why, Benjy. What is it." she said. "You mustn't cry. Caddy's not going away. See here." she said. She took up the bottle and took the stopper out and held it to my nose. "Sweet. Smell. Good."

I went away and I didn't hush, and she held the bottle in her hand, looking at me.

"Oh." she said. She put the bottle down and came and put her arms around me. "So that was it. And you were trying to tell Caddy and you couldn't tell her. You wanted to, but you couldn't, could you. Of course Caddy wont. Of course Caddy wont. Just wait till I dress."

Caddy dressed and took up the bottle again and we went down to the kitchen.

"Dilsey." Caddy said. "Benjy's got a present for you." She stooped down and put the bottle in my hand. "Hold it out to Dilsey, now." Caddy held my hand out and Dilsey took the bottle.

"Well I'll declare." Dilsey said. "If my baby aint give Dilsey a bottle of perfume. Just look here, Roskus."

Caddy smelled like trees. "We dont like perfume ourselves." Caddy said.

She smelled like trees.

"Come on, now." Dilsey said. "You too big to sleep with folks. You a big boy now. Thirteen years old. Big enough to sleep by yourself in Uncle Maury's room." Dilsey said.

Uncle Maury was sick. His eye was sick, and his mouth. Versh took his supper up to him on the tray.

"Maury says he's going to shoot the scoundrel." Father said. "I told him he'd better not mention it to Patterson before hand." He drank.

"Jason." Mother said.

"Shoot who, Father." Quentin said. "What's Uncle Maury going to shoot him for."

"Because he couldn't take a little joke." Father said.

"Jason." Mother said. "How can you. You'd sit right there and see Maury shot down in ambush, and laugh."

"Then Maury'd better stay out of ambush." Father said.

"Shoot who, Father." Quentin said. "Who's Uncle Maury going to shoot."

"Nobody." Father said. "I dont own a pistol."

Mother began to cry. "If you begrudge Maury your food, why aren't you man enough to say so to his face. To ridicule him before the children, behind his back."

"Of course I dont." Father said. "I admire Maury. He is invaluable to my own sense of racial superiority. I wouldn't swap Maury for a matched team. And do you know why, Quentin."

"No, sir." Quentin said.

"*Et ego in arcadia*[7] I have forgotten the latin for hay." Father said. "There, there." he said. "I was just joking." He drank and set the glass down and went and put his hand on Mother's shoulder.

"It's no joke." Mother said. "My people are every bit as well born as yours. Just because Maury's health is bad."

"Of course." Father said. "Bad health is the primary reason for all life. Created by disease, within putrefaction, into decay. Versh."

"Sir." Versh said behind my chair.

"Take the decanter and fill it."

"And tell Dilsey to come and take Benjamin up to bed." Mother said.

"You a big boy." Dilsey said. "Caddy tired sleeping with you. Hush now, so you can go to sleep." The room went away, but I didn't hush,

---

7. Sometimes attributed to Bartolomeo Schidone (1578?–1615), who wrote the words *Et in Arcadia ego* ("I [Death] am even in Arcadia") on his picture of two young shepherds contemplating a skull they are holding. Also found on a picture by Guercino (1591–1666), this phrase is sometimes altered to *Et ego in Arcadia*, "I too have lived in Arcadia," which expresses the idea of a supreme happiness now lost.

and the room came back and Dilsey came and sat on the bed, looking at me.

"Aint you going to be a good boy and hush." Dilsey said. "You aint, is you. See can you wait a minute, then."

She went away. There wasn't anything in the door. Then Caddy was in it.

"Hush." Caddy said. "I'm coming."

I hushed and Dilsey turned back the spread and Caddy got in between the spread and the blanket. She didn't take off her bathrobe.

"Now." she said. "Here I am." Dilsey came with a blanket and spread it over her and tucked it around her.

"He be gone in a minute." Dilsey said. "I leave the light on in your room."

"All right." Caddy said. She snuggled her head beside mine on the pillow. "Goodnight, Dilsey."

"Goodnight, honey." Dilsey said. The room went black. *Caddy smelled like trees.*

We looked up into the tree where she was.

"What she seeing, Versh." Frony whispered.

"Shhhhhhh." Caddy said in the tree. Dilsey said,

"You come on here." She came around the corner of the house. "Whyn't you all go on up stairs, like your paw said, stead of slipping out behind my back. Where's Caddy and Quentin."

"I told her not to climb up that tree." Jason said. "I'm going to tell on her."

"Who in what tree." Dilsey said. She came and looked up into the tree. "Caddy." Dilsey said. The branches began to shake again.

"You, Satan." Dilsey said. "Come down from there."

"Hush." Caddy said, "Dont you know Father said to be quiet." Her legs came in sight and Dilsey reached up and lifted her out of the tree.

"Aint you got any better sense than to let them come around here." Dilsey said.

"I couldn't do nothing with her." Versh said.

"What you all doing here." Dilsey said. "Who told you to come up to the house."

"She did." Frony said. "She told us to come."

"Who told you you got to do what she say." Dilsey said. "Get on home, now." Frony and T. P. went on. We couldn't see them when they were still going away.

"Out here in the middle of the night." Dilsey said. She took me up and we went to the kitchen.

"Slipping out behind my back." Dilsey said. "When you knowed it's past your bedtime."

"Shhhh, Dilsey." Caddy said. "Dont talk so loud. We've got to be quiet."

"You hush your mouth and get quiet, then." Dilsey said. "Where's Quentin."

"Quentin's mad because we had to mind me tonight." Caddy said. "He's still got T. P.'s bottle of lightning bugs."

"I reckon T. P. can get along without it." Dilsey said. "You go and find Quentin, Versh. Roskus say he seen him going towards the barn." Versh went on. We couldn't see him.

"They're not doing anything in there." Caddy said. "Just sitting in chairs and looking."

"They dont need no help from you all to do that." Dilsey said. We went around the kitchen.

Where you want to go now, Luster said. You going back to watch them knocking ball again. We done looked for it over there. Here. Wait a minute. You wait right here while I go back and get that ball. I done thought of something.

The kitchen was dark. The trees were black on the sky. Dan came waddling out from under the steps and chewed my ankle. I went around the kitchen, where the moon was. Dan came scuffling along, into the moon.

"Benjy." T. P. said in the house.

The flower tree by the parlor window wasn't dark, but the thick trees were. The grass was buzzing in the moonlight where my shadow walked on the grass.

"You, Benjy." T. P. said in the house. "Where you hiding. You slipping off. I knows it."

Luster came back. Wait, he said. Here. Dont go over there. Miss Quentin and her beau in the swing yonder. You come on this way. Come back here, Benjy.

It was dark under the trees. Dan wouldn't come. He stayed in the moonlight. Then I could see the swing and I began to cry.

Come away from there, Benjy, Luster said. You know Miss Quentin going to get mad.

It was two now, and then one in the swing. Caddy came fast, white in the darkness.

"Benjy." she said. "How did you slip out. Where's Versh."

She put her arms around me and I hushed and held to her dress and tried to pull her away.

"Why, Benjy." she said. "What is it. T. P." she called.

The one in the swing got up and came, and I cried and pulled Caddy's dress.

"Benjy." Caddy said. "It's just Charlie. Dont you know Charlie."

"Where's his nigger." Charlie said. "What do they let him run around loose for."

"Hush, Benjy." Caddy said. "Go away, Charlie. He doesn't like you." Charlie went away and I hushed. I pulled at Caddy's dress.

"Why, Benjy." Caddy said. "Aren't you going to let me stay here and talk to Charlie a while."

"Call that nigger." Charlie said. He came back. I cried louder and pulled at Caddy's dress.

"Go away, Charlie." Caddy said. Charlie came and put his hands on Caddy and I cried more. I cried loud.

"No, no." Caddy said. "No. No."

"He cant talk." Charlie said. "Caddy."

"Are you crazy." Caddy said. She began to breathe fast. "He can see. Dont. Dont." Caddy fought. They both breathed fast. "Please. Please." Caddy whispered.

"Send him away." Charlie said.

"I will." Caddy said. "Let me go."

"Will you send him away." Charlie said.

"Yes." Caddy said. "Let me go." Charlie went away. "Hush." Caddy said. "He's gone." I hushed. I could hear her and feel her chest going.

"I'll have to take him to the house." she said. She took my hand. "I'm coming." she whispered.

"Wait." Charlie said. "Call the nigger."

"No." Caddy said. "I'll come back. Come on, Benjy."

"Caddy." Charlie whispered, loud. We went on. "You better come back. Are you coming back." Caddy and I were running. "Caddy." Charlie said. We ran out into the moonlight, toward the kitchen.

"Caddy." Charlie said.

Caddy and I ran. We ran up the kitchen steps, onto the porch, and Caddy knelt down in the dark and held me. I could hear her and feel her chest. "I wont." she said. "I wont anymore, ever. Benjy. Benjy." Then she was crying, and I cried, and we held each other. "Hush." she said. "Hush. I wont anymore." So I hushed and Caddy got up and we went into the kitchen and turned the light on and Caddy took the kitchen soap and washed her mouth at the sink, hard. Caddy smelled like trees.

I kept a telling you to stay away from there, Luster said. They sat up in the swing, quick. Quentin had her hands on her hair. He had a red tie.

You old crazy loon, Quentin said. I'm going to tell Dilsey about the way you let him follow everywhere I go. I'm going to make her whip you good.

"I couldn't stop him." Luster said. "Come on here, Benjy."

"Yes you could." Quentin said. "You didn't try. You were both snooping around after me. Did Grandmother send you all out here to spy on me." She jumped out of the swing. "If you dont take him right away this minute and keep him away, I'm going to make Jason whip you."

"I cant do nothing with him." Luster said. "You try it if you think you can."

"Shut your mouth." Quentin said. "Are you going to get him away."

"Ah, let him stay." he said. He had a red tie. The sun was red on it. "Look here, Jack." He struck a match and put it in his mouth. Then he took the match out of his mouth. It was still burning. "Want to try it." he said. I went over there. "Open your mouth." he said. I opened my mouth. Quentin hit the match with her hand and it went away.

"Goddam you." Quentin said. "Do you want to get him started. Dont you know he'll beller all day. I'm going to tell Dilsey on you." She went away running.

"Here, kid." he said. "Hey. Come on back. I aint going to fool with him."

Quentin ran on to the house. She went around the kitchen.

"You played hell then, Jack." he said. "Aint you."

"He cant tell what you saying." Luster said. "He deef and dumb."

"Is." he said. "How long's he been that way."

"Been that way thirty three years today." Luster said. "Born looney. Is you one of them show folks."

"Why." he said.

"I dont ricklick seeing you around here before." Luster said.

"Well, what about it." he said.

"Nothing." Luster said. "I going tonight."

He looked at me.

"You aint the one can play a tune on that saw, is you." Luster said.

"It'll cost you a quarter to find that out." he said. He looked at me. "Why dont they lock him up." he said. "What'd you bring him out here for."

"You aint talking to me." Luster said. "I cant do nothing with him. I just come over here looking for a quarter I lost so I can go to the show tonight. Look like now I aint going to get to go." Luster looked on the ground. "You aint got no extra quarter, is you." Luster said.

"No." he said. "I aint."

"I reckon I just have to find that other one, then." Luster said. He put his hand in his pocket. "You dont want to buy no golf ball neither, does you." Luster said.

"What kind of ball." he said.

"Golf ball." Luster said. "I dont want but a quarter."

"What for." he said. "What do I want with it."

"I didn't think you did." Luster said. "Come on here, mulehead." he said. "Come on here and watch them knocking that ball. Here. Here something you can play with along with that jimson weed." Luster picked it up and gave it to me. It was bright.

"Where'd you get that." he said. His tie was red in the sun, walking.

"Found it under this here bush." Luster said. "I thought for a minute it was that quarter I lost."

He came and took it.

"Hush." Luster said. "He going to give it back when he done looking at it."

"Agnes Mabel Becky."[8] he said. He looked toward the house.

"Hush." Luster said. "He fixing to give it back."

He gave it to me and I hushed.

"Who come to see her last night." he said.

"I dont know." Luster said. "They comes every night she can climb down that tree. I dont keep no track of them."

"Damn if one of them didn't leave a track." he said. He looked at the house. Then he went and lay down in the swing. "Go away." he said. "Dont bother me."

"Come on here." Luster said. "You done played hell now. Time Miss Quentin get done telling on you."

We went to the fence and looked through the curling flower spaces. Luster hunted in the grass.

"I had it right here." he said. I saw the flag flapping, and the sun slanting on the broad grass.

"They'll be some along soon." Luster said. "There some now, but they going away. Come on and help me look for it."

We went along the fence.

"Hush." Luster said. "How can I make them come over here, if they aint coming. Wait. They'll be some in a minute. Look yonder. Here they come."

I went along the fence, to the gate, where the girls passed with their booksatchels. "You, Benjy." Luster said. "Come back here."

You cant do no good looking through the gate, T. P. said. Miss Caddy done gone long ways away. Done got married and left you. You cant do no good, holding to the gate and crying. She cant hear you.

What is it he wants, T. P. Mother said. Cant you play with him and keep him quiet.

He want to go down yonder and look through the gate, T. P. said.

---

8. The most popular contraceptive early in the twentieth century was a condom called the Merry Widow, which was sold in circular metal boxes, three to a box. The top label read "Three Merry Widows Agnes Mabel Becky."

Well, he cannot do it, Mother said. It's raining. You will just have to play with him and keep him quiet. You, Benjamin.

Aint nothing going to quiet him, T. P. said. He think if he down to the gate, Miss Caddy come back.

Nonsense, Mother said.

I could hear them talking. I went out the door and I couldn't hear them, and I went down to the gate, where the girls passed with their booksatchels. They looked at me, walking fast, with their heads turned. I tried to say, but they went on, and I went along the fence, trying to say, and they went faster. Then they were running and I came to the corner of the fence and I couldn't go any further, and I held to the fence, looking after them and trying to say.

"You, Benjy." T. P. said. "What you doing, slipping out. Dont you know Dilsey whip you."

"You cant do no good, moaning and slobbering through the fence." T. P. said. "You done skeered them chillen. Look at them, walking on the other side of the street."

How did he get out, Father said. Did you leave the gate unlatched when you came in, Jason.

Of course not, Jason said. Dont you know I've got better sense than to do that. Do you think I wanted anything like this to happen. This family is bad enough, God knows. I could have told you, all the time. I reckon you'll send him to Jackson, now. If Mr Burgess dont shoot him first.

Hush, Father said.

I could have told you, all the time, Jason said.

It was open when I touched it, and I held to it in the twilight. I wasn't crying, and I tried to stop, watching the girls coming along in the twilight. I wasn't crying.

"There he is."

They stopped.

"He cant get out. He wont hurt anybody, anyway. Come on."

"I'm scared to. I'm scared. I'm going to cross the street."

"He cant get out."

I wasn't crying.

"Dont be a fraid cat. Come on."

They came on in the twilight. I wasn't crying, and I held to the gate. They came slow.

"I'm scared."

"He wont hurt you. I pass here every day. He just runs along the fence."

They came on. I opened the gate and they stopped, turning. I was trying to say, and I caught her, trying to say, and she screamed and I was trying to say and trying and the bright shapes began to stop and I tried to get out. I tried to get it off of my face, but the bright shapes were going again. They were going up the hill to where it fell away and I tried to cry. But when I breathed in, I couldn't breathe out again to cry, and I tried to keep from falling off the hill and I fell off the hill into the bright, whirling shapes.

Here, looney, Luster said. Here come some. Hush your slobbering and moaning, now.

They came to the flag. He took it out and they hit, then he put the flag back.

"Mister." Luster said.

He looked around. "What." he said.

"Want to buy a golf ball." Luster said.

"Let's see it." he said. He came to the fence and Luster reached the ball through.

"Where'd you get it." he said.

"Found it." Luster said.

"I know that." he said. "Where. In somebody's golf bag."

"I found it laying over here in the yard." Luster said. "I'll take a quarter for it."

"What makes you think it's yours." he said.

"I found it." Luster said.

"Then find yourself another one." he said. He put it in his pocket and went away.

"I got to go to that show tonight." Luster said.

"That so." he said. He went to the table. "Fore caddie." he said. He hit.

"I'll declare." Luster said. "You fusses when you dont see them and you fusses when you does. Why cant you hush. Dont you reckon folks gets tired of listening to you all the time. Here. You dropped your jimson weed." He picked it up and gave it back to me. "You needs a new one. You bout wore that one out." We stood at the fence and watched them.

"That white man hard to get along with." Luster said. "You see him take my ball." They went on. We went on along the fence. We came to the garden and we couldn't go any further. I held to the fence and looked through the flower spaces. They went away.

"Now you aint got nothing to moan about." Luster said. "Hush up. I the one got something to moan over, you aint. Here. Whyn't you hold on to that weed. You be bellering about it next." He gave me the flower. "Where you heading now."

Our shadows were on the grass. They got to the trees before we did. Mine got there first. Then we got there, and then the shadows were gone. There was a flower in the bottle. I put the other flower in it.

"Aint you a grown man, now." Luster said. "Playing with two weeds in a bottle. You know what they going to do with you when

Miss Cahline die. They going to send you to Jackson, where you belong. Mr Jason say so. Where you can hold the bars all day long with the rest of the looneys and slobber. How you like that."

Luster knocked the flowers over with his hand. "That's what they'll do to you at Jackson when you starts bellering."

I tried to pick up the flowers. Luster picked them up, and they went away. I began to cry.

"Beller." Luster said. "Beller. You want something to beller about. All right, then. Caddy." he whispered. "Caddy. Beller now. Caddy."

"Luster." Dilsey said from the kitchen.

The flowers came back.

"Hush." Luster said. "Here they is. Look. It's fixed back just like it was at first. Hush, now."

"You, Luster." Dilsey said.

"Yessum." Luster said. "We coming. You done played hell. Get up." He jerked my arm and I got up. We went out of the trees. Our shadows were gone.

"Hush." Luster said. "Look at all them folks watching you. Hush."

"You bring him on here." Dilsey said. She came down the steps.

"What you done to him now." she said.

"Aint done nothing to him." Luster said. "He just started bellering."

"Yes you is." Dilsey said. "You done something to him. Where you been."

"Over yonder under them cedars." Luster said.

"Getting Quentin all riled up." Dilsey said. "Why cant you keep him away from her. Dont you know she dont like him where she at."

"Got as much time for him as I is." Luster said. "He aint none of my uncle."

"Dont you sass me, nigger boy." Dilsey said.

"I aint done nothing to him." Luster said. "He was playing there, and all of a sudden he started bellering."

"Is you been projecking with his graveyard." Dilsey said.

"I aint touched his graveyard." Luster said.

"Dont lie to me, boy." Dilsey said. We went up the steps and into the kitchen. Dilsey opened the firedoor and drew a chair up in front of it and I sat down. I hushed.

What you want to get her started for, Dilsey said. Whyn't you keep him out of there.

He was just looking at the fire, Caddy said. Mother was telling him his new name. We didn't mean to get her started.

I knows you didn't, Dilsey said. Him at one end of the house and her at the other. You let my things alone, now. Dont you touch nothing till I get back.

"Aint you shamed of yourself." Dilsey said. "Teasing him." She set the cake on the table.

"I aint been teasing him." Luster said. "He was playing with that bottle full of dogfennel and all of a sudden he started up bellering. You heard him."

"You aint done nothing to his flowers." Dilsey said.

"I aint touched his graveyard." Luster said. "What I want with his truck. I was just hunting for that quarter."

"You lost it, did you." Dilsey said. She lit the candles on the cake. Some of them were little ones. Some were big ones cut into little pieces. "I told you to go put it away. Now I reckon you want me to get you another one from Frony."

"I got to go to that show, Benjy or no Benjy." Luster said. "I aint going to follow him around day and night both."

"You going to do just what he want you to, nigger boy." Dilsey said. "You hear me."

"Aint I always done it." Luster said. "Dont I always does what he wants. Dont I, Benjy."

"Then you keep it up." Dilsey said. "Bringing him in here, bawling and getting her started too. You all go ahead and eat this cake, now, before Jason come. I dont want him jumping on me about a cake I bought with my own money. Me baking a cake here, with him counting every egg that comes into this kitchen. See can you let him alone now, less you dont want to go to that show tonight."

Dilsey went away.

"You cant blow out no candles." Luster said. "Watch me blow them out." He leaned down and puffed his face. The candles went away. I began to cry. "Hush." Luster said. "Here. Look at the fire whiles I cuts this cake."

I could hear the clock, and I could hear Caddy standing behind me, and I could hear the roof. It's still raining, Caddy said. I hate rain. I hate everything. And then her head came into my lap and she was crying, holding me, and I began to cry. Then I looked at the fire again and the bright, smooth shapes went again. I could hear the clock and the roof and Caddy.

I ate some cake. Luster's hand came and took another piece. I could hear him eating. I looked at the fire.

A long piece of wire came across my shoulder. It went to the door, and then the fire went away. I began to cry.

"What you howling for now." Luster said. "Look there." The fire was there. I hushed. "Cant you set and look at the fire and be quiet like mammy told you." Luster said. "You ought to be ashamed of yourself. Here. Here's you some more cake."

"What you done to him now." Dilsey said. "Cant you never let him alone."

"I was just trying to get him to hush up and not sturb Miss Cahline." Luster said. "Something got him started again."

"And I know what that something name." Dilsey said. "I'm going to get Versh to take a stick to you when he comes home. You just trying yourself. You been doing it all day. Did you take him down to the branch."

"Nome." Luster said. "We been right here in this yard all day, like you said."

His hand came for another piece of cake. Dilsey hit his hand. "Reach it again, and I chop it right off with this here butcher knife." Dilsey said. "I bet he aint had one piece of it."

"Yes he is." Luster said. "He already had twice as much as me. Ask him if he aint."

"Reach hit one more time." Dilsey said. "Just reach it."

That's right, Dilsey said. I reckon it'll be my time to cry next. Reckon Maury going to let me cry on him a while, too.

His name's Benjy now, Caddy said.

How come it is, Dilsey said. He aint wore out the name he was born with yet, is he.

Benjamin came out of the bible, Caddy said. It's a better name for him than Maury was.

How come it is, Dilsey said.

Mother says it is, Caddy said.

Huh, Dilsey said. Name aint going to help him. Hurt him, neither. Folks dont have no luck, changing names. My name been Dilsey since fore I could remember and it be Dilsey when they's long forgot me.

How will they know it's Dilsey, when it's long forgot, Dilsey, Caddy said.

It'll be in the Book, honey, Dilsey said. Writ out.[9]

Can you read it, Caddy said.

Wont have to, Dilsey said. They'll read it for me. All I got to do is say he here.

The long wire came across my shoulder, and the fire went away. I began to cry.

Dilsey and Luster fought.

"I seen you." Dilsey said. "Oho, I seen you." She dragged Luster out of the corner, shaking him. "Wasn't nothing bothering him, was they. You just wait till your pappy come home. I wish I was young like I use to be, I'd tear them years right off your head. I good mind to lock you up in that cellar and not let you go to that show tonight, I sho is."

"Ow, mammy." Luster said. "Ow, mammy."

9. See Revelation 20.12, 15.

I put my hand out to where the fire had been.

"Catch him." Dilsey said. "Catch him back."

My hand jerked back and I put it in my mouth and Dilsey caught me. I could still hear the clock between my voice. Dilsey reached back and hit Luster on the head. My voice was going loud every time.

"Get that soda." Dilsey said. She took my hand out of my mouth. My voice went louder then and my hand tried to go back to my mouth, but Dilsey held it. My voice went loud. She sprinkled soda on my hand.

"Look in the pantry and tear a piece off of that rag hanging on the nail." she said. "Hush, now. You dont want to make your maw sick again, does you. Here, look at the fire. Dilsey make your hand stop hurting in just a minute. Look at the fire." She opened the fire door. I looked at the fire, but my hand didn't stop and I didn't stop. My hand was trying to go to my mouth, but Dilsey held it.

She wrapped the cloth around it. Mother said,

"What is it now. Cant I even be sick in peace. Do I have to get up out of bed to come down to him, with two grown negroes to take care of him."

"He all right now." Dilsey said. "He going to quit. He just burnt his hand a little."

"With two grown negroes, you must bring him into the house, bawling." Mother said. "You got him started on purpose, because you know I'm sick." She came and stood by me. "Hush." she said. "Right this minute. Did you give him this cake."

"I bought it." Dilsey said. "It never come out of Jason's pantry. I fixed him some birthday."

"Do you want to poison him with that cheap store cake." Mother said. "Is that what you are trying to do. Am I never to have one minute's peace."

"You go on back up stairs and lay down." Dilsey said. "It'll quit smarting him in a minute now, and he'll hush. Come on, now."

"And leave him down here for you all to do something else to." Mother said. "How can I lie there, with him bawling down here. Benjamin. Hush this minute."

"They aint nowhere else to take him." Dilsey said. "We aint got the room we use to have. He cant stay out in the yard, crying where all the neighbors can see him."

"I know, I know." Mother said. "It's all my fault. I'll be gone soon, and you and Jason will both get along better." She began to cry.

"You hush that, now." Dilsey said. "You'll get yourself down again. You come on back up stairs. Luster going to take him to the liberry and play with him till I get his supper done."

Dilsey and Mother went out.

"Hush up." Luster said. "You hush up. You want me to burn your other hand for you. You aint hurt. Hush up."

"Here." Dilsey said. "Stop crying, now." She gave me the slipper, and I hushed. "Take him to the liberry." she said. "And if I hear him again, I going to whip you myself."

We went to the library. Luster turned on the light. The windows went black, and the dark tall place on the wall came and I went and touched it. It was like a door, only it wasn't a door.

The fire came behind me and I went to the fire and sat on the floor, holding the slipper. The fire went higher. It went onto the cushion in Mother's chair.

"Hush up." Luster said. "Cant you never get done for a while. Here I done built you a fire, and you wont even look at it."

Your name is Benjy, Caddy said. Do you hear. Benjy. Benjy.

Dont tell him that, Mother said. Bring him here.

Caddy lifted me under the arms.

Get up, Mau——I mean Benjy, she said.

Dont try to carry him, Mother said. Cant you lead him over here. Is that too much for you to think of.

I can carry him, Caddy said. "Let me carry him up, Dilsey."

"Go on, Minute." Dilsey said. "You aint big enough to tote a flea. You go on and be quiet, like Mr Jason said."

There was a light at the top of the stairs. Father was there, in his shirt sleeves. The way he looked said Hush. Caddy whispered,

"Is Mother sick."

Versh set me down and we went into Mother's room. There was a fire. It was rising and falling on the walls. There was another fire in the mirror. I could smell the sickness. It was on a cloth folded on Mother's head. Her hair was on the pillow. The fire didn't reach it, but it shone on her hand, where her rings were jumping.

"Come and tell Mother goodnight." Caddy said. We went to the bed. The fire went out of the mirror. Father got up from the bed and lifted me up and Mother put her hand on my head.

"What time is it." Mother said. Her eyes were closed.

"Ten minutes to seven." Father said.

"It's too early for him to go to bed." Mother said. "He'll wake up at daybreak, and I simply cannot bear another day like today."

"There, there." Father said. He touched Mother's face.

"I know I'm nothing but a burden to you." Mother said. "But I'll be gone soon. Then you will be rid of my bothering."

"Hush." Father said. "I'll take him downstairs a while." He took me up. "Come on, old fellow. Let's go down stairs a while. We'll have to be quiet while Quentin is studying, now."

Caddy went and leaned her face over the bed and Mother's hand came into the firelight. Her rings jumped on Caddy's back.

Mother's sick, Father said. Dilsey will put you to bed. Where's Quentin.

Versh getting him, Dilsey said.

Father stood and watched us go past. We could hear Mother in her room. Caddy said "Hush." Jason was still climbing the stairs. He had his hands in his pockets.

"You all must be good tonight." Father said. "And be quiet, so you wont disturb Mother."

"We'll be quiet." Caddy said. "You must be quiet now, Jason." she said. We tiptoed.

We could hear the roof. I could see the fire in the mirror too. Caddy lifted me again.

"Come on, now." she said. "Then you can come back to the fire. Hush, now."

"Candace." Mother said.

"Hush, Benjy." Caddy said. "Mother wants you a minute. Like a good boy. Then you can come back. Benjy."

Caddy let me down, and I hushed.

"Let him stay here, Mother. When he's through looking at the fire, then you can tell him."

"Candace." Mother said. Caddy stooped and lifted me. We staggered. "Candace." Mother said.

"Hush." Caddy said. "You can still see it. Hush."

"Bring him here." Mother said. "He's too big for you to carry. You must stop trying. You'll injure your back. All of our women have prided themselves on their carriage. Do you want to look like a washerwoman."

"He's not too heavy." Caddy said. "I can carry him."

"Well, I dont want him carried, then." Mother said. "A five year old child. No, no. Not in my lap. Let him stand up."

"If you'll hold him, he'll stop." Caddy said. "Hush." she said. "You can go right back. Here. Here's your cushion. See."

"Dont, Candace." Mother said.

"Let him look at it and he'll be quiet." Caddy said. "Hold up just a minute while I slip it out. There, Benjy. Look."

I looked at it and hushed.

"You humor him too much." Mother said. "You and your father both. You dont realise that I am the one who has to pay for it. Damuddy spoiled Jason that way and it took him two years to outgrow it, and I am not strong enough to go through the same thing with Benjamin."

"You dont need to bother with him." Caddy said. "I like to take care of him. Dont I. Benjy."

"Candace." Mother said. "I told you not to call him that. It was bad enough when your father insisted on calling you by that silly nickname, and I will not have him called by one. Nicknames are vulgar. Only common people use them. Benjamin." she said.

"Look at me." Mother said.

"Benjamin." she said. She took my face in her hands and turned it to hers.

"Benjamin." she said. "Take that cushion away, Candace."

"He'll cry." Caddy said.

"Take that cushion away, like I told you." Mother said. "He must learn to mind."

The cushion went away.

"Hush, Benjy." Caddy said.

"You go over there and sit down." Mother said. "Benjamin." She held my face to hers.

"Stop that." she said. "Stop it."

But I didn't stop and Mother caught me in her arms and began to cry, and I cried. Then the cushion came back and Caddy held it above Mother's head. She drew Mother back in the chair and Mother lay crying against the red and yellow cushion.

"Hush, Mother." Caddy said. "You go up stairs and lay down, so you can be sick. I'll go get Dilsey." She led me to the fire and I looked at the bright, smooth shapes. I could hear the fire and the roof.

Father took me up. He smelled like rain.

"Well, Benjy." he said. "Have you been a good boy today."

Caddy and Jason were fighting in the mirror.

"You, Caddy." Father said.

They fought. Jason began to cry.

"Caddy." Father said. Jason was crying. He wasn't fighting any-more, but we could see Caddy fighting in the mirror and Father put me down and went into the mirror and fought too. He lifted Caddy up. She fought. Jason lay on the floor, crying. He had the scissors in his hand. Father held Caddy.

"He cut up all Benjy's dolls." Caddy said. "I'll slit his gizzle."

"Candace." Father said.

"I will." Caddy said. "I will." She fought. Father held her. She kicked at Jason. He rolled into the corner, out of the mirror. Father brought Caddy to the fire. They were all out of the mirror. Only the fire was in it. Like the fire was in a door.

"Stop that." Father said. "Do you want to make Mother sick in her room."

Caddy stopped. "He cut up all the dolls Mau—— Benjy and I made." Caddy said. "He did it just for meanness."

"I didn't." Jason said. He was sitting up, crying. "I didn't know they were his. I just thought they were some old papers."

"You couldn't help but know." Caddy said. "You did it just "

"Hush." Father said. "Jason." he said.

"I'll make you some more tomorrow." Caddy said. "We'll make a lot of them. Here, you can look at the cushion, too."

Jason came in.

I kept telling you to hush, Luster said.

What's the matter now, Jason said.

"He just trying hisself." Luster said. "That the way he been going on all day."

"Why dont you let him alone, then." Jason said. "If you cant keep him quiet, you'll have to take him out to the kitchen. The rest of us cant shut ourselves up in a room like Mother does."

"Mammy say keep him out the kitchen till she get supper." Luster said.

"Then play with him and keep him quiet." Jason said. "Do I have to work all day and then come home to a mad house." He opened the paper and read it.

You can look at the fire and the mirror and the cushion too, Caddy said. You wont have to wait until supper to look at the cushion, now. We could hear the roof. We could hear Jason too, crying loud beyond the wall.

Dilsey said, "You come, Jason. You letting him alone, is you."

"Yessum." Luster said.

"Where Quentin." Dilsey said. "Supper near bout ready."

"I dont know'm." Luster said. "I aint seen her."

Dilsey went away. "Quentin." she said in the hall. "Quentin. Supper ready."

We could hear the roof. Quentin smelled like rain, too.

What did Jason do, he said.

He cut up all Benjy's dolls, Caddy said.

Mother said to not call him Benjy, Quentin said. He sat on the rug by us. I wish it wouldn't rain, he said. You cant do anything.

You've been in a fight, Caddy said. Haven't you.

It wasn't much, Quentin said.

You can tell it, Caddy said. Father'll see it.

I dont care, Quentin said. I wish it wouldn't rain.

Quentin said, "Didn't Dilsey say supper was ready."

"Yessum." Luster said. Jason looked at Quentin. Then he read the paper again. Quentin came in. "She say it bout ready." Luster said. Quentin jumped down in Mother's chair. Luster said,

"Mr Jason."

"What." Jason said.

"Let me have two bits." Luster said.

"What for." Jason said.

"To go to the show tonight." Luster said.

"I thought Dilsey was going to get a quarter from Frony for you." Jason said.

"She did." Luster said. "I lost it. Me and Benjy hunted all day for that quarter. You can ask him."

"Then borrow one from him." Jason said. "I have to work for mine." He read the paper. Quentin looked at the fire. The fire was in her eyes and on her mouth. Her mouth was red.

"I tried to keep him away from there." Luster said.

"Shut your mouth." Quentin said. Jason looked at her.

"What did I tell you I was going to do if I saw you with that show fellow again." he said. Quentin looked at the fire. "Did you hear me." Jason said.

"I heard you." Quentin said. "Why dont you do it, then."

"Dont you worry." Jason said.

"I'm not." Quentin said. Jason read the paper again.

I could hear the roof. Father leaned forward and looked at Quentin. Hello, he said. Who won.

"Nobody." Quentin said. "They stopped us. Teachers."

"Who was it." Father said. "Will you tell."

"It was all right." Quentin said. "He was as big as me."

"That's good." Father said. "Can you tell what it was about."

"It wasn't anything." Quentin said. "He said he would put a frog in her desk and she wouldn't dare to whip him."

"Oh." Father said. "She. And then what."

"Yes, sir." Quentin said. "And then I kind of hit him."

We could hear the roof and the fire, and a snuffling outside the door.

"Where was he going to get a frog in November." Father said.

"I dont know, sir." Quentin said.

We could hear them.

"Jason." Father said. We could hear Jason.

"Jason." Father said. "Come in here and stop that."

We could hear the roof and the fire and Jason.

"Stop that, now." Father said. "Do you want me to whip you again." Father lifted Jason up into the chair by him. Jason snuffled. We could hear the fire and the roof. Jason snuffled a little louder.

"One more time." Father said. We could hear the fire and the roof.

Dilsey said, All right. You all can come on to supper.

Versh smelled like rain. He smelled like a dog, too. We could hear the fire and the roof.

We could hear Caddy walking fast. Father and Mother looked at the door. Caddy passed it, walking fast. She didn't look. She walked fast.

"Candace." Mother said. Caddy stopped walking.

"Yes, Mother." she said.

"Hush, Caroline." Father said.

"Come here." Mother said.

"Hush, Caroline." Father said. "Let her alone."

Caddy came to the door and stood there, looking at Father and Mother. Her eyes flew at me, and away. I began to cry. It went loud and I got up. Caddy came in and stood with her back to the wall, looking at me. I went toward her, crying, and she shrank against the wall and I saw her eyes and I cried louder and pulled at her dress. She put her hands out but I pulled at her dress. Her eyes ran.

Versh said, Your name Benjamin now. You know how come your name Benjamin now. They making a bluegum[1] *out of you. Mammy say in old time your granpaw changed nigger's name, and he turn preacher, and when they look at him, he bluegum too. Didn't use to be bluegum, neither. And when family woman look him in the eye in the full of the moon, chile born bluegum. And one evening, when they was about a dozen them bluegum chillen running around the place, he never come home. Possum hunters found him in the woods, et clean. And you know who et him. Them bluegum chillen did.*

We were in the hall. Caddy was still looking at me. Her hand was against her mouth and I saw her eyes and I cried. We went up the stairs. She stopped again, against the wall, looking at me and I cried and she went on and I came on, crying, and she shrank against the wall, looking at me. She opened the door to her room, but I pulled at her dress and we went to the bathroom and she stood against the door, looking at me. Then she put her arm across her face and I pushed at her, crying.

What are you doing to him, Jason said. Why cant you let him alone.

I aint touching him, Luster said. He been doing this way all day long. He needs whipping.

He needs to be sent to Jackson, Quentin said. How can anybody live in a house like this.

If you dont like it, young lady, you'd better get out, Jason said.

I'm going to, Quentin said. Dont you worry.

Versh said, "You move back some, so I can dry my legs off." He shoved me back a little. "Dont you start bellering, now. You can still see it. That's all you have to do. You aint had to be out in the rain like I is. You's born lucky and dont know it." He lay on his back before the fire.

---

1. A person who has bluish gums and whose bite, according to superstition, is poisonous.

"You know how come your name Benjamin now." Versh said. "Your mamma too proud for you. What mammy say."

"You be still there and let me dry my legs off." Versh said. "Or you know what I'll do. I'll skin your rinktum."

We could hear the fire and the roof and Versh.

Versh got up quick and jerked his legs back. Father said, "All right, Versh."

"I'll feed him tonight." Caddy said. "Sometimes he cries when Versh feeds him."

"Take this tray up." Dilsey said. "And hurry back and feed Benjy."

"Dont you want Caddy to feed you." Caddy said.

Has he got to keep that old dirty slipper on the table, Quentin said. Why dont you feed him in the kitchen. It's like eating with a pig.

If you dont like the way we eat, you'd better not come to the table, Jason said.

Steam came off of Roskus. He was sitting in front of the stove. The oven door was open and Roskus had his feet in it. Steam came off the bowl. Caddy put the spoon into my mouth easy. There was a black spot on the inside of the bowl.

Now, now, Dilsey said. He aint going to bother you no more.

It got down below the mark. Then the bowl was empty. It went away. "He's hungry tonight." Caddy said. The bowl came back. I couldn't see the spot. Then I could. "He's starved, tonight." Caddy said. "Look how much he's eaten."

Yes he will, Quentin said. You all send him out to spy on me. I hate this house. I'm going to run away.

Roskus said, "It going to rain all night."

You've been running a long time, not to've got any further off than mealtime, Jason said.

See if I dont, Quentin said.

"Then I dont know what I going to do." Dilsey said. "It caught me in the hip so bad now I cant scarcely move. Climbing them stairs all evening."

Oh, I wouldn't be surprised, Jason said. I wouldn't be surprised at anything you'd do.

Quentin threw her napkin on the table.

Hush your mouth, Jason, Dilsey said. She went and put her arm around Quentin. Sit down, honey, Dilsey said. He ought to be shamed of hisself, throwing what aint your fault up to you.

"She suiting again, is she." Roskus said.

"Hush your mouth." Dilsey said.

Quentin pushed Dilsey away. She looked at Jason. Her mouth was red. She picked up her glass of water and swung her arm back, looking at Jason. Dilsey caught her arm. They fought. The glass broke on the table, and the water ran into the table. Quentin was running.

"Mother's sick again." Caddy said.

"Sho she is." Dilsey said. "Weather like this make anybody sick. When you going to get done eating, boy."

Goddam you, Quentin said. Goddam you. We could hear her running on the stairs. We went to the library.

Caddy gave me the cushion, and I could look at the cushion and the mirror and the fire.

"We must be quiet while Quentin's studying." Father said. "What are you doing, Jason."

"Nothing." Jason said.

"Suppose you come over here to do it, then." Father said.

Jason came out of the corner.

"What are you chewing." Father said.

"Nothing." Jason said.

"He's chewing paper again." Caddy said.

"Come here, Jason." Father said.

Jason threw into the fire. It hissed, uncurled, turning black. Then it was gray. Then it was gone. Caddy and Father and Jason were in Mother's chair. Jason's eyes were puffed shut and his mouth moved, like tasting. Caddy's head was on Father's shoulder. Her hair was like fire, and little points of fire were in her eyes, and I went and Father lifted me into the chair too, and Caddy held me. She smelled like trees.

She smelled like trees. In the corner it was dark, but I could see the window. I squatted there, holding the slipper. I couldn't see it, but my hands saw it, and I could hear it getting night, and my hands saw the slipper but I couldn't see myself, but my hands could see the slipper, and I squatted there, hearing it getting dark.

Here you is, Luster said. Look what I got. He showed it to me. You know where I got it. Miss Quentin give it to me. I knowed they couldn't keep me out. What you doing, off in here. I thought you done slipped back out doors. Aint you done enough moaning and slobbering today, without hiding off in this here empty room, mumbling and taking on. Come on here to bed, so I can get up there before it starts. I cant fool with you all night tonight. Just let them horns toot the first toot and I done gone.

We didn't go to our room.

"This is where we have the measles." Caddy said. "Why do we have to sleep in here tonight."

"What you care where you sleep." Dilsey said. She shut the door and sat down and began to undress me. Jason began to cry. "Hush." Dilsey said.

"I want to sleep with Damuddy." Jason said.

"She's sick." Caddy said. "You can sleep with her when she gets well. Cant he, Dilsey."

"Hush, now." Dilsey said. Jason hushed.

"Our nighties are here, and everything." Caddy said. "It's like moving."

"And you better get into them." Dilsey said. "You be unbuttoning Jason."

Caddy unbuttoned Jason. He began to cry.

"You want to get whipped." Dilsey said. Jason hushed.

Quentin, Mother said in the hall.

What, Quentin said beyond the wall. We heard Mother lock the door. She looked in our door and came in and stooped over the bed and kissed me on the forehead.

When you get him to bed, go and ask Dilsey if she objects to my having a hot water bottle, Mother said. Tell her that if she does, I'll try to get along without it. Tell her I just want to know.

Yessum, Luster said. Come on. Get your pants off.

Quentin and Versh came in. Quentin had his face turned away. "What are you crying for." Caddy said.

"Hush." Dilsey said. "You all get undressed, now. You can go on home, Versh."

I got undressed and I looked at myself, and I began to cry. Hush, Luster said. Looking for them aint going to do no good. They're gone. You keep on like this, and we aint going have you no more birthday. He put my gown on. I hushed, and then Luster stopped, his head toward the window. Then he went to the window and looked out. He came back and took my arm. Here she come, he said. Be quiet, now. We went to the window and looked out. It came out of Quentin's window and climbed across into the tree. We watched the tree shaking. The shaking went down the tree, then it came out and we watched it go away across the grass. Then we couldn't see it. Come on, Luster said. There now. Hear them horns. You get in that bed while my foots behaves.

There were two beds. Quentin got in the other one. He turned his face to the wall. Dilsey put Jason in with him. Caddy took her dress off.

"Just look at your drawers." Dilsey said. "You better be glad your maw aint seen you."

"I already told on her." Jason said.

"I bound you would." Dilsey said.

"And see what you got by it." Caddy said. "Tattletale."

"What did I get by it." Jason said.

"Whyn't you get your nightie on." Dilsey said. She went and helped Caddy take off her bodice and drawers. "Just look at you." Dilsey said. She wadded the drawers and scrubbed Caddy behind with them. "It done soaked clean through onto you." she said. "But you wont get no bath this night. Here." She put Caddy's nightie on her and Caddy climbed into the bed and Dilsey went to the door and stood with her hand on the light. "You all be quiet now, you hear." she said.

"All right." Caddy said. "Mother's not coming in tonight." she said. "So we still have to mind me."

"Yes." Dilsey said. "Go to sleep, now."

"Mother's sick." Caddy said. "She and Damuddy are both sick."

"Hush." Dilsey said. "You go to sleep."

The room went black, except the door. Then the door went black. Caddy said, "Hush, Maury" putting her hand on me. So I stayed hushed. We could hear us. We could hear the dark.

It went away, and Father looked at us. He looked at Quentin and Jason, then he came and kissed Caddy and put his hand on my head.

"Is Mother very sick." Caddy said.

"No." Father said. "Are you going to take good care of Maury."

"Yes." Caddy said.

Father went to the door and looked at us again. Then the dark came back, and he stood black in the door, and then the door turned black again. Caddy held me and I could hear us all, and the darkness, and something I could smell. And then I could see the windows, where the trees were buzzing. Then the dark began to go in smooth, bright shapes, like it always does, even when Caddy says that I have been asleep.

June Second, 1910.

When the shadow of the sash appeared on the curtains it was between seven and eight oclock and then I was in time again, hearing the watch. It was Grandfather's and when Father gave it to me he said I give you the mausoleum of all hope and desire; it's rather excruciating-ly[1] apt that you will use it to gain the reducto absurdum[2] of all human experience which can fit your individual needs no better than it fitted his or his father's. I give it to you not that you may remember time, but that you might forget it now and then for a moment and not spend all your breath trying to conquer it. Because no battle is ever won he said. They are not even fought. The field only reveals to man his own folly and despair, and victory is an illusion of philosophers and fools.

It was propped against the collar box and I lay listening to it. Hearing it, that is. I dont suppose anybody ever deliberately listens to a watch or a clock. You dont have to. You can be oblivious to the

---

1. Faulkner uses the unusual hyphen to suggest a particular pronunciation, stressing the "ly."
2. A corruption of the Latin phrase *reductio ad absurdum*.

sound for a long while, then in a second of ticking it can create in
the mind unbroken the long diminishing parade of time you didn't
hear. Like Father said down the long and lonely light-rays you
might see Jesus walking, like. And the good Saint Francis that said
Little Sister Death, that never had a sister.[3]

Through the wall I heard Shreve's bed-springs and then his slippers on the floor hishing. I got up and went to the dresser and slid
my hand along it and touched the watch and turned it face-down
and went back to bed. But the shadow of the sash was still there
and I had learned to tell almost to the minute, so I'd have to turn
my back to it, feeling the eyes animals used to have in the back of
their heads when it was on top, itching. It's always the idle habits
you acquire which you will regret. Father said that. That Christ
was not crucified: he was worn away by a minute clicking of little
wheels. That had no sister.

And so as soon as I knew I couldn't see it, I began to wonder what
time it was. Father said that constant speculation regarding the
position of mechanical hands on an arbitrary dial which is a symp-
tom of mind-function. Excrement Father said like sweating. And I
saying All right. Wonder. Go on and wonder.

If it had been cloudy I could have looked at the window, thinking
what he said about idle habits. Thinking it would be nice for them
down at New London[4] if the weather held up like this. Why shouldn't
it? The month of brides, the voice that breathed[5] *She ran right out
of the mirror, out of the banked scent. Roses. Roses. Mr and Mrs Jason
Richmond Compson announce the marriage of.* Roses. Not virgins
like dogwood, milkweed. I said I have committed incest, Father I
said. Roses. Cunning and serene. If you attend Harvard one year, but
dont see the boat-race, there should be a refund. Let Jason have it.
Give Jason a year at Harvard.

Shreve stood in the door, putting his collar on, his glasses glinting rosily, as though he had washed them with his face. "You taking
a cut this morning?"

"Is it that late?"

He looked at his watch. "Bell in two minutes."

"I didn't know it was that late." He was still looking at the watch,
his mouth shaping. "I'll have to hustle. I cant stand another cut.
The dean told me last week——" He put the watch back into his
pocket. Then I quit talking.

"You'd better slip on your pants and run," he said. He went out.

---

3. As he was dying, Saint Francis of Assisi is reputed to have said, "Welcome my sister
   death."
4. Town in Connecticut where the annual Harvard-Yale boat race is held.
5. Later Quentin completes this phrase, "The voice that breathed o'er Eden." See the first
   line of "Holy Matrimony," a poem by John Keble. See also Genesis 3.8.

I got up and moved about, listening to him through the wall. He entered the sitting-room, toward the door.

"Aren't you ready yet?"

"Not yet. Run along. I'll make it."

He went out. The door closed. His feet went down the corridor. Then I could hear the watch again. I quit moving around and went to the window and drew the curtains aside and watched them running for chapel, the same ones fighting the same heaving coatsleeves, the same books and flapping collars flushing past like debris on a flood, and Spoade. Calling Shreve my husband. Ah let him alone, Shreve said, if he's got better sense than to chase after the little dirty sluts, whose business. In the South you are ashamed of being a virgin. Boys. Men. They lie about it. Because it means less to women, Father said. He said it was men invented virginity not women. Father said it's like death: only a state in which the others are left and I said, But to believe it doesn't matter and he said, That's what's so sad about anything: not only virginity and I said, Why couldn't it have been me and not her who is unvirgin and he said, That's why that's sad too; nothing is even worth the changing of it, and Shreve said if he's got better sense than to chase after the little dirty sluts and I said Did you ever have a sister? Did you? Did you?

Spoade was in the middle of them like a terrapin in a street full of scuttering dead leaves, his collar about his ears, moving at his customary unhurried walk. He was from South Carolina, a senior. It was his club's boast that he never ran for chapel and had never got there on time and had never been absent in four years and had never made either chapel or first lecture with a shirt on his back and socks on his feet. About ten oclock he'd come in Thompson's, get two cups of coffee, sit down and take his socks out of his pocket and remove his shoes and put them on while the coffee cooled. About noon you'd see him with a shirt and collar on, like anybody else. The others passed him running, but he never increased his pace at all. After a while the quad was empty.

A sparrow slanted across the sunlight, onto the window ledge, and cocked his head at me. His eye was round and bright. First he'd watch me with one eye, then flick! and it would be the other one, his throat pumping faster than any pulse. The hour began to strike. The sparrow quit swapping eyes and watched me steadily with the same one until the chimes ceased, as if he were listening too. Then he flicked off the ledge and was gone.

It was a while before the last stroke ceased vibrating. It stayed in the air, more felt than heard, for a long time. Like all the bells that ever rang still ringing in the long dying light-rays and Jesus and Saint Francis talking about his sister. Because if it were just to hell;

if that were all of it. Finished. If things just finished themselves. Nobody else there but her and me. If we could just have done something so dreadful that they would have fled hell except us. *I have committed incest I said Father it was I it was not Dalton Ames* And when he put Dalton Ames. Dalton Ames. Dalton Ames. When he put the pistol in my hand I didn't. That's why I didn't. He would be there and she would and I would. Dalton Ames, Dalton Ames. Dalton Ames. If we could have just done something so dreadful and Father said That's sad too people cannot do anything that dreadful they cannot do anything very dreadful at all they cannot even remember tomorrow what seemed dreadful today and I said, You can shirk all things and he said, Ah can you. And I will look down and see my murmuring bones and the deep water like wind, like a roof of wind, and after a long time they cannot distinguish even bones upon the lonely and inviolate sand. Until on the Day when He says Rise[6] only the flat-iron would come floating up. It's not when you realise that nothing can help you—religion, pride, anything— it's when you realise that you dont need any aid. Dalton Ames. Dalton Ames. Dalton Ames. If I could have been his mother lying with open body lifted laughing, holding his father with my hand refraining, seeing, watching him die before he lived. *One minute she was standing in the door*

I went to the dresser and took up the watch, with the face still down. I tapped the crystal on the corner of the dresser and caught the fragments of glass in my hand and put them into the ashtray and twisted the hands off and put them in the tray. The watch ticked on. I turned the face up, the blank dial with little wheels clicking and clicking behind it, not knowing any better. Jesus walking on Galilee and Washington not telling lies. Father brought back a watch-charm from the Saint Louis Fair[7] to Jason: a tiny opera glass into which you squinted with one eye and saw a skyscraper, a ferris wheel all spidery, Niagara Falls on a pinhead. There was a red smear on the dial. When I saw it my thumb began to smart. I put the watch down and went into Shreve's room and got the iodine and painted the cut. I cleaned the rest of the glass out of the rim with a towel.

I laid out two suits of underwear, with socks, shirts, collars and ties, and packed my trunk. I put in everything except my new suit and an old one and two pairs of shoes and two hats, and my books. I carried the books into the sitting-room and stacked them on the table, the ones I had brought from home and the ones *Father said it used to be a gentleman was known by his books; nowadays he is*

6. See Revelation 20.13.
7. Louisiana Purchase Exposition, 1904, held to celebrate the centennial of the Louisiana Purchase. This fair did much to popularize the automobile.

known by the ones he has not returned and locked the trunk and addressed it. The quarter hour sounded. I stopped and listened to it until the chimes ceased.

I bathed and shaved. The water made my finger smart a little, so I painted it again. I put on my new suit and put my watch on and packed the other suit and the accessories and my razor and brushes in my hand bag, and folded the trunk key into a sheet of paper and put it in an envelope and addressed it to Father, and wrote the two notes and sealed them.

The shadow hadn't quite cleared the stoop. I stopped inside the door, watching the shadow move. It moved almost perceptibly, creeping back inside the door, driving the shadow back into the door. *Only she was running already when I heard it. In the mirror she was running before I knew what it was. That quick her train caught up over her arm she ran out of the mirror like a cloud, her veil swirling in long glints her heels brittle and fast clutching her dress onto her shoulder with the other hand, running out of the mirror the smells roses roses the voice that breathed o'er Eden. Then she was across the porch I couldn't hear her heels then in the moonlight like a cloud, the floating shadow of the veil running across the grass, into the bellowing. She ran out of her dress, clutching her bridal, running into the bellowing where T. P. in the dew Whooey Sassprilluh Benjy under the box bellowing. Father had a V-shaped silver cuirass on his running chest*

Shreve said, 'Well, you didn't. . . . Is it a wedding or a wake?"

"I couldn't make it," I said.

"Not with all that primping. What's the matter? You think this was Sunday?'

"I reckon the police wont get me for wearing my new suit one time," I said.

"I was thinking about the Square students. They'll think you go to Harvard. Have you got too proud to attend classes too?"

"I'm going to eat first." The shadow on the stoop was gone. I stepped into sunlight, finding my shadow again. I walked down the steps just ahead of it. The half hour went. Then the chimes ceased and died away.

Deacon wasn't at the postoffice either. I stamped the two envelopes and mailed the one to Father and put Shreve's in my inside pocket, and then I remembered where I had last seen the Deacon. It was on Decoration Day, in a G.A.R.[8] uniform, in the middle of the parade. If you waited long enough on any corner you would see him in whatever parade came along. The one before was on Columbus'

---

8. Grand Army of the Republic, a veterans organization formed at the end of the Civil War. *Decoration Day*: a day set apart for decorating the graves of soldiers who died in the Civil War; formal celebration began May 30, 1868, as Memorial Day.

or Garibaldi's[9] or somebody's birthday. He was in the Street Sweepers' section,[1] in a stovepipe hat, carrying a two inch Italian flag, smoking a cigar among the brooms and scoops. But the last time was the G.A.R. one, because Shreve said:

"There now. Just look at what your grandpa did to that poor old nigger."

"Yes," I said. "Now he can spend day after day marching in parades. If it hadn't been for my grandfather, he'd have to work like whitefolks."

I didn't see him anywhere. But I never knew even a working nigger that you could find when you wanted him, let alone one that lived off the fat of the land. A car came along. I went over to town and went to Parker's and had a good breakfast. While I was eating I heard a clock strike the hour. But then I suppose it takes at least one hour to lose time in, who has been longer than history getting into the mechanical progression of it.

When I finished breakfast I bought a cigar. The girl said a fifty cent one was the best, so I took one and lit it and went out to the street. I stood there and took a couple of puffs, then I held it in my hand and went on toward the corner. I passed a jeweller's window, but I looked away in time. At the corner two bootblacks caught me, one on either side, shrill and raucous, like blackbirds. I gave the cigar to one of them, and the other one a nickel. Then they let me alone. The one with the cigar was trying to sell it to the other for the nickel.

There was a clock, high up in the sun, and I thought about how, when you dont want to do a thing, your body will try to trick you into doing it, sort of unawares. I could feel the muscles in the back of my neck, and then I could hear my watch ticking away in my pocket and after a while I had all the other sounds shut away, leaving only the watch in my pocket. I turned back up the street, to the window. He was working at the table behind the window. He was going bald. There was a glass in his eye—a metal tube screwed into his face. I went in.

The place was full of ticking, like crickets in September grass, and I could hear a big clock on the wall above his head. He looked up, his eye big and blurred and rushing beyond the glass. I took mine out and handed it to him.

"I broke my watch."

He flipped it over in his hand. "I should say you have. You must have stepped on it."

9. Giuseppe Garibaldi (1807–1882) was a freedom fighter, general, and nationalist leader in Italy.
1. The section of the parade where street sweepers walked to sweep up after the horses.

"Yes, sir. I knocked it off the dresser and stepped on it in the dark. It's still running though."

He pried the back open and squinted into it. "Seems to be all right. I cant tell until I go over it, though. I'll go into it this afternoon."

"I'll bring it back later," I said. "Would you mind telling me if any of those watches in the window are right?"

He held my watch on his palm and looked up at me with his blurred rushing eye.

"I made a bet with a fellow," I said. "And I forgot my glasses this morning."

"Why, all right," he said. He laid the watch down and half rose on his stool and looked over the barrier. Then he glanced up at the wall. "It's twen——"

"Dont tell me," I said, "please sir. Just tell me if any of them are right."

He looked at me again. He sat back on the stool and pushed the glass up onto his forehead. It left a red circle around his eye and when it was gone his whole face looked naked. "What're you celebrating today?" he said. "That boat race aint until next week, is it?"

"No, sir. This is just a private celebration. Birthday. Are any of them right?"

"No. But they haven't been regulated and set yet. If you're thinking of buying one of them——"

"No, sir. I dont need a watch. We have a clock in our sitting room. I'll have this one fixed when I do." I reached my hand.

"Better leave it now."

"I'll bring it back later." He gave me the watch. I put it in my pocket. I couldn't hear it now, above all the others. "I'm much obliged to you. I hope I haven't taken up your time."

"That's all right. Bring it in when you are ready. And you better put off this celebration until after we win that boat race."

"Yes, sir. I reckon I had."

I went out, shutting the door upon the ticking. I looked back into the window. He was watching me across the barrier. There were about a dozen watches in the window, a dozen different hours and each with the same assertive and contradictory assurance that mine had, without any hands at all. Contradicting one another. I could hear mine, ticking away inside my pocket, even though nobody could see it, even though it could tell nothing if anyone could.

And so I told myself to take that one. Because Father said clocks slay time. He said time is dead as long as it is being clicked off by little wheels; only when the clock stops does time come to life. The hands were extended, slightly off the horizontal at a faint angle, like a gull tilting into the wind. Holding all I used to be sorry about

like the new moon holding water,[2] niggers say. The jeweller was
working again, bent over his bench, the tube tunnelled into his face.
His hair was parted in the center. The part ran up into the bald
spot, like a drained marsh in December.

I saw the hardware store from across the street. I didn't know you
bought flat-irons by the pound.

"Maybe you want a tailor's goose,"[3] the clerk said. "They weigh
ten pounds." Only they were bigger than I thought. So I got two six-
pound little ones, because they would look like a pair of shoes wrapped
up. They felt heavy enough together, but I thought again how Father
had said about the reducto absurdum of human experience, thinking
how the only opportunity I seemed to have for the application of
Harvard. Maybe by next year; thinking maybe it takes two years in
school to learn to do that properly.

But they felt heavy enough in the air. A car came. I got on. I
didn't see the placard on the front. It was full, mostly prosperous
looking people reading newspapers. The only vacant seat was
beside a nigger. He wore a derby and shined shoes and he was holding a dead cigar stub. I used to think that a Southerner had to be
always conscious of niggers. I thought that Northerners would
expect him to. When I first came East I kept thinking You've got to
remember to think of them as colored people not niggers, and if it
hadn't happened that I wasn't thrown with many of them, I'd have
wasted a lot of time and trouble before I learned that the best way
to take all people, black or white, is to take them for what they
think they are, then leave them alone. That was when I realised
that a nigger is not a person so much as a form of behavior; a sort of
obverse reflection of the white people he lives among. But I thought
at first that I ought to miss having a lot of them around me because
I thought that Northerners thought I did, but I didn't know that I
really had missed Roskus and Dilsey and them until that morning
in Virginia. The train was stopped when I waked and I raised the
shade and looked out. The car was blocking a road crossing, where
two white fences came down a hill and then sprayed outward and
downward like part of the skeleton of a horn, and there was a nigger on a mule in the middle of the stiff ruts, waiting for the train to
move. How long he had been there I didn't know, but he sat strad-
dle of the mule, his head wrapped in a piece of blanket, as if they
had been built there with the fence and the road, or with the hill,
carved out of the hill itself, like a sign put there saying You are
home again. He didn't have a saddle and his feet dangled almost to
the ground. The mule looked like a rabbit. I raised the window.

2. If the horns of the crescent moon are turned up so that they will "hold water," the
weather will be dry; otherwise, it will pour out water, and there will be rain.
3. A tailor's pressing iron, which holds hot water.

"Hey, Uncle," I said. "Is this the way?"

"Suh?" He looked at me, then he loosened the blanket and lifted it away from his ear.

"Christmas gift!" I said.

"Sho comin, boss. You done caught me, aint you."

"I'll let you off this time."[4] I dragged my pants out of the little hammock and got a quarter out. "But look out next time. I'll be coming back through here two days after New Year, and look out then." I threw the quarter out the window. "Buy yourself some Santy Claus."

"Yes, suh," he said. He got down and picked up the quarter and rubbed it on his leg. "Thanky, young marster. Thanky." Then the train began to move. I leaned out the window, into the cold air, looking back. He stood there beside the gaunt rabbit of a mule, the two of them shabby and motionless and unimpatient. The train swung around the curve, the engine puffing with short, heavy blasts, and they passed smoothly from sight that way, with that quality about them of shabby and timeless patience, of static serenity: that blending of childlike and ready incompetence and paradoxical reliability that tends and protects them it loves out of all reason and robs them steadily and evades responsibility and obligations by means too barefaced to be called subterfuge even and is taken in theft or evasion with only that frank and spontaneous admiration for the victor which a gentleman feels for anyone who beats him in a fair contest, and withal a fond and unflagging tolerance for whitefolks' vagaries like that of a grandparent for unpredictable and troublesome children, which I had forgotten. And all that day, while the train wound through rushing gaps and along ledges where movement was only a laboring sound of the exhaust and groaning wheels and the eternal mountains stood fading into the thick sky, I thought of home, of the bleak station and the mud and the niggers and country folks thronging slowly about the square, with toy monkeys and wagons and candy in sacks and roman candles sticking out, and my insides would move like they used to do in school when the bell rang.

I wouldn't begin counting until the clock struck three. Then I would begin, counting to sixty and folding down one finger and thinking of the other fourteen fingers waiting to be folded down, or thirteen or twelve or eight or seven, until all of a sudden I'd realise silence and the unwinking minds, and I'd say "Ma'am?" "Your name is Quentin, isn't it?" Miss Laura would say. Then more silence and the cruel unwinking minds and hands jerking into the silence. "Tell

---

4. On Christmas Day, or during the following week, custom held that the first person to say "Christmas gift" was entitled to a small gift of money or food.

Quentin who discovered the Mississippi River, Henry." "DeSoto."
Then the minds would go away, and after a while I'd be afraid I had
gotten behind and I'd count fast and fold down another finger, then
I'd be afraid I was going too fast and I'd slow up, then I'd get afraid
and count fast again. So I never could come out even with the bell,
and the released surging of feet moving already, feeling earth in the
scuffed floor, and the day like a pane of glass struck a light, sharp
blow, and my insides would move, sitting still. *Moving sitting still.*
My bowels moved for thee. One minute she was standing in the door.
Benjy. Bellowing. Benjamin the child of mine old age[5] bellowing.
Caddy! Caddy!

I'm going to run away. He began to cry she went and touched him.
Hush. I'm not going to. Hush. He hushed. Dilsey.

He smell what you tell him when he want to. Dont have to listen
nor talk.

Can he smell that new name they give him? Can he smell bad
luck?

What he want to worry about luck for? Luck cant do him no hurt.

What they change his name for then if aint trying to help his luck?
The car stopped, started, stopped again. Below the window I
watched the crowns of people's heads passing beneath new straw
hats not yet unbleached. There were women in the car now, with
market baskets, and men in work-clothes were beginning to out-
number the shined shoes and collars.

The nigger touched my knee. "Pardon me," he said. I swung my
legs out and let him pass. We were going beside a blank wall, the
sound clattering back into the car, at the women with market baskets on their knees and a man in a stained hat with a pipe stuck in
the band. I could smell water, and in a break in the wall I saw a
glint of water and two masts, and a gull motionless in midair, like
on an invisible wire between the masts, and I raised my hand and
through my coat touched the letters I had written. When the car
stopped I got off.

The bridge was open to let a schooner through. She was in tow,
the tug nudging along under her quarter, trailing smoke, but the
ship herself was like she was moving without visible means. A man
naked to the waist was coiling down a line on the fo'c's'le head. His
body was burned the color of leaf tobacco. Another man in a straw
hat without any crown was at the wheel. The ship went through the
bridge, moving under bare poles like a ghost in broad day, with
three gulls hovering above the stern like toys on invisible wires.

When it closed I crossed to the other side and leaned on the rail
above the boathouses. The float was empty and the doors were

5. See Genesis 21.7.

closed. Crew just pulled in the late afternoon now, resting up before. The shadow of the bridge, the tiers of railing, my shadow leaning flat upon the water, so easily had I tricked it that would not quit me. At least fifty feet it was, and if I only had something to blot it into the water, holding it until it was drowned, the shadow of the package like two shoes wrapped up lying on the water. Niggers say a drowned man's shadow was watching for him in the water all the time. It twinkled and glinted, like breathing, the float slow like breathing too, and debris half submerged, healing out to the sea and the caverns and the grottoes of the sea. The displacement of water is equal to the something of something.[6] Reducto absurdum of all human experience, and two six-pound flat-irons weigh more than one tailor's goose. What a sinful waste Dilsey would say. Benjy knew it when Damuddy died. He cried. *He smell hit. He smell hit.*

The tug came back downstream, the water shearing in long rolling cylinders, rocking the float at last with the echo of passage, the float lurching onto the rolling cylinder with a plopping sound and a long jarring noise as the door rolled back and two men emerged, carrying a shell. They set it in the water and a moment later Bland came out, with the sculls. He wore flannels, a gray jacket and a stiff straw hat. Either he or his mother had read somewhere that Oxford students pulled in flannels and stiff hats, so early one March they bought Gerald a one pair shell and in his flannels and stiff hat he went on the river. The folks at the boathouse threatened to call a policeman, but he went anyway. His mother came down in a hired auto, in a fur suit like an arctic explorer's, and saw him off in a twenty-five mile wind and a steady drove of ice floes like dirty sheep. Ever since then I have believed that God is not only a gentleman and a sport; he is a Kentuckian too. When he sailed away she made a detour and came down to the river again and drove along parallel with him, the car in low gear. They said you couldn't have told they'd ever seen one another before, like a King and Queen, not even looking at one another, just moving side by side across Massachusetts on parallel courses like a couple of planets.

He got in and pulled away. He pulled pretty well now. He ought to. They said his mother tried to make him give rowing up and do something else the rest of his class couldn't or wouldn't do, but for once he was stubborn. If you could call it stubbornness, sitting in his attitudes of princely boredom, with his curly yellow hair and his violet eyes and his eyelashes and his New York clothes, while his mamma was telling us about Gerald's horses and Gerald's niggers and

6. While bathing, Archimedes of Syracuse (287–212 B.C.) noticed that he displaced water equal in volume to his own body; he formulated the principle that when a body floats in a liquid, its weight is equal to the weight of liquid displaced, and that when it is immersed, its weight is diminished by that amount.

Gerald's women. Husbands and fathers in Kentucky must have been awful glad when she carried Gerald off to Cambridge. She had an apartment over in town, and Gerald had one there too, besides his rooms in college. She approved of Gerald associating with me because I at least revealed a blundering sense of noblesse oblige by getting myself born below Mason and Dixon, and a few others whose Geography met the requirements (minimum). Forgave, at least. Or condoned. But since she met Spoade coming out of chapel one He said she couldn't be a lady no lady would be out at that hour of the night she never had been able to forgive him for having five names, including that of a present English ducal house. I'm sure she solaced herself by being convinced that some misfit Maingault or Mortemar[7] had got mixed up with the lodge-keeper's daughter. Which was quite probable, whether she invented it or not. Spoade was the world's champion sitter-around, no holds barred and gouging discretionary.

The shell was a speck now, the oars catching the sun in spaced glints, as if the hull were winking itself along him along.[8] *Did you ever have a sister? No but they're all bitches. Did you ever have a sister? One minute she was. Bitches. Not bitch one minute she stood in the door* Dalton Ames. Dalton Ames. Dalton Shirts. I thought all the time they were khaki, army issue khaki, until I saw they were of heavy Chinese silk or finest flannel because they made his face so brown his eyes so blue. Dalton Ames. It just missed gentility. Theatrical fixture. Just papier-mache, then touch. Oh. Asbestos. Not quite bronze. *But wont see him at the house.*

Caddy's a woman too remember. She must do things for women's reasons too.

Why wont you bring him to the house, Caddy? Why must you do like nigger women do in the pasture the ditches the dark woods hot hidden furious in the dark woods.

And after a while I had been hearing my watch for some time and I could feel the letters crackle through my coat, against the railing, and I leaned on the railing, watching my shadow, how I had tricked it. I moved along the rail, but my suit was dark too and I could wipe my hands, watching my shadow, how I had tricked it. I walked it into the shadow of the quai. Then I went east.

Harvard my Harvard boy Harvard harvard That pimple-faced infant she met at the field-meet with colored ribbons. Skulking along the fence trying to whistle her out like a puppy. Because they

---

7. Names for European aristocracy.
8. Noel Polk describes his restoration of "along him" to "along" as an important way of accenting "the contrast between Quentin's obsession with drowning in the peaceful grottoes of the sea and the extroverted Gerald Bland's capacity to glide smoothly along the water's surface."

couldn't cajole him into the diningroom Mother believed he had
some sort of spell he was going to cast on her when he got her
alone. Yet any blackguard *He was lying beside the box under the
window bellowing* that could drive up in a limousine with a flower
in his buttonhole. *Harvard. Quentin this is Herbert. My Harvard
boy. Herbert will be a big brother has already promised Jason*

Hearty, celluloid like a drummer.[9] Face full of teeth white but
not smiling. *I've heard of him up there.* All teeth but not smiling.
You going to drive?

Get in Quentin.

You going to drive.

*It's her car aren't you proud of your little sister owns first auto in
town Herbert his present. Louis has been giving her lessons every
morning didn't you get my letter* Mr and Mrs Jason Richmond
Compson announce the marriage of their daughter Candace to Mr
Sydney Herbert Head on the twenty-fifth of April one thousand
nine hundred and ten at Jefferson Mississippi. At home after the
first of August number Something Something Avenue South Bend
Indiana. Shreve said Aren't you even going to open it? *Three days.
Times. Mr and Mrs Jason Richmond Compson* Young Lochinvar[1]
rode out of the west a little too soon, didn't he?

I'm from the south. You're funny, aren't you.

O yes I knew it was somewhere in the country.

You're funny, aren't you. You ought to join the circus.

I did. That's how I ruined my eyes watering the elephant's fleas.
Three times These country girls. You cant ever tell about them,
can you. Well, any way Byron never had his wish,[2] thank God. *But
not hit a man in glasses* Aren't you even going to open it? *It lay on
the table a candle burning at each corner upon the envelope tied in
a soiled pink garter two artificial flowers. Not hit a man in glasses.*

Country people poor things they never saw an auto before lots of
them honk the horn Candace so *She wouldn't look at me* they'll
get out of the way *wouldn't look at me* your father wouldn't like it
if you were to injure one of them I'll declare your father will simply
have to get an auto now I'm almost sorry you brought it down Herbert I've enjoyed it so much of course there's the carriage but so
often when I'd like to go out Mr Compson has the darkies doing
something it would be worth my head to interrupt he insists that
Roskus is at my call all the time but I know what that means I know

9. Traveling salesman.
1. See Sir Walter Scott, "Marmion," which was once used in many elementary school-
   books. In the fifth canto, Lochinvar, the hero, rescues his fair Ellen, who is about to be
   married to a "laggard in love and a dastard in war." Lochinvar arrives at the bridal
   feast, claims the lady, swings her onto his horse, and rides off with her.
2. Contrary to Quentin's remark, most scholars now believe it probable that the relationship between Byron and his half-sister, Augusta Leigh, was consummated.

how often people make promises just to satisfy their consciences are you going to treat my little baby girl that way Herbert but I know you wont Herbert has spoiled us all to death Quentin did I write you that he is going to take Jason into his bank when Jason finishes high school Jason will make a splendid banker he is the only one of my children with any practical sense you can thank me for that he takes after my people the others are all Compson *Jason furnished the flour. They made kites on the back porch and sold them for a nickel a piece, he and the Patterson boy. Jason was treasurer.*

There was no nigger in this car, and the hats unbleached as yet flowing past under the window. Going to Harvard. We have sold Benjy's *He lay on the ground under the window, bellowing. We have sold Benjy's pasture so that Quentin may go to Harvard* a brother to you. Your little brother.

You should have a car it's done you no end of good dont you think so Quentin I call him Quentin at once you see I have heard so much about him from Candace.

Why shouldn't you I want my boys to be more than friends yes Candace and Quentin more than friends *Father I have committed* what a pity you had no brother or sister *No sister no sister had no sister* Dont ask Quentin he and Mr Compson both feel a little insulted when I am strong enough to come down to the table I am going on nerve now I'll pay for it after it's all over and you have taken my little daughter away from me *My little sister had no.*[3] *If I could say Mother. Mother*

Unless I do what I am tempted to and take you instead I dont think Mr Compson could overtake the car.

Ah Herbert Candace do you hear that *She wouldn't look at me soft stubborn jaw-angle not back-looking* You needn't be jealous though it's just an old woman he's flattering a grown married daughter I cant believe it.

Nonsense you look like a girl you are lots younger than Candace color in your cheeks like a girl *A face reproachful tearful an odor of camphor and of tears a voice weeping steadily and softly beyond the twilit door the twilight-colored smell of honeysuckle. Bringing empty trunks down the attic stairs they sounded like coffins French Lick.*[4] *Found not death at the salt lick*

Hats not unbleached and not hats. In three years I can not wear a hat. I could not. Was. Will there be hats then since I was not and not Harvard then. Where the best of thought Father said clings like dead ivy vines upon old dead brick. Not Harvard then. Not to me, anyway. Again. Sadder than was. Again. Saddest of all. Again.

---

3. See Song of Solomon 8.8: "We have a little sister, and she hath no breasts: what shall we do for our sister in the day when she shall be spoken for?"
4. Resort town in southern Indiana.

Spoade had a shirt on; then it must be. When I can see my shadow again if not careful that I tricked into the water shall tread again upon my impervious shadow.[5] But no sister. I wouldn't have done it. *I wont have my daughter spied on* I wouldn't have.

How can I control any of them when you have always taught them to have no respect for me and my wishes I know you look down on my people but is that any reason for teaching my children my own children I suffered for to have no respect Trampling my shadow's bones into the concrete with hard heels and then I was hearing the watch, and I touched the letters through my coat.

I will not have my daughter spied on by you or Quentin or anybody no matter what you think she has done

At least you agree there is reason for having her watched

I wouldn't have I wouldn't have. *I know you wouldn't I didn't mean to speak so sharply but women have no respect for each other for themselves*

But why did she The chimes began as I stepped on my shadow, but it was the quarter hour. The Deacon wasn't in sight anywhere. *think I would have could have*

She didn't mean that that's the way women do things it's because she loves Caddy

The street lamps would go down the hill then rise toward town I walked upon the belly of my shadow. I could extend my hand beyond it. *feeling Father behind me beyond the rasping darkness of summer and August the street lamps* Father and I protect women from one another from themselves our women *Women are like that they dont acquire knowledge of people we are for that they are just born with a practical fertility of suspicion that makes a crop every so often and usually right they have an affinity for evil for supplying whatever the evil lacks in itself for drawing it about them instinctively as you do bed-clothing in slumber fertilising the mind for it until the evil has served its purpose whether it ever existed or no* He was coming along between a couple of freshmen. He hadn't quite recovered from the parade, for he gave me a salute, a very superior-officerish kind.

"I want to see you a minute," I said, stopping.

"See me? All right. See you again, fellows," he said, stopping and turning back; "glad to have chatted with you." That was the Deacon, all over. Talk about your natural psychologists. They said he hadn't missed a train at the beginning of school in forty years, and that he could pick out a Southerner with one glance. He never missed, and once he had heard you speak, he could name your state. He had a

---

5. In superstition, if you step on your own shadow, you will die.

regular uniform he met trains in, a sort of Uncle Tom's cabin outfit, patches and all.

"Yes, suh. Right dis way, young marster, hyer we is," taking your bags. "Hyer, boy, come hyer and git dese grips." Whereupon a moving mountain of luggage would edge up, revealing a white boy of about fifteen, and the Deacon would hang another bag on him somehow and drive him off. "Now, den, dont you drap hit. Yes, suh, young marster, jes give de old nigger yo room number, and hit'll be done got cold dar when you arrives."

From then on until he had you completely subjugated he was always in or out of your room, ubiquitous and garrulous, though his manner gradually moved northward as his raiment improved, until at last when he had bled you until you began to learn better he was calling you Quentin or whatever, and when you saw him next he'd be wearing a cast-off Brooks suit and a hat with a Princeton club I forget which band that someone had given him and which he was pleasantly and unshakably convinced was a part of Abe Lincoln's military sash. Someone spread the story years ago, when he first appeared around college from wherever he came from, that he was a graduate of the divinity school. And when he came to understand what it meant he was so taken with it that he began to retail the story himself, until at last he must have come to believe he really had. Anyway he related long pointless anecdotes of his undergraduate days, speaking familiarly of dead and departed professors by their first names, usually incorrect ones. But he had been guide mentor and friend to unnumbered crops of innocent and lonely freshmen, and I suppose that with all his petty chicanery and hypocrisy he stank no higher in heaven's nostrils than any other.

"Haven't seen you in three-four days," he said, staring at me from his still military aura. "You been sick?"

"No. I've been all right. Working, I reckon. I've seen you, though."

"Yes?"

"In the parade the other day."

"Oh, that. Yes, I was there. I dont care nothing about that sort of thing, you understand, but the boys likes to have me with them, the vet'runs does. Ladies wants all the old vet'runs to turn out, you know. So I has to oblige them."

"And on that Wop holiday too," I said. "You were obliging the W. C. T. U.[6] then, I reckon."

"That? I was doing that for my son-in-law. He aims to get a job on the city forces. Street cleaner. I tells him all he wants is a broom to sleep on. You saw me, did you?"

6. Women's Christian Temperance Union. *Wop holiday:* Quentin's term for Columbus Day.

"Both times. Yes."

"I mean, in uniform. How'd I look?"

"You looked fine. You looked better than any of them. They ought to make you a general, Deacon."

He touched my arm, lightly, his hand that worn, gentle quality of niggers' hands. "Listen. This aint for outside talking. I dont mind telling you because you and me's the same folks, come long and short." He leaned a little to me, speaking rapidly, his eyes not looking at me. "I've got strings out, right now. Wait till next year. Just wait. Then see where I'm marching. I wont need to tell you how I'm fixing it; I say, just wait and see, my boy." He looked at me now and clapped me lightly on the shoulder and rocked back on his heels, nodding at me. "Yes, sir. I didn't turn Democrat three years ago for nothing. My son-in-law on the city; me——Yes, sir. If just turning Democrat'll make that son of a bitch go to work. . . . And me: just you stand on that corner yonder a year from two days ago, and see."

"I hope so. You deserve it, Deacon. And while I think about it——" I took the letter from my pocket. "Take this around to my room tomorrow and give it to Shreve. He'll have something for you. But not till tomorrow, mind."

He took the letter and examined it. "It's sealed up."

"Yes. And it's written inside, Not good until tomorrow."

"H'm," he said. He looked at the envelope, his mouth pursed. "Something for me, you say?"

"Yes. A present I'm making you."

He was looking at me now, the envelope white in his black hand, in the sun. His eyes were soft and irisless and brown, and suddenly I saw Roskus watching me from behind all his whitefolks' claptrap of uniforms and politics and Harvard manner, diffident, secret, inarticulate and sad. "You aint playing a joke on the old nigger, is you?"

"You know I'm not. Did any Southerner ever play a joke on you?"

"You're right. They're fine folks. But you cant live with them."

"Did you ever try?" I said. But Roskus was gone. Once more he was that self he had long since taught himself to wear in the world's eye, pompous, spurious, not quite gross.

"I'll confer to your wishes, my boy."

"Not until tomorrow, remember."

"Sure," he said; "understood, my boy. Well——"

"I hope——" I said. He looked down at me, benignant, profound. Suddenly I held out my hand and we shook, he gravely, from the pompous height of his municipal and military dream. "You're a good fellow, Deacon. I hope. . . . You've helped a lot of young fellows, here and there."

"I've tried to treat all folks right," he said. "I draw no petty social lines. A man to me is a man, wherever I find him."

"I hope you'll always find as many friends as you've made."

"Young fellows. I get along with them. They dont forget me, neither," he said, waving the envelope. He put it into his pocket and
buttoned his coat. "Yes, sir," he said. "I've had good friends."

The chimes began again, the half hour. I stood in the belly of my
shadow and listened to the strokes spaced and tranquil along the
sunlight, among the thin, still little leaves. Spaced and peaceful and
serene, with that quality of autumn always in bells even in the month
of brides. *Lying on the ground under the window bellowing*   He took
one look at her and knew. Out of the mouths of babes.[7] *The street
lamps*   The chimes ceased. I went back to the postoffice, treading
my shadow into pavement. *go down the hill then they rise toward town
like lanterns hung one above another on a wall.* Father said because
she loves Caddy she loves people through their shortcomings. Uncle
Maury straddling his legs before the fire must remove one hand long
enough to drink Christmas. Jason ran on, his hands in his pockets
fell down and lay there like a trussed fowl until Versh set him up.
*Whyn't you keep them hands outen your pockets when you running
you could stand up then*   Rolling his head in the cradle rolling it flat
across the back. Caddy told Jason and Versh that the reason Uncle
Maury didn't work was that he used to roll his head in the cradle
when he was little.

Shreve was coming up the walk, shambling, fatly earnest, his
glasses glinting beneth the running leaves like little pools.

"I gave Deacon a note for some things. I may not be in this afternoon, so dont you let him have anything until tomorrow, will you?

"All right." He looked at me. "Say, what're you doing today, anyhow?
All dressed up and mooning around like the prologue to a suttee.
Did you go to Psychology this morning?"

"I'm not doing anything. Not until tomorrow, now."

"What's that you got there?"

"Nothing. Pair of shoes I had half-soled. Not until tomorrow, you
hear?"

"Sure. All right. Oh, by the way, did you get a letter off the table
this morning?"

"No."

"It's there. From Semiramis.[8] Chauffeur brought it before ten
oclock."

"All right. I'll get it. Wonder what she wants now."

"Another band recital, I guess. Tumpty ta ta Gerald blah. 'A little
louder on the drum, Quentin'. God, I'm glad I'm not a gentleman."
He went on, nursing a book, a little shapeless, fatly intent. *The*

7. See Matthew 21.16 and Psalms 8.2.
8. A famous Assyrian queen.

street lamps do you think so because one of our forefathers was a governor and three were generals and Mother's werent

any live man is better than any dead man but no live or dead man is very much better than any other live or dead man *Done in Mother's mind though. Finished. Finished. Then we were all poisoned* you are confusing sin and morality women dont do that your mother is thinking of morality whether it be sin or not has not occurred to her

Jason I must go away you keep the others I'll take Jason and go where nobody knows us so he'll have a chance to grow up and forget all this the others dont love me they have never loved anything with that streak of Compson selfishness and false pride Jason was the only one my heart went out to without dread

nonsense Jason is all right I was thinking that as soon as you feel better you and Caddy might go up to French Lick

and leave Jason here with nobody but you and the darkies

she will forget him then all the talk will die away *found not death at the salt licks*

maybe I could find a husband for her *not death at the salt licks*

The car came up and stopped. The bells were still ringing the half hour. I got on and it went on again, blotting the half hour. No: the three quarters. Then it would be ten minutes anyway. To leave Harvard *your mother's dream for sold Benjy's pasture for*

what have I done to have been given children like these Benjamin was punishment enough and now for her to have no more regard for me her own mother I've suffered for her dreamed and planned and sacrificed I went down into the valley[9] yet never since she opened her eyes has she given me one unselfish thought at times I look at her I wonder if she can be my child except Jason he has never given me one moment's sorrow since I first held him in my arms I knew then that he was to be my joy and my salvation[1] I thought that Benjamin was punishment enough for any sins I have committed I thought he was my punishment for putting aside my pride and marrying a man who held himself above me I dont complain I loved him above all of them because of it because my duty though Jason pulling at my heart all the while but I see now that I have not suffered enough I see now that I must pay for your sins as well as mine what have you done what sins have your high and mighty people visited upon me but you'll take up for them you always have found excuses for your own blood only Jason can do wrong because he is more Bascomb than Compson while your own daughter my little daughter my baby girl she is she is no better than

9. See Psalms 23.4.
1. See Psalms 51.2.

that when I was a girl I was unfortunate I was only a Bascomb I was taught that there is no halfway ground that a woman is either a lady or not but I never dreamed when I held her in my arms that any daughter of mine could let herself dont you know I can look at her eyes and tell you may think she'd tell you but she doesn't tell things she is secretive you dont know her I know things she's done that I'd die before I'd have you know that's it go on criticise Jason accuse me of setting him to watch her as if it were a crime while your own daughter can I know you dont love him that you wish to believe faults against him you never have yes ridicule him as you always have Maury you cannot hurt me any more than your children already have and then I'll be gone and Jason with no one to love him shield him from this I look at him every day dreading to see this Compson blood beginning to show in him at last with his sister slipping out to see what do you call it then have you ever laid eyes on him will you even let me try to find out who he is it's not for myself I couldn't bear to see him it's for your sake to protect you but who can fight against bad blood you wont let me try we are to sit back with our hands folded while she not only drags your name in the dirt but corrupts the very air your children breathe Jason you must let me go away I cannot stand it let me have Jason and you keep the others they're not my flesh and blood like he is strangers nothing of mine and I am afraid of them I can take Jason and go where we are not known I'll go down on my knees and pray for the absolution of my sins that he may escape this curse try to forget that the others ever were

If that was the three quarters, not over ten minutes now. One car had just left, and people were already waiting for the next one. I asked, but he didn't know whether another one would leave before noon or not because you'd think that interurbans. So the first one was another trolley. I got on. You can feel noon. I wonder if even miners in the bowels of the earth. That's why whistles: because people that sweat, and if just far enough from sweat you wont hear whistles and in eight minutes you should be that far from sweat in Boston. Father said a man is the sum of his misfortunes. One day you'd think misfortune would get tired, but then time is your misfortune Father said. A gull on an invisible wire attached through space dragged. You carry the symbol of your frustration into eternity. Then the wings are bigger Father said only who can play a harp.

I could hear my watch whenever the car stopped, but not often they were already eating *Who would play a* Eating the business of eating inside of you space too space and time confused Stomach saying noon brain saying eat oclock All right I wonder what time it is what of it. People were getting out. The trolley didn't stop so often now, emptied by eating.

Then it was past. I got off and stood in my shadow and after a while a car came along and I got on and went back to the interurban station. There was a car ready to leave, and I found a seat next the window and it started and I watched it sort of frazzle out into slack tide flats, and then trees. Now and then I saw the river and I thought how nice it would be for them down at New London if the weather and Gerald's shell going solemnly up the glinting forenoon and I wondered what the old woman would be wanting now, sending me a note before ten oclock in the morning. What picture of Gerald I to be one of the *Dalton Ames oh asbestos Quentin has shot* background. Something with girls in it. Women do have *always his voice above the gabble voice that breathed* an affinity for evil, for believing that no woman is to be trusted, but that some men are too innocent to protect themselves. Plain girls. Remote cousins and family friends whom mere acquaintanceship invested with a sort of blood obligation noblesse oblige. And she sitting there telling us before their faces what a shame it was that Gerald should have all the family looks because a man didn't need it, was better off without it but without it a girl was simply lost. Telling us about Gerald's women in a *Quentin has shot Herbert he shot his voice through the floor of Caddy's room* tone of smug approbation. "When he was seventeen I said to him one day 'What a shame that you should have a mouth like that it should be on a girl's face' and can you imagine. *the curtains leaning in on the twilight upon the odor of the apple tree her head against the twilight her arms behind her head kimono-winged the voice that breathed o'er eden clothes upon the bed by the nose seen above the apple* what he said? just seventeen, mind. 'Mother' he said 'it often is'." And him sitting there in attitudes regal watching two or three of them through his eyelashes. They gushed like swallows swooping his eyelashes. Shreve said he always had *Are you going to look after Benjy and Father*

The less you say about Benjy and Father the better when have you ever considered them Caddy

Promise

You needn't worry about them you're getting out in good shape

Promise I'm sick you'll have to promise wondered who invented that joke but then he always had considered Mrs Bland a remarkably preserved woman he said she was grooming Gerald to seduce a duchess sometime. She called Shreve that fat Canadian youth twice she arranged a new room-mate for me without consulting me at all, once for me to move out, once for

He opened the door in the twilight. His face looked like a pumpkin pie.

"Well, I'll say a fond farewell. Cruel fate may part us, but I will never love another. Never."

"What are you talking about?"

"I'm talking about cruel fate in eight yards of apricot silk and more metal pound for pound than a galley slave and the sole owner and proprietor of the unchallenged peripatetic john of the late Confederacy." Then he told me how she had gone to the proctor to have him moved out and how the proctor had revealed enough low stubbornness to insist on consulting Shreve first. Then she suggested that he send for Shreve right off and do it, and he wouldn't do that, so after that she was hardly civil to Shreve. "I make it a point never to speak harshly of females," Shreve said, "but that woman has got more ways like a bitch than any lady in these sovereign states and dominions." and now Letter on the table by hand, command orchid scented colored If she knew I had passed almost beneath the window knowing it there without   My dear Madam I have not yet had an opportunity of receiving your communication but I beg in advance to be excused today or yesterday and tomorrow or when As I remember that the next one is to be how Gerald throws his nigger downstairs and how the nigger plead to be allowed to matriculate in the divinity school to be near marster marse gerald and How he ran all the way to the station beside the carriage with tears in his eyes when marse gerald rid away I will wait until the day for the one about the sawmill husband came to the kitchen door with a shotgun Gerald went down and bit the gun in two and handed it back and wiped his hands on a silk handkerchief threw the handkerchief in the stove I've only heard that one twice

shot him through the   I saw you come in here so I watched my chance and came along thought we might get acquainted have a cigar

Thanks I dont smoke

No things must have changed up there since my day mind if I light up

Help yourself

Thanks I've heard a lot I guess your mother wont mind if I put the match behind the screen will she a lot about you Candace talked about you all the time up there at the Licks   I got pretty jealous I says to myself who is this Quentin anyway I must see what this animal looks like because I was hit pretty hard see soon as I saw the little girl I dont mind telling you it never occurred to me it was her brother she kept talking about she couldn't have talked about you any more if you'd been the only man in the world husband wouldn't have been in it you wont change your mind and have a smoke

I dont smoke

In that case I wont insist even though it is a pretty fair weed cost me twenty-five bucks a hundred wholesale friend of in Havana yes I guess there are lots of changes up there I keep promising myself a visit but I never get around to it been hitting the ball now for ten years I cant get away from the bank during school fellow's habits change things that seem important to an undergraduate you know tell me about things up there

I'm not going to tell Father and Mother if that's what you are getting at Not going to tell not going to oh that that's what you are talking about is it you understand that I dont give a damn whether you tell or not understand that a thing like that unfortunate but no police crime I wasn't the first or the last I was just unlucky you might have been luckier

You lie

Keep your shirt on I'm not trying to make you tell anything you dont want to meant no offense of course a young fellow like you would consider a thing of that sort a lot more serious than you will in five years

I dont know but one way to consider cheating I dont think I'm likely to learn different at Harvard

We're better than a play you must have made the Dramat well you're right no need to tell them we'll let bygones be bygones eh no reason why you and I should let a little thing like that come between us I like you Quentin I like your appearance you dont look like these other hicks I'm glad we're going to hit it off like this I've promised your mother to do something for Jason but I would like to give you a hand too Jason would be just as well off here but there's no future in a hole like this for a young fellow like you

Thanks you'd better stick to Jason he'd suit you better than I would I'm sorry about that business but a kid like I was then I never had a mother like yours to teach me the finer points it would just hurt her unnecessarily to know it yes you're right no need to that includes Candace of course

I said Mother and Father

Look here take a look at me how long do you think you'd last with me

I wont have to last long if you learned to fight up at school too try and see how long I would

You damned little what do you think you're getting at

Try and see

My God the cigar what would your mother say if she found a blister on her mantel just in time too look here Quentin we're about to do something we'll both regret I like you liked you as soon as I saw you I says he must be a damned good fellow whoever he is or Candace wouldn't be so keen on him listen I've been out in the world now for ten years things dont matter so much then you'll find that out let's you and I get together on this thing sons of old Harvard and all I guess I wouldn't know the place now best place for a young fellow in the world I'm going to send my sons there give them a better chance than I had wait dont go yet let's discuss this thing a young man gets these ideas and I'm all for them does him good while he's in school forms his character good for tradition the school but when he gets out into the world he'll have to get his the best way he can because he'll find that everybody else is doing the same thing and be damned to here let's shake hands and let bygones be bygones for your mother's sake remember her health come on give me your hand here look at it it's just out of convent look not a blemish not even been creased yet see here

To hell with your money

No no come on I belong to the family now see I know how it is with a young fellow he has lots of private affairs it's always pretty hard to get the old man to stump up for I know haven't I been there and not so long ago either but now I'm getting married and all specially up there come on dont be a fool listen when we get a chance for a real talk I want to tell you about a little widow over in town

I've heard that too keep your damned money

Call it a loan then just shut your eyes a minute and you'll be fifty

Keep your hands off of me you'd better get that cigar off the mantel

Tell and be damned then see what it gets you if you were not a damned fool you'd have seen that I've got them too tight for any half-baked Galahad of a brother your mother's told me about your sort with your head swelled up come in oh come in dear Quentin and I were just getting acquainted talking about Harvard did you want me cant stay away from the old man can she

Go out a minute Herbert I want to talk to Quentin

Come in come in let's all have a gabfest and get acquainted I was just telling Quentin

Go on Herbert go out a while

Well all right then I suppose you and bubber do want to see one another once more eh

You'd better take that cigar off the mantel

Right as usual my boy then I'll toddle along let them order you around while they can Quentin after day after tomorrow it'll be pretty please to the old man wont it dear give us a kiss honey

Oh stop that save that for day after tomorrow

I'll want interest then dont let Quentin do anything he cant finish oh by the way did I tell Quentin the story about the man's parrot and what happened to it a sad story remind me of that think of it yourself ta-ta see you in the funnypaper

Well

Well

What are you up to now

Nothing

You're meddling in my business again didn't you get enough of that last summer

Caddy you've got fever   *You're sick how are you sick*

   I'm just sick. I cant ask.

   Shot his voice through the

Not that blackguard Caddy

Now and then the river glinted beyond things in sort of swooping glints, across noon and after. Good after now, though we had passed where he was still pulling upstream majestical in the face of god gods. Better. Gods. God would be canaille too in Boston in Massachusetts. Or maybe just not a husband. The wet oars winking him along in bright winks and female palms. Adulant. Adulant if not a husband he'd ignore God. *That blackguard, Caddy*   The river glinted away beyond a swooping curve.

   I'm sick you'll have to promise

   Sick how are you sick

   I'm just sick I cant ask anybody yet promise you will

   If they need any looking after it's because of you how are you sick Under the window we could hear the car leaving for the station, the 8:10 train. To bring back cousins. Heads. Increasing himself head by head but not barbers. Manicure girls. We had a blood horse once. In the stable yes, but under leather a cur. *Quentin has shot all of their voices through the floor of Caddy's room*

The car stopped. I got off, into the middle of my shadow. A road crossed the track. There was a wooden marquee with an old man eating something out of a paper bag, and then the car was out of hearing too. The road went into trees, where it would be shady, but June foliage in New England not much thicker than April at home. I could see a smoke stack. I turned my back to it, tramping my shadow into the dust. *There was something terrible in me sometimes at night I could see it grinning at me I could see it through them grinning at me through their faces it's gone now and I'm sick*

   Caddy

   Dont touch me just promise

   If you're sick you cant

   Yes I can after that it'll be all right it wont matter dont let them send him to Jackson promise

   I promise Caddy Caddy

   Dont touch me dont touch me

   What does it look like Caddy

   What

   That that grins at you that thing through them

I could still see the smoke stack. That's where the water would be, healing out to the sea and the peaceful grottoes. Tumbling peacefully they would, and when He said Rise only the flat irons.

When Versh and I hunted all day we wouldn't take any lunch, and at twelve oclock I'd get hungry. I'd stay hungry until about one, then all of a sudden I'd even forget that I wasn't hungry anymore. *The street lamps go down the hill then heard the cargo down the hill. The chair-arm flat cool smooth under my forehead shaping the chair the apple tree leaning on my hair above the eden clothes by the nose seen* You've got fever I felt it yesterday it's like being near a stove.

Dont touch me.

Caddy you cant do it if you are sick. That blackguard.

I've got to marry somebody. *Then they told me the bone would have to be broken again*

At last I couldn't see the smoke stack. The road went beside a wall. Trees leaned over the wall, sprayed with sunlight. The stone was cool. Walking near it you could feel the coolness. Only our country was not like this country. There was something about just walking through it. A kind of still and violent fecundity that satisfied even bread-hunger like. Flowing around you, not brooding and nursing every niggard stone. Like it were put to makeshift for enough green to go around among the trees and even the blue of distance not that rich chimaera. *told me the bone would have to be broken again and inside me it began to say Ah Ah Ah and I began to sweat. What do I care I know what a broken leg is all it is it wont be anything I'll just have to stay in the house a little longer that's all and my jaw-muscles getting numb and my mouth saying Wait Wait just a minute through the sweat ah ah ah behind my teeth and Father damn that horse damn that horse. Wait it's my fault. He came along the fence every morning with a basket toward the kitchen dragging a stick along the fence every morning I dragged myself to the window cast and all and laid for him with a piece of coal Dilsey said you goin to ruin yoself aint you you got no mo sense than that not fo days since you bruck hit. Wait I'll get used to it in a minute wait just a minute I'll get*

Even sound seemed to fail in this air, like the air was worn out with carrying sounds so long. A dog's voice carries further than a train, in the darkness anyway. And some people's. Niggers. Louis Hatcher never even used his horn carrying it and that old lantern. I said, "Louis, when was the last time you cleaned that lantern?"

"I cleant hit a little while back. You member when all dat flood-watter wash dem folks away up yonder? I cleant hit dat ve'y day. Old woman and me settin fo de fire dat night and she say 'Louis, whut you gwine do ef dat flood git out dis fur?' and I say 'Dat's a fack. I reckon I had better clean dat lantun up.' So I cleant hit dat night."

"That flood was way up in Pennsylvania," I said. "It couldn't ever have got down this far."

"Dat's whut you says," Louis said. "Watter kin git des ez high en wet in Jefferson ez hit kin in Pennsylvaney, I reckon. Hit's de folks dat says de high watter cant git dis fur dat comes floatin out on de ridge-pole, too."

"Did you and Martha get out that night?"

"We done jest dat. I cleant dat lantun and me and her sot de balance of de night on top o dat knoll back de graveyard. En ef I'd a knowed of aihy one higher, we'd a been on hit instead."

"And you haven't cleaned that lantern since then."

"Whut I want to clean hit when dey aint no need?"

"You mean, until another flood comes along?"

"Hit kep us outen dat un."

"Oh, come on, Uncle Louis," I said.

"Yes, suh. You do yo way en I do mine. Ef all I got to do to keep outen de high watter is to clean dis yere lantun, I wont quoil wid no man."

"Unc' Louis wouldn't ketch nothin wid a light he could see by," Versh said.

"I wuz huntin possums in dis country when dey was still drowndin nits in yo pappy's head wid coal oil, boy," Louis said. "Ketchin um, too."

"Dat's de troof," Versh said. "I reckon Unc' Louis done caught mo possums than aihy man in dis country."

"Yes, suh," Louis said. "I got plenty light fer possums to see, all right. I aint heard none o dem complainin. Hush, now. Dar he. Whooey. Hum awn, dawg." And we'd sit in the dry leaves that whispered a little with the slow respiration of our waiting and with the slow breathing of the earth and the windless October, the rank smell of the lantern fouling the brittle air, listening to the dogs and to the echo of Louis' voice dying away. He never raised it, yet on a still night we have heard it from our front porch. When he called the dogs in he sounded just like the horn he carried slung on his shoulder and never used, but clearer, mellower, as though his voice were a part of darkness and silence, coiling out of it, coiling   into   it again.   WhoOoooo.   WhoOoooo. WhoOooooooooooooooo.

Got to marry somebody

  Have there been very many Caddy

  I dont know too many will you look after Benjy and Father

  You dont know whose it is then does he know

  Dont touch me will you look after Benjy and Father

I began to feel the water before I came to the bridge. The bridge was of gray stone, lichened, dappled with slow moisture where the fungus crept. Beneath it the water was clear and still in the shadow, whispering and clucking about the stone in fading swirls of spinning sky. *Caddy that*

  I've got to marry somebody Versh told me about a man who mutilated himself. He went into the woods and did it with a razor, sitting in a ditch. A broken razor flinging them backward over his shoulder the same motion complete the jerked skein of blood backward not looping. But that's not it. It's not not having them. It's never to have had them then I could say O That That's Chinese I dont know Chinese. And Father said it's because you are a virgin: dont you see? Women are never virgins. Purity is a negative state and therefore contrary to nature. It's nature is hurting you not Caddy and I said That's just words and he said So is virginity and I said you dont know. You cant know and he said Yes. On the instant when we come to realise that tragedy is second-hand.

Where the shadow of the bridge fell I could see down for a long way, but not as far as the bottom. When you leave a leaf in water a long time after a while the tissue will be gone and the delicate fibers waving slow as the motion of sleep. They dont touch one another, no matter how knotted up they once were, no matter how close they lay once to the bones. And maybe when He says Rise the eyes will come floating up too, out of the deep quiet and the sleep, to look on glory. And after a while the flat irons would come floating up. I hid them under the end of the bridge and went back and leaned on the rail.

I could not see the bottom, but I could see a long way into the motion of the water before the eye gave out, and then I saw a shadow hanging like a fat arrow stemming into the current. Mayflies skimmed in and out of the shadow of the bridge just above the surface. *If it could just be a hell beyond that: the clean flame*[2] *the two of us more than dead. Then you will have only me then only me then the two of us amid the pointing and the horror beyond the clean flame* The arrow increased without motion, then in a quick swirl the trout lipped a fly beneath the surface with that sort of gigantic delicacy of an elephant picking up a peanut. The fading vortex drifted away down stream and then I saw the arrow again, nose into the current, wavering delicately to the motion of the water above which the May flies slanted and poised. *Only you and me then amid the pointing and the horror walled by the clean flame*

The trout hung, delicate and motionless among the wavering shadows. Three boys with fishing poles came onto the bridge and we leaned on the rail and looked down at the trout. They knew the fish. He was a neighborhood character.

"They've been trying to catch that trout for twenty-five years. There's a store in Boston offers a twenty-five dollar fishing rod to anybody that can catch him."

"Why dont you all catch him, then? Wouldn't you like to have a twenty-five dollar fishing rod?"

2. See Luke 16.24–25.

"Yes," they said. They leaned on the rail, looking down at the trout. "I sure would," one said.

"I wouldn't take the rod," the second said. "I'd take the money instead."

"Maybe they wouldn't do that," the first said. "I bet he'd make you take the rod."

"Then I'd sell it."

"You couldn't get twenty-five dollars for it."

"I'd take what I could get, then. I can catch just as many fish with this pole as I could with a twenty-five dollar one." Then they talked about what they would do with twenty-five dollars. They all talked at once, their voices insistent and contradictory and impatient, making of unreality a possibility, then a probability, then an incontrovertible fact, as people will when their desires become words.

"I'd buy a horse and wagon," the second said.

"Yes you would," the others said.

"I would. I know where I can buy one for twenty-five dollars. I know the man."

"Who is it?"

"That's all right who it is. I can buy it for twenty-five dollars."

"Yah," the others said. "He dont know any such thing. He's just talking."

"Do you think so?" the boy said. They continued to jeer at him, but he said nothing more. He leaned on the rail, looking down at the trout which he had already spent, and suddenly the acrimony, the conflict, was gone from their voices, as if to them too it was as though he had captured the fish and bought his horse and wagon, they too partaking of that adult trait of being convinced of anything by an assumption of silent superiority. I suppose that people, using themselves and each other so much by words, are at least consistent in attributing wisdom to a still tongue, and for a while I could feel the other two seeking swiftly for some means by which to cope with him, to rob him of his horse and wagon.

"You couldn't get twenty-five dollars for that pole," the first said. "I bet anything you couldn't."

"He hasn't caught that trout yet," the third said suddenly, then they both cried:

"Yah, what'd I tell you? What's the man's name? I dare you to tell. There aint any such man."

"Ah, shut up," the second said. "Look. Here he comes again." They leaned on the rail, motionless, identical, their poles slanting slenderly in the sunlight, also identical. The trout rose without haste, a shadow in faint wavering increase; again the little vortex faded slowly downstream. "Gee," the first one murmured.

"We dont try to catch him anymore," he said. "We just watch Boston folks that come out and try."

"Is he the only fish in this pool?"

"Yes. He ran all the others out. The best place to fish around here is down at the Eddy."

"No it aint," the second said. "It's better at Bigelow's Mill two to one." Then they argued for a while about which was the best fishing and then left off all of a sudden to watch the trout rise again and the broken swirl of water suck down a little of the sky. I asked how far it was to the nearest town. They told me.

"But the closest car line is that way," the second said, pointing back down the road. "Where are you going?"

"Nowhere. Just walking."

"You from the college?"

"Yes. Are there any factories in that town?"

"Factories?" They looked at me.

"No," the second said. "Not there." They looked at my clothes. "You looking for work?"

"How about Bigelow's Mill?" the third said. "That's a factory."

"Factory my eye. He means a sure enough factory."

"One with a whistle," I said. "I haven't heard any one oclock whistles yet."

"Oh," the second said. "There's a clock in the unitarial steeple. You can find out the time from that. Haven't you got a watch on that chain?"

"I broke it this morning." I showed them my watch. They examined it gravely.

"It's still running," the second said. "What does a watch like that cost?"

"It was a present," I said. "My father gave it to me when I graduated from high school."

"Are you a Canadian?" the third said. He had red hair.

"Canadian?"

"He dont talk like them," the second said. "I've heard them talk. He talks like they do in minstrel shows."

"Say," the third said. "Aint you afraid he'll hit you?"

"Hit me?"

"You said he talks like a colored man."

"Ah, dry up," the second said. "You can see the steeple when you get over that hill there."

I thanked them. "I hope you have good luck. Only dont catch that old fellow down there. He deserves to be let alone."

"Cant anybody catch that fish," the first said. They leaned on the rail, looking down into the water, the three poles like three slanting threads of yellow fire in the sun. I walked upon my shadow, tramping it into the dappled shade of trees again. The road curved, mounting away from the water. It crossed the hill, then descended winding, carrying the eye, the mind on ahead beneath a still green tunnel, and the square cupola above the trees and the round eye of the clock but far enough. I sat down at the roadside. The grass was ankle deep, myriad. The shadows on the road were as still as if they had been put there with a stencil, with slanting pencils of sunlight. But it was only a train, and after a while it died away beyond the trees, the long sound, and then I could hear my watch and the train dying away, as though it were running through another month or another summer somewhere, rushing away under the poised gull and all things rushing. Except Gerald. He would be sort of grand too, pulling in lonely state across the noon, rowing himself right out of noon, up the long bright air like an apotheosis, mounting into a drowsing infinity where only he and the gull, the one terrifically motionless, the other in a steady and measured pull and recover that partook of inertia itself, the world punily beneath their shadows on the sun. *Caddy that blackguard that blackguard Caddy*

Their voices came over the hill, and the three slender poles like balanced threads of running fire. They looked at me passing, not slowing.

"Well," I said. "I dont see him."

"We didn't try to catch him," the first said. "You cant catch that fish."

"There's the clock," the second said, pointing. "You can tell the time when you get a little closer."

"Yes," I said. "All right." I got up. "You all going to town?"

"We're going to the Eddy for chub," the first said.

"You cant catch anything at the Eddy," the second said.

"I guess you want to go to the mill, with a lot of fellows splashing and scaring all the fish away."

"You cant catch any fish at the Eddy."

"We wont catch none nowhere if we dont go on," the third said.

"I dont see why you keep on talking about the Eddy," the second said. "You cant catch anything there."

"You dont have to go," the first said. "You're not tied to me."

"Let's go to the mill and go swimming," the third said.

"I'm going to the Eddy and fish," the first said. "You can do as you please."

"Say, how long has it been since you heard of anybody catching a fish at the Eddy?" the second said to the third.

"Let's go to the mill and go swimming," the third said. The cupola sank slowly beyond the trees, with the round face of the clock far enough yet. We went on in the dappled shade. We came to an orchard, pink and white. It was full of bees; already we could hear them.

"Let's go to the mill and go swimming," the third said. A lane turned off beside the orchard. The third boy slowed and halted. The first went on, flecks of sunlight slipping along the pole across his shoulder and down the back of his shirt. "Come on," the third said. The second boy stopped too. *Why must you marry somebody Caddy*

Do you want me to say it do you think that if I say it it wont be

"Let's go up to the mill," he said. "Come on."

The first boy went on. His bare feet made no sound, falling softer than leaves in the thin dust. In the orchard the bees sounded like a wind getting up, a sound caught by a spell just under crescendo and sustained. The lane went along the wall, arched over, shattered with bloom, dissolving into trees. Sunlight slanted into it, sparse and eager. Yellow butterflies flickered along the shade like flecks of sun.

"What do you want to go to the Eddy for?" the second boy said. "You can fish at the mill if you want to."

"Ah, let him go," the third said. They looked after the first boy. Sunlight slid patchily across his walking shoulders, glinting along the pole like yellow ants.

"Kenny," the second said. *Say it to Father will you I will am my fathers Progenitive I invented him created I him Say it to him it will not be for he will say I was not and then you and I since philoprogenitive*

"Ah, come on," the third boy said. "They're already in." They looked after the first boy. "Yah," they said suddenly, "go on then, mamma's boy. If he goes swimming he'll get his head wet and then he'll get a licking." They turned into the lane and went on, the yellow butterfies slanting about them along the shade.

it is because there is nothing else I believe there is something else but there may not be and then I You will find that even injustice is scarcely worthy of what you believe yourself to be He paid me no attention, his jaw set in profile, his face turned a little away beneath his broken hat.

"Why dont you go swimming with them?" I said. *that blackguard Caddy*

Were you trying to pick a fight with him were you

A liar and a scoundrel Caddy was dropped from his club for cheating at cards got sent to Coventry[3] caught cheating at midterm exams and expelled

3. To send one to "Coventry" is to take no notice of him, to make him feel that he is in disgrace by ignoring him. It is said that the citizens of Coventry once had so great a dislike of soldiers that a woman seen speaking to one was instantly ostracized; hence when a soldier was sent to Coventry, he was cut off from all social intercourse.

Well what about it I'm not going to play cards with

"Do you like fishing better than swimming?" I said. The sound of the bees diminished, sustained yet, as though instead of sinking into silence, silence merely increased between us, as water rises. The road curved again and became a street between shady lawns with white houses. *Caddy that blackguard can you think of Benjy and Father and do it not of me*

What else can I think about what else have I thought about The boy turned from the street. He climbed a picket fence without looking back and crossed the lawn to a tree and laid the pole down and climbed into the fork of the tree and sat there, his back to the road and the dappled sun motionless at last upon his white shirt, *else have I thought about I cant even cry I died last year I told you I had but I didn't know then what I meant I didn't know what I was saying* Some days in late August at home are like this, the air thin and eager like this, with something in it sad and nostalgic and familiar. Man the sum of his climatic experiences Father said. Man the sum of what have you. A problem in impure properties carried tediously to an unvarying nil: stalemate of dust and desire, *but now I know I'm dead I tell you*

Then why must you listen we can go away you and Benjy and me where nobody knows us where The buggy was drawn by a white horse, his feet clopping in the thin dust; spidery wheels chattering thin and dry, moving uphill beneath a rippling shawl of leaves. Elm. No: ellum. Ellum.

On what on your school money the money they sold the pasture for so you could go to Harvard dont you see you've got to finish now if you dont finish he'll have nothing

Sold the pasture His white shirt was motionless in the fork, in the flickering shade. The wheels were spidery. Beneath the sag of the buggy the hooves neatly rapid like the motions of a lady doing embroidery, diminishing without progress like a figure on a treadmill being drawn rapidly offstage. The street turned again. I could see the white cupola, the round stupid assertion of the clock. *Sold the pasture*

Father will be dead in a year they say if he doesn't stop drinking and he wont stop he cant stop since I since last summer and then they'll send Benjy to Jackson I cant cry I cant even cry one minute she was standing in the door the next minute he was pulling at her dress and bellowing his voice hammered back and forth between the walls in waves and she shrinking against the wall getting smaller and smaller with her white face her eyes like thumbs dug into it until he pushed her out of the room his voice hammering back and forth as though its own momentum would not let it stop as though there were no place for it in silence bellowing

When you opened the door a bell tinkled, but just once, high and clear and small in the neat obscurity above the door, as though it were gauged and tempered to make that single clear small sound so as not to wear the bell out nor to require the expenditure of too much silence in restoring it when the door opened upon the recent warm scent of baking; a little dirty child with eyes like a toy bear's and two patent-leather pigtails.

"Hello, sister." Her face was like a cup of milk dashed with coffee in the sweet warm emptiness. "Anybody here?"

But she merely watched me until a door opened and the lady came. Above the counter where the ranks of crisp shapes behind the glass her neat gray face her hair tight and sparse from her neat gray skull, spectacles in neat gray rims riding approaching like something on a wire, like a cash box in a store. She looked like a librarian. Something among dusty shelves of ordered certitudes long divorced from reality, desiccating peacefully, as if a breath of that air which sees injustice done

"Two of these, please, ma'am."

From under the counter she produced a square cut from a newspaper and laid it on the counter and lifted the two buns out. The little girl watched them with still and unwinking eyes like two currants floating motionless in a cup of weak coffee Land of the kike home of the wop. Watching the bread, the neat gray hands, a broad gold band on the left forefinger, knuckled there by a blue knuckle.

"Do you do your own baking, ma'am?"

"Sir?" she said. Like that. Sir? Like on the stage. Sir? "Five cents. Was there anything else?"

"No, ma'am. Not for me. This lady wants something." She was not tall enough to see over the case, so she went to the end of the counter and looked at the little girl.

"Did you bring her in here?"

"No, ma'am. She was here when I came."

"You little wretch," she said. She came out around the counter, but she didn't touch the little girl. "Have you got anything in your pockets?"

"She hasn't got any pockets," I said. "She wasn't doing anything. She was just standing here, waiting for you."

"Why didn't the bell ring, then?" She glared at me. She just needed a bunch of switches, a blackboard behind her 2 x 2 e 5. "She'll hide it under her dress and a body'd never know it. You, child. How'd you get in here?"

The little girl said nothing. She looked at the woman, then she gave me a flying black glance and looked at the woman again. "Them foreigners," the woman said. "How'd she get in without the bell ringing?"

"She came in when I opened the door," I said. "It rang once for both of us. She couldn't reach anything from here, anyway. Besides, I dont think she would. Would you, sister?" The little girl looked at me, secretive, contemplative. "What do you want? bread?"

She extended her fist. It uncurled upon a nickel, moist and dirty, moist dirt ridged into her flesh. The coin was damp and warm. I could smell it, faintly metallic.

"Have you got a five cent loaf, please, ma'am?"

From beneath the counter she produced a square cut from a newspaper sheet and laid it on the counter and wrapped a loaf into it. I laid the coin and another one on the counter. "And another one of those buns, please, ma'am."

She took another bun from the case. "Give me that parcel," she said. I gave it to her and she unwrapped it and put the third bun in and wrapped it and took up the coins and found two coppers in her apron and gave them to me. I handed them to the little girl. Her fingers closed about them, damp and hot, like worms.

"You going to give her that bun?" the woman said.

"Yessum," I said. "I expect your cooking smells as good to her as it does to me."

I took up the two packages and gave the bread to the little girl, the woman all iron-gray behind the counter, watching us with cold certitude. "You wait a minute," she said. She went to the rear. The door opened again and closed. The little girl watched me, holding the bread against her dirty dress.

"What's your name?" I said. She quit looking at me, but she was still motionless. She didn't even seem to breathe. The woman returned. She had a funny looking thing in her hand. She carried it sort of like it might have been a dead pet rat.

"Here," she said. The child looked at her. "Take it," the woman said, jabbing it at the little girl. "It just looks peculiar. I calculate you wont know the difference when you eat it. Here. I cant stand here all day." The child took it, still watching her. The woman rubbed her hands on her apron. "I got to have that bell fixed," she said. She went to the door and jerked it open. The little bell tinkled once, faint and clear and invisible. We moved toward the door and the woman's peering back.

"Thank you for the cake," I said.

"Them foreigners," she said, staring up into the obscurity where the bell tinkled. "Take my advice and stay clear of them, young man."

"Yessum," I said. "Come on, sister." We went out. "Thank you, ma'am."

She swung the door to, then jerked it open again, making the bell give forth its single small note. "Foreigners," she said, peering up at the bell.

We went on. "Well," I said. "How about some ice cream?" She was eating the gnarled cake. "Do you like ice cream?" She gave me a black still look, chewing. "Come on."

We came to the drugstore and had some ice cream. She wouldn't put the loaf down. "Why not put it down so you can eat better?" I said, offering to take it. But she held to it, chewing the ice cream like it was taffy. The bitten cake lay on the table. She ate the ice cream steadily, then she fell to on the cake again, looking about at the showcases. I finished mine and we went out.

"Which way do you live?" I said.

A buggy, the one with the white horse it was. Only Doc Peabody is fat. Three hundred pounds. You ride with him on the uphill side, holding on. Children. Walking easier than holding uphill. *Seen the doctor yet   have you seen   Caddy*

I dont have to I cant ask now afterward it will be all right it wont matter

Because women so delicate so mysterious Father said. Delicate equilibrium of periodical filth between two moons balanced. Moons he said full and yellow as harvest moons her hips thighs. Outside outside of them always but. Yellow. Feet soles with walking like. Then know that some man that all those mysterious and imperious concealed. With all that inside of them shapes an outward suavity waiting for a touch to. Liquid putrefaction like drowned things floating like pale rubber flabbily filled getting the odor of honeysuckle all mixed up.

"You'd better take your bread on home, hadn't you?"

She looked at me. She chewed quietly and steadily; at regular intervals a small distension passed smoothly down her throat. I opened my package and gave her one of the buns. "Goodbye," I said.

I went on. Then I looked back. She was behind me. "Do you live down this way?" She said nothing. She walked beside me, under my elbow sort of, eating. We went on. It was quiet, hardly anyone about *getting the odor of honeysuckle all mixed She would have told me not to let me sit there on the steps hearing her door twilight slamming hearing Benjy still crying Supper she would have to come down then getting honeysuckle all mixed up in it*   We reached the corner.

"Well, I've got to go down this way," I said. "Goodbye." She stopped too. She swallowed the last of the cake, then she began on the bun, watching me across it. "Goodbye," I said. I turned into the street and went on, but I went to the next corner before I stopped.

"Which way do you live?" I said. "This way?" I pointed down the street. She just looked at me. "Do you live over that way? I bet you live close to the station, where the trains are. Dont you?" She just looked at me, serene and secret and chewing. The street was empty both ways, with quiet lawns and houses neat among the trees, but no one at all except back there. We turned and went back. Two men sat in chairs in front of a store.

"Do you all know this little girl? She sort of took up with me and I cant find where she lives."

They quit looking at me and looked at her.

"Must be one of them new Italian families," one said. He wore a rusty frock coat. "I've seen her before. What's your name, little girl?" She looked at them blackly for a while, her jaws moving steadily. She swallowed without ceasing to chew.

"Maybe she cant speak English," the other said.

"They sent her after bread," I said. "She must be able to speak something."

"What's your pa's name?" the first said. "Pete? Joe? name John huh?" She took another bite from the bun.

"What must I do with her?" I said. "She just follows me. I've got to get back to Boston."

"You from the college?"

"Yes, sir. And I've got to get on back."

"You might go up the street and turn her over to Anse. He'll be up at the livery stable. The marshal."

"I reckon that's what I'll have to do," I said. "I've got to do something with her. Much obliged. Come on, sister."

We went up the street, on the shady side, where the shadow of the broken façade blotted slowly across the road. We came to the livery stable. The marshal wasn't there. A man sitting in a chair tilted in the broad low door, where a dark cool breeze smelling of ammonia blew among the ranked stalls, said to look at the postoffice. He didn't know her either.

"Them furriners. I cant tell one from another. You might take her across the tracks where they live, and maybe somebody'll claim her."

We went to the postoffice. It was back down the street. The man in the frock coat was opening a newspaper.

"Anse just drove out of town," he said. "I guess you'd better go down past the station and walk past them houses by the river. Somebody there'll know her."

"I guess I'll have to," I said. "Come on, sister." She pushed the last piece of the bun into her mouth and swallowed it. "Want another?" I said. She looked at me, chewing, her eyes black and unwinking and friendly. I took the other two buns out and gave her one and bit into the other. I asked a man where the station was and he showed me. "Come on, sister."

We reached the station and crossed the tracks, where the river was. A bridge crossed it, and a street of jumbled frame houses followed the river, backed onto it. A shabby street, but with an air heterogeneous and vivid too. In the center of an untrimmed plot enclosed by a fence of gaping and broken pickets stood an ancient lopsided surrey and a weathered house from an upper window of which hung a garment of vivid pink.

"Does that look like your house?" I said. She looked at me over the bun. "This one?" I said, pointing. She just chewed, but it seemed to me that I discerned something affirmative, acquiescent even if it wasn't eager, in her air. "This one?" I said. "Come on, then." I entered the broken gate. I looked back at her. "Here?" I said. "This look like your house?"

She nodded her head rapidly, looking at me, gnawing into the damp halfmoon of the bread. We went on. A walk of broken random flags, speared by fresh coarse blades of grass, led to the broken stoop. There was no movement about the house at all, and the pink garment hanging in no wind from the upper window. There was a bell pull with a porcelain knob, attached to about six feet of wire when I stopped pulling and knocked. The little girl had the crust edgeways in her chewing mouth.

A woman opened the door. She looked at me, then she spoke rapidly to the little girl in Italian, with a rising inflexion, then a pause, interrogatory. She spoke to her again, the little girl looking at her across the end of the crust, pushing it into her mouth with a dirty hand.

"She says she lives here," I said. "I met her down town. Is this your bread?"

"No spika," the woman said. She spoke to the little girl again. The little girl just looked at her.

"No live here?" I said. I pointed to the girl, then at her, then at the door. The woman shook her head. She spoke rapidly. She came to the edge of the porch and pointed down the road, speaking.

I nodded violently too. "You come show?" I said. I took her arm, waving my other hand toward the road. She spoke swiftly, pointing. "You come show," I said, trying to lead her down the steps.

"Si, si," she said, holding back, showing me whatever it was. I nodded again.

"Thanks. Thanks. Thanks." I went down the steps and walked toward the gate, not running, but pretty fast. I reached the gate and stopped and looked at her for a while. The crust was gone now, and she looked at me with her black, friendly stare. The woman stood on the stoop, watching us.

"Come on, then," I said. "We'll have to find the right one sooner or later."

She moved along just under my elbow. We went on. The houses all seemed empty. Not a soul in sight. A sort of breathlessness that empty houses have. Yet they couldn't all be empty. All the different rooms, if you could just slice the walls away all of a sudden. Madam, your daughter, if you please. No. Madam, for God's sake, your daughter. She moved along just under my elbow, her shiny tight pigtails, and then the last house played out and the road curved out of sight beyond a wall, following the river. The woman was emerging from the broken gate, with a shawl over her head and clutched under her chin. The road curved on, empty. I found a coin and gave it to the little girl. A quarter. "Goodbye, sister," I said. Then I ran.

I ran fast, not looking back. just before the road curved away I looked back. She stood in the road, a small figure clasping the loaf of bread to her filthy little dress, her eyes still and black and unwinking. I ran on.

A lane turned from the road. I entered it and after a while I slowed to a fast walk. The lane went between back premises— unpainted houses with more of those gay and startling colored garments on lines, a barn broken-backed, decaying quietly among rank orchard trees, unpruned and weed-choked, pink and white and murmurous with sunlight and with bees. I looked back. The entrance to the lane was empty. I slowed still more, my shadow pacing me, dragging its head through the weeds that hid the fence.

The lane went back to a barred gate, became defunctive in grass, a mere path scarred quietly into new grass. I climbed the gate into a woodlot and crossed it and came to another wall and followed that one, my shadow behind me now. There were vines and creepers where at home would be honeysuckle. Coming and coming especially in the dusk when it rained, getting honeysuckle all mixed up in it as though it were not enough without that, not unbearable enough. *What did you let him for kiss kiss*

I didn't let him I made him watching me getting mad What do you think of that? Red print of my hand coming up through her face like turning a light on under your hand her eyes going bright

It's not for kissing I slapped you. Girl's elbows at fifteen Father said you swallow like you had a fishbone in your throat what's the matter with you and Caddy across the table not to look at me. It's for letting it be some darn town squirt I slapped you you will will you now I guess you say calf rope. My red hand coming up out of her face. What do you think of that scouring her head into the. Grass sticks criss-crossed into the flesh tingling scouring her head. Say calf rope say it

I didn't kiss a dirty girl like Natalie anyway The wall went into shadow, and then my shadow, I had tricked it again. I had forgot about the river curving along the road. I climbed the wall. And then she watched me jump down, holding the loaf against her dress.

I stood in the weeds and we looked at one another for a while.

"Why didn't you tell me you lived out this way, sister?" The loaf was wearing slowly out of the paper; already it needed a new one. "Well, come on then and show me the house." *not a dirty girl like Natalie. It was raining we could hear it on the roof, sighing through the high sweet emptiness of the barn.*

There? touching her

Not there

There? not raining hard but we couldn't hear anything but the roof and if it was my blood or her blood

She pushed me down the ladder and ran off and left me Caddy did

Was it there it hurt you when Caddy did ran off was it there

Oh She walked just under my elbow, the top of her patent leather head, the loaf fraying out of the newspaper.

"If you dont get home pretty soon you're going to wear that loaf out. And then what'll your mamma say?" *I bet I can lift you up*

You cant I'm too heavy

Did Caddy go away did she go to the house you cant see the barn from our house did you ever try to see the barn from

It was her fault she pushed me she ran away

I can lift you up see how I can

Oh her blood or my blood Oh We went on in the thin dust, our feet silent as rubber in the thin dust where pencils of sun slanted in the trees. And I could feel water again running swift and peaceful in the secret shade.

"You live a long way, dont you. You're mighty smart to go this far to town by yourself." *It's like dancing sitting down did you ever dance sitting down? We could hear the rain, a rat in the crib, the empty barn vacant with horses. How do you hold to dance do you hold like this*

Oh

I used to hold like this you thought I wasn't strong enough didn't you

Oh Oh Oh Oh

I hold to use like this I mean did you hear what I said I said

oh oh oh oh

The road went on, still and empty, the sun slanting more and more. Her stiff little pigtails were bound at the tips with bits of crimson cloth. A corner of the wrapping flapped a little as she walked, the nose of the loaf naked. I stopped.

"Look here. Do you live down this road? We haven't passed a house in a mile, almost."

She looked at me, black and secret and friendly.

"Where do you live, sister? Dont you live back there in town?"

There was a bird somewhere in the woods, beyond the broken and infrequent slanting of sunlight.

"Your papa's going to be worried about you. Dont you reckon you'll get a whipping for not coming straight home with that bread?"

The bird whistled again, invisible, a sound meaningless and profound, inflexionless, ceasing as though cut off with the blow of a knife, and again, and that sense of water swift and peaceful above secret places, felt, not seen not heard.

"Oh, hell, sister." About half the paper hung limp. "That's not doing any good now." I tore it off and dropped it beside the road. "Come on. We'll have to go back to town. We'll go back along the river."

We left the road. Among the moss little pale flowers grew, and the sense of water mute and unseen. *I hold to use like this I mean I use to hold She stood in the door looking at us her hands on her hips*

You pushed me it was your fault it hurt me too

We were dancing sitting down I bet Caddy cant dance sitting down

Stop that stop that

I was just brushing the trash off the back of your dress

You keep your nasty old hands off of me it was your fault you pushed me down I'm mad at you

I don't care she looked at us stay mad she went away We began to hear the shouts, the splashings; I saw a brown body gleam for an instant.

Stay mad. My shirt was getting wet and my hair. Across the roof hearing the roof loud now I could see Natalie going through the garden among the rain. Get wet I hope you catch pneumonia go on home Cowface. I jumped hard as I could into the hogwallow the mud yellowed up to my waist stinking I kept on plunging until I fell down and rolled over in it "Hear them in swimming, sister? I wouldn't mind doing that myself." *If I had time. When I have time. I could hear my watch, mud was warmer than the rain it smelled awful. She had her back turned I went around in front of her. You know what I was doing? She turned her back I went around in front of her the rain creeping into the mud flatting her bodice through her dress it smelled horrible. I was hugging her that's what I was doing. She turned her back I went around in front of her. I was hugging her I tell you.*

I dont give a damn what you were doing

You dont you dont I'll make you I'll make you give a damn. She hit my hands away I smeared mud on her with the other hand I couldn't feel the wet smacking of her hand I wiped mud from my legs smeared it on her wet hard turning body hearing her fingers going into my face but I couldn't feel it even when the rain began to taste sweet on my lips

They saw us from the water first, heads and shoulders. They yelled and one rose squatting and sprang among them. They looked like beavers, the water lipping about their chins, yelling.

"Take that girl away! What did you want to bring a girl here for? Go on away!"

"She wont hurt you. We just want to watch you for a while."

They squatted in the water. Their heads drew into a clump, watching us, then they broke and rushed toward us, hurling water with their hands. We moved quick.

"Look out, boys; she wont hurt you."

"Go on away, Harvard!" It was the second boy, the one that thought the horse and wagon back there at the bridge. "Splash them, fellows!"

"Let's get out and throw them in," another said. "I aint afraid of any girl."

"Splash them! Splash them!" They rushed toward us, hurling water. We moved back. "Go on away!" they yelled. "Go on away!"

We went away. They huddled just under the bank, their slick heads in a row against the bright water. We went on. "That's not for us, is it." The sun slanted through to the moss here and there, leveller. "Poor kid, you're just a girl." Little flowers grew among the moss, littler than I had ever seen. "You're just a girl. Poor kid." There was a path, curving along beside the water. Then the water was still again, dark and still and swift. "Nothing but a girl. Poor sister." *We lay in the wet grass panting the rain like cold shot on my back. Do you care now do you do you*

My Lord we sure are in a mess get up. Where the rain touched my forehead it began to smart my hand came red away streaking off pink in the rain. Does it hurt

Of course it does what do you reckon

I tried to scratch your eyes out my Lord we sure do stink we better try to wash it off in the branch "There's town again, sister. You'll have to go home now. I've got to get back to school. Look how late it's getting. You'll go home now, wont you?" But she just looked at me with her black, secret, friendly gaze, the half-naked loaf clutched to her breast. "It's wet. I thought we jumped back in time." I took my handkerchief and tried to wipe the loaf, but the crust began to come off, so I stopped. "We'll just have to let it dry itself. Hold it like this." She held it like that. It looked kind of like rats had been eating it now.   *and the water building and building up the squatting back the sloughed mud stinking surfaceward pocking the pattering surface like grease on a hot stove. I told you I'd make you*

I dont give a goddam what you do

Then we heard the running and we stopped and looked back and saw him coming up the path running, the level shadows flicking upon his legs.

"He's in a hurry. We'd——" then I saw another man, an oldish man running heavily, clutching a stick, and a boy naked from the waist up, clutching his pants as he ran.

"There's Julio," the little girl said, and then I saw his Italian face and his eyes as he sprang upon me. We went down. His hands were jabbing at my face and he was saying something and trying to bite me, I reckon, and then they hauled him off and held him heaving and thrashing and yelling and they held his arms and he tried to kick me until they dragged him back. The little girl was howling, holding the loaf in both arms. The half naked boy was darting and jumping up and down, clutching his trousers and someone pulled me up in time to see another stark naked figure come around the tranquil bend in the path running and change direction in mid-stride and leap into the woods, a couple of garments rigid as boards behind it. Julio still struggled. The man who had pulled me up said, "Whoa, now. We got you." He wore a vest but no coat. Upon it was a metal shield. In his other hand he clutched a knotted, polished stick.

"You're Anse, aren't you?" I said. "I was looking for you. What's the matter?"

"I warn you that anything you say will be used aganst you," he said. "You're under arrest."

"I killa heem," Julio said. He struggled. Two men held him. The little girl howled steadily, holding the bread. "You steala my seester," Julio said. "Let go, meesters."

"Steal his sister?" I said. "Why, I've been——"

"Shet up," Anse said. "You can tell that to Squire."

"Steal his sister?" I said. Julio broke from the men and sprang at me again, but the marshal met him and they struggled until the other two pinioned his arms again. Anse released him, panting.

"You durn furriner," he said. "I've a good mind to take you up too, for assault and battery." He turned to me again. "Will you come peaceable, or do I handcuff you?"

"I'll come peaceable," I said. "Anything, just so I can find some-one——do something with——Stole his sister," I said. "Stole his——"

"I've warned you," Anse said. "He aims to charge you with medi-tated criminal assault. Here, you, make that gal shut up that noise."

"Oh," I said. Then I began to laugh. Two more boys with plas-tered heads and round eyes came out of the bushes, buttoning shirts that had already dampened onto their shoulders and arms, and I tried to stop the laughter, but I couldn't.

"Watch him, Anse, he's crazy, I believe."

"I'll h-have to qu-quit," I said. "It'll stop in a mu-minute. The other time it said ah ah ah," I said, laughing. "Let me sit down a while." I sat down, they watching me, and the little girl with her streaked face and the gnawed looking loaf, and the water swift and peaceful below the path. After a while the laughter ran out. But my throat wouldn't quit trying to laugh, like retching after your stomach is empty.

"Whoa, now," Anse said. "Get a grip on yourself."

"Yes," I said, tightening my throat. There was another yellow butterfly, like one of the sunflecks had come loose. After a while I didn't have to hold my throat so tight. I got up. "I'm ready. Which way?"

We followed the path, the two others watching Julio and the little girl and the boys somewhere in the rear. The path went along the river to the bridge. We crossed it and the tracks, people coming to the doors to look at us and more boys materialising from somewhere until when we turned into the main street we had quite a procession. Before the drug store stood an auto, a big one, but I didn't recognise them until Mrs Bland said,

"Why, Quentin! Quentin Compson!" Then I saw Gerald, and Spoade in the back seat, sitting on the back of his neck. And Shreve. I didn't know the two girls.

"Quentin Compson!" Mrs Bland said.

"Good afternoon," I said, raising my hat. "I'm under arrest. I'm sorry I didn't get your note. Did Shreve tell you?"

"Under arrest?" Shreve said. "Excuse me," he said. He heaped himself up and climbed over their feet and got out. He had on a pair of my flannel pants, like a glove. I didn't remember forgetting them. I didn't remember how many chins Mrs Bland had, either. The prettiest girl was with Gerald in front, too. They watched me through veils, with a kind of delicate horror. "Who's under arrest?" Shreve said. "What's this, mister?"

"Gerald," Mrs Bland said. "Send these people away. You get in this car, Quentin."

Gerald got out. Spoade hadn't moved.

"What's he done, Cap?" he said. "Robbed a hen house?"

"I warn you," Anse said. "Do you know the prisoner?"

"Know him," Shreve said. "Look here——"

"Then you can come along to the squire's. You're obstructing justice. Come along." He shook my arm.

"Well, good afternoon," I said. "I'm glad to have seen you all. Sorry I couldn't be with you."

"You, Gerald," Mrs Bland said.

"Look here, constable," Gerald said.

"I warn you you're interfering with an officer of the law," Anse said. "If you've anything to say, you can come to the squire's and make cognizance of the prisoner." We went on. Quite a procession now, Anse and I leading. I could hear them telling them what it was, and Spoade asking questions, and then Julio said something violently in Italian and I looked back and saw the little girl standing at the curb, looking at me with her friendly, inscrutable regard.

"Git on home," Julio shouted at her. "I beat hell outa you."

We went down the street and turned into a bit of lawn in which, set back from the street, stood a one storey building of brick trimmed with white. We went up the rock path to the door, where Anse halted everyone except us and made them remain outside. We entered, a bare room smelling of stale tobacco. There was a sheet iron stove in the center of a wooden frame filled with sand,[4] and a faded map on the wall and the dingy plat of a township. Behind a scarred littered table a man with a fierce roach of iron gray hair peered at us over steel spectacles.

"Got him, did ye, Anse?" he said.

"Got him, Squire."

He opened a huge dusty book and drew it to him and dipped a foul pen into an inkwell filled with what looked like coal dust.

"Look here, mister," Shreve said.

"The prisoner's name," the squire said. I told him. He wrote it slowly into the book, the pen scratching with excruciating deliberation.

"Look here, mister," Shreve said. "We know this fellow. We——"

"Order in the court," Anse said.

"Shut up, bud," Spoade said. "Let him do it his way. He's going to anyhow."

"Age," the squire said. I told him. He wrote that, his mouth moving as he wrote. "Occupation." I told him. "Harvard student, hey?" he said. He looked up at me, bowing his neck a little to see over the spectacles. His eyes were clear and cold, like a goat's. "What are you up to, coming out here kidnapping children?"

"They're crazy, Squire," Shreve said. "Whoever says this boy's kidnapping——"

Julio moved violently. "Crazy?" he said. "Dont I catcha heem, eh? Dont I see weetha my own eyes——"

"You're a liar," Shreve said. "You never——"

"Order, order," Anse said, raising his voice.

"You fellers shet up," the squire said. "If they dont stay quiet, turn'em out, Anse." They got quiet. The squire looked at Shreve, then at Spoade, then at Gerald. "You know this young man?" he said to Spoade.

"Yes, your honor," Spoade said. "He's just a country boy in school up there. He dont mean any harm. I think the marshal'll find it's a mistake. His father's a congregational minister."

4. The sand provided protection from fire caused by stray coals.

"H'm," the squire said. "What was you doing, exactly?" I told him, he watching me with his cold, pale eyes. "How about it, Anse?"

"Might have been," Anse said. "Them durn furriners."

"I American," Julio said. "I gotta da pape'."

"Where's the gal?"

"He sent her home," Anse said.

"Was she scared or anything?"

"Not till Julio there jumped on the prisoner. They were just walking along the river path, towards town. Some boys swimming told us which way they went."

"It's a mistake, Squire," Spoade said. "Children and dogs are always taking up with him like that. He cant help it."

"H'm," the squire said. He looked out of the window for a while. We watched him. I could hear Julio scratching himself. The squire looked back.

"Air you satisfied the gal aint took any hurt, you, there?"

"No hurt now," Julio said sullenly.

"You quit work to hunt for her?"

"Sure I quit. I run. I run like hell. Looka here, looka there, then man tella me he seen him giva her she eat. She go weetha."

"H'm," the squire said. "Well, son, I calculate you owe Julio something for taking him away from his work."

"Yes, sir," I said. "How much?"

"Dollar, I calculate."

I gave Julio a dollar.

"Well," Spoade said. "If that's all——I reckon he's discharged, your honor?"

The squire didn't look at him. "How far'd you run him, Anse?"

"Two miles, at least. It was about two hours before we caught him."

"H'm," the squire said. He mused a while. We watched him, his stiff crest, the spectacles riding low on his nose. The yellow shape of the window grew slowly across the floor, reached the wall, climbing. Dust motes whirled and slanted. "Six dollars."

"Six dollars?" Shreve said. "What's that for?"

"Six dollars," the squire said. He looked at Shreve a moment, then at me again.

"Look here," Shreve said.

"Shut up," Spoade said. "Give it to him, bud, and let's get out of here. The ladies are waiting for us. You got six dollars?"

"Yes," I said. I gave him six dollars.

"Case dismissed," he said.

"You get a receipt," Shreve said. "You get a signed receipt for that money."

The squire looked at Shreve mildly. "Case dismissed," he said without raising his voice.

"I'll be damned——" Shreve said.

"Come on here," Spoade said, taking his arm. "Good afternoon, Judge. Much obliged." As we passed out the door Julio's voice rose again, violent, then ceased. Spoade was looking at me, his brown eyes quizzical, a little cold. "Well, bud, I reckon you'll do your girl chasing in Boston after this."

"You damned fool," Shreve said. "What the hell do you mean anyway, straggling off here, fooling with these damn wops?"

"Come on," Spoade said. "They must be getting impatient."

Mrs Bland was talking to them. They were Miss Holmes and Miss Daingerfield and they quit listening to her and looked at me again with that delicate and curious horror, their veils turned back upon their little white noses and their eyes fleeing and mysterious beneath the veils.

"Quentin Compson," Mrs Bland said. "What would your mother say. A young man naturally gets into scrapes, but to be arrested on foot by a country policeman. What did they think he'd done, Gerald?"

"Nothing," Gerald said.

"Nonsense. What was it, you, Spoade?"

"He was trying to kidnap that little dirty girl, but they caught him in time," Spoade said.

"Nonsense," Mrs Bland said, but her voice sort of died away and she stared at me for a moment, and the girls drew their breaths in with a soft concerted sound. "Fiddlesticks," Mrs Bland said briskly. "If that isn't just like these ignorant lowclass Yankees. Get in, Quentin."

Shreve and I sat on two small collapsible seats. Gerald cranked the car and got in and we started.

"Now, Quentin, you tell me what all this foolishness is about," Mrs Bland said. I told them, Shreve hunched and furious on his little seat and Spoade sitting again on the back of his neck beside Miss Daingerfield.

"And the joke is, all the time Quentin had us all fooled," Spoade said. "All the time we thought he was the model youth that anybody could trust a daughter with, until the police showed him up at his nefarious work."

"Hush up, Spoade," Mrs Bland said. We drove down the street and crossed the bridge and passed the house where the pink garment hung in the window. "That's what you get for not reading my note. Why didn't you come and get it? Mr MacKenzie says he told you it was there."

"Yessum. I intended to, but I never went back to the room."

"You'd have let us sit there waiting I dont know how long, if it hadn't been for Mr MacKenzie. When he said you hadn't come back, that left an extra place, so we asked him to come. We're very glad to have you anyway, Mr MacKenzie." Shreve said nothing. His arms were folded and he glared straight ahead past Gerald's cap. It was a cap for motoring in England. Mrs Bland said so. We passed that house, and three others, and another yard where the little girl stood by the gate. She didn't have the bread now, and her face looked like it had been streaked with coal-dust. I waved my hand, but she made no reply, only her head turned slowly as the car passed, following us with her unwinking gaze. Then we ran beside the wall, our shadows running along the wall, and after a while we passed a piece of torn newspaper lying beside the road and I began to laugh again. I could feel it in my throat and I looked off into the trees where the afternoon slanted, thinking of afternoon and of the bird and the boys in swimming. But still I couldn't stop it and then I knew that if I tried too hard to stop it I'd be crying and I thought about how I'd thought about I could not be a virgin, with so many of them walking along in the shadows and whispering with their soft girlvoices lingering in the shadowy places and the words coming out and perfume and eyes you could feel not see, but if it was that simple to do it wouldn't be anything and if it wasn't anything, what was I and then Mrs Bland said, "Quentin? Is he sick, Mr MacKenzie?" and then Shreve's fat hand touched my knee and Spoade began talking and I quit trying to stop it.

"If that hamper is in his way, Mr MacKenzie, move it over on your side. I brought a hamper of wine because I think young gentlemen should drink wine, although my father, Gerald's grandfather" *ever do that Have you ever done that In the gray darkness a little light her hands locked about*

"They do, when they can get it," Spoade said. "Hey, Shreve?" *her knees her face looking at the sky the smell of honeysuckle upon her face and throat*

"Beer, too," Shreve said. His hand touched my knee again. I moved my knee again, *like a thin wash of lilac colored paint talking about him bringing*

"You're not a gentleman," Spoade said. *him between us until the shape of her blurred not with dark*

"No. I'm Canadian," Shreve said. *talking about him the oar blades winking him along winking the Cap made for motoring in England and all time rushing beneath and they two blurred within the other forever more he had been in the army had killed men*

"I adore Canada," Miss Daingerfield said. "I think it's marvellous."

"Did you ever drink perfume?" Spoade said. *with one hand he could lift her to his shoulder and run with her running Running*

"No," Shreve said, *running the beast with two backs*[5] *and she blurred in the winking oars running the swine of Euboeleus running coupled within how many Caddy*

"Neither did I," Spoade said. *I dont know too many there was something terrible in me terrible in me Father I have committed Have you ever done that We didnt we didnt do that did we do that*

"and Gerald's grandfather always picked his own mint before breakfast, while the dew was still on it. He wouldn't even let old Wilkie touch it do you remember Gerald but always gathered it himself and made his own julep. He was as crotchety about his julep as an old maid, measuring everything by a recipe in his head. There was only one man he ever gave that recipe to; that was" *we did how can you not know it if youll just wait Ill tell you how it was it was a crime we did a terrible crime it cannot be hid you think it can but wait   Poor Quentin youve never done that have you   and Ill tell you how it was Ill tell Father then itll have to be because you love Father then well have to go away amid the pointing and the horror the clean flame Ill make you say we did Im stronger than you Ill make you know we did you thought it was them but it was me listen I fooled you all the time it was me you thought I was in the house where that damn honeysuckle trying not to think the swing the cedars the secret surges the breathing locked drinking the wild breath the yes Yes Yes yes* "never be got to drink wine himself, but he always said that a hamper what book did you read that in the one where Gerald's rowing suit of wine was a necessary part of any gentlemen's picnic basket" *did you love them Caddy did you love them When they touched me I died*

one minute she was standing there the next he was yelling and pulling at her dress they went into the hall and up the stairs yelling and shoving at her up the stairs to the bathroom door and stopped her back against the door and her arm across her face yelling and trying to shove her into the bathroom when she came in to supper T. P. was feeding him he started again just whimpering at first until she touched him then he yelled she stood there her eyes like cornered rats then I was running in the gray darkness it smelled of rain and all flower scents the damp warm air released and crickets

---

5. In *Othello*, Iago uses this expression to describe lovemaking. *Euboeleus:* When Persephone was carried off by Pluto, a swineherd called Eubuleus was herding his swine at the spot, and his herd was engulfed in the chasm down which Pluto vanished with Persephone. In an ancient Greek fertility rite, Eubuleus's fate was recalled by flinging pigs into the chasms of Demeter and Persephone. Women then fetched the decayed remains and, after a purity ritual, sowed the flesh with seeds in the ground to secure a good crop and ensure human fertility. Cakes of dough in the shape of serpents and phalli were cast into the caverns to symbolize fertility.

sawing away in the grass pacing me with a small travelling island of silence Fancy watched me across the fence blotchy like a quilt on a line I thought damn that nigger he forgot to feed her again I ran down the hill in that vacuum of crickets like a breath travelling across a mirror she was lying in the water her head on the sand spit the water flowing about her hips there was a little more light in the water her skirt half saturated flopped along her flanks to the waters motion in heavy ripples going nowhere renewed themselves of their own movement I stood on the bank I could smell the honeysuckle on the water gap the air seemed to drizzle with honeysuckle and with the rasping of crickets a substance you could feel on the flesh

is Benjy still crying

I dont know yes I dont know

poor Benjy

I sat down on the bank the grass was damp a little then I found my shoes wet

get out of that water are you crazy

but she didnt move her face was a white blur framed out of the blur of the sand by her hair

get out now

she sat up then she rose her skirt flopped against her draining she climbed the bank her clothes flopping sat down

why dont you wring it out do you want to catch cold

yes

the water sucked and gurgled across the sand spit and on in the dark among the willows across the shallow the water rippled like a piece of cloth holding still a little light as water does

hes crossed all the oceans all around the world

then she talked about him clasping her wet knees her face tilted back in the gray light the smell of honeysuckle there was a light in mothers room and in Benjys where T. P. was putting him to bed

do you love him

her hand came out I didnt move it fumbled down my arm and she held my hand flat against her chest her heart thudding

no no

did he make you then he made you do it let him he was stronger than you and he tomorrow Ill kill him I swear I will father neednt know until afterward and then you and I nobody need ever know we can take my school money we can cancel my matriculation Caddy you hate him dont you dont you

she held my hand against her chest her heart thudding I turned and caught her arm

Caddy you hate him dont you

she moved my hand up against her throat her heart was hammering there

poor Quentin

her face looked at the sky it was low so low that all smells and sounds of night seemed to have been crowded down like under a slack tent especially the honeysuckle it had got into my breathing it was on her face and throat like paint her blood pounded against my hand I was leaning on my other arm it began to jerk and jump and I had to pant to get any air at all out of that thick gray honeysuckle

yes I hate him I would die for him Ive already died for him I die for him over and over again everytime this goes

when I lifted my hand I could still feel crisscrossed twigs and grass burning into the palm

poor Quentin

she leaned back on her arms her hands locked about her knees

youve never done that have you

what done what

that what I have what I did

yes yes lots of times with lots of girls

then I was crying her hand touched me again and I was crying against her damp blouse then she lying on her back looking past my head into the sky I could see a rim of white under her irises I opened my knife do you remember the day damuddy died when you sat down in the water in your drawers

yes

I held the point of the knife at her throat

it wont take but a second just a second then I can do mine I can do mine then

all right can you do yours by yourself

yes the blades long enough Benjys in bed by now

yes

it wont take but a second Ill try not to hurt

all right

will you close your eyes

no like this youll have to push it harder

touch your hand to it

but she didnt move her eyes were wide open looking past my head at the sky

Caddy do you remember how Dilsey fussed at you because your drawers

were muddy

dont cry

Im not crying Caddy

push it are you going to

do you want me to
yes push it
touch your hand to it
dont cry poor Quentin
but I couldnt stop she held my head against her damp hard breast
I could hear her heart going firm and slow now not hammering
and the water gurgling among the willows in the dark and waves of
honeysuckle coming up the air my arm and shoulder were twisted
under me
what is it what are you doing
her muscles gathered I sat up
its my knife I dropped it
she sat up
what time is it
I dont know
she rose to her feet I fumbled along the ground
Im going let it go
to the house
I could feel her standing there I could smell her damp clothes
feeling her there
its right here somewhere
let it go you can find it tomorrow come on
wait a minute Ill find it
are you afraid to
here it is it was right here all the time
was it come on
I got up and followed we went up the hill the crickets hushing before
us its funny how you can sit down and drop something and have to
hunt all around for it
the gray it was gray with dew slanting up into the gray sky then the
trees beyond
damn that honeysuckle I wish it would stop
you used to like it
we crossed the crest and went on toward the trees she walked into
me she gave over a little the ditch was a black scar on the gray grass
she walked into me again she looked at me and gave over we reached
the ditch
lets go this way
what for
lets see if you can still see Nancys bones I havent thought to look in
a long time have you
it was matted with vines and briers dark
they were right here you cant tell whether you see them or not can
you
stop Quentin

come on
the ditch narrowed closed she turned toward the trees
stop Quentin
Caddy
I got in front of her again
Caddy
stop it
I held her
Im stronger than you
she was motionless hard unyielding but still
I wont fight stop youd better stop
Caddy dont Caddy
it wont do any good dont you know it wont let me go
the honeysuckle drizzled and drizzled I could hear the crickets
watching us in a circle she moved back went around me on toward
the trees
you go on back to the house you neednt come
I went on
why dont you go on back to the house
damn that honeysuckle
we reached the fence she crawled through I crawled through when
I rose from stooping he was coming out of the trees into the gray
toward us coming toward us tall and flat and still even moving like
he was still she went to him
this is Quentin Im wet Im wet all over you dont have to if you dont
want to
their shadows one shadow her head rose it was above his on the sky
higher their two heads
you dont have to if you dont want to
then not two heads the darkness smelled of rain of damp grass and
leaves the gray light drizzling like rain the honeysuckle coming up
in damp waves I could see her face a blur against his shoulder he
held her in one arm like she was no bigger than a child he extended
his hand
glad to know you
we shook hands then we stood there her shadow high against his
shadow
one shadow
whatre you going to do Quentin
walk a while I think Ill go through the woods to the road and come
back through town
I turned away going
goodnight
Quentin

I stopped
what do you want
in the woods the tree frogs were going smelling rain in the air
they sounded like toy music boxes that were hard to turn and the
honeysuckle come here
what do you want
come here Quentin
I went back she touched my shoulder leaning down her shadow the
blur of her face leaning down from his high shadow I drew back
look out
you go on home
Im not sleepy Im going to take a walk
wait for me at the branch
Im going for a walk
Ill be there soon wait for me you wait
no Im going through the woods
I didnt look back the tree frogs didnt pay me any mind the gray
light like moss in the trees drizzling but still it wouldnt rain after a
while I turned went back to the edge of the woods as soon as I got
there I began to smell honeysuckle again I could see the lights on
the courthouse clock and the glare of town the square on the sky
and the dark willows along the branch and the light in mothers
windows the light still on in Benjys room and I stooped through the
fence and went across the pasture running I ran in the gray grass
among the crickets the honeysuckle getting stronger and stronger
and the smell of water then I could see the water the color of gray
honeysuckle I lay down on the bank with my face close to the
ground so I couldnt smell the honeysuckle I couldnt smell it then
and I lay there feeling the earth going through my clothes listening
to the water and after a while I wasnt breathing so hard and I lay
there thinking that if I didnt move my face I wouldnt have to
breathe hard and smell it and then I wasnt thinking about anything
at all she came along the bank and stopped I didnt move
its late you go on home
what
you go on home its late
all right
her clothes rustled I didnt move they stopped rustling
are you going in like I told you
I didnt hear anything
Caddy
yes I will if you want me to I will
I sat up she was sitting on the ground her hands clasped about her
knee

go on to the house like I told you
yes Ill do anything you want me to anything yes
she didnt even look at me I caught her shoulder and shook her hard
you shut up
I shook her
you shut up you shut up
yes
she lifted her face then I saw she wasnt even looking at me at all I
could see that white rim
get up
I pulled her she was limp I lifted her to her feet
go on now
was Benjy still crying when you left
go on
we crossed the branch the roof came in sight then the windows
upstairs
hes asleep now
I had to stop and fasten the gate she went on in the gray light the
smell of rain and still it wouldnt rain and honeysuckle beginning to
come from the garden fence beginning she went into the shadow I
could hear her feet then
Caddy
I stopped at the steps I couldnt hear her feet
Caddy
I heard her feet then my hand touched her not warm not cool just
still
her clothes a little damp still
do you love him now
not breathing except slow like far away breathing
Caddy do you love him now
I dont know
outside the gray light the shadows of things like dead things in
stagnant water
I wish you were dead
do you you coming in now
are you thinking about him now
I dont know
tell me what youre thinking about tell me
stop stop Quentin
you shut up you shut up you hear me you shut up are you going to
shut up
all right I will stop well make too much noise
Ill kill you do you hear
lets go out to the swing theyll hear you here
Im not crying do you say Im crying

no hush now well wake Benjy up
you go on into the house go on now
I am dont cry Im bad anyway you cant help it
theres a curse on us its not our fault is it our fault
hush come on and go to bed now
you cant make me theres a curse on us
finally I saw him he was just going into the barbershop he looked
out I went on and waited
Ive been looking for you two or three days
you wanted to see me
Im going to see you
he rolled the cigarette quickly with about two motions he struck
the match with his thumb
we cant talk here suppose I meet you somewhere
Ill come to your room are you at the hotel
no thats not so good you know that bridge over the creek in there
back of
yes all right
at one oclock right
yes
I turned away
Im obliged to you
look
I stopped looked back
she all right
he looked like he was made out of bronze his khaki shirt
she need me for anything now
Ill be there at one
she heard me tell T. P. to saddle Prince at one oclock she kept
watching
me not eating much she came
too
what are you going to do
nothing cant I go for a ride if I want to
youre going to do something what is it
none of your business whore whore
T. P. had Prince at the side door
I wont want him Im going to walk
I went down the drive and out the gate I turned into the lane then I
ran before I reached the bridge I saw him leaning on the rail the
horse was hitched in the woods he looked over his shoulder then he
turned his back he didnt look up until I came onto the bridge and
stopped he had a piece of bark in his hands breaking pieces from it
and dropping them over the rail into the water
I came to tell you to leave town

he broke a piece of bark deliberately dropped it carefully into the
water

watched it float away

I said you must leave town

he looked at me

did she send you to me

I say you must go not my father not anybody I say it

listen save this for a while I want to know if shes all right have they
been bothering her up there

thats something you dont need to trouble yourself about

then I heard myself saying Ill give you until sundown to leave town

he broke a piece of bark and dropped it into the water then he laid
the bark on the rail and rolled a cigarette with those two swift motions
spun the match over the rail

what will you do if I dont leave

Ill kill you dont think that just because I look like a kid to you

the smoke flowed in two jets from his nostrils across his face

how old are you

I began to shake my hands were on the rail I thought if I hid them
hed know why

Ill give you until tonight

listen buddy whats your name Benjys the natural isnt he

you are

Quentin

my mouth said it I didnt say it at all

Ill give you till sundown

Quentin

he raked the cigarette ash carefully off against the rail he did it slowly
and carefully like sharpening a pencil my hands had quit shaking

listen no good taking it so hard its not your fault kid it would have
been some other fellow

did you ever have a sister did you

no but theyre all bitches

I hit him my open hand beat the impulse to shut it to his face his
hand moved as fast as mine the cigarette went over the rail I swung
with the other hand he caught it too before the cigarette reached the
water he held both my wrists in the same hand his other hand flicked
to his armpit under his coat behind him the sun slanted and a bird
singing somewhere beyond the sun we looked at one another while
the bird singing he turned my hands loose

look here

he took the bark from the rail and dropped it into the water it
bobbed up the current took it floated away his hand lay on the rail
holding the pistol loosely we waited

you cant hit it now
no
it floated on it was quite still in the woods I heard the bird again
and the water afterward the pistol came up he didnt aim at all the
bark disappeared then pieces of it floated up spreading he hit two
more of them pieces of bark no bigger than silver dollars
thats enough I guess
he swung the cylinder out and blew into the barrel a thin wisp of
smoke dissolved he reloaded the three chambers shut the cylinder
he handed it to me butt first
what for I wont try to beat that
youll need it from what you said Im giving you this one because
youve seen what itll do
to hell with your gun
I hit him I was still trying to hit him long after he was holding my
wrists but I still tried then it was like I was looking at him through
a piece of colored glass I could hear my blood and then I could see
the sky again and branches against it and the sun slanting through
them and he holding me on my feet
did you hit me
I couldnt hear
what
yes how do you feel
all right let go
he let me go I leaned against the rail
do you feel all right
let me alone Im all right
can you make it home all right
go on let me alone
youd better not try to walk take my horse
no you go on
you can hang the reins on the pommel and turn him loose hell go
back to the stable
let me alone you go on and let me alone
I leaned on the rail looking at the water I heard him untie the horse
and ride off and after a while I couldnt hear anything but the water
and then the bird again I left the bridge and sat down with my back
against a tree and leaned my head against the tree and shut my eyes
a patch of sun came through and fell across my eyes and I moved a
little further around the tree I heard the bird again and the water
and then everything sort of rolled away and I didnt feel anything at
all I felt almost good after all those days and the nights with honeysuckle coming up out of the darkness into my room where I was trying to sleep even when after a while I knew that he hadnt hit me

that he had lied about that for her sake too and that I had just passed out like a girl but even that didnt matter anymore and I sat there against the tree with little flecks of sunlight brushing across my face like yellow leaves on a twig listening to the water and not thinking about anything at all even when I heard the horse coming fast I sat there with my eyes closed and heard its feet bunch scuttering the hissing sand and feet running and her hard running hands fool fool are you hurt

I opened my eyes her hands running on my face

I didnt know which way until I heard the pistol I didnt know where I didnt think he and you running off slipping

I didnt think he would have

she held my face between her hands bumping my head against the tree

stop stop that

I caught her wrists

quit that quit it

I knew he wouldnt I knew he wouldnt

she tried to bump my head against the tree

I told him never to speak to me again I told him

she tried to break her wrists free

let me go

stop it Im stronger than you stop it now

let me go Ive got to catch him and ask his let me go Quentin please let me go let me go

all at once she quit her wrists went lax

yes I can tell him I can make him believe anytime I can make him Caddy

she hadnt hitched Prince he was liable to strike out for home if the notion took him

anytime he will believe me

do you love him Caddy

do I what

she looked at me then everything emptied out of her eyes and they looked

like the eyes in statues blank and unseeing and serene

put your hand against my throat

she took my hand and held it flat against her throat

now say his name

Dalton Ames

I felt the first surge of blood there it surged in strong accelerating beats

say it again

her face looked off into the trees where the sun slanted and where the bird say it again

Dalton Ames

her blood surged steadily beating and beating against my hand

It kept on running for a long time, but my face felt cold and sort of dead, and my eye, and the cut place on my finger was smarting again. I could hear Shreve working the pump, then he came back with the basin and a round blob of twilight wobbling in it, with a yellow edge like a fading balloon, then my reflection. I tried to see my face in it.

"Has it stopped?" Shreve said. "Give me the rag." He tried to take it from my hand.

"Look out," I said. "I can do it. Yes, it's about stopped now." I dipped the rag again, breaking the balloon. The rag stained the water. "I wish I had a clean one."

"You need a piece of beefsteak for that eye," Shreve said. "Damn if you wont have a shiner tomorrow. The son of a bitch," he said.

"Did I hurt him any?" I wrung out the handkerchief and tried to clean the blood off of my vest.

"You cant get that off," Shreve said. "You'll have to send it to the cleaner's. Come on, hold it on your eye, why dont you."

"I can get some of it off," I said. But I wasn't doing much good. "What sort of shape is my collar in?"

"I dont know," Shreve said. "Hold it against your eye. Here."

"Look out," I said. "I can do it. Did I hurt him any?"

"You may have hit him. I may have looked away just then or blinked or something. He boxed the hell out of you. He boxed you all over the place. What did you want to fight him with your fists for? You goddam fool. How do you feel?"

"I feel fine," I said. "I wonder if I can get something to clean my vest."

"Oh, forget your damn clothes. Does your eye hurt?"

"I feel fine," I said. Everything was sort of violet and still, the sky green paling into gold beyond the gable of the house and a plume of smoke rising from the chimney without any wind. I heard the pump again. A man was filling a pail, watching us across his pumping shoulder. A woman crossed the door, but she didn't look out. I could hear a cow lowing somewhere.

"Come on," Shreve said. "Let your clothes alone and put that rag on your eye. I'll send your suit out first thing tomorrow."

"All right. I'm sorry I didn't bleed on him a little, at least."

"Son of a bitch," Shreve said. Spoade came out of the house, talking to the woman I reckon, and crossed the yard. He looked at me with his cold, quizzical eyes.

"Well, bud," he said, looking at me, "I'll be damned if you dont go to a lot of trouble to have your fun. Kidnapping, then fighting. What do you do on your holidays? burn houses?"

"I'm all right," I said. "What did Mrs Bland say?"

"She's giving Gerald hell for bloodying you up. She'll give you hell for letting him, when she sees you. She dont object to the fighting, it's the blood that annoys her. I think you lost caste with her a little by not holding your blood better. How do you feel?"

"Sure," Shreve said. "If you cant be a Bland, the next best thing is to commit adultery with one or get drunk and fight him, as the case may be."

"Quite right," Spoade said. "But I didn't know Quentin was drunk."

"He wasn't," Shreve said. "Do you have to be drunk to want to hit that son of a bitch?"

"Well, I think I'd have to be pretty drunk to try it, after seeing how Quentin came out. Where'd he learn to box?"

"He's been going to Mike's every day, over in town," I said.

"He has?" Spoade said. "Did you know that when you hit him?"

"I dont know," I said. "I guess so. Yes."

"Wet it again," Shreve said. "Want some fresh water?"

"This is all right," I said. I dipped the cloth again and held it to my eye. "Wish I had something to clean my vest." Spoade was still watching me.

"Say," he said. "What did you hit him for? What was it he said?"

"I dont know. I dont know why I did."

"The first I knew was when you jumped up all of a sudden and said, 'Did you ever have a sister? did you?' and when he said No, you hit him. I noticed you kept on looking at him, but you didn't seem to be paying any attention to what anybody was saying until you jumped up and asked him if he had any sisters."

"Ah, he was blowing off as usual," Shreve said, "about his women. You know: like he does, before girls, so they dont know exactly what he's saying. All his damn innuendo and lying and a lot of stuff that dont make sense even. Telling us about some wench that he made a date with to meet at a dance hall in Atlantic City and stood her up and went to the hotel and went to bed and how he lay there being sorry for her waiting on the pier for him, without him there to give her what she wanted. Talking about the body's beauty and the sorry ends thereof and how tough women have it, without anything else they can do except lie on their backs. Leda lurking in the bushes, whimpering and moaning for the swan, see.[6] The son of a bitch. I'd hit him myself. Only I'd grabbed up her damn hamper of wine and done it if it had been me."

6. In Greek mythology, Zeus, while in the form of a swan, impregnates Leda, a Spartan queen.

"Oh," Spoade said, "the champion of dames. Bud, you excite not only admiration, but horror." He looked at me, cold and quizzical. "Good God," he said.

"I'm sorry I hit him," I said. "Do I look too bad to go back and get it over with?"

"Apologies, hell," Shreve said. "Let them go to hell. We're going to town."

"He ought to go back so they'll know he fights like a gentleman," Spoade said. "Gets licked like one, I mean."

"Like this?" Shreve said. "With his clothes all over blood?"

"Why, all right," Spoade said. "You know best."

"He cant go around in his undershirt," Shreve said. "He's not a senior yet. Come on, let's go to town."

"You needn't come," I said. "You go on back to the picnic."

"Hell with them," Shreve said. "Come on here."

"What'll I tell them?" Spoade said. "Tell them you and Quentin had a fight too?"

"Tell them nothing," Shreve said. "Tell her her option expired at sunset. Come on, Quentin. I'll ask that woman where the nearest interurban——"

"No," I said. "I'm not going back to town."

Shreve stopped, looking at me. Turning his glasses looked like small yellow moons.

"What are you going to do?"

"I'm not going back to town yet. You go on back to the picnic. Tell them I wouldn't come back because my clothes were spoiled."

"Look here," he said. "What are you up to?"

"Nothing. I'm all right. You and Spoade go on back. I'll see you tomorrow." I went on across the yard, toward the road.

"Do you know where the station is?" Shreve said.

"I'll find it. I'll see you all tomorrow. Tell Mrs Bland I'm sorry I spoiled her party." They stood watching me. I went around the house. A rock path went down to the road. Roses grew on both sides of the path. I went through the gate, onto the road. It dropped downhill, toward the woods, and I could make out the auto beside the road. I went up the hill. The light increased as I mounted, and before I reached the top I heard a car. It sounded far away across the twilight and I stopped and listened to it. I couldn't make out the auto any longer, but Shreve was standing in the road before the house, looking up the hill. Behind him the yellow light lay like a wash of paint on the roof of the house. I lifted my hand and went on over the hill, listening to the car. Then the house was gone and I stopped in the green and yellow light and heard the car growing louder and louder, until just as it began to die away it ceased all together. I waited until I heard it start again. Then I went on.

As I descended the light dwindled slowly, yet at the same time without altering its quality, as if I and not light were changing, decreasing, though even when the road ran into trees you could have read a newspaper. Pretty soon I came to a lane. I turned into it. It was closer and darker than the road, but when it came out at the trolley stop—another wooden marquee—the light was still unchanged. After the lane it seemed brighter, as though I had walked through night in the lane and come out into morning again. Pretty soon the car came. I got on it, they turning to look at my eye, and found a seat on the left side.

The lights were on in the car, so while we ran between trees I couldn't see anything except my own face and a woman across the aisle with a hat sitting right on top of her head, with a broken feather in it, but when we ran out of the trees I could see the twilight again, that quality of light as if time really had stopped for a while, with the sun hanging just under the horizon, and then we passed the marquee where the old man had been eating out of the sack, and the road going on under the twilight, into twilight and the sense of water peaceful and swift beyond. Then the car went on, the draft building steadily up in the open door until it was drawing steadily through the car with the odor of summer and darkness except honeysuckle. Honeysuckle was the saddest odor of all, I think. I remember lots of them. Wistaria was one. On the rainy days when Mother wasn't feeling quite bad enough to stay away from the windows we used to play under it. When Mother stayed in bed Dilsey would put old clothes on us and let us go out in the rain because she said rain never hurt young folks. But if Mother was up we always began by playing on the porch until she said we were making too much noise, then we went out and played under the wistaria frame.

This was where I saw the river for the last time this morning, about here. I could feel water beyond the twilight, smell. When it bloomed in the spring and it rained the smell was everywhere you didn't notice it so much at other times but when it rained the smell began to come into the house at twilight either it would rain more at twilight or there was something in the light itself but it always smelled strongest then until I would lie in bed thinking when will it stop when will it stop. The draft in the door smelled of water, a damp steady breath. Sometimes I could put myself to sleep saying that over and over until after the honeysuckle got all mixed up in it the whole thing came to symbolise night and unrest I seemed to be lying neither asleep nor awake looking down a long corridor of gray

halflight where all stable things had become shadowy paradoxical
all I had done shadows all I had felt suffered taking visible form
antic and perverse mocking without relevance inherent themselves
with the denial of the significance they should have affirmed thinking I was I was not who was not was not who.

I could smell the curves of the river beyond the dusk and I saw
the last light supine and tranquil upon tideflats like pieces of broken mirror, then beyond them lights began in the pale clear air,
trembling a little like butterflies hovering a long way off. Benjamin
the child of. How he used to sit before that mirror. Refuge unfailing
in which conflict tempered silenced reconciled. Benjamin the child
of mine old age held hostage into Egypt.[7] O Benjamin. Dilsey said
it was because Mother was too proud for him? They come into
white people's lives like that in sudden sharp black trickles that
isolate white facts for an instant in unarguable truth like under a
microscope; the rest of the time just voices that laugh when you see
nothing to laugh at, tears when no reason for tears. They will bet
on the odd or even number of mourners at a funeral. A brothel full
of them in Memphis went into a religious trance ran naked into the
street. If took three policemen to subdue one of them. Yes Jesus O
good man Jesus O that good man.

The car stopped. I got out, with them looking at my eye. When
the trolley came it was full. I stopped on the back platform.

"Seats up front," the conductor said. I looked into the car. There
were no seats on the left side.

"I'm not going far," I said. "I'll just stand here."

We crossed the river. The bridge, that is, arching slow and high
into space, between silence and nothingness where lights—yellow
and red and green—trembled in the clear air, repeating themselves.

"Better go up front and get a seat," the conductor said.

"I get off pretty soon," I said. "A couple of blocks."

I got off before we reached the postoffice. They'd all be sitting
around somewhere by now though, and then I was hearing my
watch and I began to listen for the chimes and I touched Shreve's
letter through my coat, the bitten shadows of the elms flowing upon
my hand. And then as I turned into the quad the chimes did begin
and I went on while the notes came up like ripples on a pool and
passed me and went on, saying Quarter to what? All right. Quarter
to what.

Our windows were dark. The entrance was empty. I walked close
to the left wall when I entered, but it was empty: just the stairs

7. See Genesis 42–44.

curving up into shadows echoes of feet in the sad generations like
light dust upon the shadows, my feet waking them like dust, lightly
to settle again.

I could see the letter before I turned the light on, propped against
a book on the table so I would see it. Calling him my husband. And
then Spoade said they were going somewhere, would not be back
until late, and Mrs Bland would need another cavalier. But I would
have seen him and he cannot get another car for an hour because
after six oclock. I took out my watch and listened to it clicking
away, not knowing it couldn't even lie. Then I laid it face up on the
table and took Mrs Bland's letter and tore it across and dropped
the pieces into the waste basket and took off my coat, vest, collar, tie
and shirt. The tie was spoiled too, but then niggers. Maybe a pattern
of blood he could call that the one Christ was wearing. I found the
gasoline in Shreve's room and spread the vest on the table, where it
would be flat, and opened the gasoline.

*the first car in town a girl Girl that's what Jason couldn't bear smell
of gasoline making him sick then got madder than ever because a girl
Girl had no sister but Benjamin Benjamin the child of my sorrowful*[8]
if I'd just had a mother so I could say Mother Mother It took a lot of
gasoline, and then I couldn't tell if it was still the stain or just the
gasoline. It had started the cut to smarting again so when I went to
wash I hung the vest on a chair and lowered the light cord so that
the bulb would be drying the splotch. I washed my face and hands,
but even then I could smell it within the soap stinging, constricting
the nostrils a little. Then I opened the bag and took the shirt and
collar and tie out and put the bloody ones in and closed the bag,
and dressed. While I was brushing my hair the half hour went. But
there was until the three quarters anyway, except suppose   *seeing
on the rushing darkness only his own face no broken feather unless
two of them but not two like that going to Boston the same night then
my face his face for an instant across the crashing when out of darkness two lighted windows in rigid fleeing crash gone his face and
mine just I see saw did I see not goodbye the marquee empty of eating
the road empty in darkness in silence the bridge arching into silence
darkness sleep the water peaceful and swift not goodbye*

I turned out the light and went into my bedroom, out of the gasoline but I could still smell it. I stood at the window the curtains
moved slow out of the darkness touching my face like someone
breathing asleep, breathing slow into the darkness again, leaving
the touch.   *After they had gone up stairs Mother lay back in her
chair, the camphor handkerchief to her mouth. Father hasn't moved*

8. See Genesis 35.18.

he still sat beside her holding her hand the bellowing hammering away like no place for it in silence When I was little there was a picture in one of our books, a dark place into which a single weak ray of light came slanting upon two faces lifted out of the shadow. *You know what I'd do if I were King?* she never was a queen or a fairy she was always a king or a giant or a general *I'd break that place open and drag them out and I'd whip them good* It was torn out, jagged out. I was glad. I'd have to turn back to it until the dungeon was Mother herself she and Father upward into weak light holding hands and us lost somewhere below even them without even a ray of light. Then the honeysuckle got into it. As soon as I turned off the light and tried to go to sleep it would begin to come into the room in waves building and building up until I would have to pant to get any air at all out of it until I would have to get up and feel my way like when I was a little boy *hands can see touching in the mind shaping unseen door Door now nothing hands can see* My nose could see gasoline, the vest on the table, the door. The corridor was still empty of all the feet in sad generations seeking water. *yet the eyes unseeing clenched like teeth not disbelieving doubting even the absence of pain shin ankle knee the long invisible flowing of the stair-railing where a misstep in the darkness filled with sleeping Mother Father Caddy Jason Maury door I am not afraid only Mother Father Caddy Jason Maury geting so far ahead sleeping I will sleep fast when I door Door door* It was empty too, the pipes, the porcelain, the stained quiet walls, the throne of contemplation. I had forgotten the glass, but I could *hands can see cooling fingers invisible swan-throat where less than Moses rod[9] the glass touch tentative not to drumming lean cool throat drumming cooling the metal the glass full overfull cooling the glass the fingers flushing sleep leaving the taste of dampened sleep in the long silence of the throat* I returned up the corridor, waking the lost feet in whispering battalions in the silence, into the gasoline, the watch telling its furious lie on the dark table. Then the curtains breathing out of the dark upon my face, leaving the breathing upon my face. A quarter hour yet. And then I'll not be. The peacefullest words. Peacefullest words. *Non fui. Sum. Fui. Non sum.*[1] Somewhere I heard bells once. Mississippi or Massachusetts. I was. I am not. Massachusetts or Mississippi. Shreve has a bottle in his trunk. *Aren't you even going to open it* Mr and Mrs Jason Richmond Compson announce the *Three times. Days. Aren't you even going to open it* marriage of their daughter Candace *that liquor teaches you to confuse the means with the end* I am. Drink.

9. See Exodus 17.6 and Numbers 20.11.
1. I was not. I am. I was. I am not. (Latin.)

I was not. Let us sell Benjy's pasture so that Quentin may go to
Harvard and I may knock my bones together and together. I will be
dead in. Was it one year Caddy said. Shreve has a bottle in his
trunk. Sir I will not need Shreve's I have sold Benjy's pasture and I
can be dead in Harvard Caddy said in the caverns and the grottoes
of the sea tumbling peacefully to the wavering tides because Harvard is such a fine sound forty acres is no high price for a fine sound.
A fine dead sound we will swap Benjy's pasture for a fine dead sound.
It will last him a long time because he cannot hear it unless he can
smell it *as soon as she came in the door he began to cry* I thought
all the time it was just one of those town squirts that Father was
always teasing her about until. I didn't notice him any more than
any other stranger drummer or what thought they were army shirts
until all of a sudden I knew he wasn't thinking of me at all as a
potential source of harm but was thinking of her when he looked at
me was looking at me through her like through a piece of colored
glass *why must you meddle with me dont you know it wont do any
good I thought you'd have left that for Mother and Jason*

 did Mother set Jason to spy on you I wouldn't have.

 *Women only use other people's codes of honor it's because she
loves Caddy* staying downstairs even when she was sick so Father
couldn't kid Uncle Maury before Jason Father said Uncle Maury
was too poor a classicist to risk the blind immortal boy in person he
should have chosen Jason because Jason would have made only the
same kind of blunder Uncle Maury himself would have made not
one to get him a black eye the Patterson boy was smaller than Jason
too they sold the kites for a nickel a piece until the trouble over
finances Jason got a new partner still smaller one small enough
anyway because T. P. said Jason still treasurer but Father said why
should Uncle Maury work if he Father could support five or six niggers that did nothing at all but sit with their feet in the oven he
certainly could board and lodge Uncle Maury now and then and
lend him a little money who kept his Father's belief in the celestial
derivation of his own species at such a fine heat then Mother would
cry and say that Father believed his people were better than hers
that he was ridiculing Uncle Maury to teach us the same thing she
couldn't see that Father was teaching us that all men are just
accumulations dolls stuffed with sawdust swept up from the trash
heaps where all previous dolls had been thrown away the sawdust
flowing from what wound in what side[2] that not for me died not. It

2. See John 19.34. Compare with the hymn "Rock of Ages," written by Augustus Mon-
tague Toplady.

used to be I thought of death as a man something like Grandfather a friend of his a kind of private and particular friend like we used to think of Grandfather's desk not to touch it not even to talk loud in the room where it was I always thought of them as being together somewhere all the time waiting for old Colonel Sartoris to come down and sit with them waiting on a high place beyond cedar trees Colonel Sartoris was on a still higher place looking out across at something and they were waiting for him to get done looking at it and come down Grandfather wore his uniform and we could hear the murmur of their voices from beyond the cedars they were always talking and Grandfather was always right

The three quarters began. The first note sounded, measured and tranquil, serenely peremptory, emptying the unhurried silence for the next one and that's it if people could only change one another forever that way merge like a flame swirling up for an instant then blown cleanly out along the cool eternal dark instead of lying there trying not to think of the swing until all cedars came to have that vivid dead smell of perfume that Benjy hated so. Just by imagining the clump it seemed to me that I could hear whispers secret surges smell the beating of hot blood under wild unsecret flesh watching against red eyelids the swine untethered in pairs rushing coupled into the sea[3] and he we must just stay awake and see evil done for a little while its not always and i it doesnt have to be even that long for a man of courage and he do you consider that courage and i yes sir dont you and he every man is the arbiter of his own virtues whether or not you consider it courageous is of more importance than the act itself than any act otherwise you could not be in earnest and i you dont believe i am serious and he i think you are too serious to give me any cause for alarm you wouldnt have felt driven to the expedient of telling me you had committed incest otherwise and i i wasnt lying i wasnt lying and he you wanted to sublimate a piece of natural human folly into a horror and then exorcise it with truth and i it was to isolate her out of the loud world so that it would have to flee us of necessity and then the sound of it would be as though it had never been and he did you try to make her do it and i i was afraid to i was afraid she might and then it wouldnt have done any good but if i could tell you we did it would have been so and then the others wouldnt be so and then the world would roar away and he and now this other you are not lying now either but you are still blind to what is in yourself to that part of general truth the sequence of natural events and their causes which shadows

3. See Matthew 8.28–32; Luke 8.26–34.

every mans brow even benjys you are not thinking of finitude you are contemplating an apotheosis in which a temporary state of mind will become symmetrical above the flesh and aware both of itself and of the flesh it will not quite discard you will not even be dead and i temporary and he you cannot bear to think that someday it will no longer hurt you like this now were getting at it you seem to regard it merely as an experience that will whiten your hair overnight so to speak without altering your appearance at all you wont do it under these conditions it will be a gamble and the strange thing is that man who is conceived by accident and whose every breath is a fresh cast with dice already loaded against him will not face that final main which he knows before hand he has assuredly to face without essaying expedients ranging all the way from violence to petty chicanery that would not deceive a child until someday in very disgust he risks everything on a single blind turn of a card no man ever does that under the first fury of despair or remorse or bereavement he does it only when he has realised that even the despair or remorse or bereavement is not particularly important to the dark diceman and i temporary and he it is hard believing to think that a love or a sorrow is a bond purchased without design and which matures willynilly and is recalled without warning to be replaced by whatever issue the gods happen to be floating at the time no you will not do that until you come to believe that even she was not quite worth despair perhaps and i i will never do that nobody knows what i know and he i think youd better go on up to cambridge right away you might go up into maine for a month you can afford it if you are careful it might be a good thing watching pennies has healed more scars than jesus and i suppose i realise what you believe i will realise up there next week or next month and he then you will remember that for you to go to harvard has been your mothers dream since you were born and no compson has ever disappointed a lady and i temporary it will be better for me for all of us and he every man is the arbiter of his own virtues but let no man prescribe for another mans wellbeing and i temporary and he was the saddest word of all there is nothing else in the world its not despair until time its not even time until it was

The last note sounded. At last it stopped vibrating and the darkness was still again. I entered the sitting room and turned on the light. I put my vest on. The gasoline was faint now, barely noticeable, and in the mirror the stain didn't show. Not like my eye did, anyway. I put on my coat. Shreve's letter crackled through the cloth and I took it out and examined the address, and put it in my side pocket. Then I carried the watch into Shreve's room and put it in his drawer and went to my room and got a fresh handkerchief and went to the door and put my hand on the light switch. Then I remembered I hadn't brushed my teeth, so I had to open the bag again. I found my toothbrush and got some of Shreve's paste and went out and brushed my teeth. I squeezed the brush as dry as I could and put it back in the bag and shut it, and went to the door again. Before I snapped the light out I looked around to see if there was anything else, then I saw that I had forgotten my hat. I'd have to go by the postoffice and I'd be sure to meet some of them, and they'd think I was a Harvard Square student making like he was a senior. I had forgotten to brush it too, but Shreve had a brush, so I didn't have to open the bag any more.

April Sixth, 1928.

Once a bitch always a bitch, what I say. I says you're lucky if her playing out of school is all that worries you. I says she ought to be down there in that kitchen right now, instead of up there in her room, gobbing paint on her face and waiting for six niggers that cant even stand up out of a chair unless they've got a pan full of bread and meat to balance them, to fix breakfast for her. And Mother says,

"But to have the school authorities think that I have no control over her, that I cant——"

"Well," I says. "You cant can you? You never have tried to do anything with her," I says. "How do you expect to begin this late, when she's seventeen years old?"

She thought about that for a while.

"But to have them think that . . . I didn't even know she had a report card. She told me last fall that they had quit using them this year. And now for Professor Junkin to call me on the telephone and tell me if she's absent one more time, she will have to leave school. How does she do it? Where does she go? You're down town all day; you ought to see her if she stays on the streets."

"Yes," I says. "If she stayed on the streets. I dont reckon she'd be playing out of school just to do something she could do in public," I says.

"What do you mean?" she says.

"I dont mean anything," I says. "I just answered your question." Then she begun to cry again, talking about how her own flesh and blood rose up to curse her.

"You asked me," I says.

"I dont mean you," she says. "You are the only one of them that isn't a reproach to me."

"Sure," I says. "I never had time to be. I never had time to go to Harvard or drink myself into the ground. I had to work. But of course if you want me to follow her around and see what she does, I can quit the store and get a job where I can work at night. Then I can watch her during the day and you can use Ben for the night shift."

"I know I'm just a trouble and a burden to you," she says, crying on the pillow.

"I ought to know it," I says. "You've been telling me that for thirty years. Even Ben ought to know it now. Do you want me to say anything to her about it?"

"Do you think it will do any good?" she says.

"Not if you come down there interfering just when I get started," I says. "If you want me to control her, just say so and keep your hands off. Everytime I try to, you come butting in and then she gives both of us the laugh."

"Remember she's your own flesh and blood," she says.

"Sure," I says, "that's just what I'm thinking of—flesh. And a little blood too, if I had my way. When people act like niggers, no matter who they are the only thing to do is treat them like a nigger."

"I'm afraid you'll lose your temper with her," she says.

"Well," I says. "You haven't had much luck with your system. You want me to do anything about it, or not? Say one way or the other; I've got to get on to work."

"I know you have to slave your life away for us," she says. "You know if I had my way, you'd have an office of your own to go to, and hours that became a Bascomb. Because you are a Bascomb, despite your name. I know that if your father could have foreseen——"

"Well," I says, "I reckon he's entitled to guess wrong now and then, like anybody else, even a Smith or a Jones." She begun to cry again.

"To hear you speak bitterly of your dead father," she says.

"All right," I says, "all right. Have it your way. But as I haven't got an office, I'll have to get on to what I have got. Do you want me to say anything to her?"

"I'm afraid you'll lose your temper with her," she says.

"All right," I says. "I wont say anything, then."

"But something must be done," she says. "To have people think I permit her to stay out of school and run about the streets, or that I cant prevent her doing it. . . . Jason, Jason," she says. "How could you. How could you leave me with these burdens."

"Now, now," I says. "You'll make yourself sick. Why dont you either lock her up all day too, or turn her over to me and quit worrying over her?"

"My own flesh and blood," she says, crying. So I says,

"All right. I'll tend to her. Quit crying, now."

"Dont lose your temper," she says. "She's just a child, remember."

"No," I says. "I wont." I went out, closing the door.

"Jason," she says. I didn't answer. I went down the hall. "Jason," she says beyond the door. I went on down stairs. There wasn't anybody in the diningroom, then I heard her in the kitchen. She was trying to make Dilsey let her have another cup of coffee. I went in.

"I reckon that's your school costume, is it?" I says. "Or maybe today's a holiday?"

"Just a half a cup, Dilsey," she says. "Please."

"No, suh," Dilsey says. "I aint gwine do it. You aint got no business wid mo'n one cup, a seventeen year old gal, let lone whut Miss Cahline say. You go on and git dressed for school, so you kin ride to town wid Jason. You fixin to be late again."

"No she's not," I says. "We're going to fix that right now." She looked at me, the cup in her hand. She brushed her hair back from her face, her kimono slipping off her shoulder. "You put that cup down and come in here a minute," I says.

"What for?" she says.

"Come on," I says. "Put that cup in the sink and come in here."

"What you up to now, Jason?" Dilsey says.

"You may think you can run over me like you do your grandmother and everybody else," I says. "But you'll find out different. I'll give you ten seconds to put that cup down like I told you."

She quit looking at me. She looked at Dilsey. "What time is it, Dilsey?" she says. "When it's ten seconds, you whistle. Just a half a cup, Dilsey, pl——"

I grabbed her by the arm. She dropped the cup. It broke on the floor and she jerked back, looking at me, but I held her arm. Dilsey got up from her chair.

"You, Jason," she says.

"You turn me loose," Quentin says. "I'll slap you."

"You will, will you?" I says. "You will will you?" She slapped at me. I caught that hand too and held her like a wildcat. "You will, will you?" I says. "You think you will?"

"You, Jason!" Dilsey says. I dragged her into the diningroom. Her kimono came unfastened, flapping about her, dam near naked. Dilsey came hobbling along. I turned and kicked the door shut in her face.

"You keep out of here," I says.

Quentin was leaning against the table, fastening her kimono. I looked at her.

"Now," I says. "I want to know what you mean, playing out of school and telling your grandmother lies and forging her name on your report and worrying her sick. What do you mean by it?"

She didn't say anything. She was fastening her kimono up under her chin, pulling it tight around her, looking at me. She hadn't got around to painting herself yet and her face looked like she had polished it with a gun rag. I went and grabbed her wrist. "What do you mean?" I says.

"None of your damn business," she says. "You turn me loose."

Dilsey came in the door. "You, Jason," she says.

"You get out of here, like I told you," I says, not even looking back. "I want to know where you go when you play out of school," I says. "You keep off the streets, or I'd see you. Who do you play out with? Are you hiding out in the woods with one of those dam slick-headed jellybeans? Is that where you go?"

"You—you old goddam!" she says. She fought, but I held her. "You damn old goddam!" she says.

"I'll show you," I says. "You may can scare an old woman off, but I'll show you who's got hold of you now." I held her with one hand, then she quit fighting and watched me, her eyes getting wide and black.

"What are you going to do?" she says.

"You wait until I get this belt out and I'll show you," I says, pulling my belt out. Then Dilsey grabbed my arm.

"Jason," she says. "You, Jason! Aint you shamed of yourself."

"Dilsey," Quentin says. "Dilsey."

"I aint gwine let him," Dilsey says. "Dont you worry, honey." She held to my arm. Then the belt came out and I jerked loose and flung her away. She stumbled into the table. She was so old she couldn't do any more than move hardly. But that's all right: we need somebody in the kitchen to eat up the grub the young ones cant tote off. She came hobbling between us, trying to hold me again. "Hit me, den," she says, "ef nothin else but hittin somebody wont do you. Hit me," she says.

"You think I wont?" I says.

"I dont put no devilment beyond you," she says. Then I heard Mother on the stairs. I might have known she wasn't going to keep out of it. I let go. She stumbled back against the wall, holding her kimono shut.

"All right," I says. "We'll just put this off a while. But dont think you can run it over me. I'm not an old woman, nor an old half dead nigger, either. You dam little slut," I says.

"Dilsey," she says. "Dilsey, I want my mother."

Dilsey went to her. "Now, now," she says. "He aint gwine so much as lay his hand on you while Ise here." Mother came on down the stairs.

"Jason," she says. "Dilsey."

"Now, now," Dilsey says. "I aint gwine let him tech you." She put her hand on Quentin. She knocked it down.

"You damn old nigger," she says. She ran toward the door.

"Dilsey," Mother says on the stairs. Quentin ran up the stairs, passing her. "Quentin," Mother says. "You, Quentin." Quentin ran on. I could hear her when she reached the top, then in the hall. Then the door slammed.

Mother had stopped. Then she came on. "Dilsey," she says.

"All right," Dilsey says. "Ise comin. You go on and git dat car and wait now," she says, "so you kin cahy her to school."

"Dont you worry," I says. "I'll take her to school and I'm going to see that she stays there. I've started this thing, and I'm going through with it."

"Jason," Mother says on the stairs.

"Go on, now," Dilsey says, going toward the door. "You want to git her started too? Ise comin, Miss Cahline."

I went on out. I could hear them on the steps. "You go on back to bed now," Dilsey was saying. "Dont you know you aint feeling well enough to git up yet? Go on back, now. I'm gwine to see she gits to school in time."

I went on out the back to back the car out, then I had to go all the way round to the front before I found them.

"I thought I told you to put that tire on the back of the car," I says.

"I aint had time," Luster says. "Aint nobody to watch him till mammy git done in de kitchen."

"Yes," I says. "I feed a whole dam kitchen full of niggers to follow around after him, but if I want an automobile tire changed, I have to do it myself."

"I aint had nobody to leave him wid," he says. Then he begun moaning and slobbering.

"Take him on round to the back," I says. "What the hell makes you want to keep him around here where people can see him?" I made them go on, before he got started bellowing good. It's bad enough on Sundays, with that dam field full of people that haven't got a side show and six niggers to feed, knocking a dam oversize mothball around. He's going to keep on running up and down that fence and bellowing every time they come in sight until first thing I know they're going to begin charging me golf dues, then Mother and Dilsey'll have to get a couple of china door knobs and a walking stick and work it out, unless I play at night with a lantern. Then they'd send us all to Jackson, maybe. God knows, they'd hold Old Home week when that happened.

I went on back to the garage. There was the tire, leaning against the wall, but be damned if I was going to put it on. I backed out and turned around. She was standing by the drive. I says,

"I know you haven't got any books: I just want to ask you what you did with them, if it's any of my business. Of course I haven't got any right to ask," I says. "I'm just the one that paid $11.65 for them last September."

"Mother buys my books," she says. "There's not a cent of your money on me. I'd starve first."

"Yes?" I says. "You tell your grandmother that and see what she says. You dont look all the way naked," I says, "even if that stuff on your face does hide more of you than anything else you've got on."

"Do you think your money or hers either paid for a cent of this?" she says.

"Ask your grandmother," I says. "Ask her what became of those checks. You saw her burn one of them, as I remember." She wasn't even listening, with her face all gummed up with paint and her eyes hard as a fice dog's.

"Do you know what I'd do if I thought your money or hers either bought one cent of this?" she says, putting her hand on her dress.

"What would you do?" I says. "Wear a barrel?"

"I'd tear it right off and throw it into the street," she says. "Dont you believe me?"

"Sure you would," I says. "You do it every time."

"See if I wouldn't," she says. She grabbed the neck of her dress in both hands and made like she would tear it.

"You tear that dress," I says, "and I'll give you a whipping right here that you'll remember all your life."

"See if I dont," she says. Then I saw that she really was trying to tear it, to tear it right off of her. By the time I got the car stopped and grabbed her hands there was about a dozen people looking. It made me so mad for a minute it kind of blinded me.

"You do a thing like that again and I'll make you sorry you ever drew breath," I says.

"I'm sorry now," she says. She quit, then her eyes turned kind of funny and I says to myself if you cry here in this car, on the street, I'll whip you. I'll wear you out. Lucky for her she didn't, so I turned her wrists loose and drove on. Luckily we were near an alley, where I could turn into the back street and dodge the square. They were already putting the tent up in Beard's lot. Earl had already given me the two passes for our show windows. She sat there with her face turned away, chewing her lip. "I'm sorry now," she says. "I dont see why I was ever born."

"And I know of at least one other person that dont understand all he knows about that," I says. I stopped in front of the school house. The bell had rung, and the last of them were just going in. "You're on time for once, anyway," I says. "Are you going in there and stay there, or am I coming with you and make you?" She got out and banged the door. "Remember what I say," I says. "I mean it. Let me hear one more time that you are slipping up and down back alleys with one of those dam squirts."

She turned back at that, "I dont slip around," she says, "I dare anybody to know everything I do."

"And they all know it, too," I says. "Everybody in this town knows what you are. But I wont have it anymore, you hear? I dont care what you do, myself," I says. "But I've got a position in this town, and I'm not going to have any member of my family going on like a nigger wench. You hear me?"

"I dont care," she says. "I'm bad and I'm going to hell, and I dont care. I'd rather be in hell than anywhere where you are."

"If I hear one more time that you haven't been to school, you'll wish you were in hell," I says. She turned and ran on across the yard. "One more time, remember," I says. She didn't look back.

I went to the postoffice and got the mail and drove on to the store and parked. Earl looked at me when I came in. I gave him a chance to say something about my being late, but he just said,

"Those cultivators have come. You'd better help Uncle Job put them up."

I went on to the barn, where old Job was uncrating them, at the rate of about three bolts to the hour.

"You ought to be working for me," I says. "Every other no-count nigger in town eats in my kitchen."

"I works to suit de man whut pays me Sat'dy night," he says. "When I does dat, it dont leave me a whole lot of time to please other folks." He screwed up a nut. "Aint nobody works much in dis country cep de boll-weevil, noways," he says.

"You'd better be glad you're not a boll-weevil waiting on those cultivators," I says. "You'd work yourself to death before they'd be ready to prevent you."

"Dat's de troof," he says. "Boll-weevil got tough time. Work ev'y day in de week out in de hot sun, rain er shine. Aint got no front porch to set on en watch de wattermilyuns growin en Sat'dy dont mean nothin a-tall to him."

"Saturday wouldn't mean nothing to you, either," I says, "if it depended on me to pay you wages. Get those things out of the crates now and drag them inside."

I opened her letter first and took the check out. Just like a woman. Six days late. Yet they try to make men believe that they're capable of conducting a business. How long would a man that thought the first of the month came on the sixth last in business. And like as not, when they sent the bank statement out, she would want to know why I never deposited my salary until the sixth. Things like that never occur to a woman.

"I had no answer to my letter about Quentin's easter dress. Did it arrive all right? I've had no answer to the last two letters I wrote her, though the check in the second one was cashed with the other check. Is she sick? Let me know at once or I'll come there and see for myself. You promised you would let me know when she needed things. I will expect to hear from you before the 10th. No you'd better wire me at once. You are opening my letters to her. I know that as well as if I were looking at you. You'd better wire me at once about her to this address."

About that time Earl started yelling at Job, so I put them away and went over to try to put some life into him. What this country needs is white labor. Let these dam trifling niggers starve for a couple of years, then they'd see what a soft thing they have.

Along toward ten oclock I went up front. There was a drummer there. It was a couple of minutes to ten, and I invited him up the street to get a dope.[1] We got to talking about crops.

"There's nothing to it," I says. "Cotton is a speculator's crop. They fill the farmer full of hot air and get him to raise a big crop for them to whipsaw[2] on the market, to trim the suckers with. Do you think the farmer gets anything out of it except a red neck and a hump in his back? You think the man that sweats to put it into the ground gets a red cent more than a bare living," I says. "Let him make a big crop and it wont be worth picking; let him make a small crop and he wont have enough to gin. And what for? so a bunch of dam eastern jews I'm not talking about men of the Jewish religion," I says. "I've known some jews that were fine citizens. You might be one yourself," I says.

"No," he says. "I'm an American."

"No offense," I says. "I give every man his due, regardless of religion or anything else. I have nothing against jews as an individual," I says. "It's just the race. You'll admit that they produce nothing. They follow the pioneers into a new country and sell them clothes."

"You're thinking of Armenians," he says, "aren't you. A pioneer wouldn't have any use for new clothes."

"No offense," I says. "I dont hold a man's religion against him."

"Sure," he says. "I'm an American. My folks have some French blood, why I have a nose like this. I'm an American, all right."

"So am I," I says. "Not many of us left. What I'm talking about is the fellows that sit up there in New York and trim the sucker gamblers."

1. The first edition reads "coca-cola," for which "dope" was a slang term.
2. To win two bets at one time, as in a gambling game; here, the cotton market.

"That's right," he says. "Nothing to gambling, for a poor man. There ought to be a law against it."

"Dont you think I'm right?" I says.

"Yes," he says. "I guess you're right. The farmer catches it coming and going."

"I know I'm right," I says. "It's a sucker game, unless a man gets inside information from somebody that knows what's going on. I happen to be associated with some people who're right there on the ground. They have one of the biggest manipulators in New York for an adviser. Way I do it," I says, "I never risk much at a time. It's the fellow that thinks he knows it all and is trying to make a killing with three dollars that they're laying for. That's why they are in the business."

Then it struck ten. I went up to the telegraph office. It opened up a little, just like they said. I went into the corner and took out the telegram again, just to be sure. While I was looking at it a report came in. It was up two points. They were all buying. I could tell that from what they were saying. Getting aboard. Like they didn't know it could go but one way. Like there was a law or something against doing anything but buying. Well, I reckon those eastern jews have got to live too. But I'll be damned if it hasn't come to a pretty pass when any dam foreigner that cant make a living in the country where God put him, can come to this one and take money right out of an American's pockets. It was up two points more. Four points. But hell, they were right there and knew what was going on. And if I wasn't going to take the advice, what was I paying them ten dollars a month for. I went out, then I remembered and came back and sent the wire. "All well. Q writing today."

"Q?" the operator says.

"Yes," I says. "Q. Cant you spell Q?"

"I just asked to be sure," he says.

"You send it like I wrote it and I'll guarantee you to be sure," I says. "Send it collect."

"What you sending, Jason?" Doc Wright says, looking over my shoulder. "Is that a code message to buy?"

"That's all right about that," I says. "You boys use your own judgment. You know more about it than those New York folks do."

"Well, I ought to," Doc says. "I'd a saved money this year raising it at two cents a pound."

Another report came in. It was down a point.

"Jason's selling," Hopkins says. "Look at his face."

"That's all right about what I'm doing," I says. "You boys follow your own judgment. Those rich New York jews have got to live like everybody else," I says.

I went on back to the store. Earl was busy up front. I went on back to the desk and read Lorraine's letter. "Dear daddy wish you

were here. No good parties when daddys out of town I miss my
sweet daddy." I reckon she does. Last time I gave her forty dollars.
Gave it to her. I never promise a woman anything nor let her know
what I'm going to give her. That's the only way to manage them.
Always keep them guessing. If you cant think of any other way to
surprise them, give them a bust in the jaw.

I tore it up and burned it over the spittoon. I make it a rule never
to keep a scrap of paper bearing a woman's hand, and I never write
them at all. Lorraine is always after me to write to her but I says
anything I forgot to tell you will save till I get to Memphis again but
I says I dont mind you writing me now and then in a plain envelope,
but if you ever try to call me up on the telephone, Memphis wont
hold you I says. I says when I'm up there I'm one of the boys, but I'm
not going to have any woman calling me on the telephone. Here I
says, giving her the forty dollars. If you ever get drunk and take a
notion to call me on the phone, just remember this and count ten
before you do it.

"When'll that be?" she says.

"What?" I says.

"When you're coming back," she says.

"I'll let you know," I says. Then she tried to buy a beer, but I
wouldn't let her. "Keep your money," I says. "Buy yourself a dress
with it." I gave the maid a five, too. After all, like I say money has no
value; it's just the way you spend it. It dont belong to anybody, so
why try to hoard it. It just belongs to the man that can get it and
keep it. There's a man right here in Jefferson made a lot of money
selling rotten goods to niggers, lived in a room over the store about
the size of a pigpen, and did his own cooking. About four or five
years ago he was taken sick. Scared the hell out of him so that
when he was up again he joined the church and bought himself a
Chinese missionary, five thousand dollars a year. I often think how
mad he'll be if he was to die and find out there's not any heaven,
when he thinks about that five thousand a year. Like I say, he'd better go on and die now and save money.

When it was burned good I was just about to shove the others
into my coat when all of a sudden something told me to open Quentin's before I went home, but about that time Earl started yelling for
me up front, so I put them away and went and waited on the dam
redneck while he spent fifteen minutes deciding whether he wanted
a twenty cent hame string or a thirty-five cent one.

"You'd better take that good one," I says, "How do you fellows
ever expect to get ahead, trying to work with cheap equipment?"

"If this one aint any good," he says, "why have you got it on sale?"

"I didn't say it wasn't any good," I says. "I said it's not as good as
that other one."

"How do you know it's not," he says. "You ever use airy one of them?"

"Because they dont ask thirty-five cents for it," I says. "That's how I know it's not as good."

He held the twenty cent one in his hands, drawing it through his fingers. "I reckon I'll take this hyer one," he says. I offered to take it and wrap it, but he rolled it up and put it in his overalls. Then he took out a tobacco sack and finally got it untied and shook some coins out. He handed me a quarter. "That fifteen cents will buy me a snack of dinner," he says.

"All right," I says. "You're the doctor. But dont come complaining to me next year when you have to buy a new outfit."

"I aint makin next year's crop yit," he says. Finally I got rid of him, but every time I took that letter out something would come up. They were all in town for the show, coming in in droves to give their money to something that brought nothing to the town and wouldn't leave anything except what those grafters in the Mayor's office will split among themselves, and Earl chasing back and forth like a hen in a coop, saying "Yes, ma'am, Mr Compson will wait on you. Jason, show this lady a churn or a nickel's worth of screen hooks."

Well, Jason likes work. I says no I never had university advantages because at Harvard they teach you how to go for a swim at night without knowing how to swim and at Sewanee they dont even teach you what water is.[3] I says you might send me to the state University; maybe I'll learn how to stop my clock with a nose spray and then you can send Ben to the Navy I says or to the cavalry anyway, they use geldings in the cavalry. Then when she sent Quentin home for me to feed too I says I guess that's right too, instead of me having to go way up north for a job they sent the job down here to me and then Mother begun to cry and I says it's not that I have any objection to having it here; if it's any satisfaction to you I'll quit work and nurse it myself and let you and Dilsey keep the flour barrel full, or Ben. Rent him out to a sideshow; there must be folks somewhere that would pay a dime to see him, then she cried more and kept saying my poor afflicted baby and I says yes he'll be quite a help to you when he gets his growth not being more than one and a half times as high as me now and she says she'd be dead soon and then we'd all be better off and so I says all right, all right, have it your way. It's your grandchild, which is more than any other grandparents it's got can say for certain. Only I says it's only a question of time. If you believe she'll do what she says and not try to see it, you fool yourself because the first time that was the Mother kept on saying thank God you are not a Compson except in name, because

3. Jason's father went to the University of the South, also known as Sewanee.

you are all I have left now, you and Maury and I says well I could
spare Uncle Maury myself and then they came and said they were
ready to start. Mother stopped crying then. She pulled her veil
down and we went down stairs. Uncle Maury was coming out of the
diningroom, his handkerchief to his mouth. They kind of made a
lane and we went out the door just in time to see Dilsey driving Ben
and T. P. back around the corner. We went down the steps and got
in. Uncle Maury kept saying Poor little sister, poor little sister, talking around his mouth and patting Mother's hand. Talking around
whatever it was.

"Have you got your band on?" she says. "Why dont they go on,
before Benjamin comes out and makes a spectacle. Poor little boy.
He doesn't know. He cant even realise."

"There, there," Uncle Maury says, patting her hand, talking
around his mouth. "It's better so. Let him be unaware of bereavement until he has to."

"Other women have their children to support them in times like
this." Mother says.

"You have Jason and me," he says.

"It's so terrible to me," she says. "Having the two of them like
this, in less than two years."

"There, there." he says. After a while he kind of sneaked his hand
to his mouth and dropped them out the window. Then I knew what
I had been smelling. Clove stems.[4] I reckon he thought that the
least he could do at Father's or maybe the sideboard thought it was
still Father and tripped him up when he passed. Like I say, if he
had to sell something to send Quentin to Harvard we'd all been a
dam sight better off if he'd sold that sideboard and bought himself
a one-armed strait jacket with part of the money. I reckon the reason all the Compson gave out before it got to me like Mother says,
is that he drank it up. At least I never heard of him offering to sell
anything to send me to Harvard.

So he kept on patting her hand and saying "Poor little sister,"
patting her hand with one of the black gloves that we got the bill
for four days later because it was the twenty-sixth because it was
the same day one month that Father went up there and got it and
brought it home and wouldn't tell anything about where she was or
anything and Mother crying and saying "And you didn't even see
him? You didn't even try to get him to make any provision for it?"
and Father says "No she shall not touch his money not one cent of
it" and Mother says "He can be forced to by law. He can prove nothing, unless——Jason Compson," she says. "Were you fool enough
to tell——"

4. Cloves were often used to conceal the odor of alcohol on the breath.

"Hush, Caroline," Father says, then he sent me to help Dilsey get that old cradle out of the attic and I says,

"Well, they brought my job home tonight" because all the time we kept hoping they'd get things straightened out and he'd keep her because Mother kept saying she would at least have enough regard for the family not to jeopardise my chance after she and Quentin had had theirs.

"And whar else do she belong?" Dilsey says. "Who else gwine raise her cep me? Aint I raised ev'y one of y'all?"

"And a dam fine job you made of it," I says. "Anyway it'll give her something to sure enough worry over now." So we carried the cradle down and Dilsey started to set it up in her old room. Then Mother started sure enough.

"Hush, Miss Cahline," Dilsey says. "You gwine wake her up."

"In there?" Mother says. "To be contaminated by that atmosphere? It'll be hard enough as it is, with the heritage she already has."

"Hush," Father says. "Dont be silly."

"Why aint she gwine sleep in here," Dilsey says. "In the same room whar I put her maw to bed ev'y night of her life since she was big enough to sleep by herself."

"You dont know," Mother says. "To have my own daughter cast off by her husband. Poor little innocent baby," she says, looking at Quentin. "You will never know the suffering you've caused."

"Hush, Caroline," Father says.

"What you want to go on like that fo Jason fer?" Dilsey says.

"I've tried to protect him," Mother says. "I've always tried to protect him from it. At least I can do my best to shield her."

"How sleepin in dis room gwine hurt her, I like to know," Dilsey says.

"I cant help it," Mother says. "I know I'm just a troublesome old woman. But I know that people cannot flout God's laws with impunity."

"Nonsense," Father says. "Fix it in Miss Caroline's room then, Dilsey."

"You can say nonsense," Mother says. "But she must never know. She must never even learn that name. Dilsey, I forbid you ever to speak that name in her hearing. If she could grow up never to know that she had a mother, I would thank God."

"Dont be a fool," Father says.

"I have never interfered with the way you brought them up," Mother says. "But now I cannot stand anymore. We must decide this now, tonight. Either that name is never to be spoken in her hearing, or she must go, or I will go. Take your choice."

"Hush," Father says. "You're just upset. Fix it in here, Dilsey."

"En you's about sick too," Dilsey says. "You looks like a hant. You git in bed and I'll fix you a toddy and see kin you sleep. I bet you aint had a full night's sleep since you lef."

"No," Mother says. "Dont you know what the doctor says? Why must you encourage him to drink? That's what's the matter with him now. Look at me, I suffer too, but I'm not so weak that I must kill myself with whiskey."

"Fiddlesticks," Father says. "What do doctors know? They make their livings advising people to do whatever they are not doing at the time, which is the extent of anyone's knowledge of the degenerate ape. You'll have a minister in to hold my hand next." Then Mother cried, and he went out. Went down stairs, and then I heard the sideboard. I woke up and heard him going down again. Mother had gone to sleep or something, because the house was quiet at last. He was trying to be quiet too, because I couldn't hear him, only the bottom of his nightshirt and his bare legs in front of the sideboard.

Dilsey fixed the cradle and undressed her and put her in it. She never had waked up since he brought her in the house.

"She pretty near too big fer hit," Dilsey says. "Dar now. I gwine spread me a pallet right acrost de hall, so you wont need to git up in de night."

"I wont sleep," Mother says. "You go on home. I wont mind. I'll be happy to give the rest of my life to her, if I can just prevent——"

"Hush, now," Dilsey says. "We gwine take keer of her. En you go on to bed too," she says to me. "You got to go to school tomorrow."

So I went out, then Mother called me back and cried on me a while.

"You are my only hope," she says. "Every night I thank God for you." While we were waiting there for them to start she says Thank God if he had to be taken too, it is you left me and not Quentin. Thank God you are not a Compson, because all I have left now is you and Maury and I says, Well I could spare Uncle Maury myself. Well, he kept on patting her hand with his black glove, talking away from her. He took them off when his turn with the shovel came. He got up near the first, where they were holding the umbrellas over them, stamping every now and then and trying to kick the mud off their feet and sticking to the shovels so they'd have to knock it off, making a hollow sound when it fell on it, and when I stepped back around the hack I could see him behind a tombstone, taking another one out of a bottle. I thought he never was going to stop because I had on my new suit too, but it happened that there wasn't much mud on the wheels yet, only Mother saw it and says I dont know when you'll ever have another one and Uncle Maury says, "Now, now. Dont you worry at all. You have me to depend on, always."

And we have. Always. The fourth letter was from him. But there wasn't any need to open it. I could have written it myself, or recited it to her from memory, adding ten dollars just to be safe. But I had a hunch about that other letter. I just felt that it was about time she was up to some of her tricks again. She got pretty wise after that first time. She found out pretty quick that I was a different breed of cat from Father. When they begun to get it filled up toward the top Mother started crying sure enough, so Uncle Maury got in with her and drove off. He says You can come in with somebody: they'll be glad to give you a lift. I'll have to take your mother on and I thought about saying, Yes you ought to brought two bottles instead of just one only I thought about where we were, so I let them go on. Little they cared how wet I got, because then Mother could have a whale of a time being afraid I was taking pneumonia.

Well, I got to thinking about that and watching them throwing dirt into it, slapping it on anyway like they were making mortar or something or building a fence, and I began to feel sort of funny and so I decided to walk around a while. I thought that if I went toward town they'd catch up and be trying to make me get in one of them, so I went on back toward the nigger graveyard. I got under some cedars, where the rain didn't come much, only dripping now and then, where I could see when they got through and went away. After a while they were all gone and I waited a minute and came out.

I had to follow the path to keep out of the wet grass so I didn't see her until I was pretty near there, standing there in a black cloak, looking at the flowers. I knew who it was right off, before she turned and looked at me and lifted up her veil.

"Hello, Jason," she says, holding out her hand. We shook hands.

"What are you doing here?" I says. "I thought you promised her you wouldn't come back here. I thought you had more sense than that."

"Yes?" she says. She looked at the flowers again. There must have been fifty dollars' worth. Somebody had put one bunch on Quentin's. "You did?" she says.

"I'm not surprised though," I says. "I wouldn't put anything past you. You dont mind anybody. You dont give a dam about anybody."

"Oh," she says, "that job." She looked at the grave. "I'm sorry about that, Jason."

"I bet you are," I says. "You'll talk mighty meek now. But you needn't have come back. There's not anything left. Ask Uncle Maury, if you dont believe me."

"I dont want anything," she says. She looked at the grave. "Why didn't they let me know?" she says. "I just happened to see it in the paper. On the back page. Just happened to."

I didn't say anything. We stood there, looking at the grave, and then I got to thinking about when we were little and one thing and another and I got to feeling funny again, kind of mad or something, thinking about now we'd have Uncle Maury around the house all the time, running things like the way he left me to come home in the rain by myself. I says,

"A fine lot you care, sneaking in here soon as he's dead. But it wont do you any good. Dont think that you can take advantage of this to come sneaking back. If you cant stay on the horse you've got, you'll have to walk," I says. "We dont even know your name at that house," I says. "Do you know that? We dont even know your name. You'd be better off if you were down there with him and Quentin," I says. "Do you know that?"

"I know it," she says. "Jason," she says, looking at the grave, "if you'll fix it so I can see her a minute I'll give you fifty dollars."

"You haven't got fifty dollars," I says.

"Will you?" she says, not looking at me.

"Let's see it," I says. "I dont believe you've got fifty dollars."

I could see where her hands were moving under her cloak, then she held her hand out. Dam if it wasn't full of money. I could see two or three yellow ones.[5]

"Does he still give you money?" I says. "How much does he send you?"

"I'll give you a hundred," she says. "Will you?"

"Just a minute," I says. "And just like I say. I wouldn't have her know it for a thousand dollars."

"Yes," she says. "Just like you say do it. Just so I see her a minute. I wont beg or do anything. I'll go right on away."

"Give me the money," I says.

"I'll give it to you afterward," she says.

"Dont you trust me?" I says.

"No," she says. "I know you. I grew up with you."

"You're a fine one to talk about trusting people," I says. "Well," I says. "I got to get on out of the rain. Goodbye." I made to go away.

"Jason," she says. I stopped.

"Yes?" I says. "Hurry up. I'm getting wet."

"All right," she says. "Here." There wasn't anybody in sight. I went back and took the money. She still held to it. "You'll do it?" she says, looking at me from under the veil. "You promise?"

"Let go," I says. "You want somebody to come along and see us?"

She let go. I put the money in my pocket. "You'll do it, Jason?" she says. "I wouldn't ask you, if there was any other way."

5. Also called "yellow backs." Bank notes, especially gold certificates.

"You dam right there's no other way," I says. "Sure I'll do it. I said I would, didn't I? Only you'll have to do just like I say, now."

"Yes," she says. "I will." So I told her where to be, and went to the livery stable. I hurried and got there just as they were unhitching the hack. I asked if they had paid for it yet and he said No and I said Mrs Compson forgot something and wanted it again, so they let me take it. Mink was driving. I bought him a cigar, so we drove around until it begun to get dark on the back streets where they wouldn't see him. Then Mink said he'd have to take the team on back and so I said I'd buy him another cigar and so we drove into the lane and I went across the yard to the house. I stopped in the hall until I could hear Mother and Uncle Maury upstairs, then I went on back to the kitchen. She and Ben were there with Dilsey. I said Mother wanted her and I took her into the house. I found Uncle Maury's raincoat and put it around her and picked her up and went back to the lane and got in the hack. I told Mink to drive to the depot. He was afraid to pass the stable, so we had to go the back way and I saw her standing on the corner under the light and I told Mink to drive close to the walk and when I said Go on, to give the team a bat. Then I took the raincoat off of her and held her to the window and Caddy saw her and sort of jumped forward.

"Hit 'em, Mink!" I says, and Mink gave them a cut and we went past her like a fire engine. "Now get on that train like you promised," I says. I could see her running after us through the back window. "Hit 'em again," I says. "Let's get on home." When we turned the corner she was still running.

And so I counted the money again that night and put it away, and I didn't feel so bad. I says I reckon that'll show you. I reckon you'll know now that you cant beat me out of a job and get away with it. It never occurred to me she wouldn't keep her promise and take that train. But I didn't know much about them then; I didn't have any more sense than to believe what they said, because the next morning dam if she didn't walk right into the store, only she had sense enough to wear the veil and not speak to anybody. It was Saturday morning, because I was at the store, and she came right on back to the desk where I was, walking fast.

"Liar," she says. "Liar."

"Are you crazy?" I says. "What do you mean? coming in here like this?" She started in, but I shut her off. I says, "You already cost me one job; do you want me to lose this one too? If you've got anything to say to me, I'll meet you somewhere after dark. What have you got to say to me?" I says. "Didn't I do everything I said? I said see her a minute, didn't I? Well, didn't you?" She just stood there looking at me, shaking like an ague-fit, her hands clenched and kind of jerking. "I did just what I said I would," I says. "You're the one that lied.

You promised to take that train. Didn't you? Didn't you promise? If you think you can get that money back, just try it," I says. "If it'd been a thousand dollars, you'd still owe me after the risk I took. And if I see or hear you're still in town after number 17 runs," I says, "I'll tell Mother and Uncle Maury. Then hold your breath until you see her again." She just stood there, looking at me, twisting her hands together.

"Damn you," she says. "Damn you."

"Sure," I says. "That's all right too. Mind what I say, now. After number 17, and I tell them."

After she was gone I felt better. I says I reckon you'll think twice before you deprive me of a job that was promised me. I was a kid then. I believed folks when they said they'd do things. I've learned better since. Besides, like I say I guess I dont need any man's help to get along I can stand on my own feet like I always have. Then all of a sudden I thought of Dilsey and Uncle Maury. I thought how she'd get around Dilsey and that Uncle Maury would do anything for ten dollars. And there I was, couldn't even get away from the store to protect my own Mother. Like she says, if one of you had to be taken, thank God it was you left me I can depend on you and I says well I dont reckon I'll ever get far enough from the store to get out of your reach. Somebody's got to hold on to what little we have left, I reckon.

So as soon as I got home I fixed Dilsey. I told Dilsey she had leprosy and I got the bible and read where a man's flesh rotted off and I told her that if she ever looked at her or Ben or Quentin they'd catch it too. So I thought I had everything all fixed until that day when I came home and found Ben bellowing. Raising hell and nobody could quiet him. Mother said, Well, get him the slipper then. Dilsey made out she didn't hear. Mother said it again and I says I'd go I couldn't stand that dam noise. Like I say I can stand lots of things I dont expect much from them but if I have to work all day long in a dam store dam if I dont think I deserve a little peace and quiet to eat dinner in. So I says I'd go and Dilsey says quick, "Jason!"

Well, like a flash I knew what was up, but just to make sure I went and got the slipper and brought it back, and just like I thought, when he saw it you'd thought we were killing him. So I made Dilsey own up, then I told Mother. We had to take her up to bed then, and after things got quieted down a little I put the fear of God into Dilsey. As much as you can into a nigger, that is. That's the trouble with nigger servants, when they've been with you for a long time they get so full of self importance that they're not worth a dam. Think they run the whole family.

"I like to know whut's de hurt in lettin dat po chile see her own baby," Dilsey says. "If Mr Jason was still here hit ud be different."

"Only Mr Jason's not here," I says. "I know you wont pay me any mind, but I reckon you'll do what Mother says. You keep on worrying her like this until you get her into the graveyard too, then you can fill the whole house full of ragtag and bobtail. But what did you want to let that dam boy see her for?"

"You's a cold man, Jason, if man you is," she says. "I thank de Lawd I got mo heart dan dat, even ef hit is black."

"At least I'm man enough to keep that flour barrel full," I says. "And if you do that again, you wont be eating out of it either."

So the next time I told her that if she tried Dilsey again, Mother was going to fire Dilsey and send Ben to Jackson and take Quentin and go away. She looked at me for a while. There wasn't any street light close and I couldn't see her face much. But I could feel her looking at me. When we were little when she'd get mad and couldn't do anything about it her upper lip would begin to jump. Everytime it jumped it would leave a little more of her teeth showing, and all the time she'd be as still as a post, not a muscle moving except her lip jerking higher and higher up her teeth. But she didn't say anything. She just said,

"All right. How much?"

"Well, if one look through a hack window was worth a hundred," I says. So after that she behaved pretty well, only one time she asked to see a statement of the bank account.

"I know they have Mother's indorsement on them," she says. "But I want to see the bank statement. I want to see myself where those checks go."

"That's in Mother's private business," I says. "If you think you have any right to pry into her private affairs I'll tell her you believe those checks are being misappropriated and you want an audit because you dont trust her."

She didn't say anything or move. I could hear her whispering Damn you oh damn you oh damn you.

"Say it out," I says. "I dont reckon it's any secret what you and I think of one another. Maybe you want the money back," I says.

"Listen, Jason," she says. "Dont lie to me now. About her. I wont ask to see anything. If that isn't enough, I'll send more each month. Just promise that she'll——that she——You can do that. Things for her. Be kind to her. Little things that I cant, they wont let. . . . But you wont. You never had a drop of warm blood in you. Listen,' she says. "If you'll get Mother to let me have her back, I'll give you a thousand dollars."

"You haven't got a thousand dollars," I says. "I know you're lying now."

"Yes I have. I will have. I can get it."

"And I know how you'll get it," I says. "You'll get it the same way you got her. And when she gets big enough——" Then I thought she really was going to hit at me, and then I didn't know what she was going to do. She acted for a minute like some kind of a toy that's wound up too tight and about to burst all to pieces.

"Oh, I'm crazy," she says. "I'm insane. I cant take her. Keep her. What am I thinking of. Jason," she says, grabbing my arm. Her hands were hot as fever. "You'll have to promise to take care of her, to—— She's kin to you; your own flesh and blood. Promise, Jason. You have Father's name: do you think I'd have to ask him twice? once, even?"

"That's so," I says. "He did leave me something. What do you want me to do," I says. "Buy an apron and a go-cart? I never got you into this," I says. "I run more risk than you do, because you haven't got anything at stake. So if you expect——"

"No," she says, then she begun to laugh and to try to hold it back all at the same time. "No. I have nothing at stake," she says, making that noise, putting her hands to her mouth. "Nuh-nuh-nothing," she says.

"Here," I says. "Stop that!"

"I'm tr-trying to," she says, holding her hands over her mouth. "Oh God, oh God."

"I'm going away from here," I says. "I cant be seen here. You get on out of town now, you hear?"

"Wait," she says, catching my arm. "I've stopped. I wont again. You promise, Jason?" she says, and me feeling her eyes almost like they were touching my face. "You promise? Mother——that money——if sometimes she needs things——If I send checks for her to you, other ones besides those, you'll give them to her? You wont tell? You'll see that she has things like other girls?"

"Sure," I says, "As long as you behave and do like I tell you."

And so when Earl came up front with his hat on he says, "I'm going to step up to Rogers' and get a snack. We wont have time to go home to dinner, I reckon."

"What's the matter we wont have time?" I says.

"With this show in town and all," he says. "They're going to give an afternoon performance too, and they'll all want to get done trading in time to go to it. So we'd better just run up to Rogers'."

"All right," I says. "It's your stomach. If you want to make a slave of yourself to your business, it's all right with me."

"I reckon you'll never be a slave to any business," he says.

"Not unless it's Jason Compson's business," I says.

So when I went back and opened it the only thing that surprised me was it was a money order not a check. Yes, sir. You cant trust a one of them. After all the risk I'd taken, risking Mother finding out about her coming down here once or twice a year sometimes, and me having to tell Mother lies about it. That's gratitude for you. And I wouldn't put it past her to try to notify the postoffice not to let anyone except her cash it. Giving a kid like that fifty dollars. Why I never saw fifty dollars until I was twenty-one years old, with all the other boys with the afternoon off and all day Saturday and me working in a store. Like I say, how can they expect anybody to control her, with her giving her money behind our backs. She has the same home you had I says, and the same raising. I reckon Mother is a better judge of what she needs than you are, that haven't even got a home. "If you want to give her money," I says, "you send it to Mother, dont be giving it to her. If I've got to run this risk every few months, you'll have to do like I say, or it's out."

And just about the time I got ready to begin on it because if Earl thought I was going to dash up the street and gobble two bits worth of indigestion on his account he was bad fooled. I may not be sitting with my feet on a mahogany desk but I am being payed for what I do inside this building and if I cant manage to live a civilised life outside of it I'll go where I can. I can stand on my own feet; I dont need any man's mahogany desk to prop me up. So just about the time I got ready to start I'd have to drop everything and run to sell some redneck a dime's worth of nails or something, and Earl up there gobbling a sandwich and half way back already, like as not, and then I found that all the blanks were gone. I remembered then that I had aimed to get some more, but it was too late now, and then I looked up and there she came. In the back door. I heard her asking old Job if I was there. I just had time to stick them in the drawer and close it.

She came around to the desk. I looked at my watch.

"You been to dinner already?" I says. "It's just twelve; I just heard it strike. You must have flown home and back."

"I'm not going home to dinner," she says. "Did I get a letter today?"

"Were you expecting one?" I says. "Have you got a sweetie that can write?"

"From Mother," she says. "Did I get a letter from Mother?" she says, looking at me.

"Mother got one from her," I says. "I haven't opened it. You'll have to wait until she opens it. She'll let you see it, I imagine."

"Please, Jason," she says, not paying any attention. "Did I get one?"

"What's the matter?" I says. "I never knew you to be this anxious about anybody. You must expect some money from her."

"She said she——" she says. "Please, Jason," she says. "Did I?"

"You must have been to school today, after all," I says. "Somewhere where they taught you to say please. Wait a minute, while I wait on that customer."

I went and waited on him. When I turned to come back she was out of sight behind the desk. I ran. I ran around the desk and caught her as she jerked her hand out of the drawer. I took the letter away from her, beating her knuckles on the desk until she let go.

"You would, would you?" I says.

"Give it to me," she says. "You've already opened it. Give it to me. Please, Jason. It's mine. I saw the name."

"I'll take a hame string to you," I says. "That's what I'll give you. Going into my papers."

"Is there some money in it?" she says, reaching for it. "She said she would send me some money. She promised she would. Give it to me."

"What do you want with money?" I says.

"She said she would," she says. "Give it to me. Please, Jason. I wont ever ask you anything again, if you'll give it to me this time."

"I'm going to, if you'll give me time," I says. I took the letter and the money order out and gave her the letter. She reached for the money order, not hardly glancing at the letter. "You'll have to sign it first," I says.

"How much is it?" she says.

"Read the letter," I says. "I reckon it'll say."

She read it fast, in about two looks.

"It dont say," she says, looking up. She dropped the letter to the floor. "How much is it?"

"It's ten dollars," I says.

"Ten dollars?" she says, staring at me.

"And you ought to be dam glad to get that," I says. "A kid like you. What are you in such a rush for money all of a sudden for?"

"Ten dollars?" she says, like she was talking in her sleep. "Just ten dollars?" She made a grab at the money order. "You're lying," she says. "Thief!" she says. "Thief!"

"You would, would you?" I says, holding her off.

"Give it to me!" she says. "It's mine. She sent it to me. I will see it. I will."

"You will?" I says, holding her. "How're you going to do it?"

"Just let me see it, Jason," she says. "Please. I wont ask you for anything again."

"Think I'm lying, do you?" I says. "Just for that you wont see it."

"But just ten dollars," she says. "She told me she——she told me——Jason, please please please. I've got to have some money. I've just got to. Give it to me, Jason. I'll do anything if you will."

"Tell me what you've got to have money for," I says.

"I've got to have it," she says. She was looking at me. Then all of a sudden she quit looking at me without moving her eyes at all. I knew she was going to lie. "It's some money I owe," she says. "I've got to pay it. I've got to pay it today."

"Who to?" I says. Her hands were sort of twisting. I could watch her trying to think of a lie to tell. "Have you been charging things at stores again?" I says. "You needn't bother to tell me that. If you can find anybody in this town that'll charge anything to you after what I told them, I'll eat it."

"It's a girl," she says. "It's a girl. I borrowed some money from a girl. I've got to pay it back. Jason, give it to me. Please. I'll do anything. I've got to have it. Mother will pay you. I'll write to her to pay you and that I wont ever ask her for anything again. You can see the letter. Please, Jason. I've got to have it."

"Tell me what you want with it, and I'll see about it," I says. "Tell me." She just stood there, with her hands working against her dress. "All right," I says. "If ten dollars is too little for you, I'll just take it home to Mother, and you know what'll happen to it then. Of course, if you're so rich you dont need ten dollars——"

She stood there, looking at the floor, kind of mumbling to herself. "She said she would send me some money. She said she sends money here and you say she dont send any. She said she's sent a lot of money here. She says it's for me. That it's for me to have some of it. And you say we haven't got any money."

"You know as much about that as I do," I says. "You've seen what happens to those checks."

"Yes," she says, looking at the floor. "Ten dollars," she says. "Ten dollars."

"And you'd better thank your stars it's ten dollars," I says. "Here," I says. I put the money order face down on the desk, holding my hand on it. "Sign it."

"Will you let me see it?" she says. "I just want to look at it. Whatever it says, I wont ask for but ten dollars. You can have the rest. I just want to see it."

"Not after the way you've acted," I says. "You've got to learn one thing, and that is that when I tell you to do something, you've got it to do. You sign your name on that line."

She took the pen, but instead of signing it she just stood there with her head bent and the pen shaking in her hand. Just like her mother. "Oh, God," she says, "oh, God."

"Yes," I says. "That's one thing you'll have to learn if you never learn anything else. Sign it now, and get on out of here."

She signed it. "Where's the money?" she says. I took the order and blotted it and put it in my pocket. Then I gave her the ten dollars.

"Now you go on back to school this afternoon, you hear?" I says.
She didn't answer. She crumpled the bill up in her hand like it was
a rag or something and went on out the front door just as Earl came
in. A customer came in with him and they stopped up front. I gathered up the things and put on my hat and went up front.

"Been much busy?" Earl says.

"Not much," I says. He looked out the door.

"That your car over yonder?" he says. "Better not try to go out
home to dinner. We'll likely have another rush just before the show
opens. Get you a lunch at Rogers' and put a ticket in the drawer."

"Much obliged," I says. "I can still manage to feed myself, I
reckon."

And right there he'd stay, watching that door like a hawk until I
came through it again. Well, he'd just have to watch it for a while; I
was doing the best I could. The time before I says that's the last one
now; you'll have to remember to get some more right away. But who
can remember anything in all this hurrah. And now this dam show
had to come here the one day I'd have to hunt all over town for a
blank check, besides all the other things I had to do to keep the
house running, and Earl watching the door like a hawk.

I went to the printing shop and told him I wanted to play a joke
on a fellow, but he didn't have anything. Then he told me to have a
look in the old opera house, where somebody had stored a lot of
papers and junk out of the old Merchants' and Farmers' Bank when
it failed, so I dodged up a few more alleys so Earl couldn't see me
and finally found old man Simmons and got the key from him and
went up there and dug around. At last I found a pad on a Saint
Louis bank. And of course she'd pick this one time to look at it
close. Well, it would have to do. I couldn't waste any more time
now.

I went back to the store. "Forgot some papers Mother wants to go
to the bank," I says. I went back to the desk and fixed the check.
Trying to hurry and all, I says to myself it's a good thing her eyes
are giving out, with that little whore in the house, a Christian for-
bearing woman like Mother. I says you know just as well as I do
what she's going to grow up into but I says that's your business, if
you want to keep her and raise her in your house just because of
Father. Then she would begin to cry and say it was her own flesh
and blood so I just says All right. Have it your way. I can stand it if
you can.

I fixed the letter up again and glued it back and went out.

"Try not to be gone any longer than you can help," Earl says.

"All right," I says. I went to the telegraph office. The smart boys
were all there.

"Any of you boys made your million yet?" I says.

"Who can do anything, with a market like that?" Doc says.

"What's it doing?" I says. I went in and looked. It was three points under the opening. "You boys are not going to let a little thing like the cotton market beat you, are you?" I says. "I thought you were too smart for that."

"Smart, hell," Doc says. "It was down twelve points at twelve oclock. Cleaned me out."

"Twelve points?" I says. "Why the hell didn't somebody let me know? Why didn't you let me know?" I says to the operator.

"I take it as it comes in," he says. "I'm not running a bucket shop."[6]

"You're smart, aren't you?" I says. "Seems to me, with the money I spend with you, you could take time to call me up. Or maybe your dam company's in a conspiracy with those dam eastern sharks."

He didn't say anything. He made like he was busy.

"You're getting a little too big for your pants," I says. "First thing you know you'll be working for a living."

"What's the matter with you?" Doc says. "You're still three points to the good."

"Yes," I says. "If I happened to be selling. I haven't mentioned that yet, I think. You boys all cleaned out?"

"I got caught twice," Doc says. "I switched just in time."

"Well," I. O. Snopes says, "I've picked hit; I reckon taint no more than fair fer hit to pick me once in a while."

So I left them buying and selling among themselves at a nickel a point. I found a nigger and sent him for my car and stood on the corner and waited. I couldn't see Earl looking up and down the street, with one eye on the clock, because I couldn't see the door from here. After about a week he got back with it.

"Where the hell have you been?" I says. "Riding around where the wenches could see you?"

"I come straight as I could," he says. "I had to drive clean around the square, wid all dem wagons."

I never found a nigger yet that didn't have an airtight alibi for whatever he did. But just turn one loose in a car and he's bound to show off. I got in and went on around the square. I caught a glimpse of Earl in the door across the square.

I went straight to the kitchen and told Dilsey to hurry up with dinner.

"Quentin aint come yit," she says.

"What of that?" I says. "You'll be telling me next that Luster's not quite ready to eat yet. Quentin knows when meals are served in this house. Hurry up with it, now."

6. A fraudulent securities brokerage.

Mother was in her room. I gave her the letter. She opened it and took the check out and sat holding it in her hand. I went and got the shovel from the corner and gave her a match. "Come on," I says. "Get it over with. You'll be crying in a minute."

She took the match, but she didn't strike it. She sat there, looking at the check. Just like I said it would be.

"I hate to do it," she says. "To increase your burden by adding Quentin. . . ."

"I guess we'll get along," I says. "Come on. Get it over with."

But she just sat there, holding the check.

"This one is on a different bank," she says. "They have been on an Indianapolis bank."

"Yes," I says. "Women are allowed to do that too."

"Do what?" she says.

"Keep money in two different banks," I says.

"Oh," she says. She looked at the check a while. "I'm glad to know she's so . . . she has so much. . . . God sees that I am doing right," she says.

"Come on," I says. "Finish it. Get the fun over."

"Fun?" she says. "When I think——"

"I thought you were burning this two hundred dollars a month for fun," I says. "Come on, now. Want me to strike the match?"

"I could bring myself to accept them," she says. "For my children's sake. I have no pride."

"You'd never be satisfied," I says. "You know you wouldn't. You've settled that once, let it stay settled. We can get along."

"I leave everything to you," she says. "But sometimes I become afraid that in doing this I am depriving you all of what is rightfully yours. Perhaps I shall be punished for it. If you want me to, I will smother my pride and accept them."

"What would be the good in beginning now, when you've been destroying them for fifteen years?" I says. "If you keep on doing it, you have lost nothing, but if you'd begin to take them now, you'll have lost fifty thousand dollars. We've got along so far, haven't we?" I says. "I haven't seen you in the poorhouse yet."

"Yes," she says. "We Bascombs need nobody's charity. Certainly not that of a fallen woman."

She struck the match and lit the check and put it in the shovel, and then the envelope, and watched them burn.

"You dont know what it is," she says. "Thank God you will never know what a mother feels."

"There are lots of women in this world no better than her," I says.

"But they are not my daughters," she says. "It's not myself," she says. "I'd gladly take her back, sins and all, because she is my flesh and blood. It's for Quentin's sake."

Well, I could have said it wasn't much chance of anybody hurting Quentin much, but like I say I dont expect much but I do want to eat and sleep without a couple of women squabbling and crying in the house.

"And yours," she says. "I know how you feel toward her."

"Let her come back," I says, "far as I'm concerned."

"No," she says. "I owe that to your father's memory."

"When he was trying all the time to persuade you to let her come home when Herbert threw her out?" I says.

"You dont understand," she says. "I know you dont intend to make it more difficult for me. But it's my place to suffer for my children," she says. "I can bear it."

"Seems to me you go to a lot of unnecessary trouble doing it," I says. The paper burned out. I carried it to the grate and put it in. "It just seems a shame to me to burn up good money," I says.

"Let me never see the day when my children will have to accept that, the wages of sin," she says. "I'd rather see even you dead in your coffin first."

"Have it your way," I says. "Are we going to have dinner soon?" I says. "Because if we're not, I'll have to go on back. We're pretty busy today." She got up. "I've told her once," I says. "It seems she's waiting on Quentin or Luster or somebody. Here, I'll call her. Wait." But she went to the head of the stairs and called.

"Quentin aint come yit," Dilsey says.

"Well, I'll have to get on back," I says. "I can get a sandwich downtown. I dont want to interfere with Dilsey's arrangements," I says. Well, that got her started again, with Dilsey hobbling and mumbling back and forth, saying,

"All right, all right, Ise puttin hit on fast as I kin."

"I try to please you all," Mother says. "I try to make things as easy for you as I can."

"I'm not complaining, am I?" I says. "Have I said a word except I had to go back to work?"

"I know," she says. "I know you haven't had the chance the others had, that you've had to bury yourself in a little country store. I wanted you to get ahead. I knew your father would never realise that you were the only one who had any business sense, and then when everything else failed I believed that when she married, and Herbert . . . after his promise——"

"Well, he was probably lying too," I says. "He may not have even had a bank. And if he had, I dont reckon he'd have to come all the way to Mississippi to get a man for it."

We ate a while. I could hear Ben in the kitchen, where Luster was feeding him. Like I say, if we've got to feed another mouth and she wont take that money, why not send him down to Jackson. He'll be happier there, with people like him. I says God knows there's little enough room for pride in this family, but it dont take much pride to not like to see a thirty year old man playing around the yard with a nigger boy, running up and down the fence and lowing like a cow whenever they play golf over there. I says if they'd sent him to Jackson at first we'd all be better off today. I says, you've done your duty by him; you've done all anybody can expect of you and more than most folks would do, so why not send him there and get that much benefit out of the taxes we pay. Then she says, "I'll be gone soon. I know I'm just a burden to you" and I says "You've been saying that so long that I'm beginning to believe you" only I says you'd better be sure and not let me know you're gone because I'll sure have him on number seventeen that night and I says I think I know a place where they'll take her too and the name of it's not Milk street and Honey avenue[7] either. Then she begun to cry and I says All right all right I have as much pride about my kinfolks as anybody even if I dont always know where they come from.

We ate for a while. Mother sent Dilsey to the front to look for Quentin again.

"I keep telling you she's not coming to dinner," I says.

"She knows better than that," Mother says. "She knows I dont permit her to run about the streets and not come home at meal time. Did you look good, Dilsey?"

"Dont let her, then," I says.

"What can I do," she says. "You have all of you flouted me. Always."

"If you wouldn't come interfering, I'd make her mind," I says. "It wouldn't take me but about one day to straighten her out."

"You'd be too brutal with her," she says. "You have your Uncle Maury's temper."

That reminded me of the letter. I took it out and handed it to her. "You wont have to open it," I says. "The bank will let you know how much it is this time."

"It's addressed to you," she says.

"Go on and open it," I says. She opened it and read it and handed it to me.

"'My dear young nephew,' it says,

'You will be glad to learn that I am now in a position to avail myself of an opportunity regarding which, for reasons which I shall make obvious to you, I shall not go into details until I have an opportunity to divulge it to you in a more secure manner. My business experience has taught me to be chary of committing anything of a confidential nature to any more concrete medium

7. See Exodus 3.8, 17.

than speech, and my extreme precaution in this instance should give you some inkling of its value. Needless to say, I have just completed a most exhaustive examination of all its phases, and I feel no hesitancy in telling you that it is that sort of golden chance that comes but once in a lifetime, and I now see clearly before me that goal toward which I have long and unflaggingly striven: i.e., the ultimate solidification of my affairs by which I may restore to its rightful position that family of which I have the honor to be the sole remaining male descendant; that family in which I have ever included your lady mother and her children.

'As it so happens, I am not quite in a position to avail myself of this opportunity to the uttermost which it warrants, but rather than go out of the family to do so, I am today drawing upon your Mother's bank for the small sum necessary to complement my own initial investment, for which I herewith enclose, as a matter of formality, my note of hand at eight percent. per annum. Needless to say, this is merely a formality, to secure your Mother in the event of that circumstance of which man is ever the plaything and sport. For naturally I shall employ this sum as though it were my own and so permit your Mother to avail herself of this opportunity which my exhaustive investigation has shown to be a bonanza—if you will permit the vulgarism—of the first water and purest ray serene.[8]

'This is in confidence, you will understand, from one business man to another; we will harvest our own vineyards, eh? And knowing your Mother's delicate health and that timorousness which such delicately nurtured Southern ladies would naturally feel regarding matters of business, and their charming proneness to divulge unwittingly such matters in conversation, I would suggest that you do not mention it to her at all. On second thought, I advise you not to do so. It might be better to simply restore this sum to the bank at some future date, say, in a lump sum with the other small sums for which I am indebted to her, and say nothing about it at all. It is our duty to shield her from the crass material world as much as possible.

'Your affectionate Uncle,
'Maury L. Bascomb.'"

"What do you want to do about it?" I says, flipping it across the table.

"I know you grudge what I give him," she says.

"It's your money," I says. "If you want to throw it to the birds even, it's your business."

---

8. See Thomas Gray, "Elegy Written in a Country Churchyard," line 53.

"He's my own brother," Mother says. "He's the last Bascomb. When we are gone there wont be any more of them."

"That'll be hard on somebody, I guess," I says. "All right, all right," I says. "It's your money. Do as you please with it. You want me to tell the bank to pay it?"

"I know you begrudge him," she says. "I realise the burden on your shoulders. When I'm gone it will be easier on you."

"I could make it easier right now," I says. "All right, all right, I wont mention it again. Move all bedlam in here if you want to."

"He's your own brother," she says. "Even if he is afflicted."

"I'll take your bank book," I says. "I'll draw my check today."

"He kept you waiting six days," she says. "Are you sure the business is sound? It seems strange to me that a solvent business cannot pay its employees promptly."

"He's all right," I says. "Safe as a bank. I tell him not to bother about mine until we get done collecting every month. That's why it's late sometimes."

"I just couldn't bear to have you lose the little I had to invest for you," she says. "I've often thought that Earl is not a good business man. I know he doesn't take you into his confidence to the extent that your investment in the business should warrant. I'm going to speak to him."

"No, you let him alone," I says. "It's his business."

"You have a thousand dollars in it."

"You let him alone," I says. "I'm watching things. I have your power of attorney. It'll be all right."

"You dont know what a comfort you are to me," she says. "You have always been my pride and joy, but when you came to me of your own accord and insisted on banking your salary each month in my name, I thanked God it was you left me if they had to be taken."

"They were all right," I says. "They did the best they could, I reckon."

"When you talk that way I know you are thinking bitterly of your father's memory," she says. "You have a right to, I suppose. But it breaks my heart to hear you."

I got up. "If you've got any crying to do," I says, "you'll have to do it alone, because I've got to get on back. I'll get the bank book."

"I'll get it," she says.

"Keep still," I says. "I'll get it." I went up stairs and got the bank book out of her desk and went back to town. I went to the bank and deposited the check and the money order and the other ten, and stopped at the telegraph office. It was one point above the opening. I had already lost thirteen points, all because she had to come helling in there at twelve, worrying me about that letter.

"What time did that report come in?" I says.

"About an hour ago," he says.

"An hour ago?" I says. "What are we paying you for?" I says. "Weekly reports? How do you expect a man to do anything? The whole dam top could blow off and we'd not know it."

"I dont expect you to do anything," he says. "They changed that law making folks play the cotton market."

"They have?" I says. "I hadn't heard. They must have sent the news out over the Western Union."

I went back to the store. Thirteen points. Dam if I believe anybody knows anything about the dam thing except the ones that sit back in those New York offices and watch the country suckers come up and beg them to take their money. Well, a man that just calls shows he has no faith in himself, and like I say if you aren't going to take the advice, what's the use in paying money for it. Besides, these people are right up there on the ground; they know everything that's going on. I could feel the telegram in my pocket. I'd just have to prove that they were using the telegraph company to defraud. That would constitute a bucket shop. And I wouldn't hesitate that long, either. Only be damned if it doesn't look like a company as big and rich as the Western Union could get a market report out on time. Half as quick as they'll get a wire to you saying Your account closed out. But what the hell do they care about the people. They're hand in glove with that New York crowd. Anybody could see that.

When I came in Earl looked at his watch. But he didn't say anything until the customer was gone. Then he says,

"You go home to dinner?"

"I had to go to the dentist," I says because it's not any of his business where I eat but I've got to be in the store with him all the afternoon. And with his jaw running off after all I've stood. You take a little two by four country storekeeper like I say it takes a man with just five hundred dollars to worry about it fifty thousand dollars' worth.

"You might have told me," he says. "I expected you back right away."

"I'll trade you this tooth and give you ten dollars to boot, any time," I says. "Our agreement was an hour for dinner," I says, "and if you dont like the way I do, you know what you can do about it."

"I've known that some time," he says. "If it hadn't been for your mother I'd have done it before now, too. She's a lady I've got a lot of sympathy for, Jason. Too bad some other folks I know cant say as much."

"Then you can keep it," I says. "When we need any sympathy I'll let you know in plenty of time."

"I've protected you about that business a long time, Jason," he says.

"Yes?" I says, letting him go on. Listening to what he would say before I shut him up.

"I believe I know more about where that automobile came from than she does."

"You think so, do you?" I says. "When are you going to spread the news that I stole it from my mother?"

"I dont say anything," he says. "I know you have her power of attorney. And I know she still believes that thousand dollars is in this business."

"All right," I says. "Since you know so much, I'll tell you a little more: go to the bank and ask them whose account I've been depositing a hundred and sixty dollars on the first of every month for twelve years."

"I dont say anything," he says. "I just ask you to be a little more careful after this."

I never said anything more. It doesn't do any good. I've found that when a man gets into a rut the best thing you can do is let him stay there. And when a man gets it in his head that he's got to tell something on you for your own good, goodnight. I'm glad I haven't got the sort of conscience I've got to nurse like a sick puppy all the time. If I'd ever be as careful over anything as he is to keep his little shirt tail full of business from making him more than eight percent. I reckon he thinks they'd get him on the usury law if he netted more than eight percent. What the hell chance has a man got, tied down in a town like this and to a business like this. Why I could take his business in one year and fix him so he'd never have to work again, only he'd give it all away to the church or something. If there's one thing gets under my skin, it's a dam hypocrite. A man that thinks anything he dont understand all about must be crooked and that first chance he gets he's morally bound to tell the third party what's none of his business to tell. Like I say if I thought every time a man did something I didn't know all about he was bound to be a crook, I reckon I wouldn't have any trouble finding something back there on those books that you wouldn't see any use for running and telling somebody I thought ought to know about it, when for all I knew they might know a dam sight more about it now than I did, and if they didn't it was dam little of my business anyway and he says, "My books are open to anybody. Anybody that has any claim or believes she has any claim on this business can go back there and welcome."

"Sure, you wont tell," I says. "You couldn't square your conscience with that. You'll just take her back there and let her find it. You wont tell, yourself."

"I'm not trying to meddle in your business," he says. "I know you missed out on some things like Quentin had. But your mother has had a misfortunate life too, and if she was to come in here and ask me why you quit, I'd have to tell her. It aint that thousand dollars. You know that. It's because a man never gets anywhere if fact and his ledgers dont square. And I'm not going to lie to anybody, for myself or anybody else."

"Well, then," I says. "I reckon that conscience of yours is a more valuable clerk than I am; it dont have to go home at noon to eat. Only dont let it interfere with my appetite," I says, because how the hell can I do anything right, with that dam family and her not making any effort to control her nor any of them like that time when she happened to see one of them kissing Caddy and all next day she went around the house in a black dress and a veil and even Father couldn't get her to say a word except crying and saying her little daughter was dead and Caddy about fifteen then only in three years she'd been wearing haircloth or probably sandpaper at that rate. Do you think I can afford to have her running about the streets with every drummer that comes to town, I says, and them telling the new ones up and down the road where to pick up a hot one when they made Jefferson. I haven't got much pride, I cant afford it with a kitchen full of niggers to feed and robbing the state asylum of its star freshman. Blood, I says, governors and generals. It's a dam good thing we never had any kings and presidents; we'd all be down there at Jackson chasing butterflies. I says it'd be bad enough if it was mine; I'd at least be sure it was a bastard to begin with, and now even the Lord doesn't know that for certain probably.

So after a while I heard the band start up, and then they begun to clear out. Headed for the show, every one of them. Haggling over a twenty cent hame string to save fifteen cents, so they can give it to a bunch of Yankees that come in and pay maybe ten dollars for the privilege. I went on out to the back.

"Well," I says. "If you dont look out, that bolt will grow into your hand. And then I'm going to take an axe and chop it out. What do you reckon the boll-weevils'll eat if you dont get those cultivators in shape to raise them a crop?" I says, "sage grass?"

"Dem folks sho do play dem horns," he says. "Tell me man in dat show kin play a tune on a handsaw. Pick hit like a banjo."

"Listen," I says. "Do you know how much that show'll spend in this town? About ten dollars," I says. "The ten dollars Buck Turpin has in his pocket right now."

"Whut dey give Mr Buck ten dollars fer?" he says.

"For the privilege of showing here," I says. "You can put the balance of what they'll spend in your eye."

"You mean dey pays ten dollars jest to give dey show here?" he says.

"That's all," I says, "And how much do you reckon——"

"Gret day," he says. "You mean to tell me dey chargin um to let um show here? I'd pay ten dollars to see dat man pick dat saw, ef I had to. I figures dat tomorrow mawnin I be still owin um nine dollars and six bits at dat rate."

And then a Yankee will talk your head off about niggers getting ahead. Get them ahead, what I say. Get them so far ahead you cant find one south of Louisville with a blood hound. Because when I told him about how they'd pick up Saturday night and carry off at least a thousand dollars out of the county, he says,

"I dont begridge um. I kin sho afford my two bits."

"Two bits hell," I says. "That dont begin it. How about the dime or fifteen cents you'll spend for a dam two cent box of candy or something. How about the time you're wasting right now, listening to that band."

"Dat's de troof," he says. "Well, ef I lives twell night hit's gwine to be two bits mo dey takin out of town, dat's sho."

"Then you're a fool," I says.

"Well," he says. "I dont spute dat neither. Ef dat uz a crime, all chain-gangs wouldn't be black."

Well, just about that time I happened to look up the alley and saw her. When I stepped back and looked at my watch I didn't notice at the time who he was because I was looking at the watch. It was just two thirty, forty-five minutes before anybody but me expected her to be out. So when I looked around the door the first thing I saw was the red tie he had on and I was thinking what the hell kind of a man would wear a red tie. But she was sneaking along the alley, watching the door, so I wasn't thinking anything about him until they had gone past. I was wondering if she'd have so little respect for me that she'd not only play out of school when I told her not to, but would walk right past the store, daring me not to see her. Only she couldn't see into the door because the sun fell straight into it and it was like trying to see through an automobile searchlight, so I stood there and watched her go on past, with her face painted up like a dam clown's and her hair all gummed and twisted and a dress that if a woman had come out doors even on Gayoso or Beale[9] street when I was a young fellow with no more than that to cover her legs and behind, she'd been thrown in jail. I'll be damned if they dont dress like they were trying to make every man they passed on the street want to reach out and clap his hand on it. And so I was thinking what kind of a dam man would wear a red tie when all of a sudden I knew he was one of those show folks well as if she'd told me. Well, I can stand a lot; if I couldn't dam if I wouldn't be in a hell of a fix, so when they turned the corner I jumped down and

9. Streets in Memphis.

followed. Me, without any hat, in the middle of the afternoon, having to chase up and down back alleys because of my mother's good
name. Like I say you cant do anything with a woman like that, if
she's got it in her. If it's in her blood, you cant do anything with her.
The only thing you can do is to get rid of her, let her go on and live
with her own sort.

I went on to the street, but they were out of sight. And there I
was, without any hat, looking like I was crazy too. Like a man would
naturally think, one of them is crazy and another one drowned himself and the other one was turned out into the street by her husband,
what's the reason the rest of them are not crazy too. All the time I
could see them watching me like a hawk, waiting for a chance to
say Well I'm not surprised I expected it all the time the whole family's crazy. Selling land to send him to Harvard and paying taxes
to support a state University all the time that I never saw except
twice at a baseball game and not letting her daughter's name be
spoken on the place until after a while Father wouldn't even come
down town anymore but just sat there all day with the decanter I
could see the bottom of his nightshirt and his bare legs and hear
the decanter clinking until finally T. P. had to pour it for him and
she says You have no respect for your Father's memory and I says I
dont know why not it sure is preserved well enough to last only if
I'm crazy too God knows what I'll do about it just to look at water
makes me sick and I'd just as soon swallow gasoline as a glass of
whiskey and Lorraine telling them he may not drink but if you dont
believe he's a man I can tell you how to find out she says If I catch
you fooling with any of these whores you know what I'll do she says
I'll whip her grabbing at her I'll whip her as long as I can find her
she says and I says if I dont drink that's my business but have you
ever found me short I says I'll buy you enough beer to take a bath in
if you want it because I've got every respect for a good honest whore
because with Mother's health and the position I try to uphold to
have her with no more respect for what I try to do for her than
to make her name and my name and my Mother's name a byword in
the town.

She had dodged out of sight somewhere. Saw me coming and
dodged into another alley, running up and down the alleys with a
dam show man in a red tie that everybody would look at and think
what kind of a dam man would wear a red tie. Well, the boy kept
speaking to me and so I took the telegram without knowing I had
taken it. I didn't realise what it was until I was signing for it, and I
tore it open without even caring much what it was. I knew all the
time what it would be, I reckon. That was the only thing else that
could happen, especially holding it up until I had already had the
check entered on the pass book.

I dont see how a city no bigger than New York can hold enough people to take the money away from us country suckers. Work like hell all day every day, send them your money and get a little piece of paper back, Your account closed at 20.62. Teasing you along, letting you pile up a little paper profit, then bang! Your account closed at 20.62. And if that wasn't enough, paying ten dollars a month to somebody to tell you how to lose it fast, that either dont know anything about it or is in cahoots with the telegraph company. Well, I'm done with them. They've sucked me in for the last time. Any fool except a fellow that hasn't got any more sense than to take a jew's word for anything could tell the market was going up all the time, with the whole dam delta about to be flooded again and the cotton washed right out of the ground like it was last year. Let it wash a man's crop out of the ground year after year, and them up there in Washington spending fifty thousand dollars a day keeping an army in Nicarauga[1] or some place. Of course it'll overflow again, and then cotton'll be worth thirty cents a pound. Well, I just want to hit them one time and get my money back. I dont want a killing; only these small town gamblers are out for that, I just want my money back that these dam jews have gotten with all their guaranteed inside dope. Then I'm through; they can kiss my foot for every other red cent of mine they get.

I went back to the store. It was half past three almost. Dam little time to do anything in, but then I am used to that. I never had to go to Harvard to learn that. The band had quit playing. Got them all inside now, and they wouldn't have to waste any more wind. Earl says,

"He found you, did he? He was in here with it a while ago. I thought you were out back somewhere."

"Yes," I says. "I got it. They couldn't keep it away from me all afternoon. The town's too small. I've got to go out home a minute," I says. "You can dock me if it'll make you feel any better."

"Go ahead," he says, "I can handle it now. No bad news, I hope."

"You'll have to go to the telegraph office and find that out," I says. "They'll have time to tell you. I haven't."

"I just asked," he says. "Your mother knows she can depend on me."

"She'll appreciate it," I says. "I wont be gone any longer than I have to."

"Take your time," he says. "I can handle it now. You go ahead."

I got the car and went home. Once this morning, twice at noon, and now again, with her and having to chase all over town and

---

1. Noel Polk has changed this spelling to correspond with the manuscript version, which reflects Jason's pronunciation of Nicaragua.

having to beg them to let me eat a little of the food I am paying for. Sometimes I think what's the use of anything. With the precedent I've been set I must be crazy to keep on. And now I reckon I'll get home just in time to take a nice long drive after a basket of tomatoes or something and then have to go back to town smelling like a camphor factory so my head wont explode right on my shoulders. I keep telling her there's not a dam thing in that aspirin except flour and water for imaginary invalids. I says you dont know what a headache is. I says you think I'd fool with that dam car at all if it depended on me. I says I can get along without one I've learned to get along without lots of things but if you want to risk yourself in that old wornout surrey with a halfgrown nigger boy all right because I says God looks after Ben's kind, God knows He ought to do something for him but if you think I'm going to trust a thousand dollars' worth of delicate machinery to a halfgrown nigger or a grown one either, you'd better buy him one yourself because I says you like to ride in the car and you know you do.

Dilsey said she was in the house. I went on into the hall and listened, but I didn't hear anything. I went up stairs, but just as I passed her door she called me.

"I just wanted to know who it was," she says. "I'm here alone so much that I hear every sound."

"You dont have to stay here," I says. "You could spend the whole day visiting like other women, if you wanted to." She came to the door.

"I thought maybe you were sick," she says. "Having to hurry through your dinner like you did."

"Better luck next time," I says. "What do you want?"

"Is anything wrong?" she says.

"What could be?" I says. "Cant I come home in the middle of the afternoon without upsetting the whole house?"

"Have you seen Quentin?" she says.

"She's in school," I says.

"It's after three," she says. "I heard the clock strike at least a half an hour ago. She ought to be home by now."

"Ought she?" I says. "When have you ever seen her before dark?"

"She ought to be home," she says. "When I was a girl——"

"You had somebody to make you behave yourself," I says. "She hasn't."

"I cant do anything with her," she says. "I've tried and I've tried."

"And you wont let me, for some reason," I says. "So you ought to be satisfied." I went on to my room. I turned the key easy and stood there until the knob turned. Then she says,

"Jason."

"What," I says.

"I just thought something was wrong."

"Not in here," I says. "You've come to the wrong place."

"I dont mean to worry you," she says.

"I'm glad to hear that," I says. "I wasn't sure. I thought I might have been mistaken. Do you want anything?"

After a while she says, "No. Not any thing." Then she went away. I took the box down and counted out the money and hid the box again and unlocked the door and went out. I thought about the camphor, but it would be too late now, anyway. And I'd just have one more round trip. She was at her door, waiting.

"You want anything from town?" I says.

"No," she says. "I dont mean to meddle in your affairs. But I dont know what I'd do if anything happened to you, Jason."

"I'm all right," I says. "Just a headache."

"I wish you'd take some aspirin," she says. "I know you're not going to stop using the car."

"What's the car got to do with it?" I says. "How can a car give a man a headache?"

"You know gasoline always made you sick," she says. "Ever since you were a child. I wish you'd take some aspirin."

"Keep on wishing it," I says. "It wont hurt you."

I got in the car and started back to town. I had just turned onto the street when I saw a ford coming helling toward me. All of a sudden it stopped. I could hear the wheels sliding and it slewed around and backed and whirled and just as I was thinking what the hell they were up to, I saw that red tie. Then I recognised her face looking back through the window. It whirled into the alley. I saw it turn again, but when I got to the back street it was just disappearing, running like hell.

I saw red. When I recognised that red tie, after all I had told her, I forgot about everything. I never thought about my head even until I came to the first forks and had to stop. Yet we spend money and spend money on roads and dam if it isn't like trying to drive over a sheet of corrugated iron roofing. I'd like to know how a man could be expected to keep up with even a wheelbarrow. I think too much of my car; I'm not going to hammer it to pieces like it was a ford. Chances were they had stolen it, anyway, so why should they give a dam. Like I say blood always tells. If you've got blood like that in you, you'll do anything. I says whatever claim you believe she has on you has already been discharged; I says from now on you have only yourself to blame because you know what any sensible person would do. I says if I've got to spend half my time being a dam detective, at least I'll go where I can get paid for it.

So I had to stop there at the forks. Then I remembered it. It felt like somebody was inside with a hammer, beating on it. I says I've

tried to keep you from being worried by her; I says far as I'm concerned, let her go to hell as fast as she pleases and the sooner the
better. I says what else do you expect except every dam drummer
and cheap show that comes to town because even these town jellybeans give her the go-by now. You dont know what goes on I says,
you dont hear the talk that I hear and you can just bet I shut them
up too. I says my people owned slaves here when you all were running
little shirt tail country stores and farming land no nigger would
look at on shares.

If they ever farmed it. It's a good thing the Lord did something
for this country; the folks that live on it never have. Friday afternoon, and from right here I could see three miles of land that
hadn't even been broken, and every able bodied man in the county
in town at that show. I might have been a stranger starving to
death, and there wasn't a soul in sight to ask which way to town
even. And she trying to get me to take aspirin. I says when I eat
bread I'll do it at the table. I says you always talking about how
much you give up for us when you could buy ten new dresses a year
on the money you spend for those dam patent medicines. It's not
something to cure it I need it's just a even break not to have to have
them but as long as I have to work ten hours a day to support a
kitchen full of niggers in the style they're accustomed to and send
them to the show where every other nigger in the county, only he
was late already. By the time he got there it would be over.

After a while he got up to the car and when I finally got it through
his head if two people in a ford had passed him, he said yes. So I went
on, and when I came to where the wagon road turned off I could see
the tire tracks. Ab Russell was in his lot, but I didn't bother to ask
him and I hadn't got out of sight of his barn hardly when I saw the
ford. They had tried to hide it. Done about as well at it as she did at
everything else she did. Like I say it's not that I object to so much;
maybe she cant help that, it's because she hasn't even got enough
consideration for her own family to have any discretion. I'm afraid
all the time I'll run into them right in the middle of the street or
under a wagon on the square, like a couple of dogs.

I parked and got out. And now I'd have to go way around and
cross a plowed field, the only one I had seen since I left town, with
every step like somebody was walking along behind me, hitting me
on the head with a club. I kept thinking that when I got across the
field at least I'd have something level to walk on, that wouldn't jolt
me every step, but when I got into the woods it was full of under-
brush and I had to twist around through it, and then I came to a
ditch full of briers. I went along it for a while, but it got thicker and
thicker, and all the time Earl probably telephoning home about
where I was and getting Mother all upset again.

When I finally got through I had had to wind around so much that I had to stop and figure out just where the car would be. I knew they wouldn't be far from it, just under the closest bush, so I turned and worked back toward the road. Then I couldn't tell just how far I was, so I'd have to stop and listen, and then with my legs not using so much blood, it all would go into my head like it would explode any minute, and the sun getting down just to where it could shine straight into my eyes and my ears ringing so I couldn't hear anything. I went on, trying to move quiet, then I heard a dog or something and I knew that when he scented me he'd have to come helling up, then it would be all off.

I had gotten beggar lice and twigs and stuff all over me, inside my clothes and shoes and all, and then I happened to look around and I had my hand right on a bunch of poison oak. The only thing I couldn't understand was why it was just poison oak and not a snake or something. So I didn't even bother to move it. I just stood there until the dog went away. Then I went on.

I didn't have any idea where the car was now. I couldn't think about anything except my head, and I'd just stand in one place and sort of wonder if I had really seen a ford even, and I didn't even care much whether I had or not. Like I say, let her lay out all day and all night with everthing in town that wears pants, what do I care. I dont owe anything to anybody that has no more consideration for me, that wouldn't be a dam bit above planting that ford there and making me spend a whole afternoon and Earl taking her back there and showing her the books just because he's too dam virtuous for this world. I says you'll have one hell of a time in heaven, without anybody's business to meddle in only dont you ever let me catch you at it I says, I close my eyes to it because of your grandmother, but just you let me catch you doing it one time on this place, where my mother lives. These dam little slick haired squirts, thinking they are raising so much hell, I'll show them something about hell I says, and you too. I'll make him think that dam red tie is the latch string to hell, if he thinks he can run the woods with my niece.

With the sun and all in my eyes and my blood going so I kept thinking every time my head would go on and burst and get it over with, with briers and things grabbing at me, then I came onto the sand ditch where they had been and I recognised the tree where the car was, and just as I got out of the ditch and started running I heard the car start. It went off fast, blowing the horn. They kept oh blowing it, like it was saying Yah. Yah. Yaaahhhhhhhh, going out of sight. I got to the road just in time to see it go out of sight.

By the time I got up to where my car was, they were clean out of sight, the horn still blowing. Well, I never thought anything about it except I was saying Run. Run back to town. Run home and try to convince Mother that I never saw you in that car. Try to make her believe that I dont know who he was. Try to make her believe that I didn't miss ten feet of catching you in that ditch. Try to make her believe you were standing up, too.

It kept on saying Yahhhhh, Yahhhhh, Yaaahhhhhhhhh, getting fainter and fainter. Then it quit, and I could hear a cow lowing up at Russell's barn. And still I never thought. I went up to the door and opened it and raised my foot. I kind of thought then that the car was leaning a little more than the slant of the road would be, but I never found it out until I got in and started off.

Well, I just sat there. It was getting on toward sundown, and town was about five miles. They never even had guts enough to puncture it, to jab a hole in it. They just let the air out. I just stood there for a while, thinking about that kitchen full of niggers and not one of them had time to lift a tire onto the rack and screw up a couple of bolts. It was kind of funny because even she couldn't have seen far enough ahead to take the pump out on purpose, unless she thought about it while he was letting out the air maybe. But what it probably was was somebody took it out and gave it to Ben to play with for a squirt gun because they'd take the whole car to pieces if he wanted it and Dilsey says, Aint nobody teched yo car. What we want to fool with hit fer? and I says You're a nigger. You're lucky, do you know it? I says I'll swap with you any day because it takes a white man not to have anymore sense than to worry about what a little slut of a girl does.

I walked up to Russell's. He had a pump. That was just an oversight on their part, I reckon. Only I still couldn't believe she'd have had the nerve to. I kept thinking that. I dont know why it is I cant seem to learn that a woman'll do anything. I kept thinking, Let's forget for a while how I feel toward you and how you feel toward me: I just wouldn't do you this way. I wouldn't do you this way no matter what you had done to me. Because like I say blood is blood and you cant get around it. It's not playing a joke that any eight year old boy could have thought of, it's letting your own uncle be laughed at by a man that would wear a red tie. They come into town and call us all a bunch of hicks and think it's too small to hold them. Well he doesn't know just how right he is. And her too. If that's the way she feels about it, she'd better keep right on going and a dam good riddance.

I stopped and returned Russell's pump and drove on to town. I went to the drugstore and got a shot[2] and then I went to the telegraph office. It had closed at 20.21, forty points down. Forty times five dollars; buy something with that if you can, and she'll say, I've

---

2. The first edition reads "coca-cola," for which "shot" was a slang term.

got to have it I've just got to and I'll say that's too bad you'll have to try somebody else, I haven't got any money; I've been too busy to make any.

I just looked at him.

"I'll tell you some news," I says. "You'll be astonished to learn that I am interested in the cotton market," I says. "That never occurred to you, did it?"

"I did my best to deliver it," he says. "I tried the store twice and called up your house, but they didn't know where you were," he says, digging in the drawer.

"Deliver what?" I says. He handed me a telegram. "What time did this come?" I says.

"About half past three," he says.

"And now it's ten minutes past five," I says.

"I tried to deliver it," he says. "I couldn't find you."

"That's not my fault, is it?" I says. I opened it, just to see what kind of a lie they'd tell me this time. They must be in one hell of a shape if they've got to come all the way to Mississippi to steal ten dollars a month. Sell, it says. The market will be unstable, with a general downward tendency. Do not be alarmed following government report.

"How much would a message like this cost?" I says. He told me.

"They paid it," he says.

"Then I owe them that much," I says. "I already knew this. Send this collect," I says, taking a blank. Buy, I wrote, Market just on point of blowing its head off. Occasional flurries for purpose of hooking a few more country suckers who haven't got in to the telegraph office yet. Do not be alarmed. "Send that collect," I says.

He looked at the message, then he looked at the clock. "Market closed an hour ago," he says.

"Well," I says. "That's not my fault either. I didn't invent it; I just bought a little of it while under the impression that the telegraph company would keep me informed as to what it was doing."

"A report is posted whenever it comes in," he says.

"Yes," I says. "And in Memphis they have it on a blackboard every ten seconds," I says. "I was within sixty-seven miles of there once this afternoon."

He looked at the message. "You want to send this?" he says.

"I still haven't changed my mind," I says. I wrote the other one out and counted the money. "And this one too, if you're sure you can spell b-u-y."

I went back to the store. I could hear the band from down the street. Prohibition's a fine thing. Used to be they'd come in Saturday with just one pair of shoes in the family and him wearing them, and they'd go down to the express office and get his package; now they all go to the show barefooted, with the merchants in the door like a row of tigers or something in a cage, watching them pass. Earl says,

"I hope it wasn't anything serious."

"What?" I says. He looked at his watch. Then he went to the door and looked at the courthouse clock. "You ought to have a dollar watch," I says. "It wont cost you so much to believe it's lying each time."

"What?" he says.

"Nothing," I says. "Hope I haven't inconvenienced you."

"We were not busy much," he says. "They all went to the show. It's all right."

"If it's not all right," I says, "you know what you can do about it."

"I said it was all right," he says.

"I heard you," I says. "And if it's not all right, you know what you can do about it."

"Do you want to quit?" he says.

"It's not my business," I says. "My wishes dont matter. But dont get the idea that you are protecting me by keeping me."

"You'd be a good business man if you'd let yourself, Jason," he says.

"At least I can tend to my own business and let other people's alone," I says.

"I dont know why you are trying to make me fire you," he says. "You know you could quit anytime and there wouldn't be any hard feelings between us."

"Maybe that's why I dont quit," I says. "As long as I tend to my job, that's what you are paying me for." I went on to the back and got a drink of water and went on out to the back door. Job had the cultivators all set up at last. It was quiet there, and pretty soon my head got a little easier. I could hear them singing now, and then the band played again. Well, let them get every quarter and dime in the county; it was no skin off my back. I've done what I could; a man that can live as long as I have and not know when to quit is a fool. Especially as it's no business of mine. If it was my own daughter now it would be different, because she wouldn't have time to; she'd have to work some to feed a few invalids and idiots and niggers, because how could I have the face to bring anybody there. I've too much respect for anybody to do that. I'm a man, I can stand it, it's my own flesh and blood and I'd like to see the color of the man's eyes that would speak disrespectful of any woman that was my friend it's these dam good women that do it I'd like to see the good, church-going woman that's half as square as Lorraine, whore or no whore. Like I say if I was to get married you'd go up like a balloon and you know it and she says I want you to be happy to have a family of your own not to slave your life away for us. But I'll be gone soon and then you can take a wife but you'll never find a woman who is worthy of you and I says yes I could. You'd get right up out of your grave you know you would. I says no thank you I have all the women I can take care of now if I married a wife she'd probably turn out to be a hophead or something. That's all we lack in this family, I says.

The sun was down beyond the Methodist church now, and the pigeons were flying back and forth around the steeple, and when the band stopped I could hear them cooing. It hadn't been four months since Christmas, and yet they were almost as thick as ever. I reckon Parson Walthall was getting a belly full of them now. You'd have thought we were shooting people, with him making speeches and even holding onto a man's gun when they came over. Talking about peace on earth good will toward all and not a sparrow can fall to earth.[3] But what does he care how thick they get, he hasn't got anything to do: what does he care what time it is. He pays no taxes, he doesn't have to see his money going every year to have the courthouse clock cleaned to where it'll run. They had to pay a man forty-five dollars to clean it. I counted over a hundred half-hatched pigeons on the ground. You'd think they'd have sense enough to leave town. It's a good thing I dont have anymore ties than a pigeon, I'll say that.

The band was playing again, a loud fast tune, like they were breaking up. I reckon they'd be satisfied now. Maybe they'd have enough music to entertain them while they drove fourteen or fifteen miles home and unharnessed in the dark and fed the stock and milked. All they'd have to do would be to whistle the music and tell the jokes to the live stock in the barn, and then they could count up how much they'd made by not taking the stock to the show too. They could figure that if a man had five children and seven mules, he cleared a quarter by taking his family to the show. Just like that. Earl came back with a couple of packages.

"Here's some more stuff going out," he says. "Where's Uncle Job?"

"Gone to the show, I imagine," I says. "Unless you watched him."

"He doesn't slip off," he says. "I can depend on him."

"Meaning me by that," I says.

He went to the door and looked out, listening.

"That's a good band," he says. "It's about time they were breaking up, I'd say."

"Unless they're going to spend the night there," I says. The swallows had begun, and I could hear the sparrows beginning to swarm

---

3. Matthew 10.29: "Are not two sparrows sold for a farthing? Yet one of them shall not fall on the ground without your Father."

in the trees in the courthouse yard. Every once in a while a bunch of them would come swirling around in sight above the roof, then go away. They are as big a nuisance as the pigeons, to my notion. You cant even sit in the courthouse yard for them. First thing you know, bing. Right on your hat. But it would take a millionaire to afford to shoot them at five cents a shot. If they'd just put a little poison out there in the square, they'd get rid of them in a day, because if a merchant cant keep his stock from running around the square, he'd better try to deal in something besides chickens, something that dont eat, like plows or onions. And if a man dont keep his dogs up, he either dont want it or he hasn't any business with one. Like I say if all the businesses in a town are run like country businesses, you're going to have a country town.

"It wont do you any good if they have broke up," I says. "They'll have to hitch up and take out to get home by midnight as it is."

"Well," he says. "They enjoy it. Let them spend a little money on a show now and then. A hill farmer works pretty hard and gets mighty little for it."

"There's no law making them farm in the hills," I says. "Or anywhere else."

"Where would you and me be, if it wasn't for the farmers?" he says.

"I'd be home right now," I says. "Lying down, with an ice pack on my head."

"You have these headaches too often," he says. "Why dont you have your teeth examined good? Did he go over them all this morning?"

"Did who?" I says.

"You said you went to the dentist this morning."

"Do you object to my having the headache on your time?" I says. "Is that it?" They were crossing the alley now, coming up from the show.

"There they come," he says. "I reckon I better get up front." He went on. It's a curious thing how, no matter what's wrong with you, a man'll tell you to have your teeth examined and a woman'll tell you to get married. It always takes a man that never made much at any thing to tell you how to run your business, though. Like these college professors without a whole pair of socks to his name, telling you how to make a million in ten years, and a woman that couldn't even get a husband can always tell you how to raise a family.

Old man Job came up with the wagon. After a while he got through wrapping the lines around the whip socket.

"Well," I says. "Was it a good show?"

"I aint been yit," he says. "But I kin be arrested in dat tent tonight, dough."

"Like hell you haven't," I says. "You've been away from here since three oclock. Mr Earl was just back here looking for you."

"I been tendin to my business," he says. "Mr Earl knows whar I been."

"You may can fool him," I says. "I wont tell on you."

"Den he's de onliest man here I'd try to fool," he says. "Whut I want to waste my time foolin a man whut I dont keer whether I sees him Sat'dy night er not? I wont try to fool you," he says. "You too smart fer me. Yes, suh," he says, looking busy as hell, putting five or six little packages into the wagon. "You's too smart fer me. Aint a man in dis town kin keep up wid you fer smartness. You fools a man whut so smart he cant even keep up wid hisself," he says, getting in the wagon and unwrapping the reins.

"Who's that?" I says.

"Dat's Mr Jason Compson," he says. "Git up dar, Dan!"

One of the wheels was just about to come off. I watched to see if he'd get out of the alley before it did. Just turn any vehicle over to a nigger, though. I says that old rattletrap's just an eyesore, yet you'll keep it standing there in the carriage house a hundred years just so that boy can ride to the cemetery once a week. I says he's not the first fellow that'll have to do things he doesn't want to. I'd make him ride in that car like a civilised man or stay at home. What does he know about where he goes or what he goes in, and us keeping a carriage and a horse so he can take a ride on Sunday afternoon.

A lot Job cared whether the wheel came off or not, long as he wouldn't have too far to walk back. Like I say the only place for them is in the field, where they'd have to work from sunup to sundown. They cant stand prosperity or an easy job. Let one stay around white people for a while and he's not worth killing. They get so they can outguess you about work before your very eyes, like Roskus the only mistake he ever made was he got careless one day and died. Shirking and stealing and giving you a little more lip and a little more lip until some day you have to lay them out with a scantling or something. Well, it's Earl's business. But I'd hate to have my business advertised over this town by an old doddering nigger and a wagon that you thought every time it turned a corner it would come all to pieces.

The sun was all high up in the air now, and inside it was beginning to get dark. I went up front. The square was empty. Earl was back closing the safe, and then the clock begun to strike.

"You lock the back door?" he says. I went back and locked it and came back. "I suppose you're going to the show tonight," he says. "I gave you those passes yesterday, didn't I?"

"Yes," I says. "You want them back?"

"No, no," he says. "I just forgot whether I gave them to you or not. No sense in wasting them."

He locked the door and said Goodnight and went on. The sparrows were still rattling away in the trees, but the square was empty except for a few cars. There was a ford in front of the drugstore, but I didn't even look at it. I know when I've had enough of anything. I dont mind trying to help her, but I know when I've had enough. I guess I could teach Luster to drive it, then they could chase her all day long if they wanted to, and I could stay home and play with Ben.

I went in and got a couple of cigars. Then I thought I'd have another headache shot for luck, and I stood and talked with them a while.

"Well," Mac says. "I reckon you've got your money on the Yankees this year."

"What for?" I says.

"The Pennant," he says. "Not anything in the league can beat them."

"Like hell there's not," I says. "They're shot," I says. "You think a team can be that lucky forever?"

"I dont call it luck," Mac says.

"I wouldn't bet on any team that fellow Ruth played on," I says. "Even if I knew it was going to win."

"Yes?" Mac says.

"I can name you a dozen men in either league who're more valuable than he is," I says.

"What have you got against Ruth?" Mac says.

"Nothing," I says. "I haven't got any thing against him. I dont even like to look at his picture." I went on out. The lights were coming on, and people going along the streets toward home. Sometimes the sparrows never got still until full dark. The night they turned on the new lights around the courthouse it waked them up and they were flying around and blundering into the lights all night long. They kept it up two or three nights, then one morning they were all gone. Then after about two months they all came back again.

I drove on home. There were no lights in the house yet, but they'd all be looking out the windows, and Dilsey jawing away in the kitchen like it was her own food she was having to keep hot until I got there. You'd think to hear her that there wasn't but one supper in the world, and that was the one she had to keep back a few minutes on my account. Well at least I could come home one time without finding Ben and that nigger hanging on the gate like a bear and a monkey in the same cage. Just let it come toward sundown and he'd head for the gate like a cow for the barn, hanging onto it and bobbing his head and sort of moaning to himself. That's a hog for punishment for you. If what had happened to him for fooling with open gates had happened to me, I never would want to see another one. I often wondered what he'd be thinking about, down there at the gate, watching the girls going home from school, trying to want something he couldn't even remember he didn't and couldn't want any longer. And what he'd think when they'd be undressing him and he'd happen to take a look at himself and begin to cry like he'd do. But like I say they never did enough of that. I says I know what you need you need what they did to Ben then you'd behave. And if you dont know what that was I says, ask Dilsey to tell you.

There was a light in Mother's room. I put the car up and went on into the kitchen. Luster and Ben were there.

"Where's Dilsey?" I says. "Putting supper on?"

"She up stairs wid Miss Cahline," Luster says. "Dey been goin hit. Ever since Miss Quentin come home. Mammy up there keepin um fum fightin. Is dat show come, Mr Jason?"

"Yes," I says.

"I thought I heard de band," he says. "Wish I could go," he says. "I could ef I jes had a quarter."

Dilsey came in. "You come, is you?" she says. "Whut you been up to dis evenin? You knows how much work I got to do; whyn't you git here on time?"

"Maybe I went to the show," I says. "Is supper ready?"

"Wish I could go," Luster says. "I could ef I jes had a quarter."

"You aint got no bisiness at no show," Dilsey says. "You go on in de house and set down," she says. "Dont you go up stairs and git um started again, now."

"What's the matter?" I says.

"Quentin come in a while ago and says you been follerin her around all evenin and den Miss Cahline jumped on her. Whyn't you let her alone? Cant you live in de same house wid yo own blood niece widout quoilin?"

"I cant quarrel with her," I says, "because I haven't seen her since this morning. What does she say I've done now? made her go to school? That's pretty bad," I says.

"Well, you tend to yo business and let her lone," Dilsey says. "I'll take keer of her ef you'n Miss Cahline'll let me. Go on in dar now and behave yoself twell I git supper on."

"Ef I jes had a quarter," Luster says, "I could go to dat show."

"En ef you had wings you could fly to heaven," Dilsey says. "I dont want to hear another word about dat show."

"That reminds me," I says. "I've got a couple of tickets they gave me." I took them out of my coat.

"You fixin to use um?" Luster says.

"Not me," I says. "I wouldn't go to it for ten dollars."

"Gimme one of um, Mr Jason," he says.

"I'll sell you one," I says. "How about it?"

"I aint got no money," he says.

"That's too bad," I says. I made to go out.

"Gimme one of um, Mr Jason," he says. "You aint gwine need um bofe."

"Hush yo mouf," Dilsey says. "Dont you know he aint gwine give nothin away?"

"How much you want fer hit?" he says.

"Five cents," I says.

"I aint got dat much," he says.

"How much you got?" I says.

"I aint got nothin," he says.

"All right," I says. I went on.

"Mr Jason," he says.

"Whyn't you hush up?" Dilsey says, "He jes teasin you. He fixin to use dem tickets hisself. Go on, Jason, and let him lone."

"I dont want them," I says. I came back to the stove. "I came in here to burn them up. But if you want to buy one for a nickel?" I says, looking at him and opening the stove lid.

"I aint got dat much," he says.

"All right," I says. I dropped one of them in the stove.

"You, Jason," Dilsey says. "Aint you shamed?"

"Mr Jason," he says. "Please, suh. I'll fix dem tires ev'y day fer a mont."

"I need the cash," I says. "You can have it for a nickel."

"Hush, Luster," Dilsey says. She jerked him back. "Go on," she says. "Drop hit in. Go on. Git hit over with."

"You can have it for a nickel," I says.

"Go on," Dilsey says. "He aint got no nickel. Go on. Drop hit in."

"All right," I says. I dropped it in and Dilsey shut the stove.

"A big growed man like you," she says. "Git on outen my kitchen. Hush," she says to Luster. "Dont you git Benjy started. I'll git you a quarter fum Frony tonight and you kin go tomorrow night. Hush up, now."

I went on into the living room. I couldn't hear anything from upstairs. I opened the paper. After a while Ben and Luster came in. Ben went to the dark place on the wall where the mirror used to be, rubbing his hands on it and slobbering and moaning. Luster began punching at the fire.

"What're you doing?" I says. "We dont need any fire tonight."

"I tryin to keep him quiet," he says. "Hit always cold Easter," he says.

"Only this is not Easter," I says. "Let it alone."

He put the poker back and got the cushion out of Mother's chair and gave it to Ben, and he hunkered down in front of the fireplace and got quiet.

I read the paper. There hadn't been a sound from upstairs when Dilsey came in and sent Ben and Luster on to the kitchen and said supper was ready.

"All right," I says. She went out. I sat there, reading the paper. After a while I heard Dilsey looking in at the door.

"Whyn't you come on and eat?" she says.

"I'm waiting for supper," I says.

"Hit's on the table," she says. "I done told you."

"Is it?" I says. "Excuse me. I didn't hear anybody come down."

"They aint comin," she says. "You come on and eat, so I can take something up to them."

"Are they sick?" I says. "What did the doctor say it was? Not Smallpox, I hope."

"Come on here, Jason," she says. "So I kin git done."

"All right," I says, raising the paper again. "I'm waiting for supper now."

I could feel her watching me at the door. I read the paper.

"Whut you want to act like this fer?" she says. "When you knows how much bother I has anyway."

"If Mother is any sicker than she was when she came down to dinner, all right," I says. "But as long as I am buying food for people younger than I am, they'll have to come down to the table to eat it. Let me know when supper's ready," I says, reading the paper again. I heard her climbing the stairs, dragging her feet and grunting and groaning like they were straight up and three feet apart. I heard her at Mother's door, then I heard her calling Quentin, like the door was locked, then she went back to Mother's room and then Mother went and talked to Quentin. Then they came down stairs. I read the paper.

Dilsey came back to the door. "Come on," she says, "fo you kin think up some mo devilment. You just tryin yoself tonight."

I went to the diningroom. Quentin was sitting with her head bent. She had painted her face again. Her nose looked like a porcelain insulator.

"I'm glad you feel well enough to come down," I says to Mother.

"It's little enough I can do for you, to come to the table," she says. "No matter how I feel. I realise that when a man works all day he likes to be surrounded by his family at the supper table. I want to please you. I only wish you and Quentin got along better. It would be easier for me."

"We get along all right," I says. "I dont mind her staying locked up in her room all day if she wants to. But I cant have all this whoop-de-do and sulking at mealtimes. I know that's a lot to ask her, but I'm that way in my own house. Your house, I meant to say."

"It's yours," Mother says. "You are the head of it now."

Quentin hadn't looked up. I helped the plates and she begun to eat.

"Did you get a good piece of meat?" I says. "If you didn't, I'll try to find you a better one."

She didn't say anything.

"I say, did you get a good piece of meat?" I says.

"What?" she says. "Yes. It's all right."

"Will you have some more rice?" I says.

"No," she says.

"Better let me give you some more," I says.

"I dont want any more," she says.

"Not at all," I says. "You're welcome."

"Is your headache gone?" Mother says.

"Headache?" I says.

"I was afraid you were developing one," she says. "When you came in this afternoon."

"Oh," I says. "No, it didn't show up. We stayed so busy this afternoon I forgot about it."

"Was that why you were late?" Mother says. I could see Quentin listening. I looked at her. Her knife and fork were still going, but I caught her looking at me, then she looked at her plate again. I says,

"No. I loaned my car to a fellow about three oclock and I had to wait until he got back with it." I ate for a while.

"Who was it?" Mother says.

"It was one of those show men," I says. "It seems his sister's husband was out riding with some town woman, and he was chasing them."

Quentin sat perfectly still, chewing.

"You ought not to lend your car to people like that," Mother says. "You are too generous with it. That's why I never call on you for it if I can help it."

"I was beginning to think that myself, for a while," I says. "But he got back, all right. He says he found what he was looking for."

"Who was the woman?" Mother says.

"I'll tell you later," I says. "I dont like to talk about such things before Quentin."

Quentin had quit eating. Every once in a while she'd take a drink of water, then she'd sit there crumbling a biscuit up, her face bent over her plate.

"Yes," Mother says. "I suppose women who stay shut up like I do have no idea what goes on in this town."

"Yes," I says. "They dont."

"My life has been so different from that," Mother says. "Thank God I dont know about such wickedness. I dont even want to know about it. I'm not like most people."

I didn't say any more. Quentin sat there, crumbling the biscuit until I quit eating. Then she says,

"Can I go now?" without looking at anybody.

"What?" I says. "Sure, you can go. Were you waiting on us?"

She looked at me. She had crumpled all the bread, but her hands still went on like they were crumpling it yet and her eyes looked like they were cornered or something and then she started biting her mouth like it ought to have poisoned her, with all that red lead.

"Grandmother," she says. "Grandmother——"

"Did you want something else to eat?" I says.

"Why does he treat me like this, Grandmother?" she says. "I never hurt him."

"I want you all to get along with one another," Mother says. "You are all that's left now, and I do want you all to get along better."

"It's his fault," she says. "He wont let me alone, and I have to. If he doesn't want me here, why wont he let me go back to——"

"That's enough," I says. "Not another word."

"Then why wont he let me alone?" she says. "He——he just——"

"He is the nearest thing to a father you've ever had," Mother says. "It's his bread you and I eat. It's only right that he should expect obedience from you."

"It's his fault," she says. She jumped up. "He makes me do it. If he would just——" she looked at us, her eyes cornered, kind of jerking her arms against her sides.

"If I would just what?" I says.

"Whatever I do, it's your fault," she says. "If I'm bad, it's because I had to be. You made me. I wish I was dead. I wish we were all dead." Then she ran. We heard her run up the stairs. Then a door slammed.

"That's the first sensible thing she ever said," I says.

"She didn't go to school today," Mother says.

"How do you know?" I says. "Were you down town?"

"I just know," she says. "I wish you could be kinder to her."

"If I did that I'd have to arrange to see her more than once a day," I says. "You'll have to make her come to the table every meal. Then I could give her an extra piece of meat every time."

"There are little things you could do," she says.

"Like not paying any attention when you ask me to see that she goes to school?" I says.

"She didn't go to school today," she says. "I just know she didn't. She says she went for a car ride with one of the boys this afternoon and you followed her."

"How could I," I says, "when somebody had my car all afternoon? Whether or not she was in school today is already past," I says. "If you've got to worry about it, worry about next Monday."

"I wanted you and she to get along with one another," she says. "But she has inherited all of the headstrong traits. Quentin's too. I thought at the time, with the heritage she would already have, to give her that name, too. Sometimes I think she is the judgment of both of them upon me."

"Good Lord," I says. "You've got a fine mind. No wonder you keep yourself sick all the time."

"What?" she says. "I dont understand."

"I hope not," I says. "A good woman misses a lot she's better off without knowing."

"They were both that way," she says. "They would make interest with your father against me when I tried to correct them. He was always saying they didn't need controlling, that they already knew what cleanliness and honesty were, which was all that anyone could hope to be taught. And now I hope he's satisfied."

"You've got Ben to depend on," I says. "Cheer up."

"They deliberately shut me out of their lives," she says. "It was always her and Quentin. They were always conspiring against me. Against you too, though you were too young to realise it. They always looked on you and me as outsiders, like they did your Uncle Maury. I always told your father that they were allowed too much freedom, to be together too much. When Quentin started to school we had to let her go the next year, so she could be with him. She couldn't bear for any of you to do anything she couldn't. It was vanity in her, vanity and false pride. And then when her troubles began I knew that Quentin would feel that he had to do something just as bad. But I didn't believe that he would have been so selfish as to——I didn't dream that he——"

"Maybe he knew it was going to be a girl," I says. "And that one more of them would be more than he could stand."

"He could have controlled her," she says. "He seemed to be the only person she had any consideration for. But that is a part of the judgment too, I suppose."

"Yes," I says. "Too bad it wasn't me instead of him. You'd be a lot better off."

"You say things like that to hurt me," she says. "I deserve it though. When they began to sell the land to send Quentin to Harvard I told your father that he must make an equal provision for you. Then when Herbert offered to take you into the bank I said, Jason is provided for now, and when all the expense began to pile up and I was forced to sell our furniture and the rest of the pasture, I wrote her at once because I said she will realise that she and

Quentin have had their share and part of Jason's too and that it depends on her now to compensate him. I said she will do that out of respect for her father. I believed that, then. But I'm just a poor old woman; I was raised to believe that people would deny themselves for their own flesh and blood. It's my fault. You were right to reproach me."

"Do you think I need any man's help to stand on my feet?" I says. "Let alone a woman that cant name the father of her own child."

"Jason," she says.

"All right," I says. "I didn't mean that. Of course not."

"If I believed that were possible, after all my suffering."

"Of course it's not," I says. "I didn't mean it."

"I hope that at least is spared me," she says.

"Sure it is," I says. "She's too much like both of them to doubt that."

"I couldn't bear that," she says.

"Then quit thinking about it," I says. "Has she been worrying you any more about getting out at night?"

"No. I made her realise that it was for her own good and that she'd thank me for it some day. She takes her books with her and studies after I lock the door. I see the light on as late as eleven oclock some nights."

"How do you know she's studying?" I says.

"I dont know what else she'd do in there alone," she says. "She never did read any."

"No," I says. "You wouldn't know. And you can thank your stars for that," I says. Only what would be the use in saying it aloud. It would just have her crying on me again.

I heard her go up stairs. Then she called Quentin and Quentin says What? through the door. "Goodnight," Mother says. Then I heard the key in the lock, and Mother went back to her room.

When I finished my cigar and went up, the light was still on. I could see the empty keyhole, but I couldn't hear a sound. She studied quiet. Maybe she learned that in school. I told Mother goodnight and went on to my room and got the box out and counted it again. I could hear the Great American Gelding snoring away like a planing mill. I read somewhere they'd fix men that way to give them women's voices. But maybe he didn't know what they'd done to him. I dont reckon he even knew what he had been trying to do, or why Mr Burgess knocked him out with the fence picket. And if they'd just sent him on to Jackson while he was under the ether, he'd never have known the difference. But that would have been too simple for a Compson to think of. Not half complex enough. Having to wait to do it at all until he broke out and tried to run a little girl down on the street with her own father looking at him.

Well, like I say they never started soon enough with their cutting, and they quit too quick. I know at least two more that needed something like that, and one of them not over a mile away, either. But then I dont reckon even that would do any good. Like I say once a bitch always a bitch. And just let me have twenty-four hours without any dam New York jew to advise me what it's going to do. I dont want to make a killing; save that to suck in the smart gamblers with. I just want an even chance to get my money back. And once I've done that they can bring all Beale street and all bedlam in here and two of them can sleep in my bed and another one can have my place at the table too.

April Eighth, 1928.

The day dawned bleak and chill, a moving wall of gray light out of the northeast which, instead of dissolving into moisture, seemed to disintegrate into minute and venomous particles, like dust that, when Dilsey opened the door of the cabin and emerged, needled laterally into her flesh, precipitating not so much a moisture as a substance partaking of the quality of thin, not quite congealed oil. She wore a stiff black straw hat perched upon her turban, and a maroon velvet cape with a border of mangy and anonymous fur above a dress of purple silk, and she stood in the door for a while with her myriad and sunken face lifted to the weather, and one gaunt hand flac-soled as the belly of a fish, then she moved the cape aside and examined the bosom of her gown.

The gown fell gauntly from her shoulders, across her fallen breasts, then tightened upon her paunch and fell again, ballooning a little above the nether garments which she would remove layer by layer as the spring accomplished and the warm days, in color regal and moribund. She had been a big woman once but now her skeleton rose, draped loosely in unpadded skin that tightened again upon a paunch almost dropsical, as though muscle and tissue had been courage or fortitude which the days or the years had consumed until only the indomitable skeleton was left rising like a ruin or a landmark above the somnolent and impervious guts, and above that the collapsed face that gave the impression of the bones themselves being outside the flesh, lifted into the driving day with an expression at once fatalistic and of a child's astonished disappointment, until she turned and entered the house again and closed the door.

The earth immediately about the door was bare. It had a patina, as though from the soles of bare feet in generations, like old silver or the walls of Mexican houses which have been plastered by hand. Beside the house, shading it in summer, stood three mulberry trees, the fledged leaves that would later be broad and placid as the palms of hands streaming flatly undulant upon the driving air. A pair of jaybirds came up from nowhere, whirled up on the blast like gaudy scraps of cloth or paper and lodged in the mulberries, where they swung in raucous tilt and recover, screaming into the wind that ripped their harsh cries onward and away like scraps of paper or of cloth in turn. Then three more joined them and they swung and tilted in the wrung branches for a time, screaming. The door of the cabin opened and Dilsey emerged once more, this time in a man's felt hat and an army overcoat, beneath the frayed skirts of which her blue gingham dress fell in uneven balloonings, streaming too about her as she crossed the yard and mounted the steps to the kitchen door.

A moment later she emerged, carrying an open umbrella now, which she slanted ahead into the wind, and crossed to the wood-pile and laid the umbrella down, still open. Immediately she caught at it and arrested it and held to it for a while, looking about her. Then she closed it and laid it down and stacked stovewood into her crooked arm, against her breast, and picked up the umbrella and got it open at last and returned to the steps and held the wood pre-cariously balanced while she contrived to close the umbrella, which she propped in the corner just within the door. She dumped the wood into the box behind the stove. Then she removed the overcoat and hat and took a soiled apron down from the wall and put it on and built a fire in the stove. While she was doing so, rattling the grate bars and clattering the lids, Mrs Compson began to call her from the head of the stairs.

She wore a dressing gown of quilted black satin, holding it close under her chin. In the other hand she held a red rubber hot water bottle and she stood at the head of the back stairway, calling "Dilsey" at steady and inflectionless intervals into the quiet stairwell that descended into complete darkness, then opened again where a gray window fell across it. "Dilsey," she called, without inflection or emphasis or haste, as though she were not listening for a reply at all. "Dilsey."

Dilsey answered and ceased clattering the stove, but before she could cross the kitchen Mrs Compson called her again, and before she crossed the diningroom and brought her head into relief against the gray splash of the window, still again.

"All right," Dilsey said. "All right, here I is. I'll fill hit soon ez I git some hot water." She gathered up her skirts and mounted the stairs, wholly blotting the gray light. "Put hit down dar en g'awn back to bed."

"I couldn't understand what was the matter," Mrs Compson said. "I've been lying awake for an hour at least, without hearing a sound from the kitchen."

"You put hit down and g'awn back to bed," Dilsey said. She toiled painfully up the steps, shapeless, breathing heavily. "I'll have de fire gwine in a minute, en de water hot in two mo."

"I've been lying there for an hour, at least," Mrs Compson said. "I thought maybe you were waiting for me to come down and start the fire."

Dilsey reached the top of the stairs and took the water bottle. "I'll fix hit in a minute," she said. "Luster overslep dis mawnin, up half de night at dat show. I gwine build de fire myself. Go on now, so you wont wake de others twell I ready."

"If you permit Luster to do things that interfere with his work, you'll have to suffer for it yourself," Mrs Compson said. "Jason wont like this if he hears about it. You know he wont."

"'Twusn't none of Jason's money he went on," Dilsey said. "Dat's one thing sho." She went on down the stairs. Mrs Compson returned to her room. As she got into bed again she could hear Dilsey yet descending the stairs with a sort of painful and terrific slowness that would have become maddening had it not presently ceased beyond the flapping diminishment of the pantry door.

She entered the kitchen and built up the fire and began to prepare breakfast. In the midst of this she ceased and went to the window and looked out toward her cabin, then she went to the door and opened it and shouted into the driving weather.

"Luster!" she shouted, standing to listen, tilting her face from the wind. "You, Luster!" She listened, then as she prepared to shout again Luster appeared around the corner of the kitchen.

"Ma'am?" he said innocently, so innocently that Dilsey looked down at him, for a moment motionless, with something more than mere surprise.

"Whar you at?" she said.

"Nowhere," he said. "Jes in de cellar."

"Whut you doin in de cellar?" she said. "Dont stand dar in de rain, fool," she said.

"Aint doin nothin," he said. He came up the steps.

"Dont you dare come in dis do widout a armful of wood," she said. "Here I done had to tote yo wood en build yo fire bofe. Didn't I tole you not to leave dis place last night befo dat woodbox wus full to de top?"

"I did," Luster said. "I filled hit."

"Whar hit gone to, den?"

"I dont know'm. I aint teched hit."

"Well, you git hit full up now," she said. "And git on up dar en see bout Benjy."

She shut the door. Luster went to the woodpile. The five jaybirds whirled over the house, screaming, and into the mulberries again.

He watched them. He picked up a rock and threw it. "Whoo," he said. "Git on back to hell, whar you belong at. 'Taint Monday yit."[1]

He loaded himself mountainously with stove wood. He could not see over it, and he staggered to the steps and up them and blundered crashing against the door, shedding billets. Then Dilsey came and opened the door for him and he blundered across the kitchen. "You, Luster!" she shouted, but he had already hurled the wood into the box with a thunderous crash. "Hah!" he said.

"Is you tryin to wake up de whole house?" Dilsey said. She hit him on the back of his head with the flat of her hand. "Go on up dar and git Benjy dressed, now."

"Yessum," he said. He went toward the outer door.

"Whar you gwine?" Dilsey said.

"I thought I better go round de house en in by de front, so I wont wake up Miss Cahline en dem."

"You go on up dem back stairs like I tole you en git Benjy's clothes on him," Dilsey said. "Go on, now."

"Yessum," Luster said. He returned and left by the diningroom door. After a while it ceased to flap. Dilsey prepared to make biscuit. As she ground the sifter steadily above the bread board, she sang, to herself at first, something without particular tune or words, repetitive, mournful and plaintive, austere, as she ground a faint, steady snowing of flour onto the bread board. The stove had begun to heat the room and to fill it with murmurous minors of the fire, and presently she was singing louder, as if her voice too had been thawed out by the growing warmth, and then Mrs Compson called her name again from within the house. Dilsey raised her face as if her eyes could and did penetrate the walls and ceiling and saw the old woman in her quilted dressing gown at the head of the stairs, calling her name with machinelike regularity.

"Oh, Lawd," Dilsey said. She set the sifter down and swept up the hem of her apron and wiped her hands and caught up the bottle from the chair on which she had laid it and gathered her apron about the handle of the kettle which was now jetting faintly. "Jes a minute," she called. "De water jes dis minute got hot."

It was not the bottle which Mrs Compson wanted, however, and clutching it by the neck like a dead hen Dilsey went to the foot of the stairs and looked upward.

"Aint Luster up dar wid him?" she said.

"Luster hasn't been in the house. I've been lying here listening for him. I knew he would be late, but I did hope he'd come in time

---

1. In folk belief, jaybirds go to hell on Friday and come out on Monday. Some say the jaybirds sold themselves to the devil for an ear of corn and are obliged to take a grain of sand to him to make his fire hot. Others regard the jaybirds as the devil's messengers, who tell him of people's sins.

to keep Benjamin from disturbing Jason on Jason's one day in the week to sleep in the morning."

"I dont see how you expect anybody to sleep, wid you standin in de hall, holl'in at folks fum de crack of dawn," Dilsey said. She began to mount the stairs, toiling heavily. "I sont dat boy up dar half an hour ago."

Mrs Compson watched her, holding the dressing gown under her chin. "What are you going to do?" she said.

"Gwine git Benjy dressed en bring him down to de kitchen, whar he wont wake Jason en Quentin," Dilsey said.

"Haven't you started breakfast yet?"

"I'll tend to dat too," Dilsey said. "You better git back in bed twell Luster make yo fire. Hit cold dis mawnin."

"I know it," Mrs Compson said. "My feet are like ice. They were so cold they waked me up." She watched Dilsey mount the stairs. It took her a long while. "You know how it frets Jason when breakfast is late," Mrs Compson said.

"I cant do but one thing at a time," Dilsey said. "You git on back to bed, fo I has you on my hands dis mawnin too."

"If you're going to drop everything to dress Benjamin, I'd better come down and get breakfast. You know as well as I do how Jason acts when it's late."

"En who gwine eat yo messin?" Dilsey said. "Tell me dat. Go on now," she said, toiling upward. Mrs Compson stood watching her as she mounted, steadying herself against the wall with one hand, holding her skirts up with the other.

"Are you going to wake him up just to dress him?" she said.

Dilsey stopped. With her foot lifted to the next step she stood there, her hand against the wall and the gray splash of the window behind her, motionless and shapeless she loomed.

"He aint awake den?" she said.

"He wasn't when I looked in," Mrs Compson said. "But it's past his time. He never does sleep after half past seven. You know he doesn't."

Dilsey said nothing. She made no further move, but though she could not see her save as a blobby shape without depth, Mrs Compson knew that she had lowered her face a little and that she stood now like cows do in the rain, holding the empty water bottle by its neck.

"You're not the one who has to bear it," Mrs Compson said. "It's not your responsibility. You can go away. You dont have to bear the brunt of it day in and day out. You owe nothing to them, to Mr Compson's memory. I know you have never had any tenderness for Jason. You've never tried to conceal it."

Dilsey said nothing. She turned slowly and descended, lowering her body from step to step, as a small child does, her hand against the wall. "You go on and let him alone," she said. "Dont go in dar no mo, now. I'll send Luster up soon as I find him. Let him alone, now."

She returned to the kitchen. She looked into the stove, then she drew her apron over her head and donned the overcoat and opened the outer door and looked up and down the yard. The weather drove upon her flesh, harsh and minute, but the scene was empty of all else that moved. She descended the steps, gingerly, as if for silence, and went around the corner of the kitchen. As she did so Luster emerged quickly and innocently from the cellar door.

Dilsey stopped. "Whut you up to?" she said.

"Nothin," Luster said. "Mr Jason say fer me to find out whar dat water leak in de cellar fum."

"En when wus hit he say fer you to do dat?" Dilsey said. "Last New Year's day, wasn't hit?"

"I thought I jes be lookin whiles dey sleep," Luster said. Dilsey went to the cellar door. He stood aside and she peered down into the obscurity odorous of dank earth and mold and rubber.

"Huh," Dilsey said. She looked at Luster again. He met her gaze blandly, innocent and open. "I dont know whut you up to, but you aint got no business doin hit. You jes tryin me too dis mawnin cause de others is, aint you? You git on up dar en see to Benjy, you hear?"

"Yessum," Luster said. He went on toward the kitchen steps, swiftly.

"Here," Dilsey said. "You git me another armful of wood while I got you."

"Yessum," he said. He passed her on the steps and went to the woodpile. When he blundered again at the door a moment later, again invisible and blind within and beyond his wooden avatar, Dilsey opened the door and guided him across the kitchen with a firm hand.

"Jes thow hit at dat box again," she said. "Jes thow hit."

"I got to," Luster said, panting. "I cant put hit down no other way."

"Den you stand dar en hold hit a while," Dilsey said. She unloaded him a stick at a time. "Whut got into you dis mawnin? Here I sont you fer wood en you aint never brought mo'n six sticks at a time to save yo life twell today. Whut you fixin to ax me kin you do now? Aint dat show lef town yit?"

"Yessum. Hit done gone."

She put the last stick into the box. "Now you go on up dar wid Benjy, like I tole you befo," she said. "And I dont want nobody else yellin down dem stairs at me twell I rings de bell. You hear me."

"Yessum," Luster said. He vanished through the swing door. Dilsey put some more wood in the stove and returned to the bread board. Presently she began to sing again.

The room grew warmer. Soon Dilsey's skin had taken on a rich, lustrous quality as compared with that as of a faint dusting of wood ashes which both it and Luster's had worn as she moved about the kitchen, gathering about her the raw materials of food, coordinating the meal. On the wall above a cupboard, invisible save at night, by lamp light and even then evincing an enigmatic profundity because it had but one hand, a cabinet clock ticked, then with a preliminary sound as if it had cleared its throat, struck five times.

"Eight oclock," Dilsey said. She ceased and tilted her head upward, listening. But there was no sound save the clock and the fire. She opened the oven and looked at the pan of bread, then stooping she paused while someone descended the stairs. She heard the feet cross the diningroom, then the swing door opened and Luster entered, followed by a big man who appeared to have been shaped of some substance whose particles would not or did not cohere to one another or to the frame which supported it. His skin was dead looking and hairless; dropsical too, he moved with a shambling gait like a trained bear. His hair was pale and fine. It had been brushed smoothly down upon his brow like that of children in daguerrotypes. His eyes were clear, of the pale sweet blue of cornflowers, his thick mouth hung open, drooling a little.

"Is he cold?" Dilsey said. She wiped her hands on her apron and touched his hand.

"Ef he aint, I is," Luster said. "Always cold Easter. Aint never seen hit fail. Miss Cahline say ef you aint got time to fix her hot water bottle to never mind about hit."

"Oh, Lawd," Dilsey said. She drew a chair into the corner between the woodbox and the stove. The man went obediently and sat in it. "Look in de dinin room and see whar I laid dat bottle down," Dilsey said. Luster fetched the bottle from the diningroom and Dilsey filled it and gave it to him. "Hurry up, now," she said. "See ef Jason wake now. Tell em hit's all ready."

Luster went out. Ben sat beside the stove. He sat loosely, utterly motionless save for his head, which made a continual bobbing sort of movement as he watched Dilsey with his sweet vague gaze as she moved about. Luster returned.

"He up," he said. "Miss Cahline say put hit on de table." He came to the stove and spread his hands palm down above the firebox. "He up, too," he said. "Gwine hit wid bofe feet dis mawnin."

"Whut's de matter now?" Dilsey said. "Git away fum dar. How kin I do anything wid you standin over de stove?"

"I cold," Luster said.

"You ought to thought about dat whiles you wus down dar in dat cellar;" Dilsey said. "Whut de matter wid Jason?"

"Sayin me en Benjy broke dat winder in his room."

"Is dey one broke?" Dilsey said.

"Dat's whut he sayin," Luster said. "Say I broke hit."

"How could you, when he keep hit locked all day en night?"

"Say I broke hit chunkin rocks at hit," Luster said.

"En did you?"

"Nome," Luster said.

"Dont lie to me, boy," Dilsey said.

"I never done hit," Luster said. "Ask Benjy ef I did. I aint stud'in dat winder."

"Who could a broke hit, den?" Dilsey said. "He jes tryin hisself, to wake Quentin up," she said, taking the pan of biscuits out of the stove.

"Reckin so," Luster said. "Dese funny folks. Glad I aint none of em."

"Aint none of who?" Dilsey said. "Lemme tell you somethin, nigger boy, you got jes es much Compson devilment in you es any of em. Is you right sho you never broke dat window?"

"Whut I want to break hit fur?"

"Whut you do any of yo devilment fur?" Dilsey said. "Watch him now, so he cant burn his hand again twell I git de table set."

She went to the diningroom, where they heard her moving about, then she returned and set a plate at the kitchen table and set food there. Ben watched her, slobbering, making a faint, eager sound.

"All right, honey," she said. "Here yo breakfast. Bring his chair, Luster." Luster moved the chair up and Ben sat down, whimpering and slobbering. Dilsey tied a cloth about his neck and wiped his mouth with the end of it. "And see kin you keep fum messin up his clothes one time," she said, handing Luster a spoon.

Ben ceased whimpering. He watched the spoon as it rose to his mouth. It was as if even eagerness were musclebound in him too, and hunger itself inarticulate, not knowing it is hunger. Luster fed him with skill and detachment. Now and then his attention would return long enough to enable him to feint the spoon and cause Ben to close his mouth upon the empty air, but it was apparent that Luster's mind was elsewhere. His other hand lay on the back of the chair and upon that dead surface it moved tentatively, delicately, as if he were picking an inaudible tune out of the dead void, and once he even forgot to tease Ben with the spoon while his fingers teased out of the slain wood a soundless and involved arpeggio until Ben recalled him by whimpering again.

In the diningroom Dilsey moved back and forth. Presently she rang a small clear bell, then in the kitchen Luster heard Mrs Compson and Jason descending, and Jason's voice, and he rolled his eyes whitely with listening.

"Sure, I know they didn't break it," Jason said. "Sure, I know that. Maybe the change of weather broke it."

"I dont see how it could have," Mrs Compson said. "Your room stays locked all day long, just as you leave it when you go to town. None of us ever go in there except Sunday, to clean it. I dont want you to think that I would go where I'm not wanted, or that I would permit anyone else to."

"I never said you broke it, did I?" Jason said.

"I dont want to go in your room," Mrs Compson said. "I respect anybody's private affairs. I wouldn't put my foot over the threshold, even if I had a key."

"Yes," Jason said. "I know your keys wont fit. That's why I had the lock changed. What I want to know is, how that window got broken."

"Luster say he didn't do hit," Dilsey said.

"I knew that without asking him," Jason said. "Where's Quentin?" he said.

"Where she is ev'y Sunday mawnin," Dilsey said. "Whut got into you de last few days, anyhow?"

"Well, we're going to change all that," Jason said. "Go up and tell her breakfast is ready."

"You leave her alone now, Jason," Dilsey said. "She gits up fer breakfast ev'y week mawnin, en Miss Cahline lets her stay in bed ev'y Sunday. You knows dat."

"I cant keep a kitchen full of niggers to wait on her pleasure, much as I'd like to," Jason said. "Go and tell her to come down to breakfast."

"Aint nobody have to wait on her," Dilsey said. "I puts her breakfast in de warmer en she——"

"Did you hear me?" Jason said.

"I hears you," Dilsey said. "All I been hearin, when you in de house. Ef hit aint Quentin er yo maw, hit's Luster en Benjy. Whut you let him go on dat way fer, Miss Cahline?"

"You'd better do as he says," Mrs Compson said. "He's head of the house now. It's his right to require us to respect his wishes. I try to do it, and if I can, you can too."

"'Taint no sense in him bein so bad tempered he got to make Quentin git up jes to suit him," Dilsey said. "Maybe you think she broke dat window."

"She would, if she happened to think of it," Jason said. "You go and do what I told you."

"En I wouldn't blame her none ef she did," Dilsey said, going toward the stairs. "Wid you naggin at her all de blessed time you in de house."

"Hush, Dilsey," Mrs Compson said. "It's neither your place nor mine to tell Jason what to do. Sometimes I think he is wrong, but I try to obey his wishes for you all's sakes. If I'm strong enough to come to the table, Quentin can too."

Dilsey went out. They heard her mounting the stairs. They heard her a long while on the stairs.

"You've got a prize set of servants," Jason said. He helped his mother and himself to food. "Did you ever have one that was worth killing? You must have had some before I was big enough to remember."

"I have to humor them," Mrs Compson said. "I have to depend on them so completely. It's not as if I were strong. I wish I were. I wish I could do all the house work myself. I could at least take that much off your shoulders."

"And a fine pigsty we'd live in, too," Jason said. "Hurry up, Dilsey," he shouted.

"I know you blame me," Mrs Compson said, "for letting them off to go to church today."

"Go where?" Jason said. "Hasn't that damn show left yet?"

"To church," Mrs Compson said. "The darkies are having a special Easter service. I promised Dilsey two weeks ago that they could get off."

"Which means we'll eat cold dinner," Jason said, "or none at all."

"I know it's my fault," Mrs Compson said. "I know you blame me."

"For what?" Jason said. "You never resurrected Christ, did you?"

They heard Dilsey mount the final stair, then her slow feet overhead.

"Quentin," she said. When she called the first time Jason laid his knife and fork down and he and his mother appeared to wait across the table from one another in identical attitudes; the one cold and shrewd, with close-thatched brown hair curled into two stubborn hooks, one on either side of his forehead like a bartender in caricature, and hazel eyes with black-ringed irises like marbles, the other cold and querulous, with perfectly white hair and eyes pouched and baffled and so dark as to appear to be all pupil or all iris.

"Quentin," Dilsey said. "Get up, honey. Dey waitin breakfast on you."

"I cant understand how that window got broken," Mrs Compson said. "Are you sure it was done yesterday? It could have been like that a long time, with the warm weather. The upper sash, behind the shade like that."

"I've told you for the last time that it happened yesterday," Jason said. "Dont you reckon I know the room I live in? Do you reckon I could have lived in it a week with a hole in the window you could stick your hand. . . ." his voice ceased, ebbed, left him staring at his mother with eyes that for an instant were quite empty of anything. It was as though his eyes were holding their breath, while his mother looked at him, her face flaccid and querulous, interminable, clairvoyant yet obtuse. As they sat so Dilsey said,

"Quentin. Dont play wid me, honey. Come on to breakfast, honey. Dey waitin fer you."

"I cant understand it," Mrs Compson said. "It's just as if somebody had tried to break into the house——" Jason sprang up. His chair crashed over backward. "What——" Mrs Compson said, staring at him as he ran past her and went jumping up the stairs, where he met Dilsey. His face was now in shadow, and Dilsey said.

"She sullin. Yo maw aint unlocked——" But Jason ran on past her and along the corridor to a door. He didn't call. He grasped the knob and tried it, then he stood with the knob in his hand and his head bent a little, as if he were listening to something much further away than the dimensioned room beyond the door, and which he already heard. His attitude was that of one who goes through the motions of listening in order to deceive himself as to what he already hears. Behind him Mrs Compson mounted the stairs, calling his name. Then she saw Dilsey and she quit calling him and began to call Dilsey instead.

"I told you she aint unlocked dat do yit," Dilsey said.

When she spoke he turned and ran toward her, but his voice was quiet, matter of fact. "She carry the key with her?" he said. "Has she got it now, I mean, or will she have——"

"Dilsey," Mrs Compson said on the stairs.

"Is which?" Dilsey said. "Whyn't you let——"

"The key," Jason said. "To that room. Does she carry it with her all the time. Mother." Then he saw Mrs Compson and he went down the stairs and met her. "Give me the key," he said. He fell to pawing at the pockets of the rusty black dressing sacque she wore. She resisted.

"Jason," she said. "Jason! Are you and Dilsey trying to put me to bed again?" she said, trying to fend him off. "Cant you even let me have Sunday in peace?"

"The key," Jason said, pawing at her. "Give it here." He looked back at the door, as if he expected it to fly open before he could get back to it with the key he did not yet have.

"You, Dilsey!" Mrs Compson said, clutching her sacque about her.

"Give me the key, you old fool!" Jason cried suddenly. From her pocket he tugged a huge bunch of rusted keys on an iron ring like a mediaeval jailer's and ran back up the hall with the two women behind him.

"You, Jason!" Mrs Compson said. "He will never find the right one," she said. "You know I never let anyone take my keys, Dilsey," she said. She began to wail.

"Hush," Dilsey said. "He aint gwine do nothin to her. I aint gwine let him."

"But on Sunday morning, in my own house," Mrs Compson said. "When I've tried so hard to raise them christians. Let me find the right key, Jason," she said. She put her hand on his arm. Then she began to struggle with him, but he flung her aside with a motion of his elbow and looked around at her for a moment, his eyes cold and harried, then he turned to the door again and the unwieldy keys.

"Hush," Dilsey said. "You, Jason!"

"Something terrible has happened," Mrs Compson said, wailing again. "I know it has. You, Jason," she said, grasping at him again. "He wont even let me find the key to a room in my own house!"

"Now, now," Dilsey said. "Whut kin happen? I right here. I aint gwine let him hurt her. Quentin," she said, raising her voice, "dont you be skeered, honey, I'se right here."

The door opened, swung inward. He stood in it for a moment, hiding the room, then he stepped aside. "Go in," he said in a thick, light voice. They went in. It was not a girl's room. It was not any-body's room, and the faint scent of cheap cosmetics and the few feminine objects and the other evidences of crude and hopeless efforts to feminise it but added to its anonymity, giving it that dead and stereotyped transience of rooms in assignation houses. The bed had not been disturbed. On the floor lay a soiled undergarment of cheap silk a little too pink, from a half open bureau drawer dangled a single stocking. The window was open. A pear tree grew there, close against the house. It was in bloom and the branches scraped and rasped against the house and the myriad air, driving in the window, brought into the room the forlorn scent of the blossoms.

"Dar now," Dilsey said. "Didn't I told you she all right?"

"All right?" Mrs Compson said. Dilsey followed her into the room and touched her.

"You come on and lay down, now," she said. "I find her in ten minutes."

Mrs Compson shook her off. "Find the note," she said. "Quentin left a note when he did it."

"All right," Dilsey said. "I'll find hit. You come on to yo room, now."

"I knew the minute they named her Quentin this would happen," Mrs Compson said. She went to the bureau and began to turn over the scattered objects there—scent, bottles, a box of powder, a chewed pencil, a pair of scissors with one broken blade lying upon a darned scarf dusted with powder and stained with rouge. "Find the note," she said.

"I is," Dilsey said. "You come on, now. Me and Jason'll find hit. You come on to yo room."

"Jason," Mrs Compson said. "Where is he?" She went to the door. Dilsey followed her on down the hall, to another door. It was closed. "Jason," she called through the door. There was no answer. She tried the knob, then she called him again. But there was still no answer, for he was hurling things backward out of the closet, garments, shoes, a suitcase. Then he emerged carrying a sawn section of tongue-and-groove planking and laid it down and entered the closet again and emerged with a metal box. He set it on the bed and stood looking at the broken lock while he dug a keyring from his pocket and selected a key, and for a time longer he stood with the selected key in his hand, looking at the broken lock. Then he put the keys back in his pocket and carefully tilted the contents of the box out upon the bed. Still carefully he sorted the papers, taking them up one at a time and shaking them. Then he upended the box and shook it too and slowly replaced the papers and stood again, looking at the broken lock, with the box in his hands and his head bent. Outside the window he heard some jaybirds swirl shrieking past and away, their cries whipping away along the wind, and an automobile passed somewhere and died away also. His mother spoke his name again beyond the door, but he didn't move. He heard Dilsey lead her away up the hall, and then a door closed. Then he replaced the box in the closet and flung the garments back into it and went down stairs to the telephone. While he stood there with the receiver to his ear waiting Dilsey came down the stairs. She looked at him, without stopping, and went on.

The wire opened. "This is Jason Compson," he said, his voice so harsh and thick that he had to repeat himself. "Jason Compson," he said, controlling his voice. "Have a car ready, with a deputy, if you cant go, in ten minutes. I'll be there——What?——Robbery. My house. I know who it——Robbery, I say. Have a car read——What? Aren't you a paid law enforcement——Yes, I'll be there in five minutes. Have that car ready to leave at once. If you dont, I'll report it to the governor."

He clapped the receiver back and crossed the diningroom, where the scarce broken meal lay cold now on the table, and entered the kitchen. Dilsey was filling the hot water bottle. Ben sat, tranquil and empty. Beside him Luster looked like a fice dog, brightly watchful. He was eating something. Jason went on across the kitchen.

"Aint you going to eat no breakfast?" Dilsey said. He paid her no attention. "Go on en eat yo breakfast, Jason." He went on. The outer door banged behind him. Luster rose and went to the window and looked out.

"Whoo," he said. "Whut happenin up dar? He been beatin Miss Quentin?"

"You hush yo mouf," Dilsey said. "You git Benjy started now en I beat yo head off. You keep him quiet es you kin twell I git back, now." She screwed the cap on the bottle and went out. They heard her go up the stairs, then they heard Jason pass the house in his car. Then there was no sound in the kitchen save the simmering murmur of the kettle and the clock.

"You know whut I bet?" Luster said. "I bet he beat her. I bet he knock her in de head en now he gone fer de doctor. Dat's whut I bet." The clock tick-tocked, solemn and profound. It might have been the dry pulse of the decaying house itself, after a while it whirred and cleared its throat and struck six times. Ben looked up at it, then he looked at the bulletlike silhouette of Luster's head in the window and he begun to bob his head again, drooling. He whimpered.

"Hush up, looney," Luster said without turning. "Look like we aint gwine git to go to no church today." But Ben sat in the chair, his big soft hands dangling between his knees, moaning faintly. Suddenly he wept, a slow bellowing sound, meaningless and sustained. "Hush," Luster said. He turned and lifted his hand. "You want me to whup you?" But Ben looked at him, bellowing slowly with each expiration. Luster came and shook him. "You hush dis minute!" he shouted. "Here," he said. He hauled Ben out of the chair and dragged the chair around facing the stove and opened the door to the firebox and shoved Ben into the chair. They looked like a tug nudging at a clumsy tanker in a narrow dock. Ben sat down again facing the rosy door. He hushed. Then they heard the clock again, and Dilsey slow on the stairs. When she entered he began to whimper again. Then he lifted his voice.

"Whut you done to him?" Dilsey said. "Why cant you let him lone dis mawnin, of all times?"

"I aint doin nothin to him," Luster said. "Mr Jason skeered him, dat's whut hit is. He aint kilt Miss Quentin, is he?"

"Hush, Benjy," Dilsey said. He hushed. She went to the window and looked out. "Is it quit rainin?" she said.

"Yessum," Luster said. "Quit long time ago."

"Den y'all go out do's a while," she said. "I jes got Miss Cahline quiet now."

"Is we gwine to church?" Luster said.

"I let you know bout dat when de time come. You keep him away fum de house twell I calls you."

"Kin we go to de pastuh?" Luster said.

"All right. Only you keep him away fum de house. I done stood all I kin."

"Yessum," Luster said. "Whar Mr Jason gone, mammy?"

"Dat's some mo of yo business, aint it?" Dilsey said. She began to clear the table. "Hush, Benjy. Luster gwine take you out to play."

"Whut he done to Miss Quentin, mammy?" Luster said.

"Aint done nothin to her. You all git on outen here."

"I bet she aint here," Luster said.

Dilsey looked at him. "How you know she aint here?"

"Me and Benjy seed her clamb out de window last night. Didn't us, Benjy?"

"You did?" Dilsey said, looking at him.

"We sees her doin hit ev'y night," Luster said. "Clamb right down dat pear tree."

"Dont you lie to me, nigger boy," Dilsey said.

"I aint lyin. Ask Benjy ef I is."

"Whyn't you say somethin about it, den?"

"'Twarn't none o my business," Luster said. "I aint gwine git mixed up in white folks' business. Come on here, Benjy, les go out do's."

They went out. Dilsey stood for a while at the table, then she went and cleared the breakfast things from the diningroom and ate her breakfast and cleaned up the kitchen. Then she removed her apron and hung it up and went to the foot of the stairs and listened for a moment. There was no sound. She donned the overcoat and the hat and went across to her cabin.

The rain had stopped. The air now drove out of the southeast, broken overhead into blue patches. Upon the crest of a hill beyond the trees and roofs and spires of town sunlight lay like a pale scrap of cloth, was blotted away. Upon the air a bell came, then as if at a signal, other bells took up the sound and repeated it.

The cabin door opened and Dilsey emerged, again in the maroon cape and the purple gown, and wearing soiled white elbow-length gloves and minus her headcloth now. She came into the yard and called Luster. She waited a while, then she went to the house and around it to the cellar door, moving close to the wall, and looked into the door. Ben sat on the steps. Before him Luster squatted on the damp floor. He held a saw in his left hand, the blade sprung a little by pressure of his hand, and he was in the act of striking the blade with the worn wooden mallet with which she had been making beaten biscuit for more than thirty years. The saw gave forth a single sluggish twang that ceased with lifeless alacrity, leaving the blade in a thin clean curve between Luster's hand and the floor. Still, inscrutable, it bellied.

"Dat's de way he done hit," Luster said. "I jes aint foun de right thing to hit it wid."

"Dat's whut you doin, is it?" Dilsey said. "Bring me dat mallet," she said.

"I aint hurt hit," Luster said.

"Bring hit here," Dilsey said. "Put dat saw whar you got hit first."

He put the saw away and brought the mallet to her. Then Ben wailed again, hopeless and prolonged. It was nothing. Just sound. It might have been all time and injustice and sorrow become vocal for an instant by a conjunction of planets.

"Listen at him," Luster said. "He been gwine on dat way ev'y since you sont us outen de house. I dont know whut got in to him dis mawnin."

"Bring him here," Dilsey said.

"Come on, Benjy," Luster said. He went back down the steps and took Ben's arm. He came obediently, wailing, that slow hoarse sound that ships make, that seems to begin before the sound itself has started, seems to cease before the sound itself has stopped.

"Run and git his cap," Dilsey said. "Dont make no noise Miss Cahline kin hear. Hurry, now. We already late."

"She gwine hear him anyhow, ef you dont stop him," Luster said.

"He stop when we git off de place," Dilsey said. "He smellin hit. Dat's whut hit is."

"Smell whut, mammy?" Luster said.

"You go git dat cap," Dilsey said. Luster went on. They stood in the cellar door, Ben one step below her. The sky was broken now into scudding patches that dragged their swift shadows up out of the shabby garden, over the broken fence and across the yard. Dilsey stroked Ben's head, slowly and steadily, smoothing the bang upon his brow. He wailed quietly, unhurriedly. "Hush," Dilsey said. "Hush, now. We be gone in a minute. Hush, now." He wailed quietly and steadily.

Luster returned, wearing a stiff new straw hat with a colored band and carrying a cloth cap. The hat seemed to isolate Luster's skull in the beholder's eye as a spotlight would, in all its individual planes and angles. So peculiarly individual was its shape that at first glance the hat appeared to be on the head of someone standing immediately behind Luster. Dilsey looked at the hat.

"Whyn't you wear yo old hat?" she said.

"Couldn't find hit," Luster said.

"I bet you couldn't. I bet you fixed hit last night so you couldn't find hit. You fixin to ruin dat un."

"Aw, mammy," Luster said. "Hit aint gwine rain."

"How you know? You go git dat old hat en put dat new un away."

"Aw, mammy."

"Den you go git de umbreller."

"Aw, mammy."

"Take yo choice," Dilsey said. "Git yo old hat, er de umbreller. I dont keer which."

Luster went to the cabin. Ben wailed quietly.

"Come on," Dilsey said. "Dey kin ketch up wid us. We gwine to hear de singin." They went around the house, toward the gate. "Hush," Dilsey said from time to time as they went down the drive.

They reached the gate. Dilsey opened it. Luster was coming down the drive behind them, carrying the umbrella. A woman was with him. "Here dey come," Dilsey said. They passed out the gate. "Now, den," she said. Ben ceased. Luster and his mother overtook them. Frony wore a dress of bright blue silk and a flowered hat. She was a thin woman, with a flat, pleasant face.

"You got six weeks' work right dar on yo back," Dilsey said. "Whut you gwine do ef hit rain?"

"Git wet, I reckon," Frony said. "I aint never stopped no rain yit."

"Mammy always talkin bout hit gwine rain," Luster said.

"Ef I dont worry bout y'all, I dont know who is," Dilsey said. "Come on, we already late."

"Rev'un Shegog gwine preach today," Frony said.

"Is?" Dilsey said. "Who him?"

"He fum Saint Looey," Frony said. "Dat big preacher."

"Huh," Dilsey said. "Whut dey needs is a man kin put de fear of God into dese here triflin young niggers."

"Rev'un Shegog kin do dat," Frony said. "So dey tells."

They went on along the street. Along its quiet length white people in bright clumps moved churchward, under the windy bells, walking now and then in the random and tentative sun. The wind was gusty, out of the southeast, chill and raw after the warm days.

"I wish you wouldn't keep on bringin him to church, mammy," Frony said. "Folks talkin."

"Whut folks?" Dilsey said.

"I hears em," Frony said.

"And I knows whut kind of folks," Dilsey said. "Trash white folks. Dat's who it is. Thinks he aint good enough fer white church, but nigger church aint good enough fer him."

"Dey talks, jes de same," Frony said.

"Den you send um to me," Dilsey said. "Tell um de good Lawd dont keer whether he bright er not. Dont nobody but white trash keer dat."

A street turned off at right angles, descending, and became a dirt road. On either hand the land dropped more sharply; a broad flat dotted with small cabins whose weathered roofs were on a level with the crown of the road. They were set in small grassless plots littered with broken things, bricks, planks, crockery, things of a once utilitarian value. What growth there was consisted of rank weeds and the trees were mulberries and locusts and sycamores—trees that partook also of the foul desiccation which surrounded the houses; trees whose very burgeoning seemed to be the sad and stubborn remnant of September, as if even spring had passed them by, leaving them to feed upon the rich and unmistakable smell of negroes in which they grew.

From the doors negroes spoke to them as they passed, to Dilsey usually:

"Sis' Gibson! How you dis mawnin?"

"I'm well. Is you well?"

"I'm right well, I thank you."

They emerged from the cabins and struggled up the shaling levee to the road—men in staid, hard brown or black, with gold watch chains and now and then a stick; young men in cheap violent blues or stripes and swaggering hats; women a little stiffly sibilant, and children in garments bought second hand of white people, who looked at Ben with the covertness of nocturnal animals:

"I bet you wont go up en tech him."

"How come I wont?"

"I bet you wont. I bet you skeered to."

"He wont hurt folks. He des a looney."

"How come a looney wont hurt folks?"

"Dat un wont. I teched him."

"I bet you wont now."

"Case Miss Dilsey lookin."

"You wont no ways."

"He dont hurt folks. He des a looney."

And steadily the older people speaking to Dilsey, though, unless they were quite old, Dilsey permitted Frony to respond.

"Mammy aint feelin well dis mawnin."

"Dat's too bad. But Rev'un Shegog'll kyo dat. He'll give her de comfort en de unburdenin."

The road rose again, to a scene like a painted backdrop. Notched into a cut of red clay crowned with oaks the road appeared to stop short off, like a cut ribbon. Beside it a weathered church lifted its crazy steeple like a painted church, and the whole scene was as flat and without perspective as a painted cardboard set upon the ultimate edge of the flat earth, against the windy sunlight of space and April and a midmorning filled with bells. Toward the church they thronged with slow sabbath deliberation, the women and children went on in, the men stopped outside and talked in quiet groups until the bell ceased ringing. Then they too entered.

The church had been decorated, with sparse flowers from kitchen gardens and hedgerows, and with streamers of colored crepe paper. Above the pulpit hung a battered Christmas bell, the accordion sort that collapses. The pulpit was empty, though the choir was already in place, fanning themselves although it was not warm.

Most of the women were gathered on one side of the room. They were talking. Then the bell struck one time and they dispersed to their seats and the congregation sat for an instant, expectant.

The bell struck again one time. The choir rose and began to sing and the congregation turned its head as one as six small children—four girls with tight pigtails bound with small scraps of cloth like butterflies, and two boys with close napped heads—entered and marched up the aisle, strung together in a harness of white ribbons and flowers, and followed by two men in single file. The second man was huge, of a light coffee color, imposing in a frock coat and white tie. His head was magisterial and profound, his neck rolled above his collar in rich folds. But he was familiar to them, and so the heads were still reverted when he had passed, and it was not until the choir ceased singing that they realised that the visiting clergyman had already entered, and when they saw the man who had preceded their minister enter the pulpit still ahead of him an indescribable sound went up, a sigh, a sound of astonishment and disappointment.

The visitor was undersized, in a shabby alpaca coat. He had a wizened black face like a small, aged monkey. And all the while that the choir sang again and while the six children rose and sang in thin, frightened, tuneless whispers, they watched the insignificant looking man sitting dwarfed and countrified by the minister's imposing bulk, with something like consternation. They were still looking at him with consternation and unbelief when the minister rose and introduced him in rich, rolling tones whose very unction served to increase the visitor's insignificance.

"En dey brung dat all de way fum Saint Looey," Frony whispered.

"I've knowed de Lawd to use cuiser tools dan dat," Dilsey said. "Hush, now," she said to Ben. "Dey fixin to sing again in a minute."

When the visitor rose to speak he sounded like a white man. His voice was level and cold. It sounded too big to have come from him and they listened at first through curiosity, as they would have to a monkey talking. They began to watch him as they would a man on a tight rope. They even forgot his insignificant appearance in the virtuosity with which he ran and poised and swooped upon the cold inflectionless wire of his voice, so that at last, when with a sort of swooping glide he came to rest again beside the reading desk with one arm resting upon it at shoulder height and his monkey body as reft of all motion as a mummy or an emptied vessel, the congregation sighed as if it waked from a collective dream and moved a little in its seats. Behind the pulpit the choir fanned steadily. Dilsey whispered, "Hush, now. Dey fixin to sing in a minute."

Then a voice said, "Brethren."

The preacher had not moved. His arm lay yet across the desk, and he still held that pose while the voice died in sonorous echoes between the walls. It was as different as day and dark from his former tone, with a sad, timbrous quality like an alto horn, sinking into their hearts and speaking there again when it had ceased in fading and cumulate echoes.

"Brethren and sisteren," it said again. The preacher removed his arm and he began to walk back and forth before the desk, his hands clasped behind him, a meagre figure, hunched over upon itself like that of one long immured in striving with the implacable earth, "I got the recollection and the blood of the Lamb!"[2] He tramped steadily back and forth beneath the twisted paper and the Christmas bell, hunched, his hands clasped behind him. He was like a worn small rock whelmed by the successive waves of his voice. With his body he seemed to feed the voice that, succubus like, had fleshed its teeth in him. And the congregation seemed to watch with its own eyes while the voice consumed him, until he was nothing and they were nothing and there was not even a voice but instead their hearts were speaking to one another in chanting measures beyond the need for words, so that when he came to rest against the reading desk, his monkey face lifted and his whole attitude that of a serene, tortured crucifix that transcended its shabbiness and insignificance and made it of no moment, a long moaning expulsion of breath rose from them, and a woman's single soprano: "Yes, Jesus!"

As the scudding day passed overhead the dingy windows glowed and faded in ghostly retrograde. A car passed along the road outside, laboring in the sand, died away. Dilsey sat bolt upright, her hand on Ben's knee. Two tears slid down her fallen cheeks, in and out of the myriad coruscations of immolation and abnegation and time.

"Brethren," the minister said in a harsh whisper, without moving.

"Yes, Jesus!" the woman's voice said, hushed yet.

"Breddren en sistuhn!" His voice rang again, with the horns. He removed his arm and stood erect and raised his hands. "I got de ricklickshun en de blood of de Lamb!" They did not mark just when his intonation, his pronunciation, became negroid, they just sat swaying a little in their seats as the voice took them into itself.

"When de long, cold——Oh, I tells you, breddren, when de long, cold. . . . I sees de light en I sees de word,[3] po sinner! Dey passed away in Egypt, de swingin chariots; de generations passed away.[4] Wus a rich man: whar he now, O breddren? Wus a po man: whar he now, O sistuhn?[5] Oh I tells you, ef you aint got de milk en de dew of de old salvation when de long, cold years rolls away!"

2. See Revelation 7.14.
3. See John 1.1–4.
4. See Genesis 50.22–26.
5. See Luke 16.19–24.

"Yes, Jesus!"

"I tells you, breddren, en I tells you, sistuhn, dey'll come a time. Po sinner sayin Let me lay down wid de Lawd, lemme lay down my load. Den whut Jesus gwine say, O breddren? O sistuhn? Is you got de ricklickshun en de Blood of de Lamb? Case I aint gwine load down heaven!"

He fumbled in his coat and took out a handkerchief and mopped his face. A low concerted sound rose from the congregation: "Mmm-mmmmmmmmmmmm!" The woman's voice said, "Yes, Jesus! Jesus!"

"Breddren! Look at dem little chillen settin dar. Jesus wus like dat once. He mammy suffered de glory en de pangs. Sometime maybe she helt him at de nightfall, whilst de angels singin him to sleep; maybe she look out de do en see de Roman po-lice passin." He tramped back and forth, mopping his face. "Listen, breddren! I sees de day. Ma'y settin in de do wid Jesus on her lap, de little Jesus. Like dem chillen dar, de little Jesus. I hears de angels singin de peaceful songs en de glory; I sees de closin eyes; sees Mary jump up, sees de sojer face: We gwine to kill! We gwine to kill! We gwine to kill yo little Jesus! I hears de weepin en de lamentation of de po mammy widout de salvation en de word of God!"[6]

"Mmmmmmmmmmmmmmmmmm! Jesus! Little Jesus!" and another voice, rising:

"I sees, O Jesus! Oh I sees!" and still another, without words, like bubbles rising in water.

"I sees hit, breddren! I sees hit! Sees de blastin, blindin sight! I sees Calvary, wid de sacred trees, sees de thief en de murderer en de least of dese; I hears de boastin en de braggin: Ef you be Jesus, lif up yo tree en walk![7] I hears de wailin of women en de evenin lamentations; I hears de weepin en de cryin en de turnt-away face of God: dey done kilt Jesus; dey done kilt my Son!"

"Mmmmmmmmmmmmmmm. Jesus! I sees, O Jesus!"

"O blind sinner! Breddren, I tells you; sistuhn, I says to you, when de Lawd did turn His mighty face, say, Aint gwine overload heaven! I can see de widowed God shet His do; I sees de whelmin flood roll between; I sees de darkness en de death everlastin upon de generations. Den, lo! Breddren! Yes, breddren! Whut I see? Whut I see, O sinner? I sees de resurrection en de light; sees de meek Jesus sayin Dey kilt me dat ye shall live again; I died dat dem whut sees en believes shall never die.[8] Breddren, O breddren! I sees de doom crack en de golden horns shoutin down de glory,[9] en de arisen dead whut got de blood en de ricklickshun of de Lamb!"

6. See Matthew 2.16
7. See Matthew 27.39–44 and Mark 2.9.
8. See John 11.25–26; Romans 5.8; I Corinthians 15.22.
9. See Revelation 8.

In the midst of the voices and the hands Ben sat, rapt in his sweet blue gaze. Dilsey sat bolt upright beside, crying rigidly and quietly in the annealment and the blood of the remembered Lamb.

As they walked through the bright noon, up the sandy road with the dispersing congregation talking easily again group to group, she continued to weep, unmindful of the talk.

"He sho a preacher, mon! He didn't look like much at first, but hush!"

"He seed de power en de glory."

"Yes, suh. He seed hit. Face to face he seed hit."

Dilsey made no sound, her face did not quiver as the tears took their sunken and devious courses, walking with her head up, making no effort to dry them away even.

"Whyn't you quit dat, mammy?" Frony said. "Wid all dese people lookin. We be passin white folks soon."

"I've seed de first en de last," Dilsey said. "Never you mind me."[1]

"First en last whut?" Frony said.

"Never you mind," Dilsey said. "I seed de beginnin, en now I sees de endin."

Before they reached the street though she stopped and lifted her skirt and dried her eyes on the hem of her topmost underskirt. Then they went on. Ben shambled along beside Dilsey, watching Luster who anticked along ahead, the umbrella in his hand and his new straw hat slanted viciously in the sunlight, like a big foolish dog watching a small clever one. They reached the gate and entered. Immediately Ben began to whimper again, and for a while all of them looked up the drive at the square, paintless house with its rotting portico.

"Whut's gwine on up dar today?" Frony said. "Somethin is."

"Nothin," Dilsey said. "You tend to yo business en let de whitefolks tend to deir'n."

"Somethin is," Frony said. "I heard him first thing dis mawnin. 'Taint none of my business, dough."

"En I knows whut, too," Luster said.

"You knows mo dan you got any use fer," Dilsey said. "Aint you jes heard Frony say hit aint none of yo business? You take Benjy on to de back and keep him quiet twell I put dinner on."

"I knows whar Miss Quentin is," Luster said.

"Den jes keep hit," Dilsey said. "Soon es Quentin need any of yo egvice, I'll let you know. Y'all g'awn en play in de back, now."

"You know whut gwine happen soon es dey start playin dat ball over yonder," Luster said.

---

1. See Revelation 22.13.

"Dey wont start fer a while yit. By dat time T. P. be here to take him ridin. Here, you gimme dat new hat."

Luster gave her the hat and he and Ben went on across the back yard. Ben was still whimpering, though not loud. Dilsey and Frony went to the cabin. After a while Dilsey emerged, again in the faded calico dress, and went to the kitchen. The fire had died down. There was no sound in the house. She put on the apron and went up stairs. There was no sound anywhere. Quentin's room was as they had left it. She entered and picked up the undergarment and put the stocking back in the drawer and closed it. Mrs Compson's door was closed. Dilsey stood beside it for a moment, listening. Then she opened it and entered, entered a pervading reek of camphor. The shades were drawn, the room in halflight, and the bed, so that at first she thought Mrs Compson was asleep and was about to close the door when the other spoke.

"Well?" she said. "What is it?"

"Hit's me," Dilsey said. "You want anything?"

Mrs Compson didn't answer. After a while, without moving her head at all, she said: "Where's Jason?"

"He aint come back yit," Dilsey said. "Whut you want?"

Mrs Compson said nothing. Like so many cold, weak people, when faced at last by the incontrovertible disaster she exhumed from somewhere a sort of fortitude, strength. In her case it was an unshakable conviction regarding the yet unplumbed event. "Well," she said presently. "Did you find it?"

"Find whut? Whut you talkin about?"

"The note. At least she would have enough consideration to leave a note. Even Quentin did that."

"Whut you talkin about?" Dilsey said. "Dont you know she all right? I bet she be walkin right in dis do befo dark."

"Fiddlesticks," Mrs Compson said. "It's in the blood. Like uncle, like niece. Or mother. I dont know which would be worse. I dont seem to care."

"Whut you keep on talkin that way fur?" Dilsey said. "Whut she want to do anything like that fur?"

"I dont know. What reason did Quentin have? Under God's heaven what reason did he have? It cant be simply to flout and hurt me. Whoever God is, He would not permit that. I'm a lady. You might not believe that from my offspring, but I am."

"You des wait en see," Dilsey said. "She be here by night, right dar in her bed." Mrs Compson said nothing. The camphor soaked cloth lay upon her brow. The black robe lay across the foot of the bed. Dilsey stood with her hand on the door knob.

"Well," Mrs Compson said. "What do you want? Are you going to fix some dinner for Jason and Benjamin, or not?"

"Jason aint come yit," Dilsey said. "I gwine fix somethin. You sho you dont want nothin? Yo bottle still hot enough?"

"You might hand me my bible."

"I give hit to you dis mawnin, befo I left."

"You laid it on the edge of the bed. How long did you expect it to stay there?"

Dilsey crossed to the bed and groped among the shadows beneath the edge of it and found the bible, face down. She smoothed the bent pages and laid the book on the bed again. Mrs Compson didn't open her eyes. Her hair and the pillow were the same color, beneath the wimple of the medicated cloth she looked like an old nun praying. "Dont put it there again," she said, without opening her eyes. "That's where you put it before. Do you want me to have to get out of bed to pick it up?"

Dilsey reached the book across her and laid it on the broad side of the bed. "You cant see to read, noways," she said. "You want me to raise de shade a little?"

"No. Let them alone. Go on and fix Jason something to eat."

Dilsey went out. She closed the door and returned to the kitchen. The stove was almost cold. While she stood there the clock above the cupboard struck ten times. "One oclock," she said aloud. "Jason aint comin home. Ise seed de first en de last," she said, looking at the cold stove. "I seed de first en de last." She set out some cold food on a table. As she moved back and forth she sang, a hymn. She sang the first two lines over and over to the complete tune. She arranged the meal and went to the door and called Luster, and after a time Luster and Ben entered. Ben was still moaning a little, as to himself.

"He aint never quit," Luster said.

"Y'all come on en eat," Dilsey said. "Jason aint comin to dinner." They sat down at the table. Ben could manage solid food pretty well for himself, though even now, with cold food before him, Dilsey tied a cloth about his neck. He and Luster ate. Dilsey moved about the kitchen, singing the two lines of the hymn which she remembered. "Y'all kin g'awn en eat," she said. "Jason aint comin home."

He was twenty miles away at that time. When he left the house he drove rapidly to town, overreaching the slow sabbath groups and the peremptory bells along the broken air. He crossed the empty square and turned into a narrow street that was abruptly quieter even yet, and stopped before a frame house and went up the flower bordered walk to the porch.

Beyond the screen door people were talking. As he lifted his hand to knock he heard steps, so he withheld his hand until a big man in black broadcloth trousers and a stiff bosomed white shirt without collar opened the door. He had vigorous untidy iron-gray hair and his gray eyes were round and shiny like a little boy's. He took Jason's hand and drew him into the house, still shaking it.

"Come right in," he said. "Come right in."

"You ready to go now?" Jason said.

"Walk right in," the other said, propelling him by the elbow into a room where a man and a woman sat. "You know Myrtle's husband, dont you? Jason Compson, Vernon."

"Yes," Jason said. He did not even look at the man, and as the sheriff drew a chair across the room the man said,

"We'll go out so you can talk. Come on, Myrtle."

"No, no," the sheriff said. "You folks keep your seat. I reckon it aint that serious, Jason? Have a seat."

"I'll tell you as we go along," Jason said. "Get your hat and coat."

"We'll go out," the man said, rising.

"Keep your seat," the sheriff said. "Me and Jason will go out on the porch."

"You get your hat and coat," Jason said. "They've already got a twelve hour start." The sheriff led the way back to the porch. A man and a woman passing spoke to him. He responded with a hearty florid gesture. Bells were still ringing, from the direction of the section known as Nigger Hollow. "Get your hat, Sheriff," Jason said. The sheriff drew up two chairs.

"Have a seat and tell me what the trouble is."

"I told you over the phone," Jason said, standing. "I did that to save time. Am I going to have to go to law to compel you to do your sworn duty?"

"You sit down and tell me about it," the sheriff said. "I'll take care of you all right."

"Care, hell," Jason said. "Is this what you call taking care of me?"

"You're the one that's holding us up," the sheriff said. "You sit down and tell me about it."

Jason told him, his sense of injury and impotence feeding upon its own sound, so that after a time he forgot his haste in the violent cumulation of his self justification and his outrage. The sheriff watched him steadily with his cold shiny eyes.

"But you dont know they done it," he said. "You just think so."

"Dont know?" Jason said. "When I spent two damn days chasing her through alleys, trying to keep her away from him, after I told her what I'd do to her if I ever caught her with him, and you say I dont know that that little b——"

"Now, then," the sheriff said. "That'll do. That's enough of that." He looked out across the street, his hands in his pockets.

"And when I come to you, a commissioned officer of the law," Jason said.

"That show's in Mottson this week," the sheriff said.

"Yes," Jason said. "And if I could find a law officer that gave a solitary damn about protecting the people that elected him to office, I'd be there too by now." He repeated his story, harshly recapitulant, seeming to get an actual pleasure out of his outrage and impotence. The sheriff did not appear to be listening at all.

"Jason," he said. "What were you doing with three thousand dollars hid in the house?"

"What?" Jason said. "That's my business where I keep my money. Your business is to help me get it back."

"Did your mother know you had that much on the place?"

"Look here," Jason said. "My house has been robbed. I know who did it and I know where they are. I come to you as the commissioned officer of the law, and I ask you once more, are you going to make any effort to recover my property, or not?"

"What do you aim to do with that girl, if you catch them?"

"Nothing," Jason said. "Not anything. I wouldn't lay my hand on her. The bitch that cost me a job, the one chance I ever had to get ahead, that killed my father and is shortening my mother's life every day and made my name a laughing stock in the town. I wont do anything to her," he said. "Not anything."

"You drove that girl into running off, Jason," the sheriff said.

"How I conduct my family is no business of yours," Jason said. "Are you going to help me or not?"

"You drove her away from home," the sheriff said. "And I have some suspicions about who that money belongs to that I dont reckon I'll ever know for certain."

Jason stood, slowly wringing the brim of his hat in his hands. He said quietly: "You're not going to make any effort to catch them for me?"

"That's not any of my business, Jason. If you had any actual proof, I'd have to act. But without that I dont figger it's any of my business."

"That's your answer, is it?" Jason said. "Think well, now."

"That's it, Jason."

"All right," Jason said. He put his hat on. "You'll regret this. I wont be helpless. This is not Russia, where just because he wears a little metal badge, a man is immune to law." He went down the steps and got in his car and started the engine. The sheriff watched him drive away, turn, and rush past the house toward town.

The bells were ringing again, high in the scudding sunlight in bright disorderly tatters of sound. He stopped at a filling station and had his tires examined and the tank filled.

"Gwine on a trip, is you?" the negro asked him. He didn't answer. "Look like hit gwine fair off, after all," the negro said.

"Fair off, hell." Jason said. "It'll be raining like hell by twelve oclock." He looked at the sky, thinking about rain, about the slick clay roads, himself stalled somewhere miles from town. He thought about it with a sort of triumph, of the fact that he was going to miss dinner, that by starting now and so serving his compulsion of haste, he would be at the greatest possible distance from both towns when noon came. It seemed to him that in this circumstance was giving him a break, so he said to the negro:

"What the hell are you doing? Has somebody paid you to keep this car standing here as long as you can?"

"Dis here ti' aint got no air a-tall in hit," the negro said.

"Then get the hell away from there and let me have that tube," Jason said.

"Hit up now," the negro said, rising. "You kin ride now."

Jason got in and started the engine and drove off. He went into second gear, the engine spluttering and gasping, and he raced the engine, jamming the throttle down and snapping the choker in and out savagely. "It's going to rain," he said. "Get me half way there, and rain like hell." And he drove on out of the bells and out of town, thinking of himself slogging through the mud, hunting a team. "And every damn one of them will be at church." He thought of how he'd find a church at last and take a team and of the owner coming out, shoutin' at him and of himself striking the man down. "I'm Jason Compson. See if you can stop me. See if you can elect a man to office that can stop me," he said, thinking of himself entering the courthouse with a file of soldiers and dragging the sheriff out. "Thinks he can sit with his hands folded and see me lose my job. I'll show him about jobs." Of his niece he did not think at all, nor of the arbitrary valuation of the money. Neither of them had had entity or individuality for him for ten years: together they merely symbolised the job in the bank of which he had been deprived before he ever got it.

The air brightened, the running shadow patches were now the obverse, and it seemed to him that the fact that the day was clearing was another cunning stroke on the part of the foe, the fresh battle toward which he was carrying ancient wounds. From time to time he passed churches, unpainted frame buildings with sheet iron steeples, surrounded by tethered teams and shabby motorcars, and it seemed to him that each of them was a picketpost where the rear guards of Circumstance peeped fleetingly back at him. "And damn You, too," he said. "See if You can stop me;" thinking of himself, his file of soldiers with the manacled sheriff in the rear, dragging Omnipotence down from his throne, if necessary; of the embattled legions of both hell and heaven through which he tore his way and put his hands at last on his fleeing niece.

The wind was out of the southeast. It blew steadily upon his cheek. It seemed that he could feel the prolonged blow of it sinking through his skull, and suddenly with an old premonition he clapped the brakes on and stopped and sat perfectly still. Then he lifted his hand to his neck and began to curse, and sat there, cursing in a harsh whisper. When it was necessary for him to drive for any length of time he fortified himself with a handkerchief soaked in camphor, which he would tie about his throat when clear of town, thus inhaling the fumes, and he got out and lifted the seat cushion on the chance that there might be a forgotten one there. He looked beneath both seats and stood again for a while, cursing, seeing himself mocked by his own triumphing. He closed his eyes, leaning on the door. He could return and get the forgotten camphor, or he could go on. In either case, his head would be splitting, but at home he could be sure of finding camphor on Sunday, while if he went on he could not be sure. But if he went back, he would be an hour and a half later in reaching Mottson. "Maybe I can drive slow," he said. "Maybe I can drive slow, thinking of something else. . . ."

He got in and started. "I'll think of something else," he said, so he thought about Lorraine. He imagined himself in bed with her, only he was just lying beside her, pleading with her to help him, then he thought of the money again, and that he had been outwitted by a woman, a girl. If he could just believe it was the man who had robbed him. But to have been robbed of that which was to have compensated him for the lost job, which he had acquired through so much effort and risk, by the very symbol of the lost job itself, and worst of all, by a bitch of a girl. He drove on, shielding his face from the steady wind with the corner of his coat.

He could see the opposed forces of his destiny and his will drawing swiftly together now, toward a junction that would be irrevocable; he became cunning. I cant make a blunder, he told himself. There would be just one right thing, without alternatives: he must do that. He believed that both of them would know him on sight, while he'd have to trust to seeing her first, unless the man still wore the red tie. And the fact that he must depend on that red tie seemed to be the sum of the impending disaster; he could almost smell it, feel it above the throbbing of his head.

He crested the final hill. Smoke lay in the valley, and roofs, a spire or two above trees. He drove down the hill and into the town, slowing, telling himself again of the need for caution, to find where the tent was located first. He could not see very well now, and he knew that it was the disaster which kept telling him to go directly and get something for his head. At a filling station they told him that the tent was not up yet, but that the show cars were on a siding at the station. He drove there.

Two gaudily painted pullman cars stood on the track. He reconnoitred them before he got out. He was trying to breathe shallowly, so that the blood would not beat so in his skull. He got out and went along the station wall, watching the cars. A few garments hung out of the windows, limp and crinkled, as though they had been recently laundered. On the earth beside the steps of one sat three canvas chairs. But he saw no sign of life at all until a man in a dirty apron came to the door and emptied a pan of dishwater with a broad gesture, the sunlight glinting on the metal belly of the pan, then entered the car again.

Now I'll have to take him by surprise, before he can warn them, he thought. It never occurred to him that they might not be there, in the car. That they should not be there, that the whole result should not hinge on whether he saw them first or they saw him first, would be opposed to all nature and contrary to the whole rhythm of events. And more than that: he must see them first, get the money back, then what they did would be of no importance to him, while otherwise the whole world would know that he, Jason Compson, had been robbed by Quentin, his niece, a bitch.

He reconnoitred again. Then he went to the car and mounted the steps, swiftly and quietly, and paused at the door. The galley was dark, rank with stale food. The man was a white blur, singing in a cracked, shaky tenor. An old man, he thought, and not as big as I am. He entered the car as the man looked up.

"Hey?" the man said, stopping his song.

"Where are they?" Jason said. "Quick, now. In the sleeping car?"

"Where's who?" the man said.

"Dont lie to me," Jason said. He blundered on in the cluttered obscurity.

"What's that?" the other said. "Who you calling a liar?" and when Jason grasped his shoulder he exclaimed, "Look out, fellow!"

"Dont lie," Jason said. "Where are they?"

"Why, you bastard," the man said. His arm was frail and thin in Jason's grasp. He tried to wrench free, then he turned and fell to scrabbling on the littered table behind him.

"Come on," Jason said. "Where are they?"

"I'll tell you where they are," the man shrieked. "Lemme find my butcher knife."

"Here," Jason said, trying to hold the other. "I'm just asking you a question."

"You bastard," the other shrieked, scrabbling at the table. Jason tried to grasp him in both arms, trying to prison the puny fury of him. The man's body felt so old, so frail, yet so fatally singlepurposed that for the first time Jason saw clear and unshadowed the disaster toward which he rushed.

"Quit it!" he said. "Here. Here! I'll get out. Give me time, and I'll get out."

"Call me a liar," the other wailed. "Lemme go. Lemme go just one minute. I'll show you."

Jason glared wildly about, holding the other. Outside it was now bright and sunny, swift and bright and empty, and he thought of the people soon to be going quietly home to Sunday dinner, decorously festive, and of himself trying to hold the fatal, furious little old man whom he dared not release long enough to turn his back and run.

"Will you quit long enough for me to get out?" he said. "Will you?" But the other still struggled, and Jason freed one hand and struck him on the head. A clumsy, hurried blow, and not hard, but the other slumped immediately and slid clattering among pans and buckets to the floor. Jason stood above him, panting, listening. Then he turned and ran from the car. At the door he restrained himself and descended more slowly and stood there again. His breath made a hah hah hah sound and he stood there trying to repress it, darting his gaze this way and that, when at a scuffling sound behind him he turned in time to see the little old man leaping awkwardly and furiously from the vestibule, a rusty hatchet high in his hand.

He grasped at the hatchet, feeling no shock but knowing that he was falling, thinking So this is how it'll end, and he believed that he was about to die and when something crashed against the back of his head he thought How did he hit me there? Only maybe he hit me a long time ago, he thought, And I just now felt it, and he thought Hurry. Hurry. Get it over with, and then a furious desire not to die seized him and he struggled, hearing the old man wailing and cursing in his cracked voice.

He still struggled when they hauled him to his feet, but they held him and he ceased.

"Am I bleeding much?" he said. "The back of my head. Am I bleeding?" He was still saying that while he felt himself being propelled rapidly away, heard the old man's thin furious voice dying away behind him. "Look at my head," he said. "Wait, I——"

"Wait, hell," the man who held him said. "That damn little wasp'll kill you. Keep going. You aint hurt."

"He hit me," Jason said. "Am I bleeding?"

"Keep going," the other said. He led Jason on around the corner of the station, to the empty platform where an express truck stood, where grass grew rigidly in a plot bordered with rigid flowers and a sign in electric lights: Keep your on Mottson, the gap filled by a human eye with an electric pupil. The man released him.

"Now," he said. "You get on out of here and stay out. What were you trying to do? commit suicide?"

"I was looking for two people," Jason said. "I just asked him where they were."

"Who you looking for?"

"It's a girl," Jason said. "And a man. He had on a red tie in Jefferson yesterday. With this show. They robbed me."

"Oh," the man said. "You're the one, are you. Well, they aint here."

"I reckon so," Jason said. He leaned against the wall and put his hand to the back of his head and looked at his palm. "I thought I was bleeding," he said. "I thought he hit me with that hatchet."

"You hit your head on the rail," the man said. "You better go on. They aint here."

"Yes. He said they were not here. I thought he was lying."

"Do you think I'm lying?" the man said.

"No," Jason said. "I know they're not here."

"I told him to get the hell out of there, both of them," the man said. "I wont have nothing like that in my show. I run a respectable show, with a respectable troupe."

"Yes," Jason said. "You dont know where they went?"

"No. And I dont want to know. No member of my show can pull a stunt like that. You her . . . brother?"

"No," Jason said. "It dont matter. I just wanted to see them. You sure he didn't hit me? No blood, I mean."

"There would have been blood if I hadn't got there when I did. You stay away from here, now. That little bastard'll kill you. That your car yonder?"

"Yes."

"Well, you get in it and go back to Jefferson. If you find them, it wont be in my show. I run a respectable show. You say they robbed you?"

"No," Jason said. "It dont make any difference." He went to the car and got in. What is it I must do? he thought. Then he remembered. He started the engine and drove slowly up the street until he found a drugstore. The door was locked. He stood for a while with his hand on the knob and his head bent a little. Then he turned away and when a man came along after a while he asked if there was a drugstore open anywhere, but there was not. Then he asked when the northbound train ran, and the man told him at two thirty. He crossed the pavement and got in the car again and sat there. After a while two negro lads passed. He called to them.

"Can either of you boys drive a car?"

"Yes, suh."

"What'll you charge to drive me to Jefferson right away?"

They looked at one another, murmuring.

"I'll pay a dollar," Jason said.

They murmured again. "Couldn't go fer dat," one said.

"What will you go for?"

"Kin you go?" one said.

"I cant git off," the other said. "Whyn't you drive him up dar? You aint got nothin to do."

"Yes I is."

"Whut you got to do?"

They murmured again, laughing.

"I'll give you two dollars," Jason said. "Either of you."

"I cant git away neither," the first said.

"All right," Jason said. "Go on."

He sat there for some time. He heard a clock strike the half hour, then people began to pass, in Sunday and easter clothes. Some looked at him as they passed, at the man sitting quietly behind the wheel of a small car, with his invisible life ravelled out about him like a wornout sock, and went on. After a while a negro in overalls came up.

"Is you de one wants to go to Jefferson?" he said.

"Yes," Jason said. "What'll you charge me?"

"Fo dollars."

"Give you two."

"Cant go fer no less'n fo." The man in the car sat quietly. He wasn't even looking at him. The negro said, "You want me er not?"

"All right," Jason said. "Get in."

He moved over and the negro took the wheel. Jason closed his eyes. I can get something for it at Jefferson, he told himself, easing himself to the jolting, I can get something there. They drove on, along the streets where people were turning peacefully into houses and Sunday dinners, and on out of town. He thought that. He wasn't thinking of home, where Ben and Luster were eating cold dinner at the kitchen table. Something—the absence of disaster, threat, in any constant evil—permitted him to forget Jefferson as any place which he had ever seen before, where his life must resume itself.

When Ben and Luster were done Dilsey sent them outdoors. "And see kin you let him alone twell fo oclock. T. P. be here den."

"Yessum," Luster said, They went out. Dilsey ate her dinner and cleared up the kitchen. Then she went to the foot of the stairs and listened, but there was no sound. She returned through the kitchen and out the outer door and stopped on the steps. Ben and Luster were not in sight, but while she stood there she heard another sluggish twang from the direction of the cellar door and she went to the door and looked down upon a repetition of the morning's scene.

"He done hit jes dat way," Luster said. He contemplated the motionless saw with a kind of hopeful dejection. "I aint got de right thing to hit it wid yit," he said.

"En you aint gwine find hit down here, neither," Dilsey said. "You take him on out in de sun. You bofe get pneumonia down here on dis wet flo."

She waited and watched them cross the yard toward a clump of cedar trees near the fence. Then she went on to her cabin.

"Now, dont you git started," Luster said. "I had enough trouble wid you today." There was a hammock made of barrel staves slatted into woven wires. Luster lay down in the swing, but Ben went on vaguely and purposelessly. He began to whimper again. "Hush, now," Luster said. "I fixin to whup you." He lay back in the swing. Ben had stopped moving, but Luster could hear him whimpering. "Is you gwine hush, er aint you?" Luster said. He got up and followed and came upon Ben squatting before a small mound of earth. At either end of it an empty bottle of blue glass that once contained poison was fixed in the ground. In one was a withered stalk of jimson weed. Ben squatted before it, moaning, a slow, inarticulate sound. Still moaning he sought vaguely about and found a twig and put it in the other bottle. "Whyn't you hush?" Luster said. "You want me to give you somethin to sho nough moan about? Sposin I does dis." He knelt and swept the bottle suddenly up and behind him. Ben ceased moaning. He squatted, looking at the small depression where the bottle had sat, then as he drew his lungs full Luster brought the bottle back into view. "Hush!" he hissed. "Dont you dast to beller! Dont you. Dar hit is. See? Here. You fixin to start ef you stays here. Come on, les go see ef dey started knockin ball yit." He took Ben's arm and drew him up and they went to the fence and stood side by side there, peering between the matted honeysuckle not yet in bloom.

"Dar," Luster said. "Dar come some. See um?"

They watched the foursome play onto the green and out, and move to the tee and drive. Ben watched, whimpering, slobbering. When the foursome went on he followed along the fence, bobbing and moaning. One said,

"Here, caddie. Bring the bag."

"Hush, Benjy," Luster said, but Ben went on at his shambling trot, clinging to the fence, wailing in his hoarse, hopeless voice. The man played and went on, Ben keeping pace with him until the fence turned at right angles, and he clung to the fence, watching the people move on and away.

"Will you hush now?" Luster said. "Will you hush now?" He shook Ben's arm. Ben clung to the fence, wailing steadily and hoarsely. "Aint you gwine stop?" Luster said. "Or is you?" Ben gazed through the fence. "All right, den," Luster said. "You want somethin to beller about?" He looked over his shoulder, toward the house. Then he whispered: "Caddy! Beller now. Caddy! Caddy! Caddy!"

A moment later, in the slow intervals of Ben's voice, Luster heard Dilsey calling. He took Ben by the arm and they crossed the yard toward her.

"I tole you he warn't gwine stay quiet," Luster said.

"You vilyun!" Dilsey said. "Whut you done to him?"

"I aint done nothin. I tole you when dem folks start play in, he git started up."

"You come on here," Dilsey said. "Hush, Benjy. Hush, now." But he wouldn't hush. They crossed the yard quickly and went to the cabin and entered. "Run git dat shoe," Dilsey said. "Dont you sturb Miss Cahline, now. Ef she say anything, tell her I got him. Go on, now; you kin sho do dat right, I reckon." Luster went out. Dilsey led Ben to the bed and drew him down beside her and she held him, rocking back and forth, wiping his drooling mouth upon the hem of her skirt. "Hush, now," she said, stroking his head. "Hush. Dilsey got you." But he bellowed slowly, abjectly, without tears; the grave hopeless sound of all voiceless misery under the sun. Luster returned, carrying a white satin slipper. It was yellow now, and cracked, and soiled, and when they gave it into Ben's hand he hushed for a while. But he still whimpered, and soon he lifted his voice again.

"You reckon you kin find T. P.?" Dilsey said.

"He say yistiddy he gwine out to St John's today. Say he be back at fo."

Dilsey rocked back and forth, stroking Ben's head.

"Dis long time, O Jesus," she said. "Dis long time."

"I kin drive dat surrey, mammy," Luster said.

"You kill bofe y'all," Dilsey said. "You do hit fer devilment. I knows you got plenty sense to. But I cant trust you. Hush, now," she said. "Hush. Hush."

"Nome I wont," Luster said. "I drives wid T. P." Dilsey rocked back and forth, holding Ben. "Miss Cahline say ef you cant quiet him, she gwine git up en come down en do hit."

"Hush, honey," Dilsey said, stroking Ben's head. "Luster, honey," she said. "Will you think about yo ole mammy en drive dat surrey right?"

"Yessum," Luster said. "I drive hit jes like T. P."

Dilsey stroked Ben's head, rocking back and forth. "I does de bes I kin," she said. "Lawd knows dat. Go git it, den," she said, rising. Luster scuttled out. Ben held the slipper, crying. "Hush, now. Luster gone to git de surrey en take you to de graveyard. We aint gwine risk gittin yo cap," she said. She went to a closet contrived of a calico curtain hung across a corner of the room and got the felt hat she had worn. "We's down to worse'n dis, ef folks jes knowed," she said. "You's de Lawd's chile, anyway. En I be His'n too, fo long, praise Jesus. Here." She put the hat on his head and buttoned his coat. He wailed steadily. She took the slipper from him and put it away and they went out. Luster came up, with an ancient white horse in a battered and lopsided surrey.

"You gwine be careful, Luster?" she said.

"Yessum," Luster said. She helped Ben into the back seat. He had ceased crying, but now he began to whimper again.

"Hit's his flower," Luster said. "Wait, I'll git him one."

"You set right dar," Dilsey said. She went and took the cheek-strap. "Now, hurry en git him one." Luster ran around the house, toward the garden. He came back with a single narcissus.

"Dat un broke," Dilsey said. "Whyn't you git him a good un?"

"Hit de onliest one I could find," Luster said, "Y'all took all of um Friday to dec'rate de church. Wait, I'll fix hit." So while Dilsey held the horse Luster put a splint on the flower stalk with a twig and two bits of string and gave it to Ben. Then he mounted and took the reins. Dilsey still held the bridle.

"You knows de way now?" she said. "Up de street, round de square, to de graveyard, den straight back home."

"Yessum," Luster said. "Hum up, Queenie."

"You gwine be careful, now?"

"Yessum." Dilsey released the bridle.

"Hum up, Queenie," Luster said.

"Here," Dilsey said. "You han me dat whup."

"Aw, mammy," Luster said.

"Give hit here," Dilsey said, approaching the wheel. Luster gave it to her reluctantly.

"I wont never git Queenie started now."

"Never you mind about dat," Dilsey said. "Queenie know mo bout whar she gwine dan you does. All you got to do es set dar en hold dem reins. You knows de way, now?"

"Yessum. Same way T. P. goes ev'y Sunday."

"Den you do de same thing dis Sunday."

"Cose I is. Aint I drove fer T. P. mo'n a hund'ed times?"

"Den do hit again," Dilsey said. "G'awn, now. En ef you hurts Benjy, nigger boy, I dont know whut I do. You bound fer de chain gang, but I'll send you dar fo even chain gang ready fer you."

"Yessum," Luster said. "Hum up, Queenie."

He flapped the lines on Queenie's broad back and the surrey lurched into motion.

"You, Luster!" Dilsey said.

"Hum up, dar!" Luster said. He flapped the lines again. With subterranean rumblings Queenie jogged slowly down the drive and turned into the street, where Luster exhorted her into a gait resembling a prolonged and suspended fall in a forward direction.

Ben quit whimpering. He sat in the middle of the seat, holding the repaired flower upright in his fist, his eyes serene and ineffable. Directly before him Luster's bullet head turned backward continually until the house passed from view, then he pulled to the side of the street and while Ben watched him he descended and broke a switch from a hedge. Queenie lowered her head and fell to cropping the grass until Luster mounted and hauled her head up and harried her into motion again, then he squared his elbows and with the switch and the reins held high he assumed a swaggering attitude out of all proportion to the sedate clopping of Queenie's hooves and the organlike basso of her internal accompaniment. Motors passed them, and pedestrians; once a group of half grown negroes:

"Dar Luster. Whar you gwine, Luster? To de boneyard?"

"Hi," Luster said. "Aint de same boneyard y'all headed fer. Hum up, elefump."

They approached the square, where the Confederate soldier gazed with empty eyes beneath his marble hand in wind and weather. Luster took still another notch in himself and gave the impervious Queenie a cut with the switch, casting his glance about the square. "Dar Mr Jason car," he said, then he spied another group of negroes. "Les show dem niggers how quality does, Benjy," he said. "Whut you say?" He looked back. Ben sat, holding the flower in his fist, his gaze empty and untroubled. Luster hit Queenie again and swung her to the left at the monument.

For an instant Ben sat in an utter hiatus. Then he bellowed. Bellow on bellow, his voice mounted, with scarce interval for breath. There was more than astonishment in it, it was horror; shock; agony eyeless, tongueless; just sound, and Luster's eyes backrolling for a white instant. "Gret God," he said. "Hush! Hush! Gret God!" He whirled again and struck Queenie with the switch. It broke and he cast it away and with Ben's voice mounting toward its unbelievable crescendo Luster caught up the end of the reins and leaned forward as Jason came jumping across the square and onto the step.

With a backhanded blow he hurled Luster aside and caught the reins and sawed Queenie about and doubled the reins back and slashed her across the hips. He cut her again and again, into a plunging gallop, while Ben's hoarse agony roared about them, and swung her about to the right of the monument. Then he struck Luster over the head with his fist.

"Dont you know any better than to take him to the left?" he said. He reached back and struck Ben, breaking the flower stalk again. "Shut up!" he said. "Shut up!" He jerked Queenie back and jumped down. "Get to hell on home with him. If you ever cross that gate with him again, I'll kill you!"

"Yes, suh!" Luster said. He took the reins and hit Queenie with the end of them. "Git up! Git up, dar! Benjy, fer God's sake!"

Ben's voice roared and roared. Queenie moved again, her feet began to clop-clop steadily again, and at once Ben hushed. Luster looked quickly back over his shoulder, then he drove on. The broken flower drooped over Ben's fist and his eyes were empty and blue and serene again as cornice and façade flowed smoothly once more from left to right, post and tree, window and doorway and signboard each in its ordered place.

New York, N.Y.
October 1928

BACKGROUNDS AND CONTEXTS

Contemporary Reception

The story goes that one day in the winter of 1929 a young editor named Lenore Marshall came into her employer's office at the newly-established publishing house of Cape & Smith and announced that she had just found a "work of genius." Harrison Smith asked what it was about, and she had to confess that she didn't yet know. She had only just started, yet even after she had finished the book and confirmed her sense of its power, Marshall admitted that she couldn't really answer Smith's question.[1] Her reaction to *The Sound and the Fury* would be repeated in the months to come: many of the novel's reviewers simply rejected it out of hand, and even those who liked it would acknowledge their own sense of bafflement.

Hal Smith had worked with Faulkner at Harcourt, Brace, which had just published the first of the Yoknapatawpha novels under the title *Sartoris*, a scaled-down version of the book Faulkner had written as *Flags in the Dust*. Smith knew what his new firm was getting. This novelist would have to create his own audience, but Smith also knew that a good publisher might help the process along, and sent the manuscript to another writer on his list. The Tennessee-born Evelyn Scott is now largely forgotten, but her 1929 Civil War panorama *The Wave* was one of that year's bestsellers, and Smith massaged her enthusiasm into a promotional pamphlet that he distributed to booksellers and critics. Her essay is in places overwritten, but it nevertheless provides the most sympathetic early account of *The Sound and the Fury*, one that both offers a sharp reading of Benjy's narrative and registers the novel's avoidance of explicit moral commentary.

Still, the book's reception can best be described as mixed. Most of its reviewers were young and one might have expected their sympathy; but while almost all of them recognized its ambition, some found its material sordid and others couldn't shake their belief that its modernist experimentation was little more than a stunt. The pieces I've selected to accompany Scott's each touch on a different aspect of the novel. Henry Nash Smith, later famous for his *Virgin Land: The American West as Symbol and Myth* (1950), concentrated on the tension in Faulkner's work between the regional and the universal. The poet and translator Dudley Fitts recognized both the novel's debt to Joyce, and the technical

---

1. Malcolm Cowley, *The Faulkner-Cowley File: Letters and Memories, 1944–1962* (New York: Viking P, 1966), 4.

skill with which Faulkner had made stream-of-consciousness his own. The young Welsh novelist Richard Hughes, whose own masterful *A High Wind in Jamaica* (1929) had just appeared, offered a preface to the English edition that in essence told the reader to stick with it; the book's difficulty had a purpose. And finally, Edward Crickmay's account echoed Lenore Marshall's. Even a second reading wasn't enough to say just what the book was about, but though many critics might "be indifferent or contemptuous or openly hostile," *The Sound and the Fury* would outlive its day.

EVELYN SCOTT

On William Faulkner's
The Sound and the Fury[†]

In this age of superlatives, one craves, despite one's disbelief in the supposed justification for censorships, a prohibition of some sort against the insincere employment of adjectives that, in an era of selection, carry rare meaning. One longs for measure in judgment. One desires above all a body of real criticism which will save the worthy artist from a careless allotment, before the public, with those whose object in writing is a purely commercial one. The sane critic, the critic who is careful of his words through his very generosity in recognizing valid talent, exists. But one doubts if the public in general has time to discriminate between the praise bestowed by such a critic, and the panegyrics of mere publicity. I want to write something about *The Sound and the Fury* before the fanfare in print can greet even the ears of the author. There will be many, I am sure, who, without this assistance, will make the discovery of the book as an important contribution to the permanent literature of fiction. I shall be pleased, however, if some others, lacking the opportunity for investigating individually the hundred claims to greatness which America makes every year in the name of art, may be led, through these comments, to a perusal of this unique and distinguished novel. The publishers, who are so much to be congratulated for presenting a little known writer with the dignity of recognition which his talent deserves, call this book 'overwhelmingly powerful and even monstrous.' Powerful it is; and it may even be described as 'monstrous' in all its implications of tragedy; but such tragedy has a noble essence.

[†] From a pamphlet accompanying the first American edition of *The Sound and the Fury* (New York: Jonathan Cape and Harrison Smith, 1929). Evelyn Scott, critically successful Tennessee-born author (1893–1963) of *The Narrow House* (1921) and *The Wave* (1929). [*Editor's note.*]

The question has been put by a contemporary critic, a genuine philosopher reviewing the arts, as to whether there exists for this age of disillusion with religion, dedication to the objective program of scientific inventiveness and general rejection of the teleology which placed man emotionally at the center of his universe, the spirit of which great tragedy is the expression. *The Sound and the Fury* seems to me to offer a reply. Indeed I feel that however sophisticated the argument of theology, man remains, in his heart, in that important position. What he seeks now is a fresh justification for the presumption of his emotions; and his present tragedy is in a realization of the futility, up to date, of his search for another, intellectually appropriate embodiment of the god that lives on, however contradicted by 'reason.'

William Faulkner, the author of this tragedy, which has all the spacious proportions of Greek art, may not consider his book in the least expressive of the general dilemma to which I refer, but that quality in his writings which the emotionally timid will call 'morbid,' seems to me reflected from the impression, made on a sensitive and normally egoistic nature, of what is in the air. Too proud to solve the human problem evasively through any of the sleight-of-hand of puerile surface optimism, he embraces, to represent life, figures that do indeed symbolize a kind of despair; but not the despair that depresses or frustrates. His pessimism as to fact, and his acceptance of all the morally inimical possibilities of human nature, is unwavering. The result is, nonetheless, the reassertion of humanity in defeat that is, in the subjective sense, a triumph. This is no Pyrrhic victory made in debate with those powers of intelligence that may be used to destroy. It is the conquest of nature by art. Or rather, the refutation, by means of a work of art, of the belittling of the materialists; and the work itself is in that category of facts which popular scientific thinking has made an ultimate. Here is beauty sprung from the perfect *realization* of what a more limiting morality would describe as ugliness. Here is a humanity stripped of most of what was claimed for it by the Victorians, and the spectacle is moving as no sugar-coated drama ever could be. The result for the reader, if he is like myself, is an exaltation of faith in mankind. It is faith without, as yet, an argument; but it is the same faith which has always lived in the most ultimate expression of the human spirit.

The Sound and the Fury is the story of the fall of a house, the collapse of a provincial aristocracy in a final debacle of insanity, recklessness, psychological perversion. The method of presentation is, as far as I know, unique. Book I is a statement of the tragedy as seen through the eyes of a thirty-three-year-old idiot son of the house, Benjy. Benjy is beautiful, as beautiful as one of the helpless angels, and the more so for the slightly repellent earthiness that is his. He is a better idiot than Dostoyevsky's because his simplicity is more convincingly united with the basic animal simplicity of creatures untried by the standards of a conscious and calculating humanity. It is as if, indeed, Blake's Tiger had been framed before us by the same Hand that made the Lamb, and, in opposition to Blake's conception, endowed with the same soul. Innocence is terrible as well as pathetic—and Benjy is terrible, sometimes terrifying. He is a Christ symbol, yet not, even in the way of the old orthodoxies, Christly. A Jesus asks for a conviction of sin and a confession before redemption. He acknowledges this as in his own history, tempting by the Devil the prelude to his renunciation. In every subtle sense, sin is the desire to sin, the awareness of sin, an assertion in innuendo that, by the very statement of virtue, sin *is*. Benjy is no saint with a wounded ego his own gesture can console. He is not anything—nothing with a name. He is alive. He can suffer. The simplicity of his suffering, the absence, for him, of any compensating sense of drama, leave him as naked of self-flattery as was the first man. Benjy is like Adam, with all he remembers in the garden and one foot in hell on earth. This was where knowledge began, and for Benjy time is too early for any spurious profiting by knowledge. It is a little as if the story of Hans Andersen's Little Mermaid had been taken away from the nursery and sentiment and made rather diabolically to grow up. Here is the Little Mermaid on the way to find her soul in an uncouth and incontinent body—but there is no happy ending. Benjy, born male and made neuter, doesn't want a soul. It is being thrust upon him, but only like a horrid bauble which he does not recognize. He holds in his hands—in his heart, exposed to the reader—something frightening, unnamed—*pain!* Benjy lives deeply in the senses. For the remainder of what he sees as life, he lives as crudely as in allegory, vicariously, through uncritical perception of his adored sister (she smells to him like 'leaves') and, in such emotional absolutism, traces for us her broken marriage, her departure forever from an unlovely home, her return by proxy in the person of her illegitimate daughter, Quentin, who, for Benjy, takes the mother's place.

Book II of the novel deals with another—the original Quentin, for whom the baby girl of later events is named. This section, inferior, I think, to the Benjy motive, though fine in part, describes in the terms of free association with which Mr Joyce is recreating vocabularies, the final day in this life of Quentin, First, who is contemplating suicide. Quentin is a student at Harvard at the time, the last wealth of the family—some property that has been nominally Benjy's having been sold to provide him with an education. Quentin is oversensitive, introvert, pathologically devoted to his sister, and his determination to commit suicide is his protest against her disgrace.

In Book III we see the world in terms of the petty, sadistic lunacy of Jason; Jason, the last son of the family, the stay-at-home, the failure, clerking in a country store, for whom no Harvard education was provided. William Faulkner has that general perspective in viewing particular events which lifts the specific incident to the dignity of catholic significance, while all the vividness of an unduplicable personal drama is retained. He senses the characteristic compulsions to action that make a fate. Jason is a devil. Yet, since the author has compelled you to the vision of the gods, he is a devil whom you compassionate. Younger than the other brothers, Jason, in his twenties, is tyrannically compensating for the sufferings of jealousy by persecution of his young niece, Caddie's daughter, Quentin, by petty thievery, by deception practiced against his weak mother, by meanest torment of that marvelously accurately conceived young negro, Luster, keeper, against all his idle, pleasure-loving inclinations of the witless Benjy. Jason is going mad. He knows it—not as an intellectual conclusion, for he holds up all the emotional barriers against reflection and self-investigation. Jason knows madness as Benjy knows the world and the smell of leaves and the leap of the fire in the grate and the sounds of himself, his own howls, when Luster teases him. Madness for Jason is a blank, immediate state of soul, which he feels encroaching on his meager, objectively considered universe. He is in an agony of inexplicable anticipation of disaster for which his cruelties afford him no relief.

The last Book is told in the third person by the author. In its pages we are to see this small world of failure in its relative aspect. Especial privilege, we are allowed to meet face to face, Dilsey, the old colored woman, who provides the beauty of coherence against the background of struggling choice. Dilsey isn't searching for a soul. She *is* the soul. She is the conscious human accepting the limitations of herself, the iron boundaries of circumstance, and still, to the best of her ability, achieving a holy compromise for aspiration.

People seem very frequently to ask of a book a 'moral.' There is no moral statement in *The Sound and the Fury*, but moral conclusions can be drawn from it as surely as from 'life,' because, as fine art, it is life organized to make revelation fuller. Jason is, in fair measure, the young South, scornful of outworn tradition, scornful indeed of all tradition, as of the ideal which has betrayed previous generations to the hope of perfection. He, Jason, would tell you, as so many others do today, that he sees things 'as they are.' There is no 'foolishness' about him, no 'bunk.' A spade is a spade, as unsuggestive as things must be in an age which prizes radios and motor cars not as means, but as ends for existence. You have 'got to show him.' Where there is proof in dollars and cents, or what they can buy, there is nothing. Misconceiving even biology, Jason would probably regard individualism of a crass order as according to nature. Jason is a martyr. He is a completely rational being. There is something exquisitely stupid in this degree of commonsense which cannot grasp the fact that ratiocination cannot proceed without presumptions made on the emotional acceptance of a state antedating reason. Jason argues, as it were, from nothing to nothing. In this *reductio ad absurdum* he annihilates himself, even his vanity. And he runs amok, with his conclusion that one gesture is as good as another, that there is only drivelling self-deception to juxtapose to his tin-pot Nietzscheanism— actually the most romantic attitude of all.

But there is Dilsey, without so much as a theory to controvert theory, stoic as some immemorial carving of heroism, going on, doing the best she can, guided only by instinct and affection and the self-respect she will not relinquish—the ideal of herself to which she conforms irrationally, which makes her life something whole, while her 'white folks' accept their fragmentary state, disintegrate. And she recovers for us the spirit of tragedy which the patter of cynicism has often made seem lost.

HENRY NASH SMITH

[Three Southern Novels]†

William Faulkner's novel calls for a re-examination of our premises. It raises at least two perplexing questions: first, does an unmistakably provincial locale make a book a provincial piece of writing? and secondly, what evidences of provincialism might one expect in the style of a novel written by a man who has, in the trite phrase, sunk his roots into the soil?

The first question suggests some consideration of a new Southwestern book, *Dobe Walls*.[1] Stanley Vestal's novel, for all its wealth of frontier incident and description, is perfectly conventional in its plot, its technique, and its heroine; only in some of the men (Bob Thatcher for instance) does the influence of the Frontier on character become evident. *Dobe Walls* escapes from the here and now of life; it is a historical tale with unusually authentic information about the period and the region it treats. In this respect it is vastly different

---

† From "Review of *The Sound and the Fury*," *Southwest Review* 15.1 (Autumn 1929): iii–iv. Reprinted by permission of *Southwest Review*.
1. Stanley Vestal (1887–1957), popular historian and novelist of the American West. *'Dobe Walls: a Story of Kit Carson's Southwest* (1929). [*Editor*]

from *The Sound and the Fury*, which is concerned with a regional tradition only as it appears in the present, and from Mr Faulkner's earlier novels, which often lean toward satire. Yet both novels have a regional setting, and both authors are residents of the provinces. Are both books to be related to the 'new provincialism'?

The question of a provincial style is even more involved. One may always be suspicious when talk grows as theoretical as discussions of the 'rhythm of a landscape' or 'the spacious gesture of the frontier' tend to become. It seems entirely possible that some of us have been misled by an analogy, and have wandered a little into realms of speculation. Upholders of the idea of universal standards not dependent upon a genius of the age or a genius of the place have always been uneasy in the presence of such theories; and perhaps they are nearer right than we. Or maybe we are both right, but have not yet found the reconciling 'nevertheless'.

Let me, therefore, deliver myself from both points of view on the subject of *The Sound and the Fury*. No matter how universal the standard, there are certain pages in this novel which are very near great literature. I refer, for instance, to the character of Jason Compson, Senior, in which the typical cynicism of a decadent aristocracy is merged with—perhaps grows out of—an intensely individual delineation. They praise Chaucer for taking a stock character like Criseyde and, without losing typical traits, making her a person; for writing that half-allegory, half-comedy, the *Nonne Preestes Tale*, in which a remarkable verisimilitude alternates with the complete fantasy of the beast fable as colors play back and forth with the shifting light on changeable silk. In both of these respects *The Sound and the Fury* will easily bear comparison with the verses of the fat customs officer himself.

From another 'universal' standpoint—the traditional definition of tragedy—Faulkner's achievement is also remarkable. Pity and fear are not often more poignantly aroused than they are in the scene where Candace Compson stands cursing her brother for the devil he is. The subject, too, is of an imposing magnitude; for as the story spreads its fragments before the reader there emerges the spectacle of a civilization uprooted and left to die. Scope such as this is not usual in American novels.

Faulkner's handling of the tradition of the Old South, nevertheless, is distinctly related to provincialism. He has realized minutely and understandingly a given milieu and a given tradition—to all intents and purposes, the milieu of Oxford, Mississippi, where the author has lived most of his life, and the tradition of the ante-bellum aristocracy. He has avoided the mere sophistication which sometimes is evident in his earlier novels, and is certainly at the farthest remove from a metropolitan smartness. That he has borrowed the stream-of-consciousness technique from Europe seems to me of minor importance: to say the least, he has modified it to his own use and has refused to be tyrannized by conventions, even the conventions of revolt.

In short, by the only definition that means very much, Mr Faulkner is a provincial writer. He belongs to the South, if not to the Southwest. Though he is not a folklorist, though he is more concerned with life than with regionalism, his book has shown unguessed possibilities in the treatment of provincial life without loss of universality.

DUDLEY FITTS

Two Aspects of Telemachus†

[Both *The Sound and the Fury* and *Look Homeward, Angel*] deal with the South, the theme of both is the decadence of a family, and both are unusually rhetorical. *The Sound and the Fury* treats imbecility, incest, alcoholism, and insanity; it is almost unreadable. The vices celebrated in *Look Homeward, Angel*[1] are less extravagant, though no less pernicious; the book is perhaps too readable. In each case, the striking characteristic is the style. The books are really not novels, but declamations. The effects are emotional, not cerebral. Mr Faulkner and Mr Wolfe are poets, and they write in the manner of poets.

The Sound and the Fury is the story of a degenerate Mississippi family, dropped piecemeal from the minds of the agonists. The book begins in the chaotic brain of Benjy, a man of thirty, a mute whose mind has never developed. For ninety delirious pages the story unfolds in the disordered consciousness of an idiot. Benjy lacks time-sense, and is incapable of relating impressions; Benjy lacks judgment, and cannot distinguish between significant and insignificant, actual, remembered, and imaginary; and, of course, Benjy's mind-words are the mind-words of a child. It is through this medium that Mr Faulkner has chosen to introduce his characters, sketch the necessary background, and supply us with tags and motives for the ensuing narrative. He has been courageous, but I question the practicability of his device. The deliberate obscurity of the opening pages repels rather than invites; and when the reader perseveres, he struggles out at the other end of Benjy's maunderings with

---

† From *Hound and Horn* 3 (April–June 1930): 445–50.
1. Thomas Wolfe (1900–1938), North Carolina–born novelist of *Look Homeward, Angel* (1929) and *Of Time and the River* (1935). [*Editor's note.*]

no clearer an idea of what has happened, or may be expected to happen, than he had when he entered.[2] Once this section is traversed, however, the going is easier. There is still considerable incoherence: Mr Faulkner is fond of the psychological throwback and the technic perfected in the Gæa episode of *Ulysses*; but in spite of these interruptions the story marches on vigorously and intelligibly. By the time he has reached the last pages, the reader is somewhat astonished to discover that he is being held by the force of narrative alone; and even more astonished when he realizes that the narrative is straight from the old school of melodrama—nothing more nor less than the pursuit-on-wheels of eloping lovers. And this after so much agony in stony places! Almost what the movie-blurbs would call 'a gripping story.' Especially in the last pages, once the stylistic surface has been penetrated, the scenario atmosphere is unmistakable; and looking back, the reader recovers and reaffirms a suspicion which was always felt: that the men and women of *The Sound and the Fury* are not real men and women at all, but dramatic clichés for all their individuality of vice and action. Only the idiot Benjy is realized; Caddy and Quentin and Dilsey and Miss Caroline and Jason are melodrama types.

The style, then. It is the study of Mr Faulkner's style, the consideration of the book as a rhetorical exercise, as a declamation, that repays the reader. Joyce is the ultimate source, obviously; but the Joycean technic has been pretty thoroughly absorbed, integrated with the author's sensibility. Much of the time the writing is on two or more concurrent planes; and Mr Faulkner's skill in avoiding the clash, while preserving the identity, of each tone is noteworthy. A typical passage (not, by the way, from the idiot's stream-of-consciousness) illustrates his method admirably:

> 'and Gerald's grandfather always picked his own mint before breakfast while the dew was still on it. He wouldnt even let old Wilkie touch it do you remember Gerald but always gathered it himself and made his own julep. He was as crochety about his julep as an old maid, measuring everything by a recipe in his head. There was only one man he ever gave that recipe to; that was' *we did how can you not know it if you'll just wait I'll tell you how it was it was a crime we did a terrible crime it cannot be hid you think it can but wait Poor Quentin youve never done*

2. I can speak only for myself, of course. Nevertheless, armed though I was with eagerness and the best of will, I tried four times to finish the first section, and each time either fell asleep or started gnawing at the wallpaper after ten pages. It was at dawn on S. Swithin's that I finally arrived at what I think is the solution: let the reader start the book at page 93, putting off the introduction until the end. In this way he will not only reassemble the chronology of the narrative, but, thoroughly acquainted with most of the characters, he will better appreciate the significance of Benjy's meditations. In the event of a reprinting I recommend this arrangement.

that have you and I'll tell you how it was I'll tell Father then itll have to be because you love Father then we'll have to go away amid the pointing and the horror the clean flame I'll make you say we did I'm stronger than you I'll make you know we did you thought it was them but it was me listen I fooled you all the time it was me you thought I was in the house where that damn honey- suckle trying not to think the swing the cedars the secret surges the breathing locked drinking the wild breath the yes Yes Yes yes 'never be got to drink wine himself, but he always said that a hamper what book did you read that in where Geralds rowing suit of wine was a necessary part of any gentleman's picnic basket' *did you love them Caddy did you love them When they touched me I died.*

While this is by no means an original technic, it is nevertheless beautifully employed. The diction is generally natural (although I suspect a certain stagey cleverness in the interjection of 'what book . . . rowing suit' into the progressing statement 'he always said that a hamper of wine was necessary': it is improbable that two voices would combine so happily as to result in the amusing 'Ger- alds rowing suit of wine'); the expression of the subjective stream is balanced, rhythmic, intense, and at the same time lacking in affectation. The prose owes a great deal to Joyce—possibly too much;[3] but the individual impetus of Mr Faulkner's sensibility is unmistakable.

*   *   *

The shadow of Joyce is heavy upon Mr Faulkner and Mr Wolfe, as, indeed, it is heavy upon us all. Directly or indirectly, we owe to *Ulysses* most of what is fine, as well as much that is false, in our new technic. Most of all we are indebted for the revival of interest in technic *per se*. The day of the Sententious Illiterates—the Ander- sons, the Dreisers, the Lewises, and the Lawrences: ('It don't make no difference how you say a thing, so long as you got a thing to say')—is already part of last year's calendar. We know that in order to say anything, we must first of all learn to write. The instrument is too precious to abuse. And, whether we care to admit it or not, Joyce has been teaching us all over again its uses, old and new. Ulysses is still looking for a Telemachus.

3. *Cf. Ulysses*, p. 732 (1st edition, 1922): '. . . and then I asked him with my eyes to ask again yes and then he asked me would I yes to say yes my mountain flower and first I put my arms around him yes and drew him down to me so he could feel my breasts all perfume yes and his heart was going like mad and yes I said yes I will Yes.'

RICHARD HUGHES

Introduction to *The Sound and the Fury*[†]

There is a story told of a celebrated Russian dancer, who was asked by someone what she meant by a certain dance. She answered with some exasperation, 'If I could say it in so many words, do you think I should take the very great trouble of dancing it?'

It is an important story, because it is the valid explanation of obscurity in art. A method involving apparent obscurity is surely justified when it is the clearest, the simplest, the only method possible of saying in full what the writer has to say.

This is the case with *The Sound and the Fury*. I shall not attempt to give either a summary or an explanation of it: for if I could say in three pages what takes Mr. Faulkner three hundred there would obviously be no need for the book. All I propose to do is to offer a few introductory, and desultory, comments, my chief purpose being to encourage the reader. For the general reader is quite rightly a little shy of apparently difficult writing. Too often it is used, not because of its intrinsic necessity, but to drape the poverty of the writer: too often the reader, after drilling an arduous passage through the strata of the mountain, finds only the mouse, and has little profit but his exercise.

As a result of several such fiascos I myself share this initial prejudice. Yet I have read *The Sound and the Fury* three times now, and that not in the least for exercise, but for pure pleasure.

Mr. Faulkner's method in this book is successful, but it is none the less curious. The first seventy pages are told by a congenital imbecile, a man of thirty-three whose development has not advanced beyond babyhood. Benjy has no sense of time: his only thought-process is associative: the event of the day, then, and what it reminds him of in the past are all one to him: the whole of his thirty-three years are present to him in one uninterrupted and streamless flood. This enables the author to begin by giving a general and confused picture of his whole subject. He offers a certain amount of help to the understanding, it is true, in that he changes from roman to italic type whenever there is a change in time: but even then I defy an ordinary reader to disentangle the people and events concerned at a first reading. But the beauty of it is this: there is no need to disentangle anything. If one ceases to make the effort, one soon finds that this strange rigmarole holds one's attention on

---

[†] From *The Sound and the Fury* (London: Chatto & Windus, 1931), vii–ix. Reprinted by permission of David Higham Associates. Hughes (1900–1976) was an English novelist best known for *A High Wind in Jamaica* (1929). [Editor's note.]

its own merits. Vague forms of people and events, apparently unrelated, loom out of the fog and disappear again. One is seeing the
world through the eyes of an idiot: but so clever is Mr. Faulkner
that, for the time being at least, one is content to do so.

With the second part the fog begins to clear. The narrator now is
one of these vague figures, a brother Quentin, who committed suicide at Harvard in 1910: and he describes with a beautiful sense of
ironical tragedy and ironical farce his last day alive. With the third
and fourth parts, which return to the present day, the fog rolls
away altogether, the formless, sizeless, positionless shapes looming
through it condense to living people: the story quickens. It is here
this curious method is finally justified: for one finds, in a flash, that
one knows all about them, that one has understood more of Benjy's
sound and fury than one had realized: the whole story becomes
actual to one at a single moment. It is impossible to describe the
effect produced, because it is unparalleled; the thoughtful reader
must find it for himself.

It will be seen to be a natural corollary that one can read this
book a second time at least. The essential quality of a book that can
be read again and again, it seems to me, is that it shall appear different at every reading—that it shall, in short, be a new book. (Poetry
has this quality, particularly.) When one comes to read Benjy's tale
a second time, knowing the story, knowing the family; knowing
that the name Quentin covers two people, uncle and niece; knowing Benjy's passionate animal devotion to his sister Caddy, which
makes him haunt the golf-course in the hope of hearing the word
which is her name, and haunt the gate from which he can see the
children coming home from school, in the hope she will be among
them again—it is then one begins to realize with what consummate
contrapuntal skill these drivellings have been composed, with what
exquisite care their pattern fits together.

EDWARD CRICKMAY

Review of *The Sound and the Fury*[†]

Those who read Mr William Faulkner's *Soldiers' Pay* will in some
measure be prepared for the poignant and bewildering experiences
offered by *The Sound and the Fury*. It is not a book for every novel
reader; indeed, I think Mr Faulkner should consider himself lucky
if he finds a hundred discerning readers in this country. But he
may console himself with the thought that *Ulysses* had considerably

† From "Review of *The Sound and the Fury*," *Sunday Referee* (London), April 26, 1931: 9.

fewer genuine appreciators on its first appearance. I am not going to insist too strongly on a parallel between *The Sound and the Fury* and *Ulysses;* but the influence of Mr James Joyce is so strongly marked on the first hundred pages of Mr Faulkner's new novel that one cannot let it pass without special notice. In my opinion *The Sound and the Fury* is an even tougher proposition for the general novel reader than *Ulysses.* To begin with, its outline is less strongly drawn and the emotions in which it deals are not so universal. Nevertheless, Mr Faulkner's book, however strange and obscure it may appear, is one of the most important experiments in creative form and approach I have read for ten years; I hesitate in saying one of the most important achievements only because—although I have read the book twice—I have not yet completely grasped its inner significance. Laying the book aside for a second time, I feel that I have passed through one of the strangest experiences of my life—an experience which can only be paralleled in actual life by walking through a darkness which is lit fitfully by an electric storm and from which isolated figures emerge for a moment and disappear. That is precisely the effect the first part of the book left upon me. The early introduction to the narrative is made by Benjy, a congenital imbecile of thirty-three who has no time sense and who reacts naïvely to the surging of memory from a timeless flood of experiences. It is, I think, quite impossible, to disentangle any clear lines of movement or any consistent action from Benjy's wanderings; but characters now and then stand out with an almost supra-natural power, as, for instance, the sister, Candy, a superb sketch in idiot chiaroscuro. From Benjy we are taken back eighteen years and plunged into the last day of a young Harvard man's life. He commits suicide under the spell of reaction to sexual crime; and then the story is in some measure rounded off and completed by a third part. But long before the end is reached the reader has made the fullest contact with the characters. Benjy's confused and distorted images of fog have gained in outline and substance, but they have gained immeasurably in creative significance by being first passed through the corridors of an imbecile mind. It will be interesting to know how the English public receives this strange and disturbing novel. I imagine that the popular public—and its fuglemen, the popular critics—will be indifferent or contemptuous or openly hostile; yet it is my conviction that *The Sound and the Fury* will exert a powerful influence on those handful of readers who can see deeper than the mirror of fashionable and commercial art forms permits. For myself, I hold that *The Sound and the Fury* will outlive most of the works that at present loom so large, for its influence will be educative and thus create a wider circle of appreciators for its own authentic creative viewpoint.

The Writer and His Work

The documents collected here speak to two things. First, they detail Faulkner's work on *The Sound and the Fury* in 1928 and 1929. His letters are on the whole unrevealing, he did not keep a diary or notebook, and we know little about his day-to-day progress on the manuscript. Still, we do have a few of his thoughts on the new book, along with an account of its publication as written by his friend and agent, Ben Wasson. A fellow Mississippian who had recently moved to New York, Wasson worked over the novel's proofs and tried to regularize some of its strangeness, which Faulkner then had to restore. Second, these selections define Faulkner's continued involvement with the novel and its characters, for the Compsons kept on living and developing in his mind for many years to come, as though they couldn't be confined to the ordered place in which the book had left them.

As I noted in introducing this volume, *The Sound and the Fury* began as a short story called "Twilight"—so Faulkner said, at any rate, and so he wrote on the first page of his manuscript. However, no such story exists among his papers, and the manuscript itself has from the beginning the scale and proportion of the novel we know. At around the same time, Faulkner had two other pieces about the Compson children in hand. One of them, "A Justice," uses Quentin's first-person narration to frame a tale about Indian life in Yoknapatawpha County, one told by an old man of mixed race named Sam Fathers. Faulkner would return to Sam Fathers some years later, in "Lion" and "The Old People," stories in which he again takes Quentin as his narrator. By the time he revised these pieces for *Go Down, Moses*, however, he had put them into the third person and conceived of a new protagonist, the young woodsman Isaac McCaslin. The other early Compson story presents a different case. Quentin is once more the narrator, and the relations and temperaments of the three older Compson children (Benjy doesn't appear) are very much the same as they are in the novel; Caddy is similarly commanding and fearless, Jason querulous and mean. As such, the story appears to supplement the picture of them in *The Sound and the Fury*, yet this Quentin has survived to adulthood. The character is the same but his fate is different, and we must wonder whether this alternate version was conceived before or after Faulkner had killed him off. Unfortunately, no definitive paper trail exists, though the novelist must have liked the tale's sense of ghostly possibility. It wasn't published until 1931, and if consistency had mattered to him he could have changed it.

In Faulkner's mind, at least, the character would go on living. Readers have long argued whether the Quentin of *Absalom, Absalom!* is the same as that of *The Sound and the Fury*, and about the degree to which those novels need to be read together. Certainly there are discrepancies between them; the boy in the later book seems to have no siblings. Yet as he talks through the night in an icy Harvard dormitory, trying to define the meaning of the South for his Canadian roommate, he does return to many of the issues that troubled his earlier self: to brothers and sisters and the threat of a sexual attraction that one can neither admit nor suppress. My own judgment is that *The Sound and the Fury* can be read, as it was written, without any knowledge at all of its successor. But *Absalom, Absalom!* stands in dialogue with that earlier book. The side-shadows afforded by its predecessor help justify its sublime but febrile rhetoric, and our knowledge of Quentin's suicide adds an extra note of desperation to his concluding claim that he doesn't hate his native place.

The novelist knew that his work was difficult, and spoke at times of wishing that the technology of his day would allow Benjy's chapter to be printed in different colored inks, with each color representing a different time in the character's mind. He tried to interest Random House in the idea, and in 1933 he even drafted two introductions for it.[1] But the project fell through, and his manuscript pages then sat in the company's files until 1946, when they were pulled out for possible use in the new Modern Library edition of the novel. When Faulkner reread them, however, he wrote to his publisher that he had "forgotten what smug false sentimental windy shit it was," and added that he would pay double his promised fee *not* to use them.[2] They weren't published until the 1970s, but have since become crucial in many critical accounts of the novel. Even more crucial, however, is the Appendix he wrote for Malcolm Cowley's *Portable Faulkner*. I've included the relevant correspondence with Cowley, and then the Appendix itself, whose high-flown language follows the Compsons out through World War II. Faulkner told the editor that he should have "done this when I wrote the book. Then the whole thing would have fallen into pattern like a jigsaw puzzle."[3] For years the paperback edition of the novel *began* with the Appendix; some later ones put it at the end, and the current Vintage edition omits it entirely. No serious reader can entirely avoid it; and yet many find that its post-facto account of the characters' motivations distorts the novel of 1929. Those interested in the issue will find their best guide in Stacy Burton's essay in this volume's selection of criticism.

Faulkner's increasing fame brought with it the burden of speaking about his work, but while he often resisted such invitations he did agree to an interview with the *Paris Review*. He spoke at West Point and on several tours as a cultural ambassador for the State Department, and in

---

1. The project has since been realized, in a two-volume, 2012 edition of the novel prepared by Noel Polk and Stephen M. Ross for the Folio Society.
2. See Joseph Blotner, ed., *Selected Letters of William Faulkner* (New York: Random House, 1977), 235.
3. See p. 257 of this Norton Critical Edition.

1957–58 gave a series of seminars at the University of Virginia. In all these sessions he referred to his characters as if they were actual people, people in whom he was still interested and of whom he had always been fond. Sentimental? No. But his words are indeed full of sentiment, the sentiment of an aging man looking back on his work, his life, and beginning to realize just what he had accomplished.

WILLIAM FAULKNER

Selected Letters[†]

To Mrs. Walter B. McLean, Memphis

Wednesday [probably Oct. 1928]   New York City
                                                  c/o Ben Wasson[1]
                                                  146 MacDougal St.

Dear Aunt Bama—

* * * Harcourt Brace & Co bought me from Liveright. Much, much nicer there. Book will be out in Feb. Also another one, the damndest book I ever read.[2] I dont believe anyone will publish it for 10 years. Harcourt swear they will, but I dont believe it.

Having a rotten time, as usual. I hate this place.

Love to Uncle Walter, and to you as ever.

William Faulkner

To Alfred Harcourt, New York

18 Feb. 1929   Oxford, Miss.

Dear Mr Harcourt—

My copies of SARTORIS came promptly. I like the appearance of the book very much indeed. Will you let me take this opportunity to thank the office, as well as yourself? I had intended writing my thanks sooner, but I have got involved in another novel, and I have been behind in correspondence since.

About the Sound & Fury ms. That is all right. I did not believe that anyone would publish it; I had no definite plan to submit it to

---

† From *Selected Letters of William Faulkner*, ed. Joseph Blotner (New York: Random House, 1977). Copyright © 1977 by Jill Faulkner Summers. Used by permission of W. W. Norton & Company, Inc., and Random House, an imprint of The Random House Publishing Group, a division of Random House LLC. All rights reserved. The exact locations of the manuscripts and typescripts of Faulkner's letters are indicated in Blotner's edition.

1. A friend from the University of Mississippi, Wasson was acting as Faulkner's literary agent.

2. *The Sound and the Fury.*

anyone. I told Hal about it once and he dared me to bring it to him. And so it really was to him that I submitted it, more as a curiosity than aught else. I am sorry it did not go over with you all, but I will not say I did not expect that result. Thank you for delivering it to him.[3]

Spring has come here—a false one, of course; just enough to catch fruit trees and flowers with their pants down about next month. It's nice while it lasts, though.

Sincerely,
[s] William Faulkner
[t] Wm Faulkner.

On June 20, 1929, Faulkner married Estelle Oldham Franklin. While they were honeymooning in Pascagoula, Mississippi, he received the proofs of The Sound and the Fury, *which Wasson had partially edited.*

To Ben Wasson, New York

[early summer, 1929]   Pascagoula, Miss.

Dear Ben—

Thank you for the letter.

I received the proof. It seemed pretty tough to me, so I corrected it as written, adding a few more italics where the original seemed obscure on second reading. Your reason for the change, i.e., that with italics only 2 different dates were indicated I do not think sound for 2 reasons. First, I do not see that the use of breaks clarifies it any more; second, there are more than 4 dates involved. The ones I recall off-hand are: Damuddy dies. Benjy is 3. (2) His name is changed. He is 5. (3) Caddy's wedding. He is 14. (4) He tries to rape a young girl and is castrated. 15. (5) Quentin's death. (6) His father's death. (7) A visit to the cemetery at 18. (7) [*sic*]. The day of the anecdote, he is 33. These are just a few I recall. So your reason explodes itself.

But the main reason is, a break indicates an objective change in tempo, while the objective picture here should be a continuous whole, since the thought transference is subjective; i. e., in Ben's mind and not in the reader's eye. I think italics are necessary to establish for the reader Benjy's confusion; that unbroken-surfaced

---

3. Harrison Smith ["Hal"] was leaving Harcourt, Brace to become a partner in the firm of Cape and Smith, which would publish *The Sound and the Fury* on Oct. 7, 1929.

confusion of an idiot which is outwardly a dynamic and logical coherence. To gain this, by using breaks it will be necessary to write an induction for each transference. I wish publishing was advanced enough to use colored ink for such, as I argued with you and Hal in the speak-easy that day. But the form in which you now have it is pretty tough. It presents a most dull and poorly articulated picture to my eye. If something must be done, it were better to re-write this whole section objectively, like the 4th section. I think it is rotten, as is. But if you wont have it so, I'll just have to save the idea until publishing grows up to it. Anyway, change all the italics. You overlooked one of them. Also, the parts written in italics will all have to be punctuated again. You'd better see to that, since you're all for coherence. And dont make any more additions to the script, bud. I know you mean well, but so do I. I effaced the 2 or 3 you made.

We have a very pleasant place on the beach here. I swim and fish and row a little. Estelle sends love.

I hope you will think better of this. Your reason above disproves itself. I purposely used italics for both actual scenes and remembered scenes for the reason, not to indicate the different dates of happenings, but merely to permit the reader to anticipate a thought-transference, letting the recollection postulate its own date. Surely you see this.

Bill

The following fragment comes from one of the letters Faulkner subsequently sent to Wasson in the process of revision.

To Ben Wasson, New York

[early summer, 1929]   [Oxford]

Italics here indicate a speech by one person within a speech by another, so as not to use quotes within quotes, my use of italics has been too without definite plan, I suppose i.e., they do not always indicate a thought transference as in this case, but the only other manner of doing this paragraph seems clumsy still to me, since it breaks the questions interminably of Mrs Compson's drivelling talk if set like the below:

'. . . You must think, Mother said.
'Hold still now, Versh said. He put etc.
'Some day I'll be gone etc., Mother said.
'Now stop, Versh said.
'Come here and kiss . . . Mother said.

. . . .
Galley 6
Set first three lines of new scene in italics. Transference indi-
cated then. I should have done this, but missed it. Sorry.
. . . .

Excuse recent letter. Didnt mean to be stubborn and inconsider-
ate. Believe I am right, tho. And I was not blaming you with it. I
just went to you with it because I think you are more interested in
the book than anyone there, and I know that us both think alike
about it, as we already argued this very point last fall. Excuse it
anyway. Estelle sends regards.

Love to all.
Bill

BEN WASSON

[Publishing *The Sound and the Fury*]†

The morning after I completed my work,[1] and after a night of mild
celebration, Bill came to my room as usual, though this time somewhat earlier than had become his custom. He didn't greet me with
his softly spoken "good morning" but merely tossed a large obviously
filled envelope on the bed. "Read this one, Bud," he said. "It's a real
son of a bitch."

I removed the manuscript and read the title on the first page: *The
Sound and the Fury*.

"This one's the greatest I'll ever write. Just read it," he said, and
abruptly left.

The next morning he again arrived. I had stayed up late, enthralled
with his magnificent new manuscript. It left me emotionally stirred
for many hours. After telling him so, I said that the sheer technical
outrageousness and freshness of the Benjy section made it hard to
follow. He said he knew that it was demanding.

"If I could only get it printed the way it ought to be with different
color types for the different times in Benjy's section recording the
flow of events for him, it would make it simpler, probably. I don't
reckon, though, it'll ever be printed that way, and this'll have to be
the best, with the italics indicating the changes of events."

† From *Count No 'Count: Flashbacks to Faulkner* (Jackson: UP of Mississippi, 1983), 84–
97. Copyright © 1983 by the University Press of Mississippi. Reprinted by permission of
the publisher.
1. Wasson had been working on the manuscript of *Flags in the Dust*, which Harcourt
published January 31, 1929, as *Sartoris*. The full text as Faulkner wrote it was not published with his original title until 1973 by Random House.

He was planning to leave the next day for Oxford. He asked me to take the manuscript to Hal Smith, since he was afraid to leave it in his or my place. He asked that Hal give him a quick decision. And he also requested that I take some watercolor sketches he had painted for possible use on the jacket of *Sartoris*, the name either he, Hal, or I had suggested as the title to replace *Flags in the Dust*. The sketches showed different versions of a black plowing with a mule, the earth being turned over, and, overhead, a blue-washed sky. It was a rather colorful job, but Harcourt, much to Bill's regret, did not accept it. When I delivered the manuscript of *Sound*, Hal ordered that it be placed in a safe.

On what was supposedly Bill's last night in New York during that visit, a few of us celebrated again. We were always celebrating something or other: an arrival, a departure, a completed picture, a just-finished book or story, or the sale of a poem or manuscript.

On this night, I noticed Bill's body had become less slim and he was wearing his moustache thicker than usual. Throughout the years, he kept his hair about the same length, but from time to time he altered the style of his moustache and occasionally grew a beard.

I left the celebration earlier than the others, either because I wanted to do some polishing on my own manuscript or because I had imbibed too much white wine. In the morning, I was awakened by a faint tapping on the door. I opened it and Bill came in, his expression woebegone.

"I got my pocket picked or lost my pocketbook," he said, and turned his back to me. "Kick me." He turned to me again. "Anyhow, it's vanished. I wonder if you'd go with me to see Hal and try to get him to let me have money enough to get back to Mississippi?"

Hal was amused by the story. Lyle Saxon and Bill Spratling felt that Bill should have an extra amount of money for his train ride south, and they scrounged around and fattened his new wallet.

As I bade him good-bye at the station, he thanked me and said: "Let me know about *The Sound and the Fury*. I'm counting on that one."

Now to squeeze together as closely as I can—and without too much verbosity—events that took place before Bill and I were together again. These events had a great bearing on our relationship and the future of his career as a writer.

Just before Christmas, 1928, Hal Smith broke away from Harcourt, Brace, and, with the English publisher, Jonathan Cape, formed a new firm, Cape and Smith. The departure of Smith from Harcourt was not pleasant. It left ripples of discord and enmity in its wake. Harcourt was particularly incensed at the departure of Louise Bonino, who was to become a mainstay of the new firm.

*   *   *

One of Hal's first talks with me was about the manuscript of *The Sound and the Fury.* "If it's as marvelous as you say it is, I want it for our first list," he said. So I went to Harcourt, Brace, where it was released to me because they had decided it was too poor a publishing risk.

*   *   *

Hal placed the manuscript of *The Sound and the Fury* in the capable hands of Robert Ballou, technical manager, who, as soon as possible, sent it to a printer. The printer returned galley proofs, and Hal grew more excited about the novel. Lenore Marshall, who was in the editorial department, thought it an extraordinary piece of writing and fell in with the small group of admirers.

Then I had a new idea. Evelyn Scott, a distinguished though unconventional lady from Tennessee, whose novels are now sadly neglected and mostly forgotten, was a blue ribbon author on the first list of Cape and Smith. Her big novel about the Civil War, *The Wave,* led the list, and Hal persuaded the prestigious Literary Guild to announce it as one of its choices. The guild's imprimatur added great distinction to any book, fiction or nonfiction. I suggested to Hal that he have Miss Scott read the galley proof and give us her opinion. My hunch was that she would like it. Hal readily agreed, so after telephoning, I took it to her.

*   *   *

"I'll read it right away and write you what I think of it," she told me as our interview ended.

In a few days, a messenger brought me a package containing the *Sound* galleys. When I extracted them and read her enclosed letter, I rushed downstairs to Hal's office with it. Her enthusiastic and understanding remarks also excited Hal. He rubbed his nose and squinted his eyes at me: "Go see her again and thank her for this fine letter. See if she won't write more in detail about the second part of the manuscript. She seems to skimp over it."

"That'll be a lot of trouble for Miss Scott," I said.

"If her additional comments are as penetrating, tell her we'll make all of it into a handsome pamphlet, of course featuring her as its author, and we'll distribute it with the compliments of Cape and Smith to critics and book dealers and send it out with our salesmen. Go telephone her now. We'll talk money later."

That's what I did and what Evelyn Scott did and what Hal Smith did, and it all added up to a fine publicity brochure, tastefully designed by Arthur Hawkins and disseminated as Hal suggested.

* * *

I read the galley proofs of *Sound* before forwarding them to Bill. I was reading mostly for typographical errors and misspellings. In reading the Benjy section I arrogantly and heedlessly and, yes, igno-rantly, decided I could improve the method of telling and do some-thing about the italics. I don't recall what I did, but when Bill received the proofs he wrote me an angry letter, asking that the section be set in type as he had indicated and written it, with no more tampering on my part. Obviously and plainly he was indignant with me. Later he wrote a less harsh letter about the matter, but this was the first time I had been on the receiving end of his lightning bolts of wrath.

I wasn't stupid enough to try to defend what I had done, and when Bill wrote me that he knew I meant well, he couldn't have put it more scathingly. It was, though, the only unpleasantness between us, and neither of us, in the years that followed, ever referred to it.

* * *

WILLIAM FAULKNER

That Evening Sun†

I

Monday is no different from any other weekday in Jefferson now. The streets are paved now, and the telephone and electric compa-nies are cutting down more and more of the shade trees—the water oaks, the maples and locusts and elms—to make room for iron poles bearing clusters of bloated and ghostly and bloodless grapes, and we have a city laundry which makes the rounds on Monday morning, gathering the bundles of clothes into bright-colored, specially-made

† First published as "That Evening Sun Go Down" in the *American Mercury* (March 1931). Revised as "That Evening Sun" for *These Thirteen* (1931), and reprinted in *Col-lected Stories* (New York: Random House, 1950), from which the text in this Norton Critical Edition is drawn. Copyright © 1931 and renewed 1959 by William Faulkner. Used by permission of W. W. Norton & Company, Inc., Curtis Brown Group Ltd., Lon-don, on behalf of The Estate of William Faulkner, and Random House, an imprint of The Random House Publishing Group, and division of Random House LLC. All rights reserved. The title comes from W. C. Handy's "St. Louis Blues" (1914), whose most famous version is the 1925 recording by Bessie Smith, with the young Louis Armstrong on cornet. Handy's lyrics begin:

> I hate to see that evenin' sun go down
> I hate to see that evenin' sun go down
> 'Cause my baby, he done lef this town.
> Feelin' tomorrow lak ah feel today.
> Feel tomorrow lak ah feel today.
> I'll pack my trunk, make my getaway.

motor cars: the soiled wearing of a whole week now flees apparition-like behind alert and irritable electric horns, with a long diminishing noise of rubber and asphalt like tearing silk, and even the Negro women who still take in white people's washing after the old cus-tom, fetch and deliver it in automobiles.

But fifteen years ago, on Monday morning the quiet, dusty, shady streets would be full of Negro women with, balanced on their steady, turbaned heads, bundles of clothes tied up in sheets, almost as large as cotton bales, carried so without touch of hand between the kitchen door of the white house and the blackened washpot beside a cabin door in Negro Hollow.

Nancy[1] would set her bundle on the top of her head, then upon the bundle in turn she would set the black straw sailor hat which she wore winter and summer. She was tall, with a high, sad face sunken a little where her teeth were missing. Sometimes we would go a part of the way down the lane and across the pasture with her, to watch the balanced bundle and the hat that never bobbed nor wavered, even when she walked down into the ditch and up the other side and stooped through the fence. She would go down on her hands and knees and crawl through the gap, her head rigid, uptilted, the bun-dle steady as a rock or a balloon, and rise to her feet again and go on.

Sometimes the husbands of the washing women would fetch and deliver the clothes, but Jesus never did that for Nancy, even before father told him to stay away from our house, even when Dilsey was sick and Nancy would come to cook for us.

And then about half the time we'd have to go down the lane to Nancy's cabin and tell her to come on and cook breakfast. We would stop at the ditch, because father told us to not have anything to do with Jesus—he was a short black man, with a razor scar down his face—and we would throw rocks at Nancy's house until she came to the door, leaning her head around it without any clothes on.

"What yawl mean, chunking my house?" Nancy said. "What you little devils mean?"

"Father says for you to come on and get breakfast," Caddy said. "Father says it's over a half an hour now, and you've got to come this minute."

"I aint studying no breakfast," Nancy said. "I going to get my sleep out."

"I bet you're drunk," Jason said. "Father says you're drunk. Are you drunk, Nancy?"

---

1. *The Sound and the Fury* contains several references to the bones of a figure named Nancy. The bones there belong to a horse, but readers of this story will catch the echo, and shiver.

"Who says I is?" Nancy said. "I got to get my sleep out. I aint studying no breakfast."

So after a while we quit chunking the cabin and went back home. When she finally came, it was too late for me to go to school. So we thought it was whisky until that day they arrested her again and they were taking her to jail and they passed Mr Stovall. He was the cashier in the bank and a deacon in the Baptist church, and Nancy began to say:

"When you going to pay me, white man? When you going to pay me, white man? It's been three times now since you paid me a cent—" Mr Stovall knocked her down, but she kept on saying, "When you going to pay me, white man? It's been three times now since—" until Mr Stovall kicked her in the mouth with his heel and the marshal caught Mr Stovall back, and Nancy lying in the street, laughing. She turned her head and spat out some blood and teeth and said, "It's been three times now since he paid me a cent."

That was how she lost her teeth, and all that day they told about Nancy and Mr Stovall, and all that night the ones that passed the jail could hear Nancy singing and yelling. They could see her hands holding to the window bars, and a lot of them stopped along the fence, listening to her and to the jailer trying to make her stop. She didn't shut up until almost daylight, when the jailer began to hear a bumping and scraping upstairs and he went up there and found Nancy hanging from the window bar. He said that it was cocaine and not whisky, because no nigger would try to commit suicide unless he was full of cocaine, because a nigger full of cocaine wasn't a nigger any longer.

The jailer cut her down and revived her; then he beat her, whipped her. She had hung herself with her dress. She had fixed it all right, but when they arrested her she didn't have on anything except a dress and so she didn't have anything to tie her hands with and she couldn't make her hands let go of the window ledge. So the jailer heard the noise and ran up there and found Nancy hanging from the window, stark naked, her belly already swelling out a little, like a little balloon.

When Dilsey was sick in her cabin and Nancy was cooking for us, we could see her apron swelling out; that was before father told Jesus to stay away from the house. Jesus was in the kitchen, sitting behind the stove, with his razor scar on his black face like a piece of dirty string. He said it was a watermelon that Nancy had under her dress.

"It never come off of your vine, though," Nancy said.

"Off of what vine?" Caddy said.

"I can cut down the vine it did come off of," Jesus said.

"What makes you want to talk like that before these chillen?" Nancy said. "Whyn't you go on to work? You done et. You want Mr Jason to catch you hanging around his kitchen, talking that way before these chillen?"

"Talking what way?" Caddy said. "What vine?"

"I cant hang around white man's kitchen," Jesus said. "But white man can hang around mine. White man can come in my house, but I cant stop him. When white man want to come in my house, I aint got no house. I cant stop him, but he cant kick me outen it. He cant do that."

Dilsey was still sick in her cabin. Father told Jesus to stay off our place. Dilsey was still sick. It was a long time. We were in the library after supper.

"Isn't Nancy through in the kitchen yet?" mother said. "It seems to me that she has had plenty of time to have finished the dishes."

"Let Quentin go and see," father said. "Go and see if Nancy is through, Quentin. Tell her she can go on home."

I went to the kitchen. Nancy was through. The dishes were put away and the fire was out. Nancy was sitting in a chair, close to the cold stove. She looked at me.

"Mother wants to know if you are through," I said.

"Yes," Nancy said. She looked at me. "I done finished." She looked at me.

"What is it?" I said. "What is it?"

"I aint nothing but a nigger," Nancy said. "It aint none of my fault."

She looked at me, sitting in the chair before the cold stove, the sailor hat on her head. I went back to the library. It was the cold stove and all, when you think of a kitchen being warm and busy and cheerful. And with a cold stove and the dishes all put away, and nobody wanting to eat at that hour.

"Is she through?" mother said.

"Yessum," I said.

"What is she doing?" mother said.

"She's not doing anything. She's through."

"I'll go and see," father said.

"Maybe she's waiting for Jesus to come and take her home," Caddy said.

"Jesus is gone," I said. Nancy told us how one morning she woke up and Jesus was gone.

"He quit me," Nancy said. "Done gone to Memphis, I reckon. Dodging them city *po*-lice for a while, I reckon."

"And a good riddance," father said. "I hope he stays there."

"Nancy's scaired of the dark," Jason said.

"So are you," Caddy said.

"I'm not," Jason said.

"Scairy cat," Caddy said.

"I'm not," Jason said.

"You, Candace!" mother said. Father came back.

"I am going to walk down the lane with Nancy," he said. "She says that Jesus is back."

"Has she seen him?" mother said.

"No. Some Negro sent her word that he was back in town. I wont be long."

"You'll leave me alone, to take Nancy home?" mother said. "Is her safety more precious to you than mine?"

"I wont be long," father said.

"You'll leave these children unprotected, with that Negro about?"

"I'm going too," Caddy said. "Let me go, Father."

"What would he do with them, if he were unfortunate enough to have them?" father said.

"I want to go, too," Jason said.

"Jason!" mother said. She was speaking to father. You could tell that by the way she said the name. Like she believed that all day father had been trying to think of doing the thing she wouldn't like the most, and that she knew all the time that after a while he would think of it. I stayed quiet, because father and I both knew that mother would want him to make me stay with her if she just thought of it in time. So father didn't look at me. I was the oldest. I was nine and Caddy was seven and Jason was five.

"Nonsense," father said. "We wont be long."

Nancy had her hat on. We came to the lane. "Jesus always been good to me," Nancy said. "Whenever he had two dollars, one of them was mine." We walked in the lane. "If I can just get through the lane," Nancy said, "I be all right then."

The lane was always dark. "This is where Jason got scared on Hallowe'en," Caddy said.

"I didn't," Jason said.

"Cant Aunt Rachel do anything with him?" father said. Aunt Rachel was old. She lived in a cabin beyond Nancy's, by herself. She had white hair and she smoked a pipe in the door, all day long; she didn't work any more. They said she was Jesus' mother. Sometimes she said she was and sometimes she said she wasn't any kin to Jesus.

"Yes, you did," Caddy said. "You were scairder than Frony. You were scairder than T.P. even. Scairder than niggers."

"Cant nobody do nothing with him," Nancy said. "He say I done woke up the devil in him and aint but one thing going to lay it down again."

"Well, he's gone now," father said. "There's nothing for you to be afraid of now. And if you'd just let white men alone."

"Let what white men alone?" Caddy said. "How let them alone?"

"He aint gone nowhere," Nancy said. "I can feel him. I can feel him now, in this lane. He hearing us talk, every word, hid somewhere, waiting. I aint seen him, and I aint going to see him again but once more, with that razor in his mouth. That razor on that string down his back, inside his shirt. And then I aint going to be even surprised."

"I wasn't scaired," Jason said.

"If you'd behave yourself, you'd have kept out of this," father said. "But it's all right now. He's probably in St. Louis now. Probably got another wife by now and forgot all about you."

"If he has, I better not find out about it," Nancy said. "I'd stand there right over them, and every time he wropped her, I'd cut that arm off. I'd cut his head off and I'd slit her belly and I'd shove—"

"Hush," father said.

"Slit whose belly, Nancy?" Caddy said.

"I wasn't scaired," Jason said. "I'd walk right down this lane by myself."

"Yah," Caddy said. "You wouldn't dare to put your foot down in it if we were not here too."

II

Dilsey was still sick, so we took Nancy home every night until mother said, "How much longer is this going on? I to be left alone in this big house while you take home a frightened Negro?"

We fixed a pallet in the kitchen for Nancy. One night we waked up, hearing the sound. It was not singing and it was not crying, coming up the dark stairs. There was a light in mother's room and we heard father going down the hall, down the back stairs, and Caddy and I went into the hall. The floor was cold. Our toes curled away from it while we listened to the sound. It was like singing and it wasn't like singing, like the sounds that Negroes make.

Then it stopped and we heard father going down the back stairs, and we went to the head of the stairs. Then the sound began again, in the stairway, not loud, and we could see Nancy's eyes halfway up the stairs, against the wall. They looked like cat's eyes do, like a big cat against the wall, watching us. When we came down the steps to where she was, she quit making the sound again, and we stood there until father came back up from the kitchen, with his pistol in his hand. He went back down with Nancy and they came back with Nancy's pallet.

We spread the pallet in our room. After the light in mother's room went off, we could see Nancy's eyes again, "Nancy," Caddy whispered, "are you asleep, Nancy?"

Nancy whispered something. It was oh or no, I dont know which. Like nobody had made it, like it came from nowhere and went nowhere, until it was like Nancy was not there at all; that I had looked so hard at her eyes on the stairs that they had got printed on my eyeballs, like the sun does when you have closed your eyes and there is no sun. "Jesus," Nancy whispered. "Jesus."

"Was it Jesus?" Caddy said. "Did he try to come into the kitchen?"

"Jesus," Nancy said. Like this: Jeeeeeeeeeeeeeeeesus, until the sound went out, like a match or a candle does.

"It's the other Jesus she means," I said.

"Can you see us, Nancy?" Caddy whispered. "Can you see our eyes too?"

"I aint nothing but a nigger," Nancy said. "God knows. God knows."

"What did you see down there in the kitchen?" Caddy whispered. "What tried to get in?"

"God knows," Nancy said. We could see her eyes. "God knows."

Dilsey got well. She cooked dinner. "You'd better stay in bed a day or two longer," father said.

"What for?" Dilsey said. "If I had been a day later, this place would be to rack and ruin. Get on out of here now and let me get my kitchen straight again."

Dilsey cooked supper too. And that night, just before dark, Nancy came into the kitchen.

"How do you know he's back?" Dilsey said. "You aint seen him."

"Jesus is a nigger," Jason said.

"I can feel him," Nancy said. "I can feel him laying yonder in the ditch."

"Tonight?" Dilsey said. "Is he there tonight?"

"Dilsey's a nigger too," Jason said.

"You try to eat something," Dilsey said.

"I dont want nothing," Nancy said.

"I aint a nigger," Jason said,

"Drink some coffee," Dilsey said. She poured a cup of coffee for Nancy. "Do you know he's out there tonight? How come you know it's tonight?"

"I know," Nancy said. "He's there, waiting. I know. I done lived with him too long. I know what he is fixing to do fore he know it himself."

"Drink some coffee," Dilsey said. Nancy held the cup to her mouth and blew into the cup. Her mouth pursed out like a spreading adder's, like a rubber mouth, like she had blown all the color out of her lips with blowing the coffee.

"I aint a nigger," Jason said. "Are you a nigger, Nancy?"

"I hellborn, child," Nancy said. "I wont be nothing soon. I going back where I come from soon."

III

She began to drink the coffee. While she was drinking, holding the cup in both hands, she began to make the sound again. She made the sound into the cup and the coffee splashed out onto her hands and her dress. Her eyes looked at us and she sat there, her elbows on her knees, holding the cup in both hands, looking at us across the wet cup, making the sound. "Look at Nancy," Jason said. "Nancy cant cook for us now. Dilsey's got well now."

"You hush up," Dilsey said. Nancy held the cup in both hands, looking at us, making the sound, like there were two of them: one looking at us and the other making the sound. "Whyn't you let Mr Jason telefoam the marshal?" Dilsey said. Nancy stopped then, holding the cup in her long brown hands. She tried to drink some coffee again, but it sploshed out of the cup, onto her hands and her dress, and she put the cup down. Jason watched her.

"I cant swallow it," Nancy said. "I swallows but it wont go down me."

"You go down to the cabin," Dilsey said. "Frony will fix you a pallet and I'll be there soon."

"Wont no nigger stop him," Nancy said.

"I aint a nigger," Jason said. "Am I, Dilsey?"

"I reckon not," Dilsey said. She looked at Nancy. "I dont reckon so. What you going to do, then?"

Nancy looked at us. Her eyes went fast, like she was afraid there wasn't time to look, without hardly moving at all. She looked at us, at all three of us at one time. "You member that night I stayed in yawls' room?" she said. She told about how we waked up early the next morning, and played. We had to play quiet, on her pallet, until father woke up and it was time to get breakfast. "Go and ask your maw to let me stay here tonight," Nancy said. "I wont need no pallet. We can play some more."

Caddy asked mother. Jason went too. "I cant have Negroes sleeping in the bedrooms," mother said. Jason cried. He cried until mother said he couldn't have any dessert for three days if he didn't stop. Then Jason said he would stop if Dilsey would make a chocolate cake. Father was there.

"Why dont you do something about it?" mother said. "What do we have officers for?"

"Why is Nancy afraid of Jesus?" Caddy said. "Are you afraid of father, mother?"

"What could the officers do?" father said. "If Nancy hasn't seen him, how could the officers find him?"

"Then why is she afraid?" mother said.

"She says he is there. She says she knows he is there tonight."

"Yet we pay taxes," mother said. "I must wait here alone in this big house while you take a Negro woman home."

"You know that I am not lying outside with a razor," father said.

"I'll stop if Dilsey will make a chocolate cake," Jason said. Mother told us to go out and father said he didn't know if Jason would get a chocolate cake or not, but he knew what Jason was going to get in about a minute. We went back to the kitchen and told Nancy.

"Father said for you to go home and lock the door, and you'll be all right," Caddy said. "All right from what, Nancy? Is Jesus mad at you?" Nancy was holding the coffee cup in her hands again, her elbows on her knees and her hands holding the cup between her knees. She was looking into the cup. "What have you done that made Jesus mad?" Caddy said. Nancy let the cup go. It didn't break on the floor, but the coffee spilled out, and Nancy sat there with her hands still making the shape of the cup. She began to make the sound again, not loud. Not singing and not unsinging. We watched her.

"Here," Dilsey said. "You quit that, now. You get aholt of yourself. You wait here. I going to get Versh to walk home with you." Dilsey went out.

We looked at Nancy. Her shoulders kept shaking, but she quit making the sound. We watched her. "What's Jesus going to do to you?" Caddy said. "He went away."

Nancy looked at us. "We had fun that night I stayed in yawls' room, didn't we?"

"I didn't," Jason said. "I didn't have any fun."

"You were asleep in mother's room," Caddy said. "You were not there."

"Let's go down to my house and have some more fun," Nancy said.

"Mother wont let us," I said. "It's too late now."

"Dont bother her," Nancy said. "We can tell her in the morning. She wont mind."

"She wouldn't let us," I said.

"Dont ask her now," Nancy said. "Dont bother her now."

"She didn't say we couldn't go," Caddy said.

"We didn't ask," I said.

"If you go, I'll tell," Jason said.

"We'll have fun," Nancy said. "They won't mind, just to my house. I been working for yawl a long time. They won't mind."

"I'm not afraid to go," Caddy said. "Jason is the one that's afraid. He'll tell."

"I'm not," Jason said.

"Yes, you are," Caddy said. "You'll tell."

"I won't tell," Jason said. "I'm not afraid."

"Jason ain't afraid to go with me," Nancy said. "Is you, Jason?"

"Jason is going to tell," Caddy said. The lane was dark. We passed the pasture gate. "I bet if something was to jump out from behind that gate, Jason would holler."

"I wouldn't," Jason said. We walked down the lane. Nancy was talking loud.

"What are you talking so loud for, Nancy?" Caddy said.

"Who; me?" Nancy said. "Listen at Quentin and Caddy and Jason saying I'm talking loud."

"You talk like there was five of us here," Caddy said. "You talk like father was here too."

"Who; me talking loud, Mr Jason?" Nancy said.

"Nancy called Jason 'Mister,'" Caddy said.

"Listen how Caddy and Quentin and Jason talk," Nancy said.

"We're not talking loud," Caddy said. "You're the one that's talking like father—"

"Hush," Nancy said; "hush, Mr Jason."

"Nancy called Jason 'Mister' aguh—"

"Hush," Nancy said. She was talking loud when we crossed the ditch and stooped through the fence where she used to stoop through with the clothes on her head. Then we came to her house. We were going fast then. She opened the door. The smell of the house was like the lamp and the smell of Nancy was like the wick, like they were waiting for one another to begin to smell. She lit the lamp and closed the door and put the bar up. Then she quit talking loud, looking at us.

"What're we going to do?" Caddy said.

"What do yawl want to do?" Nancy said.

"You said we would have some fun," Caddy said.

There was something about Nancy's house; something you could smell besides Nancy and the house. Jason smelled it, even. "I don't want to stay here," he said. "I want to go home."

"Go home, then," Caddy said.

"I don't want to go by myself," Jason said.

"We're going to have some fun," Nancy said.

"How?" Caddy said.

Nancy stood by the door. She was looking at us, only it was like she had emptied her eyes, like she had quit using them. "What do you want to do?" she said.

"Tell us a story," Caddy said. "Can you tell a story?"

"Yes," Nancy said.

"Tell it," Caddy said. We looked at Nancy. "You don't know any stories."

"Yes," Nancy said. "Yes, I do."

She came and sat in a chair before the hearth. There was a little fire there. Nancy built it up, when it was already hot inside. She built a good blaze. She told a story. She talked like her eyes looked, like her eyes watching us and her voice talking to us did not belong to her. Like she was living somewhere else, waiting somewhere else. She was outside the cabin. Her voice was inside and the shape of her, the Nancy that could stoop under a barbed wire fence with a bundle of clothes balanced on her head as though without weight, like a balloon, was there. But that was all. "And so this here queen come walking up to the ditch, where that bad man was hiding. She was walking up to the ditch, and she say, 'If I can just get past this here ditch,' was what she say . . ."

"What ditch?" Caddy said. "A ditch like that one out there? Why did a queen want to go into a ditch?"

"To get to her house," Nancy said. She looked at us. "She had to cross the ditch to get into her house quick and bar the door."

"Why did she want to go home and bar the door?" Caddy said.

IV

Nancy looked at us. She quit talking. She looked at us. Jason's legs stuck straight out of his pants where he sat on Nancy's lap. "I don't think that's a good story," he said. "I want to go home."

"Maybe we had better," Caddy said. She got up from the floor. "I bet they are looking for us right now." She went toward the door.

"No," Nancy said. "Don't open it." She got up quick and passed Caddy. She didn't touch the door, the wooden bar.

"Why not?" Caddy said.

"Come back to the lamp," Nancy said. "We'll have fun. You don't have to go."

"We ought to go," Caddy said. "Unless we have a lot of fun." She and Nancy came back to the fire, the lamp.

"I want to go home," Jason said. "I'm going to tell."

"I know another story," Nancy said. She stood close to the lamp. She looked at Caddy, like when your eyes look up at a stick balanced on your nose. She had to look down to see Caddy, but her eyes looked like that, like when you are balancing a stick.

"I won't listen to it," Jason said. "I'll bang on the floor."

"It's a good one," Nancy said. "It's better than the other one."

"What's it about?" Caddy said. Nancy was standing by the lamp. Her hand was on the lamp, against the light, long and brown.

"Your hand is on that hot globe," Caddy said. "Don't it feel hot to your hand?"

Nancy looked at her hand on the lamp chimney. She took her hand away, slow. She stood there, looking at Caddy, wringing her long hand as though it were tied to her wrist with a string.

"Let's do something else," Caddy said.

"I want to go home," Jason said.

"I got some popcorn," Nancy said. She looked at Caddy and then at Jason and then at me and then at Caddy again. "I got some popcorn."

"I don't like popcorn," Jason said. "I'd rather have candy."

Nancy looked at Jason. "You can hold the popper." She was still wringing her hand; it was long and limp and brown.

"All right," Jason said. "I'll stay a while if I can do that. Caddy can't hold it. I'll want to go home again if Caddy holds the popper."

Nancy built up the fire. "Look at Nancy putting her hands in the fire," Caddy said. "What's the matter with you, Nancy?"

"I got popcorn," Nancy said. "I got some." She took the popper from under the bed. It was broken. Jason began to cry.

"Now we can't have any popcorn," he said.

"We ought to go home, anyway," Caddy said. "Come on, Quentin."

"Wait," Nancy said; "wait. I can fix it. Don't you want to help me fix it?"

"I don't think I want any," Caddy said. "It's too late now."

"You help me, Jason," Nancy said. "Don't you want to help me?"

"No," Jason said. "I want to go home."

"Hush," Nancy said; "hush. Watch. Watch me. I can fix it so Jason can hold it and pop the corn." She got a piece of wire and fixed the popper.

"It won't hold good," Caddy said.

"Yes, it will," Nancy said. "Yawl watch. Yawl help me shell some corn."

The popcorn was under the bed too. We shelled it into the popper and Nancy helped Jason hold the popper over the fire.

"It's not popping," Jason said. "I want to go home."

"You wait," Nancy said. "It'll begin to pop. We'll have fun then." She was sitting close to the fire. The lamp was turned up so high it was beginning to smoke.

"Why don't you turn it down some?" I said.

"It's all right," Nancy said. "I'll clean it. Yawl wait. The popcorn will start in a minute."

"I don't believe it's going to start," Caddy said. "We ought to start home, anyway. They'll be worried."

"No," Nancy said. "It's going to pop. Dilsey will tell um yawl with me. I been working for yawl long time. They won't mind if yawl at my house. You wait, now. It'll start popping any minute now."

Then Jason got some smoke in his eyes and he began to cry. He dropped the popper into the fire. Nancy got a wet rag and wiped Jason's face, but he didn't stop crying.

"Hush," she said. "Hush." But he didn't hush. Caddy took the popper out of the fire.

"It's burned up," she said. "You'll have to get some more popcorn, Nancy."

"Did you put all of it in?" Nancy said.

"Yes," Caddy said. Nancy looked at Caddy. Then she took the popper and opened it and poured the cinders into her apron and began to sort the grains, her hands long and brown, and we watching her.

"Haven't you got any more?" Caddy said.

"Yes," Nancy said; "yes. Look. This here ain't burnt. All we need to do is—"

"I want to go home," Jason said. "I'm going to tell."

"Hush," Caddy said. We all listened. Nancy's head was already turned toward the barred door, her eyes filled with red lamplight. "Somebody is coming," Caddy said.

Then Nancy began to make that sound again, not loud, sitting there above the fire, her long hands dangling between her knees; all of a sudden water began to come out on her face in big drops, running down her face, carrying in each one a little turning ball of firelight like a spark until it dropped off her chin. "She's not crying," I said.

"I ain't crying," Nancy said. Her eyes were closed. "I ain't crying. Who is it?"

"I don't know," Caddy said. She went to the door and looked out. "We've got to go now," she said. "Here comes father."

"I'm going to tell," Jason said. "Yawl made me come."

The water still ran down Nancy's face. She turned in her chair. "Listen. Tell him. Tell him we going to have fun. Tell him I take good care of yawl until in the morning. Tell him to let me come home with yawl and sleep on the floor. Tell him I won't need no pallet. We'll have fun. You member last time how we had so much fun?"

"I didn't have fun," Jason said. "You hurt me. You put smoke in my eyes. I'm going to tell."

V

Father came in. He looked at us. Nancy did not get up.

"Tell him," she said.

"Caddy made us come down here," Jason said. "I didn't want to."

Father came to the fire. Nancy looked up at him. "Can't you go to Aunt Rachel's and stay?" he said. Nancy looked up at father, her hands between her knees. "He's not here," father said. "I would have seen him. There's not a soul in sight."

"He in the ditch," Nancy said. "He waiting in the ditch yonder."

"Nonsense," father said. He looked at Nancy. "Do you know he's there?"

"I got the sign," Nancy said.

"What sign?"

"I got it. It was on the table when I come in. It was a hogbone, with blood meat still on it, laying by the lamp. He's out there. When yawl walk out that door, I gone."

"Gone where, Nancy?" Caddy said.

"I'm not a tattletale," Jason said.

"Nonsense," father said.

"He out there," Nancy said. "He looking through that window this minute, waiting for yawl to go. Then I gone."

"Nonsense," father said. "Lock up your house and we'll take you on to Aunt Rachel's."

"'Twont do no good," Nancy said. She didn't look at father now, but he looked down at her, at her long, limp, moving hands. "Putting it off wont do no good."

"Then what do you want to do?" father said.

"I don't know," Nancy said. "I can't do nothing. Just put it off. And that don't do no good. I reckon it belong to me. I reckon what I going to get ain't no more than mine."

"Get what?" Caddy said. "What's yours?"

"Nothing," father said. "You all must get to bed."

"Caddy made me come," Jason said.

"Go on to Aunt Rachel's," father said.

"It won't do no good," Nancy said. She sat before the fire, her elbows on her knees, her long hands between her knees. "When even your own kitchen wouldn't do no good. When even if I was sleeping on the floor in the room with your chillen, and the next morning there I am, and blood—"

"Hush," father said. "Lock the door and put out the lamp and go to bed."

"I scared of the dark," Nancy said. "I scared for it to happen in the dark."

"You mean you're going to sit right here with the lamp lighted?" father said. Then Nancy began to make the sound again, sitting before the fire, her long hands between her knees. "Ah, damnation," father said. "Come along, chillen. It's past bedtime."

"When yawl go home, I gone," Nancy said. She talked quieter now, and her face looked quiet, like her hands. "Anyway, I got my coffin money saved up with Mr. Lovelady." Mr. Lovelady was a short, dirty man who collected the Negro insurance, coming around to the cabins or the kitchens every Saturday morning, to collect fifteen cents. He and his wife lived at the hotel. One morning his wife committed suicide. They had a child, a little girl. He and the child went away. After a week or two he came back alone. We would see him going along the lanes and the back streets on Saturday mornings.

"Nonsense," father said. "You'll be the first thing I'll see in the kitchen tomorrow morning."

"You'll see what you'll see, I reckon," Nancy said. "But it will take the Lord to say what that will be."

VI

We left her sitting before the fire.

"Come and put the bar up," father said. But she didn't move. She didn't look at us again, sitting quietly there between the lamp and the fire. From some distance down the lane we could look back and see her through the open door.

"What, Father?" Caddy said. "What's going to happen?"

"Nothing," father said. Jason was on father's back, so Jason was the tallest of all of us. We went down into the ditch. I looked at it, quiet. I couldn't see much where the moonlight and the shadows tangled.

"If Jesus is hid here, he can see us, cant he?" Caddy said.

"He's not there," father said. "He went away a long time ago."

"You made me come," Jason said, high; against the sky it looked like father had two heads, a little one and a big one. "I didn't want to."

We went up out of the ditch. We could still see Nancy's house and the open door, but we couldn't see Nancy now, sitting before the fire with the door open, because she was tired, "I just done got tired," she said. "I just a nigger. It ain't no fault of mine."

But we could hear her, because she began just after we came up out of the ditch, the sound that was not singing and not unsinging. "Who will do our washing now, Father?" I said.

"I'm not a nigger," Jason said, high and close above father's head.

"You're worse," Caddy said, "you are a tattletale. If something was to jump out, you'd be scairder than a nigger."

"I wouldn't," Jason said.

"You'd cry," Caddy said.

"Caddy," father said.

"I wouldn't!" Jason said.

"Scairy cat," Caddy said.

"Candace!" father said.

WILLIAM FAULKNER

An Introduction for *The Sound and the Fury*†

For a new edition of *The Sound and the Fury* which was announced in 1933 but was never published, William Faulkner wrote an introduction

---

† From "An Introduction for *The Sound and the Fury*," ed. James B. Meriwether, *The Southern Review* 8 (N.S., 1972): 705–10. Copyright © 1972 by the Estate of William Faulkner. Reprinted by permission of Nicholas G. Meriwether, Literary Executor for James B. Meriwether. As printed here, Faulkner's typescript has been reproduced exactly, except for the correction of five obvious typing errors: 708.27 withoyt] without; 708.32 agao] ago; 709.10 begn] began; 709.19 give] given; 710.11 withoyt] without.

that for years was supposed to have survived only in an incomplete four-page typescript which he preserved among his papers. The recent discovery of the missing first page makes possible the publication here, for the first time, of a Faulkner document of unique critical and biographical significance.

* * *

I wrote this book and learned to read. I had learned a little about writing from Soldiers' Pay—how to approach language, words: not with seriousness so much, as an essayist does, but with a kind of alert respect, as you approach dynamite; even with joy, as you approach women: perhaps with the same secretly unscrupulous intentions. But when I finished The Sound and the Fury I discovered that there is actually something to which the shabby term Art not only can, but must, be applied. I discovered then that I had gone through all that I had ever read, from Henry James through Henty to newspaper murders, without making any distinction or digesting any of it, as a moth or a goat might. After The Sound and The Fury and without heeding to open another book and in a series of delayed repercussions like summer thunder, I discovered the Flauberts and Dostoievskys and Conrads whose books I had read ten years ago. With The Sound and the Fury I learned to read and quit reading, since I have read nothing since.

Nor do I seem to have learned anything since. While writing Sanctuary, the next novel to The Sound and the Fury, that part of me which learned as I wrote, which perhaps is the very force which drives a writer to the travail of invention and the drudgery of putting seventy-five or a hundred thousand words on paper, was absent because I was still reading by repercussion the books which I had swallowed whole ten years and more ago. I learned only from the writing of Sanctuary that there was something missing; something which The Sound and the Fury gave me and Sanctuary did not. When I began As I Lay Dying I had discovered what it was and knew that it would be also missing in this case because this would be a deliberate book. I set out deliberately to write a tour-de-force. Before I ever put pen to paper and set down the first word, I knew what the last word would be and almost where the last period would fall. Before I began I said, I am going to write a book by which, at a pinch, I can stand or fall if I never touch ink again. So when I finished it the cold satisfaction was there, as I had expected, but as I had also expected the other quality which The Sound and the Fury had given me was absent: that emotion definite and physical and yet nebulous to describe:

that ecstasy, that eager and joyous faith and anticipation of surprise which the yet unmarred sheet beneath my hand held inviolate and unfailing, waiting for release. It was not there in As I Lay Dying. I said, It is because I knew too much about this book before I began to write it. I said, More than likely I shall never again have to know this much about a book before I begin to write it, and next time it will return. I waited almost two years, then I began Light in August, knowing no more about it than a young woman, pregnant, walking along a strange country road. I thought, I will recapture it now, since I know no more about this book than I did about The Sound and the Fury when I sat down before the first blank page.

It did not return. The written pages grew in number. The story was going pretty well. I would sit down to it each morning without reluctance yet still without that anticipation and that joy which alone ever made writing pleasure to me. The book was almost finished before I acquiesced to the fact that it would not recur, since I was now aware before each word was written down just what the people would do, since now I was deliberately choosing among possibilities and probabilities of behavior and weighing and measuring each choice by the scale of the Jameses and Conrads and Balzacs. I knew that I had read too much, that I had reached that stage which all young writers must pass through, in which he believes that he has learned too much about his trade. I received a copy of the printed book and I found that I didn't even want to see what kind of jacket Smith had put on it. I seemed to have a vision of it and the other ones subsequent to The Sound and The Fury ranked in order upon a shelf while I looked at the titled backs of them with a flagging attention which was almost distaste, and upon which each succeeding title registered less and less, until at last Attention itself seemed to say, Thank God I shall never need to open any one of them again. I believed that I knew then why I had not recaptured that first ecstasy, and that I should never again recapture it; that whatever novels I should write in the future would be written without reluctance, but also without anticipation or joy: that in the Sound and The Fury I had already put perhaps the only thing in literature which would ever move me very much: Caddy climbing the pear tree to look in the window at her grandmother's funeral while Quentin and Jason and Benjy and the negroes looked up at the muddy seat of her drawers.

This is the only one of the seven novels which I wrote without any accompanying feeling of drive or effort, or any following feeling of exhaustion or relief or distaste. When I began it I had no plan at all. I wasn't even writing a book. I was thinking of books, publication, only in the reverse, in saying to myself, I wont have to worry about publishers liking or not liking this at all. Four years before I had written Soldiers' Pay. It didn't take long to write and it got published quickly and made me about five hundred dollars. I said, Writing novels is easy. You dont make much doing it, but it is easy. I wrote Mosquitoes. It wasn't quite so easy to write and it didn't get published quite as quickly and it made me about four hundred dollars. I said, Apparently there is more to writing novels, being a novelist, than I thought. I wrote Sartoris. It took much longer, and the publisher refused it at once. But I continued to shop it about for three years with a stubborn and fading hope, perhaps to justify the time which I had spent writing it. This hope died slowly, though it didn't hurt at all. One day I seemed to shut a door between me and all publishers' addresses and book lists. I said to myself, Now I can write. Now I can make myself a vase like that which the old Roman kept at his bedside and wore the rim slowly away with kissing it.[1] So I, who had never had a sister and was fated to lose my daughter in infancy, set out to make myself a beautiful and tragic little girl.

WILLIAM FAULKNER

An Introduction to *The Sound and the Fury*[†]

For a new edition of *The Sound and the Fury* that was to be published by Random House, Faulkner wrote, during the summer of 1933, an introduction that survives in several partial and complete manuscript and typescript drafts. One of them, apparently the last, was published in the *Southern Review* 8 (N.S., Autumn 1972), 705–10. The following longer and quite different version also merits publication in its own right, and it is at least possible that it was written later, rather than earlier, than the one that has been published.

* * *

Art is no part of southern life. In the North it seems to be different. It is the hardest minor stone in Manhattan's foundation. It is a part of the glitter or shabbiness of the streets. The arrowing buildings rise out of it and because of it, to be torn down and arrow again.

---

1. Faulkner alludes to a scene in the first chapter of Henryk Sienkiewicz's historical novel *Quo Vadis* (1895).

† From William Faulkner, "An Introduction to *The Sound and the Fury*," *Missisippi Quarterly* 26 (Summer 1973): 410–15. Copyright © 1973 by Mrs. Jill Faulkner Summers, Executrix for the Estate of William Faulkner. Reprinted by permission of W. W. Norton & Company, Inc.

There will be people leading small bourgeois lives (those countless and almost invisible bones of its articulation, lacking any one of which the whole skeleton might collapse) whose bread will derive from it—polyglot boys and girls progressing from tenement schools to editorial rooms and art galleries; men with grey hair and paunches who run linotype machines and take up tickets at concerts and then go sedately home to Brooklyn and suburban stations where children and grandchildren await them—long after the descendants of Irish politicians and Neapolitan racketeers are as forgotten as the wild Indians and the pigeon.

And of Chicago too: of that rhythm not always with harmony or tune; lusty, loudvoiced, always changing and always young; drawing from a river basin which is almost a continent young men and women into its living unrest and then spewing them forth again to write Chicago in New England and Virginia and Europe. But in the South art, to become visible at all, must become a ceremony, a spectacle; something between a gypsy encampment and a church bazaar given by a handful of alien mummers who must waste themselves in protest and active self-defense until there is nothing left with which to speak—a single week, say, of furious endeavor for a show to be held on Friday night and then struck and vanished, leaving only a paint-stiffened smock or a worn out typewriter ribbon in the corner and perhaps a small bill for cheesecloth or bunting in the hands of an astonished and bewildered tradesman.

Perhaps this is because the South (I speak in the sense of the indigenous dream of any given collection of men having something in common, be it only geography and climate, which shape their economic and spiritual aspirations into cities, into a pattern of houses or behavior) is old since dead. New York, whatever it may believe of itself, is young since alive; it is still a logical and unbroken progression from the Dutch. And Chicago even boasts of being young. But the South, as Chicago is the Middlewest and New York the East, is dead, killed by the Civil War. There is a thing known whimsically as the New South to be sure, but it is not the south. It is a land of Immigrants who are rebuilding the towns and cities into replicas of towns and cities in Kansas and Iowa and Illinois, with skyscrapers and striped canvas awnings instead of wooden balconies, and teaching the young men who sell the gasoline and the waitresses in the restaurants to say O yeah? and to speak with hard r's, and hanging over the intersections of quiet and shaded streets where no one save Northern tourists in Cadillacs and Lincolns ever pass at a gait faster than a horse trots, changing red-and-green lights and savage and peremptory bells.

Yet this art, which has no place in southern life, is almost the sum total of the Southern artist. It is his breath, blood, flesh, all. Not so much that it is forced back upon him or that he is forced bodily into it by the circumstance; forced to choose, lady and tiger fashion, between being an artist and being a man. He does it deliberately; he wishes it so. This has always been true of him and of him alone. Only Southerners have taken horsewhips and pistols to editors about the treatment or maltreatment of their manuscript. This—the actual pistols—was in the old days, of course, we no longer succumb to the impulse. But it is still there, still within us.

Because it is himself that the Southerner is writing about, not about his environment: who has, figuratively speaking, taken the artist in him in one hand and his milieu in the other and thrust the one into the other like a clawing and spitting cat into a croker sack. And he writes. We have never got and probably will never get, anywhere with music or the plastic forms. We need to talk, to tell, since oratory is our heritage. We seem to try in the simple furious breathing (or writing) span of the individual to draw a savage indictment of the contemporary scene or to escape from it into a make-believe region of swords and magnolias and mockingbirds which perhaps never existed anywhere. Both of the courses are rooted in sentiment; perhaps the ones who write savagely and bitterly of the incest in clayfloored cabins are the most sentimental. Anyway, each course is a matter of violent partizanship, in which the writer unconsciously writes into every line and phrase his violent despairs and rages and frustrations or his violent prophesies of still more violent hopes. That cold intellect which can write with calm and complete detachment and gusto of its contemporary scene is not among us; I do not believe there lives the Southern writer who can say without lying that writing is any fun to him. Perhaps we do not want it to be.

I seem to have tried both of the courses. I have tried to escape and I have tried to indict. After five years I look back at *The Sound and The Fury* and see that that was the turning point: in this book I did both at one time. When I began the book, I had no plan at all. I wasn't even writing a book. Previous to it I had written three novels, with progressively decreasing ease and pleasure, and reward or emolument. The third one was shopped about for three years during which I sent it from publisher to publisher with a kind of stubborn and fading hope of at least justifying the paper I had used and the time I had spent writing it. This hope must have died at last, because one day it suddenly seemed as if a door had clapped silently and forever to between me and all publishers' addresses and booklists and I said to myself, Now I can write. Now I can just write. Whereupon I, who had three brothers and no sisters and was destined to lose my first daughter in infancy, began to write about a little girl.

I did not realise then that I was trying to manufacture the sister which I did not have and the daughter which I was to lose, though the former might have been apparent from the fact that Caddy had three brothers almost before I wrote her name on paper. I just began to write about a brother and a sister splashing one another in the brook and the sister fell and wet her clothing and the smallest brother cried, thinking that the sister was conquered or perhaps hurt. Or perhaps he knew that he was the baby and that she would quit whatever water battles to comfort him. When she did so, when she quit the water fight and stooped in her wet garments above him, the entire story, which is all told by that same little brother in the first section, seemed to explode on the paper before me.

I saw that peaceful glinting of that branch was to become the dark, harsh flowing of time sweeping her to where she could not return to comfort him, but that just separation, division, would not be enough, not far enough. It must sweep her into dishonor and shame too. And that Benjy must never grow beyond this moment; that for him all knowing must begin and end with that fierce, panting, paused and stooping wet figure which smelled like trees. That he must never grow up to where the grief of bereavement could be leavened with understanding and hence the alleviation of rage as in the case of Jason, and of oblivion as in the case of Quentin.

I saw that they had been sent to the pasture to spend the afternoon to get them away from the house during the grandmother's funeral in order that the three brothers and the nigger children could look up at the muddy seat of Caddy's drawers as she climbed the tree to look in the window at the funeral, without then realising the symbology of the soiled drawers, for here again hers was the courage which was to face later with honor the shame which she was to engender, which Quentin and Jason could not face: the one taking refuge in suicide, the other in vindictive rage which drove him to rob his bastard niece of the meagre sums which Caddy could send her. For I had already gone on to night and the bedroom and Dilsey with the mudstained drawers scrubbing the naked backside of that doomed little girl—trying to cleanse with the sorry byblow of its soiling that body, flesh, whose shame they symbolised and prophesied, as though she already saw the dark future and the part she was to play in it trying to hold that crumbling household together.

Then the story was complete, finished. There was Dilsey to be the future, to stand above the fallen ruins of the family like a ruined chimney, gaunt, patient and indomitable; and Benjy to be the past. He had to be an idiot so that, like Dilsey, he could be impervious to the future, though unlike her by refusing to accept it at all. Without thought or comprehension; shapeless, neuter, like something eye-less and voiceless which might have lived, existed merely because of its ability to suffer, in the beginning of life; half fluid, groping: a pallid and helpless mass of all mindless agony under sun, in time yet not of it save that he could nightly carry with him that fierce, courageous being who was to him but a touch and a sound that may be heard on any golf links and a smell like trees, into the slow bright shapes of sleep.

The story is all there, in the first section as Benjy told it. I did not try deliberately to make it obscure; when I realised that the story might be printed, I took three more sections, all longer than Benjy's, to try to clarify it. But when I wrote Benjy's section, I was not writing it to be printed. If I were to do it over now I would do it differently, because the writing of it as it now stands taught me both how to write and how to read, and even more: It taught me what I had already read, because on completing it I discovered, in a series of repercussions like summer thunder, the Flauberts and Conrads and Turgenievs which as much as ten years before I had consumed whole and without assimilating at all, as a moth or a goat might. I have read nothing since; I have not had to. And I have learned but one thing since about writing. That is, that the emotion definite and physical and yet nebulous to describe which the writing of Benjy's section of *The Sound and The Fury* gave me—that ecstasy, that eager and joy-ous faith and anticipation of surprise which the yet unmarred sheets beneath my hand held inviolate and unfailing—will not return. The unreluctance to begin, the cold satisfaction in work well and ardu-ously done, is there and will continue to be there as long as I can do it well. But that other will not return. I shall never know it again.

So I wrote Quentin's and Jason's sections, trying to clarify Ben-jy's. But I saw that I was merely temporising; That I should have to get completely out of the book. I realised that there would be com-pensations, that in a sense I could then give a final turn to the screw and extract some ultimate distillation. Yet it took me better than a month to take pen and write *The day dawned bleak and chill* before I did so. There is a story somewhere about an old Roman who kept at his bedside a Tyrrhenian vase which he loved and the rim of which he wore slowly away with kissing it.[1] I had made myself a vase, but I suppose I knew all the time that I could not live forever inside of it, that perhaps to have it so that I too could lie in bed and look at it would be better; surely so when that day should come when not only the ecstasy of writing would be gone, but the unre-luctance and the something worth saying too. It's fine to think that

---

1. Faulkner alludes to a scene in the first chapter of Henryk Sienklewicz's historical novel *Quo Vadis* (1895).

you will leave something behind you when you die, but it's better to have made something you can die with. Much better the muddy bottom of a little doomed girl climbing a blooming pear tree in April to look in the window at the funeral.
Oxford.
19 August, 1933.

WILLIAM FAULKNER

Letters to Malcolm Cowley about
The Portable Faulkner†

Thursday [20 Sept. 1945]

Dear Cowley:

* * *

Suppose you used the last section, the Dilsey one, of SOUND & FURY, and suppose (if there is time: I am leaving here Monday for Mississippi) I wrote a page or two of synopsis to preface it, a condensation of the first 3 sections, which simply told why and when (and who she was) and how a 17 year old girl robbed a bureau drawer of hoarded money and climbed down a drain pipe and ran off with a carnival pitchman.

* * *

To Malcolm Cowley
Thursday [18 Oct. 1945]

Cher Maitre:

Here it is.[1] I should have done this when I wrote the book. Then the whole thing would have fallen into pattern like a jigsaw puzzle when the magician's wand touched it.

NOTE: I dont have a copy of TSATF, so if you find discrepancies in chronology (various ages of people, etc) or in the sum of money Quentin stole from her uncle Jason, discrepancies which are too

---

† *From Selected Letters of William Faulkner,* ed. Joseph Blotner (New York: Random House, 1977), 202 and 205. Copyright © 1977 by Jill Faulkner Summers. Used by permission of W. W. Norton & Company, Inc. and Random House, an imprint of The Random House Publishing Group, a division of Random House LLC. All rights reserved. Malcolm Cowley (1898–1989), editor and critic, whose 1946 *Portable Faulkner* was essential in both reviving Faulkner's work and making readers see the Yoknapatawpha novels and stories as a coherent whole. Author of *Exile's Return* (1933), *And I Worked at the Writer's Trade* (1978), among other works.

1. The "Appendix/Compson: 1699–1945" that Faulkner had written instead of the brief synopsis of *The Sound and the Fury* he had proposed in his letter of September 20.

glaring to leave in and which you dont want to correct yourself, send it back to me with a note. As I recall, no definite sum is ever mentioned in the book, and if the book says TP is 12, not 14, you can change that in this appendix.

I think this is all right, it took me about a week to get Hollywood out of my lungs, but I am still writing all right, I believe. The hell of it though, letting me get my hand into it, as was, your material was getting too long; now all you have is still more words. But I think this belongs in your volume. What about dropping DEATH DRAG, if something must be eliminated? That was just a tale, could have happened anywhere, could have been printed as happening anywhere by simply changing the word Jefferson where it occurs, once only I think.

Let me know what you think of this. I think it is really pretty good, to stand as it is, as a piece without implications. Maybe I am just happy that that damned west coast place has not cheapened my soul as much as I probably believed it was going to do.

Faulkner

[in ink:] I may get up east some time this fall. Will let you know.

WILLIAM FAULKNER

Appendix:
Compson
1699–1945[†]

IKKEMOTUBBE. A dispossessed American king. Called "l'Homme" (and sometimes "de l'homme") by his fosterbrother, a Chevalier of France, who had he not been born too late could have been among the brightest in that glittering galaxy of knightly blackguards who were Napoleon's marshals, who thus translated the Chickasaw title meaning "The Man"; which translation Ikkemotubbe, himself a man of wit and imagination as well as a shrewd judge of character, including his own, carried one step further and anglicised it to "Doom." Who granted out of his vast lost domain a solid square mile of virgin North Mississippi dirt as truly angled as the four corners of a card-table top (forested then because these were the old days before 1833 when the stars fell and Jefferson Mississippi was one long rambling onestorey mudchinked log building housing the Chickasaw Agent and his tradingpost store) to the grandson of a Scottish refugee who

† From *The Portable Faulkner*, ed. Malcolm Cowley (New York: Random House, 1946). Copyright © 1946 by Random House. Used by permission of W. W. Norton & Company, Inc. and Random House, an imprint of The Random House Publishing Group, a division of Random House LLC. All rights reserved.

had lost his own birthright by casting his lot with a king who himself had been dispossessed. This in partial return for the right to proceed in peace, by whatever means he and his people saw fit, afoot or a horse provided they were Chickasaw horses, to the wild western land presently to be called Oklahoma: not knowing then about the oil.

JACKSON.   A Great White Father with a sword. (An old duellist, a brawling lean fierce mangy durable imperishable old lion who set the wellbeing of the nation above the White House and the health of his new political party above either and above them all set not his wife's honor[1] but the principle that honor must be defended whether it was or not because defended it was whether or not.) Who patented sealed and countersigned the grant with his own hand in his gold tepee in Wassi Town,[2] not knowing about the oil either: so that one day the homeless descendants of the dispossessed would ride supine with drink and splendidly comatose above the dusty allotted harborage of their bones in specially built scarletpainted hearses and fire-engines.

These were Compsons:

QUENTIN MACLACHAN.   Son of a Glasgow printer, orphaned and raised by his mother's people in the Perth highlands. Fled to Carolina from Culloden Moor[3] with a claymore and the tartan he wore by day and slept under by night, and little else. At eighty, having fought once against an English king and lost, he would not make that mistake twice and so fled again one night in 1779, with his infant grandson and the tartan (the claymore had vanished, along with his son, the grandson's father, from one of Tarleton's regiments on a Georgia battlefield[4] about a year ago) into Kentucky, where a neighbor named Boon or Boone had already established a settlement.

CHARLES STUART.   Attainted and proscribed by name and grade in his British regiment. Left for dead in a Georgia swamp by his own

1. Andrew Jackson's wife, Rachel, married Jackson thinking that her first husband had divorced her, but he had not. Two years after she and Jackson married, her first husband, Lewis Robards, did obtain a divorce on grounds of desertion and adultery. She and Jackson remarried, but scandal followed them, especially after Jackson's political rise. He fought several duels over the issue, including one in 1806 with Charles Dickinson, in which Dickinson was killed.
2. Washington.
3. The site of the April 16, 1746, battle in northwest Scotland, in which British forces under the Duke of Cumberland defeated Highland Jacobite forces under Prince Charles Edward, thus ending the last armed outbreak of the Stuart cause. The battle is notorious for the slaughter of Highland wounded after the battle.
4. Banastre Tarleton (1754–1833) was a British officer during the American Revolution who led a bloody campaign through the South. The major battles were in the Carolinas, where in the Battle of Cowpens he fought against Colonel Beal's Georgians.

retreating army and then by the advancing American one, both of which were wrong. He still had the claymore even when on his homemade wooden leg he finally overtook his father and son four years later at Harrodsburg, Kentucky, just in time to bury the father and enter upon a long period of being a split personality while still trying to be the schoolteacher which he believed he wanted to be; until he gave up at last and became the gambler he actually was and which no Compson seemed to realize they all were provided the gambit was desperate and the odds long enough. Succeeded at last in risking not only his neck but the security of his family and the very integrity of the name he would leave behind him, by joining the confederation headed by an acquaintance named Wilkinson[5] (a man of considerable talent and influence and intellect and power) in a plot to secede the whole Mississippi Valley from the United States and join it to Spain. Fled in his turn when the bubble burst (as anyone except a Compson schoolteacher should have known it would), himself unique in being the only one of the plotters who had to flee the country: this not from the vengeance and retribution of the government which he had attempted to dismember, but from the furious revulsion of his late confederates now frantic for their own safety. He was not expelled from the United States, he talked himself countryless, his expulsion due not to the treason but to his having been so vocal and vociferant in the conduct of it, burning each bridge vocally behind him before he had even reached the place to build the next one: so that it was no provost marshal nor even a civic agency but his late coplotters themselves who put afoot the movement to evict him from Kentucky and the United States and, if they had caught him, probably from the world too. Fled by night, running true to family tradition, with his son and the old claymore and the tartan.

JASON LYCURGUS.   Who, driven perhaps by the compulsion of the flamboyant name given him by the sardonic embittered woodenlegged indomitable father who perhaps still believed with his heart that what he wanted to be was a classicist schoolteacher, rode up the Natchez Trace one day in 1811 with a pair of fine pistols and one meagre saddlebag on a small lightwaisted but stronghocked mare which could do the first two furlongs in definitely under the halfminute and the next two in not appreciably more, though that was all. But it was enough: who reached the Chickasaw Agency at Okatoba (which in 1860 was still called Old Jefferson) and went no further. Who within six months was the Agent's clerk and within

5. James Wilkinson (1757–1825): brigadier general who represented the U.S. in the Louisiana Purchase (1803); he was tried for his part in the Aaron Burr conspiracy but was acquitted.

twelve his partner, officially still the clerk though actually halfowner of what was now a considerable store stocked with the mare's winnings in races against the horses of Ikkemotubbe's young men which he, Compson, was always careful to limit to a quarter or at most three furlongs; and in the next year it was Ikkemotubbe who owned the little mare and Compson owned the solid square mile of land which someday would be almost in the center of the town of Jefferson, forested then and still forested twenty years later though rather a park than a forest by that time, with its slavequarters and stables and kitchengardens and the formal lawns and promenades and pavilions laid out by the same architect who built the columned porticoed house furnished by steamboat from France and New Orleans, and still the square intact mile in 1840 (with not only the little white village called Jefferson beginning to enclose it but an entire white county about to surround it because in a few years now Ikkemotubbe's descendants and people would be gone, those remaining living not as warriors and hunters but as white men—as shiftless farmers or, here and there, the masters of what they too called plantations and the owners of shiftless slaves, a little dirtier than the white man, a little lazier, a little crueller—until at last even the wild blood itself would have vanished, to be seen only occasionally in the noseshape of a Negro on a cottonwagon or a white sawmill hand or trapper or locomotive fireman), known as the Compson Domain then, since now it was fit to breed princes, statesmen and generals and bishops, to avenge the dispossessed Compsons from Culloden and Carolina and Kentucky, then known as the Governor's house because sure enough in time it did produce or at least spawn a governor—Quentin MacLachan again, after the Culloden grandfather—and still known as the Old Governor's even after it had spawned (1861) a general—(called so by predetermined accord and agreement by the whole town and county, as though they knew even then and beforehand that the old governor was the last Compson who would not fail at everything he touched save longevity or suicide)—the Brigadier Jason Lycurgus II who failed at Shiloh in '62 and failed again though not so badly at Resaca in '64, who put the first mortgage on the still intact square mile to a New England carpetbagger in '66, after the old town had been burned by the Federal General Smith and the new little town, in time to be populated mainly by the descendants not of Compsons but of Snopeses,[6] had begun to encroach and then nibble at and into it as the failed brigadier spent the next forty years selling fragments of it off to keep up the mortgage on the remainder: until one day in

6. Members of the Snopes clan play prominent roles in Faulkner's fiction, but particularly in *The Hamlet*, *The Town*, and *The Mansion*.

1900 he died quietly on an army cot in the hunting and fishing camp in the Tallahatchie River bottom where he passed most of the end of his days.

And even the old governor was forgotten now; what was left of the old square mile was now known merely as the Compson place— the weedchoked traces of the old ruined lawns and promenades, the house which had needed painting too long already, the scaling columns of the portico where Jason III (bred for a lawyer and indeed he kept an office upstairs above the Square, where entombed in dusty filingcases some of the oldest names in the county—Holston and Sutpen, Grenier and Beauchamp and Coldfield—faded year by year among the bottomless labyrinths of chancery: and who knows what dream in the perennial heart of his father, now completing the third of his three avatars—the one as son of a brilliant and gallant statesman, the second as battleleader of brave and gallant men, the third as a sort of privileged pseudo–Daniel Boone–Robinson Crusoe, who had not returned to juvenility because actually he had never left it—that that lawyer's office might again be the anteroom to the governor's mansion and the old splendor) sat all day long with a decanter of whiskey and a litter of dogeared Horaces and Livys and Catulluses,[7] composing (it was said) caustic and satiric eulogies on both his dead and his living fellowtownsmen, who sold the last of the property, except that fragment containing the house and the kitchengarden and the collapsing stables and one servant's cabin in which Dilsey's family lived, to a golfclub for the ready money with which his daughter Candace could have her fine wedding in April and his son Quentin could finish one year at Harvard and commit suicide in the following June of 1910; already known as the Old Compson place even while Compsons were still living in it on that spring dusk in 1928 when the old governor's doomed lost nameless seventeen-year-old greatgreatgranddaughter robbed her last remaining sane male relative (her uncle Jason IV) of his secret hoard of money and climbed down a rainpipe and ran off with a pitchman in a travelling streetshow, and still known as the Old Compson place long after all traces of Compsons were gone from it: after the widowed mother died and Jason IV, no longer needing to fear Dilsey now, committed his idiot brother, Benjamin, to the State Asylum in Jackson and sold the house to a countryman who operated it as a boarding house for juries and horse- and muletraders, and still known as the Old Compson place even after the boardinghouse (and presently the golfcourse too) had vanished and

7. Catullus (Gaius Valerius Catullus), ca.84–ca.54 B.C.E., a Roman poet and epigrammatist; Horace (Quintus Horatius Flaccus), 65–8 B.C.E., a Roman poet; Livy (Titus Livius), 59 B.C.E.–17 C.E., a Roman historian.

the old square mile was even intact again in row after row of small crowded jerrybuilt individuallyowned demiurban bungalows.

And these:

QUENTIN III.   Who loved not his sister's body but some concept of Compson honor precariously and (he knew well) only temporarily supported by the minute fragile membrane of her maidenhead as a miniature replica of all the whole vast globy earth may be poised on the nose of a trained seal. Who loved not the idea of the incest which he would not commit, but some presbyterian concept of its eternal punishment: he, not God, could by that means cast himself and his sister both into hell, where he could guard her forever and keep her forevermore intact amid the eternal fires. But who loved death above all, who loved only death, loved and lived in a deliberate and almost perverted anticipation of death as a lover loves and deliberately refrains from the waiting willing friendly tender incredible body of his beloved, until he can no longer bear not the refraining but the restraint and so flings, hurls himself, relinquishing, drowning. Committed suicide in Cambridge Massachusetts, June 1910, two months after his sister's wedding, waiting first to complete the current academic year and so get the full value of his paid—in-advance tuition, not because he had his old Culloden and Carolina and Kentucky grandfathers in him but because the remaining piece of the old Compson mile which had been sold to pay for his sister's wedding and his year at Harvard had been the one thing, excepting that same sister and the sight of an open fire, which his youngest brother, born an idiot, had loved.

CANDACE (CADDY).   Doomed and knew it, accepted the doom without either seeking or fleeing it. Loved her brother despite him, loved not only him but loved in him that bitter prophet and inflexible corruptless judge of what he considered the family's honor and its doom, as he thought he loved but really hated in her what he considered the frail doomed vessel of its pride and the foul instrument of its disgrace; not only this, she loved him not only in spite of but because of the fact that he himself was incapable of love, accepting the fact that he must value above all not her but the virginity of which she was custodian and on which she placed no value whatever: the frail physical stricture which to her was no more than a hangnail would have been. Knew the brother loved death best of all and was not jealous, would (and perhaps in the calculation and deliberation of her marriage did) have handed him the hypothetical hemlock. Was two months pregnant with another man's child which regardless of what its sex would be she had already named Quentin after the brother whom they both (she and her brother) knew was already the same as dead, when she married (1910) an extremely eligible young Indianian she and her mother had met while vacationing at French Lick the summer before. Divorced by him 1911. Married 1920 to a minor movingpicture magnate, Hollywood California. Divorced by mutual agreement, Mexico 1925. Vanished in Paris with the German occupation, 1940, still beautiful and probably still wealthy too since she did not look within fifteen years of her actual fortyeight, and was not heard of again. Except there was a woman in Jefferson, the county librarian, a mousesized and -colored woman who had never married, who had passed through the city schools in the same class with Candace Compson and then spent the rest of her life trying to keep *Forever Amber* in its orderly overlapping avatars and *Jurgen* and *Tom Jones*[8] out of the hands of the highschool juniors and seniors who could reach them down without even having to tip-toe from the back shelves where she herself would have to stand on a box to hide them. One day in 1943, after a week of a distraction bordering on disintegration almost, during which those entering the library would find her always in the act of hurriedly closing her desk drawer and turning the key in it (so that the matrons, wives of the bankers and doctors and lawyers, some of whom had also been in that old highschool class, who came and went in the afternoons with the copies of the *Forever Ambers* and the volumes of Thorne Smith[9] carefully wrapped from view in sheets of Memphis and Jackson newspapers, believed she was on the verge of illness or perhaps even loss of mind) she closed and locked the library in the middle of the afternoon and with her handbag clasped tightly under her arm and two feverish spots of determination in her ordinarily colorless cheeks, she entered the farmers' supply store where Jason IV had started as a clerk and where he now owned his own business as a buyer of and dealer in cotton, striding on through that gloomy cavern which only men ever entered—a cavern cluttered and walled and stalagmitehung with plows and discs and loops of tracechain and singletrees and mulecollars and sidemeat and cheap shoes and horselinament and flour and molasses, gloomy because the goods it contained were not shown but hidden rather since those who supplied Mississippi farmers or at least Negro Mississippi farmers for a share of the crop did not wish, until that crop was made and its value approximately computable, to

---

8. *Forever Amber*, a novel by Kathleen Winsor, published in 1944 and banned in Boston as obscene; *Jurgen*, a sensational novel by James Branch Cabell, published in 1919; *Tom Jones, a Foundling*, by Henry Fielding, published in 1749—all novels which she regarded as scandalous.
9. Thorne Smith, a humorous writer, 1893–1934.

show them what they could learn to want but only to supply them on specific demand with what they could not help but need—and strode on back to Jason's particular domain in the rear: a railed enclosure cluttered with shelves and pigeonholes bearing spiked dust-and-lintgathering gin receipts and ledgers and cottonsamples and rank with the blended smell of cheese and kerosene and harnessoil and the tremendous iron stove against which chewed tobacco had been spat for almost a hundred years, and up to the long high sloping counter behind which Jason stood and, not looking again at the overalled men who had quietly stopped talking and even chewing when she entered, with a kind of fainting desperation she opened the handbag and fumbled something out of it and laid it open on the counter and stood trembling and breathing rapidly while Jason looked down at it—a picture, a photograph in color clipped obviously from a slick magazine—a picture filled with luxury and money and sunlight—a Cannebière[1] backdrop of mountains and palms and cypresses and the sea, an open powerful expensive chromium-trimmed sports car, the woman's face hatless between a rich scarf and a seal coat, ageless and beautiful, cold serene and damned; beside her a handsome lean man of middleage in the ribbons and tabs of a German staffgeneral—and the mousesized mousecolored spinster trembling and aghast at her own temerity, staring across it at the childless bachelor in whom ended that long line of men who had had something in them of decency and pride even after they had begun to fail at the integrity and the pride had become mostly vanity and selfpity: from the expatriate who had to flee his native land with little else except his life yet who still refused to accept defeat, through the man who gambled his life and his good name twice and lost twice and declined to accept that either, and the one who with only a clever small quarterhorse for tool avenged his dispossessed father and grandfather and gained a principality, and the brilliant and gallant governor and the general who though he failed at leading in battle brave and gallant men at least risked his own life too in the failing, to the cultured dipsomaniac who sold the last of his patrimony not to buy drink but to give one of his descendants at least the best chance in life he could think of.

'It's Caddy!' the librarian whispered. 'We must save her!'

'It's Cad, all right,' Jason said. Then he began to laugh. He stood there laughing above the picture, above the cold beautiful face now creased and dogeared from its week's sojourn in the desk drawer and the handbag. And the librarian knew why he was laughing, who had not called him anything but Mr Compson for thirty-two years now, ever since the day in 1911 when Candace, cast off by her husband,

---

1. Main street in Marseille, France.

had brought her infant daughter home and left the child and departed by the next train, to return no more, and not only the Negro cook, Dilsey, but the librarian too divined by simple instinct that Jason was somehow using the child's life and its illegitimacy both to blackmail the mother not only into staying away from Jefferson for the rest of her life but into appointing him sole unchallengeable trustee of the money she would send for the child's maintenance, and had refused to speak to him at all since that day in 1928 when the daughter climbed down the rainpipe and ran away with the pitchman.

'Jason!' she cried. 'We must save her! Jason! Jason!'—and still crying it even when he took up the picture between thumb and finger and threw it back across the counter toward her.

'That Candace?' he said. 'Dont make me laugh. This bitch aint thirty yet. The other one's fifty now.'

And the library was still locked all the next day too when at three oclock in the afternoon, footsore and spent yet still unflagging and still clasping the handbag tightly under her arm, she turned into a neat small yard in the Negro residence section of Memphis and mounted the steps of the neat small house and rang the bell and the door opened and a black woman of about her own age looked quietly out at her. 'It's Frony, isn't it?' the librarian said. 'Dont you remember me—Melissa Meek, from Jefferson—'

'Yes,' the Negress said. 'Come in. You want to see Mama.' And she entered the room, the neat yet cluttered bedroom of an old Negro, rank with the smell of old people, old women, old Negroes, where the old woman herself sat in a rocker beside the hearth where even though it was June a fire smoldered—a big woman once, in faded clean calico and an immaculate turban wound round her head above the bleared and now apparently almost sightless eyes—and put the dogeared clipping into the black hands which, like the women of her race, were still as supple and delicately shaped as they had been when she was thirty or twenty or even seventeen.

'It's Caddy!' the librarian said. 'It is! Dilsey! Dilsey!'

'What did he say?' the old Negress said. And the librarian knew whom she meant by 'he', nor did the librarian marvel, not only that the old Negress would know that she (the librarian) would know whom she meant by the 'he', but that the old Negress would know at once that she had already shown the picture to Jason.

'Dont you know what he said?' she cried. 'When he realised she was in danger, he said it was her, even if I hadn't even had a picture to show him. But as soon as he realised that somebody, anybody, even just me, wanted to save her, would try to save her, he said it wasn't. But it is! Look at it!'

'Look at my eyes,' the old Negress said. 'How can I see that picture?'

'Call Frony!' the librarian cried. 'She will know her!' But already the old Negress was folding the clipping carefully back into its old creases, handing it back.

'My eyes aint any good anymore,' she said. 'I cant see it.'

And that was all. At six oclock she fought her way through the crowded bus terminal, the bag clutched under one arm and the return half of her roundtrip ticket in the other hand, and was swept out onto the roaring platform on the diurnal tide of a few middle-aged civilians but mostly soldiers and sailors enroute either to leave or to death and the homeless young women, their companions, who for two years now had lived from day to day in pullmans and hotels when they were lucky and in daycoaches and busses and stations and lobbies and public restrooms when not, pausing only long enough to drop their foals in charity wards or policestations and then move on again, and fought her way into the bus, smaller than any other there so that her feet touched the floor only occasionally until a shape (a man in khaki; she couldn't see him at all because she was already crying) rose and picked her up bodily and set her into a seat next the window, where still crying quietly she could look out upon the fleeing city as it streaked past and then was behind and presently now she would be home again, safe in Jefferson where life lived too with all its incomprehensible passion and turmoil and grief and fury and despair, but here at six oclock you could close the covers on it and even the weightless hand of a child could put it back among its unfeatured kindred on the quiet eternal shelves and turn the key upon it for the whole and dreamless night. *Yes* she thought, crying quietly *that was it she didn't want to see it know whether it was Caddy or not because she knows Caddy doesn't want to be saved hasn't anything anymore worth being saved for nothing worth being lost that she can lose*

JASON IV.   The first sane Compson since before Culloden and (a childless bachelor) hence the last. Logical rational contained and even a philosopher in the old stoic tradition: thinking nothing whatever of God one way or the other and simply considering the police and so fearing and respecting only the Negro woman, his sworn enemy since his birth and his mortal one since that day in 1911 when she too divined by simple clairvoyance that he was somehow using his infant niece's illegitimacy to blackmail its mother, who cooked the food he ate. Who not only fended off and held his own with Compsons but competed and held his own with the Snopeses who took over the little town following the turn of the century as the Compsons and Sartorises and their ilk faded from it (no Snopes, but Jason Compson himself who as soon as his mother died— the niece had already climbed down the rainpipe and vanished so

Dilsey no longer had either of these clubs to hold over him—committed his idiot younger brother to the state and vacated the old house, first chopping up the vast oncesplendid rooms into what he called apartments and selling the whole thing to a countryman who opened a boardinghouse in it), though this was not difficult since to him all the rest of the town and the world and the human race too except himself were Compsons, inexplicable yet quite predictable in that they were in no sense whatever to be trusted. Who, all the money from the sale of the pasture having gone for his sister's wedding and his brother's course at Harvard, used his own niggard savings out of his meagre wages as a storeclerk to send himself to a Memphis school where he learned to class and grade cotton, and so established his own business with which, following his dipsomaniac father's death, he assumed the entire burden of the rotting family in the rotting house, supporting his idiot brother because of their mother, sacrificing what pleasures might have been the right and just due and even the necessity of a thirty-year-old bachelor, so that his mother's life might continue as nearly as possible to what it had been; this not because he loved her but (a sane man always) simply because he was afraid of the Negro cook whom he could not even force to leave, even when he tried to stop paying her weekly wages; and who despite all this, still managed to save almost three thousand dollars ($2840.50) as he reported it on the night his niece stole it; in niggard and agonised dimes and quarters and halfdollars, which hoard he kept in no bank because to him a banker too was just one more Compson, but hid in a locked bureau drawer in his bedroom whose bed he made and changed himself since he kept the bedroom door locked all the time save when he was passing through it. Who, following a fumbling abortive attempt by his idiot brother on a passing female child, had himself appointed the idiot's guardian without letting their mother know and so was able to have the creature castrated before the mother even knew it was out of the house, and who following the mother's death in 1933 was able to free himself forever not only from the idiot brother and the house but from the Negro woman too, moving into a pair of offices up a flight of stairs above the supplystore containing his cotton ledgers and samples, which he had converted into a bedroom-kitchen-bath, in and out of which on weekends there would be seen a big plain friendly brazen-haired pleasantfaced woman no longer very young, in round picture hats and (in its season) an imitation fur coat, the two of them, the middleaged cottonbuyer and the woman whom the town called, simply, his friend from Memphis, seen at the local picture show on Saturday night and on Sunday morning mounting the apartment stairs with paper bags from the grocer's containing loaves and eggs and oranges and cans of soup, domestic, uxorious, connubial, until the late afternoon bus carried her back to Memphis. He was emancipated now. He was free. 'In 1865,' he would say, 'Abe Lincoln freed the niggers from the Compsons. In 1933, Jason Compson freed the Compsons from the niggers.'

BENJAMIN.   Born Maury, after his mother's only brother: a handsome flashing swaggering workless bachelor who borrowed money from almost anyone, even Dilsey although she was a Negro, explaining to her as he withdrew his hand from his pocket that she was not only in his eyes the same as a member of his sister's family, she would be considered a born lady anywhere in any eyes. Who, when at last even his mother realised what he was and insisted weeping that his name must be changed, was rechristened Benjamin by his brother Quentin (Benjamin, our lastborn, sold into Egypt). Who loved three things: the pasture which was sold to pay for Candace's wedding and to send Quentin to Harvard, his sister Candace, firelight. Who lost none of them because he could not remember his sister but only the loss of her, and firelight was the same bright shape as going to sleep, and the pasture was even better sold than before because now he and TP could not only follow timeless along the fence the motions which it did not even matter to him were humanbeings swinging golfsticks, TP could lead them to clumps of grass or weeds where there would appear suddenly in TP's hand small white spherules which competed with and even conquered what he did not even know was gravity and all the immutable laws when released from the hand toward plank floor or smokehouse wall or concrete sidewalk. Gelded 1913. Committed to the State Asylum, Jackson 1933. Lost nothing then either because, as with his sister, he remembered not the pasture but only its loss, and firelight was still the same bright shape of sleep.

QUENTIN.   The last. Candace's daughter. Fatherless nine months before her birth, nameless at birth and already doomed to be unwed from the instant the dividing egg determined its sex. Who at seventeen, on the one thousand eight hundred ninetyfifth anniversary of the day before the resurrection of Our Lord, swung herself by a rainpipe from the window of the room in which her uncle had locked her at noon, to the locked window of his own locked and empty bedroom and broke a pane and entered the window and with the uncle's firepoker burst open the locked bureau drawer and took the money (it was not $2840.50 either, it was almost seven thousand dollars and this was Jason's rage, the red unbearable fury which on that night and at intervals recurring with little or no diminishment for the next five years, made him seriously believe would at some unwarned instant destroy him, kill him as instantaneously dead as a bullet or a lightningbolt: that although he had been robbed not of a mere petty three thousand dollars but of almost seven thousand he couldn't even tell anybody; because he had been robbed of seven thousand dollars instead of just three he could not only never receive justification—he did not want sympathy—from other men unlucky enough to have one bitch for a sister and another for a niece, he couldn't even go to the police; because he had lost four thousand dollars which did not belong to him he couldn't even recover the three thousand which did since those first four thousand dollars were not only the legal property of his niece as a part of the money supplied for her support and maintenance by her mother over the last sixteen years, they did not exist at all, having been officially recorded as expended and consumed in the annual reports he submitted to the district Chancellor, as required of him as guardian and trustee by his bondsmen: so that he had been robbed not only of his thievings but his savings too, and by his own victim; he had been robbed not only of the four thousand dollars which he had risked jail to acquire but of the three thousand which he had hoarded at the price of sacrifice and denial, almost a nickel and a dime at a time, over a period of almost twenty years: and this not only by his own victim but by a child who did it at one blow, without premeditation or plan, not even knowing or even caring how much she would find when she broke the drawer open; and now he couldn't even go to the police for help: he who had considered the police always, never given them any trouble, had paid the taxes for years which supported them in parasitic and sadistic idleness; not only that, he didn't dare pursue the girl himself because he might catch her and she would talk, so that his only recourse was a vain dream which kept him tossing and sweating on nights two and three and even four years after the event, when he should have forgotten about it: of catching her without warning, springing on her out of the dark, before she had spent all the money, and murder her before she had time to open her mouth) and climbed down the same rainpipe in the dusk and ran away with the pitchman who was already under sentence for bigamy. And so vanished; whatever occupation overtook her would have arrived in no chromium Mercedes; whatever snapshot would have contained no general of staff.

And that was all. These others were not Compsons. They were black:

TP. Who wore on Memphis's Beale Street the fine bright cheap intransigent clothes manufactured specifically for him by the owners of Chicago and New York sweatshops.

FRONY.   Who married a pullman porter and went to St Louis to live and later moved back to Memphis to make a home for her mother since Dilsey refused to go further than that.

LUSTER.   A man, aged 14. Who was not only capable of the complete care and security of an idiot twice his age and three times his size, but could keep him entertained.

DILSEY.
They endured.

WILLIAM FAULKNER

Address upon Receiving the Nobel Prize for Literature[†]

STOCKHOLM, DECEMBER 10, 1950

I feel that this award was not made to me as a man, but to my work—a life's work in the agony and sweat of the human spirit, not for glory and least of all for profit, but to create out of the materials of the human spirit something which did not exist before. So this award is only mine in trust. It will not be difficult to find a dedication for the money part of it commensurate with the purpose and significance of its origin. But I would like to do the same with the acclaim too, by using this moment as a pinnacle from which I might be listened to by the young men and women already dedicated to the same anguish and travail, among whom is already that one who will some day stand here where I am standing.

Our tragedy today is a general and universal physical fear so long sustained by now that we can even bear it. There are no longer problems of the spirit. There is only the question: When will I be blown up? Because of this, the young man or woman writing today has forgotten the problems of the human heart in conflict with itself which alone can make good writing because only that is worth writing about, worth the agony and the sweat.

He must learn them again. He must teach himself that the basest of all things is to be afraid; and, teaching himself that, forget it forever, leaving no room in his workshop for anything but the old

† From *Essays, Speeches, and Public Letters*, (New York: Modern Library, 2004) 119–21. First published in *New York Herald Tribune Book Review,* January 14, 1951. Copyright © 1950 by William Faulkner. Copyright renewed 1965, 2004 by Random House. Used by permission of W. W. Norton & Company, Inc., and Random House, an imprint of The Random House Publishing Group, a division of Random House LLC. All rights reserved.

verities and truths of the heart, the old universal truths lacking
which any story is ephemeral and doomed—love and honor and pity
and pride and compassion and sacrifice. Until he does so, he labors
under a curse. He writes not of love but of lust, of defeats in which
nobody loses anything of value, of victories without hope and, worst
of all, without pity or compassion. His griefs grieve on no universal
bones, leaving no scars. He writes not of the heart but of the glands.

Until he relearns these things, he will write as though he stood
among and watched the end of man. I decline to accept the end of
man. It is easy enough to say that man is immortal simply because
he will endure: that when the last ding-dong of doom has clanged
and faded from the last worthless rock hanging tideless in the last
red and dying evening, that even then there will still be one more
sound: that of his puny inexhaustible voice, still talking. I refuse to
accept this. I believe that man will not merely endure: he will prevail. He is immortal, not because he alone among creatures has an
inexhaustible voice, but because he has a soul, a spirit capable of
compassion and sacrifice and endurance. The poet's, the writer's,
duty is to write about these things. It is his privilege to help man
endure by lifting his heart, by reminding him of the courage and
honor and hope and pride and compassion and pity and sacrifice
which have been the glory of his past. The poet's voice need not
merely be the record of man, it can be one of the props, the pillars
to help him endure and prevail.

WILLIAM FAULKNER

Interview with Jean Stein[†]

*   *   *

FAULKNER: * * * Since none of my work has met my own standards,
I must judge it on the basis of that one which caused me the most
grief and anguish, as the mother loves the child who became the
thief or murderer more than the one who became the priest.

Q: What work is that?

FAULKNER: *The Sound and the Fury.* I wrote it five separate times,
trying to tell the story, to rid myself of the dream which would
continue to anguish me until I did. It's a tragedy of two lost

† Most of this interview took place in New York early in 1956. It was first published as the
twelfth in the series "The Art of Fiction" (No. 12) in *The Paris Review*, Spring 1956.
Reprinted by permission.

women: Caddy and her daughter. Dilsey is one of my own favorite characters, because she is brave, courageous, generous, gentle and honest. She's much more brave and honest and generous than me.

Q: How did *The Sound and the Fury* begin?

FAULKNER: It began with a mental picture. I didn't realize at the time it was symbolical. The picture was of the muddy seat of a little girl's drawers in a pear tree, where she could see through a window where her grandmother's funeral was taking place and report what was happening to her brothers on the ground below. By the time I explained who they were and what they were doing and how her pants got muddy, I realized it would be impossible to get all of it into a short story and that it would have to be a book. And then I realized the symbolism of the soiled pants, and that image was replaced by the one of the fatherless and motherless girl climbing down the drainpipe to escape from the only home she had, where she had never been offered love or affection or understanding.

I had already begun to tell it through the eyes of the idiot child, since I felt that it would be more effective as told by someone capable only of knowing what happened, but not why. I saw that I had not told the story that time. I tried to tell it again, the same story through the eyes of another brother. That was still not it. I told it for the third time through the eyes of the third brother. That was still not it. I tried to gather the pieces together and fill in the gaps by making myself the spokesman. It was still not complete, not until fifteen years after the book was published, when I wrote as an appendix to another book the final effort to get the story told and off my mind, so that I myself could have some peace from it. It's the book I feel tenderest towards. I couldn't leave it alone, and I never could tell it right, though I tried hard and would like to try again, though I'd probably fail again.

Q: What emotion does Benjy arouse in you?

FAULKNER: The only emotion I can have for Benjy is grief and pity for all mankind. You can't feel anything for Benjy because he doesn't feel anything. The only thing I can feel about him personally is concern as to whether he is believable as I created him. He was a prologue like the gravedigger in the Elizabethan dramas. He serves his purpose and is gone. Benjy is incapable of good and evil because he had no knowledge of good and evil.

Q: Could Benjy feel love?

FAULKNER: Benjy wasn't rational enough even to be selfish. He was an animal. He recognized tenderness and love though he could not have named them, and it was the threat to tenderness and love that caused him to bellow when he felt the change in Caddy. He no longer had Caddy; being an idiot he was not even aware that Caddy was missing. He knew only that something was wrong, which left a vacuum in which he grieved. He tried to fill that vacuum. The only thing was he had one of Caddy's discarded slippers. The slipper was his tenderness and love, which he could not have named, but he knew only that it was missing. He was dirty because he couldn't coordinate and because dirt meant nothing to him. He could no more distinguish between dirt and cleanliness than between good and evil. The slipper gave him comfort even though he no longer remembered the person to whom it had once belonged, any more than he could remember why he grieved. If Caddy had reappeared he probably would not have known her.

Q: Does the narcissus given to Benjy have some significance?

FAULKNER: The narcissus was given to Benjy to distract his attention. It was simply a flower which happened to be handy that fifth April.[1] It was not deliberate.

WILLIAM FAULKNER

Class Conferences at the University of Virginia†

From February to June of 1957 and 1958, William Faulkner was Writer-in-Residence at the University of Virginia under a grant from the Emily Clark Balch Fund for American Literature. The following interviews are excerpted from the texts of thirty-seven group conferences in which Faulkner participated. The tapes of these discussions are now housed in the Alderman Library of the University of Virginia.

---

1. The fourth section of The Sound and the Fury is actually dated April 8.

† From Faulkner in the University: Class Conferences at the University of Virginia, 1957–1958, ed. Frederick L. Gwynn and Joseph Blotner (New York: Vintage Books, Random House, 1965; Charlottesville: The University Press of Virginia, 1959, reprinted 1977), 1–3, 6, 63–64, 84–85. © 1995 by the Rector and Visitors of the University of Virginia. Reprinted by permission of the University of Virginia Press.

February 15, 1957

Session One

Graduate Course in American Fiction

* * *

Q: Mr. Faulkner, in *The Sound and the Fury* the first three sections of that book are narrated by one of the four Compson children, and in view of the fact that Caddy figures so prominently, is there any particular reason why you didn't have a section with—giving her views or impressions of what went on?

A: That's a good question. That—the explanation of that whole book is in that. It began with the picture of the little girl's muddy drawers, climbing that tree to look in the parlor window with her brothers that didn't have the courage to climb the tree waiting to see what she saw. And I tried first to tell it with one brother, and that wasn't enough. That was Section One. I tried with another brother, and that wasn't enough. That was Section Two. I tried the third brother, because Caddy was still to me too beautiful and too moving to reduce her to telling what was going on, that it would be more passionate to see her through somebody else's eyes, I thought. And that failed and I tried myself—the fourth section—to tell what happened, and I still failed.

. . .

Q: Speaking of Caddy, is there any way of getting her back from the clutches of the Nazis, where she ends up in the Appendix?

A: I think that that would be a betrayal of Caddy, that it is best to leave her where she is. If she were resurrected there'd be something a little shabby, a little anti-climactic about it, about this. Her tragedy to me is the best I could do with it—unless, as I said, I could start over and write the book again and that can't be.

. . .

Q: Mr. Faulkner, I am interested in the symbolism in *The Sound and the Fury*, and I wasn't able to figure exactly the significance of the shadow symbol in Quentin. It's referred to over and over again: he steps in the shadow, shadow is before him, the shadow is often after him. Well then, what is the significance of this shadow?

A.: That wasn't a deliberate symbolism. I would say that that shadow that stayed on his mind so much was foreknowledge of his own death, that he was—Death is here, shall I step into it, or shall I step away from it a little longer? I won't escape it, but shall I accept it now or shall I put it off until next Friday? I think that if it had any reason that must have been it.

* * *

Q: Mr. Faulkner, I'd like to ask you about Quentin and his relationship with his father. I think many readers get the impression that Quentin is the way he is to a large extent because of his father's lack of values, or the fact that he doesn't seem to pass down to his son many values that will sustain him. Do you think that Quentin winds up the way he does primarily because of that, or are we meant to see, would you say, that the action that comes primarily from what he is, abetted by what he gets from his father?

A: The action as portrayed by Quentin was transmitted to him through his father. There was a basic failure before that. The grandfather had been a failed brigadier twice in the Civil War. It was the—the basic failure Quentin inherited through his father, or beyond his father. It was a—something had happened somewhere between the first Compson and Quentin. The first Compson was a bold ruthless man who came into Mississippi as a free forester to grasp where and when he could and wanted to, and established what should have been a princely line, and that princely line decayed.

* * *

Q: Mr. Faulkner, I've been very much interested in what it seems to me you did—maybe you didn't—in *The Sound and the Fury*, in the character of Caddy. To me she is a very sympathetic character, perhaps the most sympathetic white woman in the book, and yet we get pictures of her only through someone else's comments and most of these comments are quite [?] and wouldn't lead you to admire her on the surface, and yet I do. Did you mean for us to have this feeling for Caddy, and if so, how did you go about reducing her to the negative picture we get of her?

A: To me she was the beautiful one, she was my heart's darling. That's what I wrote the book about and I used the tools which seemed to me the proper tools to try to tell, try to draw the picture of Caddy.

* * *

March 13, 1957

Session Eight

Undergraduate Course in Contemporary Literature

Q: What is your purpose in writing into the first section of *The Sound and the Fury* passages that seem disjointed in themselves if the idea is not connected with one another?

A: That was part of the failure. It seemed to me that the book approached nearer the dream if the groundwork of it was laid by the idiot, who was incapable of relevancy. That's—I agree with you too, that's a bad method, but to me it seemed the best way to do it, that I shifted those sections back and forth to see where they went best, but my final decision was that though that was not right, that was the best to do it, that was simply the groundwork for that story, as that idiot child saw it. He himself didn't know what he was seeing. That the only thing that held him into any sort of reality, into the world at all, was the trust that he had for his sister, that he knew that she loved him and would defend him, and so she was the whole world to him, and these things were flashes that were reflected on her as in a mirror. He didn't know what they meant.

*   *   *

April 15, 1957

Session Ten

Visitors from Virginia Colleges

*   *   *

Q: In that connection, did you write it in the order in which it was published?

A: Yes. . . . I wrote the Benjy part first. That wasn't good enough so I wrote the Quentin part. That still wasn't good enough. I let Jason try it. That still wasn't enough. I let Faulkner try it and that still wasn't enough, and so about twenty years afterward I wrote an appendix still trying to make that book what—match the dream.

*   *   *

Q: Then may I ask if all of these characters in *The Sound and the Fury*—that you would call them "good people"?

A: I would call them tragic people. The good people, Dilsey, the
Negro woman, she was a good human being. That she held that
family together for not the hope of reward but just because it was
the decent and proper thing to do.

*   *   *

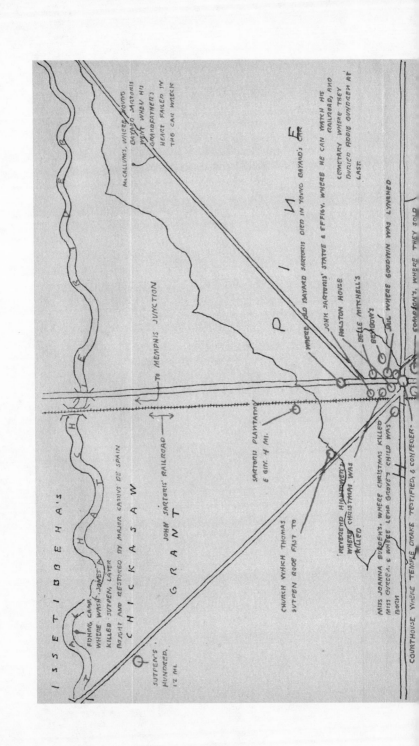

ISSETIBBEHA'S

FISHING CAMP
WHERE WASH JONES
KILLED SUTPEN, LATER
FOUGHT AND RESTORED BY MAJOR CASSIUS DE SPAIN

CHICKASAW

JOHN SARTORIS RAILROAD →

GRANT

→ To MEMPHIS JUNCTION

SUTPEN'S
HUNDRED,
12 MI.

SARTORIS PLANTATION
6 SIM. 4 MI.

CHURCH WHICH THOMAS
SUTPEN ROOF FAST TO

McCALLUMS, WHERE YOUNG
BAYARD SARTORIS
WENT WHEN HIS
GRANDFATHER'S
HEART FAILED IN
THE CAR WRECK

P I N E

WHERE OLD BAYARD SARTORIS DIED IN YOUNG BAYARD'S CAR

JOHN SARTORIS' STATUE & EFFIGY, WHERE HE CAN WATCH HIS
RAILROAD, AND
CEMETERY WHERE THEY
BURIED ADDIE BUNDREN AT
LAST

RALSTON HOUSE

BELLE MITCHELL'S

BENBOW'S

JAIL WHERE GOODWIN WAS LYNCHED

"REVEREND HIGHTOWER,"
WHERE CHRISTMAS WAS
KILLED

MISS JOANNA BURDEN'S, WHERE CHRISTMAS KILLED
MISS BURDEN & WHERE LENA GROVE'S CHILD WAS
BORN

COURTHOUSE WHERE TEMPLE DRAKE TESTIFIED, & CONFEDER-

COMPSON'S, WHERE THEY SOLD

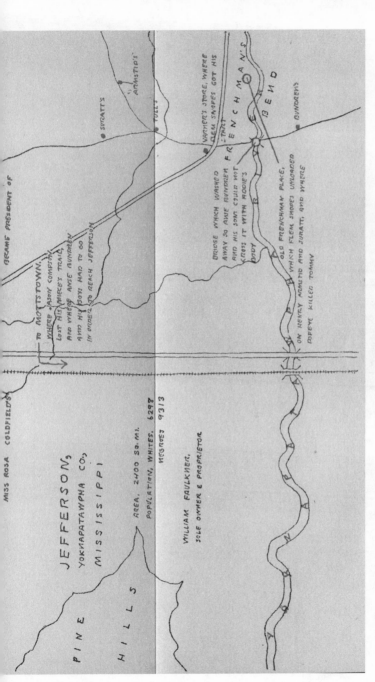

From *Absalom, Absalom!* (1936); rendered by William Faulkner. Reprinted by permission.

Cultural and Historical Contexts

Faulkner's work as a whole and *The Sound and the Fury* in particular must be read in two contexts at once: that of the international modernism of the early twentieth century, and that of American South, with all the peculiar institutions and particular burdens of its history. It's too simple to say that he uses the techniques of the one to define the meaning of the other—but for now let that judgment stand, if only as a point of departure. This section begins with C. Vann Woodward's classic statement on the distinctive character of the South as a region. It is the one part of the nation to experience the "bitter taste" of military defeat on its own soil, and in Woodward's judgment that history has produced an acute sense of the omnipresence of the past, along with a disbelief in the American creed of inevitable "progress and success." Brief excerpts from both Richard Gray and Faulkner's fellow Mississippian, William Alexander Percy, suggest the degree to which the novelist's period saw itself as living in an aftermath, a time of ghosts and ever-fading strength; Quentin Compson isn't alone in believing that he has come too late for everything. The Florida-born Lillian Smith was Faulkner's exact contemporary, and the chapter I've chosen from her 1949 autobiography, *Killers of the Dream,* describes the ideological constraints that Caddy Compson would have known and against which she rebelled.

Taken together, these writers define certain aspects of what, in his 1940 book of that title, W. J. Cash called "the mind of the South." They chart the white South's structure of feeling, the distinctive features of its consciousness. But what about consciousness itself? Faulkner has his peers in registering the flux and flow of human thought, but none of them—not Joyce or Woolf or Proust—have created characters whose minds are so troubled as that of Quentin, or as difficult to enter as that of his brother Benjy. I've provided selections from two important philosophers of mind, each of them central in shaping the way that Faulkner's contemporaries understood human consciousness, and each crucial in forming the modernist account of its workings. We have no firm evidence that Faulkner read either William James or Henri Bergson, though he did refer to the latter's *Creative Evolution* and described Quentin as cutting his psychology class at Harvard, where the work of the recently retired James held sway. Critics have long argued about the degree to which Faulkner's own representation of the inner life can be mapped onto either James or Bergson. Do the different ways that Benjy and Quentin trail their pasts behind them correspond to Bergson's sense of duration, or—given their extremity—do they perhaps deny it? What we ourselves cannot deny is that such ideas formed the zeitgeist within which Faulkner worked. These excerpts, then, can perhaps best serve as a provocation, a spur to discussion and debate.

C. VANN WOODWARD

The Irony of Southern History[†]

In a time when nationalism sweeps everything else before it, as it does at present, the regional historian is likely to be oppressed by a sense of his unimportance. America is the all-important subject, and national ideas, national institutions, and national policies are the themes that compel attention. Foreign peoples, eager to know what this New World colossus means to them and their immediate future, are impatient with details of regional variations, and Americans, intent on the need for national unity, tend to minimize their importance. New England, the West, and other regions are occasionally permitted to speak for the nation. But the South is thought to be hedged about with peculiarities that set it apart as unique. As a standpoint from which to write American history it is regarded as eccentric and, as a background for an historian, something of a handicap to be overcome.

Of the eccentric position of the South in the nation there are admittedly many remaining indications. I do not think, however, that this eccentricity need be regarded as entirely a handicap. In fact, I think that it could possibly be turned to advantage by the Southern historian, both in understanding American history and in interpreting it to non-Americans. For from a broader point of view it is not the South but America that is unique among the peoples of the world. This peculiarity arises out of the American legend of success and victory, a legend that is not shared by any other people of the civilized world. The collective will of this country has simply never known what it means to be confronted by complete frustration. Whether by luck, by abundant resources, by ingenuity, by technology, by organizing cleverness, or by sheer force of arms America has been able to overcome every major historic crisis—economic, political, or foreign—with which it has had to cope. This remarkable record has naturally left a deep imprint upon the American mind. It explains in large part the national faith in unlimited progress, in the efficacy of material means, in the importance of mass

† From *The Burden of Southern History* (Baton Rouge: Louisiana State UP, 1968), 187–91. Copyright © 1960 and 1968 by Louisiana State UP. Copyright © 1988 by C. Vann Woodward. Reprinted by permission of the publisher.

and speed, the worship of success, and the belief in the invincibility of American arms.

The legend has been supported by an unbroken succession of victorious wars. Battles have been lost, and whole campaigns—but not wars. In the course of their national history Americans, who have been called a bellicose though unmartial people, have fought eight wars, and so far without so much as one South African fiasco such as England encountered in the heyday of her power. This unique good fortune has isolated America, I think rather dangerously, from the common experience of the rest of mankind, all the great peoples of which have without exception known the bitter taste of defeat and humiliation. It has fostered the tacit conviction that American ideals, values, and principles inevitably prevail in the end. That conviction has never received a name, nor even so much explicit formulation as the old concept of Manifest Destiny. It is assumed, not discussed. And the assumption exposes us to the temptation of believing that we are somehow immune from the forces of history.

The country that has come nearest to approximating the American legend of success and victory is England. The nearness of continental rivals and the precariousness of the balance of power, however, bred in the English an historical sophistication that prevented the legend from flourishing as luxuriantly as it has in the American climate. Only briefly toward the end of the Victorian period did the legend threaten to get out of hand in England. Arnold J. Toynbee has recalled those piping days in a reminiscent passage. "I remember watching the Diamond Jubilee[1] procession myself as a small boy," he writes. "I remember the atmosphere. It was: well, here we are on the top of the world, and we have arrived at this peak to stay there—forever! There is, of course, a thing called history, but history is something unpleasant that happens to other people. We are comfortably outside all that. I am sure, if I had been a small boy in New York in 1897 I should have felt the same. Of course, if I had been a small boy in 1897 in the Southern part of the United States, I should not have felt the same; I should then have known from my parents that history had happened to my people in my part of the world."

The South has had its full share of illusions, fantasies, and pretensions, and it has continued to cling to some of them with an astonishing tenacity that defies explanation. But the illusion that "history is something unpleasant that happens to other people" is certainly not one of them—not in the face of accumulated evidence

---

1. Queen Victoria's Diamond Jubilee, 1896, celebrating the sixtieth anniversary of her ascent to the throne.

and memory to the contrary. It is true that there have been many
Southern converts to the gospel of progress and success, and there
was even a period following Reconstruction when it seemed possible that these converts might carry a reluctant region with them.
But the conversion was never anywhere near complete. Full participation in the legend of irresistible progress, success, and victory
could, after all, only be vicarious at best. For the inescapable facts
of history were that the South had repeatedly met with frustration
and failure. It had learned what it was to be faced with economic,
social, and political problems that refused to yield to all the ingenuity, patience, and intelligence that a people could bring to bear
upon them. It had learned to accommodate itself to conditions that
it swore it would never accept, and it had learned the taste left in
the mouth by the swallowing of one's own words. It had learned to
live for long decades in quite un-American poverty, and it had
learned the equally un-American lesson of submission. For the
South had undergone an experience that it could share with no
other part of America—though it is shared by nearly all the peoples
of Europe and Asia—the experience of military defeat, occupation,
and reconstruction. Nothing about this history was conducive to
the theory that the South was the darling of divine providence.

RICHARD J. GRAY

Fictions of History[†]

* * *

* * * Unlike the rest of the nation, the South had had the stunning
experience of military defeat and occupation. A whole generation of
young men had been wiped out: which is perhaps why so often in
Faulkner's narratives the living presences from the past, the keepers
of the rites who survive, are females. The men, on the other hand,
often only survive in memory and imagination: as spectres who
haunt subsequent generations with dreams of impossible daring and
glamour. Not only the dead survive in this form, however: the
Yoknapatawpha novels and stories are also populated by men—and,
to a lesser extent, women—whose experiences of war and occupation have effectively paralysed their imaginations, made it impossible for them to function as anything more than 'shadows not of flesh
and blood which had lived and died but of shadows in turn of what

† From *The Life of William Faulkner: A Critical Biography* (Cambridge, MA: Blackwell,
1996), 23–24. Copyright © Richard Gray, 1994, 1996. Reprinted with permission of
Blackwell Publishing Ltd.

were . . . shades too'. Time had become frozen for these people, even
more emphatically and traumatically than it tends to for any generation that has suffered the experience of total war. 'Many of the men
who survived that unnatural war', observed Walter Hines Page,

> unwittingly did us a greater hurt than the war itself. It gave
> every one of them the intensest experience of his life . . . Thus
> it stopped the thought of most of them as an earthquake stops
> a clock . . . they were dead men, most of them, moving among
> the living as ghosts; and yet as ghosts in a play, they held the
> stage.[1]

As a boy, Faulkner was growing up among people of the kind Page
describes here for whom, to quote Gavin Stevens, 'There's no such
thing as past'; and, significantly, he seems to have been provoked
to similar associations. A subtext of Page's account, which helps
him situate his feelings about the Civil War and his relationship to
them, is the famous speech from *Macbeth* v. v, beginning 'Tomorrow, and tomorrow, and tomorrow': in which Macbeth compares
life to 'a walking shadow' and to 'a poor player / That struts and
frets his hour upon the stage / And then is heard no more'. Nobody
who has read *The Sound and the Fury*, with its title (among other
things) borrowed from this speech, needs to be reminded of the
importance of the play for Faulkner. Not everyone, however, has
noticed that his most famous vocalization of the omnipresence of
the Civil War past in the Southern present is just as soaked in
intertextual references to *Macbeth* as Page's brief account is. In
Intruder in the Dust, Gavin Stevens, a lawyer of philosophical cast
of mind—modelled, in part, on Faulkner himself and, in part, on
his close friend and mentor, Phil Stone—observes that 'Yesterday
wont be over until tomorrow and tomorrow began ten thousand
years ago'; and this because 'for every Southern boy' there is the
dream of altering the course of Civil War battles and therefore
the course and consequences of the War itself. For them, Stevens
suggests, 'it hasn't happened yet, it hasn't even begun yet'. The passage has been frequently quoted, and for good reason: it encapsu-
lates Faulkner's sense of the interdependence and *mutually* effective
nature of past and present—in short, the dialectical nature of
history. What has been less often quoted, though, is the related
passage that follows, of which this is just a small part and the
conclusion:

---

1. Burton J. Hendrick, *The Life and Letters of Walter Hines Page*, 2 vols. (New York: Dou-
   bleday, Page & Co., 1926; rpt. 1992), vol. I, 91. Born in North Carolina, Page (1855–
   1918) became a New York–based journalist and publisher and was ambassador to Great
   Britain from 1913 until shortly before his death. [*Editor's note.*]

yesterday's sunset and yesterday's tea both are inextricable
from the scattered indestructible uninfusable grounds blown
through the endless corridors of tomorrow, into the shoes we
will have to walk in and even the sheets we will have (or try) to
sleep between: because you escape nothing, you flee nothing:
the pursuer is what is doing the running and tomorrow night is
nothing but one long sleepless wrestle with yesterday's omis-
sions and regrets.[2]

Insomnia, flight and pursuit, the endless passage of tomorrows
through which like a ghost 'you' continue to wrestle with the regrets
of yesterday: the allusions to the whole imaginative fabric of *Macbeth* are, of course, specific and appropriate to the voice that speaks
them. Gavin Stevens is a febrile, garrulous and yet introspective
man whose sense of frustration finds a convenient avenue of expression in familiar literary texts. But a more general point is being made
here too, about the way Southerners like Page and Faulkner, growing up in the region at the end of the nineteenth century, found
themselves surrounded by memories of a conflict that seemed to
compel imitation and reinvention. Those memories, apart from
nagging them, seemed to challenge the specifics of their own lives:
hence, perhaps, Faulkner's obsessive need to appropriate his own
forms of military glory, by casting himself in the role of pilot. Like
Macbeth, in fact, Southerners of Faulkner's generation felt themselves to be haunted by ghosts and, in effect, rendered impotent
by them. In their case, those ghosts came more from the general,
social and cultural past than from the personal, but the consequences were essentially the same. They felt denied the capacity for
meaningful action; they sought escape from the cunning passages
and contrived corridors of history but found, for the most part, no
way out.

* * *

---

2. William Faulkner, *Intruder in the Dust* (New York: Random House 1948; rpt. London
1949), 187–88.

WILLIAM ALEXANDER PERCY

From Lanterns on the Levee:
Recollections of a Planter's Son[†]

* * *

The desire to reminisce arises not so much I think from the number of years you may happen to have accumulated as from the number of those who meant most to you in life who have gone on the long journey. They were the bulwarks, the bright spires, the strong places. When they have gone, you are a little tired, you rest on your oars, you say to yourself: "There are no witnesses to my fine little fury, my minute heroic efforts. It is better to remember, to be sure of the good that was, rather than of the evil that is, to watch the spread and pattern of the game that is past rather than engage feebly in the present play. It was a stout world thus far, peopled with all manner of gracious and kindly and noble personages—these seem rather a pygmy tribe." After a while, particularly if you have cut no very splendid figure in the show, indulgence in this sort of communing becomes a very vice. With some addicts it takes the form of dreaming; silently—the best way, I fear—and these are mostly women; with others, of conversation, and these are mostly old men—very tiresome unless you are one too; but the most abandoned of the whole lot insist they must write it all down, and of them am I. So while the world I know is crashing to bits, and what with the noise and the cryings-out no man could hear a trumpet blast, much less an idle evening reverie, I will indulge a heart beginning to be fretful by repeating to it the stories it knows and loves of my own country and my own people. A pilgrim's script—one man's field-notes of a land not far but quite unknown—valueless except as that man loved the country he passed through and its folk, and except as he willed to tell the truth. How other, alas, than telling it!

* * *

As a class I suppose the Southern aristocrat is extinct, but what that class despised as vulgar and treasured as excellent is still

---

† From *Lanterns on the Levee: Recollections of a Planter's Son* (New York: Alfred A. Knopf, 1959), foreword, 62–63, 151, 153–54. Copyright 1941 by Alfred A. Knopf, a division of Random House, Inc. and renewed 1969 by LeRoy Pratt Percy. Used by permission of Alfred A. Knopf, a division of Random House, Inc. Percy (1885–1942) was a lawyer, landowner, and poet from Greenville, Mississippi, and uncle of the novelist Walker Percy. His father, LeRoy Percy (1860–1929), served in Washington from 1910–13 as one of Mississippi's senators before being defeated by the white supremacist demagogue James K. Vardaman. [*Editor's note.*]

despised and treasured by individuals scattered thickly from one end of the South to the other. Those individuals born into a world of tradesfolk are still aristocrats, with an uncanny ability to recognize their kind. Their distinguishing characteristic probably is that their hearts are set, not on the virtues which make surviving possible, but on those which make it worth while. They could drive tomorrow to the guillotine in Aunt Nana's shabby ante-bellum carriage with so bland and insolent an air that passing Fords would take to the alleys and a Rolls-Royce would stop dead in its tracks, realizing itself parvenu. Having neglected the virtues that have survival value, these charming people are on their way to extinction, while the vulgar are increasing and multiplying and prospering and will continue to do so until their children or their children's children, having attained security, will begin all over again to admire and cherish the forgotten virtues we were not strong enough to maintain. Perhaps in every age an aristocracy is dying and one is being born. In any event aristocratic virtues and standards themselves never die completely and never change at all. General Lee and Senator Lamar would have been at ease, even simpatico, with Pericles and Brutus and Sir Philip Sidney, as Washington was with Lafayette.

This is chilly comfort, however, to the living members of an aristocracy in the act of dying. Under the southern Valhalla the torch has been thrust, already the bastions have fallen. Watching the flames mount, we, scattered remnant of the old dispensation, smile scornfully, but grieve in our hearts. A side-show Götterdämmerung perhaps, yet who shall inherit our earth, the earth we loved? The meek? The Hagens?[1] In either event, we accept, but we do not approve.

My generation, inured to doom, wears extinction with a certain wry bravado, but it is just as well the older ones we loved are gone. They had lived, for the most part, through tragedy into poverty, which can be and usually is accomplished with dignity and a certain fine disdain. But when the last act is vulgarity, it is as hateful and confused a show as *Troilus and Cressida*.[2]

* * *

A few weeks before election day, coming back together from a hard week, Father asked me: "What do you think of it?" and I had to answer: "Not a chance." He smiled a little and said: "Right." The

1. Hagen is a thieving, treacherous figure from Norse mythology, who figures especially in Richard Wagner's 1876 opera *Götterdämmerung*. [*Editor's note.*]
2. Shakespearian tragedy (circa 1602) about the Trojan war, known for its jarring mixture of tone. [*Editor's note.*]

night the polls were closed and all Mississippi was counting ballots, Father, Mother, and I felt so relieved to be at last from under the long humiliating strain that we went to bed early and slept soundly. Father was not only defeated, but overwhelmingly. Thus at twenty-seven I became inured to defeat: I have never since expected victory.

* * *

Perhaps it is a strengthening experience to see evil triumphant, valor and goodness in the dust. But whatever the value of the experience, it is one that comes sooner or later to anyone who dares face facts. Mine came sooner because of Father's defeat. Since then I haven't expected that what should be would be and I haven't believed that virtue guaranteed any reward except itself. The good die when they should live, the evil live when they should die; heroes perish and cowards escape; noble efforts do not succeed because they are noble, and wickedness is not consumed in its own nature. Looking at truth is not at first a heartening experience—it becomes so, if at all, only with time, with infinite patience, and with the luck of a little personal happiness. When I first saw defeat as the result of a man's best efforts, I didn't like the sight, and it struck me that someone had bungled and perhaps it wasn't man.

* * *

LILLIAN SMITH

The Lessons[†]

It began so long ago, not only in the history books but in our childhood. We southerners learned our first three lessons too well.

I do not think our mothers were aware that they were teaching us lessons. It was as if they were revolving mirrors reflecting life outside the home, inside their memory, outside the home, and we were spectators entranced by the bright and terrible images we saw there. The mirror might be luminous or streaked, or so dimmed that reflections were no more than shadows, but we learned from this

† From *Killers of the Dream* (1949; rpt. New York: W. W. Norton, 1994), 83–90. Copyright © 1949, 1961 by Lillian Smith. Copyright renewed 1994 by Margaret Rose. Reprinted with permission of W. W. Norton & Company, Inc., and by McIntosh & Otis, Inc. Born in Florida, the daughter of a mill owner, Smith (1897–1966) was a writer, feminist, and fierce opponent of Jim Crow best known for *Strange Fruit* (1944), a novel about interracial romance. She also wrote *Now Is the Time* (1955), on school desegregation, and *Our Faces, Our Words* (1964) on the nonviolent resistance of the civil rights movement.

preview of the world we were born into, what was expected of us as human creatures.

We were taught in this way to love God, to love our white skin, and to believe in the sanctity of both. We learned at the same time to fear God and to think of Him as having complete power over our lives. As we were beginning to feel this power and to see it reflected in our parents, we were learning also to fear a power that was in our body and to fear dark people who were everywhere around us, though the ones who came into our homes we were taught to love.

By the time we were five years old we had learned, without hearing the words, that masturbation is wrong and segregation is right, and each had become a dread taboo that must never be broken, for we believed God, whom we feared and tried desperately to love, had made the rules concerning not only Him and our parents, but our bodies and Negroes. Therefore when we as small children crept over the race line and ate and played with Negroes or broke other segregation customs known to us, we felt the same dread fear of consequences, the same overwhelming guilt we felt when we crept over the sex line and played with our body, or thought thoughts about God or our parents that we knew we must not think. Each was a "sin," each "deserved punishment," each would receive it in this world or the next. Each was tied up with the other and all were tied close to God.

These were our first lessons. Wrapped together, they were taught us by our mother's voice, memorized with her love, patted into our lives as she rocked us to sleep or fed us. As the years passed, we learned other lessons and discovered interesting ways of cheating on them but these first rules of our life were sacred. They were taboos which we dared not break. Yet we did break them, for it was impossible to observe them. We broke the rules and told ourselves we had kept them. We were not liars; we were human, and only used the ways the human mind has of meeting an insoluble problem. We believed certain acts were so wrong that they must never be committed and then we committed them and denied to ourselves that we had done so. It worked very well. Our minds had split: hardly more than a crack at first, but we began in those early years a two-leveled existence which we have since managed quite smoothly.

The acts which we later learned were "bad" never seemed really "bad" to us; at least we could find excuses for them. But those we learned were "bad" before we were five years old were CRIMES that we could not excuse; we could only forget. Though many a southerner has lived a tough hardened life since the days his mother rocked him until his eyes were glazed with sleep, his anxiety is, even now, concerned largely with the moral junk pile which he wandered around in when a little child. But more important perhaps than the ethical residue left in our minds was the process of this learning which gave our emotions their Gothic curves.

Our first lesson about God made the deepest impression on us. We were told that He loved us, and then we were told that He would burn us in everlasting flames of hell if we displeased Him. We were told we should love Him for He gives us everything good that we have, and then we were told we should fear Him because He has the power to do evil to us whenever He cares to. We learned from this part of the lesson another: that "people," like God and parents, can love you and hate you at the same time; and though they may love you, if you displease them they may do you great injury; hence being loved by them does not give you protection from being harmed by them. We learned that They (parents) have a "right" to act in this way because God does, and that They in a sense represent God, in the family.

Sometimes, when we felt weakened by anxieties that we had no words for, and battered by impulses impossible to act out, we tried to believe that God was responsible for this miserable state of affairs and one should not be too angry with parents. At least we thought this as we grew older and it helped some of us make a far more harmonious adjustment to our parents than to God.

As the years passed, God became the mighty protagonist of ambivalence although we had not heard the word. He loomed before us as the awesome example of one who injures, even destroys, in the name of "good" those whom He loves, and does it because He has the "right" to. We tried to think of Him as our best friend because we were told that He was. Weak with fear, we told ourselves that when you break the rules you "should be punished" by Him or your parents. But a doubt, an earthy animal shrewdness, whispered that anyone who would harm us was also our enemy. Yet these whispers we dared not say aloud, or clearly to ourselves, for we feared we might drop dead if we did. Even a wispy thought or two loaded us down with unbearable guilt. As we grew older and began to value reason and knowledge and compassion, we were told that He was wise and all-loving; yet He seemed from Old Testament stories to be full of whimsies and terrifying impulses and definitely not One whom a child could talk to and expect to receive an understanding reply from.

He was Authority. And we bowed before His power with that pinched quietness of children, stoically resigning ourselves to this Force as it was interpreted by the grown folks.

But life seemed a lost battle to many of us only after we learned the lesson on the Unpardonable Sin. Then it was that man's fate, our fate certainly, was sealed. According to this lesson, received mainly at revival meetings but graven on our hearts by our parents' refusal to deny it, God forgave, if we prayed hard and piteously enough, all sins but one. This one sin "against the Holy Ghost" He would never forgive. Committing it, one lived forever among the damned. What this sin was, what the "Holy Ghost" was, no one seemed to know. Or perhaps even grown folks dared not say it aloud. But the implication was—and this was made plain—that if you did not tread softly you would commit it; the best way was never to question anything but always accept what you were told.

Love and punishment . . . redemption and the unpardonable sin. . . . He who would not harm a sparrow would burn little children in everlasting flames. . . . It added up to a terrible poetry and we learned each line by heart.

Our second lesson had to do with the body. A complicated and bewildering lesson—taught us as was our theology, in little slivers and by the unfinished sentence method. But we learned it as we learned all the rest, knowing they were important because of the anxious tones in which they were taught. This lesson, translated into words, went something like this:

"God has given you a body which you must keep clean and healthy by taking baths, eating food, exercising, and having daily elimination. It is good also to take pride in developing skills such as baseball and swimming and fighting, and natural to think a little about the clothes you wear. But the body itself is a Thing of Shame and you must never show its nakedness to anyone except to the doctor when you are sick. Indeed, you should not look at it much yourself, especially in mirrors. It is true that in a sense your body is 'yours' but it isn't yours to feel at home with. It is God's holy temple and must never be desecrated by pleasures—except the few properly introduced to you—though pain, however repulsive, you must accept as having a right to enter this temple as one accepts visits from disagreeable relatives.

"Now, parts of your body are segregated areas which you must stay away from and keep others away from. These areas you touch only when necessary. In other words, you cannot associate freely with them any more than you can associate freely with colored children.

"Especially must you be careful about what enters your body. Many things are prohibited. Among these, probably the easiest to talk about is alcohol. 'Drinking' is a symbol of an evil that begins so early in life that it may be 'inherited,' for one who 'drinks' moves almost from milk bottle to whisky bottle, from the shaky legs of a child to the shaky legs of a drunk. The word *prohibition* means a movement to prohibit strong drink but every one knows that stronger temptations are prohibited with it, just as one knows that *segregation* also shuts one away from irresistible evils. Indeed, prohibition and segregation have much to do with each other, for there are the same mysterious reasons for both of these restrictions. Food, however, is not restricted; you may eat it with a clear conscience and whenever you are hungry.

"As you are beginning to see, what enters and leaves the doors of your body is the essence of morality. Yet if you are a little girl, you should not be aware that there are certain doors. So this question of where babies come from turns into a complicated matter since it concerns both a private entrance and a semi-public exit which each human being has to make but no one wants to remember. It is true that girls are quite involved in this since most of them will some day be mothers but it is better just now for you (whether boy or girl) to accept the idea that storks bring babies, or if you prefer, that they are found in the doctor's bag. At least accept it until you are grown and can face up to the ugliness of the whole business of creation. (I have at moments wondered if moralists had only morals at heart or if they had also the self-esteem of little males in mind when they hid from children the facts of life, fearing perhaps that little females might over-value their role in this drama of creation and, turning 'uppity' as we say in Dixie, forget their inferior place in the scheme of things.)

"The truth of the matter is: the world is full of secrets and the most important are concerned with you and the feelings that roam around in you. The better part of valor is to accept these secrets and never try to find out what they are. Simply remember that morality is based on this mysterious matter of entrances and exits, and Sin hovers over all doors. Also, the Authorities are watching.

"Now, on the other hand, though your body is a thing of shame and mystery, and curiosity about it is not good, your skin is your glory and the source of your strength and pride. It is white. And, as you have heard, whiteness is a symbol of purity and excellence. Remember this: Your white skin proves that you are better than all other people on this earth. Yes, it does that. And does it simply because it is white—which, in a way, is a kind of miracle. But the Bible is full of miracles and it should not be too difficult for us to accept one more." (Southern children did not learn until years later that no one had thought much about skin color until three or four centuries ago when white folks set out from Europe to explore the earth. Nor did they know until they were grown that men in Europe and America had written books about it and a racial philosophy had developed from it which "proved" this Ptolemaic regress in which the white man was the center of the universe and all other races revolved around him in concentric circles. The racists "proved" the white man's superiority, especially the white Christian's, just as

Ptolemy long before them had proved that the earth was the center of the universe, and as the theologians of the Middle Ages proved that angels danced on the point of needles, and as Communists prove their fascinating theories that the world and all within it revolve around Marxist economics.)

"Since this is so," our lesson continued, "your skin color is a Badge of Innocence which you can wear as vaingloriously as you please because God gave it to you and hence it is good and right. It gives you priorities over colored people everywhere in the world, and especially those in the South, in matters of where you sit and stand, what part of town you live in, where you eat, the theaters you go to, the swimming pools you use, jobs, the people you love, and so on. But these matters you will learn more about as you grow older."

Exaggerated? Perhaps. Whenever one puts a belief, a way of life, into quick words of course one exaggerates. Distortion, condensation, displacement are used not only by artists and dreamers; they are used every time we speak aloud. Yet when we thought about it at all we southerners came close, in our thinking, to what I have put down here.

This process of learning was as different for each child as were his parents' vocabulary and emotional needs. We cannot wisely forget this. And we learned far more from acts than words, more from a raised eyebrow, a joke, a shocked voice, a withdrawing movement of the body, a long silence, than from long sentences. But however skillfully our grown-up minds have found euphemisms to cover brutalities and gaucheries, however widely we now separate in our memory one lesson from another to avoid their chilling implications, we accepted with scarcely a differing shade of emphasis the lesson outlines sketched here.

The lesson on segregation was only a logical extension of the lessons on sex and white superiority and God. Not only Negroes but everything dark, dangerous, evil must be pushed to the rim of one's life. Signs put over doors in the world outside and over minds seemed natural enough to children like us, for signs had already been put over forbidden areas of our body. The banning of people and books and ideas did not appear more shocking than the banning of our wishes which we learned early to send to the Dark-town of our unconscious. But we clung to the belief, as an unhappy child treasures a beloved toy, that our white skin made us "better" than all other people. And this belief comforted us, for we felt worthless and weak when confronted by Authorities who had cheapened nearly all that we held dear, except our skin color. There, in the Land of Epidermis, every one of us was a little king.

*   *   *

WILLIAM JAMES

The Stream of Consciousness[†]

* * *

The first and foremost concrete fact which everyone will affirm to belong to his inner experience is the fact that *consciousness of some sort goes on*. *'States of mind' succeed each other in him*. If we could say in English 'it thinks,' as we say 'it rains' or 'it blows,' we should be stating the fact most simply and with the minimum of assumption. As we cannot, we must simply say that *thought goes on*.

Four Characters in Consciousness.—How does it go on? We notice immediately four important characters in the process, of which it shall be the duty of the present chapter to treat in a general way:

1. Every 'state' tends to be part of a personal consciousness.
2. Within each personal consciousness states are always changing.
3. Each personal consciousness is sensibly continuous.
4. It is interested in some parts of its object to the exclusion of others, and welcomes or rejects—*chooses* from among them, in a word—all the while.

* * *

Consciousness is in constant change. I do not mean by this to say that no one state of mind has any duration—even if true, that would be hard to establish. What I wish to lay stress on is this, that *no state once gone can recur and be identical with what it was before*. Now we are seeing, now hearing; now reasoning, now willing; now recollecting, now expecting; now loving, now hating; and in a hundred other ways we know our minds to be alternately engaged. But all these are complex states, it may be said, produced by combination of simpler ones;—do not the simpler ones follow a different law? Are not the *sensations* which we get from the same object, for example, always the same? Does not the same piano-key, struck with the same force, make us hear in the same way? Does not the same grass give us the same feeling of green, the same sky the same feeling of blue, and do we not get the same olfactory sensation no matter how many times we put our nose to the same flask of cologne? It

† From *Psychology: The Briefer Course* (1892); rpt. in William James, *Writings 1878–1899* (New York: The Library of America, 1992), 152–65. William James (1842–1910), American philosopher and psychologist, Harvard professor, and brother of the novelist Henry James; he also wrote *The Varieties of Religious Experience* (1902) and *Pragmatism* (1907).

seems a piece of metaphysical sophistry to suggest that we do not; and yet a close attention to the matter shows that *there is no proof that an incoming current ever gives us just the same bodily sensation twice.*

What is got twice is the same OBJECT. We hear the same *note* over and over again; we see the same *quality* of green, or smell the same objective perfume, or experience the same *species* of pain. The realities, concrete and abstract, physical and ideal, whose permanent existence we believe in, seem to be constantly coming up again before our thought, and lead us, in our carelessness, to suppose that our 'ideas' of them are the same ideas. * * * The grass out of the window now looks to me of the same green in the sun as in the shade, and yet a painter would have to paint one part of it dark brown, another part bright yellow, to give its real sensational effect. We take no heed, as a rule; of the different way in which the same things look and sound and smell at different distances and under different circumstances. The sameness of the *things* is what we are concerned to ascertain; and any sensations that assure us of that will probably be considered in a rough way to be the same with each other. This is what makes off-hand testimony about the subjective identity of different sensations well-nigh worthless as a proof of the fact. The entire history of what is called Sensation is a commentary on our inability to tell whether two sensible qualities received apart are exactly alike. What appeals to our attention far more than the absolute quality of an impression is its *ratio* to whatever other impressions we may have at the same time. When everything is dark a somewhat less dark sensation makes us see an object white. Helmholtz[1] calculates that the white marble painted in a picture representing an architectural view by moonlight is, when seen by daylight, from ten to twenty thousand times brighter than the real moonlit marble would be, yet the latter looks white.

Such a difference as this could never have been *sensibly* learned; it had to be inferred from a series of indirect considerations. These make us believe that our sensibility is altering all the time, so that the same object cannot easily give us the same sensation over again. We feel things differently accordingly as we are sleepy or awake, hungry or full, fresh or tired; differently at night and in the morning, differently in summer and in winter; and above all, differently in childhood, manhood, and old age. And yet we never doubt that our feelings reveal the same world, with the same sensible qualities and the same sensible things occupying it. The difference

---

1. Herman von Helmholtz (1821–1894), German scientist known especially for his work on theories of vision, though he also worked on acoustics, electrodynamics, and in many other fields. [*Editor's note.*]

of the sensibility is shown best by the difference of our emotion about the things from one age to another, or when we are in different organic moods. What was bright and exciting becomes weary, flat, and unprofitable. The bird's song is tedious, the breeze is mournful, the sky is sad.

To these indirect presumptions that our sensations, following the mutations of our capacity for feeling, are always undergoing an essential change, must be added another presumption, based on what must happen in the brain. Every sensation corresponds to some cerebral action. For an identical sensation to recur it would have to occur the second time *in an unmodified brain*. But as this, strictly speaking, is a physiological impossibility, so is an unmodified feeling an impossibility; for to every brain-modification, however small, we suppose that there must correspond a change of equal amount in the consciousness which the brain subserves.

But if the assumption of 'simple sensations' recurring in immutable shape is so easily shown to be baseless, how much more baseless is the assumption of immutability in the larger masses of our thought!

For there it is obvious and palpable that our state of mind is never precisely the same. Every thought we have of a given fact is, strictly speaking, unique, and only bears a resemblance of kind with our other thoughts of the same fact. When the identical fact recurs, we *must* think of it in a fresh manner, see it under a somewhat different angle, apprehend it in different relations from those in which it last appeared. * * *

* * *

Within each personal consciousness, thought is sensibly continuous. I can only define 'continuous' as that which is without breach, crack, or division. The only breaches that can well be conceived to occur within the limits of a single mind would either be *interruptions, time*-gaps during which the consciousness went out; or they would be breaks in the content of the thought, so abrupt that what followed had no connection whatever with what went before. The proposition that consciousness feels continuous, means two things:

a. That even where there is a time-gap the consciousness after it feels as if it belonged together with the consciousness before it, as another part of the same self;

b. That the changes from one moment to another in the quality of the consciousness are never absolutely abrupt.

* * *

Consciousness does not appear to itself chopped up in bits. Such words as 'chain' or 'train' do not describe it fitly as it presents itself in the first instance. It is nothing jointed; it flows. A 'river' or a 'stream' are the metaphors by which it is most naturally described. *In talking of it hereafter, let us call it the stream of thought, of consciousness, or of subjective life.*

* * *

'Substantive' and 'Transitive' States of Mind.—When we take a general view of the wonderful stream of our consciousness, what strikes us first is the different pace of its parts. Like a bird's life, it seems to be an alternation of flights and perchings. The rhythm of language expresses this, where every thought is expressed in a sentence, and every sentence closed by a period. The resting-places are usually occupied by sensorial imaginations of some sort, whose peculiarity is that they can be held before the mind for an indefinite time, and contemplated without changing; the places of flight are filled with thoughts of relations, static or dynamic, that for the most part obtain between the matters contemplated in the periods of comparative rest.

Let us call the resting-places the 'substantive parts,' and the places of flight the 'transitive parts,' of the stream of thought. It then appears that our thinking tends at all times towards some other substantive part than the one from which it has just been dislodged. And we may say that the main use of the transitive parts is to lead us from one substantive conclusion to another.

Now it is very difficult, introspectively, to see the transitive parts for what they really are. If they are but flights to a conclusion, stopping them to look at them before the conclusion is reached is really annihilating them. Whilst if we wait till the conclusion *be* reached, it so exceeds them in vigor and stability that it quite eclipses and swallows them up in its glare. Let anyone try to cut a thought across in the middle and get a look at its section, and he will see how difficult the introspective observation of the transitive tracts is. The rush of the thought is so headlong that it almost always brings us up at the conclusion before we can arrest it. Or if our purpose is nimble enough and we do arrest it, it ceases forthwith to be itself. As a snowflake caught in the warm hand is no longer a flake but a drop, so, instead of catching the feeling of relation moving to its term, we find we have caught some substantive thing, usually the last word we were pronouncing, statically taken, and with its function, tendency, and particular meaning in the sentence quite evaporated. The attempt at introspective analysis in these cases is in fact like seizing a spinning top to catch its motion, or trying to turn up the gas quickly enough to see how the darkness looks. And the challenge to *produce* these transitive states of consciousness, which is sure to be thrown by doubting psychologists at anyone who contends for their existence, is as unfair as Zeno's treatment of the advocates of motion, when, asking them to point out in what place an arrow *is* when it moves, he argues the falsity of their thesis from their inability to make to so preposterous a question an immediate reply.[2]

＊　＊　＊

＊ ＊ ＊ [Yet] so inveterate has out habit become of recognizing the existence of the substantive parts alone, that language almost refuses to lend itself to any other use. Consider once again the analogy of the brain. We believe the brain to be an organ whose internal equilibrium is always in a state of change—the change affecting every part. The pulses of change are doubtless more violent in one place than in another, their rhythm more rapid at this time than at that. As in a kaleidoscope revolving at a uniform rate, although the figures are always rearranging themselves, there are instants during which the transformation seems minute and interstitial and almost absent, followed by others when it shoots with magical rapidity, relatively stable forms thus alternating with forms we should not distinguish if seen again; so in the brain the perpetual rearrangement must result in some forms of tension lingering relatively long, whilst others simply come and pass. But if consciousness corresponds to the fact of rearrangement itself, why, if the rearrangement stop not, should the consciousness ever cease? And if a lingering rearrangement brings with it one kind of consciousness, why should not a swift rearrangement bring another kind of consciousness as peculiar as the rearrangement itself?

It is, the reader will see, the reinstatement of the vague and inarticulate to its proper place in our mental life which I am so anxious to press on the attention. Mr. Galton and Prof. Huxley have made one step in advance in exploding the ridiculous theory of Hume and Berkeley that we can have no images but of perfectly definite things.[3] Another is made if we overthrow the equally ridiculous notion that, whilst simple objective qualities are revealed to our

2. Zeno of Elea (ca. 490 B.C.E.–ca. 430 B.C.E.). Pre-Socratic philosopher known for a series of mathematical paradoxes; the one cited by James holds that an arrow in flight is in fact motionless at any given instant of time, since it is neither moving to where it is, nor toward where it is not. [*Editor's note.*]

3. Francis Galton (1822–1911), Victorian polymath who, along with much else, coined the word "eugenics"; Thomas Henry Huxley (1825–1895), combative popularizer of Darwin; John Locke (1632–1704), English philosopher known both for his ideas of the relation of sensory perception to consciousness and as the theorist of classical liberalism; George Berkeley (1685–1753), philosopher best known for his work on the nature of perception. [*Editor's note.*]

knowledge in 'states of consciousness,' relations are not. But these reforms are not half sweeping and radical enough. What must be admitted is that the definite images of traditional psychology form but the very smallest part of our minds as they actually live. The traditional psychology talks like one who should say a river consists of nothing but pailsful, spoonsful, quartpotsful, barrelsful, and other moulded forms of water. Even were the pails and the pots all actually standing in the stream, still between them the free water would continue to flow. It is just this free water of consciousness that psychologists resolutely overlook. Every definite image in the mind is steeped and dyed in the free water that flows round it. With it goes the sense of its relations, near and remote, the dying echo of whence it came to us, the dawning sense of whither it is to lead. The significance, the value, of the image is all in this halo or penumbra that surrounds and escorts it,—or rather that is fused into one with it and has become bone of its bone and flesh of its flesh; leaving it, it is true, an image of the same *thing* it was before, but making it an image of that thing newly taken and freshly understood.

* * *

HENRI BERGSON

Duration†

The existence of which we are most assured and which we know best is unquestionably our own, for of every other object we have notions which may be considered external and superficial, whereas, of ourselves, our perception is internal and profound. What, then, do we find? In this privileged case, what is the precise meaning of the word "exist"? . . .

I find, first of all, that I pass from state to state. I am warm or cold, I am merry or sad, I work or I do nothing, I look at what is around me or I think of something else. Sensations, feelings, volitions, ideas—such are the changes into which my existence is

† Henri Bergson (1859–1941), French philosopher best known for the ideas contained in this excerpt; a determinative influence on modernist conceptions of time and consciousness. Winner of the Nobel Prize in Literature, 1927; his other important works include *Time and Free Will* (1889) and *Laughter* (1900). This selection is drawn from Richard Ellmann's and Charles Feidelson's anthology *The Modern Tradition* (New York: Oxford UP, 1965), 723–30. The first excerpt presented here comes from *Creative Evolution* (1907), trans. Arthur Michell (London: Macmillan and Co., 1911), 1–7. The second is drawn from *An Introduction to Metaphysics* (1903), trans. T. E. Hulme (New York: G. P. Putnam's Sons, 1912), 9–15, 38–39, and 59–64.

divided and which color it in turns. I change, then, without ceasing. But this is not saying enough. Change is far more radical than we are at first inclined to suppose.

For I speak of each of my states as if it formed a block and were a separate whole. I say indeed that I change, but the change seems to me to reside in the passage from one state to the next: of each state, taken separately, I am apt to think that it remains the same during all the time that it prevails. Nevertheless, a slight effort of attention would reveal to me that there is no feeling, no idea, no volition which is not undergoing change every moment: if a mental state ceased to vary, its duration would cease to flow. Let us take the most stable of internal states, the visual perception of a motionless external object. The object may remain the same, I may look at it from the same side, at the same angle, in the same light; nevertheless the vision I now have of it differs from that which I have just had, even if only because the one is an instant older than the other. My memory is there, which conveys something of the past into the present. My mental state, as it advances on the road of time, is continually swelling with the duration which it accumulates: it goes on increasing—rolling upon itself, as a snowball on the snow. Still more is this the case with states more deeply internal, such as sensations, feelings, desires, etc., which do not correspond, like a simple visual perception, to an unvarying external object. But it is expedient to disregard this uninterrupted change, and to notice it only when it becomes sufficient to impress a new attitude on the body, a new direction on the attention. Then, and then only, we find that our state has changed. The truth is that we change without ceasing, and that the state itself is nothing but change.

This amounts to saying that there is no essential difference between passing from one state to another and persisting in the same state. If the state which "remains the same" is more varied than we think, on the other hand the passing from one state to another resembles, more than we imagine, a single state being prolonged; the transition is continuous. But, just because we close our eyes to the unceasing variation of every psychical state, we are obliged, when the change has become so considerable as to force itself on our attention, to speak as if a new state were placed alongside the previous one. Of this new state we assume that it remains unvarying in its turn, and so on endlessly. The apparent discontinuity of the psychical life is then due to our attention being fixed on it by a series of separate acts: actually there is only a gentle slope; but in following the broken line of our acts of attention, we think we perceive separate steps. True, our psychic life is full of the unforeseen. A thousand incidents arise, which seem to be cut off from those which precede them, and to be disconnected from those which follow. Discontinuous though they appear, however, in point of fact they stand out against the continuity of a background on which they are designed, and to which indeed they owe the intervals that separate them; they are the beats of the drum which break forth here and there in the symphony. Our attention fixes on them because they interest it more, but each of them is borne by the fluid mass of our whole psychical existence. Each is only the best illuminated point of a moving zone which comprises all that we feel or think or will—all, in short, that we are at any given moment. It is this entire zone which in reality makes up our state. Now, states thus defined cannot be regarded as distinct elements. They continue each other in an endless flow.

But, as our attention has distinguished and separated them artificially, it is obliged next to reunite them by an artificial bond. It imagines, therefore, a formless *ego*, indifferent and unchangeable, on which it threads the psychic states which it has set up as independent entities. Instead of a flux of fleeting shades merging into each other, it perceives distinct and, so to speak, *solid* colors, set side by side like the beads of a necklace; it must perforce then suppose a thread, also itself solid, to hold the beads together. But if this colorless substratum is perpetually colored by that which covers it, it is for us, in its indeterminateness, as if it did not exist, since we only perceive what is colored, or, in other words, psychic states. As a matter of fact, this substratum has no reality; it is merely a symbol intended to recall unceasingly to our consciousness the artificial character of the process by which the attention places clean-cut states side by side, where actually there is a continuity which unfolds. If our existence were composed of separate states with an impassive ego to unite them, for us there would be no duration. For an ego which does not change does not *endure*, and a psychic state which remains the same so long as it is not replaced by the following state does not *endure* either. Vain, therefore, is the attempt to range such states beside each other on the ego supposed to sustain them: never can these solids strung upon a solid make up that duration which flows. What we actually obtain in this way is an artificial imitation of the internal life, a static equivalent which will lend itself better to the requirements of logic and language, just because we have eliminated from it the element of real time. But, as regards the psychical life unfolding beneath the symbols which conceal it, we readily perceive that time is just the stuff it is made of.

There is, moreover, no stuff more resistant nor more substantial. For our duration is not merely one infant replacing another; if it were, there would never be anything but the present—no prolonging of the past into the actual, no evolution, no concrete duration. Duration is the continuous progress of the past which gnaws into the future and which swells as it advances. And as the past grows without ceasing, so also there is no limit to its preservation. Memory . . . is not a faculty of putting away recollections in a drawer, or of inscribing them in a register. There is no register, no drawer; there is not even, properly speaking, a faculty, for a faculty works intermittently, when it will or when it can, whilst the piling up of the past upon the past goes on without relaxation. In reality, the past is preserved by itself, automatically. In its entirety, probably, it follows us at every instant; all that we have felt, thought and willed from our earliest infancy is there, leaning over the present which is about to join it, pressing against the portals of consciousness that would fain leave it outside. The cerebral mechanism is arranged just so as to drive back into the unconscious almost the whole of this past, and to admit beyond the threshold only that which can cast light on the present situation or further the action now being prepared—in short, only that which can give *useful* work. At the most, a few superfluous recollections may succeed in smuggling themselves through the half-open door. These memories, messengers from the unconscious, remind us of what we are dragging behind us unawares. But, even though we may have no distinct idea of it, we feel vaguely that our past remains present to us. What are we, in fact, what is our *character*, if not the condensation of the history that we have lived from our birth—nay, even before our birth, since we bring with us prenatal dispositions? Doubtless we think with only a small part of our past, but it is with our entire past, including the original bent of our soul, that we desire, will and act. Our past, then, as a whole, is made manifest to us in its impulse; it is felt in the form of tendency, although a small part of it only is known in the form of idea.

From this survival of the past it follows that consciousness cannot go through the same state twice. The circumstances may still be the same, but they will act no longer on the same person, since they find him at a new moment of his history. Our personality, which is being built up each instant with its accumulated experience, changes without ceasing. By changing, it prevents any state, although superficially identical with another, from ever repeating it in its very depth. That is why our duration is irreversible. We could not live over again a single moment, for we should have to begin by effacing the memory of all that had followed. Even could we erase this memory from our intellect, we could not from our will.

Thus our personality shoots, grows and ripens without ceasing. Each of its moments is something new added to what was before.

We may go further: it is not only something new, but something unforeseeable. Doubtless, my present state is explained by what was in me and by what was acting on me a moment ago. In analyzing it I should find no other elements. But even a superhuman intelligence would not have been able to foresee the simple indivisible form which gives to these purely abstract elements their concrete organization. For to foresee consists of projecting into the future what has been perceived in the past, or of imagaining for a later time a new grouping, in a new order, of elements already perceived. But that which has never been perceived, and which is at the same time simple, is necessarily unforeseeable. Now such is the case with each of our states, regarded as a moment in a history that is gradually unfolding: it is simple, and it cannot have been already perceived, since it concentrates in its indivisibility all that has been perceived and what the present is adding to it besides. It is an original moment of a no less original history.

The finished portrait is explained by the features of the model, by the nature of the artist, by the colors spread out on the palette; but, even with the knowledge of what explains it, no one, not even the artist, could have foreseen exactly what the portrait would be, for to predict it would have been to produce it before it was produced—an absurd hypothesis which is its own refutation. Even so with regard to the moments of our life, of which we are the artisans. Each of them is a kind of creation. And just as the talent of the painter is formed or deformed—in any case, is modified—under the very influence of the works he produces, so each of our states, at the moment of its issue, modifies our personality, being indeed the new form that we are just assuming. It is then right to say that what we do depends on what we are; but it is necessary to add also that we are, to a certain extent, what we do, and that we are creating ourselves continually. This creation of self by self is the more complete, the more one reasons on what one does. For reason does not proceed in such matters as in geometry, where impersonal premisses are given once for all, and an impersonal conclusion must perforce be drawn. Here, on the contrary, the same reasons may dictate to different persons, or to the same person at different moments, acts profoundly different, although equally reasonable. The truth is that they are not quite the same reasons, since they are not those of the same person, nor of the same moment. That is why we cannot deal with them in the abstract, from outside, as in geometry, nor solve for another the problems by which he is faced in life. Each must solve them from within, on his own account. But we need not go more deeply into this. We are seeking only the precise meaning that our consciousness gives to this word "exist," and we find that, for a conscious being, to exist is to change, to change is to mature, to mature is to go on creating oneself endlessly.

When I direct my attention inward to contemplate my own self (supposed for the moment to be inactive), I perceive at first, as a crust solidified on the surface, all the perceptions which come to it from the material world. These perceptions are clear, distinct, juxtaposed or juxtaposable one with another; they tend to group themselves into objects. Next, I notice the memories which more or less adhere to these perceptions and which serve to interpret them. These memories have been detached, as it were, from the depth of my personality, drawn to the surface by the perceptions which resemble them; they rest on the surface of my mind without being absolutely myself. Lastly, I feel the stir of tendencies and motor habits—a crowd of virtual actions, more or less firmly bound to these perceptions and memories. All these clearly defined elements appear more distinct from me, the more distinct they are from each other. Radiating, as they do, from within outwards, they form, collectively, the surface of a sphere which tends to grow larger and lose itself in the exterior world. But if I draw myself in from the periphery towards the center, if I search in the depth of my being that which is most uniformly, most constantly, and most enduringly myself, I find an altogether different thing.

There is, beneath these sharply cut crystals and this frozen surface, a continuous flux which is not comparable to any flux I have ever seen. There is a succession of states, each of which announces that which follows and contains that which precedes it. They can, properly speaking, only be said to form multiple states when I have already passed them and turn back to observe their tracks. Whilst I was experiencing them they were so solidly organized, so profoundly animated with a common life, that I could not have said where any one of them finished or where another commenced. In reality no one of them begins or ends, but all extend into each other.

This inner life may be compared to the unrolling of a coil, for there is no living being who does not feel himself coming gradually to the end of his role; and to live is to grow old. But it may just as well be compared to a continual rolling up, like that of a thread on a ball, for our past follows us, it swells incessantly with the present that it picks up on its way; and consciousness means memory.

But actually it is neither an unrolling nor a rolling up, for these two similes evoke the idea of lines and surfaces whose parts are homogeneous and superposable on one another. Now, there are no two identical moments in the life of the same conscious being. Take

the simplest sensation, suppose it constant, absorb in it the entire
personality: the consciousness which will accompany this sensation cannot remain identical with itself for two consecutive
moments, because the second moment always contains, over and
above the first, the memory that the first has bequeathed to it. A
consciousness which could experience two identical moments
would be a consciousness without memory. It would die and be
born again continually. In what other way could one represent
unconsciousness?

It would be better, then, to use as a comparison the myriad-tinted
spectrum, with its insensible gradations leading from one shade to
another. A current of feeling which passed along the spectrum,
assuming in turn the tint of each of its shades, would experience a
series of gradual changes, each of which would announce the one to
follow and would sum up those which preceded it. Yet even here the
successive shades of the spectrum always remain external one to
another. They are juxtaposed; they occupy space. But pure duration,
on the contrary, excludes all idea of juxtaposition, reciprocal exter-
nality, and extension.

Let us, then, rather, imagine an infinitely small elastic body, con-
tracted, if it were possible, to a mathematical point. Let this be
drawn out gradually in such a manner that from the point comes a
constantly lengthening line. Let us fix our attention not on the line
as a line, but on the action by which it is traced. Let us bear in
mind that this action, in spite of its duration, is indivisible if accomplished without stopping, that if a stopping-point is inserted, we
have two actions instead of one, that each of these separate actions
is then the indivisible operation of which we speak, and that it is
not the moving action itself which is divisible, but, rather, the sta-
tionary line it leaves behind it as its track in space. Finally, let us
free ourselves from the space which underlies the movement in
order to consider only the movement itself, the act of tension or
extension; in short, pure mobility. We shall have this time a more
faithful image of the development of our self in duration.

However, even this image is incomplete, and, indeed, every comparison will be insufficient, because the unrolling of our duration
resembles in some of its aspects the unity of an advancing movement and in others the multiplicity of expanding states; and, clearly,
no metaphor can express one of these two aspects without sacrificing the other. If I use the comparison of the spectrum with its
thousand shades, I have before me a thing already made, whilst
duration is continually in the making. If I think of an elastic which
is being stretched, or of a spring which is extended or relaxed, I
forget the richness of color, characteristic of duration that is lived,
to see only the simple movement by which consciousness passes

from one shade to another. The inner life is all this at once: variety of qualities, continuity of progress, and unity of direction. It cannot be represented by images.

But it is even less possible to represent it by *concepts*, that is by abstract, general, or simple ideas. . . .

That personality has unity cannot be denied; but such an affirmation teaches one nothing about the extraordinary nature of the particular unity presented by personality. That our self is multiple I also agree, but then it must be understood that it is a multiplicity which has nothing in common with any other multiplicity. What is really important for philosophy is to know exactly what unity, what multiplicity, and what reality superior both to abstract unity and multiplicity the multiple unity of the self actually is. Now philosophy will know this only when it recovers possession of the simple intuition of the self by the self. Then, according to the direction it chooses for its descent from this summit, it will arrive at unity or multiplicity, or at any one of the concepts by which we try to define the moving life of the self. But no mingling of these concepts would give anything which at all resembles the self that endures.

If we are shown a solid cone, we see without any difficulty how it narrows towards the summit and tends to be lost in a mathematical point, and also how it enlarges in the direction of the base into an indefinitely increasing circle. But neither the point nor the circle, nor the juxtaposition of the two on a plane, would give us the least idea of a cone. The same thing holds true of the unity and multiplicity of mental life, and of the zero and the infinite towards which empiricism and rationalism conduct personality. . . .

Let us express the same idea with more precision. If I consider duration as a multiplicity of moments bound to each other by a unity which goes through them like a thread, then, however short the chosen duration may be, these moments are unlimited in number. I can suppose them as close together as I please; there will always be between these mathematical points other mathematical points, and so on to infinity. Looked at from the point of view of multiplicity, then, duration disintegrates into a powder of moments, none of which endures, each being an instantaneity. If, on the other hand, I consider the unity which binds the moment together, this cannot endure either, since by hypothesis everything that is changing, and everything that is really durable in the duration, has been put to the account of the multiplicity of moments. As I probe more deeply into its essence, this unity will appear to me as some immobile substratum of that which is moving, as some intemporal essence of time; it is this that I shall call eternity; an eternity of death, since it is nothing else than the movement emptied of the mobility which made its life. Closely examined, the opinions of the opposing schools on the subject of duration would be seen to differ solely in this, that they attribute a capital importance to one or the other of these two concepts. Some adhere to the point of view of the multiple; they set up as concrete reality the distinct moments of a time which they have reduced to powder; the unity which enables us to call the grains a powder they hold to be much more artificial. Others, on the contrary, set up the unity of duration as concrete reality. They place themselves in the eternal. But as their eternity remains, notwithstanding, abstract, since it is empty, being the eternity of a concept which, by hypothesis, excludes from itself the opposing concept, one does not see how this eternity would permit of an indefinite number of moments coexisting in it. In the first hypothesis we have a world resting on nothing, which must end and begin again of its own accord at each instant. In the second we have an infinity of abstract eternity, about which also it is just as difficult to understand why it does not remain enveloped in itself and how it allows things to coexist with it. But in both cases, and whichever of the two metaphysics it be that one is switched into, time appears, from the psychological point of view, as a mixture of two abstractions, which admit of neither degrees nor shades. In one system as in the other, there is only one unique duration, which carries everything with it—a bottomless, bankless river, which flows without assignable force in a direction which could not be defined. Even then we can call it only a river, and the river only flows, because reality obtains from the two doctrines this concession, profiting by a moment of perplexity in their logic. As soon as they recover from this perplexity, they freeze this flux either into an immense solid sheet, or into an infinity of crystallized needles, always into a *thing* which necessarily partakes of the immobility of a *point of view*.

It is quite otherwise if we place ourselves from the first, by an effort of intuition, in the concrete flow of duration. Certainly, we shall then find no logical reason for positing multiple and diverse durations. Strictly, there might well be no other duration than our own, as, for example, there might be no other color in the world but orange. But just as a consciousness based on color, which sympathized internally with orange instead of perceiving it externally, would feel itself held between red and yellow, would even perhaps suspect beyond this last color a complete spectrum into which the continuity from red to yellow might expand naturally, so the intuition of our duration, far from leaving us suspended in the void as pure analysis would do, brings us into contact with a whole continuity of durations which we must try to follow, whether downwards or upwards; in both cases we can extend ourselves indefinitely by an increasingly violent effort, in both cases we transcend ourselves.

In the first we advance towards a more and more attenuated duration, the pulsations of which, being rapider than ours, and dividing our simple sensation, dilute its quality into quantity; at the limit would be pure homogeneity, that pure *repetition* by which we define materiality. Advancing in the other direction, we approach a duration which *strains*, contracts, and intensifies itself more and more; at the limit would be eternity. No longer conceptual eternity, which is an eternity of death, but an eternity of life. A living, and therefore still moving eternity in which our own particular duration would be included as the vibrations are in light; an eternity which would be the concentration of all duration, as materiality is its dispersion. Between these two extreme limits intuition moves, and this movement is the very essence of metaphysics.

CRITICISM

Jean-Paul Sartre wasn't yet the Sartre of history when in 1939 he wrote a brief essay on *The Sound and the Fury* for the *Nouvelle Revue Française*. He still had his future to make, and was just one of many young French intellectuals who had found a master in the slightly older Mississippian. The novel had been translated the year before by Maurice-Edgar Coindreau, the Princeton French professor who introduced both Hemingway and Faulkner to his countrymen. Sartre was in effect reviewing a new book, and his Faulkner is a modernist whose work makes nonsense of any distinction between a subject and its narrative form. But by the end of World War II, Sartre had become himself. His words had weight, and when in 1945 he met Malcolm Cowley, then at work on *The Portable Faulkner*, he told the American that "Pour les jeunes en France, Faulkner c'est un dieu."[1] That claim stands, along with *The Portable Faulkner* itself, at the start of the postwar boom in Faulkner's reputation that eventually led to the Nobel Prize.

His reputation boomed—and so did the amount written about him. From the 1950s and 1960s, the New Critical accounts by Olga Vickery and Cleanth Brooks have kept their force. Vickery in particular helps a first-time reader make sense of the novel, guiding him or her through the seeming labyrinth of Faulkner's procedures. Her essay remains the best place to begin but it is only a beginning, and the later essays presented here take up very different aspects of the novel. Donald Kartiganer's 1979 close reading may be similar in method to Brooks and Vickery, but his essay stresses the novel's fractures and tensions, its final and perhaps deliberate failure to cohere. John Irwin's *Doubling and Incest / Repetition and Revenge* remains an oddball classic of American criticism, an account of the relation between the Quentin of *The Sound and the Fury* and his later—or perhaps earlier?—iteration in *Absalom, Absalom!* Yet Irwin refuses to touch on Faulkner's own biography, and that omission is repaired in David Minter's elegant retelling of the novel's origin.

Two essays offer skeptical accounts of the novel's reputation. Eric Sundquist challenges its privileged place in both its author's oeuvre and in twentieth-century American literature as a whole, suggesting that its stature rests on the retrospective justification of Faulkner's later career. Stacy Burton uses a Foucauldian conception of authorship to strip away the mythifying crust in which Faulkner's own later comments have embedded the book. She argues that his Appendix, draft introductions, and statements in interviews have no special claim to authority; we would, she implies, do better to forget them. My own introduction to this volume suggests how little I can follow her in that—yet her bracing rigor reminds us of the care we must take with our evidence.

Anyone who reads about *The Sound and Fury* soon discovers that the novel itself has created a structural problem for its critics, divided as it is into four parts, each of them written in a different style and presented out of sequence. Most scholars move through the book

1. Malcolm Colwley, *The Faulkner–Cowley File: Letters and Memories, 1944–1962* (New York: Viking Press, 1966), 24.

section by section, day by day, and no matter how perceptive their arguments that structure can, for the reader, quickly grow enervating. I have therefore edited some of my other selections here to highlight particular sides of the novel, avoiding repetition while ensuring that all its parts receive some separate and focused treatment. For example, Richard Godden, Noel Polk, and André Bleikasten each offer remarkably rich accounts of the book as a whole. But from Godden I take only his provocative reading of Benjy's narrative, and from Polk his detailed look at Jason's voice and language; while the greatest of all Faulkner's French critics is represented by his treatment of the Reverend Shegog's sermon in the novel's conclusion.

Thadious Davis provides our best reading of the role Dilsey Gibson and her family play in the lives of their white employers, a reading that outlines the challenge they offer to the world of the Compsons themselves. John Matthews looks at the novel in relation to the popular culture of its moment, and in doing so defines the role of black vernacular speech in the novel. I have selected three very different feminist readings, by Minrose C. Gwin, Philip M. Weinstein, and Doreen Fowler. Gwin writes against the usual assumption that Faulkner has "silenced" the Compson daughter, Caddy, the only one of the four siblings without a narrative of her own. In looking at Mrs. Compson, Weinstein's broadly psychoanalytic essay suggests, along with much else, that any transhistorical conception of the maternal must be inflected by a knowledge of the character's particular time and place. Fowler's more precisely defined Lacanian account reexamines the relationship between Quentin and Caddy. And finally, Maria Truchan-Tataryn considers Benjy Compson in terms of new developments in disability studies, in the process summarizing just what was and wasn't known or believed about "idiots" in Faulkner's day.

Throughout these essays I have substituted page references to this Norton Critical Edition for the authors' original citations from earlier editions of *The Sound and the Fury*.

JEAN-PAUL SARTRE

On *The Sound and the Fury*: Time in the Work of Faulkner[†]

The first thing that strikes one in reading *The Sound and the Fury* is its technical oddity. Why has Faulkner broken up the time of his story and scrambled the pieces? Why is the first window that opens out on this fictional world the consciousness of an idiot? The reader

---

[†] From *Literary and Philosophical Essays*, trans. Annette Michelson (London: Rider, 1955), 79–87. Reprinted by permission. © Editions Gallimard 1947, 1975. First published in *La Nouvelle revue française* LII (June 1939). Page references are to this Norton Critical Edition.

is tempted to look for guide-marks and to re-establish the chronology for himself:

> Jason and Caroline Compson have had three sons and a daughter. The daughter, Caddy, has given herself to Dalton Ames and become pregnant by him. Forced to get hold of a husband quickly . . .

Here the reader stops, for he realizes he is telling another story. Faulkner did not first conceive this orderly plot so as to shuffle it afterwards like a pack of cards; he could not tell it in any other way. In the classical novel, action involves a central complication; for example, the murder of old Karamazov or the meeting of Edouard and Bernard in *The Coiners*.[1] But we look in vain for such a complication in *The Sound and the Fury*. Is it the castration of Benjy or Caddy's wretched amorous adventure or Quentin's suicide or Jason's hatred of his niece? As soon as we begin to look at any episode, it opens up to reveal behind it other episodes, all the other episodes. Nothing happens; the story does not unfold; we discover it under each word, like an obscene and obstructing presence, more or less condensed, depending upon the particular case. It would be a mistake to regard these irregularities as gratuitous exercises in virtuosity. A fictional technique always relates back to the novelist's metaphysics. The critic's task is to define the latter before evaluating the former. Now, it is immediately obvious that Faulkner's metaphysics is a metaphysics of time.

Man's misfortune lies in his being time-bound.

> . . . a man is the sum of his misfortunes. One day you'd think misfortune would get tired, but then time is your misfortune . . . (69)

Such is the real subject of the book. And if the technique Faulkner has adopted seems at first a negation of temporality, the reason is that we confuse temporality with chronology. It was man who invented dates and clocks.

> Constant speculation regarding the position of mechanical hands on an arbitrary dial which is a symptom of mind-function. Excrement Father said like sweating. (51)

In order to arrive at real time, we must abandon this invented measure which is not a measure of anything.

> . . . time is dead as long as it is being clicked off by little wheels; only when the clock stops does time come to life. (56)

---

1. Novel by Andre Gide (1861–1951; Nobel Prize, 1947) first published in French as *Les faux-monnayeurs* (1925). [*Editor's note.*]

Thus, Quentin's gesture of breaking his watch has a symbolic value; it gives us access to a time without clocks. The time of Benjy, the idiot, who does not know how to tell time, is also clockless.

What is thereupon revealed to us is the present, and not the ideal limit whose place is neatly marked out between past and future. Faulkner's present is essentially catastrophic. It is the event which creeps up on us like a thief, huge, unthinkable—which creeps up on us and then disappears. Beyond this present time there is nothing, since the future does not exist. The present rises up from sources unknown to us and drives away another present; it is forever beginning anew. "And . . . and . . . and then." Like Dos Passos, but much more discreetly, Faulkner makes an accretion of his narrative. The actions themselves, even when seen by those who perform them, burst and scatter on entering the present.

> I went to the dresser and took up the watch with the face still down. I tapped the crystal on the dresser and caught the fragments of glass in my hand and put them into the ashtray and twisted the hands off and put them in the tray. The watch ticked on. (53)

The other aspect of this present is what I shall call a sinking in. I use this expression, for want of a better one, to indicate a kind of motionless movement of this formless monster. In Faulkner's work, there is never any progression, never anything which comes from the future. The present has not first been a future possibility, and when my friend, after having been *he for whom I am waiting*, finally appears. No, to be present means to appear without any reason and to sink in. This sinking in is not an abstract view. It is within things themselves that Faulkner perceives it and tries to make it felt.

> The train swung around the curve, the engine puffing with short, heavy blasts, and they passed smoothly from sight that way, with that quality of shabby and timeless patience, of static serenity . . . (58)

And again,

> Beneath the sag of the buggy the hooves neatly rapid like motions of a lady doing embroidery, *diminishing without progress* like a figure on a treadmill being drawn rapidly off-stage. (82)[2]

It seems as though Faulkner has laid hold of a frozen speed at the very heart of things; he is grazed by congealed spurts that wane and dwindle without moving.

---

2. Italics in original. [*Editor's note.*]

This fleeting and unimaginable immobility can, however, be arrested and pondered. Quentin can say, "I broke my watch," but when he says it, his gesture is *past*. The past is named and related; it can, to a certain extent, be fixed by concepts or recognized by the heart. We pointed out earlier, in connection with *Sartoris*, that Faulkner always showed events when they were already over. In *The Sound and the Fury* everything has already happened. It is this that enables us to understand that strange remark by one of the heroes, "*Fui. Non sum.*"[3] In this sense, too, Faulkner is able to make man a sum total without a future: "The sum of his climactic experiences," "The sum of his misfortunes," "The sum of what have you." At every moment, one draws a line, since the present is nothing but a chaotic din, a future that is past. Faulkner's vision of the world can be compared to that of a man sitting in an open car and looking backwards. At every moment, formless shadows, flickerings, faint tremblings and patches of light rise up on either side of him, and only afterwards, when he has a little perspective, do they become trees and men and cars.

The past takes on a sort of super-reality; its contours are hard and clear, unchangeable. The present, nameless and fleeting, is helpless before it. It is full of gaps, and, through these gaps, things of the past, fixed, motionless and silent as judges or glances, come to invade it. Faulkner's monologues remind one of aeroplane trips full of air-pockets. At each pocket, the hero's consciousness "sinks back into the past" and rises only to sink back again. The present is not; it becomes. Everything *was*. In *Sartoris*, the past was called "the stories" because it was a matter of family memories that had been constructed, because Faulkner had not yet found his technique.

In *The Sound and the Fury* he is more individual and more undecided. But it is so strong an obsession that he is sometimes apt to disguise the present, and the present moves along in the shadow, like an underground river, and reappears only when it itself is past. When Quentin insults Bland,[4] he is not even aware of doing so; he is reliving his dispute with Dalton Ames. And when Bland punches his nose, this brawl is covered over and hidden by Quentin's past brawl with Ames. Later on, Shreve relates how Bland hit Quentin; he relates this scene because it has become a story, but while it was unfolding in the present, it was only a furtive movement, covered over by veils. Someone once told me about an old monitor who had grown senile. His memory had stopped like a broken watch; it had been arrested at his fortieth year. He was sixty, but didn't know

---

3. Latin: "I was. I am not." [*Editor's note.*]
4. Compare the dialogue with Bland inserted into the middle of the dialogue with Ames: "Did you ever have a sister?" etc., and the inextricable confusion of the two fights.

it. His last memory was that of a schoolyard and his daily walk around it. Thus, he interpreted his present in terms of his past and walked about his table, convinced that he was watching students during recreation.

Faulkner's characters are like that, only worse, for their past, which is in order, does not assume chronological order. It is, in actual fact, a matter of emotional constellations. Around a few central themes (Caddy's pregnancy, Benjy's castration, Quentin's suicide) gravitate innumerable silent masses. Whence the absurdity of the chronology of "the assertive and contradictory assurance" of the clock. The order of the past is the order of the heart. It would be wrong to think that when the present is past it becomes our closest memory. Its metamorphosis can cause it to sink to the bottom of our memory, just as it can leave it floating on the surface. Only its own density and the dramatic meaning of our life can determine at what level it will remain.

Such is the nature of Faulkner's time. Isn't there something familiar about it? This unspeakable present, leaking at every seam, these sudden invasions of the past, this emotional order, the opposite of the voluntary and intellectual order that is chronological but lacking in reality, these memories, these monstrous and discontinuous obsessions, these intermittences of the heart—are not these reminiscent of the lost and recaptured time of Marcel Proust? I am not unaware of the differences between the two; I know, for instance, that for Proust salvation lies in time itself, in the full reappearance of the past. For Faulkner, on the contrary, the past is never lost, unfortunately; it is always there, it is an obsession. One escapes from the temporal world only through mystic ecstasies. A mystic is always a man who wishes to forget something, his self or, more often, language or objective representations. For Faulkner, time must be forgotten.

> 'Quentin, I give you the mausoleum of all hope and desire; it's rather excruciatingly apt that you will use it to gain the reductio ad absurdum of all human experience which can fit your individual needs no better than it fitted his or his father's. I give it to you not that you may remember time, *but that you might forget it now and then for a moment* and not spend all your breath trying to conquer it. Because no battle is ever won he said. They are not even fought. The field only reveals to man his own folly and despair, and victory is an illusion of philosophers and fools.' (50)

It is because he has forgotten time that the hunted negro in *Light in August* suddenly achieves his strange and horrible happiness.

It's not when you realize that nothing can help you—religion, pride, anything—it's when you realize that you don't need any aid. (53)

But for Faulkner, as for Proust, time is, above all, *that which separates*. One recalls the astonishment of the Proustian heroes who can no longer enter into their past loves, of those lovers depicted in *Les Plaisirs et Les Jours*,[5] clutching their passions, afraid they will pass and knowing they will. We find the same anguish in Faulkner.

. . . people cannot do anything very dreadful at all, they cannot even remember tomorrow what seemed dreadful today . . . (53)

and

. . . a love or a sorrow is a bond purchased without design and which matures willynilly and is recalled without warning to be replaced by whatever issue the gods happen to be floating at the time . . . (118)

To tell the truth, Proust's fictional technique *should have been* Faulkner's. It was the logical conclusion of his metaphysics. But Faulkner is a lost man, and it is because he feels lost that he takes risks and pursues his thought to its uttermost consequences. Proust is a Frenchman and a classicist. The French lose themselves only a little at a time and always manage to find themselves again. Eloquence, intellectuality and a liking for clear ideas were responsible for Proust's retaining at least the semblance of chronology.

The basic reason for this relationship is to be found in a very general literary phenomenon. Most of the great contemporary authors, Proust, Joyce, Dos Passos, Faulkner, Gide, and Virginia Woolf, have tried, each in his own way, to distort time. Some of them have deprived it of its past and future in order to reduce it to the pure intuition of the instant; others, like Dos Passos, have made of it a dead and closed memory. Proust and Faulkner have simply decapitated it. They have deprived it of its future, that is, its dimension of deeds and freedom. Proust's heroes never undertake anything. They do, of course, make plans, but their plans remain stuck to them and cannot be projected like a bridge beyond the present. They are day-dreams that are put to flight by reality. The Albertine[6] who appears is not the one we were expecting, and the expectation was merely a slight, inconsequential hesitation, limited to the moment

---

5. A collection (1896) of prose pieces by Marcel Proust. [*Editor's note.*]
6. In *A la recherche du temps perdu* (*A Remembrance of Things Past*) by Proust, Albertine leaves the narrator for a lesbian affair, which only increases his obsession with her. [*Editor's note.*]

only. As to Faulkner's heroes, they never look ahead. They face back-wards as the car carries them along. The coming suicide which casts its shadow over Quentin's last day is not a human possibility; not for a second does Quentin envisage the possibility of *not* killing himself. This suicide is an immobile wall, a *thing* which he approaches back-wards, and which he neither wants to nor can conceive.

> . . . you seem to regard it merely as an experience that will whiten your hair overnight so to speak without altering your appearance at all . . . (118)

It is not an *undertaking*, but a fatality. In losing its element of possibility it ceases to exist in the future. It is already present, and Faulkner's entire art aims at suggesting to us that Quentin's monologues and his last walk *are already* his suicide. This, I think, explains the following curious paradox: Quentin thinks of his last day in the past, like someone who is remembering. But in that case, since the hero's last thoughts coincide approximately with the bursting of his memory and its annihilation, who is remembering? The inevitable reply is that the novelist's skill consists in the choice of the present moment from which he narrates the past. And Faulkner, like Salacrou in *L'Inconnu d'Arras*,[7] has chosen the infini-tesimal instant of death. Thus, when Quentin's memory begins to unravel its recollections ("Through the wall I heard Shreve's bed-springs and then his slippers on the floor hishing. I got up . . ." [51]) *he is already dead*. All this artistry and, to speak frankly, all this illusion are meant, then, merely as substitutions for the intu-ition of the future lacking in the author himself. This explains everything, particularly the irrationality of time; since the present is the unexpected, the formless can be determined only by an excess of memories. We now also understand why duration is "man's charac-teristic misfortune." If the future has reality, time withdraws us from the past and brings us nearer to the future; but if you do away with the future, time is no longer that which separates, that which cuts the present off from itself. "You cannot bear to think that some-day it will no longer hurt you like this." Man spends his life strug-gling against time, and time, like an acid, eats away at man, eats him away from himself and prevents him from fulfilling his human character. Everything is absurd. "Life is a tale told by an idiot, full of sound and fury, signifying nothing."

But is man's time without a future? I can understand that the nail's time, or the clod's or the atom's, is a perpetual present. But is man a thinking nail? If you begin by plunging him into universal

---

7. Armand Salacrou, a contemporary French dramatist (1899–1989), who wrote *L'Inconnu d'Arras*, (*The Unknown Woman from Arras*), in which a man learns of his wife's infidel-ity and kills himself. [*Editor's note.*]

time, the time of planets and nebulae, of tertiary flexures and animal species, as into a bath of sulphuric acid, then the question is settled. However, a consciousness buffeted so from one instant to another ought, *first of all*, to be a consciousness and then, *afterwards*, to be temporal; does anyone believe that time can come to it from the outside? Consciousness can "exist within time" only on condition that it becomes time as a result of the very movement by which it becomes consciousness. It must become "temporalized," as Heidegger says. We can no longer arrest man at each present and define him as "the sum of what he has." The nature of consciousness implies, on the contrary, that it project itself into the future. We can understand what it is only through what it will be. It is determined in its present being by its own possibilities. This is what Heidegger calls "the silent force of the possible." You will not recognize within yourself Faulkner's man, a creature bereft of possibilities and explicable only in terms of what he has been. Try to pin down your consciousness and probe it. You will see that it is hollow. In it you will find only the future.

I do not even speak of your plans and expectations. But the very gesture that you catch in passing has meaning for you only if you project its fulfilment out of it, out of yourself, into the not-yet. This very cup, with its bottom that you do not see—that you might see, that is, at the end of a movement you have not yet made—this white sheet of paper, whose underside is hidden (but you could turn over the sheet) and all the stable and bulky objects that surround us display their most immediate and densest qualities in the future. Man is not the sum of what he has, but the totality of what he does not yet have, of what he might have. And if we steep ourselves thus in the future, is not the formless brutality of the present thereby attenuated? The single event does not spring on us like a thief, since it is, by nature, a Having-been-future. And if a historian wishes to explain the past, must he not first seek out its future? I am afraid that the absurdity that Faulkner finds in a human life is one that he himself has put there. Not that life is not absurd, but there is another kind of absurdity.

Why have Faulkner and so many other writers chosen this particular absurdity which is so un-novelistic and so untrue? I think we should have to look for the reasons in the social conditions of our present life. Faulkner's despair seems to me to precede his metaphysics. For him, as for all of us, the future is closed. Everything we see and experience impels us to say, "This can't last." And yet change is not even conceivable, except in the form of a cataclysm. We are living in a time of impossible revolutions, and Faulkner uses his extraordinary art to describe our suffocation and a world dying of old age. I like his art, but I do not believe in his metaphysics. A closed future is still a future. "Even if human reality has nothing more 'before' it, even if 'its account is closed,' its being is still determined by this 'self-anticipation.' The loss of all hope, for example, does not deprive human reality of its possibilities; it is simply a way of *being* toward these same possibilities."[8]

OLGA W. VICKERY

The Sound and the Fury: A Study in Perspective[†]

The Sound and the Fury was the first of Faulkner's novels to make the question of form and technique an unavoidable critical issue. In any discussion of its structure the controlling assumption should be that there are plausible reasons for the particular arrangement of the four sections and for the use of the stream of consciousness technique in the first three and not in the fourth. Jean-Paul Sartre's comment that the moment the reader attempts to isolate the plot content "he notices that he is telling another story"[1] indicates the need for such an assumption, not only for any light that may be thrown on *The Sound and the Fury* but for any insight that may emerge concerning Faulkner's method and achievement.

In connection with the interdependence of the sections it has been pointed out that the water-splashing episode "presents all the main characters in situations which foreshadow the main action."[2] Equally important is the fact that the structure of the novel is paralleled by the events of the entire evening of which the water-splashing is only a part. These events reveal the typical gestures and reactions of the four children to each other and to the mysterious advent of death. They chart the range and kind of each of their responses to a new experience. In this way the evening partakes of the dual nature of the novel: primarily it is an objective, dramatic scene revealing the relations and tensions which exist among the children, but at the same time it is a study in perspective. Between the fact of Damuddy's death and the reader stands not only the

8. Heidegger, *Sein und Zeit.*

† From *The Novels of William Faulkner: A Critical Interpretation* (Baton Rouge: Louisiana State UP, 1959), 28–49. Copyright © 1959, 1964 by Louisiana State UP. Copyright © 1987, 1992 by John B. Vickery. Reprinted by permission of the publisher. Page references are to this Norton Critical Edition.

1. "Time in Faulkner. 'The Sound and the Fury'," *La Nouvelle Revue française*, 52 (June 1939) and 53 (July 1939), translated and reprinted in *William Faulkner: Two Decades of Criticism,* ed. F. J. Hoffman and O. W. Vickery (East Lansing, 1951), 180.

2. Lawrence E. Bowling, "The Technique of 'The Sound and the Fury'," *Kenyon Rev.,* 10 (Autumn 1948), reprinted in *Two Decades,* p. 177. At this point I should like to acknowledge my general indebtedness to Bowling's article. Rather than duplicate his points, I have assumed them to be established beyond the need for further elaboration. Hence my analysis largely deals with elements which he has not considered.

primitive mind of the narrator, Benjy, but the diverse attitudes of the other children and the deliberate uncommunicativeness of the adults. The result is not needless complexity or confusion but rather, in Henry James's words, "a certain fullness of truth—truth diffused, distributed and, as it were, atmospheric."[3]

Within the novel as a whole it is Caddy's surrender to Dalton Ames which serves both as the source of dramatic tension and as the focal point for the various perspectives. This is evident in the fact that the sequence of events is not caused by her act—which could be responded to in very different ways—but by the significance which each of her brothers actually attributes to it. As a result, the four sections appear quite unrelated even though they repeat certain incidents and are concerned with the same problem, namely, Caddy and her loss of virginity. Although there is a progressive revelation or rather clarification of the plot, each of the sections is itself static. The consciousness of a character becomes the actual agent illuminating and being illuminated by the central situation. Everything is immobilized in this pattern; there is no development of either character or plot in the traditional manner. This impression is reinforced not only by the shortness of time directly involved in each section but by the absence of any shifts in style of the kind that, for example, accompany the growing maturity of Cash Bundren in As I Lay Dying.

By fixing the structure while leaving the central situation ambiguous, Faulkner forces the reader to reconstruct the story and to apprehend its significance for himself. Consequently, the reader recovers the story at the same time as he grasps the relation of Benjy, Quentin, and Jason to it. This, in turn, is dependent on his comprehension of the relation between the present and the past events with which each of the first three sections deals. As he proceeds from one section to the next, there is a gradual clarification of events, a rounding out of the fragments of scenes and conversations which Benjy reports. Thus, with respect to the plot the four sections are inextricably connected, but with respect to the central situation they are quite distinct and self-sufficient. As related to the central focus, each of the first three sections presents a version of the same facts which is at once the truth and a complete distortion of the truth. It would appear, then, that the theme of The Sound and the Fury, as revealed by the structure, is the relation between the act and man's apprehension of the act, between the event and the interpretation. This relation is by no means a rigid or inelastic thing but is a matter of shifting perspective, for, in a sense, each man creates his own truth. This does not mean that truth does not exist or

3. The Art of the Novel: Critical Prefaces, ed. R. P. Blackmur (New York, 1934), 154.

that it is fragmentary or that it is unknowable; it only insists that truth is a matter of the heart's response as well as the mind's logic.

In keeping with this theme each of the first three sections presents a well demarcated and quite isolated world built around one of these splinters of truth. The fact that Benjy is dumb is symbolic of the closed nature of these worlds; communication is impossible when Caddy who is central to all three means something different to each. For Benjy she is the smell of trees; for Quentin, honor; and for Jason, money or at least the means of obtaining it. Yet these intense private dramas are taking place in a public world primarily concerned with observable behavior. Accordingly, in the fourth section we are shown what an interested but unimplicated observer would see of the Compsons. For the first time we realize that Benjy has blue eyes, that Mrs. Compson habitually wears black dressing gowns and that Jason looks somewhat like a caricature of a bartender. Moreover, since we are prevented from sharing in the consciousness and memories of the characters, Caddy is no longer an immediate center. Nevertheless, through the conflict between Jason and Miss Quentin the final repercussions of her affair penetrate into the life of Jefferson and even Mottson. And out of the Compson house, itself a symbol of isolation, one person, Dilsey, emerges to grasp the truth which must be felt as well as stated.

Out of the relation that Benjy, Quentin and Jason bear to Caddy yet another pattern emerges: a gradual progression from the completely closed and private world of the first section to the completely public world of the fourth. * * * Moreover, each of these shifts from the private to the public world is accompanied by a corresponding shift in the form of apprehension. With Benjy we are restricted entirely to sensation which cannot be communicated; quite appropriately therefore Benjy is unable to speak. * * * Quentin's world is almost as isolated and inflexible as Benjy's, but its order is based on abstractions rather than sensations. Thus, his section is filled with echoes, both literary and Biblical, phrases, names quoted out of context but falling neatly into the pattern of his thought. These echoes assume the quality of a ritual by which he attempts to conjure experience into conformity with his wishes. * * * The third section shows a greater degree of clarity though not of objectivity. The reason for this is that Jason operates in terms of a logic which forms the basis of social communication. We may not approve the direction in which his logic takes him, but that his actions are the result of clear, orderly thinking in terms of cause and effect cannot be disputed. * * * It is part of the general satiric intent of this section that Jason's obvious distortion of Caddy should be associated with logic and reason, for it throws a new perspective not only on the actions of the Compsons but on Jason, the representative of the "rational" man.

The objective nature of the fourth section precludes the use of any single level of apprehension, yet it provokes the most complex response. Dilsey * * * becomes through her actions alone the embodiment of the truth of the heart which is synonymous with morality. The acceptance of whatever time brings, the absence of questioning and petty protests, enables her to create order out of circumstance rather than in defiance of it, and in so doing she gains both dignity and significance for her life. In a sense, Dilsey represents a final perspective directed toward the past and the Compsons, but it is also the reader's perspective for which Dilsey merely provides the vantage point. This fact suggests another reason for the objective narration in this section: to use Dilsey as a point of view character would be to destroy her efficacy as the ethical norm, for that would give us but one more splinter of the truth confined and conditioned by the mind which grasped it.

Our first impression of the Benjy section is that it presents a state of utter chaos for which the only possible justification is the fact that Benjy is an idiot and therefore has a right to be confused. But out of this disorder two patterns emerge: the one, completely independent of public perspective, constitutes Benjy's world, the other serves as the author's guide for enabling the reader to grasp the fragments as a comprehensible order. With respect to the latter, Lawrence Bowling has pointed out both Faulkner's use of italics to indicate shifts in time and the fact that the reasons for such shifts occurring are easily recognizable. An object, a sound, an incident may propel the mind toward some point in the past where a similar experience took place.

Equally important is the fact that there are actually very few scenes involved despite the length of time covered. The events of 7 April 1928 are easily identified because of the prominence given to Luster in them. * * * Otherwise, there are but three extended episodes: one taking place some time in 1898, the day Damuddy died; the second occurring on the evening Benjy received his new name; and the last consisting of the scene of Caddy's wedding. * * *

With consummate skill the repetitions and identifying sensations which are used to guide the reader are also used as the basis of Benjy's own ordering of experience. Benjy's mind works not by association which is dependent, to some extent, on an ability to discriminate as well as compare but by mechanical identification. Thus, being caught on the fence while walking with Luster does not recall an associated feeling or fact but the exact replica of the incident. More important is the fact that the three deaths in the family, which Benjy senses are repetitions of each other, provoke an identical response. What he reacts to is the fact of death, or the fact of being caught on the fence. To differentiate in terms of time and circumstance is a logical matter and therefore beyond Benjy's range of apprehension.

* * *

Benjy's world is made up not only of sensations but of sensations to which he attributes an independent existence. This is further emphasized by his inflexible identification of one word with one object. Very seldom, for example, is the name of a speaker replaced by a pronoun in his section. Each person is freed from the multiplicity of descriptive relations which make him at once man and brother, father, Negro or white. For Benjy, he is forever fixed as simply Jason, Quentin or Luster. In the one scene where Benjy is brought into contact with Luster's friends, parts of the dialogue are consistently attributed to Luster, but the answers appear to come out of the air. Benjy does not know the names of these strangers and to give then an identity in terms of description is beyond his power. His literalism finds its sharpest illustration in the scene where the cries of the golfers are heard. "Caddy" can mean only one thing and elicit only one response.

Benjy both orders and evaluates his experience with this same rigidity. The objects he has learned to recognize constitute an inflexible pattern which he defends against novelty or change with every bellow in his overgrown body. At what time or under what circumstances the small mound of earth which Dilsey calls his graveyard was formed and marked with two empty bottles of blue glass holding withered stalks of jimson weed is unimportant. But that this arrangement, once established, should remain unchanged in the slightest detail is of the utmost importance. When Luster removes one of the bottles, Benjy is momentarily shocked into a silence which is immediately succeeded by the roar of protest. It is not that the bottle has any intrinsic value for Benjy, but merely that it forms part of the pattern which must not be disturbed. The fixed route to the graveyard is also sacred; Benjy is overwhelmed with horror and agony when Luster takes the wrong turn only to subside the minute the mistake is corrected.

Within this rigid world Caddy is at once the focus of order and the instrument of its destruction. The pasture, the fire and sleep, the three things Benjy loves most, are associated with her, as is illustrated by the recurrent phrase "Caddy smelled like trees," his refusal to go to sleep without her and his memory of her during the rainy evening. On that evening, for a brief moment, everything in his world was in its proper place. Caddy both realizes and respects his fear of change: while playing at the Branch she is quick to reassure him that she is not really going to run away; later, she washes off her perfume and gives the rest of it to Dilsey in order to reassure him. Even when she has accepted the inevitability of change for herself and is preparing to marry Herbert, she tries to bind Quentin to a promise of seeing that Benjy's life is not further disordered by his being committed to a mental institution. Yet what Benjy most expects of Caddy is the one thing she cannot give him, for his expectation is based on his complete indifference to or rather ignorance of time. As long as Caddy is in time, she cannot free either herself or his world from change. His dependence on her physical presence, her scent of trees, is subject to constant threats which he fends off to the best of his ability. Sin and perfume are equally resented as intrusions of change into his arbitrary and absolute pattern. Thus, Caddy, as in the Quentin section, is at once identified with the rigid order of Benjy's private world and with the disorder of actual experience. Depending on which of the two is dominant at the moment, Benjy moans or smiles serenely.

✳ ✳ ✳

Quentin too has constructed for himself a private world to which Caddy is essential, a world which is threatened and finally destroyed by her involvement in circumstance. His hopeless and endless brooding is but Benjy's moan become articulate though not rational. However, his order is based on emotions rather than sensations, on concepts rather than physical objects. And whereas Benjy is saved by being outside time, Quentin is destroyed by his excessive awareness of it. For the former, both the pattern and its disordering are eternally present as his alternation between moaning and smiling demonstrates; for the latter, the pattern has become a part of the past which cannot be recaptured and contentment has been replaced by despair. Quentin can neither accept nor reconcile himself to that change or to the possibility that a further change may make even his despair a thing of the past, and so he chooses death as a means of escaping the situation.

The structure of the section with its two sets of events, one past and the other present, reflects Quentin's problem. Throughout the day he can proceed quite mechanically with such chores as getting dressed, packing, writing letters and generally tidying up the loose ends of his life at Harvard. To a large extent he can even make the appropriate gestures and speak the proper words expected of him by others. Meanwhile, his mind is occupied with echoes of the past which make themselves felt with increasing intensity until they threaten to prevent even a mechanical attention to the details of living through that final day. Quentin cannot escape either his memories of the past or his involvement in the present.

*　*　*

The order which Quentin had once built around Caddy is as rigid and inflexible as Benjy's and it shares Benjy's fear of change and his expectation that all experience should conform to his pattern. The cause of his ineffectuality and his ultimate destruction is the fact that his system antecedes his experience and eventually is held in defiance of experience. His is an ethical order based on words, on "fine, dead sounds," the meaning of which he has yet to learn. Insofar as virginity is a concept, associated with virtue and honor, it becomes the center of Quentin's world, and since it is also physically present in Caddy, it forms a precarious link between his world and that of experience. Mr. Compson remarks that virginity is merely a transient physical state which has been given its ethical significance by men. What they have chosen to make it mean is something which is a defiance of nature, an artificial isolation of the woman. * * * Since his emotional responses center on these concepts, Quentin is quite incapable of love for any human being, even Caddy. Despite his feverish preoccupation with ethics, he is unable to perform any ethical actions himself; even his death is not so much a protest as it is simply a withdrawal. Thus, it is not the time that is out of joint but Quentin's relation to time.

*　*　*

The symbols and recurrent phrases that run through Quentin's section both intensify the emotional impact and reinforce the meaning. Such names as Jesus, St. Francis, Moses, Washington, and Byron not only add a richness of historical and literary allusion but convey the nature of Quentin's world. Into that world Benjy is admitted as "Benjamin the child of mine old age held hostage into Egypt" and Caddy as Eve or Little Sister Death. Mr. Compson forces an entry not as father or friend but as a voice which can juggle words and ideas while insisting on their emptiness. As for Quentin, he sees himself as the hero of the family drama, "the bitter prophet and inflexible corruptless judge." Part of his outrage and frustration in connection with Caddy is that neither her husband nor her lover seems worthy, in his eyes, of assuming a role in his world: Herbert is obviously despicable and Ames refuses to act in terms of Quentin's preconceptions.

The heavy, choking fragrance of honeysuckle dramatizes the conflict between his order and the blind forces of nature which constantly threaten to destroy it. Honeysuckle is the rife animality of sex, the incomprehensible and hateful world for which Caddy has abandoned his paradise, and hence it is also the symbol of his defeat. Yet honeysuckle is only a sensation, just as Caddy's affair with Ames is simply a natural event. It is Quentin who makes of the one a symbol of "night and unrest" and of the other the unforgivable sin. The references to roses have a similar function in that they too are associated with sex, but they are identified with a single scene, that of Caddy's wedding. Therefore, they are at once the symbol of the world he fears and of his irrevocable betrayal by that world.

* * *

The constant references to the shadows and the mirror emphasize the barrier between Quentin and reality. It is not only Benjy but also Quentin who sees Caddy's wedding reflected in the mirror. Caddy, however, cannot be confined to its surface; she runs not only out of the mirror but out of his and Benjy's world. Similarly, Quentin sees her and Ames not as people but as silhouettes distorted against the sky. He is lost amid these shadows, feeling that they falsify the objects they pretend to reflect, yet unable to reach out beyond them. It is significant that he sees only those aspects of Caddy as shadows which he cannot incorporate into his world: it is her love affair and her marriage which he finds perverse, mocking, denying the significance they should have affirmed. The same feeling of mockery is present in his insistence that he has tricked his shadow. A man who is dead needs no shadow, but still his accompanies him throughout the day as if it were mirroring reality when in truth it is but aping another illusion.

The number of times that the shadow images are fused with images of water indicates that death by water is Quentin's way of reconciling his two worlds, of merging shadow and reality and tempering their conflict. Whatever suggestion of purification may be present, water is primarily a symbol of oblivion for Quentin. Narcissa Benbow[4] can act as if a little water would clear her of her deed, but as Dilsey's determined scouring of Caddy's bottom shows, the stains of one's experience are not that easily removed. Both Quentin and Caddy run to the Branch to surrender themselves to its hypnotic rhythm which, like sleep, soothes the mind into unconsciousness, blurring thought and emotion, eliminating the necessity for acting. It is in the hope of making this peace eternal that Quentin surrenders his body to the water where the hard knots of circumstance will be untangled and the roof of wind will stand forever between him and the loud world.

---

4. Narcissa Benbow figures prominently in both *Flags in the Dust* and *Sanctuary*. [*Editor's note*.]

With Jason's section we enter into a world far different from Benjy's or Quentin's, yet related to theirs through Caddy. It represents a third possible way of reacting to experience, as distorted yet as "true" as the former two. Since Jason reacts logically rather than emotionally, his section offers no barriers to comprehension. His particular method of ordering and explaining his actions in terms of cause and effect, profit and loss, is all too familiar. Yet logic, presumably the basis of human communication and hence of society, isolates Jason as effectively as the moral abstractions of Quentin or the complete dependence on sensations of Benjy. In the midst of Jefferson or even his family, he is by necessity as well as by choice alone. And instead of being concerned, he glories in his self-sufficiency. * * *

One of Jason's dominant characteristics, and the main source of humor, is his pride that he has no illusions about his family or himself. The humor, however, arises not from the situation but from the way in which Jason talks about it. * * * The conviction that he alone has a firm grasp on reality results in a literalism untouched by any hint of qualification in Jason's thinking. Through it we get a new and welcome perspective on the Compsons, but it is just a perspective and not the final word that Jason makes it out to be. It is his very insistence on facing facts that causes his distorted view of Caddy, his family and the whole human race. He cannot imagine that there might be other facts, other aspects of the situation, than the ones that directly affect him; as a result, he sees certain things so clearly that all others escape him. In the process logic replaces truth, and law, justice. * * * He is not concerned with either Caddy or her daughter except as they enter into the pattern of loss and recompense and finally loss again. In short, his is a world reduced to calculation in which no subjective claims are tolerated and no margin for error allowed.

This calculating approach to experience pervades his every act, no matter how trivial. * * * It is his method of assuming control over experience by preventing himself from becoming involved in circumstances he has not foreseen. His control over the Compson house reveals the same tendency to think in terms of contracts.

Jason's concern with forms of action rather than with the actions themselves is reflected in his legalistic view of society and especially of ethics. It is on this view that the double irony of Miss Quentin's theft of his thievings hinges. He has retrieved his losses, suffered because of Caddy, at the expense of Caddy's daughter without actually breaking any law. * * * However, with her one unpremeditated act Miss Quentin destroys the work of years; more important, she is as safe from prosecution despite her heedlessness as Jason was because of all his care. Legally, she has only stolen what already belonged to her. When Jason demands an endorsement of his just indignation from the sheriff, the latter refuses to help on the basis of the very letter of the law Jason had so carefully observed. * * * During his frantic pursuit of Miss Quentin the nature of the conflict in which Jason is involved becomes explicit. He realizes that his enemy is not his niece or even the man with the red tie; rather it is "the sequence of natural events and their causes which shadows every mans [sic] brow." From the first he had distrusted everything which he could not himself control. Unlike Quentin for whom reality lay in ethical concepts, Jason had learned to believe in whatever he could hold in his hands or keep in his pocket. That alone could be protected from chance and change. * * * Yet even that is vulnerable to circumstance, to the accidental juxtaposition in place and time of a girl's whim and a man's red tie. Hence his outrage that Miss Quentin should have taken the money more or less on impulse; had her act been deliberate, calculated, he could have foreseen it and so guarded against it. The red tie becomes for him the symbol of the irrational, the antithesis of his own careful logic.

* * *

In the last section we finally emerge from the closed world of the Compson Mile into the public world as represented by Jefferson [and] * * * Dilsey emerges not only as a Negro servant in the Compson household but as a human being. With nothing to judge but her actions, with no prolonged ethical or religious polemics, her very presence enables the reader to achieve a final perspective on the lives of the Compsons. Mrs. Compson's nagging self-pity, Jason's carping exactions, Miss Quentin's thoughtlessness gain a dramatic actuality lacking while they were being filtered through an individual consciousness. Various contrasts between Dilsey and the others are delineated with striking clarity. The contrast becomes actual conflict where Dilsey and Jason are concerned. It is not only that Dilsey "survives," because, for that matter, so does Jason, but that her endurance has strength to suffer without rancor as well as to resist, to accept as well as to protest. She is the only one who challenges his word in the household, who defends the absent Caddy, Miss Quentin, Benjy and even Luster from his anger. But more important, she challenges the validity and efficacy of his world by a passive and irrational resistance to which he has no counter. That someone should work without pay is so foreign to his system that he is helpless in the face of it.

There is no doubt but that Dilsey is meant to represent the ethical norm, the realizing and acting out of one's humanity; it is from this that the Compsons have deviated, each into his separate world.

The mother and [Quentin and Jason] have abandoned their humanity for the sake of pride or vanity or self-pity. Both Benjy and Caddy are tests of the family's humanity, he simply because he is not fully human and she because her conduct creates a socio-moral hiatus between the family and Jefferson. Benjy's behavior is a constant trial to the family and to this extent counterpoints Caddy's lone disgracing act. Both challenge the family's capacity for understanding and forgiveness and the family fails both. Quite appropriately, the Compson Mile exists in an atmosphere not only of disintegration but of constriction. The property shrinks as the town begins "to encroach and then nibble at and into it" (261). The only room which seems to be lived in is Dilsey's kitchen; the others are so many private mausoleums. While each of the Compsons to some extent attempts to coerce experience and to deny his involvement in the sequence of natural events and their causes, Dilsey accepts whatever time brings. She alone never suffers that moment of rejection which is equated with death.

By working with circumstance instead of against it she creates order out of disorder; by accommodating herself to change she manages to keep the Compson household in some semblance of decency. While occupied with getting breakfast, she is yet able to start the fire in Luster's inexplicable absence, provide a hot water bottle for Mrs. Compson, see to Benjy's needs and soothe various ruffled tempers. All this despite the constant interruptions of Luster's perverseness, Benjy's moaning, Mrs. Compson's complaints, and even Jason's maniacal fury. Nor is Dilsey's attitude of acceptance confined to the minor disorders of daily tasks. The same calmness is evident with regard to Caddy's affair, Quentin's suicide and the arrival of Caddy's baby. As she herself states: she has brought up Caddy and can do the same for Miss Quentin. And if it so happens that their conduct mocks all her care and love, then it is time to find another order in the subsequent confusion. Dilsey's attitude, as she lives it, is formed by her instinctive feeling that whatever happens must be met with courage and dignity in which there is no room for passivity or pessimism.

Her ability to stand steadfast without faltering "before the hopeless juggernaut of circumstance" finds further expression in her patient preoccupation with the present, which is the only possible way of living with time. This does not imply that Dilsey is cut off from the past but only that she deals with it as it is caught up in the present without attempting to perpetuate a part of it as Quentin does, or to circumvent it as Jason tries to do. In a sense, she is a living record of all that has happened to the Compsons made significant by her own strength and courage. It is a record of pain and suffering and change but also of endurance and permanence in change.

In describing Dilsey as an ethical norm it should be stressed that she propounds no system, no code of behavior or belief, and this despite the emphasis on the Easter service which she attends. Neither in her attitude nor in the service itself is there any reference to sin and punishment but only to suffering and its surcease. At no time does Dilsey judge any of the Compsons, not even Jason, though she does object at one point to those who frown on Benjy's presence in a Negro church. But her presence enables the reader to judge not systems but actions and hence to grasp the truth instinctively: "They [Negroes] come into white people's lives like that in sudden sharp black trickles that isolate white facts for an instant in unarguable truth like under a microscope" (113). And though she does not judge, Dilsey is never deceived; her comprehension of the relations between Caddy and the rest of the family is unerring.

Dilsey's participation in the Easter service is the one meaningful ritual in the book. As she proceeds sedately from house to church, acknowledging greetings with proper reserve and dignity, she is still conscious or being, in some sense, a member of the Compson household with a certain prestige and obligations. With each member of the congregation similarly conscious of his own distinctive position in society, the Reverend Shegog begins using the magic of his voice. When he concludes, communication has been replaced by communion in which each member loses his identity but finds his humanity and the knowledge that all men are equal and brothers in their suffering.

Out of Dilsey's actions and her participation in the Easter service arise once more the simple verities of human life, "the old universal truths lacking which any story is ephemeral and doomed—love and honor and pity and pride and compassion and sacrifice."[5] It is these truths which throw the final illumination not only on Caddy and the whole sequence of events that started with her affair but also on what each of the Compsons believed her to be. The splinters of truth presented in the first three sections reverberate with the sound and the fury signifying nothing. But out of those same events, the same disorder and confusion, come Dilsey's triumph and her peace, lending significance not only to her own life but to the book as a whole.

5. The Stockholm Address. [Faulkner's speech of acceptance upon the award of the Nobel Prize for Literature—*Editor's note.*]

CLEANTH BROOKS

Man, Time, and Eternity†

* * *

The Sound and the Fury has on occasion been read as another Faulknerian document describing the fall of the Old South. Perhaps it is, but what it most clearly records is the downfall of a particular family, and the case seems rather special. The basic cause of the breakup of the Compson family—let the more general cultural causes be what they may—is the cold and self-centered mother who is sensitive about the social status of her own family, the Bascombs, who feels the birth of an idiot son as a kind of personal affront, who spoils and corrupts her favorite son, and who withholds any real love and affection from her other children and her husband. Caroline Compson is not so much an actively wicked and evil person as a cold weight of negativity which paralyzes the normal family relationships. She is certainly at the root of Quentin's lack of confidence in himself and his inverted pride. She is at least the immediate cause of her husband's breakdown into alcoholic cynicism, and doubtless she is ultimately responsible for Caddy's promiscuity. There is some evidence that Caddy's conduct was obsessive and compulsive, a flight from her family. She tells her brother Quentin: "There was something terrible in me sometimes at night I could see it grinning at me I could see it through [my lovers] grinning at me through their faces" (74).

In Faulkner's story "That Evening Sun,"[1] the events of which apparently occur in 1898, the earlier family relationships of the Compsons are revealingly portrayed. When Nancy, their Negro servant, is terrified of going home because she fears that her common-law husband is coming there to cut her throat, Mr. Compson is sympathetic and tries to be helpful. He obviously finds it difficult to take with full seriousness Nancy's irrational conviction that her man is lurking about ready to kill her, but Mr. Compson does take with great seriousness her abject terror, and he tries to find some solution that will calm her—having her stay with a friend, or putting the case before the police. But his wife, in notable contrast, is far too self-centered to view Nancy's plight with any sympathy. Nancy's terror is to Mrs. Compson simply a nuisance, and the sooner Nancy is got out of the house the better.

† From *William Faulkner: The Yoknapatawpha Country* (New Haven and London: Yale UP, 1963), 334–36, 341–44. Reprinted by permission of Louisiana State University Press. Page references are to this Norton Critical Edition.
1. See pp. 235–48 of this Norton Critical Edition.

In that story the Compson children have already assumed the personality patterns that we shall find later. Though they are too young to comprehend fully Nancy's desperation, Caddy and Quentin at least respond to the Negro woman's terror with concerned curiosity and, insofar as they are capable, sympathy. Jason is already a wretched little complainer, interested neither in Nancy nor in his brother and sister except as he may get his way by constantly threatening to "tell on" them.

Mr. Compson by 1910 was a defeated man. Perhaps he had always been a weak man, not endowed with the fighting spirit necessary to save his family. But there are plenty of indications that he was a man possessed of love and compassion. Benjy remembers a scene in which Caddy and Father and Jason were in Mother's chair. Jason had been crying, and his father was evidently comforting him. Caddy's head, Benjy remembers, was on Father's shoulder. And when Benjy himself went over to the chair, "Father lifted me into the chair too, and Caddy held me" (48). Long after Mr. Compson's death, Dilsey remembers him as a force for order in the household and reproaches Jason with the words: "if Mr Jason was still here hit ud be different" (137). And when Caddy pleads with her cold-hearted brother to be allowed to see her baby, she says to him: "You have Father's name: do you think I'd have to ask him twice? once, even?" (138). The attentive reader will have noticed that even in his drinking, Mr. Compson has evidently gone from better to worse. Caddy tells Quentin: "Father will be dead in a year they say if he doesnt stop drinking and he wont stop he cant stop since I since last summer" (82). Evidently, the knowledge of his daughter's wantonness had hit Mr. Compson hard, and his parade of cynicism about women and virginity, so much of which Quentin recalls on the day of his death, must have been in part an attempt to soften the blow for Quentin and perhaps for himself. We miss the point badly if we take it that Mr. Compson, comfortable in his cynicism, simply didn't care what his daughter did.

Quentin was apparently very close to his father and the influence of his father on him was obviously very powerful. The whole of the Quentin section is saturated with what "Father said" and with references to comparisons that Father used and observations about life that Father made. Though his father seems to have counseled acquiescence in the meaninglessness of existence, it is plain that it was from him that Quentin derived his high notion of the claims of honor. Quentin has not the slightest doubt as to what he ought to do: he ought to drive Caddy's seducer out of town, and if the seducer refuses to go, he ought to shoot him. But Quentin is not up to the heroic role. He tries, but he cannot even hurt Ames, much less kill him. Caddy sees Quentin as simply meddling in her affairs, the quixotic little brother who is to be pitied but not feared or respected.

Since *Absalom, Absalom!* was written years after *The Sound and the Fury*, we must exercise caution in using the Quentin of the later novel to throw light upon the Quentin of the earlier. But Faulkner, in choosing the character Quentin for service in *Absalom, Absalom!*, must have deemed the choice a sound one. He must have felt that the experience that Quentin was to undergo in talking with his father about the Sutpens and on his journey out to Sutpen's Hundred would be compatible with, and relevant to, what he had Quentin undergo in *The Sound and the Fury*. The Quentin of *The Sound and the Fury* would indeed have been terribly impressed by Henry Sutpen's acceptance of the heroic and tragic role thrust upon him by circumstance, and the more humiliated to have to acknowledge his own pitiful inadequacy when it became necessary to protect his own sister's honor. * * *

* * *

The downfall of the house of Compson is the kind of degeneration which can occur, and has occurred, anywhere, at any time. William Butler Yeats' play *Purgatory* [1938] is a moving dramatization of the end of a great house in Ireland. The play ends with the last member of the family, a murderous-minded old tinker, standing outside the ruins of the ancestral house; but the burning of that house and the decay of the family have no special connection with the troubles of Ireland. According to the author, the disaster resulted from a bad marriage! The real significance of the Southern setting in *The Sound and the Fury* resides, as so often elsewhere in Faulkner, in the fact that the breakdown of a family can be exhibited more poignantly and significantly in a society which is old-fashioned and in which the family is still at the center. The dissolution of the family as an institution has probably gone further in the suburban areas of California and Connecticut than it has in the small towns of Mississippi. For that very reason, what happens to the Compsons might make less noise and cause less comment, and even bring less pain to the individuals concerned, if the Compsons lived in a more progressive and liberal environment. Because the Compsons have been committed to old-fashioned ideals—close family loyalty, home care for defective children, and the virginity of unmarried daughters—the breakup of the family registers with greater impact.

The decay of the Compsons can be viewed, however, not merely with reference to the Southern past but to the contemporary American scene. It is tempting to read it as a parable of the disintegration of modern man. Individuals no longer sustained by familial and cultural unity are alienated and lost in private worlds. One thinks here not merely of Caddy, homeless, the sexual adventuress adrift in the world, or of Quentin, out of touch with reality and moving inevitably to his death, but also and even primarily of Jason, for whom the breakup of the family means an active rejection of claims and responsibilities and, with it, a sense of liberation. Jason resolves to be himself and to be self-sufficient. He says: "Besides, like I say I guess I dont need any man's help to get along I can stand on my own feet like I always have" (136). Jason prides himself in managing matters by himself and—since this is the other side of the same coin—refuses to heed the claims of anyone but himself. In his appendix Faulkner says that Jason thinks "nothing whatever of God one way or the other" but simply tries to keep clear of "the police" and fears and respects "only the Negro woman" (267), Dilsey. Jason is done with religion in every way, including its etymological sense as a "binding back." Jason is bound back to nothing. He repudiates any traditional tie. He means to be on his own and he rejects every community. The fact shows plainly in the way he conducts himself not only in his own household but also in the town of Jefferson.

The one member of the Compson household who represents a unifying and sustaining force is the Negro servant Dilsey. She tries to take care of Benjy and to give the girl Quentin the mothering she needs. In contrast to Mrs. Compson's vanity and whining self-pity, Dilsey exhibits charity and rugged good sense. She is warned by her daughter Frony that taking Benjy to church with her will provoke comments from the neighbors. "Folks talkin," Frony says; to which Dilsey answers: "Whut folks? . . . And I know whut kind of folks. Trash white folks. Dat's who it is. Thinks he aint good enough fer white church, but nigger church aint good enough fer him" (189). Frony remarks that folks talk just the same, but Dilsey has her answer: "Den you send um to me. Tell um de good Lawd dont keer whether he smart er not. Dont nobody but white trash keer dat." All of which amounts to sound manners and to sound theology as well.

Faulkner does not present Dilsey as a black fairy-godmother or as a kind of middle-aged Pollyanna full of the spirit of cheerful optimism. Even his physical description of her looks in another direction. We are told that she had once been a big woman, but now the unpadded skin is loosely draped upon "the indomitable skeleton" which is left "rising like a ruin or a landmark above the somnolent and impervious guts, and above that the collapsed face that gave the impression of the bones themselves being outside the flesh, lifted into the driving day with an expression at once fatalistic and of a child's astonished disappointment" (173). What the expression means is best interpreted by what she says and does in the novel, but the description clearly points to something other than mindless cheeriness. Dilsey's essential hopefulness has not been obliterated; she is not an embittered woman, but her optimism has been chastened by hurt and disappointment.

Faulkner does not make the mistake of accounting for Dilsey's virtues through some mystique of race in which good primitive black folk stand over against corrupt wicked white folk. Dilsey herself has no such notions. When her son Luster remarks of the Compson household: "Dese is funny folks. Glad I aint none of em," she says: "Lemme tell you somethin, nigger boy, you got jes es much Compson devilment in you es any of em" (180). She believes in something like original sin: men are not "naturally" good but require discipline and grace.

Dilsey, then, is no noble savage and no *schöne Seele*.[2] Her view of the world and mankind is thoroughly Christian, simple and limited as her theological expression of her faith would have to be. On the other hand, Dilsey is no plaster saint. She is not easy on her own children. ("Dont stand dar in de rain, fool," she tells Luster.) She does not always offer the soft answer that turneth away wrath. She rebukes Mrs. Compson with "I dont see how you expect anybody to sleep, wid you standin in de hall, holl in at folks fum de crack of dawn," and she refuses Mrs. Compson's hypocritical offer to fix breakfast, saying: "En who gwine eat yo messin? Tell me dat" (177). Dilsey's goodness is no mere goodness by, and of, nature, if one means by this a goodness that justifies a faith in man as man. Dilsey does not believe in man; she believes in God.

Dilsey's poverty and her status as a member of a deprived race do not, then, assure her nobility, but they may have had something to do with her remaining close to a concrete world of values so that she is less perverted by abstraction and more honest than are most white people in recognizing what is essential and basic. In general, Faulkner's Negro characters show less false pride, less false idealism, and more seasoned discipline in human relationships. Dilsey's race has also had something to do with keeping her close to a world still informed by religion. These matters are important: just how important they are is revealed by the emphasis Faulkner gives to the Easter service that Dilsey attends.

The Compson family—whatever may be true of the white community at large in the Jefferson of 1910—has lost its religion. Quentin's sad reveries are filled with references to Jesus and Saint Francis, but it is plain that he has retreated into some kind of Stoicism, a version which is reflected in his father's advice to him: "We must just stay awake and see evil done for a little. Quentin's reply is that "it doesn't have to be even that long for a man of courage" (176),

2. German: Beautiful soul. [*Editor's note.*]

and the act of courage in the Roman style takes Quentin into the river. Mrs. Compson, when she finds that the girl Quentin has eloped, asks Dilsey to bring her the Bible, but obviously Mrs. Compson knows nothing about either sin or redemption. Her deepest concern is with gentility and social position. And Jason, as we have seen, worships only the almighty dollar.

* * *

JOHN T. IRWIN

[Doubling and Incest in *The Sound and the Fury*]†

When Quentin demands that his father act against the seducer Dalton Ames, Quentin, by taking this initiative, is in effect trying to supplant his father, to seize his authority. But Quentin's father refuses to act, and the sense of Mr. Compson's refusal is that Quentin cannot seize his father's authority because there is no authority to seize. Quentin's alcoholic, nihilistic father presents himself as an emasculated son, ruined by General Compson's failure. Mr. Compson psychologically castrates Quentin by confronting him with a father figure, a model for manhood, who is himself a castrated son. Mr. Compson possesses no authority that Quentin could seize because what Mr. Compson inherited from the General was not power but impotence. If Quentin is a son struggling in the grip of Father Time, so is his father. And it is exactly that argument that Mr. Compson uses against Quentin. When Quentin demands that they act against the seducer, Mr. Compson answers in essence, "Do you realize how many times this has happened before and how many times it will happen again? You are seeking a once-and-for-all solution to this problem, but there are no once-and-for-all solutions. One has no force, no authority to act in this matter because one has no originality. The very repetitive nature of time precludes the existence of originality within its cycles. You cannot be the father because I am not the father—only Time is the father." When Quentin demands that they avenge Candace's virginity, his father replies, "Women are never virgins. Purity is a negative state and therefore contrary to nature. It's nature is hurting you not Caddy and I said That's just words and he said So is virginity and I said

---

† From *Doubling and Incest / Repetition and Revenge: A Speculative Reading of Faulkner* (Baltimore and London: Johns Hopkins UP, 1975) 110–13, 153–72. Copyright © 1975 by The Johns Hopkins University Press. Reprinted by permission of The Johns Hopkins University Press. Page references are to this Norton Critical Edition.

you dont know. You cant know and he said Yes. On the instant when we come to realise that tragedy is second-hand" (77). In essence Quentin's father says, "We cannot act because there exists no virginity to avenge and because there exists no authority by which we could avenge since we have no originality. We are second-hand. You are a copy of a copy. To you, a son who has only been a son, it might seem that a father has authority because he comes first, but to one who has been both a father and a son, it is clear that to come before is not necessarily to come first, that priority is not necessarily originality. My fate was determined by my father as your fate is determined by yours." Quentin's attempt to avenge his sister's lost virginity (proving thereby that it had once existed) and maintain the family honor is an attempt to maintain the possibility of "virginity" in a larger sense, the possibility of the existence of a virgin space within which one can still be first, within which one can have authority through originality, a virgin space like that Mississippi wilderness into which the first Compson (Jason Lycurgus I) rode in 1811 to seize the land later known as the Compson Domain, the land "fit to breed princes, statesmen and generals and bishops, to avenge the dispossessed Compsons from Culloden and Carolina and Kentucky" (261), just as Sutpen came to Mississippi to get land and found a dynasty that would avenge the dispossessed Sutpens of West Virginia. In a letter to Malcolm Cowley, Faulkner said that Quentin regarded Sutpen as "originless." Which is to say, that being without origin, Sutpen tries to become his own origin, his own father, an attempt implicit in the very act of choosing a father figure to replace his real father. When Quentin tells the story of the Sutpens in *Absalom*, he is not just telling his own personal story, he is telling the story of the Compson family as well.

The event that destroyed Sutpen's attempt to found a dynasty is the same event that began the decline of the Compson family—the Civil War closed off the virgin space and the time of origins, so that the antebellum South became in the minds of postwar Southerners that debilitating "golden age and lost world" in comparison with which the present is inadequate. The decline of the Compsons began with General Compson "who failed at Shiloh in '62 and failed again though not so badly at Resaca in '64, who put the first mortgage on the still intact square mile to a New England carpetbagger in '66, after the old town had been burned by the Federal General Smith and the new little town, in time to be populated mainly by the descendants not of Compsons but of Snopeses, had begun to encroach and then nibble at and into it as the failed brigadier spent the next forty years selling fragments of it off to keep up the mortgage on the remainder" (261). The last of the Compson Domain is sold by Quentin's father to send Quentin to Harvard.

Mr. Compson's denial of the existence of an authority by which he could act necessarily entails his denial of virginity, for there is no possibility of that originality from which authority springs if there is no virgin space within which one can be first. And for the same reason Quentin's obsession with Candace's loss of virginity is necessarily an obsession with his own impotence, since the absence of the virgin space renders him powerless. When Mr. Compson refuses to act against Dalton Ames, Quentin tries to force him to take some action by claiming that he and Candace have committed incest—that primal affront to the authority of the father. But where there is no authority there can be no affront, and where the father feels his own inherited impotence, he cannot believe that his son has power. Mr. Compson tells Quentin that he doesn't believe that he and Candace committed incest, and Quentin says, "If we could have just done something so dreadful and Father said That's sad too, people cannot do anything that dreadful they cannot do anything very dreadful at all they cannot even remember tomorrow what seemed dreadful today and I said, You can shirk all things and he said, Ah can you" (53). Since Mr. Compson believes that man is helpless in the grip of time, that everything is fated, there is no question of shirking or not shirking, for there is no question of willing. In discussing the revenge against time, Nietzsche speaks of those preachers of despair who say, "Alas, the stone *It was* cannot be moved" and Mr. Compson's last words in Quentin's narrative are "was the saddest word of all there is nothing else in the world its not despair until time its not even time until it was" (118).

*   *   *

Quentin's love of death incorporates his incestuous love for his sister precisely because his sister, as a substitute for Quentin's mother, is synonymous with death. On the morning of the day he dies, Quentin thinks, "I dont suppose anybody ever deliberately listens to a watch or a clock. You dont have to. You can be oblivious to the sound for a long while, then in a second of ticking it can create in the mind unbroken the long diminishing parade of time you didn't hear. Like Father said down the long and lonely lightrays you might see Jesus walking, like. And the good Saint Francis that said Little Sister Death, that never had a sister. . . . That Christ was not crucified: he was worn away by a minute clicking of little wheels. That had no sister" (50–51). Christ had no sister, but he had a mother with whom he becomes progressively identified, so that, for example, when he is taken down from sacrificing his life on the phallic tree, he is laid in his mother's lap, and the iconography of the Pietà becomes that of the Madonna and Child. As a further link between Quentin's suicide and Christ's sacrifice, we should note that the principle of sacrifice is the same as that of self-castration—the giving up of a part to save the whole, and in both sacrifice and self-castration the part is given up to save the whole from the wrath of the father. But in Christ's sacrifice and Quentin's suicide, the *son* is the part that is given up, and self-castration is death. In his discussion of the sacrifices of Isaac and Jesus, Rosolato points out that for the psychotic the notion of sacrifice becomes the fantasy of murder or suicide. The psychotic concept of sacrifice is located in the realm of an Idealized Father whose image blends the images of the Father and the Mother: "in reality, one can intervene for the other; they are interchangeable in a single ambivalence." In this situation, sacrifice "is a manner of extricating oneself from all genealogy and merging oneself with that megalomaniac and punctiform image." Rosolato adds that "to this situation central for psychosis, always in quest of an impossible sacrifice in which the subject would be himself the agent or the victim, corresponds, in myth, the connecting point of the Passion and the Sacrifice."[1] The essence of Christ's sacrifice and Quentin's suicide is that in each the subject is both the agent and the victim, at once active and passive, a conjunction of masculine and feminine.

If the Biblical context of Candace's name[2] suggests that Quentin is his sister's eunuch, then it is worth noting that in the Gospels Christ recommends that his disciples make themselves eunuchs for the kingdom of heaven: "For there are some eunuchs, which were so born from *their* mother's womb: and there are some eunuchs, which were made eunuchs of men: and there be eunuchs, which have made themselves eunuchs for the kingdom of heaven's sake. He that is able to receive *it*, let him receive *it*" (Matthew, 19:12). In Quentin's distorted version of Christ's sacrifice, what is transmitted beyond death is not the phallic power but the interruption of that power. A few months after Quentin's suicide, Candace's daughter is born, and she is named Quentin after her dead uncle. The female Quentin is an embodiment of that interruption of genealogy effected by her uncle's death, for as Faulkner says, she is "fatherless nine months before her birth, nameless at birth and already doomed to be unwed from the instant the dividing egg determined its sex" (269). There is as well in this transmission of interrupted genealogy an element of revenge, a reversal inflicted on a substitute, for as the male Quentin's death is put in the context of Christ's death and resurrection, so the female Quentin, on the day before Easter in

1. Guy Rosolato, *Essais sur le symbolique* (Paris: Gallimard, 1969), 63. [*Editor's note.*]
2. See Acts, 8:26–31, where Candace, Queen of the Ethiopians, is associated with a eunuch of great authority whom she has put in charge of all her treasures. [*Editor's note.*]

1928, escapes from the womb of the Compson home, stealing in the process the money that her Uncle Jason had withheld from her allowance—a theft that is presented as a symbolic castration of Jason (who is his father's namesake and who had his younger brother Benjy gelded) by the dead Quentin's namesake. Faulkner says of Jason, "Of his niece he did not think at all, nor the arbitrary valuation of the money. Neither of them had had entity or individuality for him for ten years; together they merely symbolized the job in the bank of which he had been deprived before he ever got it. . . . 'I'll think of something else,' he said, so he thought about Lorraine. He imagined himself in bed with her, only he was just lying beside her, pleading with her to help him, then he thought of the money again, and that he had been outwitted by a woman, a girl. If he could just believe it was the man who had robbed him. But to have been robbed of that which was to have compensated him for the lost job, which he had acquired through so much effort and risk, by the very symbol of the lost job itself, and worst of all, by a bitch of a girl" (199–200). Since Jason's friend Lorraine is a prostitute, the theft of Jason's money is a castration of his power to buy sex, and since the money that was stolen was in part money that Jason had stolen from his niece, Jason is rendered impotent, he is powerless to gain any legal redress. Jason dies a childless bachelor.

*　*　*

As a counterpoint to the transmission of interrupted physical genealogy that we find in the English runner [in *A Fable*] and the female Quentin, the two youngest male descendants of the Sutpen and Compson families, the black Jim Bond and the white Benjy Compson, are both congenital idiots whose physical condition, in this final instance of black-white doubling, evokes the traditional biological punishment of that incest from which all doubling springs. But of course, no real physical incest occurs in the Sutpen or Compson families as far as we know, so that the condition of Jim Bond and Benjy Compson is a symbol of that psychological incest that pervades both families and that makes the families in turn symbolic of a place and a time.

One could continue indefinitely multiplying examples of doubling between the stories of the Sutpen and Compson families and finding in other Faulkner novels incidents in which these doublings are doubled again, but by now we have established the outlines and the importance of a structure that is central to Faulkner's work. In this structure, the struggle between the father and the son in the incest complex is played out again and again in a series of spatial and temporal repetitions, a series of substitutive doublings and reversals in which generation in time becomes a self-perpetuating cycle of revenge on a substitute, the passing on from father to son of a fated repetition as a positive or a negative inheritance. Religion as "the longing for the father," to use Freud's phrase, attempts, successfully or not, to release man from this spirit of revenge through the mechanism of sacrifice and the alliance of the father and the son. In sacrifice, the impulses of the father against the son and those of the son against the father are simultaneously acted out on a symbolic, mediatory third term, so that the contrary impulses momentarily cancel each other out in a single act with a double psychological significance. Yet obviously, religious sacrifice as an institutionalized substitute for those impulses is also a conscious, communal preserver and transmitter of those impulses, capable at any moment of reconverting the symbolic death struggle between father and son into the real death struggle.

This structure, as I have tried to present it in all its complexity, exists in no single Faulkner novel nor in the sum total of those novels; it exists, rather, in that imaginative space that the novels create *in between* themselves by their interaction. The analysis of one novel will not reveal it, nor will it be revealed by an analysis of all the novels in a process of simple addition, for since the structure is created by means of an interplay between texts, it must be approached through a critical process that, like the solving of a simultaneous equation, oscillates between two or more texts at once. The key to the critical oscillation that I have attempted between *Absalom, Absalom!* and *The Sound and the Fury* is, of course, the figure of Quentin Compson—Quentin, whose own oscillation constantly transforms action into narration and narration into action.

It is tempting to see in Quentin a surrogate of Faulkner, a double who is fated to retell and reenact the same story throughout his life just as Faulkner seemed fated to retell in different ways the same story again and again and, insofar as narration is action, to reenact that story as well. And just as Quentin's retellings and reenactments are experienced as failures that compel him to further repetitions that will correct those failures but that are themselves experienced as failures in turn, so Faulkner's comments on his own writing express his sense of the failures of his narratives, failures that compel him to retell the story again and again. In one of his conferences at the University of Virginia, Faulkner said of the composition of *The Sound and the Fury*: "It was, I thought, a short story, something that could be done in about two pages, a thousand words, I found out it couldn't. I finished it the first time, and it wasn't right, so I wrote it again, and that was Quentin, that wasn't right. I wrote it again, that was Jason, that wasn't right, then I tried to let Faulkner do it, that still was wrong."

It is as if, in the character of Quentin, Faulkner embodied, and perhaps tried to exorcise, certain elements present in himself and in his need to be a writer. Certainly, Quentin evokes that father-son struggle that a man inevitably has with his own literary progenitors when he attempts to become an "author." He evokes as well Faulkner's apparent sense of the act of writing as a progressive dismemberment of the self in which parts of the living subject are cut off to become objectified in language, to become (from the writer's point of view) detached and deadened, drained, in that specific embodiment, of their obsessive emotional content. In this process of piecemeal self-destruction, the author, the living subject, is gradually transformed into the detached object—his books. And this process of literary self-dismemberment is the author's response to the threat of death; it is a using up, a consuming of the self in the act of writing in order to escape from that annihilation of the self that is the inevitable outcome of physical generation, to escape by means of an ablative process of artistic creation in which the self is worn away to leave only a disembodied voice on the page to survive the writer's death, a voice that represents the interruption of a physical generative power and the transmission, through the author's books, of the phallic generative power of the creative imagination. This act of writing is sacrificial and mediatory, a gradual sacrificing of the self in an attempt to attain immortality through the mediation of language. It is as well an active willing of the author's passivity in the grip of time, for since time inevitably wears away the self to nothing, that actively willed wearing away of the self in the ablative process of creation is an attempt to transform necessity into a virtue, *ananke* into *virtù*, a fate into a power. Clearly, for Faulkner, writing is a kind of doubling in which the author's self is reconstituted within the realm of language as the Other, a narcissistic mirroring of the self to which the author's reaction is at once a fascinated self-love and an equally fascinated self-hatred. In one of the conferences at Virginia Faulkner said that *Absalom* was in part "the story of Quentin Compson's hatred of the bad qualities in the country he loves." There is a sense in which that ambivalence, that "hatred of the bad qualities in the country he loves," defines as well Faulkner's novelistic effort, his relationship to a geographic and an artistic, an outer and an inner, "fatherland." The structure that we have found in the interplay between *Absalom, Absalom!* and *The Sound and the Fury* is central to Faulkner's novels precisely because it is, for Faulkner, central to the art of writing novels.

* * *

In 1933 Faulkner wrote an introduction for a new edition of *The Sound and the Fury*, an introduction that he decided not to publish and that remained unpublished for almost forty years. In it he describes the genesis of the novel:

> . . . one day it suddenly seemed as if a door had clapped silently and forever to between me and all publishers' addresses and booklists and I said to myself, Now I can write. Now I can just write. Whereupon I, who had three brothers and no sisters and was destined to lose my first daughter in infancy, began to write about a little girl.
>
> I did not realise then that I was trying to manufacture the sister which I did not have and the daughter which I was to lose, though the former might have been apparent from the fact that Caddy had three brothers almost before I wrote her name on paper. (254–55)

Later in the introduction he says that since writing *The Sound and the Fury* he learned that "the emotion definite and physical and yet nebulous to describe which the writing of Benjy's section of *The Sound and the Fury* gave me—that ecstasy, that eager and joyous faith and anticipation of surprise which the yet unmarred sheets beneath my hand held inviolate and unfailing—will not return. The unreluctance to begin, the cold satisfaction in work well and arduously done, is there and will continue to be there as long as I can do it well. But that other will not return. I shall never know it again" (256). What Faulkner describes here is the author's sense of the loss of the original virgin space ("that ecstasy, that eager and joyous faith and anticipation of surprise which the yet unmarred sheets beneath my hand held inviolate and unfailing") and his mature acceptance of repetition ("The unreluctance to begin, the cold satisfaction in work well and arduously done, is there and will continue to be there as long as I can do it well").

The introduction ends:

> There is a story somewhere about an old Roman who kept at his bedside a Tyrrhenian vase which he loved and the rim of which he wore slowly away with kissing it. I had made myself a vase, but I suppose I knew all the time that I could not live forever inside of it, that perhaps to have it so that I too could lie in bed and look at it would be better; surely so when that day should come when not only the ecstasy of writing would be gone, but the unreluctance and the something worth saying too. It's fine to think that you will leave something behind you when you die, but it's better to have made something you can die with. Much better the muddy bottom of a little doomed girl climbing a blooming pear tree in April to look in the window at the funeral. (256–57)

Faulkner revised the introduction several times. In its final version, in which Faulkner doubles Quentin's own words in the novel, the ending fuses a series of images that are separated in earlier versions:

> One day I seemed to shut a door between me and all publishers' addresses and book lists. I said to myself, Now I can write. Now I can make myself a vase like that which the old Roman kept at his bedside and wore the rim slowly away with kissing it. So I, who had never had a sister and was fated to lose my daughter in infancy, set out to make myself a beautiful and tragic little girl. (252)

Faulkner realized that it is precisely because the novelist stands outside the dark door, wanting to enter the dark room but unable to, that he *is* a novelist, that he must imagine what takes place beyond the door. Indeed, it is just that tension toward the dark room that he cannot enter that makes that room the source of all his imaginings—the womb of art. He understood that a writer's relation to his material and to the work of art is always a loss, a separation, a cutting off, a self-castration that transforms the masculine artist into the feminine-masculine vase of the work. He knew that in this act of progressive self-destruction "the author's actual self is the one that goes down," that the writer ends up identifying himself not with what remains but with what is lost, the detached object that is the work. It is precisely by a loss, by a cutting off or separation that the artist's self and his other self, the work, mutually constitute one another—loss is the very condition of their existence. Discussing the image of Candace in the stream, that "beautiful and tragic little girl" that stands for the artist's lost, other self, Faulkner said,

> I saw that peaceful glinting of that branch was to become the dark, harsh flowing of time sweeping her to where she could not return to comfort him, but that just separation, division, would not be enough, not far enough. It must sweep her into dishonor and shame too. And that Benjy must never grow beyond this moment; that for him all knowing must begin and end with that fierce, panting, paused and stooping wet figure which smelled like trees. That he must never grow up to where the grief of bereavement could be leavened with understanding and hence the alleviation of rage as in the case of Jason, and of oblivion as in the case of Quentin. (255)

DONALD M. KARTIGANER

[The Meaning of Form in *The Sound and the Fury*]†

The Sound and the Fury is the four-times-told tale that opens with a date and the disorder of an idiot's mind and concludes with "post and tree, window and doorway, and signboard, each in its ordered place" (209). But this final order is one that has meaning only for the idiot: a sequence of objects that, when viewed from one perspective rather than another, can calm Benjy into a serene silence. The reader remains in a welter of contradictory visions.

None of the four tales speaks to another, each imagined order cancels out the one that precedes it. Truth is the meaningless sum of four items that seem to have no business being added: Benjy plus Quentin plus Jason plus the "narrator." "'You bring them together,'" as Faulkner wrote in *Absalom, Absalom!*, "'. . . and . . . nothing happens.'" This atomized Southern family, caught in the conflicts of ancient honor, modern commercialism, self-pity, cynicism, diseased love, becomes Faulkner's impassioned metaphor for the modern crisis of meaning. And *The Sound and the Fury* becomes, paradoxically, a vital expression of the failure of imagination, an approximation of what, for Frank Kermode, is no novel at all: "a discontinuous unorganized middle" that lacks the beginning and end of novel-time.[1]

Neither in the figure of Caddy, for some an organizing center of the novel, nor in the well-wrought fourth narrative do we find an adequate basis of unity in the work. The former possibility has been encouraged in several places by Faulkner himself, who claimed that the story began with the image of Caddy in the tree, and that she is its center, "what I wrote the book about."[2] But rather than a means of binding the fragments together, the image is itself complicated by the fragmentation. It moves into that isolation within the memory, eternal and not quite relevant, that all the major images of the novel possess. Millgate reveals a common uneasiness about this problem: "The novel revolves upon Caddy, but Caddy herself escapes satisfactory definition."[3] The accumulation of monologues results in neither a unity of vision nor a unity of envisioners.

---

† From *The Fragile Thread: The Meaning of Form in Faulkner's Novels* (Amherst: University of Massachusetts Press, 1979), 7–22. Copyright © 1979 by the University of Massachusetts Press. Reprinted by permission of the publisher. Page references are to this Norton Critical Edition.

1. Frank Kermode, *The Sense of an Ending* (New York: Oxford UP, 1967), 140.
2. Gwynn and Blotner, *Faulkner in the University*, 6.
3. Millgate, *The Achievement of William Faulkner*, 98.

The Benjy section represents extreme objectivity, a condition impossible to the ordinary mind and far in excess of even the most naturalistic fiction. In their sections Quentin and Jason are extremely subjective, each imposing a distorted view on experience, in exact contrast to Benjy, who can abstract no order at all. The fourth section is the voice of the traditional novelist, combining in moderation the qualities of the first three sections: objective in that it seems to tell us faithfully and credibly what happens (our faith in Quentin and Jason is, of course, minimal), and at the same time interpretive but without obvious distortion. Following upon the total immersion in experience or self of the three brothers, the last section is told entirely from without, and establishes the kind of comprehensive but still fixed clarity we expect to find in fiction. And yet for those very qualities, which for many are its strengths, it does not—even as the others do not—tell us what we most need to know.

The Benjy section comes first in the novel for the simple reason that Benjy, of all the narrators, cannot lie, which is to say he cannot create. Being an idiot, Benjy is perception prior to consciousness, prior to the human need to abstract from events an intelligible order. His monologue is a series of frozen pictures, offered without bias: "Through the fence; between the curling flower spaces, I could see them hitting" (3); "'What do you want.' Jason said. He had his hands in his pockets and a pencil behind his ear" (8); "[Father] drank and set the glass down and went and put his hand on Mother's shoulder" (29). His metaphors have the status of fact: "Caddy smelled like trees" (32).

The quality of Benjy's memory is the chief indicator of his non-human perception, for he does not recollect the past: he relives it.

> "Wait a minute." Luster said. "You snagged on that nail again. Cant you never crawl through here without snagging on that nail."
>
> *Caddy uncaught me and we crawled through. Uncle Maury said to not let anybody see us, so we better stoop over, Caddy said. Stoop over, Benjy. Like this, see. We stooped over and crossed the garden, where the flowers rasped and rattled against us. The ground was hard. We climbed the fence, where the pigs were grunting and snuffing. I expect they're sorry because one of them got killed today, Caddy said. The ground was hard, churned and knotted.*
>
> *Keep your hands in your pockets, Caddy said. Or they'll get froze. You don't want your hands froze on Christmas, do you.*
>
> "It's too cold out there." Versh said. "You dont want to go out doors." (3–4)

The sequence begins in the present, April 7, 1928, with Benjy and Luster crawling through a fence to get to the branch, where Luster hopes to find a golf ball. It shifts to a winter day of Benjy's childhood, when he and Caddy are also crawling through a fence on their way to deliver a note from Uncle Maury to Mrs. Patterson. The scene shifts again to earlier the same day, before Caddy has come home from school.

These shifts are triggered by a nail, a fence, the coldness—some object or quality that abruptly springs Benjy into a different time zone, each one of which is as alive and real for Benjy as the present. Strictly speaking he "remembers" nothing. As Faulkner said of Benjy in 1955, "To that idiot, time was not a continuation, it was an instant, there was no yesterday and no tomorrow, it all is this moment, it all is [now] to him. He cannot distinguish between what was last year and what will be tomorrow, he doesn't know whether he dreamed it, or saw it."[4]

Time as duration—Bergsonian time—is what Faulkner is alluding to here; and it is this sense of time that Benjy, by virtue of his idiocy, has abandoned. Memory does not serve him as it serves the normal mind, becoming part of the mind and integral to the stream of constantly created perception that makes it up: the past which, as Bergson put it, "gnaws into the future and which swells as it advances."[5] Benjy does not recall, and therefore cannot interpret, the past from the perspective of the present; nor does the past help to determine that perspective. Instead of past and present being a continuum, each influencing the meaning of the other, they have no temporal dimension at all. They are isolated, autonomous moments that do not come "before" or "after."

This freedom from time makes Benjy a unique narrator indeed. He does not perceive reality but is at one with it; he does not need to create his life but rather possesses it with a striking immediacy. There is a timelessness in the scenes Benjy relives, but it is not the timelessness of art, abstracting time into meaning. It is the absence of the need for art.

Benjy's monologue, then, does not constitute an interpretation at all; what he tells us is life, not text. Emerging as if from the vantage point of eternal stasis, where each moment lived (whether for the first or fiftieth time) is the original moment and the only moment, unaffected by any of the others, this telling is an affront to the existence of narration or of novels. As Bleikasten says, it "is the very negation of narrative."[6] This is one of the reasons why the Benjy

4. Meriwether and Millgate, *Lion in the Garden*, 147–48.
5. Henri Bergson, *Creative Evolution*, trans. Arthur Mitchell (New York: Random House, Modern Library, 1944), 7.
6. Bleikasten, *The Most Splendid Failure*, 86.

section has such a hold on us, why we attribute to it an authority we never think of granting the others, especially the narratives of his two brothers. Spoken with the awareness that time is always present, and thus missing that sense of consecutiveness necessary to our quick understanding, Benjy's monologue is difficult; yet the cause of that difficulty persuades us that this is truth, not art.

The irony, however, and the reason why the novel does not simply end with this section, is that while Benjy is not himself formulating an interpretation, his succession of lived images passes over into *our* interpretation, becomes a temporal fiction of Compson history that is so clear it is unbelievable. Benjy's scenes, despite fractured chronology and abrupt transitions, meld into a set of clear and consistent character portraits—two-dimensional figures with the sharpness of allegorical signposts that elicit from us simplistic evaluations empty of deep moral insight. "But for the very reason for their simplicity," one critic has written, "Benjy's responses function as a quick moral index to events."[7] This is indeed the effect of Benjy's monologue and its danger.

The following passage, taken from the end of Benjy's monologue, is typical. This is the night of Damuddy's death, when Quentin, Caddy, Jason, and Benjy (between the ages of three and eight) are being put to bed:

> There were two beds. Quentin got in the other one. He turned his face to the wall. Dilsey put Jason in with him. Caddy took her dress off.
> "Just look at your drawers." Dilsey said. "You better be glad your ma aint seen you."
> "I already told on her." Jason said.
> "I bound you would." Dilsey said.
> "And see what you got by it." Caddy said. "Tattletale."
> "What did I get by it." Jason said.
> "Whyn't you get your nightie on." Dilsey said. She went and helped Caddy take off her bodice and drawers. "Just look at you." Dilsey said. She wadded the drawers and scrubbed Caddy behind with them. "It done soaked clean through onto you." she said. "But you wont get no bath this night. Here." She put Caddy's nightie on her and Caddy climbed into the bed and Dilsey went to the door and stood with her hand on the light. "You all be quiet now, you hear." she said.
> "All right." Caddy said. "Mother's not coming in tonight." she said. "So we still have to mind me."
> "Yes." Dilsey said. "Go to sleep now."

7. John W. Hunt, *William Faulkner: Art in Theological Tension* (Syracuse: Syracuse UP, 1965), 89.

"Mother's sick." Caddy said. "She and Damuddy are both sick."

"Hush." Dilsey said. "You go to sleep."

The room went black, except the door. Then the door went black. Caddy said, "Hush, Maury," putting her hand on me. So I stayed hushed. We could hear us. We could hear the dark.

It went away, and Father looked at us. He looked at Quentin and Jason, then he came and kissed Caddy and put his hand on my head.

"Is Mother very sick." Caddy said.

"No." Father said. "Are you going to take good care of Maury."

"Yes." Caddy said. (49–50)

Within the space of a single, short scene, each member of the Compson household is definitively characterized. Quentin is the figure of impotence, the one who turns his face to the wall, expressing his futile outrage at all that has gone on that day. Jason, meanness personified, has already told on Caddy—without particular benefit, although he does not realize this. Dilsey is the loyal retainer, the embodiment of responsible affection, who undresses and cleans up Caddy, and sees to it that all the children are in bed. Mother's lack of responsibility is defined by her absence: she is "sick." Father makes his appearance, to look at Jason and Quentin, and to kiss Caddy and touch Benjy (still named Maury): *almost* the responsible parent but playing his favorites and, in his last words, delegating responsibility for Benjy to Caddy. Caddy herself is love, the one who can quiet Benjy down with the touch of her hand. She is also the boldness of youth as both her dirty underwear and confident assumption of the mother's role indicate.

What is so striking about this scene is not only that the meaning of each character can be summarized in an abstract word or two, but that, although the scene comes at the end of Benjy's monologue, the characters are the same as they were in the beginning. They exhibit little change or development; nor can Benjy develop significantly his understanding of them. Each character must be himself over and over again, bearing, like a gift of birth, his inescapable moral worth.

Life—for the scenes Benjy witnesses are at one level the most authentic in the novel—retains the power of its rawness, its freedom from structure; yet simultaneously it passes into the order of our interpretation: a coherent fiction implying all-too-clear moral attitudes. And the demands of our own reader's role are such that it is impossible for us to reverse the process, to return this charged but implausible text to its state of pure presence in the mind of the nonnarrator where it originates.

The most difficult task in reading *The Sound and the Fury* is to get beyond this opening section, for finally Benjy is demonstrating poverty of the pure witness of what is unquestionably there. Benjy's monologue is never less, or more, than truth. We must pass on to the next three sections in which this truth confronts deliberate distortion: vested interests organizing, plotting—consciously or unconsciously, violently or subtly. And with these distortions the cautionary fable we have gleaned from Benjy's images collapses into new complexities: Caddy's promises succumb to need, Jason's ruthlessness turns over into psychotic paranoia, Quentin's futility rages in dreams of murder and incest.

Yet the collapse is not total, as much of the criticism of the novel attests. Not the least irony of *The Sound and the Fury* is that we are tempted most by an absolutism that the whole structure of the novel teaches us to dismiss: not because it is not true but because it is not the truth of what it means to be human in that world which, so this novel asserts, is the one that exists.

Following Benjy's freedom from time and interpretation comes the time-possessed Quentin, who wants nothing more than to *replace* life with interpretation. Reality for Quentin is primarily change—in particular the change implicit to the sexual identity of his sister Caddy—and interpretation, metaphor, is the created ground of permanence in which change is eliminated. Caddy's development from child to adolescent and her subsequent loss of virginity epitomizes that change which, in Quentin's mind, is the essence of confusion.

> until after the honeysuckle got all mixed up in it the whole thing came to symbolise night and unrest I seemed to be lying neither asleep nor awake looking down a long corridor of grey halflight where all stable things had become shadowy paradoxical all I had done shadows all I had felt suffered taking visible form antic and perverse mocking without relevance inherent themselves with the denial of the significance they should have affirmed thinking I was I was not who was not was not who. (112–13)

Against this vision of formlessness Quentin props a Byronic fable of incest between himself and Caddy, thus gilding what Father calls her "natural human folly" (117) into a horrific one. Through metaphor he informs his confusion with the clarity of hell: *"the pointing and the horror walled by the clean flame"* (77). But what is most important is that this hell, and the incest that enables Quentin and Caddy to deserve it, is purely imaginary. In the crucial interview that brings Quentin's monologue to a close, Father asks him: "did you try to make her do it and i i was afraid to i was afraid she might and then it wouldnt have done any good but if i could tell you we did it would have been so and then the others wouldnt be so and then the world would roar away" (117).

"if i could tell you we did it would have been so. . . ." It is not an actual hell reserved for actual sinners that Quentin wants, but his invented one whose unreality frees it from a confusing and disappointing world. Purity for Quentin lies in a fiction, *known* as a fiction and priding itself on its indifference to reality. He is trying to transform life from within its midst, to convert dull promiscuity to sin, his dreary frustrations into a hell of rich and well-defined despair. It is a hell necessarily unreal: actual incest with Caddy "wouldnt have done any good."

Confronted everywhere with his impotence, Quentin is desperate to believe in the power of words alone: to substitute for what-is the names of what-is-not. He wants to convince Caddy of the reality of his fantasy, not that they have literally made love but that words have a substance more real than bodies.

> . . . *I'll tell you how it was it was a crime we did a terrible crime it cannot be hid you think it can but wait Poor Quentin youve never done that have you and I'll tell you how it was I'll tell Father then itll have to be because you love Father then we'll have to go away amid the pointing and the horror the clean flame I'll make you say we did I'm stronger than you I'll make you know we did you thought it was them but it was me listen I fooled you all the time it was me* (98)

Quentin tries to get Caddy to accede to this fantasy, to see words as the originator rather than the imitator of deeds. This is Quentin's willful decadence, a version of his subsequent suicide in that it puts the world away, using metaphor as a wedge between language and life. As Mr. Compson says, Quentin is trying to make "a temporary state of mind . . . symmetrical above the flesh" (118). In this sense he is like the three young boys in Cambridge talking about what they might do with the prize money for a fish they neither have caught nor have any hope of catching: "They all talked at once, their voices insistent and contradictory and impatient, making of unreality a possibility, then a probability, then an incontrovertible fact, as people will when their desires become words" (78).

Quentin's need to alter an unbearable reality through language owes much to the teachings of his father. On the first page of Quentin's monologue we read: "Because no battle is ever won he said. They are not even fought. The field only reveals to man his own folly and despair, and victory is an illusion of philosophers and fools" (50). And shortly before the end: "Father was teaching us that all men are just accumulations dolls stuffed with sawdust swept up from the trash heaps where all previous dolls had been thrown away" (116). Mr. Compson's theme has been the futility of human action.

Anxious to believe his father is wrong, Quentin clings to the moral codes of Southern antebellum myth: if a woman has been deflowered it can only be because "he made you do it let him he was stronger than you," and a loyal brother will avenge her: "tomorrow Ill kill him I swear I will" (99). But finally this melodramatic interpretation of events will not do, and so Quentin escapes the cynicism of his father by embracing fully the idea of impotence: the pure fantasy of incest that signals the abandonment of time and his entrance into a world of words.

Quentin's behavior on June 2, 1910, parallels his quest for an irrelevant language. He moves toward a stylization of his life by separating his deeds from his purposes, the conduct of his last day from the impact of its destination. Cutting his thumb on his broken watch crystal, Quentin administers iodine in order to prevent infection; he attends to the matters of packing his belongings, writing farewell notes, stacking books, like someone going on vacation or moving to another town. At the end he carefully removes a blood stain from his vest, washes, cleans his teeth, and brushes his hat, before leaving his room to drown himself.

Both forms of metaphor, verbal and behavioral, move toward suicide. Driving words further and further from facts, style from purpose, art from meaning, Quentin is inside his death—the place without life—for much of his monologue. And yet, since the pride of his fiction-making is its admitted distance from the real, Quentin cannot help but acknowledge the agony of what is: that he has not committed incest with Caddy, that she has had several lovers, that she is pregnant with one man's child and is married to another, a "blackguard." There is in all this an affront that Quentin's artistry cannot conceal or bear. His only triumph is that he has proved his father wrong at least about one thing: "no man ever does that [commits suicide] under the first fury of despair or remorse or bereavement" (118).

The deliberate flight from fact that dominates Quentin's monologue reverses the effect of Benjy's monologue that precedes it. Benjy has made us aware of the distortions of the *literal*; his language is exact, free of bias. It is truth, not metaphor. Yet this exaggerated objectivism results in the most simplistic of moral designs. Quentin, on the other hand, has plunged into metaphor; but in doing so he reduces subjectivism to an art of decadence: "symmetrical above the flesh."

"The first sane Compson since before Culloden," Faulkner said of Jason in the Appendix to *The Sound and the Fury* written sixteen years after the novel. This is a view that has been adopted wholly or in part by many readers of the novel, although one wonders how anyone, especially Faulkner, could have considered Jason sane or rational. Surely Jason is as removed from what we generally consider sanity as any character in *The Sound and the Fury*. He is in fact far less aware of what is actually real than his brother Quentin. Such is our quickness in the twentieth century to polarize rationality and emotion, intellectual and intuitive responses, that critical interpretation of *The Sound and the Fury* has found it easy to set Jason up as its rational villain, the opposite number of the high-minded, intuitive Sartorises and Compsons, and probably, with white-trash Snopeses and invading Yankees, the secret of the fall of man in the Faulkner world. Such a thesis is hardly adequate for the kind of complexity Faulkner offers us here and elsewhere in his fiction. Faulkner may indeed be on the side of intuition, particularly as Bergson described it, but in his best work he does not demonstrate that preference by neat categories of the kind in which Jason has been pigeonholed.

A man who says, "I wouldn't bet on any team that fellow Ruth played on. . . . Even if I knew it was going to win" (165)—to pick out only one example—is hardly the epitome of cold-hearted business-like behavior. And that he could ever have "competed with and held his own with the Snopeses" (267), as Faulkner writes in the Appendix, is incredible. No man who is fooled and humiliated so many times in one day by everyone from Miss Quentin to Old Man Job is going to be a match for Flem Snopes, whose coldly analytic inhumanity has so often been wrongly identified with Jason. The latter's insistence that he would not bet on a sure winner is not only irrational, it is even the mark of a curious idealism. It is also a significant, usually ignored, side of this pathetic man who spends his Good Friday crucifying himself on the crosses he alone provides.

A psychotic, some wit once said, is a man who honestly believes that two plus two equals five; a neurotic knows very well that two plus two equals four—but it bothers him. Let this be our hint as to the difference between Jason and Quentin, for Quentin deliberately composes an incest fable in order to deal with a reality he cannot face. That it is a fable is something he himself insists on. Jason, however, confuses the real and the illusory, and is quite unaware of the way he arranges his own punishment. Standing between him and reality is his need to hold on to two opposing views of himself: one is that he is completely sufficient, the other is that he is the scapegoat of the world. On one hand Jason considers himself an effective operator, family head, market speculator, brainy swindler of Caddy and her daughter, a man of keen business sense. On the other hand he nurtures the dream of his victimization, his suffering at the hands of the Compsons, the Gibsons, his boss Earl, even the telegraph company.

Jason's entire monologue wanders through a maze of contradiction that cannot be reduced to mere hypocrisy or rationalization. With $7,000 stashed away, the accumulation of fifteen years of theft, Jason thinks "money has no value; it's just the way you spend it. It dont belong to anybody, so why try to hoard it" (128). Regretting that he must be a detective (156), he yet makes the pursuit of his niece Quentin a major project. Insisting only that she show "discretion," fearing that someday he'll find her "under a wagon on the square" (157), he nevertheless chases her far out into the country on a day when nearly everyone else is at the traveling show in town, when there is no one to see her but himself. He scoffs at Compson pride in blood (151), yet later it is his and his mother's name that Quentin is making "a byword in the town" (153). He firmly believes that it is Caddy who has deceived *him*, who has broken her promises to him, and that Quentin, in letting the air out of his tires, has given back far more than she has received: "I just wouldn't do you this way. I wouldn't do you this way no matter what you had done to me" (159). And in the midst of all this double-dealing and plain fraud, Jason can sincerely say, "If there's one thing gets under my skin, it's a damn hypocrite" (150).

Within this web of opposed purposes—is it comfort or suffering that he seeks?—Jason seems absent of any objective awareness of those realities most relevant to him. He is confusion incarnate, guilty of all he seems to hate, hating his own image in others, the least sane and the most perversely imaginative of all the Compsons. When the world threatens him with satisfaction, when his niece heeds his insistence on discretion by driving with her man friend into an abandoned countryside, Jason chases after her, contradicting his own wishes so that his pain can be adequate to his unintelligible need. Quentin creates in order to avoid suffering, Jason, to experience it.

Surely we cannot match criteria of sanity or cold logic with what goes on in Jason's mind on April 6, 1928. For Bergson, the analytic mind is capable of the "ingenious arrangement of immobilities."[8] It is the kind of perception that orders reality rather than entering into sympathetic union with it. But Jason's organization of things is so confused and contradictory that we can hardly observe in him the sense of conscious control that Bergson identifies with the analytic mind. Jason's most obvious quality, visible in all his pratfalls, is his

8. Henri Bergson, A *Study in Metaphysics: The Creative Mind,* trans. Mabelle L. Andison (Totawa, New Jersey: Littlefield, Adams & Co., 1970), 127.

inability to *utilize* reality, to make it integral to a specific design. To compare him with Faulkner's master of analytic reasoning, Flem Snopes, is to see how absurdly distant he is from Flem.

The meanness with which Jason confronts the world is the cover that scarcely conceals his lack of self-knowledge. His agony is real, but he cannot begin to explain its source or its meaning. The only language he can risk is the stream of impotent insult he inflicts on everything around him. The result, after the pathos of Benjy and the occasionally burdensome rhetorical self-indulgence of Quentin, is some uproarious invective: "I haven't got much pride, I can't afford it with a kitchen full of niggers to feed and robbing the state asylum of its star freshman. Blood, I says, governors and generals. It's a damn good thing we never had any kings and presidents; we'd all be down there at Jackson chasing butterflies" (151). Following Benjy and Quentin, this sort of thing comes as bracing, if low, comedy. And it reminds us, even in this grim study of family disintegration, of the variety of Faulkner's voices and his daring willingness to use them.

Thus Faulkner adds still one more piece to his exploration of the possibilities of vision. Still subjective, as opposed to the more objective first and fourth sections, but substantially different from Quentin's, Jason's is the mind that seems to have dissolved the boundaries of fact and invention, not as they might be dissolved in the collaboration within a supreme fiction, but as in the furthest stages of paranoia. The great irony of the section is that Jason is the one Compson who creates the appearance of ordinary social existence: he holds a job, wears a hat, visits a whorehouse regularly, and manages to fool his mother into burning what she believes are Caddy's checks. But his existence is actually a chaos of confused motion, utter disorder within the mind. Quentin, preparing methodically for suicide, is a study in contrast.

* * *

With "April Eighth 1928" the novel moves outward, away from the sealed monologues of Benjy, Quentin, and Jason. The telling of the Compson history from within passes to the telling from without. It is the last possibility Faulkner must exhaust in order to make his wasteland of sensibility complete: the traditional fictional method of the removed narrator describing objectively the characters and the events and, without a sense of excessive intrusion, interpreting them for us.

For the first time in the book we get novelistic description: weather, place, persons, the appearance of things as from the eye of a detached but interested spectator: "The day dawned bleak and chill, a moving wall of grey light out of the northeast which, instead of dissolving into moisture, seemed to disintegrate into minute and venomous particles, like dust that, when Dilsey opened the door of the cabin and emerged, needled laterally into her flesh, precipitating not so much a moisture as a substance partaking of the quality of thin, not quite congealed oil" (173). And with this description a new voice enters the novel: "She had been a big woman once but now her skeleton rose, draped loosely in unpadded skin that tightened again upon a paunch almost dropsical, as though muscle and tissue had been courage or fortitude which the days or the years had consumed until only the indomitable skeleton was left rising like a ruin or a landmark above the somnolent and impervious guts . . ." (173). It is a rhetorical voice, set apart from the chaos and the distortion we have already seen. And from its secure perch, intimate with the events yet aloof from the pain of being a Compson, this voice seeks to tell us the meaning of what has come before.

Benjy, so brilliantly rendered in his own voice in the first section, is now described from the outside.

> Luster entered, followed by a big man who appeared to have been shaped of some substance whose particles would not or did not cohere to one another or to the frame which supported it. His skin was dead looking and hairless; dropsical too, he moved with a shambling gait like a trained bear. His hair was pale and fine. It had been brushed smoothly down upon his brow like that of children in daguerrotypes. His eyes were clear, of the pale sweet blue of cornflowers, his thick mouth hung open, drooling a little. (179)

One is almost shocked by the description—is this Benjy? Having wrestled with the processes of his mind, we find this external view like the portrait of someone else, another idiot from another novel. Not only described, he is also interpreted: "Then Ben wailed again, hopeless and prolonged. It was nothing. Just sound. It might have been all time and injustice and sorrow become vocal for an instant by a conjunction of planets" (187–88).

Jason, once again in pursuit of Quentin, this time for the $7,000 she has taken from his room, is also described, "with close-thatched brown hair curled into two stubborn hooks, one on either side of his forehead like a bartender in caricature" (182), and his meaning is wrested from the confusion of his own monologue. The narrator focuses chiefly on the bank job promised Jason years ago, which he never received because of Caddy's divorce from Herbert. It is supposedly neither Quentin nor the money that he is really chasing: "they merely symbolized the job in the bank of which he had been deprived before he ever got it" (199). What has been stolen from him this time is simply "that which was to have compensated him for the lost job, which he had acquired through so much effort and risk, by the very symbol of the lost job itself" (200).

With both Benjy and Jason a great deal has been lost in the abstraction of meaning from movement. From the total immersion of the private monologue we move to the detached external view; from confused and confusing versions of reality: we get an orderly, consistent portrait of the Compson family. And yet this clarity does not explain; these interpretations of Jason and Benjy seem pale and inadequate beside their respective monologues. Can Jason's terrible confusion, for example, really be embraced by the motive attributed to him in this section? There is a curious irrelevancy here, as if in this achieved meaning one were reading about different characters entirely. And yet in the earlier monologues we have already seen the inadequacies of personal distortion and the two-dimensional clarity of pure perception.

My point here is not simply a determined refusal to admit the comprehensiveness of what I am reading. It is rather to recognize that in this fourth attempt to tell the Compson story we are still faced with the problems of the first three, namely, a failure of the creation of a sufficient form. And this failure becomes itself the form, and therefore the meaning, of *The Sound and the Fury*. The four fragments, each a fully achieved expression of voice operating within the severest limitations, remain separate and incoherent.

The fourth section is, of course, the easiest to read. It is divided into four parts: the scene in the house Easter morning, showing Dilsey at work and the discovery of the stolen money; the Easter service at church; Jason's pursuit of Quentin; and the short scene in which Luster tries to take Benjy to the graveyard through town. The polarities of Dilsey's and the Compson's existence are emphatic, especially in the juxtaposition of the Easter service, in its celebration of God's time, and Jason's mad chase, his striving in the context of human time. Dilsey, understanding the broken clock in the kitchen or the "beginning and the ending" in church, has a sure grasp of both.

Dilsey has been pointed to as the one source of value in the novel, supported by the comment in what seems to me an invariably misleading appendix, and it is clear that she embodies much that the Compsons lack, especially a sense of duty to her position as servant and her total faith in God. It is also clear that her service to the family has not been enough to save it, and that even her own children disobey her often, in certain instances emulating the Compson sin of pride. Her religious faith is remote as far as the Compsons are concerned. If the Christian myth is being put forth here as a source of order in the world, it clearly has only ironic reference to them.

"I know you blame me," Mrs. Compson said, "for letting them off to go to church today."

"Go where?" Jason said. "Hasn't that damn show left yet?" (182)

But Dilsey is irrelevant not only to the Compsons but to those assumptions of the nature of reality basic to the novel. Unlike the other members of the Compson household, and unlike the perspective implicit to this fragmented novel, Dilsey possesses a "mythic" view of the world, the assurance of an enduring order that presides over human existence, organizing it into an intelligible history. It is an order she has not invented but inherited, a traditional Christianity providing meaning and direction to her life. Outside the dissonance and distortion of the first three narratives, the grotesque visions we can never dismiss or corroborate, Dilsey's orthodoxy is a controlled and clear point of view—yet it is remote from that complexity of existence by which the novel lives.

Dilsey transcends chaos by her vision of Christian order.

"I've seed de first en de last," Dilsey said. "Never you mind me."
"First en last whut?" Frony said.
"Never you mind," Dilsey said. "I seed de beginnin, en now sees de endin." (194)

This is what Quentin wishes he could do: see in the midst of action the direction of action, understand the living moment because it is part of a history that has already, and always, ended. Dilsey has this gift because she is a Christian. She exists not as one whose life unfolds in surprise, each moment a new and frightening Now, but as one who knows every step of the way because there is in fact only one history. The traditional narrative form of this section of *The Sound and the Fury* rests on similar assumptions. Its externally placed perspective, its clear plotting, its coherent analysis of what the behavior of Benjy and Jason means—all of these are basic to a fiction that believes in endings and their power to press into service, and thus make intelligible, each single moment. Dilsey is the center of "April Eighth 1928" because she is the spiritual embodiment of the fictional tradition in which it is told.

Dilsey has what Frank Kermode calls a sense of an ending. For her, the deterioration of the Compsons only confirms the demise of the godless and prideful, and brings still nearer the moment toward which all history moves. Yet the whole of *The Sound and the Fury* does not subscribe to the implications of ending, in terms of either the resolution of action into meaning or the reconciliation of fragments into a controlling system. Dilsey's special understanding, as Frony's question makes clear—"'First en last whut?'"—is unavailable to any of the major characters in the novel. Nor is it available to the reader unless he ignores three-fourths of that novel, which flatly juxtaposes the last section against the three others that are inconsistent with it, and even confronts Dilsey (and the Easter service that articulates her mode of belief) with the spectacle of Jason's frantic chase after Quentin.[9]

Challenging Dilsey's religious vision is the same sense of time in motion, of a reality intractable to any mental construct, that lays bare the distortions of Quentin and Jason and transforms Benjy's timeless perspective, free of distortion, into a frozen imitation of experience. Neither in the Dilsey section, whatever the power of her characterization or sheer attractiveness as a human being, nor anywhere else in the novel do we see demonstrated the ability of the human imagination to render persuasively the order of things. Instead there is the sense of motion without meaning, of voices in separate rooms talking to no one: the sound and fury that fails to signify.

The Sound and the Fury reads like an anthology of fictional forms, each one of which Faulkner tests and finds wanting. The novel insists on the poverty of created meaning, although in doing so it possesses, like "The Waste Land," a power that for many readers the later works cannot equal. There is Benjy's unmediated vision of pure presence, that makes of art a kind of impertinence. There are the grotesque orderings of Quentin and Jason—one an effete escapism that seeks a reality dictated by the word, the other subjectivism crippled by paranoia. Both are parodies of the possibility that art might illuminate, not merely distort, the real. And there is the conventional nineteenth-century fiction: the orderly telling of a tale that retreats from all those suspicions of language, concept, external point of view, imposed order, that made the modern possible and necessary.

The achievement of the novel is the honesty of its experiment; we take its "failure" seriously because the attempt seems so genuine and desperate. The basic structure of a compilation of voices or discrete stories is one Faulkner returned to again and again, but never with such a candid admission of the limitations of art. Behind the novel is some as yet vague conception of what literature in the twentieth-century might be. Acknowledging, insisting on decreation, making real the time prior to prearrangement, *The Sound and the Fury* yet strives for wholeness, an articulation of design: the form not imposed like a myth from the past, but the form that is the consequence of contingent being.

9. See Bleikasten, *The Most Splendid Failure*, 184.

Nearly two decades later, Wallace Stevens expressed the hope of an age.

> To discover an order as of
> A season, to discover summer and know it,
>
> To discover winter and know it well, to find,
> Not to impose, not to have reasoned at all,
> Out of nothing to have come on major weather,
>
> It is possible, possible, possible. It must
> Be possible. It must be that in time
> The real will from its crude compoundings come[1]

The impressiveness of *The Sound and the Fury* is that it accepts nothing it cannot earn. It will have only "major weather." And so the novel sits like a stillborn colossus, always on the verge of beginning.

DAVID MINTER

Faulkner, Childhood, and the Making of *The Sound and the Fury*[†]

Early in 1928, while he was still trying to recover from Horace Liveright's rejection of *Flags in the Dust*, William Faulkner began writing stories about four children named Compson. A few months earlier, his spirits had been high. Confident that he had just finished the best book any publisher would see that year, he had begun designing a dust jacket for his third novel. His first book, *The Marble Faun*, had sold few copies, and neither of his previous novels, *Soldiers' Pay* and *Mosquitoes*, had done very well. But *Flags in the Dust* had given him a sense of great discovery, and he was counting on it to make his name for him as a writer. Following Liveright's letter, which described the novel as "diffuse and non-integral," lacking "plot, dimension and projection," Faulkner's mood became not only bitter but morbid. For several weeks he moved back and forth between threats to give up writing and take a job, and efforts to revise his manuscript or even re-write the whole thing. Yet nothing seemed to help—neither the threats, which he probably knew to be empty, nor the efforts, which left him feeling confused

---

1. "Notes Toward a Supreme Fiction," in *The Collected Poems of Wallace Stevens* (New York: Alfred A. Knopf, 1954), 403–4.
† From *American Literature* 51.3 (Durham, NC: Duke UP, 1979): 376–93. Copyright © 1979, Duke University Press. All rights reserved. Republished by permission of the copyright holder, Duke Uinversity Press. www.dukepress.edu.

and even hopeless. Finally, he decided to re-type his manuscript
and send it to Ben Wasson, a friend who had agreed to act as his
agent.[1]

The disappointment Faulkner experienced in the aftermath of
Liveright's blunt rejection was intensified by the solitude it imposed.
He had enjoyed sharing the modest success of his earlier books,
particularly with his mother, with old friends like Phil Stone, and
with his childhood sweetheart, Estelle Oldham Franklin. But
he found it impossible to share failure. "Don't Complain—Don't
Explain" was the motto his mother had hung in the family kitchen
and imprinted on the minds of her sons.[2] To her eldest son the
experience of failure proved not only more painful but more solitary than any anticipation of it. Soon he also found himself
immersed in a deep personal crisis, the contours of which remain a
mystery. Several years later he spoke to Maurice Coindreau of a
severe strain imposed by "difficulties of an intimate kind" ("des dif-
ficultes d'order intime").[3] To no one was he more specific. In a letter
to his favorite aunt, he refers to a charming, shallow woman, "Like
a lovely vase." "Thank God I've no money," he added, "or I'd marry
her."[4] But what if anything his intimate difficulties had to do with
his new love, we do not know. What we know is that the difficulties
touched much. "You know, after all," he said to an acquaintance,
"they put you in a pine box and in a few days the worms have you.
Someone might cry for a day or two and after that they've forgotten
all about you."[5]

As his depression deepened, Faulkner began reviewing his commitment to his vocation. Unable to throw it over, he determined to
alter his attitude toward it—specifically by relinquishing hope of
great recognition and reward. For several years, he had written in
order to publish. After Soldiers' Pay that had meant writing with
Horace Liveright before him. Yet, as his work had become more satisfying to him, it had become less acceptable to Liveright. Refusing
to go back to writing things he now thought "youngly glamorous,"
like Soldiers' Pay, or "trashily smart," like Mosquitoes, he decided to
go on even if it meant relinquishing his dream of success.[6]

1. See Faulkner to Liveright, Sunday,—October [16 Oct. 1927]; 30 November [1927]; and
   [mid or late Feb. 1928] in Joseph Blotner, ed., Selected Letters of William Faulkner
   (New York: Random House, 1977), 38–39. For Liveright's letter of rejection, see Joseph
   Blotner, Faulkner: A Biography (New York: Random House, 1974), 559–60.
2. Murry C. Falkner, The Falkners of Mississippi: A Memoir (Baton Rouge: Louisiana
   State UP, 1967), 9–10.
3. Maurice Coindreau, Introduction, Le bruit et la fureur (Paris: Gallimard, 1938), 14.
   See also James B. Meriwether, "Notes on the Textual History of The Sound and the
   Fury," Papers of the Bibliographical Society of America 56 (1962): 228.
4. See Faulkner to Mrs. Walter B. McLean, quoted in Blotner, Faulkner, 562–63.
5. J. W. Harmon in William Faulkner of Oxford, ed. James W. Webb and A. Wigfall Green
   (Baton Rouge: Louisiana State UP, 1965), 93–94.
6. Faulkner to Liveright [mid or late Feb. 1928], Selected Letters, 39–40.

His hope faded slowly, he recalled, but fade it did. "One day I seemed to shut a door between me and all publishers' addresses and book lists. I said to myself, Now I can write"—by which he meant that he could write for himself alone. Almost immediately he felt free. Writing "without any accompanying feeling of drive or effort, or any following feeling of exhaustion or relief or distaste," he began with no plan at all. He did not even think of his manuscript as a book. "I was thinking of books, publication, only in . . . reverse, in saying to myself, I wont have to worry about publishers liking or not liking this at all."[7]

More immediately, however, what going on and feeling free to write for himself meant was going back—not only to stories about children but to experiences from his own childhood and to characters he associated with himself and his brothers. Taking a line from "St. Louis Blues," which he had heard W. C. Handy play years before, he called the first Compson story "That Evening Sun Go Down." The second he called "A Justice." In both stories children face dark, foreboding experiences without adequate support. At the end of "A Justice" they move through a "strange, faintly sinister suspension of twilight"—an image which provided the title for another story, which Faulkner began in early spring.

Called "Twilight," the third of the Compson stories engaged him for several months, and became *The Sound and the Fury*, his first great novel. Through the earlier stories he had come to see the Compson children poised at the end of childhood and the beginning of awareness, facing scenes that lie beyond their powers of understanding and feeling emotions that lie beyond their powers of expression. In the second story, as twilight descends and their world begins to fade, loss, consternation, and bafflement become almost all they know.

This moment, which the stories discovered and the novel explores, possessed particular poignancy for Faulkner—a fact confirmed by scattered comments as well as by the deep resonance of the novel and the story of its making. "Art reminds us of our youth," Fairchild says in *Mosquitoes*, "of that age when life don't need to have her face lifted every so often for you to consider her beautiful."[8] "It's over very soon," Faulkner remarked as he observed his daughter nearing the end of her youth. "This is the end of it. She'll grow into a woman."[9] During the creation of the Compson children, he became not merely private but secretive. Even the people to whom

7. See both versions of Faulkner's Introduction to *The Sound and the Fury*, one in *The Southern Review*, 13 (Autumn 1972): and one in *The Mississippi Quarterly*, 26 (Summer 1973): 225–32; both reprinted in This Norton Critical Edition, pp. 249–57.
8. *Mosquitoes* (New York: Boni and Liveright, 1927), 319.
9. See Faulkner as quoted in Blotner, *Faulkner*, 1169.

he had talked and written most freely while working on *Flags in the Dust*—his mother and aunt, Phil Stone and Estelle Franklin—knew nothing about his new work until it was finished.[1] Although he was capable, as he once remarked, of saying almost anything in an interview, and on some subjects enjoyed contradicting himself, his comments on *The Sound and the Fury* remained basically consistent for more than thirty years. Even when the emotion they express is muted and the information they convey is limited, they show that the novel occupied a special place in his experience and in his memory. The brooding nostalgia which informs the novel also survived it: it entered interviews for years to come, and it dominated the "introduction" he wrote to *The Sound and the Fury* in the early thirties, both as emotion recalled and as emotion shared. Looking back on the painful yet splendid months of crisis during which he wrote *The Sound and the Fury*, Faulkner was able to discover emotions similar to those which that crisis enabled him to discover in childhood.

Like *Flags in the Dust*, *The Sound and the Fury* is set in Jefferson and recalls family history. The Compson family, like the Sartoris family, mirrors Faulkner's deepest sense of his family's story as a story of declension. But *The Sound and the Fury* is more bleak and more compelling. It is also more personal, primarily because the third or parental generation, which in *Flags in the Dust* is virtually deleted as having no story, plays a major role in *The Sound and the Fury*.[2] Despite its pathos, *Flags* remains almost exuberant; and despite its use of family legends, it remains open, accessible. Faulkner's changed mood, his new attitude and needs, altered not only his way of working but his way of writing. A moving story of four children and their inadequate parents, *The Sound and the Fury* is thematically regressive, stylistically and formally innovative. If being free to write for himself implied freedom to recover more personal materials, being free of concern about publishers' addresses implied freedom to become more experimental. The novel thus represented a move back toward home, family, childhood, and a move toward the interior; but it also represented an astonishing breakthrough.[3] Furthermore, both of its fundamental principles, the regressive and the innovative, possessed several corollaries. Its regressive principle we see, first, in the presence of the three Compson brothers, who recall Faulkner's own family configuration, and

1. See both versions of the Introduction to *The Sound and the Fury* cited in note 7 above; and Blotner, *Faulkner*, 570–71 and 578–80.
2. See Faulkner's explanation of his deletion of the parental generation from *Flags in the Dust* in *Faulkner in the University*, ed. Frederick L. Gwynn and Joseph Blotner (Charlottesville, Va.: UP of Virginia, 1959), 251.
3. See Conrad Aiken, "William Faulkner: The Novel as Form," in *Faulkner: A Collection of Critical Essays*, ed. R. P. Warren (Englewood Cliffs, N.J.: Prentice-Hall, 1966), 51.

second, in the use of memory and repetition as formal principles.[4] Faulkner possessed the three Compson brothers, as he later put it, almost before he put pen to paper. He took a central event and several germinating images from the death of the grandmother he and his brothers called Damuddy, after whose lingering illness and funeral they were sent from home so that it could be fumigated. For Faulkner, as for Gertrude Stein, memory is always repetition, being and living never repetition. *The Sound and the Fury*, he was fond of remarking, was a single story several times told. But memory was never for him simple repetition. He used the remembered as he used the actual: less to denominate lived events, relationships, and configurations, with their attendant attributes and emotions, than to objectify them and so be free to analyze and play with them. To place the past under the aspect of the present, the present under the aspect of the past, was to start from the regressive toward the innovative. Like the novel's regressive principle, its innovative principle possessed several corollaries, as we see, for example, in its gradual evocation of Caddy, the sister he added to memory, and in its slow progression from private toward more public worlds.[5]

The parental generation, which exists in *Flags in the Dust* only for the sake of family continuity, is crucial in *The Sound and the Fury*. Jason is aggressive in expressing the contempt he feels for his mother and especially his father. Although Benjy shares neither Jason's contempt nor the preoccupations it inspires, he does feel the vacancies his parents' inadequacies have created in his life. Although Quentin disguises his resentment, it surfaces. Like Benjy's and Quentin's obsessive attachments to Caddy, Jason's animosity toward her originates in wounds inflicted by Mr. and Mrs. Compson. In short, it is in Caddy that each brother's discontent finds its focus, as we see in their various evocations of her.

To the end of his life, Faulkner spoke of Caddy with deep devotion. She was, he suggested, both the sister of his imagination and "the daughter of his mind."[6] Born of his own discontent, she was for him "the beautiful one," his "heart's darling."[7] It was Caddy, or more precisely, Faulkner's feeling for the emerging Caddy, that

---

4. Faulkner had three brothers, of course, but during the crucial years to which his memory turned in *The Sound and the Fury*, he had only two. Leila Dean Swift, the grandmother whom the first three Falkner boys called Damuddy, died on June 1, 1907. The youngest of the four Falkner boys, Dean Swift Falkner, was born August 15, 1907. Also see Faulkner as quoted in the statement cited in note 1 [on p. 373].

5. See Aiken as cited in note 3 on p. 346.

6. See the discussions of Caddy in the Introduction cited in note 7 on p. 345; *Mosquitoes*, 339; and "Books and Things: Joseph Hergesheimer," in *William Faulkner: Early Prose and Poetry*, ed. Carvel Collins (Boston: Little, Brown, 1962), 101–103. The quoted phrase is a translation of an Italian phrase quoted in the last of these pieces, p. 102.

7. *Faulkner in the University*, 6.

turned a story called "Twilight" into a novel called *The Sound and the Fury*: "I loved her so much," he said, that "I couldn't decide to give her life just for the duration of a short story. She deserved more than that. So my novel was created, almost in spite of myself."[8]

In the same statements in which Faulkner stressed the quality of his love for Caddy, he emphasized the extent to which his novel grew as he worked on it. One source of that growth derived from Faulkner's discovery of repetition as a technical principle. Having presented Benjy's experience, he found that it was so "incomprehensible, even I could not have told what was going on then, so I had to write another chapter." The second section accordingly became both a clarification and a counterpoint to the first, just as the third became both of these to the second.[9] The story moves from the remote and strange world of Benjy's idiocy and innocence, where sensations and basic responses are all we have; through the intensely subjective as well as private world of Quentin's bizarre idealism, where thought shapes sensation and feeling into a kind of decadent poetic prose full of idiosyncratic allusions and patterns; to the more familiar, even commonsensical meanness of Jason's materialism, where rage and self-pity find expression in colloquialisms and clichés. Because it is more conventional, Jason's section is more accessible, even more public. Yet it too describes a circle of its own.[1] Wanting to move from three peculiar and private worlds toward a more public and social one, Faulkner adopted a more detached voice. The fourth section comes to us as though from "an outsider." The story, as it finally emerged, tells not only of four children and their family, but of a larger world, itself at twilight. "And that's how that book grew. That is, I wrote that same story four times. . . . That was not a deliberate *tour de force* at all, the book just grew that way. . . . I was still trying to tell one story which moved me very much and each time I failed. . . ."[2]

Given the novel's technical brilliance, it is easy to forget how simple and how moving its basic story is. In it we observe four children come of age amid the decay and dissolution of their family. It began, Faulkner recalled, with "a brother and a sister splashing one another in the brook" where they had been sent to play during the funeral of a grandmother they called Damuddy. From the play in the brook came what Faulkner several times referred to as the central image in the novel—Caddy's muddy drawers. As she clambers

---

8. See Faulkner as quoted in the translation of Maurice Coindreau's Introduction to *The Sound and the Fury*, in *The Mississippi Quarterly* 19 (Summer 1966): 109.

9. Robert A. Jelliffe, ed., *Faulkner at Nagano* (Tokyo: Kenkyusha, 1956), 104.

1. See F. H. Bradley, *Appearance and Reality* (New York: Macmillan, 1908), 346; and T. S. Eliot's note to line 142 of *The Waste Land*.

2. *Faulkner at Nagano*, 103–105.

up a tree outside the Compson home to observe the funeral inside, we and her brothers see them from below. From these episodes, Faulkner got several things: his sense of the branch as "the dark, harsh flowing of time" which was sweeping Caddy away from her brothers; his sense that the girl who had the courage to climb the tree would also find the courage to face change and loss; and his sense that the brothers who waited below would respond very differently—that Benjy would feel but never understand his loss; that Quentin would seek oblivion rather than face his; and that Jason would meet his with vindictive rage and terrible ambition.[3] The novel thus focuses not only on three brothers Faulkner possessed when he began, but also on Caddy, the figure he added to memory—which is to say, on the child whose story he never directly told as well as on those whose stories he directly tells. His decision to approach Caddy only by indirection, through the needs and demands of her brothers, was in part technical, as he repeatedly insisted. By the time he came to the fourth telling, he wanted a more detached, public voice. In addition, he thought indirection more "passionate." It was, he said, more moving to present "the shadow of the branch, and let the [reader's] mind create the tree."[4]

But in fact Caddy grew as she is presented, by indirection—in response to needs shared by Faulkner and his characters. Having discovered Benjy, in whose idiocy he saw "the blind, self-centeredness of innocence, typified by children," he "became interested in the relationship of the idiot to the world that he was in but would never be able to cope with. . . ." What particularly agitated him was where such a one as Benjy could find "the tenderness, the help, to shield him. . . ."[5] The answer he hit upon had nothing to do with Mr. and Mrs. Compson, and only a little to do with Dilsey. Mr. Compson is a weak, nihilistic alcoholic who toys with the emotions and needs of his children. Even when he feels sympathy and compassion, he fails to show it effectively. Mrs. Compson is a cold, self-involved woman who expends her energies worrying about her ailments, complaining about her life, and clinging to her notions of respectability. "If I could say Mother. Mother," Quentin says to himself. Dilsey, who distinctly recalls Mammy Caroline Barr, to whom Faulkner later dedicated *Go Down, Moses*, epitomizes the kind of Christian Faulkner most deeply

---

3. See both versions of Faulkner's Introduction, cited in note 7 on p. 345; and compare *Faulkner in the University*, 31–32.
4. *Faulkner at Nagano*, 72. Compare this statement with Mallarmé's assertion: "Nommer un objet, c'est supprimer les trois-quarts de la jouissance du poème. . . ." ["To name an object is to suppress three-fourths of the pleasure of the poem. . . ."] See also A. G. Lehmann, *The Symbolist Aesthetic in France, 1885–1895* (Oxford: Blackwell, 1950), particularly chapters 1, 2, and 6.
5. James B. Meriwether and Michael Millgate, eds., *Lion in the Garden: Interviews with William Faulkner, 1926–1962* (New York: Random House, 1968), 146.

admired. She is saved by a minimum of theology. Though her understanding is small, her wisdom and love are large. Living in the world
of the Compsons, she commits herself to the immediate; she "does
de bes'" she can to fill the vacancies left in the lives of the children
around her by their loveless and faithless parents. Since by virtue of
her love and faith she is part of a larger world, she is able not only
to help the children but "to stand above the fallen ruins of the
family. . . ."[6] She has seen, she says, the first and the last. But
Dilsey's life combines a measure of effective action with a measure of pathetic resignation. Most of Benjy's needs for tenderness
and comfort, if not help and protection, he takes to his sister. And
it was thus, Faulkner said, that "the character of his sister began
to emerge. . . ."[7] Like Benjy, Quentin and Jason also turn toward
Caddy, seeking to find in her some way of meeting needs ignored or
thwarted by their parents. Treasuring some concept of family honor
his parents seem to him to have forfeited, Quentin seeks to turn his
fair and beautiful sister into a fair, unravished, and unravishable
maiden. Lusting after an inheritance, and believing his parents to
have sold his birthright, Jason tries to make Caddy the instrument
of a substitute fortune.

The parental generation, which exists in *Flags in the Dust* only
for the sake of continuity, thus plays a crucial if destructive role in
The Sound and the Fury. Several readers have felt that Faulkner's
sympathies as a fictionist lay more with men than with women.[8]
But his fathers, at least, rarely fare better than his mothers, the
decisive direction of his sympathy being toward children, as we see
most clearly in *The Sound and the Fury*, but clearly too in works
that followed it. Jewel Bundren must live without a visible father,
while Darl discovers that in some fundamental sense he "never had
a mother." Thomas Sutpen's children live and die without an adequate father. Rosa Coldfield lives a long life only to discover that
she had lost childhood before she possessed it. Yet, even as they
resemble the deprived and often deserted or orphaned children of
Charles Dickens, Faulkner's children also resemble Hawthorne's
Pyncheons. Held without gentleness, they are still held fast. Suffering from a malady that resembles claustrophobia no less than from
fear of desertion, they find repetition easy, independence and inno-
vation almost impossible.

Although he is aggressive in expressing the hostility he feels for
his parents, Jason is never able satisfactorily to avenge himself on

---

6. See the second version of Faulkner's Introduction to *The Sound and the Fury*, cited in
   note 7, p. 367.
7. See *Lion in the Garden*, 146–47.
8. See Albert J. Guerard, *The Triumph of the Novel* (New York: Oxford UP, 1976),
   109–35.

them. Accordingly, he takes his victims where he finds them, his preference being for those who are most helpless, like Benjy and Luster, or most desperate, like Caddy. Enlarged, the contempt he feels for his family enables him to reject the past and embrace the New South, which he does without recognizing in himself vulgar versions of the materialism and self-pity that we associate with his mother. Left without sufficient tenderness and love, Quentin, Caddy, and Benjy turn toward Dilsey and each other. Without becoming aggressive, Benjy feels the vacancies his parents create in his life. All instinctively, he tries to hold fast to those moments in which Caddy meets his need for tenderness. In Quentin, we observe a very different desire: he wants to possess moments only as he would have them. Like the hero of Pound's *Cantos*, Quentin lives wondering whether any sight can be worth the beauty of his thought. His dis-ease with the immediate, which becomes a desire to escape time itself, accounts for the strange convolutions of his mind and the strange transformations of his emotions. In the end it leads him to a still harbor, where he fastidiously completes the logic of his father's life. Unlike her brothers, Caddy establishes her independence and achieves freedom. But her flight severs ties, making it impossible for her to help Quentin, comfort Benjy, or protect her daughter. Finally, freedom sweeps "her into dishonor and shame. . . ."[9] Deserted by her mother, Miss Quentin is left no one with whom to learn love, and so repeats her mother's dishonor and flight without ever knowing her tenderness. If in the story of Jason we observe the near-triumph of all that is repugnant, in the stories of Caddy and Miss Quentin we observe the degradation of all that is beautiful. No modern story has done more than theirs to explore Yeats's terrible vision of modernity in "The Second Coming," where the "best lack all conviction," while the "worst are full of passionate intensity."

Faulkner thus seems to have discovered Caddy as he presents her—through the felt needs of her brothers. Only later did he realize that he had also been trying to meet needs of his own: that in Caddy he had created the sister he had wanted but never had and the daughter he was fated to lose, "though the former might have been apparent," he added, "from the fact that Caddy had three brothers almost before I wrote her name on paper."[1] Taken together, the Compson brothers body forth needs Faulkner expressed through his creation of Caddy. In Benjy's need for tenderness we see something of the emotional confluence which precipitated the writing of *The Sound*

---

9. See the second version of Faulkner's Introduction to *The Sound and the Fury,* cited in note 7, p. 367.
1. Ibid.

and the Fury. The ecstasy and relief Faulkner associated with the writing of the novel as a whole, he associated particularly with the writing of Benjy's section.[2] In Jason's preoccupation with making a fortune, we see a vulgar version of the hope Faulkner was trying to relinquish. In Quentin's Manichaean revulsion toward all things material and physical, we see both a version of the imagination Allen Tate called "angelic" and a version of the moral sensibility that Faulkner associated with the fastidious aesthete.[3] It is more than an accident of imagery that Quentin, another of Faulkner's poets *manqués*, seeks refuge, first, in the frail "vessel" he calls Caddy, and then, in something very like the "still harbor" in which Faulkner had earlier imagined Joseph Hergesheimer submerging himself— "where the age cannot hurt him and where rumor of the world reaches him only as a far faint sound of rain."[4]

In one of his more elaborate as well as more suggestive descriptions of what the creation of Caddy meant to him, Faulkner associated her with one of his favorite images.

> I said to myself, Now I can write. Now I can make myself a vase like that which the old Roman kept at his bedside and wore the rim slowly away with kissing it. So I, who had never had a sister and was fated to lose my daughter in infancy, set out to make myself a beautiful and tragic little girl.[5]

The image of the urn or vase had turned up earlier in a review of Hergesheimer's fiction; in Faulkner's unpublished novel about Elmer Hodge; in *Mosquitoes*; and in *Flags in the Dust*. It had made a recent appearance in the letter to Aunt Bama describing his new love, and it would make several later appearances. It was an image, we may fairly assume, which possessed special force for Faulkner, and several connotations, at least three of which are of crucial significance.

The simplest of these, stressing desire for shelter or escape, Faulkner first associated with Hergesheimer's "still harbor" and later with "the classic and serene vase" which shelters Gail Hightower "from the harsh gale of living."[6] In *The Sound and the Fury* Benjy comes to us as a wholly dependent creature seeking shelter. Sentenced to stillness and silence—"like something eyeless and voiceless

2. Ibid.
3. See Allen Tate, "The Angelic Imagination," *The Man of Letters in the Modern World* (New York: Noonday Press, 1955), 113–31; Robert M. Slabey, "The 'Romanticism' of *The Sound and the Fury*," *The Mississippi Quarterly*, 16 (Summer 1963): 152–57.
4. "Books and Things: Joseph Hergesheimer," *Early Prose and Poetry*, 102.
5. See the first version of Faulkner's Introduction to *The Sound and the Fury*, cited in note 7, p. 367.
6. See the works cited in note 6, p. 347; compare *Light in August* (New York: Harrison Smith and Robert Haas, 1932), 453.

which . . . existed merely because of its ability to suffer"[7]—he is all need and all helplessness. What loss of Caddy means to him is a life of unrelieved, and for him meaningless, suffering. For Quentin, on the other hand, it means despair. In him the desire for relief and shelter becomes desire for escape. In one of the New Orleans sketches, Faulkner introduces a girl who presents herself to her lover as "Little sister Death." In an allegory written in 1926 for Helen Baird, who was busy rejecting his love, he reintroduces the figure called Little sister Death, this time in the company of a courtly knight and lover—which is, of course, one of the roles Quentin seeks to play.[8] At first all of Quentin's desire seems to focus on Caddy as the maiden of his dreams. But as his desire becomes associated with "night and unrest," Caddy begins to merge with "Little sister Death"—that is, with an incestuous love forbidden on threat of death. Rendered impotent by that threat, Quentin comes to love, not the body of his sister, nor even some concept of Compson honor, but death itself. In the end, he ceremoniously gives himself, not to Caddy, but to the river. "The saddest thing about love," says a character in *Soldiers' Pay*, "is that not only the love cannot last forever, but even the heartbreak is soon forgotten." Quentin kills himself in part as punishment for his forbidden desires; in part because Caddy proves corruptible; in part, perhaps, because he decides "that even she was not quite worth despair." But he also kills himself because he fears his own inconstancy. What he discovers in himself is deep psychological impotence. He is unable to play either of the heroic roles—as seducer or as avenger—that he deems appropriate to his fiction of himself as a gallant, chivalric lover. What he fears is that he will ultimately fail, too, in the role of the despairing lover. What he cannot abide is the prospect of a moment when Caddy's corruption no longer matters to him.[9]

Never before had Faulkner expressed anxiety so deep and diverse. In Quentin it is not only immediate failure that we observe; it is the

---

7. See the second version of Faulkner's Introduction to *The Sound and the Fury*, cited in note 7, p. 367.
8. See "The Kid Learns," in *William Faulkner: New Orleans Sketches*, ed. Carvel Collins (New York: Random House, 1958), 91. See also "Mayday," the allegory Faulkner wrote for Helen Baird, as discussed by Blotner, *Faulkner*, 510–11; by Cleanth Brooks, "The Image of Helen Baird in Faulkner's Early Poetry and Fiction." *The Sewanee Review*, 85 (Spring 1977): 220–22; and by Cleanth Brooks, *William Faulkner, Toward Yoknapatawpha and Beyond* (New Haven, Conn.: Yale UP, 1978), 47–52. A facsimile of *Mayday* edited by Carvel Collins has recently been published by the University of Notre Dame Press (1977). See also Collins, Introduction, *New Orleans Sketches*, pp. xxiv–xxv.
9. See *Soldiers' Pay* (New York: Boni and Liveright, 1926), 318. Compare Faulkner's statement, years later, to Meta Carpenter: "What is valuable is what you have lost, since then you never had the chance to wear out and so lose it shabbily. . . ." Quoted in Meta Carpenter Wilde and Orin Borsten. *A Loving Gentleman* (New York: Simon and Schuster, 1976), 317.

prospect of ultimate failure. Later, Faulkner associated the writing of *The Sound and the Fury* specifically with anxiety about a moment "when not only the ecstasy of writing would be gone, but the unreluctance and the something worth saying too."[1] Coming and going throughout his life, that anxiety came finally to haunt him. But as early as his creation of Quentin he saw clearly the destructive potential of the desire to escape it. If he wrote *The Sound and the Fury* in part to find shelter, he also wrote it knowing that he would have to emerge from it. "I had made myself a vase," he said, though "I suppose I knew all the time that I could not live forever inside of it. . . ."[2] Having finished *The Sound and the Fury*, he in fact found emergence traumatic. Still, it is probably fair to say that he knew all along what awaited him. Certainly his novel possessed other possibilities than shelter and escape for him, just as the image through which he sought to convey his sense of it possessed other connotations, including one that is clearly erotic and one that is clearly aesthetic.

The place to begin untangling the erotic is the relation between the old Roman who kept the vase at his bedside so that he could kiss it and "the withered cuckold husband that took the Decameron to bed with him every night. . . ."[3] These two figures are not only committed to a kind of substitution; they practice a kind of auto-eroticism. The old Roman is superior only if we assume that he is the maker of his vase—in which case he resembles Horace Benbow, who in *Flags in the Dust* makes an "almost perfect vase" which he keeps by his bedside and calls by his sister's name. With Horace and his vase, we might seem to have come full circle, back to Faulkner and his "heart's darling."[4] In *The Sound and the Fury* affection of brother for sister and sister for brother becomes the archetype of love; and with Caddy and Quentin, the incestuous potential of that love clearly surfaces—as it had in *Elmer, Mosquitoes,* and *Flags in the Dust*, and as it would in *Absalom, Absalom!*

The circle, however, is less perfect than it might at first appear, since at least one difference between Horace Benbow and William Faulkner is both obvious and crucial. Whereas Horace's amber vase is a substitute for a sister he has but is forbidden and fears to possess, Faulkner's is a substitute for the sister he never had. In this regard Horace Benbow is closer to Elmer Hodge, Faulkner to the sculptor named Gordon in *Mosquitoes*. Elmer is in fact a more timid as well as

---

1. See the second version of Faulkner's Introduction to *The Sound and the Fury*, cited in note 7, p. 367.
2. Ibid.
3. *Mosquitoes*, 210.
4. Compare *Flags in the Dust* (New York: Random House, 1973), 153–154, 162; and *Faulkner in the University*, 6.

an earlier version of Horace. Working with his paints—"thick-bodied and female and at the same time phallic: hermaphroditic"—Elmer creates figures he associates with something "that he dreaded yet longed for." The thing he both seeks and shuns is a "vague shape" he holds in his mind; its origins are his mother and a sister named Jo-Addie. Like Horace's, Elmer's art is devoted to imaginative possession of figures he is forbidden and fears sexually to possess.[5] When Horace calls his amber vase by his sister's name, he articulates what Elmer merely feels. Like Elmer, however, Horace makes indirect or imaginative possession a means of avoiding the fate Quentin enacts. Through their art, Elmer and Horace are able to achieve satisfaction that soothes one kind of despair without arousing guilt that might lead to another.[6]

In *Mosquitoes*, the origins of Gordon's "feminine ideal" remain obscure, though his art is quite clearly devoted to creation and possession of her. For Gordon as for Elmer and Horace, the erotic and the aesthetic are inseparable. A man is always writing, Dawson Fairchild remarks, for "some woman"; if she is not "a flesh and blood creature," she is at least "the symbol of a desire," and "she is feminine."[7] In their art Elmer and Horace work toward a figure that is actual, making art a substitute for love of a real woman. Gordon, on the other hand, associates art with an ideal whose identity remains vague. We know of it two things—that it is feminine and that it represents what Henry James called the beautiful circuit and subterfuge of thought and desire. Whereas Horace expresses his love for a real woman through his art, Gordon expresses his devotion to his sculpted ideal by pursuing, temporarily, a woman named Patricia who interests him only because she happens to resemble "the virginal breastless torso of a girl" he has already sculpted.[8] Whereas Horace is a failed, inconstant artist, Gordon is a consecrated one, the difference being that Gordon devotes his life as well as his art to pursuing the figure which exists perfectly only in thought and imagination.

On a voyage to Europe, shortly after finishing *Soldiers' Pay* and before beginning *Elmer* and *Mosquitoes*, Faulkner told William Spratling that he thought love and death the "only two basic

---

5. The *Elmer* manuscripts are in the William Faulkner Collections, University of Virginia Library. For a valuable discussion of them, see Thomas L. McHaney, "The Elmer Papers: Faulkner's Comic Portraits of the Artist," *The Mississippi Quarterly* 26 (Summer 1973): 281–311.

6. See the manuscripts cited in note 5, above, and compare *Flags in the Dust*, 153–54, 162.

7. *Mosquitoes*, 250.

8. See John Irwin, *Doubling & Incest, Repetition & Revenge* (Baltimore: Johns Hopkins UP, 1975), 160–61 [pp. 341–49 in this Norton Critical Edition]; and *Mosquitoes*, 11, 24, 28, 47–48.

compulsions on earth. . . ."[9] What engaged his imagination as much as either of these compulsions, however, was his sense of the relation of each to the other and of both to art. The amber vase Horace calls Narcissa, he also addresses "as Thou still unravished bride of quietude."[1] "There is a story somewhere," Faulkner said,

> about an old Roman who kept at his bedside a Tyrrhenian vase which he loved and the rim of which he wore slowly away with kissing it. I had made myself a vase, but I suppose I knew all the time that I could not live forever inside of it, that perhaps to have it so that I too could lie in bed and look at it would be better; surely so when that day should come when not only the ecstasy of writing would be gone, but the unreluctance and the something worth saying too. It's fine to think that you will leave something behind you when you die, but it's better to have made something you can die with.[2]

In this brief statement, the vase becomes both Caddy and *The Sound and the Fury*; both "the beautiful one" for whom he created the novel as a commodious space, and the novel in which she found protection, even privacy, as well as expression. Through its basic doubleness, the vase becomes many things: a haven or shelter into which the artist may retreat; a feminine ideal to which he gives his devotion; a work of art which he can leave behind when he is dead; and a burial urn which will contain one expression of his self as artist. If it is a mouth he may freely kiss, it is also a world in which he may find shelter; if it is a womb he may enter, it is also a space in which his troubled spirit may find both temporary rest and lasting expression.[3]

Of all his novels, it was for *The Sound and the Fury* that Faulkner felt "the most tenderness."[4] Writing it not only renewed his sense of purpose and hope;[5] it also gave him an "emotion definite and physical and yet nebulous to describe. . . ." Caught up in it, he experienced a kind of ecstasy, particularly in the "eager and joyous faith and anticipation of surprise which the yet unmarred sheets beneath my hand held inviolate and unfailing. . . ."[6] Such language may at first glance seem surprising. For *The Sound and the Fury* is, as Faulkner once noted, a "dark story of madness and hatred," and it

9. William Spratling, "Chronicle of a Friendship: William Faulkner in New Orleans," *The Texas Quarterly* 9 (Spring 1966): 38.
1. See the works cited in note 6, above.
2. See the second version of Faulkner's Introduction to *The Sound and the Fury*, cited in note 7, p. 367.
3. See Irwin, *Doubling & Incest*, 162–163.
4. *Lion in the Garden*, 147.
5. See *Faulkner in the University*, 67.
6. See the second version of Faulkner's Introduction to *The Sound and the Fury*, cited in note 7, p. 367.

clearly cost him dearly.[7] Having finished it, he moved to New York, where he continued revising it. "I worked so hard at that book," he said later, "that I doubt if there's anything in it that didn't belong there."[8] As he neared the end for which he had labored hard, he drew back, dreading completion as though it meant "cutting off the supply, destroying the source. . . ." Perhaps like Rilke and Proust, he associated "the completed" with silence.[9] Having finished his revisions, he contrived for himself an interface of silence and pain. Happening by his flat one evening, Jim Devine and Leon Scales found him alone, unconscious, huddled on the floor, empty bottles scattered around him.[1]

What *The Sound and the Fury* represented to him, however, he had anticipated in *Mosquitoes*: a work "in which the hackneyed accidents which make up this world—love and life and death and sex and sorrow—brought together by chance in perfect proportions, take on a kind of splendid and timeless beauty."[2] In the years to come, he would think of his fourth novel as a grand failure. Imperfect success would always be his ideal. To continue his effort to match his "dream of perfection," he needed dissatisfaction as well as hope. If failure might drive him to despair, success might deprive him of purpose: "it takes only one book to do it. It's not the sum of a lot of scribbling, it's one perfect book, you see. It's one single urn or shape that you want. . . ."[3]

Faulkner wanted, he once wrote Malcolm Cowley, "to be, as a private individual, abolished and voided from history." It was his aim to make his books the sole remaining sign of his life. Informing such statements is a definite need for privacy. But informing them, too, is a tacit conception of his relation to his art: that his authentic self was the self variously and nebulously yet definitely bodied forth by his fictions.[4] It is in this deeper rather than in the usual sense that his fiction is autobiographical. It is of his self expressive, which is to say, creative. "I have never known anyone," a brother wrote,

---

7. Quoted by Coindreau, Introduction to *The Sound and the Fury, The Mississippi Quarterly* 19 (Summer 1966): 109.
8. Quoted in Blotner, *Faulkner*, 589–90.
9. See W. H. Auden, Sonnet XXIII, in "In Time of War," in W. H. Auden and Christopher Isherwood, *Journey to a War* (New York: Random House, 1938). Compare Auden, Sonnet XIX in "Sonnets from China," *Collected Shorter Poems, 1927–1957* (New York: Random House, 1966). See also *Absalom, Absalom!* (New York: Random House, 1936), 373–74.
1. See Blotner, *Faulkner*, pp. 590–591.
2. *Mosquitoes*, 339.
3. *Faulkner in the University*, 65. Compare *Soldiers' Pay*, 283.
4. To Malcolm Cowley, Friday [February 11, 1949], in *The Faulkner-Cowley File* (New York: Viking Press, 1966), 126. See Irwin, *Doubling & Incest*, 171–72 [pp. 341–49 in this Norton Critical Edition].

who identified himself with his writings more than Bill did. . . .
    Sometimes it was hard to tell which was which, which one
Bill was, himself or the one in the story. And yet you knew
somehow that the two of them were the same, they were one
and inseparable.[5]

Faulkner knew that characters, "those shady but ingenious shapes,"
were a way of exploring, projecting, reaffirming both the life he
lived and the tacit, secret life underlying it. At least once he was
moved to wonder if he "had invented the world" of his fiction "or if
it had invented me. . . ."[6]
    Like indirect knowing, however, imperfect success, which implies
partial completion, carries several connotations. Both the decision
to approach Caddy only by indirection and the need to describe the
novel as a series of imperfect acts partially completed ally it with
the complex. They are in part a tribute to epistemological problems and in part a sign that beauty is difficult—that those things
most worth seeing, knowing, and saying can never be directly seen,
known, and said. But indirection and incompletion are also useful
strategies for approaching forbidden scenes, uttering forbidden
words, committing dangerous acts. For Elmer Hodge, both his sister Jo-Addie and behind her "the dark woman. The dark mother,"
are associated with a "vague shape [s]omewhere back in his mind"—
the core for him of everything he dreads and desires. Since attain-
ment, the only satisfying act, is not only dangerous but forbidden,
and therefore both can't and must be his aim, Elmer's life and art
become crude strategies of approximation. The opposite of crude,
the art of *The Sound and the Fury* is nonetheless an art of con-
cealment as well as disclosure—of delay, avoidance, evasion—
particularly where Caddy is concerned. Beyond Faulkner's sense
that indirection was more passionate lay his awareness that it was
also less dangerous. For him both desire and hesitancy touched
almost everything, making his imagination as illusive as it is allu-
sive, and his art preeminently an art of surmise and conjecture.
    In *Flags in the Dust* he had taken ingenious possession of a heri-
tage which he proceeded both to dismember and reconstruct. In
The Sound and the Fury he took possession of the pain and muted
love of his childhood—its dislocations and vacancies, its forbidden
needs and desires. The loss we observe in *The Sound and the Fury*
is associated with parental weakness and inadequacy—with parental frigidity, judgment, and rejection. In the figure of Dilsey Faulkner
re-created the haven of love he had found in Mammy Callie; in the

5. John Faulkner, *My Brother Bill* (New York: Trident Press, 1963), 275.
6. This quote is from a manuscript fragment in the Beinecke Library, Yale University. It
   is quoted in Blotner, *Faulkner*, 584.

figure of Caddy, he created one he knew only through longing. If the first of these figures is all maternal, the second is curiously mixed. In the figure of the sister he never had, we see not only a sister but a mother (the role she most clearly plays for Benjy) and a lover (the possibility most clearly forbidden). Like the emotion Faulkner experienced in writing it, the novel's central figure comes to us as one "definite and physical yet nebulous. . . ." Needing to conceal even as he disclosed her, Faulkner created in Caddy Compson a heroine who perfectly corresponds to her world: like it, she was born of regression and evasion, and like it, she transcends them.

ERIC SUNDQUIST

The Myth of *The Sound and the Fury*†

There is some irony in the fact that Faulkner's deserved public recognition came at a time (the late 1940s and on to his death) when his best work was a decade old and he was writing some of the most disappointing fiction a major novelist could conceivably write. Little that he produced after *Go Down, Moses,* including *Intruder in the Dust,* the novel that guaranteed that recognition, merits sustained attention. The larger irony is that once we begin backtracking to see where he went wrong we must return to the novel often taken to be his masterpiece. With fanfare Faulkner surely would have relished, and did his best to facilitate, *The Sound and the Fury* (1929) has become a myth. No one would want to deny its importance, but it is worthwhile considering where, exactly, that importance lies. The novel has been so thoroughly explicated that it should prove more useful to read it with an eye to its place at the starting point of Faulkner's career and in the larger self-imposed design of his fiction, a design one may certainly admire without taking altogether seriously.

   The Sound and the Fury is not, of course, the starting point of Faulkner's career. He had already written three novels: *Soldiers' Pay* (1926), a good postwar novel, which unevenly rivals Dos Passos and Hemingway; *Mosquitoes* (1927), a dismal tract on aestheticism; and *Sartoris* (1929), a minor historical novel much improved by editorial revisions that Faulkner had little to do with. Beyond that, he had written two volumes worth of *fin de siècle* poetry and a handful of short stories, some of which were later incorporated into novels,

† From *Faulkner: The House Divided* (Baltimore and London: Johns Hopkins UP, 1983), 3–7, 9–12, 13–14, 17–18, 26–27. © 1983 The Johns Hopkins University Press. Reprinted with permission of The Johns Hopkins University Press. Page references in the text are to this Norton Critical Edition.

or—in the case of *The Sound and the Fury*—blossomed into whole novels, or got added to others and then posed as novels. Without *The Sound and the Fury* and the work that followed, however, few of these earlier efforts would get more than a glance. And there is reason to believe that without Faulkner's work of the next ten years *The Sound and the Fury* would itself seem a literary curiosity, an eccentric masterpiece of experimental methods and "modernist" ideas. This states the worst case, as it were, and proposes the unknowable. But Faulkner's insistent announcements (to choose one of many examples) that the novel was "the most gallant, the most magnificent failure" of all his failed works,[1] and that he therefore loved it most, make inevitable its glamorous position at the dawn of his creation. This is not to say that *The Sound and the Fury* is not a superior novel but simply that it prefigures many problems in Faulkner's later fiction and is far too likely to appear the monumental work against which his other fiction must be judged.

Faulkner vigorously promoted this view (and apparently subscribed to it himself), and any reading of his career in whole or in part will necessarily depend on it. One may, nevertheless, accept the novel as his moment of discovered genius without concluding that it is the key to the treasure of Yoknapatawpha. It would not be apparent until 1945, when Faulkner wrote the appendix to the novel, or until after his death, when two versions of an introduction he wrote and discarded in 1933 were published, what a burden the novel would have to carry. The introduction says more eloquently what Faulkner had always said in public—that the novel was a wonderful failure, a story so great that it could not be put into words, and had produced in him an ecstasy he had never been able to recapture; but the appendix exposes something more unsettling—that the muse of Yoknapatawpha was in decline, that her author was struggling to extend his great design out of any odds and ends he could dream up. The appendix adds, in the ponderous, often absurd prose that is characteristic of Faulkner's late style, accounts of the Compson ancestors and brief surveys of the later lives of the novel's characters. Far from illuminating the novel, except in the interests of family chronicle and the retrospective purpose of Faulkner's design, it everywhere clashes with the novel, whose signal virtues create a world of timeless hallucination in which, when they are right, the words float lightly, silently through the novel's mysterious nets of consciousness, falling each into its ordered place.

---

1. Frederick L. Gwynn and Joseph L. Blotner, eds., *Faulkner in the University: Class Conferences at the University of Virginia, 1957–1958* (1958; reprint ed., New York: Vintage-Random, 1965), 61.

The novel's appendix first appeared as a set piece in Malcolm Cowley's *The Portable Faulkner*, and Faulkner claimed then that, had he written it for the novel to begin with, "the whole thing would have fallen into pattern like a jigsaw puzzle when the magician's wand touched it." He also remarked, however, that it was "a piece without implications," and later, when challenged about its apparent contradictions to the novel, he replied that the inconsistencies prove "the book is still alive after 15 years, and being still alive is growing, changing."[2] These confusing claims are entirely relevant to the larger problem of Faulkner's fictional design, in which novels simultaneously stand alone, contradict one another, or (it is said) fall into magic patterns from which no one piece of the puzzle could possibly be removed. Faulkner insisted that the appendix, when added to the novel, should appear at the beginning rather than the end (it has been published both ways) and described it at once as "the key to the whole book" and "an obituary."[3] Analogously, the more he wrote—from *Absalom, Absalom!* on, say, after he had actually drawn a map of Yoknapatawpha—the more his fiction resembled new keys to the kingdom and a record of its creative decline toward death. Nowhere is this more apparent than in *Requiem for a Nun* (1951), where Faulkner attempts to extend the story of *Sanctuary*'s main attraction in the form of a play and indulges in long, cascading prose accounts of early Yoknapatawpha in which the ancestors of many of the characters and events of his fictional career appear in a patently legendary story of The Creation. Like the appendix to *The Sound and the Fury*, these accounts intertwine fine anecdotes and exceptionally bad writing, and they indicate how fragile and disordered the vision had become. But they also present a special kind of problem to readers: If the very essence of Faulkner's design is that it will remain incomplete, if the design (like that of Thomas Sutpen or the South itself) is flawed to start with, and if its whole development expresses a falling away from that which can never be reliably or precisely articulated, how then are works that claim such failures as virtues to be rejected?

The problem, of course, is not an imposing one: bad writing is bad writing, and some of Faulkner's is very bad indeed. It can be recognized as such, just as his great design, which will continue to attract encomiums and explication, can be ignored novel by novel. Yet the risk in ignoring it altogether, a risk *The Sound and the Fury* with its drummed-up appendix perfectly represents, is that the

2. Malcolm Cowley, *The Faulkner-Cowley File: Letters and Memories, 1944–1962* (New York: Viking P, 1966), 36–37, 90.

3. *Selected Letters of William Faulkner*, ed. Joseph Blotner (New York: Random House, 1977), 220–21, 228, 237. Hereafter referred to as *Selected Letters*.

problems inherent in the greater design so resemble the problems
with individual novels, and so much become part of their avowed
thematic material, that one is left incapable of exact judgment if
they are dismissed. There is little need now for more detailed analyses of the Faulkner canon or further exposés of his philosophical
vision. The chapters that compose the second part of this study will
take up social and historical contexts that are in need of more consideration: ones in which, to be precise, Faulkner becomes a great
novelist. His explorations of the issues of race conflict and miscegenation, while they are implicit in earlier works, only come to the fore
in and after *Light in August*, and one may justly divide his career in
two, as I have done, recognizing one period to be devoted to a study
of novelistic forms and the other to carrying those developed forms
into a domain of greatest resonance. Moreover, *The Sound and
the Fury*, as my reading of it will suggest, assumes just such a position of divided sensibility when one begins to examine its place in
Faulkner's career.

There was not, of course, and there did not need to be any such
strict division in Faulkner's own mind, and the latter portion of
his career is in certain respects an extended, romantically failed
attempt to deny that there were any disjunctions whatsoever. These
kinds of characterizations may in any event seem somewhat arbitrary; others could be made and justified, but it needs to be emphasized, for example, how different *The Sound and the Fury* appears
after it is put in the context of *Absalom, Absalom!* The powerful and
instructive cross-references the later novel makes possible are what
Faulkner's whole design depends on in more demanding ways; but
leaving aside *The Unvanquished*, an addendum to *Sartoris* primarily of veiled autobiographical interest, and the sequential Snopes
trilogy, this is the only instance where anything decisive or produc-
tive gets accomplished by comparison. In *Sanctuary*, to take a striking example, Faulkner's own revisions demonstrate that the novel,
far from being ruined, is vastly improved by his discarding those
sections that most connect the character of Horace Benbow to *Sartoris* and particularly its original version, *Flags in the Dust*; whereas
Requiem for a Nun, at the opposite extreme, depends on *Sanctuary*
and fragments of other novels to such an extent as to be a vacuous
charade by itself. In this case and others, Faulkner's experimentation simply runs wild, as though its very purpose were to devise
insurmountable dangers and create a context in which the strained
forms and rhetorical excesses of earlier novels would appear to have
been marvelously checked at the point of utmost distention.

In this respect, the great design reproduces the structure of
many individual novels, where characters and stories, however the
plots may strive to entangle them, often seem to collide or to stand

in taut juxtaposition; and while this method may produce superlative results at the contained, local level of the novel, its magnification through the span of a career makes the dubious virtues of disorder and conflict far too prominent. (What it also makes prominent is the apparent necessity of the design, for with the exception of *Soldiers' Pay*, the novels having little or nothing to do with Yoknapatawpha—*Mosquitoes, Pylon, The Wild Palms*, and *A Fable*—also the least successful.) At extremity, as in *Go Down, Moses*, stories are nearly crushed together on the assumption that recurring themes and names, and the forces of rhetoric, can be made to dramatize their connection; and it is surely no coincidence that this novel marks by its precariously extenuated form the end of Faulkner's major work, as though his creative powers, after a final, draining surge, had broken under the pressures of the envisioned design. Like Cooper and Hawthorne before him, Faulkner set out to create a native American tradition, in his case by creating a whole country and people, and proceeded to do so on the modernist grounds prepared by Eliot and Joyce where tradition was a fabrication, a false and broken pattern of ruins. As these intentions became superimposed on the lost dream of the South, the design fell apart—what else could it do? And what could Faulkner do but continue adding to it, all the while assuring readers and critics that it was supposed to fall apart—what else could it do?

Despite such caveats, however, and despite his own cunning complicity in the authorial game of romantic failure, Faulkner wrote great fiction—the greatest when he wrote of the South as an explicit topic (as distinct from using it for regional atmosphere, which he always did) and, perhaps paradoxically, when his own anxieties about the value of the fictional forms he had chosen were most apparent. There is no doubt, to borrow from Martin Green's irreverent attack, that Faulkner produced "engines of mental torture, crucifixions of literary sensibility"[4]—*The Sound and the Fury* is one of them—but he did so in a fashion that, at its better moments, created unseen worlds of unimagined words, and at its best perfectly accorded with the single most agonizing experience of his region and his nation: the crisis and long aftermath of American slavery. The formal explorations his finest early novels engaged in were preparation for things to follow, a search for a way to say things that had not been said but desperately needed saying, things that for good reason could barely be said. What he had to say is implicit in *The Sound and the Fury*; what is remarkable, and what constitutes the novel's central drama, is the difficulty he had in saying it at all.

4. Martin Green, *Re-Appraisals: Some Commonsense Readings in American Literature* (New York: W. W. Norton, 1965), 194.

* * *

Faulkner's achievement, as Robert Penn Warren has written, was foremost to articulate truths about the South and Southerners that had long been "lying speechless in their experience" and to confront turbulent issues that "would not have been available, been visible in fact, without the technique" he employed.[5] This is certainly true, though it would only become visible some years after *The Sound and the Fury*, where what is speechless in the Southern experience nearly remains so and what is made available by Faulkner's technique is not immediately clear. * * *

* * *

* * * The most perplexing thing about the novel is the discrepancy between its merits and the burdensome interpretations it has inevitably had to support. It is read as an allegory of the South, an exposition of the Oedipal complex, an ironic enactment of Christ's agony, and a sustained philosophical meditation on Time. While it engages all of these issues, it illuminates none of them very exactly; rather—and here lies part of its strange magnificence—it engages these issues, allows them to invade the domain of the novel's arcane family drama, and disavows their capacity to bring the novel out of its own self-enclosing darkness. The "psychology" that is of most interest in the novel is not Benjy's or Quentin's or Jason's or Dilsey's, but the psychology of the novel as a form of containing consciousness, one that is self-contained and at the same time contains, by defining in subliminal projection, Faulkner's most significant accomplishments and their ultimate derangement. There is more to be said of this psychology, but we may note again that the "mind" the novel does not have—and will not have until Faulkner's career develops—the mind of "the South," is paradoxically the only one that fully explains, Quentin's incestuous fascination with Caddy's purity and the novel's strange obsession with her.

* * * The novel is demonstrably about failed integrity—in the Compson family, the Southern dream, the novel as a conventional form, and the "mind" of the author. All of these issues, rightly enough, appear to converge in the mind of Benjy, and the rest of the novel is a slow extraction of attention from this originating abyss. Such a narrative development produces paradoxical effects that bear on, and reappear in, all of Faulkner's work, but their most salient feature in this case is a thorough devaluation of traditional novelistic plot or action.

5. Robert Penn Warren, "Faulkner: Past and Future," in *Faulkner: A Collection of Critical Essays*, ed. Robert Penn Warren (Englewood Cliffs, NJ: Prentice-Hall, 1966), 1, 5.

Nearly everything that "happens" in the novel happens in the first section—and this is exactly what Faulkner, who largely created for readers the idolatrous admiration of Caddy Compson they have expressed, asks us to believe. The genetic myth of the novel—that "it began with the picture of the little girl's muddy drawers, climbing that tree to look in the parlor window" at her grandmother's funeral[6]—has so overwhelmed the novel itself that one no longer questions its relevance, even though there is good reason to do so. One might rather say that this scene stands in the same relation to Caddy as Caddy does to the entire novel, for we find out so little about her that we might conclude, on the basis of the action of the novel, either that she is a tender-hearted tramp or that, because she is surrounded by every conceivable form of mental and emotional instability, her own actions are justifiably inevitable. But since Caddy is not a character but an idea, an obsession in the minds of her brothers, we cannot rightly be said to find out much at all about her. Caddy is "lost" psychologically and aesthetically as well as morally: she is the very symbol of loss in Faulkner's world—the loss of innocence, integrity, chronology, personality, and dramatic unity, all the problematic virtues of his envisioned artistic design. To Benjy she smells like trees, to Quentin she is would-be lover, to Jason she is the whore mother of a whore daughter, and to Faulkner she is at once "the sister which I did not have and the daughter which I was to lose," and "a beautiful and tragic little girl" who later becomes, apparently, the mistress of a Nazi officer in occupied France.[7] There is probably no major character in literature about whom we know so little in proportion to the amount of attention she receives. This is surely no objection to the novel, but it is quite certainly a measure of its drama, which is submerged to the point of invisibility.

Because the entire intent of *The Sound and the Fury* is to sequester modes of consciousness and formally depict them as incapable of responsive interaction, however, there may be no dramaturgical objection that can stand up on the grounds the novel presents. Its avowed strategy is to divide our attention among discrete modes of narrative revelation from which the novel's plot must be drawn over the course of several readings; once that is done—or even quite aside from it—we may then pay attention, respectively, to Benjy's libidinal creativity, Quentin's psychosis, Jason's satiric viciousness, or Dilsey's humble endurance. Holding together these discrete modes of narrative experience is the figure of the doomed girl; she

6. Gwynn and Blotner, eds., *Faulkner in the University,* 1. Faulkner recounted the composition of the novel as it sprang from this image on numerous occasions.
7. Faulkner, "An Introduction to *The Sound and the Fury*," ed. James B. Meriwether, *Mississippi Quarterly* 26, no. 3 (Summer 1973): 413; Faulkner, "An Introduction for *The Sound and the Fury*," ed. James B. Meriwether, *The Southern Review*, n.s. 8, no. 4 (Autumn 1972): 710.

lives in the formal vacuum of the novel, and in doing so she represents the still point, the "innocence" of mute action the four sections break away from as they dissolve into increasingly logical and coherent forms of narration. One has only to record the scene that Faulkner maintained was the heart of the novel—

> "All right." Versh said. "You the one going to get whipped. I aint." He went and pushed Caddy up into the tree to the first limb. We watched the muddy bottom of her drawers. Then we couldn't see her. We could hear the tree thrashing. (26)

—to see how invisible Caddy truly is. Despite its marvelously elliptical portrayal of vanishing innocence and its vaguely erotic suggestion of something "dirty," this scene, without Faulkner's repeated insistence on its centrality, would itself vanish into the novel's larger pattern of glimmering memories.

If one were determined to choose any descriptive scene as central, surely either the muddying of those drawers or the wake of Caddy's deflowering or particularly her wedding (which formalizes those earlier events) would be more obvious:

> *In the mirror she was running before I knew what it was. That quick, her train caught up over her arm she ran out of the mirror like a cloud, her veil swirling in long glints her heels brittle and fast clutching her dress onto her shoulder with the other hand, running out of the mirror the smells roses roses the voice that breathed o'er Eden. Then she was across the porch I couldn't hear her heels then in the moonlight like a cloud, the floating shadow of the veil running across the grass, into the bellowing. She ran out of her dress, clutching her bridal, into the bellowing.* (54)

Here, in this lyrical passage, is the wondrous center of the book—Caddy vanishing from the mirror of Quentin's narcissism into the wrenching, mindless vacuum of Benjy's bellowing: the death of Eden, Jefferson, April 1910; and the resurrection of the Edenic myth, Faulkner, 1929, But resurrection is yet to come (April 8, 1928); there is no rising without a fall, no fall without genesis, and it is eminently just, perhaps, that the scene Faulkner grew enamoured of should appear, in the novel itself, no more consequential than others and vanish into the creative past of created loss. The genetic myth must remain mysterious, and its focal point must be projected as the one instant, the one spark that produces a whole world without necessarily resembling or defining it.

This peculiar and powerful dilemma goes to the heart of the novel, for the "loss" of Caddy (wherever one pinpoints it) represents the crucial generative event in the book—in fact, the event that forecloses generation. It is the moment of discovered grief that brings death, actual and metaphorical, into the psychological worlds of Benjy and Quentin; it is the moment of potential but elusive tragedy, envisioned deep within the novel's mind, from which the increasingly furious and distorted saga of the Compsons follows; and it is the catalytic moment of frightening disturbance that Faulkner would spend the better part of his career trying to recapture and define by transfiguring into ever more convulsive and historically search-ing dimensions. Each fragment of a scene devoted to the memory of Caddy is charged with a sure passion, at once moving and inad-equate, that derives from the fragmentation of the narrative form itself, as though her figure were receding, reappearing, and receding again in the acts of remembrance that create her doomed, ethereal life. Those scenes together often constitute so fine and so troubling a memory, and so render in prose the poetry Faulkner had never found in verse, that we may forget that much of the novel—including many of the larger scenes in which those acts of memory are embedded—appears driven to madness in the further attempt to sustain their power in dramatic form and symbolic meditation. Caddy's story, as Faulkner leaves us to divine it (and, I will suggest, as his later fiction would reimagine it), is stunning. But it is also the novel's essential paradox that the small, certain beauties of Caddy's remembered fall should seem thoroughly at odds with the rhetorical fever and philo-sophical bewilderment that event produced in her family and her creator, while at the same time appearing to be their distant, irre-vocable cause.

The last two sections of the novel may be said to suppress its great-est event altogether, for Caddy there becomes more and more mar-ginal and eventually disappears altogether from the novel's conscious attention. Caddy is "the past" to the extent that she defines remem-bered moments that have been transfigured into disembodied hallu-cinations of lost love for Benjy and Quentin, and fierce hatred of his entire family for Jason; and as she is "past," so she is as dead as Mrs. Compson makes her by ordering that her name never be spoken in the house, and as dead as Jason treats her by embezzling her money and castigating her equally promiscuous daughter. * * *

* * *

The more intently one examines any of the novel's philosophical positions or symbolic structures—most notably their correlative appearance in the ludicrous masque of the Passion—the more they reduce to seemingly unintentional parody or dissolve into a chaos of fragments. It could be argued that this is precisely the case, that the novel's strategy, in both dramatic and formal terms, is to por-tray a shattering of belief and to depict the urgent failure of modern consciousness to sustain any useful moral or temporal structures.

One might then focus attention on the various symbolic patterns—
mirrors, clocks, pear trees, Caddy, water, mud, fire, funerals, more
clocks, the Easter apparatus—and declare the novel a vast prose
poem, an interpretation of dreams, or an extended essay on *symbolism*. As Hugh Kenner rightly points out, however, Faulkner's essential
strategy (which he flamboyantly admitted on any number of occasions) "was not to symbolize (a condensing device) but to expand,
expand," and his work characteristically "prolongs what it cannot
find a way to state with concision, prolongs it until, ringed and rid-
dled with nuance, it is virtually camouflaged by patterns of circumstance."[8] Certainly, this is one of the primary effects of *The Sound
and the Fury*, especially to the extent that the novel moves with
deliberation from the static image-making capacity of Benjy's
"mind" to increasingly conscious and compulsive first-person modes
of narration, dwelling as last in the comparatively hyperbolic omniscience of the fourth section, where the crucifixion of the Compsons and the novel (and the reader) becomes most agonized. But it
is just as certainly one of the novel's most paradoxical effects that,
as it moves progressively out of its first frozen moments of lucid
astonishment, a movement required to "tell the story," it also
betrays its own proclaimed ideal and acquires the traits of bulging
prose and crude, idiosyncratic symbolism Faulkner would become
famous for, as though it were enacting its own deterioration and
failure in the very course of getting the story told.

*   *   *

Even so, the shadows of Faulkner's tragic world are here, and an
extraordinary passion, physical and intellectual, lies hidden in this
book and haunts this pair of failed sons and fathers. To speak of
Mr. Compson and Quentin in this way is appropriate not least
because their conversations, which approach and dwell in the *imaginary* whether or not we conceive of them as actually taking place,
embody in their reduction to ridiculous romantic symbolism and
whispers of gallantry the failure of a land, a people, a family—all of
them known together as "the South"—to regenerate itself. Mr.
Compson's cynical disinterest in Caddy's promiscuity and Quentin's narcissistic obsession with it represent, not opposing views,
but views that are complementary to the point of schizophrenia:
the father having renounced passion and patrimony altogether, the
son attempting psychically to totalize it, to invest an entire family
and its cultural role in an imaginary act of incest. The absence of
Caddy as a character and the fantastic character of Quentin's

---

8. Hugh Kenner, *A Homemade World: The American Modernist Writers* (New York: Alfred
    A. Knopf, 1975), 205.

passion are in this respect entangled, even indistinguishable, for the incestuous desire to father oneself or to be one's own family is here presented as correlative to, if not the cause of, the symbolic desire to absorb all creative energy into an invisible, ineffable presence—what is present only as desire, that perfect form into which all energy is channeled, all content sublimated, the vaselike erotic form Faulkner imagined his book itself to be.[9]

Quentin's suicide, therefore, should not be interpreted as a reaction against his incestuous desires or their failure to be actualized; rather, his suicide, like that of Melville's hero in *Pierre*, virtually *is* incest, the only act in which generation is thoroughly internalized (and prohibited) and the "father," as a consequence, killed. Here the rage that everywhere fractures the family and the book, the hatred of his past Quentin will deny in *Absalom, Absalom!* (or has already denied, if we merge the events of the two books), is folded into the act of love, in the bodily *image* of love: Quentin joins the water, the medium always associated with Caddy, as though he were lying down with it (one thinks of Millais's *Ophelia*), his bodily self falling to meet the enchanted corpse lying always beneath the shadowy surface of the prose. Death and love, murder and passion, are joined in incest, most of all in such an imaginary enactment and its sublimation in suicide. Quentin's death, of course, is offstage, just as invisible, in our experience of the novel, as Caddy herself; this is perfectly to the point, however, for as his reappearance in *Absalom, Absalom!* and the original stories of *Go Down, Moses* will suggest, Quentin's death, like his proscribed desires, is also *imaginary*, a symbolic distillation of the moral suicide diffused in later novels through the trauma of the Civil War, Reconstruction, broken promises, the failure of freedom and love—the encompassing drama that surrounds and defines for Faulkner the central act of grief.

The risks of such an aesthetic, one in part created retrospectively by the directions in which Faulkner was to take his initial impulses, are evident in *The Sound and the Fury*, a novel whose very essence is imaginary in that the "plot" or "story" is of almost no consequence but remains instead a way to project into actuality the inchoate states of grief and unfulfilled desire that are Faulkner's abiding subjects. Like Benjy's broken flower, his dirty slipper, and his fire, the story—by extension, the novel itself, as Faulkner would have

---

9. See Faulkner, "An Introduction to *The Sound and the Fury*," 415: "There is a story somewhere about an old Roman who kept at his bedside a Tyrrhenian vase which he loved and the rim of which he wore slowly away with kissing it. I had made myself a vase, but I suppose I knew all the time that I could not live forever inside of it, that perhaps to have it so that I could lie in bed and look at it would be better . . . it's fine to think that you will leave something behind you when you die, but its better to have made something you can die with. Much better the muddy bottom of the little doomed girl climbing a blooming pear tree in April to look in the window at the funeral."

it—is at once a memorial and a fetish; as it embodies loss without adequately containing or reproducing it, the story gets progressively more full and realistic in a traditional sense but cannot find an expression equivalent or superior to Benjy's opening inarticulate cry of Caddy's name. In the final image of Benjy circling the Confederate statue we recognize that, although the plot has unfolded and advanced, its essence still lies in section one, to which we nervously return. The returning to stillness, as to death, is the book's primary movement, and the style of Benjy's section, stillness on the point of death, enacts in narrative the hard, bright flame of symbolic intensity that Quentin imagines incest to be, and Faulkner wanted his book to be, the burning out in passionate stillness of the power to generate a family, a life, a story.

*   *   *

* * * The most vital myth of *The Sound and the Fury*—one that we can neither rely upon nor confidently gainsay—is that it made possible everything else. His next creative efforts would produce a recasting of the materials of the Southern wasteland into the bitter and hateful denunciations of *Sanctuary*, and a perfectly tuned and controlled essay on forms of grief in *As I Lay Dying*; while each of his great novels that follow would refer back implicitly or explicitly to *The Sound and the Fury*, as intimately but tenuously connected to it as the novel is to its own germinal scene and its central, invisible character. The book is its own myth, as the design of Faulkner's career came to define it, a myth of tortured innocence explicated by earlier and later novels but at the same time self-contained and—intentionally, it seems—self-defeating.

It would, perhaps, be too much to speak of the novel as a kind of womb or genesis, for its avowed depictions of luminously failed beginnings, as well as the novel's accumulated myth of ecstatic purity, suggest that nothing could ever come of it or surpass it, that it is perfectly stillborn. This is certainly not true, and Faulkner's later comparison of the novel to a "child who is an idiot or born crippled" is more to the point.[1] Like Quentin's notion of incest, the myth of the novel's perfection is half bombast and hallucination, but its importance is literally inestimable, for the simple reason that "Faulkner" can be imagined apart from it no more easily than the novel can be imagined apart from Caddy, "the beautiful one, [his] heart's darling."[2] It contains brilliant, powerful writing that Faulkner would publically declare to be his best, writing that could,

---

1. Joseph L. Fant III and Robert Ashley, eds., *Faulkner at West Point* (New York: Random House, 1964), 49.
2. Gwynn and Blotner, eds., *Faulkner in the University*, 6.

therefore, never be equalled. As though visibly enacting his own "compulsion to say everything in one sentence,"[3] and inevitably failing to do so, *The Sound and the Fury* defines his vision and its uttermost limits. It also contains the inchoate drama of the South that would mature into his best work over the course of the next decade. By the time Faulkner added the novel's appendix, that work would be several years behind him; and the design of Yoknapatawpha, obsessively recapitulating and shoring up earlier works, would more and more resemble the chaos from which it had sprung—with the paradoxical effect, of course, that only the furthering of the design could define its latent, magnificent failure and fix forever the myth of its original masterpiece.

THADIOUS M. DAVIS

[Faulkner's "Negro" in *The Sound and the Fury*][†]

* * *

In *The Sound and the Fury* Faulkner divides the southern world into black and white. He uses the black world, as he perceives it from the outside, in order to characterize the weaknesses or, more rarely, the strengths of the white world and its inhabitants. He draws extensively upon a family of black servants, the Gibsons, who are in close contact with the white Compson family. His strategy, however, depends upon the blacks and whites maintaining different attitudes and values. His blacks (primarily, but not exclusively, the Gibsons) contribute to the contrapuntal design of the novel, because their voices and actions create a meaningful contrast to the disintegrating Compsons and add greater dimension to the symbolism, themes, and narrative form.

Roskus and Dilsey Gibson are patriarch and matriarch of the black family in *The Sound and the Fury*. Their children, Versh, Frony, and T. P., and grandson, Luster, progress with the younger Compsons over the pages of the novel and history. The Gibsons take care of the Compson place and family. They play strong, supportive roles and frequently dominate the action (particularly in the first and fourth sections, in which Luster and Dilsey are central figures in the narrative present). The Gibsons function to foreshadow events, as well as to reiterate motifs. They are integral to

3. James B. Meriwether and Michael Millgate, eds., *Lion in the Garden: Interviews with William Faulkner, 1926–1962* (1968; rpt., Lincoln: U of Nebraska P, 1980), 141.
† From *Faulkner's "Negro": Art and the Southern Context* (Baton Rouge: Louisiana State UP, 1983). 70–71, 83–92, 102–111. Reprinted by perimission of the publisher. Page references are to this Norton Critical Edition.

Faulkner's formal ordering principles, and they are touchstones by which those principles become familiar to the reader.

Representing opposition to the sterility and decay evidenced by the white family, the Gibsons project a vital creativity, an inventiveness in looking at life and a spiritedness in confronting it all. Frony, for example, wears her new clothes on the climactic Easter morning even if it means getting wet, because as she states, "'I aint never stopped no rain yit.'" Like the rest of the family, she accepts the natural course of things, but does not relinquish her individual will. Frony's older brother Versh also has a level-headed approach to himself and to life. He tells Benjy, the retarded Compson son: "'You aint had to be out in the rain like I is. You's born lucky and dont know it'" (46). In other words, Benjy is born white in a region where those of his race have all the advantages. Versh quite simply places Benjy within a frame of reference that, while realistic, may be overlooked because of Benjy's idiocy. As Versh suggests, even the life of a retarded white man seems easier than that of a normal black man, because in their world blacks are circumscribed by racial restrictions to lives of hard, unrewarding work. Juxtaposed to the various kinds of lunacy demonstrated by the Compsons are the Gibsons—practical, "common-sense variety" blacks whose individual and collective voices create an eloquent contrast to the white world and form, on a level of emotion and reason, a more viable approach to life.

In the Gibson family Faulkner succeeds in capturing the symbolic and spiritual significance of a whole generation of southern blacks as they are understood by the white South. He explores the artistic possibilities inherent in traditional black life, thought, and expression. His treatment of black community suggests that the simple bonds of faith and love embodied in that community's daily relationships are ignored by the modern southerner in his search for meaning in a changing, complex society. For example, Roskus, Versh, T. P., and Luster, depicted as interchangeable elements, are present to insure the smooth operation of the place (tending the stock, driving the carriage, and caring for Benjy), but their presence also creates a sense of fused generations in a closely knit family, and of the flux of individuality bending to a stable historical community. In their closeness they represent a continuity of family that is vital to a traditional society. Dilsey at one point in Benjy's narrative remarks to the aging, arthritic Roskus, "'T. P. getting big enough to take your place'" (19). The son's carrying on for the father, assuming his responsibilities and position, is what no Compson son is able to do, and the white family is the weaker for it.

* * *

Although I have concentrated on Luster in the early segments as evidence of Faulkner's extensive use of the Negro in his creative process, I believe that throughout the novel all of the Gibsons serve structural, thematic, and symbolic functions. The Gibsons represent a picture of the Negro in the early years of the South's transition to modernity—the Negro as consciously in the shadow of the Civil War as his white counterpart and still held in a tenuous relationship to the South's cultural past and aristocratic values. Dilsey can refer as matter-of-factly to "white trash" (189) as she can to Luster's "Compson devilment" (180). The servant's sense of belonging to his "people" (his white family) evolves from a historical condition of long, close association. Even the youngest servant readily develops the traditional attitude toward his "people" and himself. Luster, for example, while driving Benjy to the graveyard, decides, "'Les show dem niggers how quality does, Benjy'" (208). Whether or not his statement is intended as an ironic reference to Benjy as "quality," Luster includes himself in the description (as exalted driver of a surrey while "dem niggers" are walking).

On the other side, the white family assumes an attitude of paternal duty and responsibility toward servants of long standing. Faulkner manipulates this pattern in *The Sound and the Fury* to reflect a specific historical and cultural place. He extends the meaning of his fiction outward from an individual family to a larger society by drawing upon the responses of white characters to blacks, particularly those whose lives over several generations carry the social history of the whites. Faulkner achieves this perspective most effectively in "April Sixth 1928," Jason's monologue, by placing Jason in open conflict with his present world and his family's legacies. Faulkner uses the Gibsons as faithful family retainers in order to shape the cultural background to which Jason reacts. Although he assigns the blacks conventional roles, Faulkner adapts them to elicit Jason's determining attitudes and his controlling patterns of action.

One of Jason's bitter harangues touches upon the relationship that normally developed between black servants and whites: "That's the trouble with nigger servants, when they've been with you for a long time they get so full of self importance that they're not worth a damn. Think they run the whole family" (136). Jason's sense of his own manhood does not allow him to admit that, at least in the case of his family, not only do the servants think they run the whole family, they actually do run it. Although his mother retains the household keys, she assumes none of the responsibility for the house. Dilsey, the black cook and housekeeper, has taken charge. Accommodations, accordingly, are made on both sides so that the household operates with some semblance of expected order. For the most part, Dilsey and Jason avoid each other because, for them, contact becomes confrontation, with authority hanging in the balance. The state of the Compson household establishes the reality of Jason's world and undermines his assertions of power and control.

Ironically, although Jason accuses the blacks of "self importance," his relationship with the Gibsons enhances his own sense of importance. His repeated references to "a whole kitchen full of niggers" reflect his personal commitment to the connection between the Gibsons and his own place in the social hierarchy. In the opening of his monologue, Jason calls attention to his "six niggers that cant even stand up out of a chair unless they've got a pan full of bread and meat to balance them" (119). This idea forms a recurrent motif. Jason adheres to old class values; he sees himself as the master who should be catered to in every way. He tells Luster, "'I feed a whole damn kitchen full of niggers to follow around after him [Benjy], but if I want an automobile tire changed, I have to do it myself'" (123). Explicitly a complaint, this statement also contains an implicit boast: that at a time when the status of the Compson males is at its lowest, Jason Compson retains servants and provides their food.

When Jason claims, "I haven't got much pride, I can't afford it with a kitchen full of niggers to feed" (151), his statement is loaded with double meanings. His disclaimer carries with it an assertion of pride in both individual and familial accomplishment. He declares his family's past connections and its continued rank. It is a way of saying that the Compsons are still important enough to maintain "six niggers." Servants, especially those inherited from a previous generation (in spite of Emancipation), validate a family's standing. Jason suggests class status in his observation of Dilsey's advancing age: "She was so old she couldn't do any more than move hardly. But that's all right: we need somebody in the kitchen to eat up the grub the young ones cant tote off" (122). Because the Compsons are "quality," they can maintain their lifelong servants even after they are too old to work. For Jason, Dilsey and the current household workers are a continuation of his family's history as landed slaveholders. He admits that this particular heritage distinguishes him and his family from most of the residents of Jefferson: "I says my people owned slaves here when you all were running little shirt tail country stores and farming land no nigger would look at on shares" (157). In light of his admission, his "kitchen full of niggers" may be interpreted as a reminder lest someone fail to comprehend his true station.

Jason emphasizes his position to whoever will listen. "'You ought to be working for me,'" he remarks to Job, a black who works for Jason's employer. "'Every other no-count nigger in town eats in my kitchen'" (125). The bragging is disguised in complaints: "I have to work ten hours a day to support a kitchen full of niggers in the style they're accustomed to and send them to the show with every other nigger in the county" (157). While he may well work ten hours a day, he burns two tickets to the show rather than give one away to Luster. The fact is that Jason continues to "feed" his blacks because for him there is no viable alternative. He has inherited, and accepted, membership (physical and psychological) in a social order once based upon wealth and class, but degenerated into empty rituals and manners—the external trappings of an old order.

Jason needs a place of his own. He desires recognition for his value and strength, because throughout his life he has been denied approval by his family and even the Gibsons. His childhood shows his exclusion from the family's affection,[1] as well as from the servants' concern. His mother insists that he is a Bascomb, but her family is of a lower class status than the Compsons, and its lone male representative, Maury, lacks economic independence, personal valor, and physical strength—character traits considered masculine in their culture. Jason's father gives him little evidence of love; in fact, whereas Mr. Compson sacrifices a portion of his land to send Quentin to Harvard and to pay for Caddy's wedding, he makes no comparable display of affection for Jason or concern for his future. As a result of his treatment, Jason is driven to prove his virility and his superiority. While his entire monologue turns upon his assertion that he is a better man than anyone else, especially his alcoholic father and suicidal brother, his protestations of superiority stem from his actual insecurity: his feeling that he has to prove his position among the other Compsons. Unfortunately, the changing society in which he lives provides no opportunity for Jason to become a man of action. His stylized reactions and invectives are the consequences of a decayed gentility that has left intact only forms, which are rendered irrational upon analysis, either because they originate in myth, prejudice, and superstition or because they have outlived the social contexts which gave them meaning.

His dwelling upon feeding so many mouths builds his self-esteem. "I'm a man, I can stand it," Jason insists (161). Nonetheless, his personal insecurities[2] about his manhood cause his vituperative attacks upon everyone around him—especially the Gibsons, who are more vulnerable as members of a lower caste and servant class. "Let these damn trifling niggers starve for a couple of years," Jason

1. Linda W. Wagner, "Jason Compson: The Demands of Honor," *Sewanee Review*, LX–XIX (Fall 1971), 560. Wagner's attempt to redeem Jason is more successful in its analysis of his childhood than in its conclusions about his generosity and kindness.

2. John Hunt, points out that throughout Jason's narrative, "'like I say,' 'what I say,' and 'I always say' drop steadily into monologue to buttress his tenuous self-confidence." *William Faulkner: Art in Theological Tension* (Syracuse: Syracuse UP, 1965), 71.

states, "then they'd see what a soft thing they have" (126). He measures his own value and manhood by his ability to feed others. He
inflates his own ego ("At least I'm man enough to keep the flour
barrel full," 137), and receives reinforcement from his mother, who
warns her granddaughter: "'He is the nearest thing to a father
you've had. . . . It's his bread you and I eat'" (170). Both Jason and
Mrs. Compson allude to the cultural meaning attached to the head
of a southern family.

Traditionally, one job expected of patriarchs of aristocratic or
well-connected families was the provision of food, not just for blood
kin, but also for members of the extended family—the numbers
(large or small) of slaves and later free servants who lived on the
"family place." The bounty of the table indicated economic and
social status. However, beginning with the Civil War, many upper-
class men lost the means of fulfilling traditional obligations. One of
the small crises of Reconstruction was the inability of the family
provider to continue feeding either relatives or the black inhabitants of the family's land. Indeed, some of these ex-slaves fed their
former masters from small vegetable gardens. Because of the massive failure of crops in the twenties (cotton destroyed by the boll
weevil, and food stuff by several disastrous floods),[3] many heads of
modern households could not provide for their own children and
kin, let alone for the blacks. The severity of the problem is suggested by Job: "'Aint nobody works much in dis country cep de boll-
weevil, nowadays'" (125).

Jason is connected to Faulkner's image of the southern patriarch,
which is generally sympathetic, but satirical as well. For example,
Jason is reminiscent of Bayard Sartoris, the aged aristocrat and
gentleman banker in *Sartoris* and *Flags in the Dust*. Bayard maintains a family of black servants after World War I, and he threatens
them in terms similar to Jason's: "'I'll be damned . . . if I haven't got
the triflingest set of folks to make a living for God ever made.
There's one thing about it: when I finally have to go to the poorhouse, every damned one of you'll be there when I come.'"[4] Bayard's
cantankerous remarks suggest that Faulkner uses him as one model
not only for Jason's paternalism toward blacks, but also for his relationship to a particular past which his attitude conveys.

---

3. Faulkner is cognizant of the boll weevil and the floods as important elements of the
setting and atmosphere. Both are synonymous with failure and precarious fortune.
Job, the black man whom Jason chides about his work, makes several references to the
effects of boll weevils on the Yoknapatawpha community (125). Louis Hatcher (in
Quentin's monologue, (75–76) talks about an earlier flood affecting Mississippi, but
Faulkner may well have been drawing upon the devastating floods of 1927.
4. William Faulkner, *Flags in the Dust* (New York: Random House, 1973), 77. The first of
Faulkner's Yoknapatawpha novels, it was initially published in a severely edited version
as *Sartoris* (1929). [*Editor's note.*]

Jason's own, more accessible, model is his father who, according to Quentin, said: "why should Uncle Maury work if he father could support five or six niggers that did nothing at all but sit with their feet in the oven he certainly could board Uncle Maury now and then lend him a little money who kept his Father's belief in the celestial derivation of his own species at such a fine heat" (116). Mr. Compson expresses in his wry way a personal satisfaction in accepting Maury Bascomb's freeloading and in supporting idle blacks. Jason, who is incapable of thinking or acting creatively, imitates his father's convictions about lazy blacks and parasitic relatives.[5] Neither father nor son is in control of his life. Traditional notions trap Mr. Compson and Jason in the pretentiousness and racism of a paternalistic system.

Jason's conduct, however, is more complexly motivated than that of his father or earlier Faulkner characters, because he exists marginally in both the family and the community and cannot reconcile his public image with his private sense of self. He feels vulnerable to public opinion ("All the time I could see them watching me like a hawk, waiting for a chance to say Well I'm not surprised I expected it all the time the whole family's crazy," 153), and obligated to maintain a public image based upon his sense of social place. The signals are his references to having gained "position in this town" (125) and those to his family's good name. In the heat of chasing his niece Quentin and the showman down alleys, Jason lets his mind wander to "Mother's health and the position I try to uphold to have her with no more respect for what I try to do for her than to make her name and my name and my Mother's name a byword in the town" (153). For all his seeming indifference to others, Jason has more than a slight regard for his standing in the community.

It takes the old family servant to give Jason his comeuppance. "'You's a cold man, Jason, if man you is,'" Dilsey judges from her privileged vantage point (137). She is unafraid to stand up to Jason. She chastises him for his behavior in general and for his treatment of Quentin in particular: "'Whyn't you let her alone? Cant you live in de same house wid you own blood niece widout quoilin?'" (166). Dilsey's long years of service allow her to take certain liberties with

5. For a discussion of Jason's relationship to his father, see Duncan Aswell, "The Recollection and the Blood: Jason's Role in *The Sound and the Fury*," *Mississippi Quarterly* XXI (Summer 1968), 211–18. Faulkner apparently based Jason's use of language on his own father, Murry Falkner. His mother, Maude Falkner, has reported that Jason "talks just like my husband did. . . . His way of talking was just like Jason's, same words and same style. All those 'you know's.' He also had an old 'nigrah' named Jobus. . . . He was always after Jobus for not working hard enough, just like in the story." See James Dahl, "A Faulkner Reminiscence: Conversations with Mrs. Maude Falkner," *Journal of Modern Literature* III (April 1974), 1028. However, because Jason echoes Mr. Compson in many ways, he may be a subtle autobiographical link to Faulkner himself, as well as to Murry Falkner.

Jason; she freely expresses her moral indignation because of her position as a servant and surrogate mother in the household. In fact, she addresses him at times as though he were still a child. ("'Go on in dar now and behave yoself twell I git supper on,'" 166). Dilsey's response to Jason is based upon familiarity. She knows him, perhaps better than he knows himself.

For such an old woman, Dilsey is a remarkably strong force. She stands firm against Jason's cruelty, though she complies with Mrs. Compson's whims. Dilsey may be enfeebled, but when necessary she confronts Jason head on: "'I dont put no devilment beyond you'" (122); "'I thank de Lawd I got mo heart dan dat, even ef hit is black'" (137). She proves to be both a restraining force and a verbal match for Jason. He, in turn, acknowledges her refusal to cower to him, and at one point he admits as much to her: "'I know you wont pay me any mind, but I reckon you'll do what Mother says'" (137). Because Dilsey has moral strength, she refuses to compromise her beliefs to satisfy Jason. Her presence in the Compson house deflates Jason's verbal assessment of his stature.

Cleanth Brooks has concluded that Jason "is bound to nothing. He repudiates any traditional tie. He means to be on his own and he rejects every community. The fact shows up plainly in the way he conducts himself not only in his own household but also in the town of Jefferson."[6] But nothing shows up plainly about Jason, as his remarks about the Gibsons make evident. If anything at all is known about Jason Compson, it is that he is not trustworthy. "Dont you trust me?" Jason asks Caddy after their father's funeral. "'No,' she says, 'I know you. I grew up with you'" (134). Jason is a master of deception, even of deceiving himself. He cannot be taken at his word. His vehement statements against family and tradition are his chief misrepresentations of the truth.

Old Job, a character comparable to the Gibsons in displaying folk wisdom, penetrates Jason's masks: "'Aint a man in dis town kin keep up wid you fer smartness. You fools a man whut so smart he cant even keep up wid hisself. . . . Dat's Mr Jason Compson'" (164). Undeceived by Jason's pretenses because he is an astute observer, Job extends the traditional intimacy and polarity between servants and masters from Jason's homelife to his work place.

Jason asserts that he is on his own even while evidencing his need for tradition. His reference to "his niggers," to his mother as a lady of quality, his treatment of his Bascomb uncle and everyone with whom he comes in contact (especially Job and blacks, Earl and his customers), all suggest Jason's conception of himself as an

6. Cleanth Brooks, *William Faulkner: The Yoknapatawpha Country* (New Haven: Yale UP, 1963), 342.

aristocrat—a position which would carry automatic validation of his worth. Moreover, what Jason vocally repudiates is any personal *need* for traditional ties, but not the ties themselves. Ironically, even his repudiation of the need is self-deceptive. Like others of his class in Faulkner's novels, Jason holds on to the memories of the past, and he does not relinquish what the past represents to those with similar memories. He hates the South, his family, and tradition a good deal less than he thinks. Even Jason's speculation on the cotton market, although suggesting Snopesism, northern material-ism, and the New South, links him to the past in which gentlemen (and potential leaders) of the Deep South had only cotton and politics as "professions" from which to amass respectable fortunes. Unlike his older brother Quentin, who searches for meaning in the tradition, Jason reveals a desperate struggle for a *place* in the tradition, because his precise relationship to his family, community, and himself is tor-tured and complex.

Far from being "the least 'Southern' of the sections," as Michael Millgate claims,[7] Jason's section is based precisely on the impor-tance of women and family, as well as the Negro, to the southern-er's sense of self and physical well-being. His monologue is intensely "southern" in its obsessions with feeding his blacks, upholding his place, protecting his mother, and cursing his victimization by his family (his father, brother, sister, and niece). Because "place" and "family" are traditionally important ways of defining self, the absence or erosion of the two precipitates an identity crisis. Jason, a constant malcontent, is not so insulated from his heritage as he would have others believe. His uncertainty about his rightful place in the Compson family, for which he does deserve measured sym-pathy, is magnified by the obvious deterioration of what family he has left to claim—a hypochondriac, an idiot, and "a hot one" (Quen-tin). Jason attempts by means of his paranoid cruelty (to Dilsey, Luster, Quentin, Mrs. Compson, and himself), his boasting lies, and his authoritative demands to negate the meaning that place and family have acquired in his culture and his personal existence. But he is unsuccessful.

The conclusion of his monologue, which occurs, appropriately, during supper, links money to the table (family position) in Jason's individual quest for place and personal status: "I just want an even chance to get my money back. And once I've done that they can bring all Beale Street and all bedlam in here and two of them can

---

7. Millgate, *The Achievement of William Faulkner*, 98. Jason is certainly as "southern" as his brother Quentin, and is not "anti-traditional," as Millgate contends, because Jason depends upon the survival of tradition to give meaning to his damaged life. For an extended analysis of Jason as southerner, see André Bleikasten, *The Most Splendid Failure: Faulkner's "The Sound and the Fury"* (Bloomington: Indiana UP, 1976), 169.

sleep in my bed and another one can have my place at the table too"
(173). "Beale Street" and "bedlam" connect blacks and idiots to the
complete downfall of the house and to the usurpation of Jason's
position as family head. He believes that retrieving the money from
his niece will redefine his status and create a place for him. But
Jason Compson has no "even chance"; the contradictions in his own
psychological makeup and the social reality of a changing culture
combine to assure his failure.

*   *   *

In "April Eighth 1928," Faulkner draws upon the distinctions,
already established in the first three monologues, between his
white and black worlds as one basis for a shift in narrative style. He
enlarges the meaning of his contrapuntal development of the Gibsons and Compsons by articulating in comprehensible detail the
reality of the blacks. By his attention to black life not only does he
make the black world intelligible, but he also makes the fractured
experiences of the white world coherent. Faulkner reenters the
white world for a fourth time, but not from the subjective perspective of a Compson. He aligns a third-person narrator with the Gibsons' angle of vision. The Gibsons, as household servants, allow, an
intimate, yet relatively objective, access to the Compsons' story; at
the same time, as blacks they define that story from an antithetical
perspective. Faulkner depends, then, upon the blacks' difference in
thought, language, and emotion to conclude his novel.

   In shaping the blacks to serve the technical demands of the
fourth part of his novel, Faulkner works through cultural and literary images. He describes the Gibsons in conventional terms, but
he transmutes traditional meanings by placing his emphasis on the
specific ways in which familiar images of blacks operate symbolically, structurally, and thematically to create a fictional reality that
is more compelling and vital than the Compsons'. By focusing on
the positive values, faith and feeling, that he associates with blacks,
Faulkner extricates his narrative from the distortions characteriz-
ing the whites in the three preceding sections and frees his vision
of blacks from the debilitating effects of stereotypes.

   The final section opens immediately with a contrast between an
image of disintegration, rain recalling the Compsons, and one of
survival, Dilsey Gibson beginning her day. The sensory description
of a rainy morning restates symbolically the theme of human fragmentation: "The day dawned bleak and chill, a moving wall of grey
light out of the northeast which, instead of dissolving into moisture, seemed to disintegrate into minute and venomous particles,
like dust that, when Dilsey opened the door . . . and emerged, needled laterally into her flesh, precipitating not so much a moisture as

a substance partaking of the quality of . . . oil" (173). A sense of the ominous overshadows the start of the day and sets the tone for the entire section; however, Dilsey appears to oppose the effects of the dismal weather.

Dilsey wears the colors and materials of royalty: "a maroon velvet cape," "a dress of purple silk" (173). She is regal and also weathered, as her "myriad and sunken face" (173) suggests. The description places her in opposition to the grey bleakness (figuratively her bright clothing) and to the image of disintegration (survival mirrored in her aged face). Faulkner builds upon Dilsey's majestic presence in establishing her position of authority in this section.

However, he attempts to substantiate Dilsey's credibility by describing her in realistic detail, seemingly based upon the appearance of older black women in his culture. For example, the richly colored cape has a border of fur that is "anonymous" and "mangy"; a "stiff black straw hat" is "perched upon her turban" (173). The result is a mixture of comic and serious modes of description. The comic mode exaggerates Dilsey's grotesque appearance ("her skeleton rose, draped loosely in unpadded skin that tightened upon a paunch almost dropsical," 173), while the serious mode emphasizes the heroic connotations ("as though muscle and tissue had been courage or fortitude," 173). The overall effect depends upon an acceptance of essentially unattractive terms for describing an admirable, aged woman: "The indomitable skeleton was left rising like a ruin or a landmark above the somnolent and impervious guts, and . . . the collapsed face that gave the impression of the bones themselves being outside the flesh" (173). Faulkner's intermingling of different elements, and perhaps even different attitudes toward Dilsey, culminates in the depiction of her expression as "at once fatalistic and of a child's astonished disappointment" (173), which, along with her dress and physical bearing, connects Dilsey to a long line of actual and fictional portraits of "mammy," the loving black servant praised for her service to a white family but often ridiculed because of her appearance.[8]

Faulkner's description of Dilsey as a mammy in voluminous skirts and headgear may rely generally upon conventional types and

8. For general discussions of "the mammy" in fiction, see Catherine Juanita Starke's chapter, "Archetypal Patterns," in *Black Portraiture in American Fiction: Stock Characters, Archetypes and Individuals* (New York: Basic Books, 1971), 125–37; and Tischler's chapter on "Faithful and Faithless Retainers," *Black Masks*, 29–49. Faulkner's brother, Murry C. Falkner, provides a personal definition of a "mammy" out of the experiences of Faulkner's family. *The Falkners of Mississippi. A Memoir* (Baton Rouge: Louisiana State UP, 1967); 13. Murry's image is based primarily upon Caroline Barr, who remained with the Falkners for over forty years. She figures in Dilsey's portrait not in physical appearance but in personal characteristics, faults, and virtues. Like Dilsey, Mammy Callie was, according to Faulkner's brother John, a combination of "shepherdess and avenging angel," "who was faithful" and "who endured." John Faulkner, *My Brother Bill, An Affectionate Reminiscence* (New York: Trident P, 1963), 48.

specifically upon his own mammy, Caroline Barr; nevertheless, his imaginative portrait transcends symbol or stylized type. His use of Dilsey is much more complex than adherence to the traditional type would allow. She is not merely a "memorial to the Negro servant" as Charles Nilon maintains.[9] Neither is she simply a matter of creating a human being as opposed to a stereotype; for instance, Vickery sees Dilsey as emerging "not only as a Negro servant in the Compson household but as a human being."[1] The implication is that a Negro servant is somehow *not* a human being.

In the fourth section, Dilsey becomes a positive representative of clear vision, just as in Benjy's section it is her husband, Roskus, who possesses clarity of vision. She embodies the cohesion of memory and activity that is vital to the work as a whole. She functions as a medium of memory, through which Faulkner filters the experience of the past. On one level, the experience of the past is that of the Compson family, while on another level, the experience is that of the three preceding narratives, with all their events and relationships distilled through one character, Dilsey. The section may not be told from inside Dilsey's consciousness, but it is told from an angle of vision which places her in the central position.

On that Easter Sunday Dilsey moves slowly; her motion is both deliberate and painful. She continues her life even though she seems distant from all those around her. Roskus is dead, and her sons do not figure in the action of Easter Sunday. Luster's age and interests separate him from his grandmother. Frony, by virtue of her position as daughter, is not Dilsey's confidante. Even the other blacks whom the Gibsons meet going to church do not seem especially close to Dilsey: "And steadily the older people speaking to Dilsey, though, unless they were quite old, Dilsey permitted Frony to respond" (190). All of these details seem to imply that Dilsey has transcended many of the ordinary aspects of social interaction.

Dilsey's isolation points to a possible reason for a third-person narrator in this section. The use of the third-person narrator does not suggest that Faulkner is incapable of presenting a sense of Dilsey's immediate impressions and thoughts; neither does it suggest that he considers the entering of a black person's consciousness condescending.[2] It appears, rather, that one technical function

9. Charles Nilon, *Faulkner and the Negro* (Citadel Press, 1965) p 101.
1. Olga M. Vickery, *The Novels of William Faulkner* (Baton Rouge: Louisiana State UP, 1959), 47.
2. Tischler, for example, notices "that it is a standard critical commentary of *The Sound and the Fury* that Faulkner fails to give Dilsey a stream-of-consciousness section parallel with that of each of the other main characters. Apparently he felt incapable of putting himself in the place of the Negro, although he chanced identifying with a woman and an idiot—a striking commentary on his belief in the remoteness of Negro psychology." *Black Masks*, 16.

of the section is the creation of the perspective of time. Faulkner creates a sense of the passing of an era, and within that perspective he presents the destruction of one family and the endurance of another.

If left still working through the immediacy of an "I" perspective in the final section, the reader would not have a sense of either the magnitude of the action or the slow, inevitable movement of time and humanity. Dilsey lends decorum and distance. Her position is a complicated one; she is a participant in the action, yet she remains outside it. She exists as a kind of sacred vessel, suggesting an experience that is both visionary and tragic. Her role on Easter is to help the reader feel the way back through the labyrinths that Dilsey's being recognizes in the Compsons' fall, but does not accept as unavoidable. Dilsey takes the reader from the level of intellectual exercise necessary to decipher and experience aesthetically the three preceding sections of the novel. Her function suggests that Faulkner envisions Dilsey (and his other blacks by extension) as existing on an intuitive, emotional level, but, at the same time, he ascribes to her a major aesthetic function.

Dilsey belongs to a dimension that assumes larger-than-life proportions quite distinct from caricature because its function has to do with the magnitude of an all-encompassing vision. Dilsey (whether or not her station in life is compatible with the burden of meaning Faulkner places on her characterization) is about vision; she does not merely stand for her own vision as an intuitive, sympathetic character, for she is also the medium for the vision of the reader. Through her the reader remembers and re-creates the novel. In effect, memory becomes a creative aesthetic process in which the reader is forced (as in *Absalom, Absalom!*) to participate in creating the experience of the novel.

Dilsey cannot emerge as a character having great psychological depth, which is the main charge made in labeling her a stereotype.[3] The reader does not know her thoughts. Nonetheless, Dilsey suggests the limitations of verbal patterns as conveyors of thought. The immediacy of thoughts and impressions properly belongs not to any character in this section but to the reader, who has Dilsey's painfully deliberate activity to help assimilate the passing of an historical moment and incorporate the perspective of time and the aging process into a total conception of meaning in the novel. Dilsey's inner life is not revealed through speech or thought, yet the reader obtains an immediate sense of the quality of her inward state. Her actions are shrouded in mystery; her motivations never clearly

---

3. See, for instance, Irene Edmonds, "Faulkner and the Black Shadow," in Rubin and Jacobs (eds.), *The Southern Renascence*, 194.

revealed. Therefore, if Dilsey ultimately becomes a positive, cohesive force in the novel, she accomplishes this feat as much by means of what her, presence encourages the reader to feel, as by the activities she performs.

In her humanity, Dilsey is responsible for emphasizing that reality is ultimately subjective and that individual meaning is noncommunicable. She also shows how in this novel reflection becomes the most valid, perhaps the only possible, means of communication. In reflecting upon Dilsey, the reader comes to terms with the external events revealed through the process of internal monologue in the first three sections. The reader abstracts meanings from the flow of events by using Dilsey as a gauge to interpret the action. Because of the introspective movement of the work, there is no fusion into objectivity without Dilsey. She makes objectivity possible by exposing the contradictory forces of the Compsons' life and suggesting the possibility of counteracting them. The funereal focus on Dilsey revives the past in the novel and the reality of the aesthetic work.

Faulkner has revealed that before he began the Easter Sunday segment of *The Sound and the Fury* he realized that he would have to get completely out of the book: "that there would be compensations, that in a sense I could then give a final turn to the screw and extract some ultimate distillation" (256). Dilsey is a vital part of that "ultimate distillation." Faulkner presents Dilsey's vision and perception as a creative center, because as Negro and other, she provides him with a way out of an artistic dilemma. Clearly, there is no resolution that Faulkner, a white southerner, could face in rendering the disintegration of the white world. Had he remained locked within the Compsons' world, he would have ended his novel in despair and nihilism, a conclusion which he could not accept. Dilsey, the embodiment of the blacks' alternative vision, rescues Faulkner from the conclusion of his own logic and the novel from fragmentation and stasis.

Faulkner specifically states, "There was Dilsey to be the future, to stand above the fallen ruins of the family like a ruined chimney, gaunt, patient and indomitable" (255). Though he speaks of Dilsey as representing the future, he compares her to "a ruined chimney," essentially a failed chimney that evokes associations with the past since it no longer serves its intended purpose. Yet that chimney is also "gaunt, patient and indomitable," certainly admirable and even virtuous because of its endurance, its ability to survive the past. By analogy, then, Dilsey may not have succeeded in holding the Compson family together, but she is the lone standard bearer of the attempt. Her tears reassure the reader that a system of morality is at work which encompasses both rewards and punishment. It is primarily an aesthetic reassurance. Dilsey's morality provides sustenance not for the white world Faulkner creates in *The Sound and the Fury,* but for the reader vicariously experiencing that world in juxtaposition to that of the imagined Negro.

Dilsey's experience on Easter morning emerges as singularly profound in the midst of the guilt-ridden, self-centered world of the Compsons. She, as Cleanth Brooks maintains, "affirms the ideal, of wholeness in a family which shows in every other member splintering and disintegration."[4] She undergoes the "annealment" extended to her by the communal religious experience. Her prophetic words, "'I've seed de first en de last. . . . I seed de beginnin and now I sees de endin'" (194), seem irrefutable because she has become, through her odyssey to church, an absolutely venerable character. In church she reveals that she possesses the faith only implied previously; there she assumes an attitude of prayer which has been persistently used in narrative to reveal thought and character with unquestionable validity.[5] Dilsey's participation in the religious service helps to establish firmly that death and disintegration need not overcome the positive forces of existence, and that the erosion of morals, values, and meaning is not universal in modern life.

Importantly, Faulkner's presentation of the Easter service assumes (and acknowledges as few writers have previously) the innate significance of the Negro's faith, which in Faulkner's version presupposes an understanding of human motivation in its simplest form. He presents a picture of right moral conduct emanating from the basic recognition of human need. He does not explore Dilsey's motivation and, consequently, exposes his acceptance of the simplicity of ethical human conduct as well as his faith in the intuitive emergence of positive moral action. Faulkner relies directly upon the Easter service and the blacks to coalesce the fragmented visions of life issuing from the various monologues and to present dramatically the thematic possibility of community, harmony, and love. In working his way out of the quandary and despair of the Compson world, Faulkner turns to his preconceived notions of the black world. He brings to his fiction a belief in black religion as a spiritual experience unifying individuals into a oneness of emotion and purpose. He sees the congregation transformed in *The Sound and the Fury*: "Their hearts were speaking to one another in chanting measures beyond the need for words" (192).

4. Cleanth Brooks, "Faulkner's Vision of Good and Evil," *The Hidden God* (New Haven: Yale UP, 1963), 22–43; rpt. in J. Robert Barth (ed.), *Religious Perspectives in Faulkner's Fiction: Yoknapatawpha and Beyond* (Notre Dame, Ind.: U of Notre Dame P, 1972), 72. Brooks treats Dilsey as a member of the Compson family.
5. Robert Scholes and Robert Kellogg, *The Nature of Narrative* (New York: Oxford UP, 1966), 200–201.

Faulkner envisions his Negro as a homogeneous, coherent social group. His picture of the Easter service prefigures his statement that Christianity shows man "how to discover himself, evolve for himself a moral, code and standard within his capacities and aspirations, by giving him a matchless example of suffering and sacrifice and the promise of hope. Writers have always drawn, and always will, on the allegories of moral consciousness."[6] In the example of the Negro's Christianity, Faulkner finds a meaningful allegory of moral consciousness.

Nevertheless, that allegory is meaningful in this novel only if the tenets of Christian faith in everlasting life can be extended to the Compsons, and they are not. Because the Reverend Shegog and his black congregation are so far removed from the white world, there is no possibility that their experience of resurrection and life can have meaning and value for Jason, Quentin, or Mrs. Compson. The Compsons lack the simplicity which Faulkner stresses as fundamental to the blacks, and to Christian faith as well. Faulkner's vision falters because he is unable to show how the Negro's experience might have meaning or bearing on the white-centered world that is his subject. The church service occurs in isolation, and it cannot be superimposed upon the fragmented Compsons. The Christian vision of the Negro is inadequate because, in its isolation, that vision is ultimately no less private (for the blacks whom it encompasses) than the visions revealed in the three monologues.

Dilsey, though she sees clearly all the actions of the past and understands their implications for the present and future, does not share her intensely private vision with anyone. It does not appear to be a matter of her inability to articulate her vision; rather Faulkner refuses to allow her to make the attempt. Even Frony, who asks, "'First en last whut?'" does not receive an answer from Dilsey. Whatever is her knowledge remains hers alone and goes untranslated for the larger world. Frony's statement to her mother, who is crying silently, suggests that what blacks experience in the privacy of their church is not to be revealed to the other world: "'Whyn't you quit dat, mammy? . . . Wid all dese people lookin. We be passin white folks soon'" (194). Dilsey initially responds, "'Never you mind. . . . I seed de beginnin, en now I sees de endin.'" However, Dilsey apparently agrees with Frony, as the narrative suggests: "Before they reached the street, though, she stopped and lifted her skirt and dried her eyes on the hem of her topmost underskirt" (194). The white world will not even see her tears—the external manifestation of her vision of tragedy.

6. Interview with Jean Stein, in Meriwether and Millgate (eds.), *Lion in the Garden*, 247.

Despite the claim by John Hunt that the Compsons could have made the same response to their condition that Dilsey makes (that is, "love, self-sacrifice, compassion, pity"),[7] the central point is that they cannot in fact make the kind of response so natural for Dilsey. Dilsey's motivation and her reactions are connected first to the relatively rudimentary or primitive Negro world that Faulkner constructs, and only after that are they connected to a larger reality. Even that reality has been refracted by Dilsey's experiences and existence as a black southerner. The Compsons react out of an orientation to life that is white, southern, and basically aristocratic; they cannot accept the simplicity of emotion or philosophy that Dilsey does. A part of their tragedy, of course, is precisely that they cannot, that they are so alienated from a world of meaning and value. The Compsons do not experience and then reject Dilsey's faith and world; there exists for them an actual inability to accept Dilsey's approach to life because her world with the black religious experience at its very center is largely unknown to them. Thus, the world of faith is inaccessible as much because its representative activity is beneath their notice as it is because of its doctrine.

* * *

ANDRÉ BLEIKASTEN

An Easter without Resurrection?[†]

A Simple Heart

From the particulars of limited individual experience the last section moves toward the universality of the mythic. Without ceasing to be a slobbering idiot, Benjy comes to stand for crucified innocence in the context of the Easter service at the Negro church; the man-child becomes an analogon of Christ. But the character in which the fusion of realism and symbolism is most successfully achieved is without any doubt Dilsey. Even though her function has often been misunderstood or overemphasized, there can be no question that she is the most memorable character in the last section. Technically, the point of view is not hers, and in dramatic terms her role is a limited one. Yet critics should not be blamed too roundly for attributing the last section to her; even Faulkner called

---

7. John Hunt, *William Faulkner: Art in Theological Tension* (Syracuse UP, 1965), 98.
† From *The Ink of Melancholy: Faulkner's Novels from* The Sound and the Fury *to* Light in August (Bloomington: Indiana UP, 1990), 134–45, 378–79. Reprinted with permission of Indiana University Press. Page references are to this Norton Critical Edition.

it "the Dilsey section."[1] The one truly admirable character in the novel, she had a special place in the writer's affections: "Dilsey is one of my favorite characters, because she is brave, courageous, generous, gentle, honest. She is much more brave and honest and generous than me."[2] She is no less admirable as a literary creation. Her portrait is so sharply individualized and her figure so warm and earthy that the charge of excessive idealization is hardly relevant. As Cleanth Brooks has rightly noted, Dilsey is "no noble savage and no *schöne Seele*."[3] Nor should she be reduced to a racial stereotype. True, she seems to fit rather nicely in the tradition of the black mammy, and her literary lineage is readily traced back to Thomas Nelson Page.[4] However, the point is that her virtues, as they are presented in the novel, owe nothing to race.[5]

That she was meant to counterbalance the Compsons is obvious enough. Her words and actions offer throughout an eloquent contrast to the behavior of her masters. In her role of faithful—though not submissive—servant, Dilsey represents the sole force for order

1. See letter to Malcolm Cowley in Joseph Blotner, ed., *Selected Letters of William Faulkner* (New York: Random House, 1977), 202.
2. James B. Meriwether and Michael Milgate, *Lion in the Garden: Interviews with William Faulkner, 1926–1962* (New York: Random House, 1968), 244–45. An early casting of Dilsey is to be found in "The Devil Beats His Wife," a story Faulkner began after his return from Europe in December 1925 but never completed. A number of critics assume that Dilsey was modeled on Caroline Barr, the "mammy" of the Faulkner family to whose memory *Go Down, Moses* was dedicated thirteen years later. The resemblances, however, are rather tenuous. Molly, Lucas Beauchamp's wife in *Go Down, Moses*, comes much closer to being a portrait of Caroline Barr.
3. Cleanth Brooks, *William Faulkner: The Yoknapatawpha Country* (New Haven: Yale UP, 1963), 343.
4. See George E. Kent's sharply critical assessment of Faulkner's "mammies" in "The Black Woman in Faulkner's Works, with the Exclusion of Dilsey," part II, *Phylon*, 36 (March 1975), 55–67.
5. This is not to say that there is no significant contrast between whites and blacks. Some of Quentin's observations aptly summarize the function of blacks in the novel: "a nigger is not a person so much as a form of behaviour; a sort of obverse reflection of the white people he lives among" (98); "They come into white people's lives like that in sudden sharp black trickles that isolate white facts for an instant in unarguable truth like under a microscope" (195). Dilsey and, to a lesser degree, her husband, her children, and grandchildren testify to the virtues which Ike McCaslin attributes to blacks in *Go Down, Moses*: endurance, pity, tolerance, fidelity, love of children (see *GDM*, p. 295). In the younger generation of the Gibsons, however, these virtues seem to be less developed than among their elders, as can be seen, for example, from Luster's occasional cruelty toward Benjy. And there is nothing to suggest that the Negroes are morally superior to the whites because they belong to a different race. Dilsey, with her customary clear-sightedness, tells her grandson Luster that he is just as fallible as his white masters: "Lemme tell you somethin, nigger boy, you got jes es much Compson devilment in you es any of em" (180). Faulkner's treatment of blacks in *The Sound and the Fury*, albeit not free of stereotypes, is never tritely sentimental, testifying to a tact and intelligence seldom found among white southern novelists. But, though the contrast between the white family and the black community provides an oblique comment upon the downfall of the Compsons, racial relationships are not central in *The Sound and the Fury* as they are in *Light in August*, *Absalom, Absalom!*, *Go Down, Moses*, and *Intruder in the Dust*.

and stability in the Compson household.[6] Not only does she see with tireless diligence and devotion to the family's material needs; she also tries, albeit with little success, to stave off the day of its disintegration. Taking on the responsibilities traditionally assumed by the mother, she comes to replace the lamentable Mrs. Compson as keeper of the house. In the later sections, she appears as Benjy's last resort,[7] and she also defends Caddy and her daughter against Jason, the usurper of paternal authority.

In the face of the whining or heinous egoism of the Compsons, Dilsey embodies the generosity of total selflessness; in contrast to Quentin's tortured idealism and Jason's sordid pragmatism, she also represents the active wisdom of simple hearts. Without fostering the slightest illusion about her exploiters, expecting no gratitude for her devotion, Dilsey accepts the world as it is, while striving as best she can to make it somewhat more habitable. Unlike the Compsons, she does not abdicate before reality nor does she refuse time, which she alone is capable of gauging and interpreting correctly:

> On the wall above a cupboard, invisible save at night, by lamp light and even then evincing an enigmatic profundity because it had but one hand, a cabinet clock ticked, then with a pre-liminary sound as if it cleared its throat, struck five times.
> "Eight oclock," Dilsey said. . . . (179)

In his rage against time, Quentin tore off the hands of his watch. The Compsons' old kitchen clock has but one hand left and its chime is out of order. Yet Dilsey does not take offense at its "lying" and automatically corrects its errors. To her, time is no matter of obsession. Not that she adjusts to it out of mere habit. Her time is not simply a "natural" phenomenon, any more than her moral qualities are "natural" virtues. Faulkner describes her as a Christian, and no analysis of the character can afford to discount the deep religious convictions attributed to her. Hers is a seemingly naive piety, a simple faith unencumbered by theological subtleties, but it gives her the courage to be and persevere which her masters lack, and provides her existence with a definite meaning and purpose.

6. In his interviews Faulkner stressed the principle of cohesion represented by Dilsey in the Compson household. See Joseph Blotner and Frederick L. Gwynn, *Faulkner in the University* (Charlottesville: U of Virginia P, 1959), 5, and *Lion in the Garden*, 126.

7. Dilsey's solicitude for Benjy is already emphasized in the first section. She is the only one to remember his thirty-third birthday and to celebrate it with a cake she buys with her own money. The manuscript of the novel includes no reference to Benjy's birth-day—an indication that in revising the section Faulkner felt the need to provide further illustration of Dilsey's kindness and so to prepare the reader for the full revelation of her personality in section 4. See Emily K. Izsak, "The Manuscript of *The Sound and the Fury*: The Revisions in the First Section," *Studies in Bibliography*, Bibliographical Society, U of Virginia, 20 (1967), 189–202.

Dilsey envisions everything in the light of the threefold mystery of the Incarnation. Passion, and Resurrection of Christ. In Benjy she sees "de Lawd's chile" (206), one of the poor in spirit promised the Kingdom of God, and for her all human suffering is justified and redeemed in the divine sacrifice commemorated during Holy Week.

Dilsey's attitude toward time proceeds quite logically from the tenets of her Christian faith. Whereas for Quentin, the incurable idealist, time is the hell of immanence, it is transfused with eternity for Dilsey. Not "a tale full of sound and fury signifying nothing," but the history of God's people. The Christ of her belief has not been "worn away by the minute clicking of little wheels" (51); his crucifixion was not a victory by time but a victory over time. Guaranteed in the past by the death and resurrection of the Son of God and in the future by the promise of His return, bounded by the Passion and the Second Coming, time regains a meaning and a direction, and each man's existence becomes again the free and responsible adventure of an individual destiny. Dilsey's Christ-centered faith allows her to adhere fully to all of time's dimensions: her answer to the past is fidelity; the present she endures with patience and humility, and armed with the theological virtue of hope, she is also able to face the future without alarm. While for Quentin there is an unbridgeable gap between the temporal and the timeless, Dilsey's eternity, instead of being an immobile splendor *above* the flux of time, is already present and at work *in* time, embodied in it just as the word was made flesh. Time, then, is no longer felt as endless and senseless repetition; nor is it experienced as an inexorable process of decay. It does have a pattern, since history has been informed from its beginnings by God's design. And it can be redeemed and vanquished, but, as T. S. Eliot puts it in the *Four Quartets*, "Only through time time is conquered."[8] Which is to say that the hour of its final defeat will be the hour of its fulfillment and reabsorption into eternity.

Firmly rooted in the eschatological doctrine of Christianity, Dilsey's concept of time is theo-logical and teleo-logical, not chronological. The assumptions on which it rests remain of course implicit, but it is in this orthodoxly Christian perspective that we are asked to interpret Dilsey's comment after Reverend Shegog's sermon: "I've seed de first en de last. . . . I seed de beginnin, en now I sees de endin" (194). Given the context of Easter in which they occur, her words obviously refer to the beginning and end of time, to the Alpha and Omega of Christ. But it goes without saying that they apply as well to the downfall of the Compsons which Dilsey has been witnessing all along. The implication is certainly not that

8. T. S. Eliot, *Collected Poems, 1909–1962* (New York: Harcourt, 1963), 178.

after all the Compsons may be saved, but what the oblique connection between the Passion Week and the family tragedy suggests is that for Dilsey the drama of the Compsons is above all one of redemption denied.

Black Easter

Yet what the Compson story means to Dilsey is not necessarily what it means to us, nor what it was meant to mean. At this point the impossibility of any final interpretation becomes obvious again. For how are we to take the many references to Christianity included in the novel? And how do they relate to this story of decline and death? One may argue that Faulkner's use of them is ironical, that they point—derisively or nostalgically—to a vanishing myth and expose its total irrelevance as far as the Compsons are concerned. Or one may interpret them in terms of paradox, the more legitimately so, it seems, as paradox has been a major mode of Judeo-Christian thought and is indeed central to Christian faith itself. According to whether irony or paradox is taken to be the clue to Faulkner's intentions, diametrically opposed interpretations of the novel will suggest themselves to the reader. But the question is one of effects rather than intentions, and it is extremely difficult to settle, since paradox and irony alike work by way of inversion.

Inversion is one of Faulkner's favorite techniques. In *The Sound and the Fury* its procedures can be traced in many places, but nowhere perhaps are they as consistently and as intriguingly used as in the episode of the Easter service.[9] With regard to the rest of the novel (and more directly to the juxtaposed Jason sequence), the episode fulfills a contrasting function homologous to that of Dilsey in relation to the other characters. And the contrast is so sharp and so unexpected that the reader is jolted into a radically different mood. It is as if a spring of pure water suddenly welled up in an arid desert, or as if the dismal clamor of the accursed family were momentarily suspended to let us listen to a gospel song. But the episode is no less surprising in the detail of its composition and the movement of its development, both of which owe a good deal of their impact to Faulkner's handling of inversion. The sequence opens rather inauspiciously with the description of the desolate setting of Dilsey's walk to the church (189–90): nothing yet heralds the upsurge of Easter joy. A sense of expectancy is soon created, however, by the gathered congregation impatiently awaiting "dat big preacher" (189) from St. Louis. But when he at last arrives, he turns out to be a shabby, monkey-faced gnome:

9. See Victor Strandberg, "Faulkner's Poor Parson and the Technique of Inversion," *Sewanee Review*, 73 (Spring 1965), 181–90.

> . . . when they saw the man who had preceded their minister
> enter the pulpit still ahead of him an indescribable sound went
> up, a sigh, a sound of astonishment and disappointment.
>   The visitor was undersized, in a shabby alpaca coat. He had
> a wizened black face like a small, aged monkey. And all the
> while that the choir sang again and while the six children rose
> and sang in thin, frightened, tuneless whispers, they watched
> the insignificant looking man sitting dwarfed and countrified
> by the minister's imposing bulk, with something like conster-
> nation. (191)

The frustration, though, is turned into starry-eyed wonderment
when the preacher begins his sermon:

> His voice was level and cold. It sounded too big to have come
> from him and they listened at first through curiosity, as they
> would have to a monkey talking. They began to watch him as
> they would a man on a tight rope. They even forgot his insig-
> nificant appearance in the virtuosity with which he ran and
> poised and swooped upon the cold inflectionless wire of his
> voice, so that at last, when with a sort of swooping glide he
> came to rest again beside the reading desk with one arm rest-
> ing upon it at shoulder height and his monkey body as reft of
> all motion as a mummy or an emptied vessel, the congregation
> sighed as if it waked from a collective dream and moved a little
> in its seats. (191)

Belying the shabbiness and grotesqueness of his physical appearance, Reverend Shegog displays the mesmerizing talents of a brilliant orator. But there is more to come: a second, even more stunning
metamorphosis occurs when the cold virtuosity of the "white" sermon suddenly bursts into the incantatory vehemence of "black"
eloquence:

> Then a voice said, "Brethren."
>   The preacher had not moved. His arm lay yet across the
> desk, and he still held that pose while the voice died in sono-
> rous echoes between the walls. It was as different as day and
> dark from his former tone, with a sad, timbrous quality like an
> alto horn, sinking into their hearts and speaking there again
> when it had ceased in fading and cumulate echoes. (191–92)

This is the moment of the decisive reversal: the preacher is no longer master of his rhetoric, nor is he anymore master of his voice.
Instead of being the flexible instrument of his eloquence, the voice,
"a voice"—having seemingly acquired a will of its own—now seizes
his body and uses it as its tool. The tightrope artist has vanished;
Shegog has become the docile servant of the Word:

He was like a worn small rock whelmed by the successive waves of his voice. With his body he seemed to feed the voice that, succubus like, had fleshed its teeth in him. And the congregation seemed to watch with its own eyes while the voice consumed him, until he was nothing and they were nothing and there was not even a voice but instead their hearts were speaking to one another in chanting measures beyond the need for words. . . . (192)

The consuming voice not only reduces the preacher to a mere medium of the Easter message; it reaches out toward the congregation and, delving into the innermost recesses of souls, unites them in a wordless chant of communion. The orderly discourse of cold reason, significantly associated with the facile tricks of "a white man" (191), has given way to the spontaneous language of the heart, a language moving paradoxically toward its own extinction as it resolves itself into "chanting measures beyond the need for words." All that "white" rhetoric could achieve was "a collective dream" (191); what is accomplished now is a truly collective experience, a welding of many into one. For the first time in the novel, separation and fragmentation are at least temporarily transcended; consciousness, instead of narrowing down to private fantasy and obsession, is expanded through the ritual reenactment of myth. In this unique instant of grace and ecstasy, all human misery is miraculously transfigured, all infirmities are forgotten, and the preacher's puny silhouette rises before the faithful like a living replica of the crucified God: "his monkey face lifted and his whole attitude that of a serene, tortured crucifix that transcended its shabbiness and insignificance and made it of no moment" (192).

The Sermon

The reader is now prepared to *listen* to the sermon itself, to its sounds and rhythms, as the congregation listens. Again there will be surprises, ruptures, reversals, but the dominant mood is at present one of trust and exaltation, any remaining doubts being swept away by the intimate certainty of redemption: "I got de ricklickshun en de blood of de Lamb" (192). Yet the sermon begins on a plaintive note, faintly recalling Quentin's obsessions with time and death: "Dey passed away in Egypt, de swinging chariots; de generations passed away. Wus a rich man: whar he now, O breddren? Wus a po man: whar he now, O sistuhn?" (192). There follows a breathless evocation of the persecuted childhood of Christ: "Breddren! Look at dem little chillen setting dar. Jesus wus like dat once. He mammy suffered de glory en de pangs. Sometime maybe she helt him at de nightfall, whilst de angels singin him to sleep; maybe she look out de do en see de Roman po-lice passin" (193). Jesus here becomes the paradigm for martyred innocence, and the relevance of this paradigm to present circumstances is poignantly emphasized by the implicit reference to Benjy, the innocent idiot, sitting amid the black community, "rapt in his sweet blue gaze" (194).

The legendary and the actual, the past and the present are thus not only contrasted, but significantly linked. Myth infuses reality: projected into an immemorial past, Benjy and Dilsey are transformed into archetypal figures through their identification with Christ and the Madonna. Conversely, the remote events of the Passion are brought back to life again and quiver with pathetic immediacy in the compelling vision of the preacher:

> "I sees hit, breddren! I sees hit! Sees de blastin, blindin sight! I sees Calvary, wid de sacred trees, sees de thief en de murderer en de least of dese; I hears de boasting en de braggin: Ef you be Jesus, lif up yo tree en walk! I hears de wailing of women en de evenin lamentations; I hear de weepin en de cryin en de turnt-away face of God: dey done kilt Jesus; dey done kilt my Son!" (193)

With the death of Christ, the sermon reaches its nadir. The preacher now witnesses the seemingly absolute triumph of Evil, and his vision becomes one of utter chaos and destruction: "I sees de whelmin flood roll between; I sees de darkness en de death everlastin upon de generations" (193). Yet this note of despair (again reminiscent of the Quentin section) is not sustained, and immediately after everything is reversed by the miracle of the Resurrection. Shadows disperse, death is forever conquered in the glory of the Second Coming:

> "I sees de resurrection en de light; sees de meek Jesus sayin Dey kilt Me dat ye shall live again; I died dat dem whut sees en believes shall never die. Breddren, O breddren! I sees de doom crack en hears de golden horns shoutin down de glory, en de arisen dead whut got de blood en de ricklickshun of de Lamb!" (193)

Although Reverend Shegog's Easter sermon only occupies a few pages in the novel, it looms very large. And while it is true that it would carry even greater weight if Faulkner had chosen to place it at the novel's close, its impact is greater than a purely structural analysis of the fourth section would lead one to expect. Literary meanings and effects are differential, to be sure, but to assess them correctly is not enough to see how they are "placed" within the text; it is also important to measure the amplitude of the differences. For the singularity here is not only one of subject and theme, nor does it merely arise from a tonal switch. A radical reversal occurs, operating on all possible levels and altering the very fiber of the novel's texture. As the narrator's own preliminary comments suggest, another *voice* takes over, which is not that of any speaker in the novel, nor that of the narrator/author—a voice enigmatically self-generated and mysteriously compelling, *the subjectless voice of myth*.

Another language is heard, unprecedented in the novel, signaled at once by the cultural-ethnic shift from "white" to "black," the emotional shift from rational coldness to spiritual fervor, and lastly by the stylistic shift from the mechanical cadences of shallow rhetoric to the entrancing rhythms of inspired speech. Not that this new language dispenses with formal devices: Shegog's sermon, so far from being an uncontrolled outpouring of emotion, is very firmly patterned and makes extensive use of rhetorical emphasis (questions and exclamations) as well as of such classical procedures as parallelism and incremental repetition (most conspicuous in the abundance of anaphoric constructions). The sermon is the ritual retelling of a mythic story fully known by all the members of the congregation: its narrative contents form a fixed sequence, and the mode of its transmission conforms likewise to a stable code. What needs to be stressed, too, is that the specific tradition to which this speech belongs is the folk tradition—well-established, particularly, in African-American culture—of the *oral* sermon.[1] Ritualized as it is, the preacher's eloquence is the eloquence of the spoken word, and Shegog's sermon reads indeed like the transcript of an oral performance. The effect is partly achieved through the faithful phonetic rendering of the black dialect. Yet Faulkner's greatest success is that he has also managed to capture the musical quality of the sermon: the "sad, timbrous quality like an alto horn, sinking into their hearts and speaking there again when it had ceased in fading and cumulate echoes" (192). More than anything else it is this musicality (i.e., that which, in his speech, belongs to another, nonverbal language) that ensures true communication between the speaker and the listeners, and among the audience itself. Myth and music cooperate in this Easter celebration to free all participants from "the need for words" as well as from the tyranny of time. Is it not precisely in their relation to time that music and myth are alike? As Claude Lévi-Strauss has noted, "it is as if music and mythology needed time only to deny it. Both, indeed, are instruments for the obliteration of time."[2]

1. On Faulkner's indebtedness to the tradition of the oral sermon, see Bruce A. Rosenberg, "The Oral Quality of Reverend Shegog's Sermon in William Faulkner's *The Sound and the Fury*," *Literatur in Wissenschaft und Unterricht*, 2 (1969), 73–88.
2. Claude Lèvi-Strauss, *The Raw and the Cooked*, trans. John and Doreen Weightman (New York: Harper and Row, 1969), 15–16.

What matters here is not so much the message conveyed as the collective ceremony of its utterance and its sharing, a ceremony allowing at once personal identity to be transcended and cultural identity to be confirmed. In contrast to the painful and derisory remembrances of the Compsons, the *commemoration* of the mythic event by the black community appears to be a victory over solitude.

The Mythic Word

Shegog's Easter sermon may be called a triumph of Faulkner's verbal virtuosity. It is noteworthy, however, that this *tour de force* was achieved through a gesture of humility. For the novelist refrained from improving on the tradition of the oral sermon as he found it. There is no literary embellishment, and there is hardly a personal touch one might attribute to the author. Shegog's sermon has been compared with records of sermons actually delivered: the difference between the latter and Faulkner's creation is barely noticeable.[3] Which is to say that, strictly speaking, it is no creation at all, but only evidence of Faulkner's extraordinary mimetic abilities. The writer here lays no claim to artistic originality, and his self-effacement is carried to such lengths that his own voice is no longer heard. Instead we are *truly* listening to the anonymous voice of an unwritten tradition, grown out of ancient roots and periodically revivified by the rites of popular piety—a voice, that is, whose authority owes nothing to the talents of an author. From *auctor* the writer has become *scriptor*, a modest scrivener scrupulously transcribing a prior text.

This is what makes the sermon a unique moment in the novel: it marks the intrusion of the spoken into the written, of the nonliterary into the literary, of the mythic into the fictional, and by the same token it also signals the writer's willing renunciation of his authorial pride and of his prerogatives as a fiction-maker (or, to put it in Heideggerian terms, his capacity to *be spoken* rather than to speak). It becomes tempting, then, to see the preacher-figure as a double of the novelist himself: do not both surrender their identity as speakers/writers to become the vehicles of an impersonal mythic voice?

Given the importance accorded to the biblical text and to the living word in the Christian—and especially in the Puritan—tradition, it is of course hardly surprising that a writer with Faulkner's background should have been fascinated with the voice of myth. In the register of the imaginary, myth is in the novel's last section what fantasy is to the prior ones. Much like fantasy, myth is

---

3. See Rosenberg, "The Oral Quality of Reverend Shegog's Sermon."

a creation of human desire negating time and death. However, as long as myth remains an object of collective belief periodically reactivated by ritual, it also fulfills a gathering function and testifies to the permanence of a shared culture. Hence the novel invokes as a last resort traditional mythic values and ritual practices, and finds them in a community in which their sacred aura has been, to all appearances, fully preserved.

Religion is *religio*, what binds man to man, man to God. The novel's last section is clearly haunted by nostalgia for religion as a binding power, but also as a way of seeing if not of knowing. The voice that takes hold of the preacher induces a vision, and this moment of vision, fully shared by the congregation, is in fact the only experience of spiritual enlightenment recorded in the whole book. Illumination or illusion? In Faulkner's text, at any rate, this capacity for vision is set against the chronic blindness of the Compsons.[4] Both Dilsey and Shegog *see*, and their vision is apparently one that goes beyond the confines of time and flesh; it brings order and significance to their lives and gives them the strength to endure pain and loss. To Dilsey, in particular, the preacher's words bring the encompassing revelation of eternity, the mystical and prophetic vision of "the beginning and the ending."

Is this to say that they embody Faulkner's novelistic "vision," and that the Easter service at the Negro church provides the key to the novel's interpretation? For those who read *The Sound and the Fury* from theological premises there is no doubt about the answer. Comparing the sermon in Faulkner's novel to the legend of the Grand Inquisitor in *The Brothers Karamazov* or to Father Mapple's sermon in *Moby-Dick*, they do not hesitate to invest it with the same central hermeneutic function: "it tells us the meaning of the various signs and symbols as on a geographical map; it tells us how to read the drama, how to interpret the characters of the plot that has been unfolding before us."[5] From there to calling *The Sound and the Fury* a Christian novel is a short step. It is one step too many, however, for although there is much to suggest such an interpretation, there is little, in the last resort, to validate it. Faulkner's work is misread as soon as it is *arrested*, and critics go astray whenever they seek to reduce its intricate web of ambiguities to a single pattern of meaning. *The Sound and the Fury* stubbornly resists any

---

4. References to empty eyes or troubled vision abound: the "blurred" eye of the jeweler (55), Caddy's eyes "like the eyes in the statues blank and unseeing and serene" (108), Benjy's vacant gaze (179, 208), not to mention the empty eyes of the Confederate soldier (208). The picture of the eye on page 202 also points to the importance of the motif of seeing/not seeing.

5. Gabriel Vahanian, *Wait without Idols* (New York: George Braziller, 1964), 111. See also Amos N. Wilder, "Faulkner and Vestigial Moralities," *Theology and Modern Literature* (Cambridge, Mass.: Harvard UP, 1958), 113–31.

attempt to dissolve its opaqueness into the reassuring clarity of an ideological statement.

That Faulkner's fiction is heavily indebted to the Christian tradition is beyond question, and the writer himself, in his interviews, freely acknowledged the debt.[6] But it is essential to relate it to the specific context of the novelist's creation: to Faulkner, Christianity was first of all an inexhaustible fund of cultural references, a treasure of images and symbols or, to borrow one of his own favorite words, an extremely useful collection of "tools." This, of course, does not settle the question of his relationship to Christianity. There is surely more than a mere craftsman's debt: myth is both the bad conscience and the Utopia of Western fiction, and for Faulkner as for many other modern novelists, the Christian myth remains an ever-present paradigm, an ordering scheme, a pattern of intelligibility toward which his fiction never ceases to move as toward a lost horizon of truth, or rather *through* which it is moving to produce its own myths. Faulkner's quest and questioning remain to a very large extent caught up in Christian modes of thought and expression, as can be even more plainly seen in later works such as *Go Down, Moses, Requiem for a Nun*, and *A Fable*. Yet Faulkner's life-long involvement with Christianity entailed no personal commitment to Christian faith, and none of his public pronouncements substantiates the claim that he considered himself a Christian writer. Besides, even if Faulkner had been an avowed believer, the relationship of his work to Christianity would still be problematical, for insofar as it is literature, it displaces the myths on which it feeds. Aspiring to turn fictions into myths, it is fated to turn myths into fictions.

The Success of Failure

"A work of literature," says Roland Barthes, "or at least of the kind that is normally considered by the critics (and this itself may be a possible definition of 'good' literature) is neither ever quite meaningless (mysterious or 'inspired') nor ever quite clear; it is, so to speak, *suspended* meaning; it offers itself to the reader as a declared system of significances, but as a signified object it eludes his grasp. This kind of *dis-appointment* or *deception* . . . inherent in the meaning explains how it is that a work of literature has such power to ask questions of the world . . . without, however, supplying any answer."[7] Faulkner's fiction fully bears out Barthes's assumptions. The wealth

---

6. See *Faulkner in the University*, 86, 117; *Lion in the Garden*, 246–47.
7. Roland Barthes, "Criticism as Language," *Times Literary Supplement* (September 27, 1963), 739–40; translated from "Qu'est-ce que la critique?" *Essais critiques* (Paris: Editions du Seuil, 1964), 256–57.

of Christian allusions we find in *The Sound and the Fury* adds immeasurably to its semantic pregnancy, but in the last analysis Christian values are neither affirmed nor denied. Episodes such as the Easter service and figures such as Dilsey are impressive evidence of Faulkner's deep understanding of Christianity, and they seem to hint at possibilities of experience which the egobound Compsons have irremediably lost. Yet, as Cleanth Brooks rightly notes, "Faulkner makes no claim for Dilsey's version of Christianity one way or the other. His presentation of it is moving and credible, but moving and credible only as an aspect of Dilsey's own mental and emotional life."[8] The reader's "disappointment" in this respect is all the greater as Faulkner's novel often *seems* to imply the existence of seizable significances: his ironies do suggest a radically negative vision, and his paradoxes bring us very close indeed to the spirit of Christianity. However, the point about Faulkner's ironies and paradoxes is that they are irreducibly *his*. Etymologically, irony implies dissembling, or feigned ignorance, and paradox refers likewise to a hidden truth. If these classical definitions are retained, Faulkner's inversions are neither ironies nor paradoxes: they are not disguised affirmations but statements of uncertainty and modes of questioning.

So the final leap is never made, nor should it be attempted by the reader. Shall we then agree with those critics to whom *The Sound and the Fury* is simply an ingenious montage of contrasting perspectives, a brilliant exercise in ambiguity? To pose the question in these terms is again to miss the point. Those who think that the novel should have a determinable sense and deplore its inconclusiveness are just as mistaken as those who assume that it has one and therefore refuse to acknowledge its indeterminacies. Both approaches fail to acknowledge the specificity of literary discourse and disregard the very impetus of Faulkner's writing. For far from being inert antinomies, its contradictions generate a field of dynamic tension and are in fact what sets his books in motion. The tension is not solved, nor can it be, but this irresolution is to be imputed neither to an incapacity to make up one's mind nor to a masochistic pursuit of failure. No more than to a Christian or a nihilistic statement should *The Sound and the Fury* be reduced to a neutral balancing of contrary views.

To Faulkner the choice was not between affirmation and denial, sense or nonsense, so much as between writing and silence. As soon as words get written, meanings are produced, that is, are both brought forth and exhibited, and the elaborately deceptive uses of language characteristic of literary discourse, far from canceling

8. Brooks, *The Yoknapatawpha Country*, 348.

significance, open up its infinite possibilities. It is true that in their different ways modern and postmodern novelists such as Beckett, Blanchot, and Robbe-Grillet (not to mention the posterity of Rimbaud among poets) have done their utmost to rarefy meaning, to bring literature as close as possible to the condition of silence, and in one sense to do so is every writer's hope. Faulkner, however, was in no way a minimalist. His literary ancestors are to be sought among the more robust of the great nineteenth-century masters, and if we relate him to his contemporaries or quasi-contemporaries, he is clearly closer to the omnivorous Joyce than to the almost anorexic Beckett. His drive was toward more and more, not less and less. And like Joyce, Faulkner pursued his quest in the teeth of absurdity. "Prendre sens dans l'insensé"[9]—to make sense of and in the senseless, to take up one's quarters where absurdity is at its thickest, is how Paul Eluard defined the function of modern literature. The definition also applies to Faulkner's design, and nowhere perhaps is this design more in evidence than in the final section of *The Sound and the Fury*. While the novel's tensions are there raised to an almost unbearable pitch, the shrill irony of its ending leaves them forever unresolved.

Yet simultaneously a countermovement develops, away from absurdity toward some tentative ordering. Faulkner's rhetoric here is both at its most ambitious and at its most humble: at its most ambitious when it gathers its energies to reassert the powers of language and the authority of the writer; at its most humble when it effaces itself behind the sacred eloquence of an Easter sermon and yields to the anonymous authority of the myth. It is most significant, too, that in this section Faulkner's inversions so often take on the colors of paradox. Given their cultural context, these paradoxes seem to call for a Christian interpretation, but one may wonder whether they do not all refer back to the central paradox of the writer's own endeavor. For the writing process also tends to operate a radical inversion of signs; it too draws strength from its weakness and glories in its want. As we have seen, Shegog, the frail vessel of the sovereign Word, may be taken for an analogon of the novelist himself, reaching the point of inspired dispossession where his individuality gives way to the "voice." And the mystical vision granted to the preacher may likewise be said to metaphorize the unmediated vision sought after by the writer. What these analogies seem to point to is the mirage of an ultimate reversal: that which would restore the absolute presence of language to itself and convert its emptiness into plenitude, its fragmentation into wholeness—fiction raised to mythos, speech raised to logos.

9. Paul Eluard, *Poésie Ininterrompue* (Paris: Gallimard, 1946), 32.

It is of course an impossible dream: the quest is never completed, the reversal forever postponed. There is no denouement, no final unknotting. The last section does not provide the hoped-for perspective from which the dissonant earlier sections could be seen as parts of a coherent and understandable whole. It only introduces us to another, less solipsistic "world," juxtaposed to the worlds of Benjy, Quentin, and Jason but incapable of holding them together. Yet even though the gap between language and meaning is always there, as readers we insist—cannot but insist, as we do with all works of art we wish to understand and make our own—that what falls apart only seems to do so and actually falls together. The illusion cannot be dispelled that the writing process has managed to create an order of its own, assigning each word and sentence to "its ordered place." And it is not just an illusion; there is indeed an order, or rather an ordering, generated out of the very vacuum of language and the very emptiness of desire. The text of *The Sound and the Fury* does hold together, and achieves admirable integrity as an aesthetic design. And while the furious and helpless voices of the Compson brothers exhaust themselves in utter solitude, the patterned incompleteness of *The Sound and the Fury* waits for readers and requires their active participation. Not that they can succeed where the author failed. But if their reading of the novel is not mindless consumption (which it can hardly be), they, too, will take part in the unending process of its production. Reading and rereading the book, they will write it again.

MINROSE C. GWIN

Hearing Caddy's Voice[†]

Caddy, as we have already seen, is first and foremost an image; she exists only in the minds and memories of her brothers. . . . She is in fact what woman has always been in man's imagination: the figure par excellence of the Other, a blank screen onto which he projects both his desires and his fears, his love and his hate. And insofar as this Other is a myth and a mirage, a mere fantasy of the Self, it is bound to be a perpetual deceit and an endless source of disappointment.

André Bleikasten,
*The Most Splendid Failure: Faulkner's
"The Sound and the Fury"*

† From *The Feminine and Faulkner: Reading (Beyond) Sexual Difference* (Knoxville: University of Tennessee Press, 1990), 34–47. Copyright © 1990 by the University of Tennessee Press. Reprinted by permission of the University of Tennessee Press. Page references are to this Norton Critical Edition.

> But what if the object began to speak?
>
> Luce Irigaray,
> *Speculum of the Other Woman*

I must begin by saying that I do not believe in Caddy Compson's silence. For if I believed in it, there would be no point in beginning at all. I will admit also that, although I do not believe that Caddy is silent, I do not understand fully what she is saying. And so I am seeking Caddy Compson, * * * straining to hear untranslatable snatches of sounds. * * * [We] listen for that of which we can hear the sense but not the substance, that which is always escaping language's appropriative gesture. Certainly this tentativeness is not an accustomed posture for those of us trained in the staid uprightness of the "objective" stance. Yet, as Jane Gallop points out in her reading of Lacan, such a (non)position as ours, vulnerable and unsettling as it is, not only allows a different relationship to the many contradictory voices of a text, but calls into question "the phallic illusions of authority" and therefore is, and must be, "profoundly feminist." Our willingness to relinquish mastery, to admit that we do not know, frees us to seek out what it *is* we do not know, to become as [Roland] Barthes would have us—rereaders rather than consumers of texts.

And so when I say I am listening for Caddy's voice as it will, I believe, float up to us muted but articulate out of the feminine space of *The Sound and the Fury*, I am saying that we are listening for what we know not and for much more than we know. Just as the inscription of woman decenters and challenges the phallocentrism of Western culture and metaphysics and its "structuring of man as the central reference point of thought, and of the phallus as the symbol of sociocultural authority," Caddy as female subject becomes * * * the discursiveness of that space which she *is* but which she also speaks out of. This is a space which expands and contracts with the force of its own motion. I do not see it as a "blank counter" or an "empty center," a "cold weight of negativity," or a "still point."[1] Indeed, by relinquishing our (imagined) mastery over it, our attempts to *fix* it, we may find ourselves being engulfed by it (much, I think, as Faulkner allowed himself to be) and losing ourselves in it and to it. We may believe ourselves in danger.

But it is then, I believe, that we may begin to hear the whisper of Caddy's voice from within the folds of Faulkner's text and from

---

1. See André Bleikasten, *The Most Splendid Failure: Faulkner's "The Sound and the Fury"* (Bloomington: Indiana UP, 1976), 58, 51; Cleanth Brooks, *William Faulkner: The Yoknapatawpha Country* (New Haven: Yale UP, 1963), 334; and Eric Sundquist, *Faulkner: The House Divided* (Baltimore: Johns Hopkins UP), 10.

within our own willingness to be absorbed into the concentric and bisexual spaces *between* the "manifest text" of Faulkner's male creative consciousness and the "unconscious discourse" of its own feminine subjectivity.[2] * * * As Faulkner disappears into the rhetoric of the text, Caddy emerges with her own language of desires, loss, subversion, and, of course, creativity.

At this point our dilemma becomes linguistic: how to converse with space, motion, force. * * * And how to listen to the language Caddy speaks, to that voice we hear between and beyond the contours of narrative—to the space which speaks both from and toward the half-light of the unconscious. In our yearning to hear that voice as it *is* (and not as we would render it through the alembic of consciousness and Being) and in our frustration at being able to catch only snatches and whispers of it, we are tempted to become like Melissa Meek, the frantic librarian, who seizes the frozen photographic image that will *place* Caddy somewhere and who cries, "It's Caddy! We must save her!" Burdened by the weight of consciousness and afraid we will not catch what it is we are meant to hear, we might hasten to fix Caddy in history and culture, in myth, as Other, as anima, as double, as nothing, as everything—and hence to erect some safe, recognizable boundaries around the feminine space of the text. Yet most of us would agree, I think, that Caddy *as character* flows beyond our ability to read her. She is *something more* than we can say, yet her presence is crucial to the deployment of language.[3]

We are like Benjy "trying to say" Caddy, but we, like Faulkner himself, always fail. Faulkner's feeling of failure (as well as his sense of the splendor of it), I believe, derives from his frustrations at "trying to say" Caddy, trying to write the female subject through a male consciousness and always failing—but *in the failure* creating the enormous bisexual tensions which play themselves out so powerfully within *The Sound and the Fury*, which in fact are essential to its subversion of the whole idea of a unified subject. We know Faulkner's passion (Bleikasten uses the term "tenderness") for Caddy, his "beautiful one," his "heart's darling." Yet we also are aware that Eric Sundquist is right in saying, "There is probably no major character in literature about whom we know so little in proportion to the amount of attention she receives."[4] I would suggest another way of seeking the mystery that is Caddy, but one which I admit will not allow us to "find" her. The inevitability of our failure, though, does not mean we should not look and listen; for in seeking Caddy as

---

2. See Robert Con Davis, ed., *Lacan and Narration: The Psychoanalytic Difference in Narrative Theory* (Baltimore: Johns Hopkins UP, 1983), 857.
3. See Julia Kristeva, *Desire in Language: A Semiotic Approach to Literature and Art*, ed. Leon S. Roudiez (New York: Columbia UP, 1980), 120. [*Editor's note.*]
4. See Bleikasten and Sundquist as cited in note 1 above. [*Editor's note.*]

feminine space and female subject-in-process we will be tracing the elusive shape of Faulkner's bisexual artistic (un)consciousness and * * * employing * * * a radical strategy of reading.

What we seek in seeking Caddy Compson is not only the language and force and mystery of woman within Faulkner's text and consciousness. This is also an inquiry into the nature of female subjectivity within a male text and the relationship of that subjectivity to what language can and cannot say. * * * Caddy's ability to speak to us as she traverses the space between presence and absence, text and nontext, the conscious and the unconscious, stretches our sense of the urgency of these questions. Simultaneously, her ability to play creatively within the bounded text of male discourse expands our sense of female energy and power, of its pressure upon the productivity of that text. Often we feel that Caddy isn't where we think she is, that her space is *somewhere else*. She is continually arising from and fading into her brothers' discourse, always in the process of emerging and disappearing in the male text. Her subjectivity, as the "punctuation" of the male discourse which bounds it, is always on the brink of *aphanisis*, fading and being lost. It thus speaks out of the play of presence and absence, moving up and down the pear tree, in and out of that hazy area between the conscious and the unconscious. * * * Benjy's final musings are indeed so strangely moving, I suggest, because they allow us to feel almost simultaneously *both* the epiphany within the maternal space created between himself and Caddy *and* its *aphanisis*:

> Father went to the door and looked at us again. Then the dark came back, and he stood black in the door, and then the door turned black again. Caddy held me and I could hear us all, and the darkness, and something I could smell. And then I could see the windows, where the trees were buzzing. Then the dark began to go in smooth, bright shapes, like it always does, even when Caddy says that I have been asleep. (50)

And yet the paradox is that Caddy *won't* fade completely; her voice and her presence emerge and reemerge throughout the narrative. She will not leave us; she rushes out of the mirror of male discourse, smelling like rain, offering Benjy's box of stars, speaking to us the language of creative play, of *différance*, of endless deconstruction and generation. Or grieving in a black raincoat, she appears suddenly out of nowhere on the periphery of the text, saying . . . what?

* * *

> "Why, Benjy." she said. She looked at me and I went and she put her arms around me. "Did you find Caddy again." she said. "Did you think Caddy had run away." (28)

Caddy's voice speaks in rhythms most of us understand, for she speaks what Kristeva has called "maternal language" out of the maternal space created in Benjy's discourse. The flatness and homogeneity of her speech evoked by punctuation and syntax have the paradoxical effect of intensifying the rhythms of mediation between self and other. * * * Hearing Caddy through the flatness of Benjy's mind, we may be reminded of the peculiar effect of hearing poetry read with a purposeful lack of expression designed to permit the language of the text to speak itself *as language*. Matthews has pointed to the fact that Benjy in his "fallen world of loss, memory, time, and grief" converts time into space.[5] I would take this idea further by suggesting that feminine space *overlays* time in the novel. * * *

Within such a space Caddy the child becomes Caddy the mother. Benjy the man is Benjy the child. Linear time is decentered and displaced by maternal space. Language is constitutive: Caddy's "saying" makes it so. Within one conversation, she makes words into exchange commodities traded for a jar of lightning bugs for Benjy and remakes grief into pleasure:

> "If I say you and T.P. can come too, will you let him hold it." Caddy said.
>
> "Aint nobody said me and T.P. got to mind you." Frony said.
>
> "If I say you dont have to, will you let him hold it." Caddy said.
>
> "All right." Frony said. "Let him hold it, T.P. We going to watch them moaning."
>
> "They aint moaning." Caddy said. "I tell you it's a party. Are they moaning, Versh." (24–25)

Linda W. Wagner writes persuasively of Caddy's attempts to "bring [Benjy] to speech" and of Caddy's roles as "creator and conveyor of language," a language of love and interconnection which is inevitably replaced by meaningless sound and fury. Matthews thinks of these initial attempts at definition and articulation as prefiguring an infinite play of meanings which suggest the inability of language to "reappropriate presence and the recognition that such a limitation opens the possibility of the endless pleasures of writing." Although Caddy's generative maternal language is eventually replaced, it is not lost. * * * Benjy has lost Caddy but he remains within her maternal discourse, for her voice has imprinted both itself and *himself* upon the receptacle of his memory. We can envision him at the state mental hospital, still hearing her speak his name and still

5. John T. Matthews, *The Play of Faulkner's Language* (Ithaca: Cornell UP, 1982), 65.

recognizing the sound of her name within language—a maternal language which traverses the chasm between her subjectivity and his. We may look at the movement of Benjy's reality within this section as illustration. At the beginning he has lost Caddy and is bellowing at the sound "caddie" and yet by the end, the maternal space of Caddy * * * has enclosed his mind with the "smooth, bright shapes" of that hazy entry to the womb-like darkness of maternal interconnection through which the boundaries between self and other are blurred. By its ability to name what is not, or what seems to be absent (Benjy's subjectivity), Caddy's maternal voice dissolves the boundary between presence and absence and thereby creates the semiotic matrix of the novel, the unconscious discourse that will go on to speak the reciprocal rhythms between the conscious and the unconscious in Quentin's tortured thoughts.

Although she is a girl and although she speaks as a girl, her voice carries this referential weight because she speaks from the *position* of the mother, whose very acts of giving birth, of gestation and nurturance, dissolve the otherness of the other. In many of the scenes created in Benjy's memory, Caddy encloses him within this maternal space which transcends the teleologies of time and loss. What Caddy's voice says out of the maternal space created for it in Benjy's mind is precisely *opposite* to what Benjy's narrative as a whole seems to be saying, i.e., that originary plenitude can never be regained, that creativity and play have given way to despair, rigidity, meaningless order—sound and fury signifying nothing.[6]

The maternal Caddy deconstructs such a message. Her voice tells another story—the creative play of *différance* within the bounded text of Benjy's mind. With her words and touch she dissolves the boundaries between herself and Benjy. His snatches of memories often end with Caddy reaffirming the maternal space that connects them. For example, Benjy remembers her persuading their mother to let her take him out in the cold, instructing the relieved Versh not to come, and then embracing him:

> He went on and we stopped in the hall and Caddy knelt and put her arms around me and her cold bright face against mine. She smelled like trees.
> "You're not a poor baby. Are you. You've got your Caddy. Haven't you got your Caddy."(6)

Caddy plays creatively within the bounds of coldness and rigidity. She speaks warmth to Benjy, even as they are being used by Maury to deliver his letter: "Keep your hands in your pockets, Caddy said.

6. More optimistically, Matthews, in *The Play of Faulkner's Language*, finds that loss opens the way to "the fun of writing" and its continual deferment, its "play of failures."

Or they'll get froze. You don't want your hands froze on Christmas, do you" (4). She connects her self to Benjy's other, even to the point of becoming other to herself, speaking of herself in the third person, connecting her desires to Benjy's, pretending, "We dont like perfume ourselves" (28). * * *

Yet just as she herself fades * * * the maternal space she creates for Benjy gives way to other more disturbing spaces, and what empowerment she receives as female subject from taking the place of the mother is punctuated by depletion and darkness. As her space constricts, we begin to see her frantic response to the necessity of remaining creative within the narrow margins allowed her own desires as a subject-in-process propelled by the motion of their force. She continues to play, but her text becomes more and more bounded. She is encircled in the concentric spaces of her own maternity created within male discourse, but also of the sexuality which transgresses that maternal space, and finally and inevitably of the patriarchal world she finds herself living within as a female subject-object. She is a subject always in the process of becoming; yet movement becomes less free and eventually, in Jason's economy, impossible.

One of the scenes most often repeated in the novel and certainly among its most central is the one in which a silenced Caddy, no longer a virgin, stands in the door, first in Benjy's and then in Quentin's memories, her eyes speaking terror and despair. Cornered by Benjy's bellowing, she is completely entrapped by male discourse, by both Benjy's inarticulate and Quentin's articulate texts of woman as other. This is a scene which Benjy recalls and then immediately repeats, and it is one which erupts again and again in Quentin's tortured thoughts. Caddy has broken the Law of the Father, that which "requires that woman maintain in her own body the material substratum of the object of desire, but that she herslf never have access to desire."[7] * * * Here she is voiceless; she becomes merely a function of the discourse of others—frozen as image, as silence. Benjy recalls the same scene in two flashes. First he recalls:

> Caddy came to the door and stood there, looking at Father and Mother. Her eyes flew at me, and away. I began to cry. It went loud and I got up. Caddy came in and stood with her back to the wall, looking at me. I went toward her, crying, and she shrank against the wall and I saw her eyes and I cried louder and pulled at her dress. She put her hands out but I pulled at her dress. Her eyes ran. (46)

7. See Luce Irigaray, *This Sex Which Is Not One*, trans. Catherine Porter and Carolyn Burke (Ithaca: Cornell UP, 1985), 188.

And then again:

> We were in the hall. Caddy was still looking at me. Her hand
> was against her mouth and I saw her eyes and I cried. We went
> up the stairs. She stopped again, against the wall, looking at
> me and I cried and she went on and I came on, crying, and she
> shrank against the wall, looking at me. She opened the door to
> her room, but I pulled at her dress and we went to the bath-
> room and she stood against the door, looking at me. Then she
> put her arm across her face and I pushed at her, crying. (46)

This is the image of Caddy silenced. She cannot remake herself
in language for Benjy. She cannot wash off or throw away her
desire. This is the moment of her entrapment, a crucial moment of
the novel and one which Quentin re-creates obsessively. If Caddy in
the pear tree is an image of her creativity and courage, of her ability
to negotiate the economies of death (that which is in the window)
and life (that which is below her, those whom she loves), then Caddy's standing in the door with eyes, "like cornered rats" as Quentin will say of a similar scene, is surely the opposite image. Caddy
speaks out of the pear tree: she speaks life to death and death to
life. She becomes, as Bleikasten shows us, a mediator between the
two.[8] Yet she is completely entrapped before Benjy's bellowing; more
devastating, she is rendered voiceless. It is significant and strangely
disturbing that these two images of Caddy, weeping after she has
entered into her first sexual relationship, are connected in Benjy's
mind by Versh's eerie tale of maternity's disastrous effects, that of
the woman's "bluegum chillen" who eat a man: *"Possum hunters
found him in the woods, et clean"* (46). Versh's story is about a woman
who has, it is implied, *"about a dozen them bluegum chillen running
around the place"* (46). This is the maternal space expanded to monstrous proportions, becoming enormously threatening and destructive to the male, just as Caddy's maternal space now threatens Benjy
because it has become also the space of female sexuality. * * *

Yet I have said that I do not believe in Caddy Compson's silence.
As female subject, she is indeed silenced at this point. But as
woman-in-effect in male discourse, as the feminine space in
Faulkner's narrative, she becomes what Irigaray calls the *"disruptive excess"* that is guilty of "jamming the theoretical machinery
itself, of suspending its pretension to the production of a truth and
of a meaning that are excessively univocal."[9] She is the text which
speaks multiplicity, maternity, sexuality, and as such she retains
not just one voice but many. They make Benjy bellow and Quentin

8. Bleikasten, *The Most Splendid Failure*, 54.
9. Irigaray, *This Sex Which Is Not One*, 78.

despair. They drive Jason to 'hatred. Their power is mammoth because they are "not one." Within the constricted space of Quentin's tortured psyche, we will hear them, like the Caddy of Benjy's maternal *chora*, fading in and out. To hear Caddy within the margins of Quentin's text will require listening to a language which transgresses the bounds of consciousness, a language which must be listened to in much the same way that Caddy listened to Benjy— beyond sound and syntax, between the lines.

* * *

PHILIP M. WEINSTEIN

"If I Could Say Mother": Construing the Unsayable about Faulknerian Maternity[†]

My title sounds insistently psychoanalytic, promising to uncover the covered-up, to find the key that will unlock the mystery and reveal its hitherto concealed treasure. This game of penetrating / mastering is itself distinctly phallic; there must be a better way to pursue the mother. I concede at the outset that I cannot say the Unsayable about Faulknerian maternity, that my argument bears most directly on the brilliantly disturbed novels between *Flags in the Dust* and *Light in August*, and that the text I shall examine at length—the source of the quotation in the title—is *The Sound and the Fury*. Faulkner's rendering of Mrs. Compson is, within the representational economy of that novel, uniquely punitive. I intend to identify the discursive model that underlies that rendering, then to reconceive the model, drawing on some contemporary feminist criticism, and finally return to Mrs. Compson. At the end I shall suggest ways in which Faulkner's texts of this troubled period are trying to say Mother and how they are succeeding.[1]

"If I could say Mother" recurs twice in Quentin's section of *The Sound and the Fury*, and in each case the phrase arises out of the memory of an April 1910 conversation between Herbert Head and Mrs. Compson:

> What a pity you had no brother or sister *No sister no sister had no sister.* Dont ask Quentin he and Mr Compson both feel a little insulted when I am strong enough to come down to the

† From *Faulkner's Subject: A Cosmos No One Owns* (New York: Cambridge UP, 1992), 29–41. Copyright © 1992 Cambridge University Press. Reprinted with the permission of Cambridge University Press. Page references are to this Norton Critical Edition.
1. I want to express here a general indebtedness to my colleague Abbe Blum, who made my path through contemporary feminist criticism more manageable.

table I am going on nerve now I'll pay for it after it's all over and you have taken my little daughter away from me *My little sister had no. If I could say Mother. Mother*

Unless I do what I am tempted to and take you instead I don't think Mr Compson could overtake the car.

Ah Herbert Candace do you hear that *She wouldn't look at me soft stubborn jaw-angle not back-looking* You needn't be jealous though it's just an old woman he's flattering a grown married daughter I cant believe it.

Nonsense you look like a girl you are lots younger than Candace color in your cheeks like a girl *A face reproachful tearful an odor of camphor and of tears a voice weeping steadily and softly beyond the twilit door the twilight-colored smell of honeysuckle.* (63)

In the second passage, near the end of Quentin's section, the smell of gasoline on his shirt reevokes this same scene of Herbert and the car, and it concludes with *"if I'd just had a mother so I could say Mother Mother"* (114).

Quentin's arresting phrase of abandonment is embedded, both times, in the context of Mrs. Compson's own fantasy return of adolescence. As she flirts with Herbert, drawing on the social model she used to know, that of the Southern belle, her son registers her maternal absence from his life. "Color in your cheeks like a girl *A face reproachful tearful an odor of camphor and of tears*": these are the only roles. Mrs. Compson can play—premarital coquetry or postmaternal grief. Her abandonment of her children emerges here as saturated in the rituals and assumptions of her own virginal past. Between her childless adolescence and her child-complicated middle age no other viable script has become available to her. Between virginal flirtation and postmaternal complaint Mrs. Compson literally has nothing else to say.

As though to emphasize the alienation of her married state, the text rarely pairs her with her husband. Faulkner often has Benjy's first memories of Mrs. Compson join her instead with Uncle Maury. The novel signals recurrently that the man most on her mind, the man she uses as a shield between herself and her husband, is Uncle Maury. In this textual sense he vies with Mr. Compson for the position of husband. (One might argue that her textual husband is her son Jason, with whom she maintains a peculiarly intense relationship. In this regard they echo Gerald Bland and his mother, also an oddly incestuous pairing in which the titular husband has been conveniently removed.)[2] In either case Mr. Compson himself is

---

2. André Bleikasten, *The Most Splendid Failure: Faulkner's "The Sound and the Fury"* (Bloomington: Indiana UP, 1976), briefly notes this point.

arguably the third male in his wife's life. Appearing most saliently
in Quentin's chapter, he registers textually more as his son's father
than as his wife's husband.

Her brother Maury seems to serve as her way of remaining a Bascomb, of refusing to consummate her entry into Compsonhood.
(My discovery at the Faulkner and Yoknapatawpha Conference in
1986 that Faulkner's family pronounces Maury as Murry, the name
of Faulkner's father, may strengthen this fantasy conflation of the
mother's brother with the mother's husband.)[3] Incestuous pairings
thus suggest themselves at the parental level as well, and Mrs.
Compson's preference for her brother leads with compelling logic
to Quentin's preference for his sister. Refusing to be a wife, Caroline Bascomb refuses to be a mother, and Caddy must therefore—
and fatally—play that role for her brothers.

The picture of Mrs. Compson that emerges is of a woman whose
life ceased to be narratable after her entry into marriage and its
sexual consequences. She has no stories to tell that can accommodate in a positive way even a grain of her postconsummation experience. Her entry into mature sexuality is swiftly followed by her exit.
Having delivered her children, she takes to her bed—the childbed,
not the marriage bed—acting like a child, exacting from her children the sustenance she should be offering them.[4]

She speaks obsessively of the rules she learned before marriage,
and of her refusal to learn anything different since:

> "Yes," Mother says. "I suppose women who stay shut up like I
> do have no idea what goes on in this town."
> "Yes," I [Jason] says, "They don't."
> "My life has been so different from that." Mother says.
> "Thank God I dont know about such wickedness. I dont even
> want to know about it. I'm not like most people." (169–70)

I am still a virgin, her camphor and tears keep saying: I don't know
anything about checks, about report cards, about business deals,
about what girls do on the street or within their own bedrooms.
Weeping and mourning, ritually heading for the cemetery throughout the novel, she registers her marital and maternal experience as
a curse that makes a mockery of all her training: "when I was a girl
I was unfortunate I was only a Bascomb I was taught that there is
no halfway ground that a woman is either a lady or not" (69).

---

3. I am indebted to conversations with James Hinkle for this information.
4. See Catherine Clément and Hélène Cixous, *The Newly Born Woman*, trans. Betsy
   Wing (Minneapolis: U of Minnesota P, 1986), 39, for a portrait of the hysteric that
   captures succinctly the economy of desire transformed into suffering that characterizes Mrs. Compson's behavior: "The hysteric . . . tries to signify eras through all the
   possible forms of anesthesia. . . . A witch in reverse, turned back within herself, she
   has put all her eroticizing into internal pain."

This rigid either-or posture indicates that it is Mrs. Compson, not her husband, who is possessed by the binarisms of the Symbolic order—but possessed by them as only someone locked into Imaginary identifications and repudiations can be. Despite John Irwin and other critics who fault Mr. Compson for not upholding paternal authority, his considerable appeal resides in his shrewd perception that a Symbolic order based upon traditional notions of morality and virginity is bankrupt, that it is an invented script. He relates to this order as a produced structure, not an inalterable essence, whereas his wife would live it as the Real itself. She thus incarnates what Roland Barthes terms the cultural code, the already known: "If we collect all such knowledge, all such vulgarisms, we create a monster, and this monster is ideology," Barthes writes. Mrs. Compson is such an ideological monster.[5]

We touch here upon the source of her failure as a mother. Deformed by her social training—a training shaped by class and race to the requirements of virginity—she abandons her own flesh and blood upon the loss of that virginity. She has outlived her image of herself. Simultaneously rushing forward to death and backward to childhood, she repeats herself and takes to black. The novel's attack upon her seems to be this: mothers are meant to nourish their young; their trucking with (male-authored) ideological scripts can only lead to overlectured and undernurtured offspring.[6]

This paradigm of ideological insistences perverting maternal function may shed light on that strange scene in which Jason wrestles with his mother over the key to Quentin's room. Noel Polk has pointed to the repression wrought into this image of the key-laden woman but there is a sexual dimension to the assault as well. Faulkner takes a full page to show us Jason all over his mother, "pawing" at her skirt, while she resists the attack. Finally, "'Give me the key, you old fool!' Jason cried suddenly. From her pocket he tugged a huge bunch of rusted keys on an iron ring like a mediaeval jailer's" (183). Pawed at, pressed, her invaded pocket reveals its

5. Roland Barthes, *S/Z*, trans. Richard Miller (New York: Hill and Wang, 1974), 97. John Irwin develops this reading of Mr. Compson throughout *Doubling and Incest / Repetition and Revenge: A Speculative Reading of Faulkner* (Baltimore: John Hopkins UP, 1975); see especially 67, 75, 110–13, and 120–22. Bleikasten, *The Most Splendid Failure*, 113, also reads the father in terms of his failure as a lawgiver.

6. This is one of the reasons that Lena Grove (not to mention Dewey Dell or Eula Varner) can be rendered with such affection: she does not meddle in the Symbolic order. Her unflappable comments about a family needing to be together "when a chap comes" (*Light in August* 18) are tonally the reverse of Mrs. Compson's outraged protestations of the flouted system. On Noel Polk cited below, see "The Dungeon Was Mother Herself: William Faulkner: 1927–1931," in Doreen Fowler and Ann J. Abadie, eds, *New Directions in Faulkner Studies: Faulkner and Yoknapatawpha, 1983* (Jackson: UP of Mississippi, 1984), 61–93.

cache of hideous keys like a grotesque parody of the children who should instead have come forth from her womb. And indeed her womb is terrifying—a space imaged here as rusted, iron, a jailer's fortress, as was also earlier implied by Quentin's image of the dark place in which he was imprisoned: "The dungeon was Mother herself" (115).

No child escapes from this dungeon, and insofar as the dungeon is a womb, no child gets fully born. In place of nourishment she feeds her children repressive ideology, and they sicken on it. From Mrs. Compson's failure to mother we move through her daughter Caddy's failure to mother and finally, reductively, into *her* daughter Quentin's refusal to conceive. "Agnes Mabel Becky," the phrase spoken by the man in the red tie upon seeing that shiny container connected with Quentin, is the term used half a century ago in the South for a three-pack of condoms.[7] Mrs. Compson's inability to nourish here literalizes into her grand-daughter's well-earned decision to seal off the reproductive functions of her womb.

Noel Polk helps us to generalize the model that Mrs. Compson fails abysmally to uphold. He writes of Faulkner's mothers of this period as "almost invariably, horrible people," failing to meet "even minimal standards of human decency, much less . . . the ideal of mother love as the epitome of selfless, unwavering care and concern." "Selfless, unwavering care and concern": this is exactly what these mothers lack; It is also what they are posited by the culture as *supposed to possess*, and what they are excoriated for not possessing. Freud writes in his study of Leonardo: "A mother's love for the infant she suckles and cares for is something far more profound than her later affection for the growing child. It is in the nature of a completely satisfying love-relation." Freud assumes, as does Faulkner, that, unlike fathers (unlike all other human beings), mothers enjoy "a completely satisfying love-relation." They *naturally* fulfill their identity in this bond with the infant. Mothers are defined as just those creatures whose subjective needs are supremely realized through the act of nurturing their own offspring.

Freed from ideology themselves, reservoirs of milk and loving kindness, mothers are meant to be sacred servants. *The Sound and the Fury* hammers this point home in the fourth chapter through the massive comparison, move for move, of Mrs. Compson with Dilsey, the latter a perfect instance of how mothers should care for offspring. And what is Dilsey's model if not the Virgin Mary herself, celebrated in the Reverend Shegog's sermon as Jesus' inexhaustibly

---

7. Paul Gaston, professor of history at the University of Virginia, supplied me with this enlightening bit of information.

loving "mammy [who] suffered de glory en de pangs," who "helt him at de nightfall, whilst de angels singing him to sleep," and who filled heaven with "de weepin en de lamentation" (193) at his death? This model of what a mother is supposed to do resonates throughout not just *The Sound and the Fury* but countless narratives in Western culture.

Such a model assumes that the Word—the realm of spirit, of the Symbolic—is articulated through a male voice, announcing the Kingdom of Heaven. Mary serves as the bodily carrier of the spirit. Her function is to nurse her infant son and to bemoan his tragic death. She emerges thus—in her role as the suffering mother, the ubiquitous Pietà of Western art—as a register for the emotional loss suffered through Christ's crucifixion. She herself has no new word to utter, but her natural care for her child is the precondition for his divine utterance in which he reveals his kinship with his father.

If we secularize this text, we arrive at something like the following. The domain of the father is the domain of the Spirit, of all Symbolic activities that make up culture and that achieve articulation in the medium of language. This domain takes the inherently binary form of language, an endless series of constructed oppositions that constitute the (male) paradigm of meaning itself. The domain of the mother, on the other hand, is the domain of the unfissured, prelinguistic body. Her function is so to nourish the child that he (the model for the child is implicitly male) becomes somatically prepared for the vertigo and alienation that accompany entry into the Symbolic order of the father. In other words, the time of bonding exists as a prelinguistic, prelogical plenitude in which mother and child are each other, in which self and world, self and other, interpenetrate. If successful, this quasi-magical bonding bequeathes to the child somatic sufficiency—bodily grounding— that enables him to sustain his later and lifelong encounter with the world outside himself, and eventually to deliver his word within that world.

The gender distinctions essential to this paradigm are common to the discourses of both Christianity and psychoanalysis. The mother is simultaneously sacred and subservient, the enabler but not the speaker of the word. If we return to Faulkner with this script in mind, we can better place the anger toward the mother that suffuses the early novels. In those novels the mother fails at her sacred bodily task. Charged with preoedipal responsibilities, she not only neglects these but barges into the terrain of the law, often in its most outdated and repressive forms. The unnourished child therefore emerges into the world too soon. He has no somatic grounding that might hold the imprint of the culture's proliferating codes, consequently no basis for stabilizing the *"maelstrom of unbearable reality."*[8] Thus we get Benjy, Quentin, Darl, Vardaman, and Joe Christmas: boy children unsure of the integrity of their own bodies, dizzyingly vulnerable to sensory overload, unable to maintain their identity within boundaries that might stabilize the relations between past and present, there and here, self and other, male and female, child and parent, brother and sister, white and black.

French and American feminists seem to agree that this male-scripted model of the nonspeaking mother is disabling rather than empowering. In "Stabat Mater" Julia Kristeva critically explores the myth of the Virgin Mary. Focusing on the iconography of breast, ears, and tears, Kristeva reads the Virgin as a figure of speechless succor. One of Kristeva's commentators, Mary Jacobus, writes:

> The function of the Virgin Mother in Western symbolic economy (according to Kristeva) is to provide an anchor for the nonverbal and for modes of signification closer to primary processes. In the face of the fascinated fear of the powerlessness of language which sustains all belief, the Mother is a necessary pendant to the Word in Christian theology—just as the fantasized preverbal mother is a means of attempting to heal the split in language, providing an image of individual signs, plenitude, and imaginary fulness.[9]

This subtext of the ideal mother as sanctuary, as preverbal plenitude, as pendant to the word and yet also a preserve against its possible emptiness, exerts a powerful punitive influence upon the representation of women in secular texts, including (as we have seen) Faulkner's texts. Kristeva, for her part, is in the difficult position of seeking to maintain the centrality of the pre-oedipal bonding without fetishizing it or making it immune to stress. Jacobus goes on to say that "for Kristeva, division is the condition of all signifying processes. No preoedipal language, no maternal discourse, can be free of this split." Kristeva enacts this, split in her essay by inserting another discourse (this one fragmented, impulsive, lyrically focused on childbirth, breastfeeding, and body parts—what she

8. William Faulkner, *"Absalom, Absalom!": The Corrected Text* (New York: Random House, 1986), 186.
9. Mary Jacobus, "Dora and the Pregnant Madonna," in *Reading Women: Essays in Feminist Criticism* (New York: Columbia UP, 1986), 137–93.

calls the "semiotic") within the surrounding "Symbolic" portion of her text.[1]

The entry of the "semiotic" into the discourse of maternity would both restore the place of the maternal body within language itself and announce that the mother's desire is, like all desire, conflicted and tension-filled, rather than speechlessly satisfied through the suckling of her son. Thus Kristeva would revise the male-coded scripting of maternal desire—what she punningly calls "pèreversion." These feminist revisions (in their insistence that women's desire exceeds malescripts for maternity, that women's desire must find a way into language, that maternity must be demythologized and approached from the perspective of the mother herself) allow us to see how gender biases in that previous script polarize Faulkner's representational strategies.

Let us now return to Mrs. Compson. What we see is a portrait of maternity crazily arrested in the "virginal" phase of the Virgin Mary model. Of the three divine components—succor, silence, and virginity—she has betrayed the two that Faulkner values and retained the one that he deconstructs. The ideal silent nourisher has degenerated into a nonnourishing nonstop talker. More, the language that pours out of her is wholly male-scripted; she speaks the defective Symbolic order at its most repressive.

Her white middle-class culture insists not merely that her desire be contained within mothering purposes. Rather, given the American South of the early twentieth century with its array of racial phobias and its constraining model of white womanhood, her desire is virtually taboo.[2] Enjoined to marry and procreate, Mrs. Compson

1. Kristeva describes the mother's extraordinary experience of one-in-two/two-in-one in terms that illuminate Faulkner's fear of and fascination with this figure: "For a mother . . . the arbitrariness that is the other (the child) goes without saying. For her the impossible is like this: it becomes one with the implacable. The other is inevitable, she seems to say, make a God of him if you like; he won't be any less natural if you do, for this other still comes from me, which is in any case not me but an endless flux of germinations. . . . This maternal quietude, more stubborn even than philosophical doubt . . . eats away at the omnipotence of the symbolic. . . . Such an attitude can be frightening if one stops to think that it may destroy everything that is specific and irreducible in the other, the child; this form of maternal love can become a straitjacket, stifling any deviant individuality. But it can also serve the speaking subject as a refuge when his symbolic carapace shatters to reveal that jagged crest where biology transpierces speech: I am thinking of moments of illness, of sexual-intellectual-physical passion, death" ("Mater" 117–18).
2. Joel Kovel's *White Racism: A Psychohistory* (New York: Random House, 1970) attempts to chart psychoanalytically this intersection of latent racial phobias and overt gender models, as these operate within American black-white relations. Winthrop Jordan's authoritatve *White over Black: American Attitudes Toward the Negro, 1550–1812* (Chapel Hill: U of North Carolina P, 1968) attends as well to the fantasy structures subtending American racism, while James Snead's *Figures of Division: William Faulkner's Major Novels* (New York: Methuen, 1986) usefully places the issue of racial polarization within the larger problematic of Western philosophy's falsely polarizing yet inescapable binarisms.

is also enjoined to abhor her status as an incarnate creature replete
with sexual organs. She may now appear to us more clearly what
she is—a socially constructed figure—taught by her culture in such
a way as to be unable to survive her own sexual initiation. The only
story she has learned is a virginal one, and on this she dwells,
within this she hides from the unbearable facts of her own parturi-
tion: a son whose idiocy indicts the very fertilization of egg by sperm;
a daughter whose burgeoning sexuality promises, at best, the
same disaster she has undergone; another son whose needs she did
not (could not) assuage, and who punished her for it by committing
suicide; and a third son whose fantasy name of Bascomb assures
her that he is hers alone: no Compson seed in him, she is still a
virgin.

Why has her adoption of the virginal script kept her from also
participating in the nurturance script? Why does the tension
(always latent) between these two "stories" become so inflamed in
Faulkner's narratives? To answer this, we might look at Faulkner's
representation of the female body in *The Sound and the Fury*. In so
doing we discover that the other story for Mrs. Compson, the nurturance story, is simply intolerable in its fetishistic focus on the
body and its linkage of fecundity with filth. The polarization of
these two narratives reveals the suffocating binarism of the culture's texts of female maturation:

> Because women so delicate so mysterious Father said. Delicate
> equilibrium of periodical filth between two moons balanced.
> Moons he said full and yellow as harvest moons her hips
> thighs. Outside outside of them always but. Yellow. Feet soles
> with walking like. Then know that some man that all those
> mysterious and imperious concealed. With all that inside of
> them shapes an outward suavity waiting for a touch to. Liquid
> putrefaction like drowned things floating like pale rubber flab-
> bily filled getting the odor of honeysuckle all mixed up. (85)

If the virginal story presupposes a blank body (a body, as Luce
Irigaray puts it, that is "pure exchange value . . . nothing but the
possibility, the place, the sign of relations between men," the body
that Quentin fantasizes here is unbearably full, though no less constructed through a male lens.[3] (How telling that Mr. rather than
Mrs. Compson speaks to Quentin of menstruation.) This "delicate"
body is more urgently imagined as huge, moonlike (moons that sway
the blood tides, moons that are her hips and thighs), filled with liquid rot, spaces that you desire to enter and in which you drown.
This is a disaster site. It is also a female womb. A place of periodical

---

3. Luce Irigaray, *Ce Sexe qui n'en est pas un* (Paris: Editions de Minuit, 1977), 181. Translation mine.

filth, this womb is obsessively scripted within an economy of decay: what could grow here? The mother's threat seems most to inhere in her leaky and fluctuating wetness, a female wetness that menaces all projects of male enclosure and mastery.

Luce Irigaray has written suggestively of the male hostility to fluidity ("La mécanique des fluides," in *Ce Sexe qui n'en pas un*), and Jane Gallop discusses her argument as follows: "Fluidity has its own properties. It is not an inadequacy in relation to solidity. In phallic fantasy, the solid-closed-virginal body is opened with violence; and blood flows. The fluid here signifies defloration, wound as proof of penetration, breaking and entering, property damage. . . . [But] menstrual blood is not a wound in the closure of the body; the menstrual flow ignores the distinction virgin//deflowered." Most of Faulkner's males recoil in horror from this female economy of the blood. *Sanctuary* and *Light in August* are concerned with male-induced penetrations of the body. The blood their male protagonists focus on is the blood they can make flow, the blood whose flowing signals male mastery of the object. Or it is the symbolic "blood" of patriarchal lineage or racial difference, not the material blood that simultaneously—and so troublingly to the male mind—carries growth and decay.[4]

A "dry" virginal script that denies desire and repudiates intercourse, a "wet" adulterate script that concedes desire and equates the fertile womb with rot and drowning: there are not other alternatives in *The Sound and the Fury*'s lexicon for constructing maternity. "I was taught that there was no halfway ground that a woman is either a lady or not" (69). In Mrs. Compson's desiccated Symbolic world, ladies and sex organs are incompatible notions. This polarization means that, here and elsewhere, Faulkner's narrative treatment of white maternity takes a schizoid form.

On one side there is the "wet" drama—always illicit, always for not-ladies—of a sexed and rebellious younger woman heading toward unsanctioned labor (Caddy, Dewey Dell, Lena, to a certain extent Temple, Charlotte, and Eula). This drama, suffused with narrative empathy, focuses intimately upon the scandal of the penetrated and/or swelling body itself. Faulkner seems mesmerized by the image of the female body escaping the propriety of its male proprietor, usually the husband/father/brother who would confine its activity within the scripts of the Symbolic order. Because that

4. Adequate consideration of this point would take more space than I can allow here. For further discussion, see chapters 2 and 4 of *Faulkner's Subject: A Cosmos No One Owns*. See also Luce Irigaray, *The Sex Which Is Not One*, trans Catherine Porter and Carolyn Burke (Ithaca: Cornell UP, 1982), esp. 83 and 93; Roland Barthes, *Roland Barthes by Roland Barthes* (New York: Farrar, Straus, and Giroux, 1977), 69; and Teresa de Lauretis, *Alice Doesn't: Feminism, Semiotics, Cinema* (Bloomington: Indiana UP, 1984) [*Editor's note.*]

order is (and needs to be shown as) without grounding, this drama is usually narrated with understanding. But the mothers-to-be in this drama are mute; they are mainly subsumed within their own bodies. When, later (as with Temple and Eula), Faulkner does endow them with speech, they have become defenders—often tragic defenders—of the Symbolic. It seems that they cannot simultaneously break the law and speak.

On the other side, there is the "dry" retrospective drama within which are imprisoned the proper wives, the repressed older women heading toward menopause and death. Mrs. Compson, Joanna Burden in her final phase, and of course Addie Bundren—a case unto herself—come to mind.[5] In general Faulkner cannot keep his narrative eye on the *same* woman moving through all the stages of the female life cycle. (Addie and Joanna cross into and out of sexual activity at the expense, so to speak, of their lives.) Maternity is thus a sort of narrative Waterloo: an incoherent zone his fiction can lead up to and away from but which none of his women can traverse and still remain themselves. Is it too much to say that once his pregnant women *deliver*, they cease to be figures of empathy or desire, for he has then entered the fantasy role of their infant needing succor? In any case, the representation of maternity ruptures on this incoherence.

With these constricting representational scripts in mind, I conclude by returning to Mrs. Compson's plight. As the quotation in my title indicates, we see her—Faulkner sees her—only through the freighted and damaged lenses of her offspring. (Indeed, psychoanalytic discourse itself, and a fortiori its commentary on the mother, has centered until recently upon the [male] child in need. What treatment the mother has received has tended to come very sharply angled.) This narrative deprivation of sympathy is decisive. Yet Mrs. Compson's gestures, when attended to against the grain of the text itself, have their pathos. Her refusal to accede to the name of Compson, for example, is heavily marked as vanity or regression, though we might also see it as a desperate attempt to preserve a shred of her own identity from the marital exchange that alters her name from that of one male to that of another. (If she were a male being exchanged, if she were Joe Christmas or Charles Etienne de St. Valery Bon, we would be invited so to read her.) Behind her tyranny within the house—she who changes others' names as though

---

5. Addie Bundren is the exception to my schema, the closest Faulkner ever comes to narrating an unco-opted female's move from virginity through intercourse and maternity and child nurturing into adulthood. This move in *As I Lay Dying*, however, is rendered as anything but continuous. Addie's remarkable awareness of body and presence of mind are premised upon the spatially and temporally unplaceable scene of her protracted dying.

in revenge for the unwanted alteration of her own—we can espy a woman with no other moves to make.

"It is our duty to shield her [your lady mother] from the crass material world as much as possible" (147), Uncle Maury writes Jason: shield her while we men invest her money in the real world of business affairs. Jason, for his part, plays the check-burning ritual upon her once a month. Men know better, they are permitted to discard when necessary the unreal rhetoric of honor (the no longer valid terms of the Symbolic). Mrs. Compson may also, at rare moments, know better—"If you want me to, I will smother my pride and accept them [the checks from Caddy]" (144)—but she remains imprisoned within her learned rhetoric, forced to believe she is repudiating her daughter's money. Born and brought up within defective male Symbolic scripts, she spends each day dying within those same scripts. "The dungeon was Mother herself," Quentin thinks; his mother is the jailer. Yes, she is the jailer, but she is also the jail and inmate. Alienated from the powers of her own body, deprived by male scripts of any language of access to her bodily desires, she is the prisoner of her own womb. The dungeon is not mother but motherhood.[6]

I have sought to indicate the ways in which Faulkner's representational strategies cannot say mother. Let me finish by suggesting that the fiction of this troubled period is nevertheless engaged, paradoxically, in "trying to say" Mother. "I was trying to say," Benjy tells us, and Faulkner invents an extraordinary rhetoric to convey to us the tangled torment of Benjy's "say." What American writer has refused more forcefully the blandishments of the "already said"? Although Faulkner never spoke of it as the Symbolic order, although he never thought of language as decisively marked by gender, although he would certainly have cringed at neologisms like phallogocentrism, in a certain sense he knew. He knew that language is the Symbolic, that it comes to us alienated from our speechless feeling, and that if words are to do more than be a shape to fill a lack, they must be tortuously reinvented, recombined, such that the "self" they articulate may appear in its incarnate, decentered, and insecurely gendered pathos. And he would have agreed with poststructuralists that, even in his most ambitious undertakings, he failed to make the words * * * ever cling to the earth.

6. Mrs. Compson's body that is not her own illustrates with uncanny aptness Foucault's claim that the body, rather than being one's private sanctuary, "is the inscribed surface of events (traced by language and dissolved by ideas), the locus of a dissociated Self (adopting the illusion of a substantial unity), and a volume in perpetual disintegration. See Michel Foucault, "Nietzsche, Genealogy, and History," in *Language, Counter-Memory, Practice: Selected Essays and Interviews of Michel Foucault*, trans. Donald E. Bouchard and Sherry Simon (Ithaca: Cornell UP, 1977), 113–38.

What he created in his most experimental early work seems to me analogous to Kristeva's "semiotic": a use of language that gets behind the crisp and repressed male structures of the Symbolic, and that is seeking (in its gaps and incoherences) to make its way back to the mother. Radically nonjudgmental, open to the confusions of past and present, self and other, Faulkner's experimental rhetoric enacts so often (within the character, within the reader) an experience of immediate, undemarcated identification. "The process of coming unalone is terrible," thinks Dewey Dell in *As I Lay Dying*. Faulkner in his early masterpieces frees language from its conventional forms of thinking and feeling in just such a way as to articulate this terrifying collapse of ego boundaries that is common to psychosis, to discovery, and to motherhood. The regressive urge of Faulkner's work of this period—its focus on assault, on overwhelming, on the unchosen—testifies to his desire to find words for the subject's inexpressible vulnerability, its boundary-riddled plight.[7]

Identification is itself primordially rooted in the infantile relation with the mother; perhaps this is why Freud was so wary of its capacity to erode ego boundaries.[8] One of his recent critics writes that for Freud, "Maturity (that is, *masculine* maturity) means being well-defended against one's past, which amounts to the same thing as having a strong capacity for resisting identification. . . . In effect, Freud's picture of maturity is of a man driven to outrun . . . identification with the body of his mother, the original unity of mother and infant."[9]

This description sounds as much like Thomas Sutpen as it sounds unlike William Faulkner. Penetrated through and through by the history of his region and his family, Faulkner outran none of it, and he invented a rhetoric unequaled in its capacity to express penetrability, the phenomenon of being wounded. The biography and the representations in the fiction give us reason to construe him as damaged by his own mother, expelled too soon, not nourished enough.[1] But if this is so, the hunger it generated was for

---

7. See *"As I Lay Dying": The Corrected Text* (New York: Random House, 1987), 56; cf. p. 160. Put too summarily, I want to argue the following: as Faulkner freed himself from his fascination with the "semiotic," as his narratorial voice took on coherence and cultural alignment, his rhetoric became increasingly predictable and his work began to lose its capacity for outrage.

8. Bleikasten has written of the relevance of Freud's "Mourning and Melancholia" to Quentin's inability to sever his "narcissistic identification with the lost object" (*Splendid* 116). In both of these accounts identification is seen as a regressive and self-damaging move.

9. Jim Swan, "Mater and Nannies: Freud's Two Mothers and the Discovery of the Oedipus Complex," *American Imago* 31 (1974): 9–10.

1. For biographical information/speculation, see David Minter, *William Faulkner: His Life and Work* (Baltimore: Johns Hopkins UP, 1980), 1–23; and Jay Martin, "'The Whole Burden of Man's History of His Impossible Heart's Desire': The Early Life of William Faulkner," *American Literature* 53 (1982): 607–29.

"chanting measures beyond the need for words" [192], and the
activity it inspired was an attempt to use words to get past the Symbolic itself, "to retrieve the plenitude of the origins," as Bleikasten
puts it, "by remembring the . . . body of the lost, forgotten, and
unforgettable mother."[2]

"There is at least one spot in every dream at which it is unplumb-
able," Freud writes in *The Interpretation of Dreams*, "a navel, as it
were, that is its point of contact with the unknown."[3] Freud's project of male autonomy makes him insist upon mystery here, but it is
possible to know what that navel connects us with. In his early
dream novels, where the experiments with language are greatest
and the psychic wounds least concealed, where the mother is punished representationally and yet sought after rhetorically, Faulkner
made that unsettling connection.

NOEL POLK

Trying Not to Say:
A Primer on the Language of
The Sound and the Fury[†]

One of the great achievements of *The Sound and the Fury* is that in
a novel which most critics now agree is centrally concerned with
language, in a novel three of whose sections are "monologues" that
make some gesture toward orality, Faulkner turns the clumsy
mechanics of the representation of that language on paper, what
Stephen Ross calls "the visual discourse of our reading,"[1] into a
highly expressive part of the language itself. At one very simple level,
reading, especially the reading of dialogue, involves translating one
sense impression into another: the author translates the aural into
the visual, readers translate the visual back into the aural—or
should, if they want to understand *The Sound and the Fury*. For
just as he plays with Benjy's hearing of the phonemes *[kædI]*, so
does Faulkner play with the way we read, with the mechanical

---

2. André Bleikasten, "In Praise of Helen," in Doreen Fowler and Ann J. Abadie, eds.,
   Faulkner and Women: Faulkner and Yoknapatawpha 1985 (Jackson: UP of Mississippi,
   1986), 140.
3. Sigmund Freud, "The Interpretation of Dreams," in the *Standard Edition of the Complete Psychological Works of Sigmund Freud*, ed. and trans. James Strachey, vols. 4–5
   (London: Hogarth Press, 1953–1974), 4: iii.
† From *New Essays on The Sound and the Fury*, ed. Noel Polk (New York: Cambridge UP,
   1993). Copyright © 1993 Cambridge University Press. Reprinted with the permission of
   Cambridge University Press. Page references to the novel are to this Norton Critical
   Edition.
1. Stephen M. Ross, *Fiction's Inexhaustible Voice: Speech and Writing in Faulkner* (Athens: U of Georgia P, 1989), 44.

signs of punctuation and spelling that harness and control, that give rhythm and shape and weight and expressive meaning to, the silent words that appear on the paper. Throughout the novel he uses an inventive array of visual devices in punctuation—or the lack of it—and spelling and grammar to help us focus on the way we comprehend language, written and oral.

Each brother, Judith Lockyer argues, "reveals an aspect of the power in language. That power is born out of the relation of language to consciousness."[2] I would suggest more: Faulkner uses the mechanics of the English language—grammar, syntax, punctuation, spelling—as a direct objective correlative to the states of each of the narrators' minds. The mechanical conventions of the writing, then, sometimes work *against the words themselves*, so that they reveal things other than what the characters are saying; they work, in fact, to reveal things that the narrators are incapable of saying or are specifically trying to keep from saying, things that have caused them pain and shame. Words are, for Quentin and Jason at any rate, lids they use to seal that pain in the unconscious, though it constantly insists on verbalizing itself. We have access to their pain largely through what they *don't* say, and also through the visual forms of the language in which Faulkner has inscribed their thoughts and feelings on paper. Benjy's section prepares us powerfully for the much more complex linguistic situations in the next three sections.

*   *   *

Jason

Jason abrupts on to the page and very nearly into the reader's ear with a very wet sense of humor so rich in the vernacular you can almost hear him speak. He may be, as Faulkner wrote sixteen years later in the Appendix, and as most commentators have taken too easily for granted, "the first sane Compson since before Culloden" (267), but his monologue is very much of a piece with those of his brothers. For all the apparent "logic" of his outpourings, he too is driven by irrational forces buried deep in his unconscious that are battering at the boundaries of articulation. His monologue is a long loud agonizing cry—Benjy's howling rage made verbal—which he sustains at such a frenetic pace to drown out the voice of his unconscious, to silence its insistent pounding at the edges of consciousness with the earsplitting volume of the sound of his own voice. As Irena Kaluža has pointed out, it is

2. Judith Lockyer, *Ordered by Words: Language and Narration in the Novels of William Faulkner* (Carbondale: Southern Illinois UP, 1991), 53.

devastatingly characteristic of Jason that he never allows his mental experience to operate beyond the conscious speech level, and always tries, by indefatigably inserting words like *because, when, where* and *if,* to organize his experience logically. But the result is far from logical, and his efforts are futile. Thus he always aspires to rationality without ever achieving it in fact.[3]

If Benjy is nonverbal and trying to say, and if Quentin is extremely verbal and trying *not* to say, trying to maintain order by keeping his words inside his head, Jason is intensely, loudly, desperately, gloriously oral. He keeps himself talking loudly so that he won't have to listen to the voices that threaten him: he drowns out one horrendous noise with an even more horrendous one.

One of the reasons Jason has been accepted as "saner" than his brothers is the relative normality of Faulkner's representation of his speech. His monologue almost completely lacks the visual markers, italics the most noticeable, of his brothers' incoherencies and psychic instabilities. It moves as much by associative logic as his brothers' monologues do, but because his psychic censor is much stronger than Quentin's, he is always able to stop himself just short of speaking that which he most fears, and thus manages to maintain a kind of control over his syntax—and so his psyche—that his brothers utterly fail at doing. But Jason cannot hide his diversionary tactics, and although Faulkner uses no italics in Jason's section, he still plays with the conventions of punctuation and representation in ways that reveal Jason's unconscious to us.

Jason's monologue can be characterized first by its defensive posture. His rhetoric is the most verbally aggressive in all of Faulkner. As Ross has noted,[4] he constantly uses his language to beat others into submission. He hardly ever engages in conversation, but rather in verbal combat, from which he can emerge a winner, because he is cleverer and quicker than most of his opponents (there are exceptions), who range from the members of his family to the functionary at the telegraph office. Although his rhetoric is aggressive, however, it emerges from a defensive mentality, perilously close to paranoia, that constantly screams self-justification. Jason is as obsessively aware of the constantly observing "eye" of his own conscience as his brothers are of the lighted window from their mother's room, and he engages a good deal of his psychic and verbal energy in defending himself from the accusations of idiocy and other forms of familial

3. Irene Kałuża, *The Functioning of Sentence Structure in the Stream-of-Consciousness Technique of William Faulkner's "The Sound and the Fury"* (Kraków: Nadładem Uniwersytetu Jagiellońskiego, 1967), 100.
4. Ross, *Fiction's Inexhaustible Voice,* 170.

and genetic insufficiency that he imagines the people of Jefferson are constantly hurling at him (153, for example); his aggressive rhetoric is, in effect, a preemptory strike. And since he knows better than anybody else those points of character and blood where he is most vulnerable, he knows how to defend himself. We can thus discover his animating fears by paying close attention to the things he defends himself against.

A second rhetorical characteristic of Jason's monologue is its almost complete dependence on cliché.[5] Quentin's highly sensitive and poetic articulations of the world about him demonstrate considerable intellectual effort to keep his mind constantly, safely, and originally engaged with the externals of his final day in Cambridge. Quite to the contrary, Jason's language, though equally engaged with externals, is filled with clichés, aphorisms pious and secular, social and personal, mindless oral formulae that he can keep firing so rapidly because they come so easily to the tongue. They never require the speaker to question whether they *mean* anything; in fact they assume he will not. They are merely noise to fill the lacks in his gaps, as Addie Bundren might put it. Though they carry a good deal of the weight of a culture's traditions (its language anyway) and profess to embody a sort of folk wisdom, they nevertheless give only the illusion of meaning. Jason is so mired in these illusions that he is not even aware when they betray him, as in this passage: "After all, like I say money has no value; it's just the way you spend it. It dont belong to anybody, so why try to hoard it. It just belongs to the man that can get it and keep it" (128). Here flatly contradictory nostrums run amok, careen carelessly into each other and demonstrate both his hypocrisy and the mindlessness of his ravings. Jason clearly does not listen to what he says, and so his "sanity" cannot be demonstrated by his language. But for his purposes the words don't have to make sense so long as they make noise: what he cannot stand is the silence in which his real topic might articulate itself.

The quality of cliché is what gives his monologue its colloquial power, its roots in the spoken dialect, and its convincing orality, but the number of clichés also suggests the degree to which, for Jason, sound and sense are separated from each other. His mouth is estranged from his mind. He works very hard to force the disengagement, as we shall see, but in spite of all his efforts, he gets so caught up in the sound of his words that he has no idea what he is saying; he loses control of his words and, no less than Quentin, of his syntax. At such times, his guard down, his mind leads him directly back

5. André Bleikasten, *The Most Splendid Failure: Faulkner's The Sound and the Fury* (Bloomington: Indiana UP, 1976), 164–5.

toward certain crucial moments in his psychic life. Like Quentin's monologue, Jason's hovers around these cruxes like moths around a flame, approaching disaster and then retreating, as the conscious and the unconscious do mortal battle with each other. Like Quentin's, Jason's guard occasionally does relax and, with his mind out of gear but his mouth constantly revving up one cliché after another, Jason rolls inevitably down the path of least resistance toward the precipitous edge, finally snatching himself safely away from it. At these moments of retreat from articulation Jason leaves huge narrative gaps that reveal his psychological preoccupations. As in the other brothers' monologues, Faulkner helps identify these preoccupations syntactically.

In certain ways he plays with the artifices of syntactical representation here more than he does in the first two monologues. Some of these ways can be demonstrated by noting a couple of differences between the 1929 Cape & Smith first edition text and the 1984 Random House New Corrected Text, which relies heavily on Faulkner's carbon typescript of the novel. Two passages are especially revelatory. The first occurs in a long funny diatribe that begins "Well, Jason likes work," and moves immediately to a by this point predictable litany into which Jason compresses all the objects of his anxieties by the same sort of fluid association characteristic of Quentin and Benjy. The association is very revealing. From this savagely ironic acceptance of his need to work, he jumps immediately to the reasons he has to work and like it, all revolving around the complex of circumstances he consciously sees as a betrayal of his chances to "get ahead" in life: Quentin's suicide, his father's death, Caddy's defalcation, Benjy's castration, and his mother's whining domination. He jokes about them to keep them at a distance:

> I says no I never had university advantages because at Harvard they teach you how to go for a swim at night without knowing how to swim and at Sewanee they dont even teach you what water is. I says you might send me to the state University; maybe I'll learn how to stop my clock with a nose spray and then you can send Ben to the Navy I says or to the cavalry anyway, they use geldings in the cavalry. Then when she sent Quentin home for me to feed too I says I guess that's right too, instead of me having to go way up north for a job they sent the job down here to me and then Mother begun to cry and I says it's not that I have any objection to having it here; if it's any satisfaction to you I'll quit work and nurse it myself and let you and Dilsey keep the flour barrel full, or Ben. Rent him out to a sideshow; there must be folks somewhere that would pay a dime to see him, then she cried more and kept saying my poor afflicted baby. (129)

Clearly Jason is in pain. Though he largely maintains control over his syntax, the energy of the passage suggests the pain is about to spill over into associations that he cannot control. He doesn't, for example, *name* Caddy, Quentin, or Father, although he does name his niece and Ben, who are the tangible, daily, reminders of his abandonment by the others. The passage continues, a few lines later:

> It's your grandchild, which is more than any other grandparents it's got can say for certain. Only I says it's only a question of time. If you believe she'll do what she says and not try to see it, you fool yourself because the first time that was the Mother kept on saying thank God you are not a Compson except in name, because you are all I have left now, you and Maury and I says well I could spare Uncle Maury myself and then they came and said they were ready to start. Mother stopped crying then. She pulled her veil down and we went down stairs. (129–30)

Jason's narrative here runs directly into, and then backs away from, a syntactical breakdown, as he realizes that he is approaching dangerously near one of his scenes of pain, his father's funeral. He still will not name Caddy, though clearly he is about to try to convince his mother that his sister will not keep her word not to see Miss Quentin. He starts to tell her how he knows Caddy won't keep her word by recalling her return to Jefferson for their father's funeral, but as he approaches the words "father's funeral," he realizes that he has entered dangerous territory:

> because the first time that was the Mother kept on saying

The Cape & Smith editors of the first edition, sensing that *something* was amiss, rendered this passage:

> because the first time that was that Mother kept on saying[6]

which neither corrects nor clarifies what is happening.[7]

Jason catches himself, just in time, from stumbling rhetorically into his father's grave. He starts to tell his mother that she can't trust Caddy because she lied "the first time" she promised never to try to see Miss Quentin again. Jason is on the verge of putting into words the scene of their confrontation over his father's grave, a scene triggered in his memory by the conversation with his mother about why he has to work, why he "likes" work. But he stalls. Faulkner's carbon typescript and his holograph manuscript render

6. Faulkner, *The Sound and the Fury* (New York: Jonathan Cape and Harrison Smith, 1929), p. 244.
7. Noel Polk, *An Editorial Handbook for William Faulkner's The Sound and the Fury* (New York: Garland 1985), 63.

this passage as it appears in the 1984 New Corrected Text, and the passage is perfectly understandable as Faulkner wrote it if we try to hear Jason stumbling over his words. A more traditional novelist, using more traditional syntactical signs, might have rendered the passage as:

> because the first time—that was—the—Mother kept on saying.

This formulation would have visually approximated the rhythms of Jason's stumbling uncertainty at how to avoid what he is afraid he is about to say. Faulkner denies us the written punctuation that tells us how to *hear* Jason as he speaks, as he rushes blindly into a danger zone, halts, backs up, tries a couple of times to start over, and then finds a safer direction to pursue, he talking not *to* but rather *about* his mother.

He leaves Caddy's perfidy as a subject, but has in fact elided his narrative directly back to the funeral of his father—Jason, Sr., for whom he is named—in as fluid an associative movement as either of his brothers manages, except that his is more evasive. He finds a way to deal with his father's funeral on that rainy day, not by talking about Caddy but by focusing humorously, if savagely, on Uncle Maury's drinking and on his feeble attempts to share in the burial in the rain. Father's funeral is the narrative locus for the next several pages, building toward that meeting with Caddy (133) at the cemetery, which he can now confront because he has constructed a self-justifying narrative framework that permits it. But his reconstruction has its own psychic rules. A telling moment occurs when he discovers that his uncle smells like clove stems, and that Maury is trying at least for the duration of the funeral to pretend that he is not drinking, though of course he is:

> I reckon he thought that the least he could do at Father's or maybe the sideboard thought it was still Father and tripped him up when he passed. (130)

This is the passage as it appears in manuscript, typescript, and the New Corrected Text; the first edition reads "at Father's funeral," which I believe indicates a misunderstanding of Faulkner's intent.[8] Jason simply will not put the words "Father's funeral" or "Father's grave" together, and again Faulkner refuses his readers the punctuation, the visual signs of reading—perhaps a dash following "Father's"—that would indicate how we are to *hear*, and so understand, what Jason is saying.

8. Ibid., 63.

Throughout these pages, which also recount Jason's and Maury's participation in the actual digging of the grave, he refers to the grave only as "it." We cannot help but remember that Jason's first appearance in the novel is in the opening pages of the Benjy section, when Mrs. Compson, Benjy, and T.P. ride the buggy through town on the way to the cemetery. They stop at the store and ask Jason to accompany them, and he refuses. He is, after all, Jason *fils*, and the pain of his father's, and his own, mortality, looms large and threatening in his imagination. The rest of the passage (from the Jason monologue) is particularly illustrative of the way Jason's mind, and his language, work:

> After a while he kind of sneaked his hand to his mouth and dropped them out the window. Then I knew what I had been smelling. Clove stems. I reckon he thought that the least he could do at Father's or maybe the sideboard thought it was still Father and tripped him up when he passed. Like I say, if he had to sell something to send Quentin to Harvard we'd all been a dam sight better off if he'd sold that sideboard and bought himself a one-armed strait jacket with part of the money. I reckon the reason all the Compson gave out before it got to me like Mother says, is that he drank it up. At least I never heard of him offering to sell anything to send me to Harvard.
>
> So he kept on patting her hand and saying "Poor little sister", patting her hand with one of the black gloves that we got the bill for four days later because it was the twenty-sixth because it was the same day one month that Father went up there and got it and brought it home and wouldn't tell anything about where she was or anything and Mother crying and saying "And you didn't even see him? You didn't even try to get him to make any provision for it?" and Father says "No she shall not touch his money not one cent of it" and Mother says "He can be forced to by law. He can prove nothing, unless——Jason Compson," she says. "Were you fool enough to tell——" (130)

Even though Jason forces a kind of logic on these associations, the passage really is a series of non sequiturs. The *becauses* are mechanical contrivances to connect them grammatically, but in fact the associations are emotional and nearly always lead him back to the same scenes of pain and conflict, whatever they happen to be. He and his mother refer to Caddy's daughter as "it," the same term he uses to refer to his father's grave, and doubtless they mean the same thing to Jason: his betrayal and abandonment by his father, his loss, like Quentin's, of an ordering center for his life. He would like to say "Father. Father."

There are similar passages in which his mother figures as the locus of a series of associated images. In the passage just cited, for example, Jason says "dam sight" rather than "damn sight," which as a visual, not an aural, distinction—eye dialect—is somewhat at odds with the intense orality of his narrative. One of the really curious orthographical features of Jason's rendered "speech" is that throughout this section Faulkner invariably employs "dam" rather than "damn" when Jason speaks on the page; that it was deliberate on Faulkner's part is suggested by the fact that when Jason quotes somebody else (Miss Quentin, twice on page 136, for example), he uses the normative "damn." The Cape & Smith first edition editors "corrected" "dam" to "damn" throughout Jason's section; when arguing for restoring Faulkner's carbon typescript reading in the New Corrected Text, I admitted that it was not clear why Faulkner did this, only that it was a demonstrable pattern, and I offered, rather feebly, the possibility that Faulkner was trying to make Jason's usage "less profane" than that of the others[9] but now that seems hardly likely. I would now suggest that Faulkner is creating a visual pun of the sort that confuses Benjy in the novel's second paragraph, and agree with Tom Bowden that the pun relies on a variety of maternal and animal-breeding meanings associated with the word "dam."[1] Faulkner uses "dam" to indicate how insistently "mother" and "sexuality" and even bestiality impinge on Jason's profanity and his attitudes, how profoundly they are related to his psychic problems; as a speaker Jason is no more aware of the difference in spelling than Benjy is of the difference between "Caddy" and "caddie," but the reader cannot escape it.

We can see how this works in another long paragraph, which occurs as Jason describes the beginnings of his futile search for his niece and the hated man in the red tie:

> I went on to the street, but they were out of sight. And there I was, without any hat, looking like I was crazy too. Like a man would naturally think, one of them is crazy and another one drowned himself and the other one was turned out into the street by her husband, what's the reason the rest of them are not crazy too. All the time I could see them watching me like a hawk, waiting for a chance to say Well I'm not surprised I expected it all the time the whole family's crazy. Selling land to send him to Harvard and paying taxes to support a state University all the time that I never saw except twice at a baseball

9. Ibid., 15–16.
1. Tom Bowden, "Functions of Leftness and 'Dam' in William Faulkner's *The Sound and the Fury.*" *Notes on Mississippi Writers* 19 (1987): 81–83.

game and not letting her daughter's name be spoken on the place until after a while Father wouldn't even come down town anymore but just sat there all day with the decanter I could see the bottom of his nightshirt and his bare legs and hear the decanter clinking until finally T. P. had to pour it for him and she says You have no respect for your Father's memory and I says I dont know why not it sure is preserved well enough to last only if I'm crazy too God knows what I'll do about it just to look at water makes me sick and I'd just as soon swallow gasoline as a glass of whiskey and Lorraine telling them he may not drink but if you dont believe he's a man I can tell you how to find out she says If I catch you fooling with any of these whores you know what I'll do she says I'll whip her grabbing at her I'll whip her as long as I can find her she says and I says if I dont drink that's my business but have you ever found me short I says I'll buy you enough beer to take a bath in if you want it because I've got every respect for a good honest whore because with Mother's health and the position I try to uphold to have her with no more respect for what I try to do for her than to make her name and my name and my Mother's name a byword in the town. (153)

This remarkable paragraph is as close to stream-of-consciousness as any in Quentin's monologue in its abandonment of all punctuation after Jason gets launched into the third sentence. As in other passages, Jason here compresses all his most threatening concerns: his father's drinking death, one brother's suicide, another's idiocy, his niece's sexual misconduct, his dalliance with his Memphis whore/girlfriend Lorraine, and his need to assert his own sexual potency, his physical mastery over women (his need to assure himself and others that he, unlike Benjy, does indeed have testicles), and, crucially, his paralyzing fear of the town's watchful eye. It is a mixture of important things, especially in the final lines where the syntax, on the verge throughout, breaks down completely: there is no object to the preposition "with," following the second "because," and no predicate to complete the clause that "because" begins. We notice this "because" since two of them, the only two in the paragraph, are jammed into this one sentence, whereas usually, as Kahiža has pointed out, Jason constantly uses such conjunctions to organize his speech, to force relationships, causes and effects, that may or may not exist; thus they signal a psychic association, if not a strictly logical or rational one. In this paragraph, "because" abrupts at us in that it becomes a psychic bridge between Lorraine and Mother: Mother equals whore.

Jason rumbles into this connection again later in a typically churning meditation:

> I'm a man, I can stand it, it's my own flesh and blood and I'd
> like to see the color of the man's eyes that would speak disre-
> spectful of any woman that was my friend it's these dam good
> women that do it I'd like to see the good, church-going woman
> that's half as square as Lorraine, whore or no whore. Like I say
> if I was to get married you'd go up like a balloon and you know
> it and she says I want you to be happy to have a family of your
> own not to slave your life away for us. But I'll be gone soon and
> then you can take a wife but you'll never find a woman who is
> worthy of you and I says yes I could. You'd get right up out of
> your grave you know you would. I says no thank you I have all
> the women I can take care of now if I married a wife she'd
> probably turn out to be a hophead or something. That's all we
> lack in this family. (161–62)

The entire paragraph moves from his resentment of his niece's
embarrassing public sexual misconduct and his irritation at having
to support her, to her mother's perfidy, which, he thinks, is why he
has to work for a living. The meditation runs from yet another
assertion of his masculinity to a cliché-ridden and phony defense of
his women friends to a cliché-ridden and phony attack on social
morality, to a defense of his secret sexual liaison with Lorraine
(secret from his mother, at any rate, and from the prying eyes of the
town). His uncontested thoughts then stampede him into a defense
of his bachelorhood, for which, he claims to have told his mother,
he blames her: "If I was to get married you'd go up like a balloon."
His reported exchanges with his mother throughout may be as
imaginary as the ones Quentin claims with their father.[2] What is
significant about Jason's "conversations," however, are the contorted
connections he makes, willy-nilly, between his bachelorhood, Lorraine, and his mother: again and again Lorraine and Mother collide,
in the deepest, least conscious, parts of Jason's mind.

Benjy's attempts to "say" get him castrated. Quentin also directly
associates sexuality, sexual shame, with language when he fantasizes castrating himself, so he can treat sexuality as he would Chinese, as a language he doesn't know (77). Like Quentin, what Jason
cannot "say," what he cannot confront in language, is how much he
both fears and desires his own castration and death: "That's a hog
for punishment for you," he says of Benjy:

> If what had happened to him for fooling with open gates had
> happened to me, I never would want to see another one. I often
> wondered what he'd be thinking about, down there at the gate,

---

2. Matthews, *Play of Faulkner's Language*, p. 103; see also François Pitavy, "Through the
Poet's Eye: A View of Quentin Compson." In André Bleikasten, *William Faulkner's The
Sound and the Fury: A Critical Casebook* (New York: Garland, 1982), p. 93.

watching the girls going home from school, trying to want something he couldn't even remember he didn't and couldn't want any longer. And what he'd think when they'd be undressing him and he'd happen to take a look at himself and begin to cry like he'd do. But like I say they never did enough of that. I says I know what you need you need what they did to Ben then you'd behave. And if you dont know what that was I says, ask Dilsey to tell you. (166)

And if they'd just sent him on to Jackson while he was under the ether, he'd never have known the difference. But that would have been too simple for a Compson to think of. Not half complex enough. Having to wait to do it at all until he broke out and tried to run a little girl down on the street with her own father looking at him. Well, like I say they never started soon enough with their cutting, and they quit too quick. I know at least two more that needed something like that, and one of them not over a mile away, either. But then I dont reckon even that would do any good. Like I say once a bitch always a bitch. (172–73)

These two startling passages—the latter close to the end of Jason's section and so part of his peroration—suggest the degree to which Jason's interlocutor throughout has been mostly himself, and he the object of his own scorn. The first passage suggests his attempt to imagine his way into the sexually safe castrated haven of Benjy's mind and, like Quentin, to imagine what it would be like not ever to have had sexual urges; he concludes that "you," his libidinous self, his id, his constant interlocutor, needs castrating. In the second passage he proposes "two more" that need cutting: "one of them . . . not over a mile away" has to be his father, whom he still will not locate verbally in the cemetery; the other, closer, can only be himself.

Thus it is not for nothing that Faulkner very carefully plants the charged word "complex" deep in the heart of Jason's final paragraph: Mother and sexuality are as essentially the subtext of his monologue as of his brothers'—Mother and sexuality and all the related substitutions and evasions that spiral outward from oedipal guilt: shame, self-loathing, the need for expiatory punishment: castration and death. No less than Quentin, Jason longs for a strong father who will force on the world a moral center around which all the fragmentation of his psychic life can cohere. If he is, as Carvel Collins argued long ago,[3] Faulkner's version of Freud's punitive superego, he also manifests his brother Quentin's essential oedipal conflicts and expresses the identical fears, though in him they emerge as rage,

3. Carvel Collins, "The Interior Monologues of The Sound and the Fury" In Alan S. Downer, ed., English Institute Essays 1952 (New York: Columbia UP, 1954), 29–56. Reprinted in James B. Meriwether, ed., The Merrill Studies in The Sound and the Fury (Columbus, Ohio: Charles E. Merrill, 1970), 59–79.

mostly at himself. He is a cauldron, a veritable inferno, of oedipal conflicts, containing within himself a raging id that has to deal with a bedridden mother whom it both desires and revolts from in shame and whom it cannot evade by substituting an absent Caddy or even the ever-present and insatiable daughter of Caddy; that must also deal with a draconian superego that insists on controlling the world, and his own libido, by punishing it appropriately—by killing it or at least castrating it—and with a surprisingly fragile ego, which no less than brother Quentin's both fears and desires castration—and death as the ultimate castration—as an appropriate punishment for one who has sinned as he has. He is therefore not so much a "negative" image of Quentin as a complete replication of his brothers, both of whom he contains within himself, along with the raging, punishing Father he so desperately longs for. This may be why he inspires in the reader the most complex response of any of the brothers.

DOREEN FOWLER

"Little Sister Death":
The Sound and the Fury
and the Denied Unconscious†

In an introduction to *The Sound and the Fury* composed in 1933, Faulkner quite uncharacteristically revealed the impulse that moved him to write his first great novel. The novel originated, he explained, in his desire to create "a beautiful and tragic little girl," who was somehow to replace two female absences: the sister he never had and the daughter he was fated to lose in infancy.[1] Caddy Compson, then, is the central focus of the novel. And yet, as critics have frequently observed, Caddy is never concretely presenced in the way that her brothers are. She is never given an interior monologue of her own; she is seen only through the gaze of her brothers, and even then only in retreat, standing in doorways, running, vanishing, forever elusive, forever just out of reach. Caddy seems, then, to be simultaneously absent and present; with her, Faulkner evokes an

---

† From *Faulkner and Psychology*, ed. Donald M. Kartiganer and Ann J. Abadie (Jackson: UP of Mississippi, 1994), 3–20. Copyright © 1994 by the University Press of Mississippi. Reprinted by permission of the publisher. Page references are to this Norton Critical Edition.

1. "Faulkner's Introduction to *The Sound and the Fury*," ed. Philip Cohen and Doreen Fowler, *American Literature* 62 (June 1990): 277. See also James B. Meriwether, "An Introduction to *The Sound and the Fury*," *Mississippi Quarterly* 26 (1973): 156–61; and James B. Meriwether, "An Introduction for *The Sound and the Fury*," *Southern Review* 8 (1972): 705–10.

absent presence, or the absent center of the novel, as André Bleikasten and John T. Matthews have observed.[2] The "absent center" is a
key term in Lacanian theory, and in order to understand how Caddy's
absence, or repression, supports masculine identity, it is useful briefly
to review Lacan's account of the origin of subjectivity.

According to Lacan, at first all children are engaged in an imaginary dyadic relation with the mother in which they find themselves
whole. During this period, no clear boundaries exist between the
child and the external world, and the child lacks any defined center
of self. For the child to acquire language, to enter the realm of the
symbolic, the child must become aware of difference. Identity comes
about only as a result of difference, only by exclusion. The appearance of the father establishes sexual difference, signified by the
phallus, the mark of the father's difference from the mother. The
father creates difference by separating the child from the maternal
body; he prohibits the merging of mother and child and denies the
child the use of the phallus to recreate this union.[3] Under the threat
of castration, the child represses the desire for unity and wholeness,
opening up the unconscious and creating the subject as lack. The
child leaves behind a state of no difference or lacks and enters the
symbolic order which is simultaneously the prohibition of incest
with the mother and the sign system that depends on the absence
of the referent.

One becomes a speaking subject, then, only through a rupture,
only by creating a vacuum where once there were plenitude and
presence. Lacan even uses the word "castration" for the relation of
subject to signifier because in the symbolic order empty discourse,
the letter of language, takes the place of authentic existence in the
world.[4] For this reason, Lacan can say the subject is that which it is

2. My interpretation owes much to the insights of other scholars; in particular, I am
   indebted to John T. Irwin's pioneering Freudian study, *Doubling and Incest/Repetition
   and Revenge* (Baltimore: Johns Hopkins UP, 1975), which draws attention to the
   importance of doubling in Faulkner's fiction; John T. Matthews's *The Play of Faulkner's
   Language* (Ithaca: Cornell UP, 1982), and André Bleikasten's *The Most Splendid Failure: Faulkner's "The Sound and the Fury"* (Bloomington: Indiana UP, 1976), both of
   which sensitively consider Caddy's focal role as the absent center of *The Sound and the
   Fury*; and Gail L. Mortimer's *Faulkner's Rhetoric of Loss: A Study in Perception and
   Meaning* (Austin: U of Texas P, 1983), which convincingly demonstrates that the per-
   ceptual habits of Faulkner's characters and narrators serve to assert control, reinforce
   boundaries, and deny interrelatedness in a world of flux.
3. It should be noted that, according to Nancy Chodorow, a woman's entry into the symbolic is different from a man's, that whereas the son is threatened with castration if he
   continues his union with the mother, the daughter is not; that the daughter instead
   identifies with the mother, and she does not enter the symbolic as wholeheartedly or as
   exclusively as the son. Moreover, the daughter, like the son, longs to recover the lost
   unity with the mother, and for the daughter this is done by becoming a mother herself
   and recreating with her child the lost tie she experienced with the mother. See *The
   Reproduction of Mothering: Psychoanalysis and the Sociology of Gender* (Berkeley: U of
   California P, 1978).
4. Jacques Lacan, *Ecrits*, trans. Alan Sheridan (London: Tavistock, 1977), 709.

not, or, to rephrase Lacan, the subject exists as a consequence of loss, the loss of the whole from which it arises. And the whole in relation to which the subject is lacking has its basis in what Freud calls "the phallic mother." The "whole" is the relationship with the preoedipal mother. Paradoxically, however, even as women represent the whole they also represent lack because the whole with which they are identified threatens to engulf and dissolve identity. As Jane Gallop helpfully explains, the maternal body "threatens to undo the achievements of repression and sublimation, threatens to return the subject to the powerlessness, intensity and anxiety of an immediate, unmediated connection with the body of the mother."[5] For this reason, then, because women are reminders of an origin in a lack of differentiation, the male's own sense of lack is projected on woman's lack of a phallus. In the words of Jacqueline Rose, woman "is the place onto which lack is projected, and through which it is simultaneously disavowed."[6] Similarly, Gallop states, "Woman is the figuration of phallic 'lack.'"[7]

In *The Sound and the Fury* Jason and Quentin are speaking subjects, who have separated from an imaginary dyadic unity, and, as a result, experience a sense of diminishment; in turn, they project these feelings of lack of being onto women, and, in particular, onto Caddy, who, as the mother-surrogate, is a reminder of a preconscious fusion. Caddy becomes the site of their own lack, the representation of their own sense of castration, which is buried in the unconscious. In this way, Caddy Compson embodies the return of the repressed. And because she represents the repressed self, her brothers' attitude toward her is contradictory. On the one hand, they desire union with her because they yearn to heal the split subject and to reexperience a lost presence and plenitude. On the other hand, they desire to confine and control Caddy, to keep conscious separate from the unconscious, to reenact the splitting that defines the boundaries of the self.

Paradoxically, both of these contradictory desires lead to feelings of nonbeing. For, if Caddy's brothers choose to embrace the symbolic, they repress the world and the mother in favor of an empty sign and experience existence as absence; on the other hand, if they elect to return to the preoedipal state, the subject merges with the other and ceases to exist.

This latter fate is dramatized in Benjy, the third Compson brother. Benjy does not exist within the symbolic order; he does not

5. Jane Gallop, *The Daughter's Seduction: Feminism and Psychoanalysis* (Ithaca: Cornell UP, 1982), 27.
6. Jacqueline Rose, "Introduction," in *Feminine Sexuality*, ed. Juliet Mitchell and Jacqueline Rose, trans. Jacqueline Rose (New York: Norton, 1982), 48.
7. Gallop, 22.

exist as an "I" separate from the other. As André Bleikasten has convincingly demonstrated, in Benjy's interior monologue, "There is no central I through whose agency his speech might be ordered and made meaningful; in like manner, there is no sense of identity to make his experience *his*."[8] Even Benjy's body seems like a collection of unrelated fragments that act independently of any central volition. He speaks of his voice, for example, as if he did not control it: "My voice was going loud every time" (40). In other words, he is not aware of his existence as separate or as an agent of action. He is not a speaking subject; rather he is a helpless, inchoate, inarticulate bundle of sensations. And Benjy's condition is directly related to his yearning for Caddy. Throughout his section, he obsessively pursues one goal: to restore a lost unity with the banished mother-figure. Benjy has not elected to separate from Caddy, the representative of a fused existence with the maternal body; rather, he is forcibly divided from her by the Law of the Father. The fence in his section functions as a concrete token of this Law; it separates him from all he desires: from his pasture, emblem of the signified, the physical world, and from the mother-surrogate, from Caddy, whose name he hears repeatedly called from the other side of the fence. On the one occasion when he finds the gate to the fence unlocked, he seizes his opportunity to act on his yearning to reexperience an unmediated connection with the body of the mother. He crosses the boundary established by the father, symbolically collapsing difference, and pursues the forbidden other, the Burgess girl, who figures the lost Caddy. For good reason, then, Benjy's recollection of running after and catching the Burgess girl merges with his memory of being anesthetized for the operation that deprives him of his male organs. The act of seizing the Burgess girl, representative of Caddy who is, in turn, the representative of the absent signified returns Benjy to a former state of indeterminacy in which consciousness is surrendered:

> They came on. I opened the gate and they stopped, turning. I was trying to say, and I caught her, trying to say, and she screamed and I was trying to say and trying and the bright shapes began to stop and I tried to get out. I tried to get it off my face, but the bright shapes were going again. They were going up the hill to where it fell away and I tried to cry. But when I breathed in, I couldn't breathe out again to cry, and I tried to keep from falling off the hill and I fell off the hill into the bright, whirling shapes. (35–36)

8. Bleikasten, 71.

By passing though the gate and expressing his desire for unity with the maternal body, Benjy has violated the Law of the Father, and the consequence of this violation is the loss of difference, figured in this instance as the loss of consciousness and the severing of the external organs which signify male difference.

While Benjy yearns to transgress boundaries, both Quentin and Jason strive, with more or less ambivalence, to maintain divisions which, by exclusion, establish difference and define the self. Because these boundaries are externalized in the shrinking Compson square mile, Quentin and Jason struggle to keep Caddy and, later, her daughter within these borders. Above all, Jason and Quentin seek to maintain the father's interdiction against merging. Thus Quentin tries to prevent Caddy from leaving the house to meet with her lover in the dark woods; and when Caddy returns from her nightly trysts, Quentin fastens the gate behind her in a futile attempt to assert difference. Similarly Quentin attempts to return the little Italian girl to her father's house.

But because Quentin and Jason see personified in Caddy and her daughter their own repressed sense of relatedness to the other, these women are identified with signs of slippage and leakage, fissures in the fence and the house—the symbols for the paternal interdiction that creates subjectivity. Again and again Caddy and her daughter are associated with windows, doors, and cracks. Each time Caddy meets to fornicate with Ames, she crawls through the fence which surrounds the Compson house. Through a window, Caddy disobediently views her grandmother's funeral; and through a window Miss Quentin escapes Jason's domination, taking with her his money, which she obtains by breaking through the locked window of his room. And when Quentin summons to mind Caddy's lost virginity, he alludes to the loss with the phrase *"One minute she was standing in the door"* (53). Just as the house and the Compson square mile attempt to assert the integrity of the self, windows, doors, and cracks expose the precariousness of this identity. These fissures metaphorically register the status of the phallus, which, in the words of Jacqueline Rose, "is a fraud."[9]

This fraudulence is the result of the loss accrued in becoming a subject. Because the speaking subject is constituted by creating absence, by repressing the original unity with the mother and the world and covering over the resulting emptiness with a sign, the subject only functions as an effect of a loss of being. This sense of a lack of integrity of being is evinced in both Quentin's and Jason's sections, where it takes the form of a sense of phallic lack or castration anxiety.

9. Rose, 40.

For example, throughout his section Quentin clearly is trying to align himself with the Law of the Father, which is signified by the phallus, but all his efforts to present himself as a man different from his own weak, ineffectual father fail; and significantly Quentin characterizes these failures as somehow feminizing him. During his humiliating confrontation with Ames, Quentin is disgusted with himself for behaving "like a girl" (108), slapping Ames with his open hand before he thinks to make a fist, fainting, and rejecting Ames's pistol and horse. Unlike Ames, who selects for their meeting place a bridge, and who has "crossed all the oceans all around the world" (99), Quentin, who loses his footing on the bridge and has to be held up by Ames, cannot bestride the waters of life.

In fact, all of the experiences which Quentin obsessively rehearses seem to culminate in failure. His sister consistently defies his interdicts; he fails to preserve her purity, his task as self-appointed surrogate-father; he fails to prevent her marriage to the odious Head; he fails to restore the little Italian girl to her father; he fails to carry out his plan of joint suicide with Caddy; and he fails ignominiously when he challenges Gerald Bland. Given these cumulative failures, it seems safe to conclude that Quentin suffers feelings of masculine inadequacy or, in Freudian terms, castration anxiety. Such feelings would explain Quentin's preoccupation with phallic symbols: the clock tower, the smoke stacks, the gun he refuses, and the knife he drops.

Like his older brother, Jason is also haunted by feelings of phallic lack.[1] One manifestation of Jason's threatened masculinity is his precarious ability to drive his automobile; for, as Jason implies when he refuses "to trust a thousand dollars' worth of delicate machinery" (155) to a black servant, only a "real man" is able to steer such a powerful machine. But in the course of Jason's pursuit of his niece and the showman, it becomes evident that he himself is not "man enough" to drive the car: its gasoline fumes reduce him to helplessness. In addition, the details of the purchase of the car—he bought the car with money given him by his mother for investment in Earl's store—also suggest a certain dependency. Moreover, if we accept Jason's car as the outward sign of his virility, his niece's and the showman's gesture of deflating the car's tires takes on suggestive sexual overtones.

Jason hungers for money for the same reason that he cherishes his car. Money helps him to counter his feelings of anxiety about

---

1. While Bleikasten notes resemblances between Jason and Quentin in *The Most Splendid Failure*, 150–52, in "Fathers in Faulkner," *The Fictional Father: Lacanian Readings of the Text*, ed. Robert Con Davis (Amherst: U of Massachusetts P, 1981), he maintains that, unlike Quentin, Jason is not threatened by feelings of impotence.

his masculine identity. For example, when Jason says to Dilsey, "At least I'm man enough to keep that flour barrel full" (137), he is using money as evidence of manhood. Money compensates him for a sense of diminishment, the same loss of father-power that Quentin feels. And if we read Jason's money as his substitute for male potency, then, when his niece steals his money, she strikes a blow against that potency. In pursuing his niece and the lost money, he is confronted with phallic symbols—"sheet iron steeples" (199) and "a spire or two above the trees" (200)—which seem to mock his lack. His feelings of impotence are dramatized when, in an attempt to forget his head pain, Jason tries to distract himself with thoughts of Lorraine. By picturing himself in bed with the prostitute, he clearly means to bolster his failing masculinity with an image of himself playing the part of the potent and phallic male, but instead in his imagined scene he is pathetic and impotent: "He imagined himself in bed with her, only he was just lying beside her, pleading with her to help him, then he thought of the money again" (200). The specter of sexual inadequacy inevitably invokes thoughts of the lost money because of the identification in Jason's mind of money with masculine potency.

Jason's failure to regain the lost money, the symbol of phallic power, ends appropriately with a symbolic castration. Jason challenges an "old man" (201), a father-figure, who wields a rusty hatchet and who causes him to fall and experience a blow to the head, an analogue, according to Freud, for castration.[2] Following this blow, Jason behaves as if he has been emasculated, abandoning his pursuit of his niece and the money, his avenue to masculine power. The ultimate sign of his emasculation is his inability to drive his car; on the trip back to Jefferson, Jason takes the back seat, and a black man drives.

For my purposes, what is most significant about these feelings of lack is the way that both Quentin and Jason attempt to evade them by projecting them on the mother or on a mother-substitute, who serves as a reminder of what they lack, the absent signified. This projection is particularly overt in Jason's section. Consumed by a sense of a lack of wholeness, Jason focuses these feelings on one central image, the lost bank job promised by Herbert Head. The job, a position of authority, serves as a symbol for the state of full phallic power that Jason aspires to. Plagued instead by feelings of loss, Jason attempts to evade these feelings by projecting them onto Caddy and, in her absence, onto her daughter. Interchangeably, then, he alludes to Caddy and his niece as "the bitch that cost me a

---

2. Sigmund Freud, *The Standard Edition of the Complete Psychological Works of Freud*, ed. and trans. James Strachey, 24 vols. (London: The Hogarth Press, 1961), 11:207.

job, the one chance I ever had to get ahead" (198). In this way, the two women become scapegoats on whom, and away from himself, Jason expels his own sense of diminishment and dispossesion. In other words, by blaming the two women, Jason denies his own lack, and these repressed feelings, the contents of his unconscious, are projected onto Caddy and her daughter.

Like Jason, Quentin also identifies women with the self's own absent center, which, if reincorporated, will blur the boundaries that define the self. In fact, Quentin's often quoted phrase, "the dungeon was Mother herself" (115), metaphorically registers this identification. The mother is a dungeon because the maternal body is a reminder of an imaginary dyadic unity in which the self is engulfed and dissolved. In the same way, Caddy, whose eyes drain of consciousness and look "like the eyes in statues blank and unseeing and serene" (108) and whose blood surges uncontrollably when she hears her lover's name, also seems to Quentin to represence the being-in-the-world that he had relegated to the unconscious. For this reason, when the adolescent Caddy and Quentin struggle together in the hogwallow, he wipes the stinking mud from his leg and smears it on Caddy, a gesture which reenacts the original displacement of the literal that made subjectivity possible.

But even as this act demonstrates Quentin's resolve to keep the other and the world out of the borders of the self, his incestuous feelings for Caddy suggest the opposite impulse, a desire to reincorporate the other into the self and recover a former completeness of being. And because such a sexual merging would blur the oppositions that define selfhood, sex and death are insistently paired throughout the novel as they are so often in literature. For example, Caddy looks in the window at her grandmother's funeral and acquires a knowledge of death at the same time as her brothers are introduced to the mysteries of sexuality as revealed in her muddy bottom. When Mrs. Compson sees her daughter kissing a boy, she wears black and announces that Caddy is dead. When Caddy sets out to meet her lover for a tryst in the dark woods, Quentin insists that first they go and look at the bones of the mare Nancy lying in a ditch. Sex and death also seem interchangeable in that both separate sleeping partners. Jason can no longer sleep with Damuddy because she is dying; Benjy can no longer sleep with Caddy because she is sexually maturing. And in Benjy's section sex and death repeatedly merge: a recollection of standing on a box to see Caddy's wedding interweaves through a memory of Caddy climbing a tree to see Damuddy's funeral. The equation of sex and death, apparent even in Shreve's sarcastic remark, "Is it a wedding or a wake?" (54), is insisted upon by Caddy who repeatedly uses death as a synonym for sexual intercourse: "yes I hate him I would die for him

Ive already died for him I die for him over and over again everytime this goes" (100).

This equation of sex and death is extended to include Caddy because, for Quentin, sex with Caddy, a mother-figure, is death, a collapse of difference. Thus Quentin finds particularly applicable to Caddy St. Francis's fond name for death, "Little Sister Death" (51), an appellation that anticipates Harry Wilbourne's expression for another mother-figure in *The Wild Palms*, the "grave-womb or womb-grave."[3] In fact, Wilbourne's notion of womb as grave is even dramatized by Quentin when his sex play with Natalie is interrupted by Caddy and he throws himself into the hogwallow in a ritual imitation of sexual intercourse: *"I jumped hard as I could into the hogwallow the mud yellowed up to my waist stinking I kept on plunging until I fell down"* (90). The hogwallow, for Quentin, figures the vagina/birth canal and also the womb where life is made, and in which the light of consciousness is extinguished, as if lost in the dark seething tumults of primal, unconscious life. Intercourse, then, is perceived as a return to the womb, a return to a fused existence in the world.

Just as the ritual intercourse with Caddy in the hogwallow is evoked in terms of death—a reversion to primal matter—so also Quentin's abortive attempt at joint suicide with Caddy simulates sexual intercourse—Quentin proposes to penetrate Caddy with his knife. At the branch, Quentin drops his knife and fails to achieve penetration, but he is determined not to fail in his last attempt to join himself with Caddy in death. Quentin's suicide simultaneously satisfies two contradictory impulses: he reassimilates his own repressed being-in-the-world, i.e., he merges with Caddy, even as he represses this being, i.e., he kills Caddy. At one level, Quentin's death by drowning is, like incest with Caddy, the mother-surrogate, an immersion of self in the dark waters of the unconscious. By drowning himself, Quentin is surrendering to the long denied forces of his own unconscious. Dissolved in water, Caddy's element, he is reabsorbed into the matrix of life, the sea (mer), the mother (mère), and he achieves the consummation he has both resisted and desired: the union of himself with Caddy, the fusion of conscious and unconscious. Conversely, by willing his own extinction, Quentin is asserting the power of the signifier over the signified, and his death becomes his victory over the body's experience, his victory over Caddy. In other words, by killing himself Quentin is also carrying out his threat to Caddy, "Ill kill you" (104).[4]

---

3. William Faulkner, *The Wild Palms* (1939; New York: Vintage, 1966), 138.
4. Both Bleikasten, *The Most Splendid Failure*, 103, and Irwin, 43, recognize that Quentin's suicide simultaneously punishes and satisfies his incestuous desire for Caddy.

Quentin's death by drowning, then, successfully enacts both his desire to commit incest with Caddy and his desire to commit joint suicide with Caddy. This proposition is supported by a brief, easily overlooked episode which occurs on the train as Quentin returns to Boston. After his humiliating defeat at the hands of Bland which merges in Quentin's mind with his failed attempt to challenge Ames, he returns alone to Boston on a trolley car. As the car moves between dark trees, with their evocation of Caddy, Quentin looks out the window, but sees only his own reflection: "The lights were on in the car, so while we ran between trees I couldn't see anything except my own face and a woman across the aisle with a hat sitting right on top of her head, with a broken feather in it" (112). In the glass, Quentin sees reflected himself and his double, or his conscious self and his repressed self. What Quentin represses is his own being-in-the-world; and, because he experiences a loss of being whether he cuts off this being or whether he reincorporates it, his double wears a hat with a broken feather. Like Benjy's broken flower, the outward sign of his castration, the broken feather externalizes Quentin's own repressed feelings of emasculation. The woman in the glass, the reflection of Quentin's own unconscious, is Caddy, the woman-figure in whom he sees himself reflected, the woman on whom he projects his own denied body. Thus, as he speeds toward Boston, intent on death, a long desired and resisted reunion, Quentin is accompanied by Caddy, his double, his sister-self, whose death is his own.[5]

Just as Caddy is Quentin's double, the external projection of Quentin's unconscious, so also is the "dirty" little Italian girl, who pursues Quentin relentlessly as he circles the Charles River. Several critics have remarked correspondences between Caddy and the foreign child.[6] Most notably, of course, Quentin calls the child "sister"; Quentin stands accused of molesting the little girl, when, in fact, it is his sister Caddy for whom Quentin harbors sexual feelings; and, in the little girl, as in Caddy, Quentin sees a reflection of himself. Like Caddy, the child is associated with doors, frames in which the self sees itself mirrored: "She came in when I opened the door. . . . [The bell] rang once for both of us" (84). The bell's one

5. The use of mirror imagery is observed by Irwin and also by Lawrance Thompson in "Mirror Analogues in *The Sound and the Fury*," *English Institute Essays*, ed. Alan Downer (New York: Columbia UP, 1954); reprinted in *William Faulkner: Three Decades of Criticism*, ed. Frederick J. Hoffman and Olga W. Vickery (New York: Harcourt, Brace, and World, 1963), 211–25. Irwin, in particular, has analyzed this imagery perceptively. However, Irwin's study is chiefly concerned with male pairings and repetitions forward in time.

6. See Matthews, 89–91; and Louise Dauner, "Quentin and the Walking Shadow," *Arizona Quarterly* 18 (1965): 159–71; reprinted in *Twentieth Century Interpretations of "The Sound and the Fury,"* ed. Michael H. Cowan (Englewood Cliffs: Prentice-Hall, 1968), 78.

ring pairs Quentin with the little girl, suggesting doubling. More specifically, the little girl, who insistently is associated with phallic symbols—her wormlike fingers, her "stiff little pigtails," the naked "nose of the loaf" (89) pressed against her dirty dress—seems to externalize Quentin's own sense of phallic lack, the lack of substance at the core of the empty signifier. The child, whose loaf with its exposed "nose" erodes in her grasp, is an image projected out of Quentin's unconscious, reflecting his own denied relatedness to the other that threatens to dissolve identity. And, as Quentin's projected self, she resembles Quentin's shadow, another projection. She "shadows" Quentin, step for step: "She moved along just under my elbow" (88). In fact, she seems almost to become Quentin's shadow: when Quentin runs from the child, he loses his shadow, but when his shadow reemerges, she suddenly reappears. "The wall went into shadow, and then my shadow, I had tricked it again," Quentin notes. "I had forgot the river curving along the road. I climbed the wall. And then she watched me jump down, holding the loaf against her dress" (88).

While John T. Irwin argues that Quentin's shadow is his masculine double and Caddy is Quentin's feminine double,[7] I propose that Caddy, Quentin's shadow, and the little foreign child are all avatars of the same figure: the absent signified, Quentin's own repressed fused existence with the world, which, if reassimilated, will collapse the distinctions that constitute identity. So Quentin's attempts to elude the child, his efforts to "trick" his shadow, and his threats to kill Caddy are all manifestations of the same deep-seated need to repress his own being-in-the-world; and when, leaning over the bridge railing, looking at his shadow spread out on the water below him, he longs to drown his shadow, it is Caddy, the reflection of the body he denies, that he seeks to drown, even as he yearns to drown in her, to reexperience the lost integration of infancy, a lost oneness with the mother. Not surprisingly, then, a Caddy-avatar, the little girl, accompanies Quentin on his river walk. Circling the water in which he intends to immerse himself, Quentin is accompanied by the girl, with her gaze as "black and unwinking . . . . and friendly" (88–89) as the "dark and still" (91) watery grave itself.

Throughout *The Sound and the Fury*, then, women are identified with a former fused existence that was banished to create identity. Once this identification is understood, certain enigmatic episodes in the novel, which have elicited little critical commentary, are readily interpreted. For example, as Quentin and "sister" walk together on the day of his suicide, they encounter several young boys at a swimming hole. Swimming naked, the boys object to a

7. Irwin, 42.

female presence and express a desire for separateness: "Take that girl away. What did you want to bring a girl here for? Go on away!" In response to this attempt to expel the girl, Quentin calls out, "She wont hurt you" (91). Quentin's four-word rejoinder provides the key to interpreting not only the boys' resistance to "sister," but also his own:[8] first, Quentin accurately assesses that the boys are threatened by the foreign girl, and, second, his brief retort partially echoes his father's diagnosis of the source of Quentin's own anguish and despair, "It's nature is hurting you, not Caddy" (77). Neither Caddy nor the little girl hurts Quentin or the boys, but these females are dreaded because they are identified with an original unity with the other and the natural world. This male identification of women, particularly mother-figures, with a fused existence in the world is dramatized when the boys hurl water—the primal substance from which all forms arise and to which they return[9]—at the girl who shadows Quentin. Like Quentin's gesture of smearing mud on Caddy, which he recalls as he and the little girl approach the swimming boys, this act of hurling water reenacts the projection on the other of the male's own repressed feeling of a lack of differentiation. Perhaps even more important, the ultimate futility of this projection is also implied in the brief scene, for, even as the boys hurl water away from themselves, they swim naked in the swimming hole in an almost ritual simulation of their preconscious existences in the wombs of their mothers. Nevertheless, because presence and identity depend on absence and negation, men persist in identifying women with their own denied being-in-the-world, and so, as Quentin and his female counterpart retreat, Quentin remarks, "Nothing but a girl. Poor sister" (91), articulating the tacit male equation of "sister," the mother-substitute, with the nothingness of nonexistence.

What is perhaps most pernicious about this projection is its effects on women themselves. While Caddy and her daughter struggle against this masculine association, nevertheless, both show signs of accepting and internalizing the male identification of them with the threat of castration and death that subtends the very constitution of identity. For example, Caddy speaks of a nightmare vision: "*There was something terrible in me sometimes at night I could see it grinning at me I could see it through them grinning at me*

---

8. In a discussion that focuses principally on the rhetorical strategies that enforce racial segregation, James A. Snead notes Quentin's desire for separateness from the female. See *Figures of Division: William Faulkner's Major Novels* (New York: Methuen, 1986), 31–32.

9. Mircea Eliade, *Patterns in Comparative Religion*, trans. Rosemary Sheed (1958; New York: New American Library, 1974), 188.

through their faces" (74). The "something terrible" which Caddy sees in herself "through them" is the interrelation of death and the constitution of the self, which men project and Caddy internalizes. Caddy's internalization of doom and loss is also evident in the novel's Appendix, published in 1946, where Caddy is last glimpsed in a photograph, seated in an expensive sports car, beside a Nazi staffgeneral. Given that the Appendix was published just after World War II, when, to an American reader, a Nazi general seemed to be the very incarnation of evil, Caddy's intimacy with the Nazi suggests that she has internalized a male projection of her own deathliness. Blamed for and even identified with the loss of being, Caddy seems to accept this attribution and thus allows herself to be possessed by this avatar of death itself. If, then, as the Appendix claims, Caddy is "lost," (267) her brothers projected this loss onto her.

Caddy's daughter is also doomed by a male projection. Blamed from birth by Jason for his own castration anxiety, Miss Quentin, like her mother, also seems to resist but finally to internalize this projection on her of absence, loss, and death; but she goes one step further than her mother and clearly identifies Jason's role in dooming her: "If I'm bad, it's because I had to be. You made me" (170).

And in light of this male identification of mothers with a relatedness that threatens to engulf and dissolve the subject, Mrs. Compson's behavior becomes readily explainable. Because she has accepted this male projection, she shuts herself up in her darkened, womb- and coffin-like room, and repeatedly predicts her death— "I'll be gone soon" (8). But, as an exponent of this male view, Mrs. Compson also intuits and articulates the often unspoken assumption of this construction of womanhood and particularly motherhood: "I know it's my fault," she says to Jason. "I know you blame me" (182).

To sum up: I have examined how in the patriarchal culture of *The Sound and the Fury* men seek to deny the loss of being that constitutes the subject by projecting this sense of loss on the mother, who recalls a preconscious fused state, a blurring of the divisions that define identity. Because of this projection, women are identified with the contents of the male's own unconscious, his own repressed being. Such an interpretation would explain why, for example, Quentin Compson responds to Caddy with such deep ambivalence, alternating between a desire to possess her and a desire to control her.

I have thus far focused my analysis on the psychological dynamics of Faulkner's characters, but, in concluding, I'd like to speculate about Faulkner's own psychic investment in *The Sound and the Fury,* More specifically, what is Faulkner's attitude toward this dynamic of repression and projection? Why do his characters practice this projection? And ultimately what is Faulkner's objective in writing this novel about a denied and desired absent center?

To respond to these questions, I refer once again to Faulkner's statement about the original impetus for writing the novel. To repeat, Faulkner explained that he wrote the novel to create "a beautiful and tragic little girl" to replace two female absences, the sister he never had and the daughter who would die days after birth. The novel originated, then, in Faulkner's own sense of feminine loss. It is possible that, for Faulkner, the absence of a sister and the death of his daughter betoken the absence of being that attends the constitution of the self. Given that this loss of being is identified with the preoedipal mother and that feelings for the mother are often displaced onto the daughter or sister, it may be that Faulkner wrote *The Sound and the Fury* out of a yearning to represence his own repressed being, which he identifies with these figures of sister and daughter.

To support this claim, I turn once again to Faulkner's 1933 Introduction to *The Sound and the Fury.* In a recently discovered early draft of the introduction, Faulkner, in an unguarded moment, reveals his own psychic involvement in the novel. While explaining that he wrote the novel to explore his own feelings for Caddy, he admits as well that he wrote himself into the novel: "I could be in it, the brother and father both. But one brother could not contain all that I could feel toward her. I gave her three: Quentin who loved her as a lover would, Jason who loved her with the same hatred of jealous and outraged pride of a father, and Benjy who loved her with the complete mindlessness of a child."[1] In this startling passage, Faulkner reveals that the Compson brothers' feelings for Caddy are his own, that he projects onto the three brothers his own deeply ambivalent feelings toward the mother-figure. And in relentlessly analyzing his feelings, Faulkner's text reveals yet another projection: onto mother-figures, particularly onto Caddy and her daughter-surrogate, the Compson brothers project their own denied unconscious. In other words, through the brothers, who represent him in the text, Faulkner makes of Caddy the projected image of his own unconscious. Such a projection would account for Caddy's elusiveness in the novel. To satisfy his conflicting desires to recover and to deny his own repressed being, Faulkner makes of Caddy an absent presence, banishing her even as he invokes her. It is no wonder, then, that Faulkner always singled out this novel as the one he

1. Quoted in Cohen and Fowler, 277.

"felt tenderest toward."[2] *The Sound and the Fury* simultaneously represses and represences Faulkner's own denied and desired unconscious, his own lost original fusion with the other that he identifies with the maternal body, with Caddy, his "heart's darling," "the beautiful one."[3]

RICHARD GODDEN

["Trying to Say": Benjamin Compson, Forming Thoughts, and the Crucible of Race][†]

Faulkner's post-publication statements about *The Sound and the Fury* swaddle the book in maidenheads: having shut his door on publishers, he "began to write about a little girl" and to "manufacture [a] sister" (255). In a further analogy for writing he cites the old Roman

> who kept at his bedside a Tyrrhenian vase which he loved and the rim of which he wore slowly away with kissing it. I had made myself a vase, but I suppose I knew all the time that I could not live forever inside of it. . . . (256)

The vase is a crackable euphemism; in *Flags in the Dust* (1927), the manuscript whose apparent rejection caused Faulkner to close his door, Horace Benbow makes a similar vessel. Having learned to blow glass in Venice, he manufactures "a small chaste shape . . . not four inches high, fragile as a silver lily and incomplete." He calls the vase Narcissa, for his sister, and is anatomically concise about the source of his skills. Of Venetian glass workers, he notes:

> They work in caves . . . down flights of stairs underground. You feel water seeping under your foot while you are reaching for the next step, and when you put your hand out to steady yourself against the wall, it's wet when you take it away. It feels just like blood.[1]

Venice and vagina elide, even as vase and hymen cross.

The pervasiveness of the hymen is reaffirmed by Faulkner's accounts of the novel's source, which places the sexuality of small girls at the first as at the last. On several occasions he insisted that

---

2. William Faulkner, *Faulkner in the University: Class Conferences at the University of Virginia, 1957–1958*, ed. Frederick L. Gwynn and Joseph Blotner (Charlottesville: U of Virginia P, 1959), 77. Page references are to this Norton Critical Edition.

3. Ibid., 6.

† From *Fictions of Labor: William Faulkner and the South's Long Revolution* (New York: Cambridge UP, 1997), 8–21. Copyright © 1997 Cambridge UP. Reprinted by permission of Cambridge University Press. Page references are to this Norton Critical Edition.

1. William Faulkner, *Flags in the Dust* (New York: Random House, 1973), 153.

the novel "began with a mental picture" (273) of Caddy's soiled undergarment up a tree; under the tree two brothers watch the stained drawers ascend. The day of the "muddy . . . drawers" is structurally central to Faulkner; his comments suggest that the four sections "grew" from a repeated attempt to explicate that "symbolical . . . picture" (273). In which case, Sartre's question retains its relevance, "Why is the first window that opens out on this fictional world the consciousness of an idiot?"[2]

It may be sufficient to say that any novel is the sum of its parts and that by April 8, 1928, much will be revealed, most of it to do with the decay of the Compson household. Traditionally, the novel's underlying inclination has been read as a movement toward clarification: from silence to articulation, from idiocy to omniscience, from discontinuous to continuous time, from Old to New South, even from id to super-ego. The interpretations proliferate, but the consensus used to have it that formally *The Sound and the Fury* reveals itself. In which case, why make exposition so difficult by starting with an idiot?

More recently, critical emphasis has shifted from presence to absence; Barthean notions of suspended meaning, and Derrida's claim for language as the infinite deferral of meaning, have been revealingly appealed to, so that generous "openness" and incompleteness as prolongation replace explication as the novel's keynote. Yet the new order, while it may privilege Benjy as a site of experimental textuality, tends to turn him into a linguistic fact rather than to address him as a fact of consciousness. The move transposes Caddy—Benjy's chief preoccupation—from sister to discourse feature. To place brother and sister in "the space of writing"[3] is to dissolve them as conscious subjects. By subjecting them to the play of language, whether as "empty signifier[s]" or Derridean "supplements,"[4] critics of a structuralist and poststructuralist persuasion have made it almost impossible to perceive them as historical subjects (language, after all, is slow to respond to historical change and fast to regress into the infinitely textual).

I make no excuse for attributing an active consciousness to Benjy. Too many readers continue to listen to the dismissals of Faulkner's Appendix (1946) and of his *Paris Review* interview (1956), or to allow an initial uncertainty to be shaped by critical accounts falling into one of two camps. The first sentimentalizes Benjy as a moral

---

2. Jean-Paul Sartre, "On *The Sound and the Fury*: Time in the Work of Faulkner." See p. 313 of this Norton Critical Edition.
3. John T. Matthews, *The Play of Faulkner's Language* (Ithaca, N.Y.: Cornell UP, 1982), 74.
4. See André Bleikasten, *The Most Splendid Failure: Faulkner's "The Sound and the Fury"* (Bloomington: Indiana UP, 1976), 56, and Matthews, *The Play of Faulkner's Language*, 25–27, 70.

touchstone, a vessel of the heart uncontaminated by intellect. To the second he is a machine—a camera with a tape recorder attached. Mystic hearts and machines are alike, indifferent to time. "Time-lessness"[5] is a fine preservative, so Faulkner credits Benjy with it and adds for good measure that he is "an animal."[6] Whatever his creator may say, Benjy is not "impervious to the future," nor as a language user can he "be the past" (255). It might be objected that to extend Benjy's sense of time on the grounds that he thinks in narrative sentences merely points up a formal limitation. The argument goes: Novelists have to use words, and Faulkner seems to have used the simplest available. Why then, if his interests were exclusively pre-linguistic, didn't he adopt an external viewpoint? The shambling idiot who walks into Dilsey's kitchen (in section four) is a far more convincing linguistic blank than the first section's approximation to imbecilic consciousness. I cannot accept that Benjy is a literary device whose linguistic habits, where they exhibit any degree of complication, are simply expressing technical limitations.

Benjy balances on the brink of silence, but he uses words which, as our only access to his imagination, are the first clue to the small girl hidden there. Once again evidence is limited. Benjy for the most part lacks most linguistic things—syntactical variants, tense changes, synonyms, negatives, exclamation and question marks are just a few of them. At his disposal he has the scaffolding of thought—ambulatory verbs, a few nouns, the simple past tense, "and," the occasional adverb, full stops. . . . Poverty or passivity are not the only conclusion that can be drawn from the list. Irena Kaluża concludes from her study of Benjy's sentence structure that he is "monolithic" and capable only of "mechanical identification."[7] What she misses is that Benjy is as rich in small sisters as he is poor in linguistic resources. Having no question or exclamation mark, he sets Caddy beyond inquiry and outrage. A basic sentence format denies complication. He has few negatives with which to exclude his sister, no causal words to explain her, and limited adjectives with which to modify her.

The degree to which Benjy's language is tailor-made to preserve a singular sister may be traced through his use of tenses. He sets two tenses aside to work exclusively in the past. More accurately, his goal is an original time almost outside time, with Caddy. My point

5. Faulkner adopts the term in "Appendix, Compson: 1699–1945."
6. James B. Meriwether and Michael Millgate, *The Lion in the Garden: Interviews with William Faulkner, 1926–1962* (Lincoln: U of Nebraska P, 1968), 240.
7. Kaluża, Irena. *The Functioning of Sentence Structure in the Stream-of-Consciousness Technique of William Faulkner's The Sound and the Fury* (Kraków: Nadładem Uniwer-sytetu Jagiellońskiego, 1967), 85.

is that this is not a passive "timelessness" but a contrivance for which he labors. Caddy alone at the branch with Benjy is an artifact that has to be invented. Benjamin is the mechanic, Faulkner the designer. Most critics fail to see the artifice under the plainness; they speak of "an objective view of the past"[8] or "a capacity for the raw intensities of pleasure and pain."[9] The greatest factor behind this assumption is passivity:

> Benjy is incapable of association of ideas; therefore his memory is stimulated by physical sensation—a sound, or a motion, or the sight of an object in the present, or in a scene being relived.[1]

I chose Edmond Volpe simply because, unfortunately, he continues to be representative. More recent criticism echoes him, having Benjy "slip from one moment of loss to another,"[2] without "faculties for controlling"[3] that slippage, because "as an idiot he simply does not know"[4] what makes him moan or stop:

> [W]hatever he experiences flashes in and out of existence, because he is totally devoid of the consciousness that is the prerequisite for an overall field of perception which would guarantee a pattern for these experiences[5]

And, as a result, "surrounded by words he cannot use, he is used by words,"[6] recording speech "verbatim, like a tape recorder, whether or not he understands its meaning";[7] the resultant transcript resembles "a Barthean *écriture degree zero* . . . writing free of social orientation."[8] To André Bleikasten shall go the summation:

> There is no central *I* through whose agency the speech might be ordered and made meaningful. . . . Hence the startling *eccentricity* of all his experiences: sensations, perceptions and emotions are accorded exactly the same status as objects and occurrences in the outer world . . . and Benjy is at least the

8. Lois Gordon, "Meaning and Myth in *The Sound and the Fury* and 'The Waste Land,'" collected in Warren French (ed.), *The Twenties* (Deadland, Fla.: Everett Edwards Inc., 1975), 272.
9. Bleikasten, *The Most Splendid Failure*, p. 71.
1. Edmond Volpe, *A Reader's Guide to William Faulkner* (London: Thames and Hudson, 1964), 90.
2. Matthews, *The Play of Faulkner's Language*, 68.
3. Walter Taylor, *Faulkner's Search for a South* (Urbana: U of Illinois P, 1983), 41.
4. Thadious Davis, *Faulkner's Negro: Art and the Southern Context* (Baton Rouge: Louisiana State UP, 1983), 77.
5. Wolfgang Iser, *The Implied Reader* (Baltimore: Johns Hopkins UP, 1974), 140.
6. Wesley Morris and Barbara Alverson Morris, *Reading Faulkner* (Madison: U of Wisconsin P, 1989), 136.
7. Stephen Ross, *Faulkner's Inexhaustible Voice: Speech and Writing in Faulkner* (Athens: U of Georgia P, 1989), 179.
8. Philip Weinstein, *Faulkner's Subject: A Cosmos No One Owns* (Cambridge: Cambridge UP, 1992), 119.

passive and incomprehensive watcher of what is happening to him.[9]

Note "passive" and "patternless"; such phrasing does not suggest how actively Benjy mixes memories. A time shift is an act of analogy that brings one time into conjunction with another; the result could be expressed as a simile in which Benjy prefers the original to the secondary term. In any comparison he will incline toward the earlier aspect; therefore, of the some 106 pieces that make up April 7, 1928, the majority occur before 1910. Preference for particular times suggests design and a capacity to draw temporal distinctions. A notional plot, even if termed "deep structure," disposes of Wolfgang Iser's idea that everything that Benjy sees is patternless and equally present.

Paul Ricoeur's account of pre-plotting may be useful here. He suggests in *Time and Narrative* that to experience is to be always and already emplotted. As cultural entities, he argues, we move among interwoven signs, rules, and norms that translate any of our actions into "a quasi-text"; these signs make up a cultural texture immanent with potential text, what he calls "(as yet) untold stories." So—our background entangles us in the prehistory of our culture's told stories:

> This "prehistory" of the story is what binds it to a larger whole and gives it a "background." This background is made up of the "living imbrication" of every lived story with every other such story. Told stories have to "emerge" from this background. With this emergence also emerges the implicit subject. We may thus say, "the story stands for the person" . . . [it follows that] narrating is a secondary process, that of "the story's becoming known." Telling, following, understanding stories is simply the "continuation" of these untold stories.[1]

Since, for Ricoeur, "untold stories" form the subtext from and through which subjects "emerge," acts of consciousness based upon them are perhaps best spoken of as "semi-conscious," or "partially articulated," intentions. I specifically avoid the terms "unconscious" and "subconscious" because, all too often, they are associated with an absence of intention. But just how "imbricated" or "intentional" can a mute with an adult body and a mental age of perhaps three be?

In answer, take the reiterated phrase "Caddy smelled like trees." It is clear from "the mental picture" which began it all that a tree dominates the "(as yet) untold stories" which make up the novel.

9. Bleikasten, *The Most Splendid Failure*, 71–72.
1. Paul Ricoeur, *Time and Narrative: Volume I* (Chicago: University of Chicago Press, 1984), 75.

The tree is particularly monumental in Benjy's experience because it describes the line between the told and the untold. Benjy was born in April 1895; his grandmother Damuddy died three years later, in 1898. The date of her death is conspicuously signaled by Caddy's subversive tree climbing. It would seem that Benjy stopped when he saw his sister's muddy drawers—that is to say, he refuses to grow mentally beyond the point at which the signs for sexuality and death enter his life. The boundary is symbolically marked by a stain over the hymen; Benjy labors to erase the mark. No word in the section antedates 1898. In 1897 he *was* the blank toward which for thirty years he has been trying to carry his sister. The tree and the stain are therefore Benjy's earliest encounter with signs. Other signs cluster near the tree: a snake slips under the house, the father's prohibition is mentioned, the name "Satan" is called by a black woman—my point is not to rehearse Faulkner's rehearsal of *Genesis* but to suggest that these "sensations" are best understood as signs imminent with rules and norms, forming a "prenarrative" whose texture Benjy appreciates. Further, because up to this moment Benjy was without words, tree climbing here marks the fall into not only a potential or "inchoate story" about sex and death but also into language. "Caddy smelled like trees" involves Benjy in much more than a favorite odor. The phrase is urgent with temporal distinctions that he must negotiate. According to the "(as yet) untold story" within whose texture Benjy's consciousness was quite literally born, the tree and the woman combine as an unsettling dryad. This tree is central to linked stories—Eden and The Fall. Its word points two ways. Its odors are sweet and stale. "Caddy smelled like trees" is not a mechanical catch phrase; it is a difficult exclusion involving harsh editing.

When one word projects diametrically opposed plots and implies two temporal layers, it is not surprising that Faulkner's attempts to mark the time shifts occurring during April 7 fail. A distinction between roman and italic script cannot signal the awkward niceties of Benjy's time scale. It is doubtful whether a range of colored inks would have done much more than help the reader to an earlier sense of the major episodes. The idea was discussed by Faulkner and his editors and dropped when printing techniques and cost proved prohibitive. But had the method been adopted, would Faulkner have printed "trees" in two colors and if so, where would the division have occurred? The absurdity of the question emphasizes the limitation of any typographical answer.

For several years I read the different print faces as encoding different times. Only gradually did it dawn on me that where the italics are brief (of no more than one or two lines), they signal a transference; this having been done, the new time reverts to roman type.

As I grew more familiar with the text, certain anomalies stood out—
unmarked shifts in continuous roman passages, typographic change
without temporal change. Initially these seemed to be errors, certainly careless and probably willful. My annoyance diminished with
a growing sense that Benjy's idiocy was more interesting than the
techniques that expressed it. By crediting the idiot with imagination, I found that anomaly became subtlety beyond the register of
typeface, Edmond Volpe has listed five unmarked shifts of scene;[2]
there are more, although given that their number is not legion it is
not important. Faulkner employs print surfaces only as a guideline.
Having introduced the problem, he leaves the reader to discover for
him- or herself the ramifications of shifting time:

> Frony said. "Is they started the funeral yet."
> "What's a funeral." Jason said.
> "Didn't mammy tell you not to tell them." Versh said.
> "Where they moans." Frony said. "They moaned two days on
> Sis Beulah Clay."
> *They moaned at Dilsey's house; Dilsey was moaning. When
> Dilsey moaned Luster said, Hush, and we hushed, and then I
> began to cry and Blue howled under the kitchen steps. Then
> Dilsey stopped and we stopped.*
> "Oh." Caddy said. "That's niggers. White folks dont have
> funerals."
> "Mammy said us not to tell them, Frony." Versh said.
> "Tell them what." Caddy said.
> *Dilsey moaned, and when it got to the place I began to cry and
> Blue howled under the steps. Luster, Frony said in the window.
> Take them down to the barn. I cant get no cooking done with all
> that racket. That hound too. Get them outen here.*
> *I aint going down there, Luster said. I might meet pappy
> down there. I seen him last night, waving his arms in the barn.*
> "I like to know why not." Frony said. "White folks dies too.
> Your grandmammy dead as any nigger can get, I reckon."
> "Dogs are dead." Caddy said. "And when Nancy fell in the
> ditch and Roskus shot her and the buzzards came and undressed
> her."
> The bones rounded out of the ditch, where the dark vines
> were in the black ditch, into the moonlight, like some of the
> shapes had stopped. Then they all stopped and it was dark, and
> when I stopped to start again I could hear Mother, and feet walk-
> ing fast away, and I could smell it. Then the room came, but
> my eyes went shut. I didn't stop. I could smell it. T.P. unpinned
> the bedclothes.
> "Hush." he said. [22–23]

2. Volpe, *A Reader's Guide to William Faulkner*, 363–64.

Frony is the first clue, by way of her relation to her brothers, the older Versh and the younger T.P. It should be noted that Faulkner uses the sequence of Benjy's attendants—first Versh, then T.P., and finally Luster—as a temporal index. At the outset, the passage is about Damuddy's death (1898); with Versh in attendance, the Compson children have been sent from their house to Dilsey's cabin, in front of which they play. The first set of italics marks a time jump, care of "moaned," whereby African American grief in 1898 shifts its object to a time as yet untraceable. The shift is brief, and the children's conversation (from 1898) continues, only to be interrupted by a further outbreak of Dilsey's moaning. Again Damuddy cannot be its object, as Frony has grown up, graduating from "playing in the dirt by the door" (22) to cookery; however, cooking proves impossible, surrounded by distress, so Frony packs Benjy off to the barn, accompanied by Luster. But Benjy, jumping time again, takes her with him (and so out of the italics), as a child. While the children, including Frony, walk, they talk about Damuddy and death in general, directing Benjy's attention to the ditch that contains Nancy's bones. Clearly, between "stopped" and "start" yet another temporal shift occurs, but without a typographical signal, posing a problem over how Benjy gets from the outbuildings to his own bedroom. Prior to mention of the ditch (and outside italics), Benjy is in 1898 with Versh. After "starting again," it is T.P. who unpins and dresses him. It follows that he has been asleep ("stopped") and has woken in another time, which a subsequent and rare negative, "It wasn't father" (23), identifies as 1912—the date of Mr. Compson's death. Fourteen years pass unregistered because Benjy goes to sleep in one panic and wakes in another. Since his first encounter with an association between Damuddy and "funeral," he has been trying to quit 1898. The result has been a sequence of deaths. Five jumps have yielded four bodies in the space of less than one page; "undressed" is the point of greatest confusion—the word is a clue pointing several ways, to the "bright, smooth shapes" that come when the child Benjy has been undressed and put to bed with Caddy, to the stained drawers that Dilsey strips from the small girl, to the increasingly fancy clothes of his sister's adolescence. Unable to orientate himself and use the clue advantageously, Benjy jumps. He travels fourteen years to discover another death. Not surprisingly, with the bones of Damuddy, Roskus, Nancy, and Mr. Compson rising from every available ditch, it is not clear to Benjy that he has moved at all.

My reading stipulates that for the most part Benjy is actively aware of the two sides of any temporal comparison; his aim is that the peaceful side cancel the less peaceful, peace for the most part being synonymous with events before 1910, the year of Caddy's marriage and subsequent departure. Often the hope is unrealized. Nonetheless, each interpolated memory is an attempt at the perfect simile that will render all time synonymous with ur-time. The perfect simile is a metaphor whose two terms have forged a unity such as "chair" and "leg" can only hint at, a unity in which the word and that for which it stands are one. The only way for the temporal simile to imply prelapsarian unanimity is for it to incline to the past. Occasionally perfection occurs. Studying the fire or near to "the smooth bright shapes" of sleep, Benjy will forget time and fail to register the words and events that happen around him. When this occurs, momentarily he is with Caddy in the garden. Because his ur-time is beyond comparison, it disposes of all linguistic analogy. Necessarily it makes no mark on the text and results in an invisible gap, or the perfect uninscribed simile. I will mark the gap (/):

> She led me to the fire and I looked at the bright, smooth shapes. I could hear the fire and the roof. /
> Father took me up. He smelled like rain.
> "Well, Benjy." he said. "Have you been a good boy today."
> Caddy and Jason were fighting in the mirror. [1900: p. 43]

or

> Quentin and Luster were playing in the dirt in front of T.P.'s house. There was a fire in the house, rising and falling, with Roskus sitting black against it. /
> "That's three, thank the Lawd." Roskus said. "I told you two years ago. They ain't no luck on this place."
> "Whyn't you get out, then." Dilsey said. She was undressing me. [1912: p. 21]

Benjy does not notice Mr. Compson enter the library or hear the fight. In Dilsey's cabin the fire absorbs whatever occurs between the idiot's entry and his preparation for bed. The intervals involved are probably considerable. By marking two gaps in the text (/), I have contravened Benjy's imagination. The discovery of a gap requires that a case be made for how Benjy was able to quit time. An unrecorded transference, once found, raises a question as to why Benjy thought two discontinuous events, one event. Faced with this issue, the editorial task very rapidly becomes historical. To see differences in undifferentiated details is to see cause and to suppose a history that is both personal and cultural. All of which is the exact opposite of what Benjy works for. By giving the reader so much to do, Faulkner absolves himself from the strain of taking away Benjy's innocence. The degrees to which any reader invents Benjy's consciousness is the degree to which the reader is stained with the fall that cognition implies.

I have overstated the case for Benjy's imagination to counter
what I take to be a wrongheaded mechanistic consensus. Therefore, before going further, I shall attempt a less polemic account of
his consciousness. April 7, 1928, like any day in Benjy's life, is full
of cues, some of which enable him to switch back toward a time
virtually prior to time. Others, because they might carry him forward to a more recent past or to the present, necessitate evasive
action, action that he frequently fails to take or that proves unsuccessful, leaving him stranded in April 7. The alternative explanation is that every day Benjy suffers a stream of mechanical
blackouts, over which he has no control and thanks to which he
finds himself randomly anywhere from 1898 to 1928. My reading
is located between the two. Benjy's control over time *is* spasmodic;
yet it is consistent enough to be spoken of as *his* control. How else,
for example, to explain the curious congruity of Caddy's loss of
virginity and Versh's story about secondhand impregnation among
bluegums?

> Caddy came to the door and stood there. . . . I went toward
> her, crying, and she shrank against the wall and I saw her eyes
> and I cried louder and pulled at her dress. She put her hands
> out but I pulled at her dress. Her eyes ran.
> *Versh said, Your name Benjamin now. You know how come
> your name Benjamin now. They making a bluegum out of you.
> Mammy say in old time your granpaw changed nigger's name,
> and he turn preacher, and when they look at him, he bluegum
> too. Didn't use to be bluegum, neither. And when family woman
> look him in the eye in the full of the moon, child born bluegum.
> And one evening, when they was about a dozen them bluegum
> chillen running around the place, he never come home. Possum
> hunters found him in the woods, et clean. And you know who et
> him. Them bluegum chillen did.* [46]

Late in the summer of 1909, Caddy lost her virginity. Benjy recognizes the loss—an insight that need not involve mysterious intuition. He does not stare at eyes because he has insight but because,
like fire and glass, the eye moves and reflects light, and at this
moment Caddy's eyes are probably moving far too fast. In any case,
the important point is that, upon his discovery of her loss of virginity, Benjy goes back almost nine years to November 1900, when his
name was changed. The shift appears to have no mechanical trig-
ger, yet there is evidence of a narrow imagination producing at least
partially conscious comparisons. Caddy's sexual change is associated with Benjy's name change, in an essentially cultural analogy
involving two impurities, so that loss of virginity is likened to loss of
a first or maiden name. Since Benjy has been named Maury after

his mother's brother, it seems that his sister's sexual activity has forced him to recognize linguistic duplicity. In effect, then, Benjy counters his disturbing insight by recalling a particular story about multiple names. A Mississippi bluegum is a black conjuror with a fatal bite. Versh's bluegum has the additional gift of magic eyes, a gift that seems to have resulted directly from a name change. Simply by looking at his congregation, the bluegum preacher can make them all, even unborn children, bluegum too. As a bluegum, then, Benjy can claim paternity over any child that his sister may have conceived in 1909. If he is bluegum, too, and can look into Caddy's shifty eyes, he will re-impregnate her in an innocent incest that involves no penetration. According to the story, Benjy is the father of Caddy's child.

The complexity of the analogy realizes a childishly simplistic purpose: Benjy wants his small sister for himself, and to that end he has engaged in "plotting"; he has invented a temporal comparison allowing him to move from an unpleasant event in 1909 to an earlier but less troubling loss. The shift works for him because, as a bluegum, Benjy can control his sister's sexuality. My attribution of an act of consciousness to Benjy—a character most typically described as "unmapped . . . [and] without the hint of a project"[3]— stems from a conviction that even those with severe learning difficulties are liable to whatever subterranean stories characterize the culture within which they pass their long childhoods.

That Benjy should play bluegum at this precise moment suggests that even a person with a mental age of perhaps three, albeit one in a thirty-three-year-old body, knows the pre-plots of his time. By means of a black mask, Benjy, at some level, intends to get his sister back, but the end of his redemptive anecdote is problematic; "old-time" refers to slavery, during which regime a master might manifest his will by canceling a slave's name, thereby consigning the slave to thing-status by severing his or her genealogical ties at the stroke of a pen. Historians refer to this as the imposition of "natal death."[4] In effect, Mrs. Compson, by removing her brother's name from her son (at the moment when his retardation is apparent), blackens her child, making him a slave to her willful preoccupation with the purity of Bascomb blood. The blackness sticks, so much so that Benjy can imagine innocent incest only from within a bluegum's black skin. It follows that sexual congress, even where only ocular, results in a guilt whose form interweaves white and black potency and ties both to death (*"Possum hunters found him in*

3. Weinstein, *Faulkner's Subject*, 119.
4. Orlando Patterson, *Slavery and Social Death: A Comparative Study* (Cambridge, Mass.: Harvard UP, 1982), 8.

the woods, et clean"). The manner of that death may yet give Benjy satisfaction, because playing bluegum involves a muted revolt against the master's or mother's will. Because Versh's story is an anecdote from slavery times, its hero can be read only as "uppity"; the preacher takes revenge on his owner by means of a look whose very existence implies untraceable sexual assaults on black, and perhaps white, women. Such a gaze is dangerous inside an institution so peculiar that no slave may look directly into a white eye for fear of punishment. The bluegum, after a successful career featuring *"about a dozen . . . chillen,"* is necessarily punished. Dilsey is the story's source (at least for Versh), and perhaps her lesson is that the bluegum dies because he is just too rebellious for a domestic servant whose life has been dedicated to sustaining a white household; but she may hand the story down because she knows that servants cannot endure masters without sustenance from a quietly subversive anecdotal tradition. Either way, the story emerges from a dense cultural web within which white and black purposes clash and cross. Furthermore, Benjy's use of the apparently simple tale is packed with "(as yet) untold stories" about seemingly necessary relationships between virginity and incest, and incest and miscegenation. I do not mean to suggest that the network is available to Benjy, but clearly his initial time jump from 1909 to 1900 *is* motivated; he achieves an act of corrective incest by means of the cultural preplots to which he has been apprenticed.

Benjy's chief purpose on April 7, 1928, is to confound his sister's growth with earlier memories. One particular cluster of episodes resists all his attempts at re-plotting: Damuddy's death (1898) and Caddy's wedding (1910) are inseparably associated. At a deeply cultural level the equation between fatality, sex, and the black constitutes a collective representation strong enough to stamp the impaired mind of an adult child. To say that Benjy has no temporal principle is to ignore his efforts to erase this particular cultural imprint. The Fall, like time and racial fear, is part of the prehistory of Faulkner's culture, and Benjy is not exempt from it. When Frony whispers to the tree-climbing Caddy in 1898, "What you seeing," Benjy answers "a wedding"; that is to say, he remembers Caddy's wedding in 1910:

> "What you seeing," Frony whispered.
>   *I saw them. Then I saw Caddy, with flowers in her hair, and a long veil like shining wind. Caddy Caddy.* [26]

Benjy's imbrication in "(as yet) untold stories" ties funerals to weddings and associates both with a tree. The association triggers an atypical sensitivity to speech; Benjy is aware not only that Frony *has* a voice, but also that she has done something to it by whispering. A time switch from death (1898) to matrimony (1910) confirms the co-presence of language and blacks within a rapidly thickening symbolic web. As he stands on a box, staring through the parlor window at his sister's reception, Benjy grows self-conscious about the noises that come from his mouth; "my throat made a sound . . . my throat keep on making a sound" (27). For a man who is unaware that he has been castrated unless he looks at himself, this is a moment of unusual perception. Funerals give way to weddings. Weddings induce words, and words about a ceremony involving sexual exchange inevitably discover a subversive black; Benjy recalls T.P.'s drunken attempts to "hush" him—the very notion of a black physically mastering a white in a basement is subversive enough, without the recollection that T.P. mocks the household patriarch, calling Mr. Compson "a sassprilluh dog, too" (26). The tangled inversion of master and servant is eventually corrected when the master's eldest son puts the black down, and the daughter leaves the reception to reembrace her brother:

> Quentin kicked T.P. and Caddy put her arms around me, and her shining veil, and I couldn't smell trees any more and I began to cry.
>   *Benjy, Caddy said, Benjy. She put her arms around me again, but I went away.* "What is it, Benjy" she said. "Is it this hat." [27]

Working backward through the associative logic within which Benjy struggles to recover Caddy (circa 1898), we see that blacks, language, sexuality, and The Fall are linked. Benjy resists their linkage. As soon as he encounters the wedding cues—a "shining veil" and the scent of 1910 flowers—he strives to convert them into a hat and some perfume worn by Caddy in 1906, when, according to Jason, she only *thought* she was grown up (27). At fourteen Caddy could still wash most of her knowledge away and restore the smell of trees, a smell that even as it comforts her idiot brother has in it, for him, a potential for temporal and narrative duplicity.

To summarize: in Benjy's consciousness, each instance of memory is an opportunity to render that moment synonymous with an initial memory. Put tersely, Benjy's mental habits center on an original image that he seeks to pre-originate—a narrative principle that Faulkner seems to espouse in his post-publication statements. Just as Benjy's thought desires to transgress its own origin, so the founding "mental picture" of the stained drawers tends to fold back into still more original images. In "An Introduction" (1933), which he did not see published, Faulkner speaks of the "unmarred sheet[s]" (250) of the manuscript or the interior of a vase. The vase has already been described as a displaced form of the sister's hymen; its male owner attempts to live inside it (Benjy pre-1898) but finds that the very act of preservation by kissing (incest) leads to erasure (Benjy post-1898). Vase, paper, and child act in very similar ways; attempting to characterize the "ecstasy," "nebulous" yet "physical," (251) that writing the Benjy section gave him, Faulkner likens the manuscript to "unmarred sheet[s] beneath my hand inviolate and unfailing" (250–51)—a complex innuendo forms, in which paper turns into the white space of a bed (Benjy's blank), while language (so black) "mars" that original purity by "marrying" it. Since, in an earlier analogy, Faulkner likened the book to a sister, writing becomes synonymous with a curiously untraceable act of incestuous miscegenation (Benjy as "bluegum")—without trace because the paper appears to absorb the black marks of the script.[5] Unpicking puns in a single strained simile may try credibility, but it is necessary in order to establish a submerged affinity between Benjy and Faulkner's associative and temporal habits—an affinity turning on the virginity of a sister.

JOHN T. MATTHEWS

Dialect and Modernism in *The Sound and the Fury*[†]

> No spika.
> *The Sound and the Fury*

> You ain't heard nothin' yet.
> *The Jazz Singer*

There is a central anomaly in the apparent indifference of *The Sound and the Fury* to representing the inner lives and points of view of the African Americans who share the Compsons' world. Although Faulkner narrates the novel through the mentalities of declined white gentility, *The Sound and the Fury* unstintingly reproduces the *sounds* of African American vernacular. In Benjy's section, black voices are as common as white, and speak to him more familiarly than any but Caddy's. Likewise, Quentin's memories of childhood, which so pointedly depend on the recollection of

---

5. Eric Sundquist proposes incest (sameness) and miscegenation (difference) as antithetical poles in Faulkner's work. Their pairing, in the character of Charles Bon, precipitates (he says) the central crisis both of *Absalom, Absalom!* and of Faulkner's South. While I have reservations about Sundquist's argument, he does isolate a conjunction that is most typically traumatic for Faulkner; that it should be not so here is a measure of how, in thinking about the writing of *The Sound and the Fury*, Faulkner adopts cognitive strategies in line with those of Benjy.

† From *William Faulkner in Venice*, ed. Rosella Mamoli Zorzi and Pia Masitro Marcolin (Venice: Marsilio Editioni, 2000), 129–40. Reprinted by permission of the editors. Page references are to this Norton Critical Edition.

spoken words, recall the co-presence of black and white speech. Even the older Quentin remains within hailing distance of voices like Deacon's, or that of the black man in Virginia waiting for the train to pass. Jason endures the insult of all sorts of voices that refuse to do his bidding, including those of his co-worker Job, his house servants, and the young men he tries to hire, all of whom talk back black to the discredited master. Meanwhile, the formal structure of *The Sound and the Fury*, moreover, directs the reader to see the Rev. Shegog's sermon as the fulfillment of the balked efforts at communication preceding it. What does it mean for Faulkner to locate in African American dialect speech the heart of his aesthetic ambition? Why does Faulkner's most massive textual effort to evade the subject of race open itself to the sounds of racialized speech? What does it mean that Faulkner's most experimental, most deliberately "artistic" and private novel is also the one most thoroughly saturated with dialect?

At one point in *The Sound and the Fury*, Quentin Compson wanders around suburban Boston and strikes up a conversation with some local boys. They comment on the oddness of his speech:

> "Are you a Canadian?" the third said. He had red hair.
> "Canadian?"
> "He dont talk like them", the second said. "I've heard them talk. He talks like they do in minstrel shows".
> "Say", the third said. "Aint you afraid he'll hit you?"
> "Hit me?"
> "You said he talks like a colored man". (79)

It is true, as several critics have noted, that the blacks in *The Sound and the Fury* speak like minstrel figures (Davis, Kodat).[1] But in the exchange above we are reminded that Faulkner's whitest of narrators—because he is Southern—also sounds like a black man, or at least like a minstrel show man. I want to argue that *The Sound and the Fury* is Faulkner's breakthrough novel in part because it confesses a social relation between the language of modernism and African American dialect. That relation—between literary language and an American dialect—itself proves dialectical because it points to the history of struggle between the races in the United States. A social dialectic of domination and resistance, of identification and subjugation, frames the verbal oppositions between standard and dialect speech, between modernist textuality and the sounds of people speaking. Faulkner discovers his voice as a novelist,

---

1. Thadious M. Davis, *Faulkner's "Negro": Art in the Southern Context* (Baton Rouge: Louisiana State University Press, 1983); Katherine Gunther Kodat, "Modernism in Black and White" (Ph.D. dissertation, Boston University, 1985).

becomes "Faulkner", in the work of realizing the modernist sensibility as a function of his region's and nation's history. The interplay of dialects in Faulkner's writing represents a complex history that brings Faulkner's voice to life as he accepts the obligation to tell about the South. Minority voices and subjects are not incidental to Faulkner's achievement; they are its foundation.

When Faulkner briefly fits Quentin with the minstrel mask, he indicates as well his own device as author for talking black. According to Michael North, such "vocal blackface"[2] signifies much more than the familiar primitivist leanings of modernists like Conrad, Gertrude Stein, or Picasso. Rather, the widespread practice of "racial ventriloquism" among modern writers aims to challenge the authority of standard English and traditional literary forms. North describes several associated effects of dialect writing in prominent modernists. Eliot and Pound, for example, who incorporate vernacular speech in their early poems and adopt dialect masks like "Ol Possum" in their private correspondence about poetry, see dialect as a way to unsettle the dominance of iambic pentameter in verse. Conrad, himself a linguistic "outsider" to his chosen English, explores the links between the practice (and defense) of "standard" English and the racial solidarity upon which it is predicated. Conrad glimpses a future creolized world culture in which English splays into accepted dialects and foreign languages mix with the Queen's tongue. Claude McKay attempts to write dialect verse but discovers that he cannot extricate dialect from the significance and value already assigned it by the dominant culture, in which it serves as an emblem of "natural" speech. For these and other writers, according to North, "[m]odernism [. . .] mimicked the strategies of dialect and aspired to become a dialect itself"; "dialect became the prototype for the most radical representational strategies of English-language modernism".

The use of dialect permitted modernist writers to signal their dissent from Victorian bourgeois mores, from the social privilege undergirding standard English, and from the imperialist power that employed it as the instrument of colonial subjugation. Conrad, one of the writers Faulkner repeatedly cited as a major influence, virtually announces the modernist project in the preface to his novella, *The Nigger of the "Narcissus"*. The novelist seeks to turn the text into a living experience for the reader: "my task which I am trying to achieve is, by the power of the written word, to make you hear, to make you feel—it is, before all, to make you *see*!" Author and audience must share a good deal for writing to achieve this

2. Michael North, *The Dialect of Modernism* (New York: Oxford University Press, 1994), 6.

immediacy; it depends on "the subtle but invincible conviction of solidarity that knits together the loneliness of innumerable hearts."[3] Readers of the modernist text learn to speak the dialect of literary experimentalism.

The modernist irony, as North elaborates it for Conrad, rests on the effort to transcend language through language. Words heated to molten transparency cool and thicken into "splendid failure". Yet the obstacle to full intelligibility in *The Nigger of the "Narcissus"*, in North's account, proves to be less metaphysical than social. It inheres in the race of the title character. The Negro James Wait cannot be properly deciphered. The narrator describes the black man's face as "pathetic and brutal; the tragic, the mysterious, the repulsive mask of a nigger's soul."[4] North concludes that "the title character of *The Nigger of the "Narcissus"* thus seems to have entered the story only to be expelled, as if to illustrate the threat that racial and cultural difference pose to the solidarity on which successful reading and writing depend".[5] Conrad both identifies with the racial outsider—as in his relation to English or his critique of imperialism—and also confronts the danger to artistic success of linguistic chaos.

Conrad reduces Wait at the moment of his death to a gibbering "nigger", not the speaker of proper English he has been, but an example of what Conrad elsewhere called "the debased jargon of niggers."[6] Notice how the following description of Wait's unintelligibility in death strikes a Shakespearean chord that Faulkner must have heard:

> James Wait rallied again. He lifted his head and turned bravely at Donkin, who saw a strange face, an unknown face, a fantastic and grimacing mask of despair and fury. Its lips moved rapidly; and hollow, moaning, whistling sounds filled the cabin with a vague mutter full of menace, complaint and desolation, like the far-off murmur of a rising wind. [. . .] It was incomprehensible and disturbing: a gibberish of emotions, a frantic dumb show of speech pleading for impossible things, promising a shadowy vengeance.[7]

Here the "despair and fury", the "dumb show of speech", mark the racial status of "debased" utterance. The evocation of the English poetic tradition signals the very source of solidarity Wait's dialect endangers. When Faulkner glosses the Compson brothers' narratives

---

3. Quoted in North, 38.
4. Quoted in North, 39.
5. Quoted in North, 40.
6. Ibid.
7. Joseph Conrad, *The Nigger of the "Narcissus"* (1898), ed. Robert Kimbrough (New York: W. W. Norton, 1978), 93.

of despair with the same passage from *Macbeth*, however, he reverses Conrad's racial polarity. In *The Sound and the Fury*, it is the erstwhile beneficiaries of a discredited social regime who tell tales signifying nothing. The "shadowy" meaning in the black man's "moaning" gains intelligibility in Faulkner's text.

If there is a black muse in *The Sound and the Fury*, it wears a minstrel mask. I am aware that identifying Faulkner's dialect effects in the novel with a form of minstrelsy risks further demeaning the work's representation of African American experience. But two recent major reconsiderations of blackface minstrelsy have complicated the meaning of one of America's earliest and most nationally characteristic popular arts. Eric Lott's *Love and Theft* (1993) and Michael Rogin's *Blackface, White Noise* (1996) each argues that some aspects of blackface minstrelsy worked in the cultural sphere to soften the rigidity of social segregation.

For Lott, minstrelsy's anti-racist potential seems most apparent in its first years, in the late 1820s and 30s, when white performers like T. D. Rice blacked up to dance Jim Crow in Northern cities. Lott insists that the peculiarly intense form of racial imitation involved in blackface constituted "a profound white investment in black culture", in which one may see in "early blackface minstrelsy the dialectical flickering of racial insult and racial envy."[8] Rogin, on the other hand, doubts the degree of racial envy in an expressive form so relentless and pointed in its ridicule of African Americans. But Rogin does appreciate the role of blackface in the movies, beginning with Al Jolson's *The Jazz Singer* and continuing through the blackface minstrel films of the 'thirties' and 'forties'.

The persistence of blackface minstrelsy in the popular imagination for more than a century and a half suggests the importance of the cultural work it performs. The history of minstrelsy throughout the nineteenth century unambiguously bears witness to the continuous racial abuse committed by the practice of blackface. But as Lott argues, such obsessive ridicule of African American slaves by whites surely sprang from deeper sources of anxiety than the simple need to reaffirm superiority over a subjugated people. One pattern for the use of blackface governs its significance as much in the 1930s as the 1830s: newcomers or outsiders to the dominant culture resort to blackface to stage the process of "Americanization". By masquerading as the disfranchised and despised, working class immigrants could imaginatively enact their own freedom to recreate themselves and accomplish assimilation. This is how blackface minstrelsy originated among the Irish of Northern cities, and it returns,

---

8. Eric Lott, *Love of Theft* (New York: Oxford University Press, 1993), 18.

according to Rogin, in the attraction of American Jews to blackface entertainment in the 1920s and 30s.

The path toward the modernization of minstrelsy led from live vaudeville to the movies, with Jewish performers prominent in both. According to Rogin, Jews were especially drawn to blackface because they saw their own ethnic alienation in the historical oppression of America's people of color. The landmark film in the tradition is *The Jazz Singer*, in which the Jewish Al Jolson plays a cantor's son, Jakie Rabinowitz, whose vocal gifts lean more toward the secular than the religious. Jakie's success singing pop carries him away from his family; his Old World father disowns him for being the first son in five generations not to serve as cantor. Eventually the prodigal returns on the eve of his father's death to sing the *Kol Nidre*. The gesture reconciles him to his father, gratifies his mother, but does not interfere with the professional career of the rapidly assimilating "Jack Robinson", who goes on to musical stage stardom.

Rogin demonstrates that the Jewish son uses blackface to enact an Oedipal rebellion against the world of his ethnic fathers. Like any number of Hollywood moviemakers, the Jolson character sets a course for assimilation and Americanization. He borrows blackface to do so, taking on the combined opprobrium and pleasure associated with the form. The black mask represents, in Rogin's reading, all that must be left behind in the passage into modern Americanized mass culture: ethnic religiosity, outdated stage forms like vaudeville, even the suddenly eclipsed silent movie. (*The Jazz Singer*, of course, is also notable for being the first sound film.) When American cinema finds its voice in 1927, it turns out to be black. Through racial cross-dressing, or cross-speaking, movies like *The Jazz Singer* could suggest a route of white escape from traditional élite culture, could suggest a site for the formation of mass culture, could render the diversity of a "mongrelized" pluralistic society through the interplay of dialect and standard speech, could practice the ritual of self-making through assumed identity, and could dramatize the process of "whitening" necessary to the transformation of Old World ethnicity into New World Americanness.

So much for what whites gain from blackface. But might not the transfer of cultural goods from black to white culture involve something more than mere borrowing? Isn't such impersonation and imitation also a kind of theft? In *The Jazz Singer*, Al Jolson resorts to blackface to gain a career, to kindle a romantic interest, to regain his mother, and finally to reconcile Gentile and Jew. Obviously, this does nothing for the racial condition of African Americans; Jolson's black double—his masked self—remains a kind of slave, subject to his bidding. The white immigrant uses blackface to accomplish assimilation, which sacrifices black assimilation in the process. From its very beginnings, minstrelsy had performed similar acts of expropriation. Lott observes that minstrelsy's cultural borrowing mystifies the material dependency of whites on commandeered black labor. That is, minstrelsy disguises white indebtedness to black labor by making blackface figures ridiculous and helpless dependents on whites. But it also encodes white guilt by re-enacting a cultural theft and placing whites in the position of dependent blacks.

In many similar ways, I wish to argue, Faulkner evokes the minstrel tradition to signal his own complex alienation from the South's dominant social and cultural traditions. The force of his disillusionment with Southern mythology makes him something of a native outsider, a kind of hypothetical person of color. One thinks forward to his article for *Ebony* magazine entitled "If I Were a Negro"[9] and in *Mosquitoes* Faulkner includes a brief self-portrait in which he casts himself as "a little kind of black man." The character hearing this description wants a nicer distinction: "'A nigger?' 'No. He was a white man, except he was awful sunburned and kind of shabby dressed.'" The minstrel elements governing the physical descriptions and dialect speech of black characters in *The Sound and the Fury* are stereotypes that betray limitations of imagination. But the limitations belong to an entire white culture that for more than a century spoke through and for blacks. As Lott says, "after minstrelsy [. . .] there could be no simple restoration of black authenticity."[1]

Faulkner reproduces minstrel and dialect forms partially and self-consciously because he senses the long history of cultural work they performed. Vocal blackface acknowledges the record of economic, social, and cultural robbery that conditions any attempt by whites in the Jim Crow South to represent and comprehend black lives. Vocal blackface points to the lack whites sensed in themselves when they projected licentiousness and pleasure-taking onto blacks. *Blacks* in blackface, such as Luster, on the other hand, suggest the growing irreverence of a people learning to speak out. Blackface measures the deep-seated artifice that helped disguise the repeated acts of dispossession, violence, denial, misrecognition, and contrition sustaining slavery and its aftermath. That "Jim Crow", the term for a system of apartheid, descends from the signature piece of minstrelsy suggests the persistence of a cultural mode laden with ideological investments. To be white is already to have entered a system of representation in which blacks are stolen from,

9. *Ebony,* September 1957.
1. Lott, 103.

subordinated, silenced, patronized, and then—perversely—envied; but to be self-consciously white, as Quentin and Faulkner learn, is to discover *within* that white identity the denial of black labor, black nurture, black expression. When Faulkner finds his voice, the year after *The Jazz Singer*, he discovers it to be black, too. The voice of the white Southerner sounds like a black man sounds, like a minstrel showman. *The Sound and the Fury* proves to be Faulkner's first talkie.

When Luster goes hunting for his missing quarter, he banters with some friends doing laundry in the branch. The patter and punchlines suggest a minstrel routine (cf. Davis 78–79), a kind of comedic *entr'acte*, but Faulkner embeds several prominent themes of historical minstrelsy in this early episode. The tone of the bit makes Luster look like a slow-witted bumbler. He lets himself get tricked out of the golfball after carelessly losing the quarter he needs for the show. When he's asked "Where bouts you lose it?" he answers, in classic simpleton fashion: "Right out this here hole in my pocket" (11). Against the broader backdrop of Luster's incessant search for missing assets, however, his exaggerated incompetence and dependence on white kindness serve to disguise serious disadvantages. The white golfer simply confiscates Luster's property, and his act confirms a whole system of unfair exchange: "White folks gives nigger money because know first white man comes along with a band going to get it all back, so nigger can go to work for some more" (10). Faulkner ventriloquizes an embarrassment over the material impoverishment of blacks by reproducing the double move of minstrelsy—to assign blame to the victim while re-enacting the victimization. The show, as white culture, steals black labor a second time.

Minstrelsy traditionally associates blackness with the indulgence of physical appetites. Such projections derive from the well-rehearsed pathology of white self-denial and hypocrisy among slaveholders, and the imagining of black bodies as sources of nurture and carnal satisfaction. Only the blacks in *The Sound and the Fury* seem to show any cravings. Luster threatens to eat Benjy's entire birthday cake himself, making literal a whole race's presumed self-indulgence, as mocked in the exaggerated mouths of blackface. (The showman tries to find room for fire in the mouth of the white spectator Benjy, but with no success.) Whites who blacked up carefully avoided smearing grease around their mouths, perhaps to emphasize the organ of ingestion associated with their models. Lott notes the "widespread preoccupation in minstrel acts with oral and genital amusement."[2]

2. Lott, 145.

Lips left unblacked also highlight the site of vocal production, blacked up sound having to pass through an encircling trace of whiteness. You may recall Faulkner's own sensuous pen-and-ink sketch of a dancing couple framed by a jazz orchestra. The animated players appear to be black, but they have white lips, as if Faulkner was conceiving blackness as blackfaceness.

At the same time, this first minstrel-like routine in the novel also allows Faulkner to voice direct black complaint about an unjust society. When one laundress observes that nobody is *making* them go to the show, another answers ruefully: "Aint yet. Aint thought of it, I reckon" (10). Nothing, even entertainment, escapes the potential for coercion in the Jim Crow South. As in post-Reconstruction blackface performed by African Americans, moreover, certain of the comedic passages in *The Sound and the Fury* ridicule white arrogance and stupidity.

Jason Compson's co-worker at Earl's hardware store also plays a minstrel defense to the bigotry directed at him. Jason's narrative makes little room for black voices, and those we hear are heavy with dialect. Job continues minstrelsy's work of turning black discomfiture into a source of amusement. Jason complains that if Job were a boll-weevil, he'd work himself to death waiting for the crops that cannot even be planted until Job finishes assembling the cultivators. Job picks up the conceit *in tempo* and wittily transforms it into a figure of economic futility, pointing out that "nobody works much in dis country cep de boll-weevil" (125). Jason means to ridicule black dependency on white productivity, one of his constant themes, but Job turns the boll-weevil into a sympathetic symbol of black farm laborers, who are forced to consume what others own, are used to working "ev'y day in de week out in de hot sun, rain er shine", are compelled to be tenants often on the move, and are oddly turned into enemies because of their very industry. Faulkner repeatedly authorizes Job's quick-witted putdowns of Jason, the best of which throws a snapper at Jim Crow injustice. When Jason calls Job a fool, he fires back: "I dont spute dat neither. Ef dat uz a crime, all chain-gangs wouldn't be black" (152). Faulkner does not let us forget, of course, that the purpose of minstrelsy was to humiliate African Americans. Job gains little dignity from his repartee, and at the one moment Luster looks most like a minstrel figure—his "eyes backrolling for a white instant" (208)—he braces to receive a blow from his white master's hand.

Faulkner's uneasy effort to speak in vocal blackface confesses the desire to locate the black voice within the white self and society, as well as to admit the inescapable falseness that marrs the effort. Dialect in *The Sound and the Fury* does not appear as itself but in opposition to "standard" English. Shegog's rhetorical effects arise from the *passage* between black and white forms. Faulkner identifies the process of dissolving between whiteface and blackface that organizes dialect plurality in *The Sound and the Fury*. Shegog at first looks too black to the congregation because of his contrast with the coffee-colored home minister. Yet when he begins speaking, he sounds too white to be black at all—like Al Jolson in *The Jazz Singer*, who even in blackface sounds white. When Shegog pauses to adjust his address, he begins to blacken his voice in order to communicate more genuinely with his audience. Yet though his new sound seems as "different as day and dark from his former tone" (191–92), the sound of his dialect lags behind: "Brethren" is what the new sermon begins with, a word that remains standard in pronunciation and orthography. "Brethren and sisteren", Shegog continues, now nodding toward the grammatical forms of dialect ("sisteren") but not the aural. Not until the congregation has already experienced the transcendence of words in the direct communication of hearts, not until Shegog already assumes the "attitude" of "a serene, tortured crucifix" does his "intonation, his pronunciation" become "negroid" (192). And when the sounds of preaching in dialect finally may be "heard" in the novel's print, the narrator, like the reader, remains at a remove, not quite able to make out why the sermon moves its listeners so fully, nor of what exactly Dilsey has seen the first and the last. The only white man present—Benjy—sits "rapt" in a "gaze" of perfect incomprehension. Faulkner refuses to dodge the fundamental inauthenticity that laces this moment of indisputable eloquence, symbolic gravity, passion.

The discomfort of Shegog's sermon for many readers, I suspect, derives from Faulkner's deliberate attempt to incorporate the burden of representational and social history in the efforts to comprehend racial difference. Notice how stagily Quentin's man on the mule appears in the Virginia countryside:

> The train was stopped when I waked and I raised the shade and looked out. The car was blocking a road crossing, where two white fences came down a hill and then sprayed outward and downward like part of the skeleton of a horn, and there was a nigger on a mule in the middle of the stiff ruts, waiting for the train to move. How long he had been there I didn't know, but he sat straddle of the mule, his head wrapped in a piece of blanket. [. . .] (57)

Quentin must raise the shade, and later the window itself, before he can communicate with this figment. It is the mule whose head is swaddled to keep it from spooking at the train, but the syntactical slippage in the referent to "his head" betrays Quentin's reflexive identification of what to him are the South's two inscrutable beasts of burden. The lines of fence form the bell of a horn, an instrument that shows up again in the comparison of Shegog's voice to an alto horn, as if this black figure comes to Quentin theatrically outlined by the traces of black music. The image of a horn's "skeleton" marks the history of black mortality that binds land, labor, and song. Later, when Luster shows up for the church service, he wears a fancy new straw hat: "the hat seemed to isolate Luster's skull in the beholder's eye as a spotlight would, in all its individual planes and angles. So peculiarly individual was its shape that at first glance the hat appeared to be on the head of someone standing immediately behind Luster" (188). Like a minstrel player spotlighted on stage, Luster's individuality is delivered by a counterfeit presence concealed behind his face. His author?

The layers of projection and artifice coloring one race's conception of the other govern the representational transactions of minstrelsy as a cultural form. Faulkner's pursuit of the 'other' silenced dialects of his fathers' world leads him, in the case of African Americans, to the tradition of minstrelsy that had become inseparably associated with white production of black speech. The consequences of this association productively help Faulkner confront the obstacles to a white male Southerner's visitation of an historically plundered and self-protective culture. The enormous richness of black folk culture, an imaginative wealth that many modernists recognized as the only legitimate source of cultural renewal and authenticity in the machine age, that richness could not be appropriated without triggering yet another round of thieving masquerade. Faulkner practices dialect writing as he deconstructs it, maintaining maximum self-critical awareness while reproducing what cannot be represented.

STACY BURTON

Rereading Faulkner: Authority, Criticism, and *The Sound and the Fury*[†]

> Once the Author is removed, the claim to decipher a text becomes
> quite futile. To give a text an Author is to impose a limit on that
> text, to furnish it with a final signified, to close the writing. Such
> a conception suits criticism very well. . . .   —Roland Barthes

Readings of *The Sound and the Fury* have been complicated by William Faulkner's extensive "supplementing" of the novel during the years between its publication in 1929 and his death in 1962. He wrote about the Compsons in short stories and *Absalom, Absalom!* in the 1930s; added an Appendix in 1946 that was published with the novel for nearly forty years; and commented on the novel extensively in interviews and classroom discussions in the 1950s. Faulkner's drafts of an introduction to the novel and letters to his editors were published posthumously. It is almost impossible to overstate the influence these later texts have had on how *The Sound and the Fury* has been understood. In Thadious Davis's phrase, readers and critics have long found it "curiously seductive" to have these words from Faulkner the Author at hand.[1]

These later texts have long been read as clarifications of—or as of a piece with—the original novel. Critics cite "That Evening Sun" (1931) in explaining the early lives of the Compson children, for instance, and generally conflate the Quentin Compson of *Absalom, Absalom!* (1936) with the version who had died a suicide in *The Sound and the Fury*.[2] The readings of *The Sound and the Fury* which have been granted virtually definitive status, however, are those found in the unfinished introductions, Appendix, letters, interviews, and classroom discussions. All of these texts come tied quite pointedly to the authority—in some cases the person—of the author. The Appendix places the characters of *The Sound and the Fury* in a larger historical framework from an omniscient position strikingly at odds with the novel's distinctly limited narrative points of view. In introduction drafts and interviews, Faulkner repeatedly claims the novel

---

† Adapted by the author for this Norton Critical Edition from *Modern Philology* 98.4 (May 2001): 604–28. Reprinted by permission of University of Chicago Press. Page references are to this Norton Critical Edition.
1. Thadious M. Davis, "Reading Faulkner's Compson Appendix: Writing History from the Margins," in *Faulkner and Ideology*, ed. Donald M. Kartiganer and Ann J. Abadie (Jackson: UP of Mississippi, 1995), 238.
2. On differing versions of Quentin, see, e.g., Cleanth Brooks, *Faulkner: The Yoknapatawpha Country* (New Haven: Yale UP, 1963), 336, and Richard Godden, *Fictions of Labor: Faulkner and the South's Long Revolution* (Cambridge: Cambridge UP, 1997), 1.

has a mysterious centrality in his career, implying that to understand it readers must do so on the author's terms. His rereadings quickly became basic premises in criticism: the idea that Benjy "loved three things: the pasture . . . his sister . . . firelight," (269) the claim that Quentin "loved not his sister's body but some concept of Compson honor precariously and (he knew well) only temporarily supported by the minute fragile membrane of her maidenhead," and the description of Caddy as the writer's "heart's darling." (263) As Philip Weinstein noted in the 1980s, "the amount of critical exegesis dependent upon" the Appendix (and, I would add, other retrospective texts) "is weighty indeed, and it is not limited to undergraduates who don't know better."[3] Godden noted the same problem in the 1990s: "Too many readers continue to listen to . . . Faulkner's Appendix (1946) and . . . his *Paris Review* interview (1956)."[4] The weight given these retrospective texts has been extraordinary: virtually all critical analyses of the novel cite them, often as authoritative sources for readers working to make sense of a difficult narrative. In over half a century of criticism, this practice has been so common that most of the best-known phrases and lines of interpretation in *The Sound and the Fury* criticism come from Faulkner's retrospective comments rather than from the novel itself. Yet critics have yet truly to examine the full implications of the exegetical role these later texts have assumed.

It is not surprising that Faulkner's rereadings of *The Sound and the Fury* had a kind of canonical status from their initial publication into the 1970s. Malcolm Cowley opens his account of working with Faulkner with an anecdote about the need for authoritative interpretation. Harrison (Hal) Smith, previously Faulkner's editor, had founded a small publishing house:

> One morning his editorial reader, Lenore Marshall, came running downstairs to say, breathlessly, "I think I have found a work of genius."
>
> Hal must have suspected that it was *The Sound and the Fury*. . . . But he only said, according to Mrs. Marshall, "What's it about?"
>
> "I don't know," she confessed. "I'm just starting it."
>
> "Finish it."
>
> She did, that day, and thereupon reported that *The Sound and the Fury* was indeed a work of genius, though she still didn't know what it was about.

3. Philip Weinstein, "'Thinking I Was I Was Not Who Was Not Was Not Who': The Vertigo of Faulknerian Identity," in *Faulkner and the Craft of Fiction*, ed. Doreen Fowler and Ann J. Abadie (Jackson: UP of Mississippi, 1989), 188.
4. Godden, 9.

Cowley invokes images—the puzzled (not to mention breathless and female) reader, the modernist genius—which are congruent with his own critical premises about authorship and the relative significance of authors and readers. Influenced by formalist aesthetics and humanism, he assumes that an author's work is characterized by unity and that the author, as creator, is the best reader of his own work. In this literary-critical context, Faulkner's retrospective texts readily achieve an authorial imprimatur comparable to that of the original novel. For Cowley, who declares the Appendix "an integral part" of the novel, they may even supersede the original, for in his view "the story lived in Faulkner's mind, where it grew and changed like every living thing."[5]

But in the wake of the last thirty years of literary theory, Faulkner's continued, largely unquestioned claim to authoritative interpretation is—at the very least—puzzling. For since the work of Roland Barthes and Michel Foucault, the critical conception of the author upon which Cowley relied has been severely qualified, if not wholly discredited. Foucault describes modernity's "author function" in terms reminiscent of Cowley's reading of Faulkner:

> the author provides the basis for explaining not only the presence of certain events in a work, but also their transformations, distortions, and diverse modifications. . . . The author also serves to neutralize the contradictions that may emerge in a series of texts: there must be—at a certain level of his thought or desire, of his consciousness or unconscious—a point where contradictions are resolved, where incompatible elements are at last tied together or organized around a fundamental or originating contradiction.

For criticism, Foucault explains, the author serves as "a certain functional principle by which . . . one impedes the free circulation, the free manipulation, the free composition, decomposition, and recomposition of fiction." The "author" is thus "the ideological figure by which one marks the manner in which we fear the proliferation of meaning."[6] Faulkner's repeated rereadings of *The Sound and the Fury*—and the authority critics have granted them—offer an apposite demonstration of the author function at work.

This bedrock layer of Faulkner criticism has remained remarkably impervious to poststructuralist thought. Even deconstructionist, feminist, materialist, and other theoretically informed readings of *The Sound and the Fury* have continued to rely upon the retrospective

5. Malcolm Cowley, *The Faulkner-Cowley File: Letters and Memories, 1944–1962* (New York: Viking, 1966), 4, 37, 41.
6. Michel Foucault, "What Is an Author?" in *The Foucault Reader*, ed. Paul Rabinow (New York: Pantheon, 1984), 111, 119.

authority of William Faulkner. There are exceptions: for example, John Matthews notes that reading the Appendix prior to the novel "short-circuit[s] the intended shock and confusion Benjy's section was . . . surely meant to produce."[7] But most critics who have reservations about the later texts make them as a caveat and proceed apace. Godden, for instance, challenges some of Faulkner's re-readings and provocatively declares that "Faulkner's post-publication statements about *The Sound and the Fury* swaddle the book in maidenheads." Yet he takes this "swaddling" to be central for understanding the novel: "Why should a sister's hymen matter so much?" frames his discussion of the novel's contradictions, which he argues "can be relocated within Faulkner, through a notion of the author as a subject who 'authors' himself by means of the story he tells."[8] The Author, it appears, never really died in Faulkner studies.

This persistent author-effect in the critical history of *The Sound and the Fury* appears especially suspect in light of the novel itself, which (as numerous critics have observed) challenges the premise that one vantage point can ever claim to tell the "true" story of human experience. The three first-person narrators speak in distinct voices, each highly subjective and self-absorbed in its own way: Benjy by mental limitations, Quentin by neurosis, Jason by defensive self-justification. The fourth narrator does not resolve them but instead demonstrates, in conjunction with them, the impossibility of an omniscient point of view. Later critics have not shared Cowley's assumptions about unity; most focus on the text's contradictions and the ways it complicates attempts at resolution and undermines attempts at closure. Peter Stoicheff, for example, quoting Foucault, writes that "the novel's exploration of language and voice implies that the author loses his very individuality, or 'endlessly disappears' in the endeavor to write."[9] *The Sound and the Fury*, contemporary critics generally agree, repeatedly undermines truth claims, orderly histories, monologues, and notions of certainty.

Mikhail Bakhtin's theories about discourse and the novel, which have proved useful in examining Faulkner's narrative practice, challenge the ways that Faulkner-as-author has been granted retrospective authority over this text. Historically, Bakhtin argues, the genre of the novel begins in modernity, when "the homogenizing power of myth over language" has been destroyed: "Language is transformed from the absolute dogma it had been within the

---

7. John Matthews, The Sound and the Fury: *Faulkner and the Lost Cause* (Boston: Twayne, 1991), 123.
8. Godden, 8, 21, 48.
9. Peter Stoicheff, "Between Originality and Indebtedness: Allegories of Authorship in Faulkner's *The Sound and the Fury*," *Modern Language Quarterly* 53.4 (1992): 453.

narrow framework of a sealed-off and impermeable monoglossia into a working hypothesis for comprehending and understanding reality."[1] It develops in a world that is fundamentally heteroglot: "The prose art presumes a deliberate feeling for the historical and social concreteness of living discourse, as well as its relativity, a feeling for its participation in historical becoming and in social struggle; it deals with discourse that is still warm from that struggle and hostility, as yet unresolved and still fraught with hostile intentions and accents; prose art finds discourse in this state and subjects it to the dynamic-unity of its own style."[2] Bakhtin's understanding of the novel's existence in a heteroglot, unfinalizable environment and his descriptions of the novelist's creative work help to illuminate both Faulkner's rereadings and critics' uncritical acceptance of them. Bakhtin's conception of discourse makes such retroactive efforts to control meaning appear quite questionable: it is difficult to see Faulkner's revisions and critical reliance upon them as anything other than repeated attempts at the final version of "the Compson story" that The Sound and the Fury proves impossible.

In effect, Faulkner's "supplements" claim monologic authority over a text characterized by heteroglossia and inconclusiveness. As Matthews says of Absalom, Absalom! and the Appendix, each of these new accounts offers a "retrospective framing" that claims to present definitive "truth" and thus to prescribe what The Sound and the Fury might mean.[3] The Appendix burdens the Compsons with a closed future that refuses other plausible readings, while the interviews insistently mythologize the novel as a failed rendition of the image of Caddy Compson. The notion Faulkner proffers of Yoknapatawpha as a "unique fictional world," as Stoicheff points out, serves as a "form of mock writerly authority," a nostalgic, "rueful gesture" toward the failed traditional ideology of the author.[4]

While novelists may attempt to speak authoritatively (and readers may listen to them as though they do), Bakhtin proposes that they cannot sustain it. In the novel the author does not occupy a discrete plane; rather "the creating consciousness stands, as it were, on the boundary line between languages and styles." The author's language is but one of many in and about the text: "Authorial speech, the speeches of narrators, inserted genres, the speech of characters are merely those fundamental compositional unities

1. M. M. Bakhtin, The Dialogic Imagination: Four Essays, trans. Caryl Emerson and Michael Holquist, ed. Holquist (Austin: U of Texas P, 1984), 60, 61.
2. Ibid., 331.
3. John Matthews, "The Rhetoric of Containment in Faulkner," in Faulkner's Discourse: An International Symposium, ed. Lothar Hönnighausen (Tübingen: M. Niemeyer, 1989), 56.
4. Stoicheff refers to Foucault and Barthes; 462. See also Minrose C. Gwin, The Feminine and Faulkner: Reading (Beyond) Sexual Difference (Knoxville: U of Tennessee P, 1990), 35–36, 48.

with whose help heteroglossia . . . can enter the novel; each of them permits a multiplicity of social voices and a wide variety of their links and interrelationships. . . . this movement of the theme . . . its dispersion into the rivulets and droplets of social heteroglossia, its dialogization—this is the basic distinguishing feature of the stylistics of the novel." The novelist, whose avowed goal is "compelling language ultimately to serve all his own intentions," does so by speaking "*through* languages" to "refract" his intentions.[5] Heteroglossia works against the writer's impulse to override other discourses and claim the authority traditionally vested in the author. Bakhtin's understanding of discourse suggests that critical discussion must approach Faulkner's supplementary narratives much more skeptically. Decades after Foucault and Barthes questioned the privilege given the authorial word, this point seems belated, but necessary. Although even Faulkner occasionally disavowed his performance as author, criticism has seldom taken note. In 1933 he drafted a story of *The Sound and the Fury*'s origin; after rereading it in 1946, he wrote: "I had forgotten what smug false sentimental windy shit it was."[6] Until his death, however, he would retell—and retail—that genesis story. That Faulkner's readers continue to take his comments authoritatively only compounds the necessity of a critique.

The title announces the claim to authority:

APPENDIX

COMPSON: 1699–1945

The inclusive dates consume the years recounted in the novel in a much larger historical continuum, while "Appendix" asserts that this text is something other than—truer than—fiction. Faulkner's blend of genealogical and encyclopedic formats implies that this text contains the true chronicle of the Compsons, beginning to end. Robert Dale Parker's comments on the "problematic relation" between *Absalom, Absalom!* and its supplementary texts apply: the latter rest "on some implied notion that the chronology holds superior authority because it comes directly from the author, who, the unspoken assumption implies, holds superior authority because in an appendix he speaks with the privileges of omniscience instead of the mediated and therefore tenuous authority of a character or even an author who speaks in the text proper."[7] An "appendix" presents

---

5. Bakhtin, *Dialogic Imagination*, 60, 263, 299, 300.
6. *Selected Letters of William Faulkner*, ed. Joseph M. Blotner (New York: Random House, 1977), 235.
7. Robert Dale Parker, "The Chronology and Genealogy of *Absalom, Absalom!*: The Authority of Fiction and the Fiction of Authority," *Studies in American Fiction* 14 (1986): 193.

itself as what Bakhtin calls "authoritative discourse": "we encounter it with its authority already fused to it." It "remains sharply demarcated, compact and inert: it demands, so to speak, not only quotation marks but a demarcation even more magisterial."[8]

Faulkner makes these claims explicit in letters to his editors, identifying the Appendix as an authoritative key designed to help "the 4 sections as they stand now fall into clarity and place" and "clear up its obscurity."[9] The impetus, he repeatedly explains, was to transform a complicated dialogic text into a monologic account, to constrain the centrifugal Compson stories until "the whole thing would [fall] into pattern like a jigsaw puzzle when the magician's wand touched it." (257) Writing to institute an authoritative rereading, Faulkner requested that the Appendix be published at the beginning of *The Sound and the Fury* to ensure that readers approached the novel with the focus he desired.[1] Publishers in the United States included the Appendix in all editions of the novel from 1946 to 1984, first at the beginning and then, from 1966 onward, at the end. The 1984 "corrected text" aimed to restore the novel to its original state and omitted the Appendix, though the paperback edition inexplicably cited Faulkner's retrospective comments of the 1950s on its jacket cover.[2] A 1992 edition included a "corrected text" of the Appendix.

Adding the Appendix had a substantial effect, one deepened by the fact that it was in the late 1940s and 1950s that Faulkner—newly rehabilitated as a literary figure—finally received widespread attention. Faulkner's new acceptance escalated further as he was made beneficiary of the new aesthetic sensibility fostered by postwar critics.[3] Little substantial criticism on *The Sound and the Fury* had been published before 1946, and with little disagreement critics followed Faulkner's lead in using it to guide their reading. Whatever reservations they had were usually relegated to footnotes or mentioned only in passing: even well into the 1980s, the "death of the author" registers nowhere.[4]

Because of the interpretive weight it has borne, the text of the Appendix requires careful examination. Faulkner presented the text to Cowley as "a piece without implications." (258) But its authoritative form, the details it emphasizes, and the narrator's often ironic tone contradict this claim: throughout the Appendix Faulkner redefines characters with a decisiveness and slant that have enormous

8. Bakhtin, *Dialogic Imagination*, 342, 343.
9. Blotner, ed., 220, 237.
1. Blotner, ed., 220–21, 228, 237.
2. Faulkner, *The Sound and the Fury: The Corrected Text* (New York: Vintage, 1987).
3. See Lawrence H. Schwartz, *Creating Faulkner's Reputation* (Knoxville: U of Tennessee P, 1988).
4. See Carl E. Rollyson, Jr., *Uses of the Past in the Novels of William Faulkner* (Ann Arbor: U of Michigan P, 1984), 79–81, 154–59.

implications. In place of the rich ambiguities of the original novel, in which characters take shape gradually through their own voices and actions juxtaposed with—and remembered through—others, the Appendix offers explicit definitions claiming the authority of retrospection. We are told with certainty that Quentin "loved death above all . . . loved only death," (263) that Jason was "[t]he first sane Compson since before Culloden. . . . Logical rational contained," (267) that Benjy "could not remember his sister but only the loss of her," (269) and that Caddy, "[d]oomed and knew it, accepted the doom without either seeking or fleeing it." (263) The brothers appear as more rigid versions of their earlier selves, and Jason's own voice echoes throughout the Appendix account of him. These definitions became central in virtually all analyses of these characters. The notion that Benjy is unable to remember, for example, became a commonplace despite the fact that the first section of the novel, set when he is thirty-three, is filled with scenes recollected from his childhood. Faulkner represents Caddy as fundamentally changed. In the magazine photo that librarian Melissa Meek discovers, Caddy looks "ageless and beautiful, cold serene and damned" (265)—more like the specter her brother Quentin envisions just prior to his suicide than the impassioned figure of the original novel.

The Appendix provides detailed historical and social contexts for the Compsons at the price of encumbering them with a genealogy of doom that renders any future or freedom impossible. At the end of *The Sound and the Fury*, "each in its ordered place" is clearly only a transient, ironic illusion. Benjy is filled with memories, Jason frantic at the thought of ruin. Quentin's voice has been so prominent that it belies his long-ago death. Caddy alone has broken out of the vortex of Compson history, while her brothers have yet to think past her. Her daughter Quentin's escape from the overbearing Jason opens the possibility of creating her own future. (Stealing back money that Caddy has sent over the years for her care makes Caddy the indirect means of her escape.) In straightening out the novel's convoluted narratives, however, Faulkner insists on precisely the kind of tidy closure that the novel itself refuses. Thus in the Appendix Jason has an approximation of what he wants, Benjy can remember nothing, the brother Quentin is forgotten. "Doom" makes Caddy the mistress of a German staff general by 1943 (a heavy-handed fate to write for a character in 1946). Denied her own section in the novel, she is denied a voice here as well, appearing only as others represent her. Davis writes that this silences Caddy's disruptive voice in the novel proper, "debasing" her "into an icon of evil" and making of her a "spectacle" of "corruption."[5] Her

5. Davis, 238, 246.

daughter Quentin remains voiceless as well. The Appendix pronounces her fated to be a mediocre echo: "whatever occupation
overtook her would have arrived in no chromium Mercedes; whatever snapshot would have contained no general of staff." (270)

Discrepancies between *The Sound and the Fury* and the Appendix troubled Cowley, but Faulkner, who wrote the later text without
rereading the novel, defended them:

> The inconsistencies in the appendix prove that to me that the
> book is still alive after 15 years, and being still alive is growing,
> changing; the appendix was done in the same heat as the book,
> even though 15 years later, and so it is the book itself which is
> inconsistent, not the appendix. That is, at the age of 30 I did
> not know these people as at 45 I now do; that I was even wrong
> now and then in the very conclusions I drew from watching
> them, and the information in which I once believed.[6]

Faulkner presents the Appendix as a totalizing image that exchanges
the vertiginous modernism of the original text for a much more
tightly constructed version of the Compson story. As Sergei Chakovsky wryly notes, the Appendix "contains the plan of *The Sound
and the Fury* as it could have been written . . . but luckily never
was." It fixes in place a very different history, bound by a closing
date. As Davis rightly points out, it "enacts a repositioning of the
author himself from the margins to the center."[7]

Faulkner's re-centering as author of *The Sound and the Fury* occurs
most emphatically in the comments he made in interviews and
classrooms in the 1950s. While a few critics caution against rely-
ing upon these comments, most take them seriously and build
key elements of their interpretations around them. In *The Play of
Faulkner's Language*, for example, Matthews writes at length on the
novel's ambiguity but does not address the issues of authority raised
by Faulkner's later texts, which he cites in framing his arguments.[8]
Like the Appendix, the comments provide succinct external character assessments in place of the novel's complex, contradictory
interior monologues. The most influential of these have been the
definition of Benjy as an "idiot" and the claim that Quentin only
imagines some events and conversations. Faulkner describes Benjy
as an "idiot" who "himself didn't know what he was seeing"[9] and as

6. Cowley, 90.
7. Chakovsky, 285; Davis, 239.
8. Matthews, *The Play*, 22, 63–64.
9. Frederick L. Gwynn and Joseph L. Blotner, eds., *Faulkner in the University: Class Con-
    ferences at the University of Virginia, 1957–1958* (Charlottesville: University of Virginia
    Press, 1959), 64.

an "animal" who "doesn't feel anything." (274) This characterization has been echoed widely in criticism, where Benjy has generally
been read as a passive slate upon which events are written—and
thus as a reliable narrator. Faulkner's claim about Quentin came
when a student asked whether a conversation in which Quentin
told his father about his (imagined) incest with Caddy had "actually" occurred. Faulkner replied: "He never did. He said, If I were
brave, I would—I might say this to my father, whether it was a lie or
not, or if I were—if I would say this to my father, maybe he would
answer me back the magic word which would relieve me of this
anguish and agony which I live with. No, they were imaginary."[1]
Critics since have relied upon this as authoritative deciphering, cit-
ing it almost as a matter of course. Stephen Ross and Noel Polk, for
instance, note it as a source of clarity in the face of ambiguity:
"Faulkner said that Quentin only imagined that he confessed
incest . . . though there is no internal evidence in the novel to determine whether Quentin is remembering or imagining."[2]

The interviews foster two crucial arguments that have become
widely accepted critical premises: first, that the genesis and thus
"conceptual or symbolic center" of *The Sound and the Fury* lie in
the image of young Caddy Compson with muddy drawers, climbing
the tree and looking in the window, and second, that the novel is a
series of frustrated attempts to tell a story that could never be made
right.[3] Faulkner first articulated these readings in introduction
drafts; in the 1950s he reiterated them often. The most detailed
genesis story appears in the *Paris Review* interview, in response to
the question "how did *The Sound and the Fury* begin?"

> It began with a mental picture. I didn't realize at the time it
> was symbolical. The picture was of the muddy seat of a little
> girl's drawers in a pear tree where she could see through a win-
> dow where her grandmother's funeral was taking place and
> report what was happening to her brothers on the ground
> below. By the time I explained who they were and what they
> were doing and how her pants got muddy, I realized it would
> be impossible to get all of it into a short story and that it would
> have to be a book. . . . I had already begun to tell it through
> the eyes of the idiot child since I felt that it would be more
> effective as told by someone capable only of knowing what
> happened, but not why. I saw that I had not told the story that

---

1. Gwynn and Blotner, eds, 262–63.
2. Matthews, *The Play*, 84; Stephen M. Ross and Noel Polk, *Reading Faulkner: "The Sound and the Fury"* (Jackson: UP of Mississippi, 1996), 149.
3. The term comes from Paul Hedeen, "A Symbolic Center in a Conceptual Country: A Gassian Rubric for *The Sound and the Fury*," *Modern Fiction Studies* 31 (1985): 641–662.

time. I tried to tell it again, the same story through the eyes of another brother. That was still not it. I told it for the third time through the eyes of a third brother. That was still not it. I tried to gather the pieces together and fill in the gaps by making myself the spokesman. It was still not complete, not until 15 years after the book was published when I wrote as an appendix to another book the final effort to get the story told and off my mind, so that I myself could have some peace from it. . . . I could never tell it right, though I tried hard and would like to try again, though I'd probably fail again. (273)

This creation myth, told nearly thirty years after the novel was published, has had an extraordinary effect. Read as ur-text rather than competing narrative, it quickly became the foundation upon which interpretations of *The Sound and the Fury* were built. Among the many readings it has influenced are those assessing the novel as a psychoanalytic account of its originary image, those seeing the Compson world as a microcosm of larger myths about loss and remembrance, those focusing on formal relationships between the novel's four parts, and those understanding the novel as an account of language's insufficiency in the face of human experience. For Godden, more recently, Faulkner's "swaddling" reads as a response to the historical contradictions that produced the novel—contradictions he could not answer—and thus remains the necessary framework for reading.[4]

Faulkner seems to want it both ways: he says that he and the Compson brothers can never quite narrate Caddy's story even as he ingrains a "true" plotline about her, consigns her to doom, and refuses to let her narrate her own story on the grounds that she is "too beautiful and too moving to reduce her to telling what was going on."[5] Particularly in a Bakhtinian context, Faulkner's words remind us in spite of themselves that there are no final words, for narratives occur in a heteroglot world in which one more story may always be told and a mythic image is a monologic, contestable gesture. In the case of *The Sound and the Fury*, as numerous critics have shown, Caddy Compson's are the most conspicuous such images and the most conspicuously absent of the not-yet-told stories.[6] Faulkner's Appendix makes Caddy into an image fixed in a photograph; his myth of origin makes her an overdetermined object. Together, these later texts demand that critics pay attention to a character they had earlier ignored and prescribe exactly how

4. Godden, 48.
5. Gwynn and Blotner, eds., 1.
6. See, e.g., Eileen Gregory, "Caddy Compson's World," in Meriwether, *Merrill Studies*, 89–101; Douglas Hill, "Faulkner's Caddy," *Canadian Review of American Studies* 7.1 (1976): 26–38; Gwin, 34–62; and Davis.

she is to be read. Faulkner's myth makes Caddy an icon, "a visual symbol of masculine desire and longing, of male need and loss."[7] As Matthews shrewdly observes, this mode of commemoration leaves "no space for Caddy's subjectivity, her version of her story."[8]

Yet Caddy's vital presence in the dialogues overheard, remembered, and imagined by the novel's narrators suggests her penultimate, barely voiced words hovering on the edges, refusing to be contained. Interestingly, critics writing about Caddy question Faulkner's retrospective narratives earlier and more insistently than other critics. Eileen Gregory, for example, opens her 1970 reading of Caddy's unconventional "vitality" by dismissing critical reliance on the Appendix as "irresponsible." Douglas Hill argues that the reader's sense of her character, as refracted through her brother's narratives, is so substantial that "the Caddy of the novel" overrides the "stock female characterizations" of the Appendix. Only by reading Caddy against Faulkner-the-author's narratives about her—by way of reader response and feminist theories—are critics able to make discursive room for her subjectivity and story in their readings of The Sound and the Fury. When they do, they find rich but elusive glimpses of a character whose language and actions (not merely presence and absence) give shape to the entire text. Indeed, Caddy's dialogic engagement with Benjy, Quentin, and Mr. Compson is so significant that Linda Wagner proposes she may plausibly be read as one of the novel's "essential narrators."[9]

Readers "may begin to hear the whisper of Caddy's voice," Minrose Gwin writes, precisely because Faulkner cannot claim traditional authority over the text.[1] Once heard, Caddy's voice refuses to heed the boundaries set by others' words. Bakhtin describes characters in Dostoevsky's fiction who "do furious battle with such definitions of their personality in the mouths of other people." Such characters "acutely sense their own inner unfinalizability, their capacity to outgrow, as it were, from within and to render untrue any externalizing and finalizing definition of them. . . . Dostoevsky's hero always seeks to destroy that framework of other people's words about him that might finalize and deaden him. Sometimes this struggle becomes an important tragic motif in the character's life."[2] While Dostoevsky, in Bakhtin's account, refuses the privileges of "literary finalization" that "the author-monologist kept for himself,"

7. Davis, 246.
8. Matthews, "The Sound," 91.
9. Gregory, 90; Hill, 37, 33; Linda W. Wagner, "Language and Act: Caddy Compson," Southern Literary Review 14.2 (1982): 61.
1. Gwin, 35.
2. Mikhail Bakhtin, Problems of Dostoevsky's Poetics, trans. and ed. Caryl Emerson (Minneapolis: U of Minnesota P, 1984), 59.

Faulkner tries, retrospectively, to retain it all.[3] Even from the margins, however, Caddy undermines efforts to control meaning in (and about) *The Sound and the Fury*. That Faulkner "could never get it right" says little if anything about Caddy's beauty, but it does say something about the ineluctable contradiction between the novel's unusual, experimental fidelity to heteroglossia and its preoccupation with a subject to whom it denies voice.

Bakhtin's account of novelistic discourse helps to explain Faulkner's attempt to be both author and giver of the final word regarding *The Sound and the Fury*. With the development of the novel comes a profound shift in authorial "positioning": "The underlying, original formal author . . . appears in a new relationship with the represented world. . . . The 'depicting' authorial language now lies on the same plane as the 'depicted' language of the hero, and may enter into dialogic relations and hybrid combinations with it (indeed, it cannot help but enter into such relations)."[4] Writing novels thus involves risking the traditional prerogatives of authorship, for it produces unreliable narrators who claim knowledge they do not have, authors who are limited readers of their own texts, and other uncertainties. Even if the writer attempts to speak authoritatively, "he knows that such language is . . . not in itself incontestable. . . . It is precisely this that defines the utterly distinctive orientation of discourse in the novel—an orientation that is contested, contestable and contesting—for this discourse cannot forget or ignore, either through naiveté or by design, the heteroglossia that surrounds it."[5] The modern novelist may pose as a traditional author, but cannot actually be one. Faulkner's retrospective narratives about *The Sound and the Fury* demonstrate this predicament particularly well. As designed, they have largely been accepted as authoritative clarification rather than as narrative, as sources of fact rather than as "competing" texts.[6] *The Sound and the Fury* has been read within the terms they establish, but they themselves have yet to be read against and contested by the original novel.

A few critics have examined the Appendix as a text preoccupied with authorship; others have suggested that it should be read as a distinct fiction. Given how it has constrained readings of *The Sound and the Fury* for over fifty years, however, the Appendix's complicated relationship with the novel is surely the more crucial topic for future study. The exegetical role played by the interview comments, which have enjoyed an even more exceptional

3. Bakhtin, *Problems of Dostoevsky's Poetics*, 58, 52.
4. Bakhtin, *Dialogic Imagination*, 27–28.
5. Ibid., 332.
6. Parker, 193.

status—much quoted, seldom discussed—merits equally rigorous consideration. The time is long overdue for readers to examine Faulkner's retrospective narratives skeptically and to contest his readings as well as (or rather than) to embrace them.

How these multiple narratives engage one another dialogically is in part the province of readers, who bring their own voices and heteroglot environments to bear as well. *The Sound and the Fury*, with its radical disjunction between narrators, and Faulkner's later narratives, with their omnipresent author-as-reader, invite and require this. Modernist novels (with their multiple narratives and time lines) exaggerate the usual process of reading by leaving many questions open-ended for the reader. *The Sound and the Fury* provokes reader participation from its first pages, for as soon as readers recognize the severe limits of Benjy's perceptions, they attempt to supplement what the narrator has to say. The result, Wolfgang Iser describes, is that the reader "experiences Benjy's perspective not only from the inside—with Benjy—but also from the outside, as he tries to understand Benjy."[7] Once initiated, this dialogic mode of reading both inside and outside becomes the way readers read the narrators and narratives that follow; the text itself establishes that no one voice has the entire story.

In this context, to grant the Appendix and interviews authoritative status is, simply, to misread badly. Putting the Appendix at the beginning of the text "short-circuited" more than just the disorienting experience of the Benjy section; it undermined the very process of reading that the novel itself instigates. For *The Sound and the Fury*, as Warwick Wadlington writes, requires considerably more than "reconstruction of an inferable narrative line," and in doing so it provocatively demonstrates that one can and must "read in several ways, and in several ways at once, with no necessity of seeing contradiction and epistemological gaps in this multiple functioning."[8] This discomfits many readers, from students unsettled by Faulkner's experimental narrative technique to Faulkner himself, wanting to set the story straight. Cheryl Lester argues that the Appendix reaches "in plural and contradictory ways in several directions at once," but most Faulkner criticism fails to take those rich ambiguities into account.[9] Rather, the aspects of the Appendix and interviews congenial to such arguments have been overshadowed almost entirely by the claims these texts make about their own authoritative status and the closure they offer.

7. Wolfgang Iser, *The Implied Reader: Patterns of Communication in Prose Fiction from Bunyan to Beckett* (Baltimore: Johns Hopkins UP, 1974), 140.
8. Wadlington, 88, 37. See also Bleikasten, "Reading Faulkner," in *New Directions in Faulkner Studies*, 1–17; and Wesley Morris with Barbara Alverson Morris, *Reading Faulkner* (Madison: U of Wisconsin P, 1989).
9. Cheryl Lester, "To Market, to Market: *The Portable Faulkner*," *Criticism* 29 (1987): 389.

Bakhtin sees this impulse to resolve contradictions and close off plots as a consequence of the novel's modernity: "[t]he absence of internal conclusiveness and exhaustiveness creates a sharp increase in demands for an *external* and *formal* completedness and exhaustiveness, especially in regard to plot-line."[1] In the case of *The Sound and the Fury*, such demands are evident across the critical spectrum. Even as he placed the Appendix at the front and rehearsed his genesis myths, Faulkner claimed—rather dubiously—to distrust the idea of an introduction: "To me, the book is its own prologue epilogue introduction preface argument and all. I doubt if any writing bloke can take seriously this or any other manifestation of the literary criticism trade."[2] But Faulkner did take the notion seriously. Such literary historical details cast the critical contradictions of modern authorship in sharp relief.

Faulkner's repeated retelling of *The Sound and the Fury* reminds us that "novelistic representation is always an open, unresolvable conflict of representations."[3] Bakhtin's theories suggest that critical discussion of *The Sound and the Fury* will inevitably read Faulkner's later texts far more dialogically—and skeptically—than in the past. The process of decentering Faulkner-as-author has been underway for some time, though criticism has been slow to notice. The most telling examples have been in readings of Caddy Compson, which have had to dismantle Faulkner's iconography in order to read her unpredictable "voice of alterity."[4] In 1957, University of Virginia graduate students astutely asked why Caddy didn't have her own section in the novel and whether there was "any way of getting her back from the clutches of the Nazis, where she ends up in the Appendix?" In response, Faulkner, the eminent visiting author, recited yet again his story of the novel's genesis and failure and spoke of Caddy as being "too beautiful" to narrate. To bring her back to life "would be a betrayal": "it is best to leave her where she is."[5] Faulkner criticism, in turn, ignored their questions and canonized his answers. But Faulkner's statements—spoken and heard as authoritative—find quite a different audience half a century later. As Matthews remarks, contemporary college students simply "will not accept Faulkner's explanation why a novel devoted to the absent nurturing female never permits her to tell her own story."[6] For

1. Bakhtin, *Dialogic Imagination*, 31.
2. Blotner, ed., 236–37.
3. David Carroll, "The Alterity of Discourse: Form, History, and the Question of the Political in M. M. Bakhtin," *Diacritics* 13.2 (1983): 77.
4. Gwin, 61.
5. Gwynn and Blotner, eds., 1.
6. John Matthews, "Text and Context: Teaching *The Sound and the Fury* after Deconstruction," in *Approaches to Teaching Faulkner's "The Sound and the Fury,"* ed. Stephen Hahn and Arthur F. Kinney (New York: MLA, 1996), 125.

readers skeptical of the author as best reader or final signified, "betrayal" far more accurately describes Faulkner's late rejection of his own experiment in modernism. Bakhtin describes the life of the literary work as one of continual creative engagement: real and represented worlds "find themselves in continual mutual interaction" as readers with "differing time-spaces" "recreate and in so doing renew the text."[7] The history of *The Sound and the Fury* criticism, from its most formalist moments to the possibilities opened by poststructuralist and feminist approaches, demonstrates this process with particular clarity. It also reveals how easily critical readings of texts can become conventionalized, and how narrow the space may be between renewing a text creatively and reifying it. The challenge of rethinking Faulkner's dialogic relationship with the novel he loved most serves as a provocative reminder that for readers, as for Benjy Compson, "each in its ordered place" (209) is an always provisional condition that time and language will change.

MARIA TRUCHAN-TATARYN

Textual Abuse: Faulkner's Benjy[†]

> Is this not the life undertaking of us all . . . to become human? . . . It can be a long and sometimes painful process. It involves . . . no longer hiding behind masks or behind the walls of fear and prejudice. It means discovering our common humanity.

> —Jean Vanier, *Becoming Human* (Toronto: Anansi, 1998)

The first section of *The Sound and the Fury* is applauded as Faulkner's most remarkable achievement. There is overwhelming consensus, in particular, acknowledging Faulkner's success in portraying the consciousness of an "idiot" in the character of Benjy Compson. Indeed, this reception exemplifies a critical cliché that has resisted notice. My intent is not to add yet another variation to the established themes of explication of Benjy but to demonstrate how unquestioning acceptance of him as a successful representation of intellectual disability reveals an underlying ableism in the literary critical endeavor and an academic acquiescence to dated socio-cultural constructions of disability. Whereas feminist and cultural theories have exposed the socio-political currency of

---

7. Bakhtin, *Dialogic Imagination*, 254, 253.
† From *Journal of Medical Humanities* 26.2/3 (Fall 2005): 159–72. Reprinted by perimission of Springer Science+Business Media. Page references are to this Norton Critical Edition.

fictional portrayals of race and gender, images of disability still remain largely unexamined. Faulkner's depiction of African-Americans, for instance, as lazy or loyal servants is unequivocally situated in an identifiable past. Irving Howe observes that "the terms in which Dilsey is conceived are thoroughly historical and by their nature become increasingly unavailable to us. . . ."[1] Similarly, Faulkner's female figures assume fresh meanings when viewed through the kaleidoscopic perspectives of gender theories. Perceptions of Benjy's character, however, have not clearly evolved in parallel ways. Despite the growth of a global disability rights movement and the development of the discipline of disability studies in the humanities, the figure of Benjy's mindless, voiceless subhumanity continues to resonate through Faulknerian scholarship as a believable portrait of disability. Interrogating this interpretation contributes to contemporary academic projects striving to mitigate entrenched biases in order to recover silenced voices, particularly the voices of those whose bodies and minds refuse to conform to prescribed norms.

Faulkner compared the artist to a carpenter who works with materials stored in the attic. His "own experience of people" is the lumber stored in his memory.[2] Both Blotner's biography of Faulkner[3] and John Cullen's recollections readily locate the source for Benjy's character in an individual well known to Faulkner's childhood community:

> He was based on Elwin Crandle (fictitious name), the son of a doctor. Although he lived to be more than thirty, his mind never did develop. Just as Benjy Compson tried to catch a little girl, Elwin Crandle chased little girls and frightened them . . . no one actually attempted to solve the problem by castration. . . . he watched us and played with his testicles all the time. The family had a difficult time keeping him under control. They would pull his dress down, and they kept him inside the high fence around their yard. Somebody looked after him all the time.[4]

Faulkner undeniably intended Benjy to represent accurately someone medically diagnosed with idiocy and inscribed in him the attributes assumed to be consistent with the diagnosis. In a 1956 interview, he admits that "the only thing I can feel about him personally is concern as to whether he is believable as I created him"

1. Irving Howe, *William Faulkner: A Critical Study* (Chicago, UP Chicago, 1975), 247.
2. John B. Cullen, *Old Times in the Faulkner Country*, in collaboration with Floyd C. Watkins (Baton Rouge: Louisiana State UP, 1975), vii.
3. Joseph Blotner, *Faulkner: A Biography*, Volume One (New York: Random House, 1974).
4. Cullen, 79–80.

[273]. The implications of idiocy, Faulkner believed, provided him with an essential tool for engineering the structure of his literary project, but the weight and richness of metaphoric expediency rested on Benjy's credibility as a mentally impaired person.

Faulkner conceived *The Sound and the Fury* in the 1920s after social Darwinism and eugenics, the progeny of the fertile union of positivism and science, had settled comfortably into the American psyche, Dr. Henry Goddard's theories still fueled fears of societal contamination by "feebleminded" procreation; social "undesirables" were often forcibly confined and sterilized.[5] In the late 19th century, Dr. Langdon Down, in keeping with the scientific method of the time in his derogation of both disability and race, classified children he studied in one asylum as "Mongoloid idiots," equating them with Mongolians who were then believed to be a less evolved human species.[6] By 1928, the term "idiot," had been appropriated by medical science to signify the most profound mental impairment. Recasting the term "idiot," as a medical label signifying a measured classification of intelligence (below twenty) did not erase the centuries of fear, ridicule and awe equated with it but rather contributed to the existing panoply of notions surrounding mental impairment. The character of Benjy reflects both this context of medicalization and the contemporary social valuation of the person with disability as infantile, dependent and subhuman.

While Faulkner recognizes the victimization suffered by those not accepted into mainstream society, he also perpetuates these constructions of disability. In *The Sound and the Fury*, others are judged by the way they approach "the idiot." Faulkner uses Benjy's inferiority to demarcate the humanity of others, but he does not illuminate Benjy's humanity. According to the much cited interview with Jean Stein vanden Heuvel, Faulkner realized the story "would be more effective as told by someone capable only of knowing what happened, but not why" [273]. The brainless Benjy develops into Faulkner's symbol of innocence and pain; "mindless at birth," utterly incapable of rational thought, Benjy functions instinctively, sensorially: "He was an animal . . . He could no more distinguish between dirt and cleanliness than between good and evil" [274]. Although Faulkner seems to indulge in characteristic hyperbole, his words indicate a clear, rational objectification of the Benjy character: "You can't feel anything for Benjy because he doesn't feel anything"

---

5. See John David Smith, *Minds Made Feeble: The Myth and Legacy of the Kallikaks* (Rockville, MD: Aspen Systems Corp., 1985) and Leila Zenderland, *Measuring Minds: Henry Herbert Goddard and the Origins of American Intelligence Testing* (Cambridge and New York: Cambridge UP, 1998).

6. Mary Beirne-Smith, James Patton, and Richard Ittenbach, eds., *Mental Retardation*, 4th ed. (Upper Saddle River, N. J.: Prentice Hall, 1994), 140.

[273]. Faulkner also conveyed a philosophical curiosity concerning idiocy: "I became interested in the relationship of the idiot to the world that he was in but would never be able to cope with."[7]

* * * Although Benjy is mute, Faulkner devised a syntactic, grammatical method to denote the mindlessness attributed to developmental disability. Further, as Michael Millgate describes in his study of the extant manuscript and prepublication material of *The Sound and the Fury* (1966), Faulkner wanted to have Benjy record events "with camera-like fidelity."[8] Before the publication of the novel by Cape and Smith, he added revisions that further illustrate his desire to remove traces of agency or understanding in Benjy. In the manuscript, for example, Benjy extends his hand to the "fire door"; when published, this passage reads "where the fire had been," removing recognition of both door and permanence of the fire behind it. "I tried to put it back" becomes "my hand tried to go back to my mouth," a revision that disengages Benjy still further from his own experience.[9] When Faulkner revised his manuscript to intensify Benjy's portrayal of mental retardation as he saw it, he added Benjy's age of thirty-three. Only a "retarded" character could fulfill Faulkner's need to convey the innocence of childhood arrested in a maturing body. Benjy also connects with traditions of literary representation; as Merritt Moseley points out, his "idiocy is . . . a literary convention."[1] Faulkner's enculturation would enable him to conflate actual people like Elwin Crandle with characters such as Wordsworth's "Idiot Boy," consequently placing among the images prescribed to developmental disability in literary works, from holy fool to demonic predator.

While Faulkner's exploitation of idiocy can be understood, if not condoned, by his historical context, his work has authorized a legacy of writing that sustains, with few exceptions, the idiot myths. For critics, Faulkner's rendering of human blankness has typified individuals medically labeled as idiots. Benjy, however, more accurately illuminates not the (lack of) subjectivity of a cognitively impaired individual in lived experience but rather imaginings projected upon a population denied agency and voice by authors of public policy as well as narrative texts. An overview of the critical literature on Benjy to date manifests not only an overwhelming admiration for the unparalleled skill with which Faulkner produced

7. Robert A. Jelliffe, ed., *Faulkner at Nagano* (Tokyo: Tokyo Kenkyusha, 1959), 104.
8. Michael Millgate, *The Achievement of William Faulkner* (New York: Random House, 1966), 301.
9. Millgate, 160.
1. Merritt Moseley, "Faulkner's Benjy, Hemingway's Jake," *College Literature* 13 (1986): 300–304.

such a plausible idiot in the character of Benjamin Compson[2] but also an ignorance of changing concepts of disability.

Critical views of Benjy have remained relatively static over time, assessing his character as an accurate representation of a person with mental retardation and tacitly agreeing with the descriptive elements that determine this reality.[3] A selection of critical texts reflects the cultural expectations fulfilled in Benjy's characterization and points out that unlike *The Sound and the Fury's* representations of race and gender, which have inspired frequent analysis in recent decades, the vexed construction of disability in Faulkner's novel persists unacknowledged.

Before gambling with the publication of *The Sound and the Fury*, Ben Wasson, Faulkner's editor and personal friend, sought the consideration of the novelist Evelyn Scott. Scott's lavish review prompted Faulkner's new editors (Cape and Smith) to commission a full length essay that would be distributed with advance copies of the book. Her literary stature at the time determined the tenor of subsequent analysis of *The Sound and the Fury* and likely played a significant role in establishing the route of Faulkner's career. Scott's description of Benjy illustrates her eloquent inclusion of so many of the perceptions held over time about developmental disability:

> Benjy is beautiful, as beautiful as one of the helpless angels, and the more so for the slightly repellent earthiness that is his . . . Innocence is terrible as well as pathetic—and Benjy is terrible, sometimes terrifying . . . He is not anything—nothing with a name. He is alive. He can suffer. The simplicity of his suffering, the absence, for him, of any compensating sense of drama, leave him as naked of self-flattery as was the first man. Benjy is like Adam, with all he remembers in the garden and one foot in hell on earth. This was where knowledge began, and for Benjy time is too early for any spurious profiting by knowledge. It is a little as if the story of Hans Anderson's Little Mermaid had been taken from the nursery and sentiment and made rather diabolically to grow up. Here is the Little Mermaid on the way to find her soul in an uncouth and incontinent body—but there is no happy ending. Benjy, born male and made neuter, doesn't want a soul. It is being thrust upon him,

2. Even two dissenting critics, W. Tilley and S. McLaughlin, merely disagree with Benjy's diagnosis of idiocy and present alternate medical criteria; they do not challenge the representation on other grounds. See Winthrop Tilley, "The Idiot Boy in Mississippi: Faulkner's *The Sound and the Fury*," *American Journal of Mental Deficiency*, 59 (1955): 374–77. See also Sara McLaughlin, "Faulkner's Faux Pax: Referring to Benjy Compson as an Idiot," *Literature and Psychology*, 33 (1987): 34–40.

3. In this paper, the term "idiot" is used since it is the modifier pervasively applied to Benjy by Faulkner and his critics.

but only like a horrid bauble which he does not recognize. He holds in his hands—in his heart, exposed to the reader— something frightening, unnamed—*pain*! Benjy lives deeply in the senses. (215–16)

Scott implies the existence of a universal prototype or ideal of idiot to which others can be compared; hence, Benjy can be a "better" idiot than Dostoyevsky's. Benjy's "beauty" is "angelic"— supernatural, divine, holy, but it fascinates because it paradoxically includes the physical—"repellent earthiness"—-the primordial nature. His approximation to a simple animal augments his credibility as an idiot. Benjy's identification with animal nature inscribes the association of disability with the carnal, the instinct, the id. Benjy encompasses the Aristotelian extremes: his innocence is both "pathetic" and "terrifying." He portends both heaven and hell. An amalgam of historic prejudices, Benjy embodies the existential angst of (disability as) pain, bereft of meaning.

* * *

Analyses of Faulkner's linguistic craft leave assumptions about "idiocy" unchallenged, even when they acknowledge the constructedness of other identities. Lynn Berk argues that Faulkner challenges traditional perspectives of meaning, leaving gender, race and class standing precariously on a fault line. He achieves this at least in part through what Berk describes as "a profound linguistic equivocation"[4] that demands collaboration; the reader must determine the signifier of the signs. Hence, even though Faulkner's once subversive treatment of Dilsey and Caddy today betrays persistent racism and sexism, new generations of readers are able to reframe the meaning and relevance of these major characters. Little equivocation, however, surrounds the representation of Benjy as an idiot. The writer's task, Berk asserts, is to articulate the meaning of language in the human experience. Thus, for Berk, Benjy's lack of language emphasizes this meaning. Dismissing interpretations of Benjy as a type of holy fool, Berk points out that "Benjy is after all an idiot and his capacity for human experience is limited . . . He is not capable of genuine human communication nor is he capable of purposeful human action".[5]

* * * [Berk's statements imply that] mental retardation or an inability to communicate in typical ways attenuates the humanity of individuals perceived to be like Benjy. Again, while we applaud

---

4. Lynn M. Berk, "A Tale Told by an Idiot: The Problem of Language in the Novels of William Faulkner," *Southern Studies*, 1 (1990): 350.
5. Berk, 338.

Faulkner's genius in manipulating language to convey speechless-
ness and a stream of consciousness that carries no engaged awareness, it is important to note the failure of Faulknerian scholarship
to query the particular socio-political investments served by the
assumption that this configured mentality reflects a lived experience of people with developmental disabilities. Unlike, for example,
the portrayal of race in Dilsey and gender in Caddy, Benjy's disability marking is rarely historically contextualized. The demonstration
of a sustained insistence on a naturalized correlation between subhuman existence and intellectual disability in critical work on *The
Sound and the Fury* from its publication in 1929 until the end of
the 20th century foregrounds the need for a disability studies reading of literature generally and Faulkner specifically. Regardless of
the cultural currents, or critical interests of the scholars, interpretations of Benjy perpetuate oppressive stereotypes of disability as
diminished in function and therefore in human worth. Benjy's
voicelessness garners particular metaphoric mileage, providing
a blank screen, as it were, onto which meaning(lessness) can be
projected.

* * * Nonetheless, Faulkner's attribution of speech to Benjy's
consciousness ostensibly grants insight (albeit fictional) into what
appears otherwise unfathomable. Does Benjy's credibility as a character then presume that an actual person could have no capacity for
thought rather than simply having a different thinking process—
one that contains a perspective others need to access? Does this
insistence on the authenticity of Benjy's portrayal of cognitive
impairment betray an academic dependence on conventional perceptions of intellectual disability as devalued personhood in order
to reinforce academic superiority? In accepting the portrayal of a
fictional character such as Benjy as realistic, the critical literature
perpetuates the dehumanizing notions of people with disabilities as
primitive or bestial instincts—unmitigated by thought.

Benjy's primitive, bestial attributes result in canine analogues[6]
that further imprint Benjy's condition on the reader's mind as not
quite human. If, as Monroe Beardsley suggests "our thinking
is directed, not by the force of the argument at hand, but by the
interest in the image in our mind,"[7] the image of Benjy as wholly
"other," barely human, but recognizably so, is still more intensely
delineated by comparisons of him to animals. The idea of the idiot

6. Morrow details Benjy's acute sense of smell, loyalty to Caddy, attachment to her slipper
and other pet dog images. See Patrick D. Morrow, "Mental Retardation in *The Sound
and the Fury* and The Last Picture Show," *RE:Artes Liberates*, 6 (1979): 4. Feldstein
describes Benjy's rituals as "Pavlovian." See Richard Feldstein, "Patterns of Idiot Consciousness," *Literature and Psychology*, 32 (1986): 16.
7. Monroe C. Beardsley, *Thinking Straight: Principles of Reasoning for Readers and Writers* (Englewood Cliffs, N.J.: Prentice Hall, 1966), 194.

as a primitive, pre-social being, as yet unevolved from an intrinsic association with the natural environment, pervades the critical oeuvre and creates an animalistic image of Benjy that, once planted, can well inform judgments of those he is presumed to represent.

Panthea Broughton argues that Benjy, "outside of human relations," serves as an "emblem of subhumanity," yet she equates Benjy's characteristics to the results of a study of people with brain damage.[8] Thus, subhumanity does not seem to obviate Benjy's relationship to human beings with brain impairment. Benjy's confinement within the fence appears to be a logical consequence of his animal qualities for Cleanth Brooks, who describes Benjy at the church service "as if he, too, understood,"[9] implying, of course, the impossibility of such understanding. Both these sentiments echo prevalent dilemmas for people with developmental disabilities. Inhuman treatment is justified by subhuman status and evidence of cognition is subsumed by a self-authorized judgment of mindlessness.

James Mellard suggests that Faulkner used Benjy "to indicate how much baser the corruption of the civilized can be than the bestiality of the natural."[1] The notion of the disabled figure as a measuring stick for the moral quality of others gains potency from the myth of the person with a developmental delay as uncontrolled natural instinct—innocently dangerous—as opposed to deliberately so. Hence the disabled figure is dehumanized both as a "bestial" entity and as the lowest denominator for evaluating human action. For Donald Kartiganer, Benjy's lack of speech, lack of emotion, lack of "human" communication and lack of awareness of time culminates in the "non-human."[2] Purely objective mechanical reporting is hardly a human characteristic, yet the reader must see through Benjy's eyes. Having vicariously been in Benjy's mind, Kartiganer is shocked by Benjy's description in the fourth section, as if the portrait was of "another idiot from another novel. Not only described, he [Benjy] is also interpreted:. . . It was nothing. Just sound".[3] * * * Once again these analyses fail to challenge the erroneous association of intellectual disability with a mental, emotional and social emptiness.

The narration with which we identify, Kartiganer implies, cannot be reconciled with the represented body of an "idiot." Nevertheless,

8. Panthea R. Broughton, *William Faulkner: The Abstract and the Actual* (Baton Rouge: Louisiana State UP, 1974), 189–90.
9. Cleanth Brooks, *William Faulkner: Toward Yoknapatawpha and Beyond* (New Haven: Yale UP, 1978), 268.
1. James M. Mellard, "Caliban as Prospero: Benjy and *The Sound and the Fury,*" *Novel: A Forum on Fiction,* 3 (1970): 243.
2. Donald M. Kartiganer, "The Meaning of Form in *The Sound and the Fury,*" in this Norton Critical Edition, 350.
3. Kartiganer, 350

the persistently avoided question is whether the deviant or subhuman external attributes seen in Benjy at this point in the narrative actually do correlate to "actual" people presumed to be the models for literary idiots. Is the person who is unable to communicate mindless? Can a human being actually be devoid of any self-awareness or emotions when conscious? The critics' failure to challenge these constructions suggests that Faulkner's creation of Benjy satisfies a social need to delineate an "other" to affirm a notion of collective sameness. As disability scholars argue, perceiving the "Benjys" in our midst affirms our normalcy. In this way Benjy's credibility as a representation of a recognizable "type" is imperative.

* * *

In the critical consensus, a dissenting voice is raised by Winthrop Tilley, who flatly rejects any hint of credibility in the character of Benjy Compson: "All things considered, Benjy seems to turn out a fabricated literary idiot whose correspondence to any idiot, living or dead, would be not only coincidental but miraculous".[4] According to Tilley, Benjy's traits are too distant from fact to be admissible. Tilley derisively underlines the failure of critics, Faulkner and the "man in the street" to distinguish between "maturity, mental deficiency and mental illness".[5] He questions "whether this stuffed idiot can, in view of his incredibility on the literal level, function acceptably on the level of symbolism".[6] The medical journal which published Tilley's essay includes an editor's note suggesting that while a literary review is not scientific, it nevertheless calls attention to the "need for clearer diagnostic concepts" in literature as well as science.[7] Tilley's analysis manifests an interrelationship among literal credibility, symbolic significance and scientific authority. The professed demarcations are often blurred. Tilley fastidiously details Faulkner's disregard for medical and legal facts while he himself strictly subscribes to a medical delineation of idiocy without consideration for the hypothetical nature of a great deal of this "knowledge" as well as its omission of individual human experience. Benjy corresponds to a pervasive cultural stereotyping of idiocy that, as Tilley demonstrates, may not reflect his medical diagnosis, but both ideologies serve to repress and oppress the labeled individual.

Like Tilley, Sara McLaughlin in "Faulkner's Faux Pas: Referring to Benjy Compson as an Idiot" protests against Benjy's label of idiot,

4. Tilley, 376.
5. Tilley, 376.
6. Tilley, 377.
7. Tilley, 374.

arguing that his behavior belies the now obsolete term and that, in fact, his symptoms correspond to autism, a condition named in 1943, well after the appearance of *The Sound and the Fury*. McLaughlin appears to agree with Tilley's contention that the characterization of the idiot in *The Sound and the Fury* is not only unrealistic but also absurd. It soon becomes apparent, however, that McLaughlin is instead corroborating Benjy's realism in terms of the diagnosis of autism. She proceeds to illustrate Benjy's autistic tendencies, contrasting his language, for example, to that of "normal" people[8] and ultimately proposing that Benjy's mother induced his condition.

Under the guise of medical authentication, McLaughlin concludes that Benjy accurately represents a person with a developmental disability: not an idiot but an "autistic person": "Faulkner has unknowingly presented one of the earliest pictures in American literature of the devastating effects autism can have on a human being—Benjy Compson".[9] Thus, McLaughlin actually reinforces the reification of people with disabilities by suggesting that the dehumanized image of developmental disability portrayed by Benjy is medically accurate, just misdiagnosed by critics.

Faulkner masterfully constructed, from his writer's attic of "experience, observation and imagination," a figure of an "idiot" that unambiguously refers to a person with a developmental disability or the diagnosis of mental retardation.[1] The success of his fictional creation as a recognizable, credible characterization is reiterated by the decades of critical literature inspired by *The Sound and the Fury* and specifically by the character of Benjamin Compson. Far from "realistically" depicting the human being with disabilities, however, Faulkner's Benjy portrays an entrenched, derogatory stereotype of disability that has served both in fiction and reality to reify and oppress a large percentage of the human population.

Scholars publishing in Evelyn Scott's wake present multifarious renditions of the same interpretations of Benjy without deviating from the notion that the representation corresponds to reality. What they have neglected to examine is the constructedness of this reality. The problem is not so much the nature of Benjy as an imaginary figure but that he is perceived to be a mimetic rendition of a person with some kind of cognitive or developmental disability, despite interpretive conflicts regarding the diagnosis and despite the development of a critical consciousness about such claims for mimesis.

---

8. McLaughlin, 35.
9. McLaughlin, 38.
1. James B. Mariwether and Michael Millgate, eds. *Lion in the Garden: Interviews with William Faulkner, 1926–1962* (New York: Random House, 1968), 248.

Unevenness in cultural responses to different kinds of "difference" is again a part of the context. When in 1929 Scott praised Faulkner's skill in shaping Benjy as not just an idiot but as *the* archetypal idiot, eugenics was at the height of its popularity in North America, fueled by fears of national degeneration caused by the unchecked breeding of the feeble-minded. Benjy fulfilled the expectations of deviancy spawned in this cultural climate of the early 20th century, manifesting the concept of a monstrosity that threatened to contaminate the troubled nation. After Nazi Germany took eugenics to its logical end in the Holocaust, the ideology lost its luster in the West—but policies of segregation and sterilization generally continued into the 1970s. Perverse, dehumanizing images of disability, unlike those of gender and race, met no prevalent counter-discourses in most communities. The subjectivities and complexities of individuals with disabilities were subsumed under a single mark of deviancy.

However slowly, changes have occurred in cultural constructions of intellectual and developmental disabilities. Since the beginning decades of the twentieth century, medical definitions of what is vulgarly understood as idiocy have undergone a series of conceptual changes. The American Association for Mental Retardation still retains mental retardation as a clinical term although it is contested both on a professional and popular level. As with contemporary definitions of disability, generally, there is no agreement on one standard term.[2] The authors of the 1994 edition of the textbook *Mental Retardation* assert that

> after navigating the maze of actual definitions, and the issues and philosophies regarding definitions and definitional practices, one may be left with solving the task of determining who is "really" mentally retarded. However, the lesson is not that new definitions are better or more accurate, but that the definition of mental retardation is totally a social and political one that rests with the powers that be, and not in the minds of the people who experience intellectual deficits.[3]

Like the term "nigger," "idiot" has been replaced by other medical terms. More recently, a growing emphasis on cultural constructions of disablement within the humanities and social sciences has catalyzed new work on concepts of intellectual and developmental

2. Current terms denoting "idiot" include mentally handicapped, mentally impaired, mentally disabled, individual with exceptional needs, educationally handicapped, intellectually handicapped, learning impaired and developmentally disabled. See Mary Beirne-Smith, James Patton, and Richard Ittenbach, eds., *Mental Retardation*, 4th ed. (Upper Saddle River, N.J.: Prentice Hall, 1994), 85. Ibid, 78.

3. Ibid, 78.

disability.[4] In the face of these changes, however, Faulkner's Benjy, described as mindless, subhuman, primordial, continues to be associated with disability and taken for an accurate representation of persons with developmental disability.

Disability stereotypes in literature reinforce "the fictions of life" configured by hegemonic social power structures. Despite the vertiginous symbolism implicit in Benjy's role, he is unequivocally apprehended not only as a literary type but also as a type of person. For the reader, the idiot does have a referent in reality—the individual with an intellectual disability. Whether consciously or not, the equation of this idiot, replete with metaphor, symbol, sub or super humanity, is made and is intended to be made with actual people labeled disabled. The figure of Benjy thus supports a vast system that profits from the subjugation of "deviance."

* * *

Faulkner's Benjy, however, also offers an opportunity to explore disability in a new way. "[T]he fictions of literature spring, not from life, but from the fictions of life, not from reality but from the gaps in reality."[5] Faulknerian scholarship has largely participated in the marginalization of a large segment of humanity. Criticism that acknowledges disability issues in Faulkner's *The Sound and the Fury*, however, may conceivably be just as influential in the process of societal inclusion of people with disabilities.

In the past decade literary scholarship from a disability perspective has burgeoned, enriching investigations of both theory and art, Students of literature in western universities are being more frequently exposed to the politicized questions posed by textual inscriptions of biological anomaly throughout literary history. Also, as the voices of a global disability movement penetrate the mainstream, contemporary authors of fiction such as Barbara Gowdy in *Mister Sandman* and Anne-Marie MacDonald in *Fall on Your Knees*[6] playfully mock literary conventions of the disability trope, creating characters that overtly reject the traditional metaphorizations these authors are positioned to claim. Reinterpreting Benjy, problematizing the idea of absence of thought in a conscious individual as a realistic possibility, invites a deeper consideration of the need to engage with diversity in human experience and its textual representation.

---

4. The *Handbook of Disability Studies*, eds., Gary L. Albrecht, Katherine D. Seelman, and Michael Bury (Thousand Oaks, CA: Sage Publications, 2001) is an example of the explosion of work in the cross-disciplinary field of disability studies.
5. André Bleikasten, ed., *William Faulkner's The Sound and the Fury: A Critical Casebook* (New York: Garland, 1982), xii.
6. See Barbara Gowdy, *Mister Sandman* (Toronto: Harper, 1995), and Anne Marie MacDonald, *Fall on Your Knees* (Toronto: Vintage, 1996).

William Faulkner: A Chronology

1897 Born William Cuthbert Falkner on September 25, in New Albany, Mississippi, first of the four sons of Maud Butler Falkner and Murry Cuthbert Falkner. Family roots are in Ripley, MS, where in 1886 his paternal great-grandfather, William Clark Falkner—plantation owner and Confederate colonel—had taken control of the local railroad.

1902 Family moves to Oxford, MS, where his grandfather, John Falkner, is a locally prominent lawyer and politician. Father goes into business and opens a livery stable. Former slave Caroline Barr ("Mammy Callie") hired to care for the children.

1903 Meets and sometimes plays with Lida Estelle Oldham (b. 1896), whom in 1929 he will marry.

1909–15 Works in father's livery stable when off from school. Starts to draw and write, and to read authors such as Twain, Shakespeare, Conrad, Balzac, and Melville. Begins to fall in love with Estelle. Friendship begins with law student Phil Stone, his first literary mentor.

1918 Estelle engaged to Cornell Franklin, a lawyer, but still talks of eloping with young "Falkner" anyway; nevertheless, she weds Franklin, by whom she will have two children. Faulkner visits Phil Stone at Yale that spring, and in July joins the Royal Air Force in Toronto, enlisting under the name "Faulkner." Discharged in December before finishing training.

1919–24 Writes poetry, publishes some of it, and briefly attends the University of Mississippi in his hometown. Called "Count No 'Count" by fellow students who find him pretentious. Visits New York and returns to job as postmaster at the university. Friendship with Sherwood Anderson in New Orleans, where he writes for local magazines. First book: *The Marble Faun*, poems, published December 1924.

1925   Begins work on novel *Mayday* (later *Soldiers' Pay*). In
         July sails to Europe on freighter; travels through Italy
         and Switzerland to Paris, and then briefly to England.
         Returns in December.

1926   *Soldiers' Pay* is published. Parents shocked at sexual
         content. Begins work on the Yoknapatawpha Cycle
         with both the unfinished *Father Abraham*, which con-
         tains the germ of his Snopes novels, and *Flags in the
         Dust*, drawing on family history. Estelle returns to
         Oxford, her marriage broken.

1927–28 *Mosquitoes* is published. *Flags in the Dust* rejected.
         His career at an impasse, writes *The Sound and the
         Fury*, working without plan or design in a state of
         never-to-be-recovered ecstasy. Estelle begins divorce
         proceedings.

1929   Publishes both *Sartoris*, a revised and cut version of
         Flags in the Dust, and *The Sound and the Fury*. Marries
         Estelle. Works on early version of *Sanctuary*, rejected as
         too scandalous to publish without fear of prosecution. In
         the fall, writes *As I Lay Dying* while working as a night
         supervisor at the University of Mississippi power plant.

1930   Purchases rundown antebellum Oxford house and
         names it Rowan Oak. Publishes *As I Lay Dying*.

1931   Revised but no less scandalous *Sanctuary* appears.
         These 13, a collection of stories, is published. Daughter
         Alabama born in January; dies after nine days. Faulkner
         drinking heavily.

1932   *Light in August* is published. Goes to California to write
         for Metro-Goldwyn-Mayer. Will work on-and-off in
         the movie industry, especially for the director Howard
         Hawks, until 1951. Father Murry Falkner dies.

1933   *A Green Bough*, a book of poetry, is published. Daugh-
         ter Jill born in June.

1934   *Doctor Martino and Other Stories* is published.

1935   *Pylon* is published. Brother Dean killed in plane crash.
         Faulkner assumes financial responsibility for Dean's
         widow and unborn child. Begins intermittent, fifteen-
         year relationship with Hawks's secretary, Meta Doherty
         Carpenter.

1936   *Absalom, Absalom!* is published.

1938   Random House publishes *The Unvanquished*, a novel
         stitched from a series of heavily revised magazine sto-
         ries about a boy's experience during the Civil War and
         after. Book sold to Hollywood, though never filmed,
         and Faulkner buys a farm with the proceeds.

1939   Random House publishes *The Wild Palms*. Faulkner
            appears on the cover of *Time* Magazine. Elected to the
            National Institute of Arts and Letters.

1940   Random House publishes *The Hamlet*, episodic first
            novel in the Snopes trilogy, again drawing on earlier
            published material. Caroline Barr dies; Faulkner gives
            the eulogy at her funeral and will dedicate to her *Go
            Down, Moses*, his cycle of stories about the black and
            white descendants of the same planter.

1942–46   Random House publishes *Go Down, Moses and Other
            Stories*. Faulkner spends much of World War II in Hol-
            lywood, working on such classic films as *The Big Sleep*
            and *Mildred Pierce*, among others. Drinks heavily, and
            notes that all his books with the exception of *Sanctuary*
            have fallen out of print. Begins to work with the critic
            Malcolm Cowley on a selection from his work.

1946   Cowley publishes *The Portable Faulkner*, including
            Faulkner's new appendix to *The Sound and the Fury*,
            "Compson 1699–1945." *The Sound and the Fury* and *As
            I Lay Dying* republished in a single volume by the Mod-
            ern Library.

1948   *Intruder in the Dust* is published. Faulkner sells film
            rights for $50,000. Elected to the American Academy
            of Arts and Letters.

1949   *Knight's Gambit*, a volume of detective stories, is pub-
            lished. Movie of *Intruder in the Dust* released, with its
            premiere held in Oxford.

1950   In May, receives the Howells Medal for Fiction from
            the American Academy of Arts and Letters. *Collected
            Stories of William Faulkner*, winner of the National Book
            Award, is published. November: announcement of
            the Nobel Prize; Faulkner travels to Sweden for prize
            ceremony.

1951   *Requiem for a Nun* is published.

1952–53   Hospitalized several times in Paris, Memphis, and New
            York for riding- and drinking-related injuries.

1954   *A Fable*, winner of the Pulitzer Prize and National
            Book Award, is published. Travels in Europe. Daughter
            Jill marries Paul D. Summers, Jr; they settle in Charlot-
            tesville, VA.

1955   *Big Woods*, a collection of hunting stories, is published.
            Increasingly involved in the civil rights movement, and
            advocates school integration.

1957–59   *The Town*, second novel of the Snopes trilogy, is pub-
            lished. Teaches at the University of Virginia and buys

a house there to be near Jill and his new grandchildren. Enjoys fox-hunting, but rides recklessly and is often hurt in falls. *The Mansion*, the final Snopes novel, is published.

1960   Mother Maud Butler Falkner dies. Faulkner divides time between Oxford and Charlottesville.

1962   Gold Medal for Fiction from the National Institute of Arts and Letters. Hospitalized several times, his riding injuries exacerbated by his drinking. *The Reivers*, winner of the Pulitzer Prize, a comic novel about a horse theft, is published in June. Faulkner dies of a heart attack on July 6 and is buried in Oxford.

Selected Bibliography

The number of articles, essays, and books written about Faulkner in the fifty years since his death is rivaled, in the study of American literature, only by those devoted to Henry James. The bibliography below is therefore highly selective. I've included those works most useful to students, with an emphasis on reference books and collections of essays, and have omitted a number of important books about the novelist that yet say little about *The Sound and the Fury* as such. Works excerpted in this Norton Critical Edition are marked with a •.

Biographical and Historical

Aiken, Charles S. *William Faulkner and the Southern Landscape*. Athens: U of Georgia P, 2009.

Blotner, Joseph. *Faulkner: A Biography*. New York: Random House. 2 vols., 1974.

• ———, ed. *Selected Letters of William Faulkner*. New York: Random House, 1977.

• ———, and Frederick L. Gwynn, eds. *Faulkner in the University: Class Conferences at the University of Virginia, 1957–1958*. Charlottesville: U of Virginia P, 1959.

• Cowley, Malcolm. *The Faulkner-Cowley File: Letters and Memories, 1944–1962*. New York: Viking P, 1966.

Doyle, Don Harrison. *Faulkner's County: The Historical Roots of Yoknapatwapha, 1540–1962*. Chapel Hill: U of North Carola P, 2001.

• Gray, Richard J., *The Life of William Faulkner: A Critical Biography*. Cambridge, MA: Blackwell, 1994.

• Meriwether, James B., ed. *Essays, Speeches & Public Letters by William Faulkner*. New York: Random House, 1965.

• ———, and Michael Millgate, eds. *Lion in the Garden: Interviews with William Faulkner, 1926–1962*. New York: Random House, 1968.

Sensibar, Judith L. *Faulkner and Love: The Women Who Shaped His Art*. New Haven: Yale UP, 2009.

Williamson, Joel. *William Faulkner and Southern History*. New York: Oxford UP, 1993.

Wolff, Sally, with Floyd C. Watkins. *Talking about William Faulkner*. Baton Rouge: Louisiana State UP, 1996.

Reference and Collections

Bassett, John, ed. *William Faulkner: The Critical Heritage*. Boston: Routledge and K. Paul, 1975.

Brown, Calvin S. *A Glossary of Faulkner's South*. New Haven: Yale UP, 1976.

Claridge, Henry, ed. *William Faulkner: Critical Assessments*. 4 vols. East Sussex: Helm Information, 1999.

Hamblin, Robert W., and Charles A. Peek, eds. *A William Faulkner Encyclopedia*. Westport, CT: Greenwood P, 1999.

Inge, M. Thomas., ed. *William Faulkner—The Contemporary Reviews*. New York: Cambridge UP, 1995.

Kinney, Arthur F., ed. *Critical Essays on William Faulkner: The Compson Family*. Boston: G.K. Hall, 1982.

————, and Stephen Hahn, eds. *Approaches to Teaching Faulkner's* The Sound and the Fury. New York: Modern Language Association of America, 1996.

Kirk, Robert W. *Faulkner's People: A Complete Guide and Index to Characters in the Fiction of William Faulkner*. Berkeley: U of California P, 1963.

Moreland, Richard C., ed. *A Companion to William Faulkner*. Malden, MA: Blackwell, 2007.

Peek, Charles A., and Robert W. Hamblin, eds. *A Companion to Faulkner Studies*. Westport, CT: Greenwood P, 2004.

• Polk, Noel, ed. *New Essays on* The Sound and the Fury. New York: Cambridge UP, 1993.

————, and Stephen M. Ross. *Reading Faulkner*. The Sound and the Fury: *Glossary and Commentary*. Jackson: UP of Mississippi, 1996.

Warren, Robert Penn, ed. *Faulkner: A Collection of Critical Essays*. Englewood Cliffs, NJ: Prentice-Hall, 1966.

Weinstein, Philip M., ed. *The Cambridge Companion to William Faulkner*. New York: Cambridge UP, 1995.

• Zorzi, Rosella Mamoli, and Pia Masiero Marcolin, eds. *William Faulkner in Venice*. Venice: Marsillo, 2000.

Books about Faulkner

Atkinson, Ted. *Faulkner and the Great Depression: Aesthetics, Ideology, and Cultural Politics*. Athens: U of Georgia P, 2006.

• Bleikasten, André. *The Ink of Melancholy: Faulkner's Novels, from* The Sound and the Fury *to Light in August*. Bloomington: Indiana UP, 1990.

• Brooks, Cleanth. *William Faulkner: The Yoknapatawpha Country*. New Haven: Yale UP, 1963.

Clarke, Deborah. *Robbing the Mother: Women in Faulkner*. Jackson: UP of Mississippi, 1994.

Coindreau, Maurice Edgar. *The Time of William Faulkner: A French View of Modern American Fiction*. Ed. and chief trans. George McMillan Reeves. Columbia: U of South Carolina P, 1971.

• Davis, Thadious M. *Faulkner's "Negro": Art and the Southern Context*. Baton Rouge: Louisiana State UP, 1983.

Fowler, Doreen. *Faulkner: The Return of the Repressed*. Charlottesville: UP of Virginia, 1997.

Glissant, Édouard. *Faulkner, Mississippi* (1996). Trans. Barbara Lewis and Thomas C. Spear. New York: Farrar, Straus and Giroux, 1999.

• Godden, Richard. *Fictions of Labor: William Faulkner and the South's Long Revolution*. Cambridge: Cambridge UP, 1997.

• Gwin, Minrose C. *The Feminine and Faulkner: Reading (Beyond) Sexual Difference*. Knoxville: U of Tennessee P, 1990.

Howe, Irving. *William Faulkner: A Critical Study*. 3rd ed. Chicago: U of Chicago P, 1975.

• Irwin, John T. *Doubling and Incest/Repetition and Revenge: A Speculative Reading of Faulkner*. Baltimore: Johns Hopkins UP, 1975.

Jehlen, Myra. *Class and Character in Faulkner's South*. New York: Columbia UP, 1976.

• Kartiganer, Donald M. *The Fragile Thread: The Meaning of Form in Faulkner's Novels*. Amherst: U of Massachusetts P, 1979.

Matthews, John T. *The Play of Faulkner's Language*. Ithaca: Cornell UP, 1982.

———. *The Sound and the Fury: Faulkner and the Lost Cause.* Boston: Twayne Publishers, 1991.
———. *William Faulkner: Seeing through the South.* Malden, MA: Wiley-Blackwell, 2009.
Millgate, Michael. *The Achievement of William Faulkner.* New York: Random House, 1966.
Minter, David. *William Faulkner, His Life and Work.* Baltimore: Johns Hopkins UP, 1980.
———. *Faulkner's Questioning Narratives: Fiction of His Major Phase, 1929–42.* Urbana: U of Illinois P, 2001.
Polk, Noel. *Children of the Dark House: Text and Context in Faulkner.* Jackson: UP of Mississippi, 1996.
Porter, Carolyn. *William Faulkner.* New York: Oxford UP, 2007.
Roberts, Diane. *Faulkner and Southern Womanhood.* Athens: U of Georgia P, 1994.
Ross, Stephen M. *Fiction's Inexhaustible Voice: Speech and Writing in Faulkner.* Athens: U of Georgia P, 1989.
• Sundquist, Eric J. *Faulkner: The House Divided.* Baltimore: Johns Hopkins UP, 1983.
Stonum, Gary Lee. *Faulkner's Career: An Internal Literary History.* Ithaca: Cornell UP, 1979.
• Vickery, Olga W. *The Novels of William Faulkner: A Critical Interpretation.* Baton Rouge: Louisiana State UP, 1959.
Wadlington, Warwick. *Reading Faulknerian Tragedy.* Ithaca: Cornell UP, 1987.
Waggoner, Hyatt Howe. *William Faulkner: From Jefferson to the World.* Lexington: U of Kentucky P, 1959.
Welty, Eudora. *On William Faulkner.* Jackson: UP of Mississippi, 2003.
• Weinstein, Philip M. *Faulkner's Subject: A Cosmos No One Owns.* New York: Cambridge UP, 1992.
———. *What Else but Love?: The Ordeal of Race in Faulkner and Morrison.* New York: Columbia UP, 1996.
———. *Becoming Faulkner: The Art and Life of William Faulkner.* New York: Oxford UP, 2010.

Articles on *The Sound and the Fury*

Essays reprinted in this Norton Critical Edition are not included in the list below.

Abate, Michelle Ann. "Reading Red: The Man with the (Gay) Red Tie in Faulkner's *The Sound and the Fury.*" *Mississippi Quarterly* 54.3, (Summer 2001).
Aiken, Conrad. "William Faulkner: The Novel as Form." *Atlantic Monthly* 47 (November 1939).
Collins, Carvel. "The Interior Monologues of *The Sound and the Fury.*" In Alan S. Downer, ed., *English Institute Essays 1952.* New York: Columbia UP, 1954.
Davis, Thadious M. "Reading Faulkner's Compson Appendix: Writing History from the Margins." In *Faulkner and Ideology,* ed. Donald M. Kartiganer and Ann J. Abadie. Jackson: UP of Mississippi, 1995.
Donaldson, Susan V. "Reading Faulkner Reading Cowley Reading Faulkner: Authority and Gender in the Compson Appendix." *Faulkner Journal* 7.1–2 (Fall 1991–Spring 1992).
Fujie, Kristin. "All Mixed Up: Female Sexuality and Race in *The Sound and the Fury.*" In Annette Trefzer and Ann J. Abadie, *Faulkner's Sexualities: Faulkner and Yoknapatwapha, 2007.* Jackson: UP of Mississippi, 2010.

Hagood, Taylor. "The Secret Machinery of Textuality, Or, What Is Benjy Compson Really Thinking?" In Annette Trefzer and Ann J. Abadie, *Faulkner and Formalism: Returns of the Text*. Jackson: UP of Mississippi, 2012.

Iser, Wolfgang. "Perception, Temporality, and Action as Modes of Subjectivity. W. Faulkner: *The Sound and the Fury*." In *The Implied Reader: Patterns of Communication in Prose Fiction from Bunyan to Beckett*. Baltimore: Johns Hopkins UP, 1974.

Lester, Cheryl. "From Place to Place in *The Sound and the Fury*: The Syntax of Interrogation." *Modern Fiction Studies* 34.2 (1988).

Meriwether, James B. "Notes on the Textual History of *The Sound and the Fury*." *Papers of the Bibliographical Society of America* 56 (1962).

Moser, Thomas C. "Faulkner's Muse: Speculations on the Genesis of *The Sound and the Fury*." In Robert M. Polhemus and Roger B. Henkle, *Critical Reconstructions: The Relationship of Fiction and Life*. Stanford: Stanford UP, 1994.

Parker, Robert Dale. "Where You Want to Go Now: Recharting the Scene Shifts in the First Section of *The Sound and the Fury*." *Faulkner Journal* 14.2 (Spring 1999).

Pryse, Marjorie. "Textual Duration against Chronological Time: Graphing Memory in Faulkner's Benjy Section." *Faulkner Journal* 25.1 (Fall 2009).

Spillers, Hortense. "Faulkner Adds Up: Reading *Absalom, Absalom!* and *The Sound and the Fury*." In Joseph R. Urgo and Ann J. Abadie, *Faulkner in America*. Jackson: UP of Mississippi, 2001.

Westbrook, Wayne W. "Skunked on the New York Cotton Exchange: What Really Happens to Jason Compson in *The Sound and the Fury*." *Southern Literary Journal* (Spring 2009).

The series of *William Faulkner: Manuscripts* (New York and London: Garland, 1987) includes a two-volume set, edited by Noel Polk, that contains a facsimile of both Faulkner's manuscript for *The Sound and the Fury* and his carbon typescript.

Three periodicals specialize in Faulkner studies: the *Faulkner Journal*; the *Mississippi Quarterly*, which regularly devotes a special issue to Faulkner's work; and the volume drawn each year from the "Faulkner and Yoknapatawpha" conference held every summer at the University of Mississippi (e.g., *Faulkner and Ideology*, above). The most comprehensive website is "William Faulkner on the Web," www.mcsr.olemiss.edu/~egjbp/faulkner/faulkner.html (accessed spring 2013).